TRUE LOVE

THE ALPINE RIDGE COMPLETE SERIES

MELANIE A. SMITH

WICKED DREAMS PUBLISHING

Published by
WICKED DREAMS PUBLISHING
info@wickeddreamspublishing.com
Boise, ID USA

Cover design, editing, and interior formatting by Wicked Dreams Publishing

eBook ISBN: 978-1-952121-90-6
Paperback ISBN: 978-1-952121-91-3
Hardcover ISBN: 978-1-952121-92-0

CONTENTS

TOUGH LOVE

RECKLESSLY IN LOVE

UNSCRIPTED LOVE

ELUSIVE LOVE

TOUGH LOVE

A STEAMY SMALL-TOWN FORCED PROXIMITY ROMANCE

CONTENT WARNING

Tough Love is a small-town forced proximity romance novel that includes elements that might not be suitable for some readers, including the use of profanity, open-door sex scenes, and other potentially sensitive topics. Visit https://melanieasmithauthor.com/tlcw.html for a full list (warning: may include spoilers).

CHAPTER ONE

MIA

"I'm sorry, Mr. Matthews, you are unable to request that Mrs. Matthews return the kidney you donated to her brother as part of your divorce settlement."

Well, that's the weirdest statement I've ever made. And, as a divorce lawyer, that's saying something.

"And why the hell not?" he asks hotly, his chubby face reddening. "You're my lawyer. Isn't your job to back me up?" He folds his arms smugly over his chest.

Luckily, I've had plenty of practice dealing with dillholes like him, so his attitude doesn't bother me in the slightest.

"That was between you and her brother. It has nothing to do with your wife, nor is it within the scope of this matter to challenge the legal agreement you almost certainly signed to undergo the procedure. If you'd like to pursue that, why don't we discuss it separately? For now, let's get back to the matter at hand."

Mr. Matthews splutters and puffs for a minute before barking out, "Fine." His beady eyes narrow at his overly made-up, soon-to-be-ex-wife sitting across the table. She's glaring back, lips pursed, not backing down from the anger he's directing her way. "Then I want the poodle."

Mrs. Matthews gasps and her hand flies to her chest. And I swear to god, if she was wearing pearls, she'd be clutching them right now. That's how scandalized she looks.

"You vindictive bastard," she seethes. "You *hate* Mr. Fluffington."

"You get the house, I get the dog," he insists.

Even I can see he's just demanding it to hurt her. I take a subtle deep breath, trying to ward off the headache forming at my temples. I shoot a firm look toward Mrs. Matthews' attorney, who couldn't look more bored if he tried, desperately trying to engage him so we can get through this debacle as quickly as possible. He pointedly avoids my gaze as the couple continues to bicker. Though he may be onto something. Some couples just need to get it out of their system before you can really get them to seriously discuss the terms of their divorce.

Mia Anderson, this is your life, I think wryly. While I'm used to it, I have to admit that this kind of shit definitely wears on you after five years straight of nothing but bitter, petty former couples trying to stick it to each other in every horrible way possible. It has certainly sucked dry my will to date. And sometimes to live. People are *mean*.

Unfortunately, the insanity continues through my usual lunchtime, so by the time we've concluded, for today anyway, I've only got about fifteen minutes before my next meeting. I head straight to the break room, hoping against hope that some of the French apple tart I made and brought in this morning is still around. Not the healthiest lunch, but it's about all I've got time for.

As soon as I enter the small room, I can see the large tray is completely empty, with barely a few crumbs left. Defeated, I sink into a chair and slump my head down on the table in the center of the room. Guess it's coffee and a granola bar for lunch. Again.

Heavy footsteps approach the room, and I lift my head tiredly. My father enters a moment later.

"Hey, pumpkin," he greets me, stopping at the coffee machine to refill his cup. "Saw you missed lunch dealing with the Matthews. I had Janice get you a chowder bowl from Ivar's. It should be in the fridge."

I leap up from the table and give him a kiss on the cheek as I make for the refrigerator.

"Thanks, Dad, you're a lifesaver."

I make a mental note to thank Janice, our office manager, later. Ivar's has my favorite chowder in all of Seattle. Which may be more due to nostalgia than it being the best, but in any case, it was exceptionally thoughtful and definitely appreciated given the circumstances.

Dad smiles as I rip the still-warm container from the fridge and dive into it before I even fully close the door.

"Can't have my star employee come to our workflow meeting with a growling stomach." He winks as he heads back out the door.

Once he's gone, I roll my eyes and sink back into my chair to finish the chowder. Star employee, my ass. More like indentured servant.

In fact, that's the very phrase I had to use to get him to allow me to schedule my first vacation since before law school. Sure, in theory our benefits include vacation time. But with a typically eighty-hour workweek and caseloads that don't allow for breaks, the job doesn't lend itself to actually using that particular perk. Though everyone else in my dad's firm has managed it since I've been here. But Dad expects more from his little pumpkin. His would-be successor.

Except, I'm not so sure that's what I want to be. I can't say I was *ever* sure, but it was a ready-made career that I turned out to be pretty good at. I didn't have any better ideas at the time anyway.

I still don't have any better ideas. Except Hawaii, that is. For a whole week. With my best friend. I'd go with a boyfriend, except I don't have one of those.

Haven't in years. Another concession to the job, if the job itself didn't already make me leery of ever getting married. It's all very catch-22.

I check the clock on my phone, realizing it's time for the meeting. I down the last of the chowder in one go and head to the conference room. Five days. Just five more days and I get a whole week off.

I just manage to make it out of work in time to meet my best friend, Joanie, at a pub in Fremont for drinks.

"You look like shit," Joanie greets me as I join her at the two-seater high-top table she's snagged. Happy hour is almost over, which usually means the place starts to empty out. But not tonight. It's still packed even though it's just after eight o'clock.

I glare at her as I remove my suit jacket. It's the beginning of March, so it was still crisp enough outside to need it. But it's roasting in here. I can only hope I don't have sweat stains on my silk shirt to add to Joanie's assessment of my looks.

"Thanks for noticing," I reply sarcastically.

I eye her dark brown hair and blue eyes that almost make us look like sisters. Except where I'm tall and curvy, she's short and thin. And she's always so put together, even after a long day at work. Tonight is no exception, and her fuchsia suit is both in style and flawless, same as her slicked-back ponytail and immaculate makeup that both seem like they were just done in a salon.

I'm rumpled, I'm sure my waves are even frizzier than they were when I left in a hurry this morning, and I can't remember the last time I wore makeup.

"How do you always look so put together? I mean, really, where do you even find the time?"

She grins widely. "I don't sleep."

I huff out a dry laugh and shake my head. "Bet your clients love that," I reply drolly, dropping my eyes to the bar menu. I need something, even if it is just greasy appetizers.

Our waitress pops by and we order our drinks and apps. Once she's gone, I set the menu down and let out a big sigh.

"Rough day?" she teases.

I give her a sharp look. "It's a day ending in 'y' isn't it?"

"Just remember: This time next week, we'll be soaking up the sun, drinking piña coladas oceanside, checking out all the gorgeous guys surfing ..." She trails off and closes her eyes, a blissful smile spreading over her face.

"I'm living for it, Jo. Living. For. It."

Her eyes pop open. "I'm still shocked your old man allowed it," she admits, tapping her French-manicured nails on the tabletop.

"Me too. But I'm more shocked we were both able to get the time off."

She shrugs. "I'm a criminal defense attorney. It's not exactly seasonal work, so I may as well take time off when I damn well feel like it. Besides, there are, what, more than a dozen partners in my firm? They'll figure it out."

Joanie and I have been besties since our first day of law school. Out of the dozens of women in our class, for some reason we just clicked. It could be that she's as sharp-witted as I am sarcastic. Like two flavors of the same dessert, we complement each other's snarkiness.

"Wish I could say the same for my dad's firm. He wants to keep it small, but he also doesn't know how to turn work down. I'm fucking exhausted, Jo. And I honestly won't be surprised if he changes his mind or, at the very least, decides I should take some work with me."

She shakes her head and wags a finger. "Nuh-uh. In fact, I'm going to teach you a word that will help you deal with that."

Curious, I gesture for her to go on.

She takes a deep breath. "NO," she barks sharply. Then she gestures to me. "Now you try."

I narrow my eyes at her and she laughs. "Ha ha," I snip drily. "Mia doesn't know how to say no. Very funny."

"It's funny 'cause it's truueee," she singsongs.

The waitress delivers our drinks and apps, but I hesitate before diving in.

"All right, fine," I agree. "But only with my dad. I'm not a complete doormat." I take a sip of my cocktail to hide my blush at admitting that I am a total pushover when it comes to my father. I'm too old to still care so much what he wants, to be so needy of his approval, and it's embarrassing.

Joanie winks at me. "I know that, babe. We wouldn't be friends if you were. I'm just giving you a hard time." She lifts her glass and throws up her other finger. "Speaking of which, I am definitely planning on some hard times while we're there, if you know what I mean." She wiggles her eyebrows, then takes a sip of her drink, and I can't help laughing.

"And that's why I booked separate rooms," I remind her. "Just, you know, try not to abandon me the whole time, okay?"

Joanie tilts her head. "Or you could get some too," she suggests.

"I could," I agree. "But I probably won't. I mean, how do you jump someone you just met like that?" I'm no prude, far from it, but I've never managed casual hookups. Maybe it takes me too long to warm up to someone. Maybe I'm too high-strung. I don't know.

"Booze," she says simply. She puts a jalapeño popper in her mouth and chews thoughtfully for a minute. "Look, babe. Life is short. You're almost thirty. I get that our jobs are demanding and finding time for relationships is hard, but don't deprive yourself. If you want sex, go out and get it. It doesn't need to be a big deal."

"Oh god, I'm almost thirty," I gasp.

She cackles. "You forgot? Your birthday is next month, babe."

"I ..." A chilling sensation settles in my stomach. "Yes, I forgot." It comes out a whisper. Because I'm floored. I've been so busy, and I never really focus on my birthday. But I'm turning thirty.

My twenties are almost gone.

Holy. Fucking. Shit.

"You okay over there?" she asks, eyeing me suspiciously.

I raise my eyes back up to meet hers. "I ... don't know," I admit.

"Early life crisis?" she asks knowingly. Joanie is two years older than me, so she's been there.

"I just … holy shit, Jo, what am I even doing with my life? I've wasted my twenties!"

Joanie considers me for a minute. "Not yet, Mia. Not yet." She raises one slender eyebrow and gives me a feline grin. And I know she's already thinking of what she can do for our vacation to end my twenties with a bang. Or, given her history, lots of bangs.

I'm not sure I'm ready for whatever I just unleashed.

But I'm about to be thirty.

Holy.

Fucking.

Shit.

I can't stop thinking those three words.

I always thought my twenties were going to be the highlight of my life. My teens were just awkward and I was so focused on getting into a good college, then succeeding there. But when I finally finished my education and graduated law school, I thought sure, it would be a lot of work, but I'd have my own money for the first time. I'd have more freedom. More confidence. More fun traveling, dating, going out to nice restaurants, and all the other great perks of being an independent adult.

Looking back though, pretty much none of that except the money happened. Everything else was usurped by the almighty case load.

If I felt overworked before, now I'm just pissed. I wasted my twenties on a fucking *job*? One I'm not even sure I care all that much about, at the end of the day? Holy. Fucking. Shit.

Ready or not, Joanie is right. It's about damn time I stopped wasting my life.

Even though my flight isn't until Sunday, I leave early Saturday morning. The plan is to go visit my Gran overnight to avoid my dad and any potential last-minute trip-ruining surprises. I'm leaving so early because I know he is still sleeping after having schmoozed one of our higher-profile clients late into Friday night.

Yes, that's right, I still live with my parents. And I'm almost thirty.

To be fair, "with" isn't exactly right. My parents have a house on Mercer Island. Their lot is huge, for the area anyway, and there's a separate guest house that I moved into when I finished school. It just made sense, since I knew I'd be working for my dad. They had an empty guest house. I needed a place to live. And it would allow us to discuss cases on the commute. Never a moment wasted, that's Dad's motto.

I'm definitely not wasting any this morning. I'm not just dodging Dad, I also haven't seen Gran in weeks. I usually visit every other weekend, as I'm able, but my schedule seems to keep getting worse and worse, so it's been nearly two months.

She's probably my favorite person ever though, since she pretty much raised me and my sister while Dad ran his firm and Mom built her small accounting business once we were in school. She's equal parts sugar and sass, and I never realize how much I miss her until I break free of Seattle and start the two-hour drive into the Cascades to her tiny cabin in the equally tiny former gold mining town of Alpine Ridge.

Deep in the mountains between Leavenworth and Ellensburg, it was originally a vacation home that she moved into once Gramps passed about five years ago. It's rife with memories of my sister and I going there with our parents every summer for hiking, visiting the enchanting Bavarian village that is Leavenworth, Washington, and heading to Lake Wenatchee to camp and play in the water.

At the second thought of my sister, I shake my head. Even after a year and a half of heading up here without her, it's still weird. Carrie's in graduate school, which has pretty much held all of her attention these past eighteen months. In some ways I miss her, but in others it's a relief. She's the baby of the family and she acts like it. I've never been one to care about all the material possessions our parents' success has brought, but Carrie loves being spoiled. And boy does Dad love spoiling her. Rotten.

Still, it hurts every time I arrive and watch Gran's eyes land on the passenger seat, hoping her other granddaughter will visit.

Today is no exception, as I pull up to Gran sitting on her porch swing, and her eyes look first to that empty seat before connecting with mine. A lighter blue than my own, they're not the eyes of an eighty-two-year-old woman. They've always radiated youthful energy and intelligence and the spark that is my Gran. The one constant light in my life.

I practically hop out of the car and launch myself into her arms.

"Oh, Gran," I sigh, my voice wavering with all of the emotion of our reunion. It doesn't help that I couldn't stop thinking about my own struggles the whole way here.

"Hi, honey," she greets me, squeezing me tight against her small frame.

I feel something brush against my leg and look down to see Simba, her fat old tabby cat, looking up at me and purring. With a laugh, I break free and reach down to scratch the back of his head.

"Hey, fatty," I purr back at him. He happily rubs his face into my hand.

"You smell good, honey. New perfume?" Gran asks, watching me pet the cat with a smile.

I look back up at her. "Nope. I made cinnamon buns. Want one? You're looking a little thin." I give her a wink.

Gran chuckles. "You're a bad influence, Mia. Whatever am I going to do with you?"

"You know you love it," I joke, heading back down the steps to retrieve the pan from the car, along with the bag I'll need while I'm here. I leave my suitcases for Hawaii in the trunk.

She goes into the house and I follow, setting my bag on the couch as I head into the kitchen with the pan. Gran is already pulling out plates and glasses when I set it down on the small island countertop.

Peeling back the foil gets Gran's attention, and she inhales deeply, closes her eyes, and sighs.

"Those smell amazing," she says with a sigh. Then she gives me a sharp look. "I only break my diet for your pastries, Mia."

"I'm … sorry?" I reply hesitantly.

Gran scoops up a cinnamon bun and takes a huge bite. "Don't be," she mumbles around the doughy, sugary concoction. "It was a compliment."

With a chuckle, I retrieve a pitcher of orange juice from the fridge and fill our glasses.

"Then you're welcome," I tell her, leaning in to grab my own pastry.

The warmth and spices fill my mouth and my heart. There's nothing quite like baked goods to make you forget everything else.

Gran sets down her half-finished roll, wipes her fingers on a napkin, and takes a sip of juice.

"So, are you excited for your trip?" she asks politely.

"I am," I reply with a half-distracted smile.

Because while I am looking forward to it, I still can't stop thinking about the bigger issue. That taking this trip is just the first step toward the kind of life I really want. One where I'm free to do what I like, when I like.

"Then why do you seem so out of sorts?" she asks shrewdly, taking another bite of her cinnamon bun.

I plop the remains of mine down on the plate and suck the sugar crystals off my fingers.

"God, Gran, how do you do that?" I ask, irritated. Even though I know the answer. She just gets me. Always has.

"What's bothering you, honey?" she asks, walking to the small oak dining table on the other side of the kitchen and settling down. I follow, settling in the chair across from her.

"I'm going to be thirty next month," I say, as if that explains everything.

"Yes, I'm aware," she replies drily. "And goodness if that doesn't make me feel old." She pauses. "Is that how you're feeling?"

I tip my head from side to side. "Sort of," I admit. "But it's less about the age and more about everything I've missed out on that I should've done by now."

"Ah," she says knowingly, folding her hands in her lap and giving me a classic Gran look. "Yes, I was wondering when you would get there."

My eyebrows jump in shock. "Pardon me?"

Gran tips her head to the side and sighs. "Oh, honey. You've always been the apple of your father's eye. His pride and joy. But you live to please him, Mia. I knew someday you'd realize that it's your own desires that matter."

There she goes again, getting straight to my exact issue without me having to explain. And even though Joanie has already given me the "seize the day" lecture, something about Gran's blunt insight breaks the dam of emotion inside of me. All the times I've put his wishes first. All the times I didn't bother figuring out my own. All the time wasted on something that's brought me nothing but stress. I put a hand to my mouth as tears well in my eyes. She stands, opening her arms to me. I rise to meet her, wrapping myself in the warmth of her love and affection.

"It's okay, honey, let it out," she urges, rubbing small circles into my back.

I'm not a sobber. And I've never been comfortable showing emotion. So the tears stream out silently, and I only shake a little as I let Gran hold me, as I allow myself to feel the grief of losing such a large part of my life to the desire to make my dad happy.

Finally, I pull away, wiping at my face. "It's not Dad's fault, really," I say, my voice thick with tears. "I just didn't know what else to do. It seemed like the easiest path. But now, I see it was a mistake. A big one. How did I not see that before?"

Gran shakes her head and swipes a hand over my cheek. "You weren't ready. And between you and me, your mother and father are very similar in their selfishness, Mia. I hate to say that about my own daughter and my son-in-law, but they've always been very focused on their own paths, in how their success makes them feel and look. It was natural that your success would make them feel even more validated," she explains. "I guess what I'm saying is, it's made me sad to watch them put their feelings above yours. And it *is* their fault, at least in part. They should've thought more about what was best for *you*. But making mistakes is what growing up is all about. It's what you learn from them that matters most."

I sniff deeply, considering her words. She's not wrong. I've always known that Mom and Dad's influence is where Carrie got her selfish, appearance-focused side.

"Thanks for saying that, Gran. But at the end of the day, I could've said no. I could've made my own way. This is on me."

"Well, whatever you decide to do, you know I'm always here for you," she tells me.

I look at her skeptically. "Even if I decide to quit and move out of the guest house?" I ask. I'm not sure that I'm there yet, because I know how that will go down with both of my parents, Dad especially. Even though I'm almost certain it's what I want. That it's what's best for me.

"I'd be disappointed if you didn't," she says with a twinkle in her eye. "And you always have a room here if you need it." Her tone and words tell me she also knows exactly what will happen if I go that path.

"Thank you," I reply sincerely. "I'm just worried about what I might lose to gain a life that might not be any better."

"You never know until you try."

"But I feel so ungrateful, Gran. I make good money. My future is secure. I want for nothing."

Sorrow fills my grandmother's eyes. "Oh, honey," she breathes. "There's so much more to want that you don't even know is out there yet."

Tears fill my eyes, and I blink hard against them. "What? Cool places to see? Men to … have fun with?" I barely stop myself from saying "men to fuck" in front of my grandmother. "I don't know, Gran. What if it's not worth what I'll be giving up?"

Gran's aged hands wrap around my own. "What if it is?"

I don't have an answer for that, but I know she wasn't really asking for one, because she continues.

"I know you're struggling, and I know this is difficult, but I'm honestly pleased you've finally gotten here. So I'm going to give you some tough love." She looks me square in the eye. "It's the journey, child. The journey of finding yourself, what you want, that's worth it. Not the places you'll see, or the men that will woo you, though those experiences are priceless too. If you're not living a life that's true to yourself just because it's easier, then you're simply not living. So. Now that you've realized what's been going on, even if you don't quit and move out, by the time you come see me again, I want you to have done *something*. Even if it's small. Something that puts you back in the driver's seat of your own life. Do you understand?"

Through the tears that are still stinging my eyes, I burst out laughing. "You're giving me homework?" I ask incredulously. I bend over, clutching my stomach as the laughter rolls through me. It's so *Gran*. This time when I straighten up, I'm wiping away tears of laughter.

Gran's hands are on her hips and she's giving me a stern look.

"You're darn right I am," she says firmly. "This is progress, honey, and I'm not letting you back down now."

This time it's with a smile that I wrap my arms around her. "Thanks, Gran."

She leans in and holds me tight. I don't ask why she didn't challenge me to find my independence sooner. I know I needed to be the one who came to this realization. And it feels good to know that I'm not making something out of nothing, that Gran saw it too — and was apparently waiting for me to see it as well. Waiting to help me live my own life.

The affirmation has done wonders for my state of mind. And by the time I head to the airport on Sunday morning, I'm not just ready for a Hawaiian vacation. I'm ready for the next phase of my life. My real life.

CHAPTER TWO

NATE

"Thank you, Nate, I don't know what I'd do without you," Dorothy says as I finish putting her groceries away.

"You'd manage just fine," I reply, same as I do every Sunday afternoon.

She pats me on the arm and tries to hand me money. Same as always. And I pretend like I don't see it. Same as always.

"At least stay for tea," she insists, relenting and lifting the kettle from the stove to fill it with water.

"Make that coffee, and you have a deal," I agree with a smile. But on my way past the stove toward the dining room table, I get a whiff of something unusual. I turn back to her. "Do I smell … cinnamon rolls?"

Dorothy presses her lips together, looking guilty as sin. "Good lord, were you a bloodhound in a previous life?" she asks, shaking her head.

She flips the burner on for the kettle, then opens the oven door, pulling out a foil-covered tray.

"That's not a baking tray. You were hiding those from me, weren't you?" I accuse her with a teasing smile as I go sit down.

"Unsuccessfully, it would seem," she replies drily. "I take it that you don't want one, then?" I give her a look and she waves me off. "Fine, you eat like a Tibetan monk if you wish. But at least let *me* enjoy myself once in a while."

She puts one on a plate for herself and starts the coffee maker, then joins me at the dining table. I watch her as she starts to eat the pastry. She does look happy. And it does look good. Nothing like the subpar grocery store fare that's pretty much all there is within Dorothy's ability to drive to.

"Where'd you even get that?" I tease. There's another good reason I don't mind doing Dorothy's weekly shopping. Knowing she's been struggling with fatigue and sleeplessness, having some control over what she can eat helps me help her. And we both know she'd eat way too much sugar if left to her own devices.

She sets it down and primly wipes her hands on her napkin. "Mia was here. She left this morning. Shame you weren't here a little earlier. I would've loved to introduce you two." She gives me a pointed look.

One I ignore. Same as always when she tries to get me interested in one of her granddaughters. Or any woman, for that matter. I've explained enough that's not where I'm at right now.

The kettle whistles, saving me from further questioning and my own thoughts, and Dorothy starts to rise, but I gesture that I'll get it.

"So why didn't she do your shopping this week, then?" I ask as I prepare her usual chamomile, then pour myself a cup of coffee. I return, setting her cup down near her to steep, and I take a sip of my own black, fully caffeinated goodness.

"She was barely here for a whole day. I didn't want to bother her," Dorothy deflects, taking the last bite of her treat.

I raise an eyebrow and lean in. "You still haven't told your family, have you?"

Dorothy sighs heavily and finishes chewing before answering.

"There's nothing to tell." She shrugs indifferently.

I scoff. "That's because you're too stubborn to see a doctor."

Her face splits in a smile. "Well, I'm talking to one now — doesn't that count?"

She's suddenly all innocence and sunshine and I can't help chuckling.

"You know it doesn't," I reply.

I haven't practiced medicine for years, and she knows full well that I'm not the kind of doctor she needs.

Simba chooses that moment to jump into my lap, distracting me with the cute. I cuddle him against me, rubbing a finger under his chin until he purrs happily.

Dorothy pulls her cup toward her, dipping the teabag in and out of the hot water before taking a sip.

"I'm sure it's nothing," she says dismissively. "I'm just getting older."

"Maybe. Maybe not. Have you been taking your vitals like I asked?"

The embarrassed look she gives me over another sip says she hasn't.

With a sigh, I rise. "I'll go get the bag out of my truck."

I head outside and grab the black bag I always keep behind the passenger seat, then head back in.

I wash and prep a thermometer and, with a sigh, she opens up and lets me put it under her tongue. I take her blood pressure while it reads and my eyebrows immediately shoot up.

"You're one-seventy-two over one-oh-eight," I tell her. I yank the thermometer out of her mouth. "And you're hovering around a hundred." My eyes snap up to hers. "How are you feeling right now?"

"Still just very tired," she admits. "And I guess I have been feeling a bit warm today."

"Any shortness of breath? Chest pain? Arm? Jaw?" I persist.

She shakes her head. "Nothing like that," she assures me. "I'm probably just worn down."

My turn to shake my head. "From what? You don't go anywhere. Your granddaughter visiting wasn't stressful, was it?"

"Lord, no. Quite the opposite. It always does wonders for me to see Mia."

I give her a look. "Are you telling me you felt *worse* before that?"

"I … yes, this week hasn't been great," she admits.

I pack my instruments back into my bag. "All right, let's go. Emergency room time, young lady."

She smiles, as she always does when I call her that. "Is that really necessary? Why don't I just call in for an appointment this week?"

I hold out a hand to her. "It's necessary. They won't even take appointments until tomorrow, and you'd be lucky to get in anytime soon. We could take you to an urgent care clinic, but the only one around is farther than the hospital. Your vitals are concerning, Dorothy. You need to get checked out as soon as possible."

She takes my hand with a resigned expression, allowing me to help her to her feet. "Fine, if we must, we must," she says with a sigh. "Let's get it over with."

Turns out the sweet and feisty old lady I love gets extremely crotchety when forced to do what she knows she needs to in order to take care of herself, because she refuses to speak to me the whole way to the hospital and through check-in. Doesn't bother me. I may not be an ER doc, but I know a person in distress when I see one.

And the only thought running through my head while I sit in the waiting room is that I should've insisted sooner. Because medical training aside, the waiting part is always the worst. The not knowing. Replaying the past few months of memories in my head, reflecting on her decreased energy, her clear discomfort, and I'm fairly certain she's lost weight too.

It also kind of pisses me off that her family hasn't noticed. To my knowledge, only the one grandkid even visits, and that's only every few weeks or less. And never for long at once. Never long enough to see past the front I'd bet dollars to donuts Dorothy puts on to keep them from realizing that something is wrong. Then she'd have to admit it to herself too.

I'm surprised she's let me as close as she has, but then, she has to have *someone* to rely on. And it's not like I have anything else going on at the moment.

I'm brought out of my thoughts by a nurse approaching purposefully. I stand to meet her.

"Mr. Edwards?" she confirms.

I nod. "Is Dorothy all right?"

"Why don't you come see for yourself? She's asked for you." The slender brunette turns away with a gesture to follow, so I do.

They have Dorothy in a room not far in, hooked into an IV and monitor, looking every bit as cross as she did on the trip here.

I nod my thanks to the nurse as she leaves us alone.

"Looks like they plan to keep you around for a bit," I remark drily, leaning against the doorframe.

"Guess so," she grumbles. "Even though my EKG is fine apparently, and the fever is mild, they took about a gallon of blood and are going to do some chest X-rays."

"That all sounds pretty standard," I assure her. "I wouldn't be too worried."

She hasn't outright said it, not that Dorothy ever would, but I can only assume she hasn't seen a doctor yet because she's afraid of what they might find. So my guess is she's afraid that all these tests mean something bad.

"Pardon me," a voice says from behind me.

I shift upright and turn to see a doctor with a clipboard, clearly looking to get in the room. I step just inside to let him by.

"Mrs. Lewis," he greets her. "I'm Dr. Jacobson." He glances between her and me.

"He can stay," she says, answering his silent question. "Out with it."

Dr. Jacobson turns an amused glance back toward her. "All right, then. Your blood pressure is high. Your fever, while low grade, is still concerning, especially since you tested negative for flu and you don't have any other symptoms that would point us toward a likely culprit. Given your issues the last few weeks, I'd like to get those chest X-rays as soon as possible, and we'll likely need to keep you overnight for observation."

"Overnight? Really? It's just a little fever," she protests.

"Mrs. Lewis, you told the nurse you've been tired for weeks —"

"Months," I interject. "With sleep issues, night sweats, and intermittent high BP. And possible weight loss."

Dr. Jacobson turns to me and raises an eyebrow. "Are you in the medical field, son?"

I bristle at the condescension, since he's *maybe* ten years older than my forty-two years, though I get it. I was around assholes like him long enough to know the drill. Hell, I *was* one of those assholes.

"Retired," I return with as much vitriol as I can inject into the word while flexing every not-inconsiderable muscle in my upper body. While I haven't played this game for years, apparently I'm still not able to resist a little pushback on a challenge.

He makes an indistinct noise of dismissal and turns back to Dorothy. "That all true, Mrs. Lewis?"

"Yes, yes, I'd forgotten about the night sweats."

"So you don't have them every night?"

"No."

"How often?"

She rolls her eyes and sighs. "Once or twice a week? I don't know. I don't sleep well enough to get them anymore."

Dr. Jacobson frowns deeply. Bad poker face for an ER doc. I, on the other hand, keep a straight face even though I'm just as concerned. Probably more so.

"And the weight loss?"

"Just a few pounds," she snaps impatiently. Geez, I've never seen her this cranky.

"How many over the last six months, would you say?"

"Oh, I don't know, ten pounds or so?"

Okay, that shoots my eyebrows up. The woman is five-four, maybe, and has been on the slender side as long as I've known her, putting her not much over a hundred pounds. That's a huge loss for such a tiny person. Especially one who can put away cinnamon rolls like there's no tomorrow. So, her appetite is still good. There's that, at least.

Dorothy answers a few more questions and the X-ray tech comes just as they're wrapping up. I have a seat in the guest chair and wait for her to return.

She comes back looking extra disgruntled from the poking and prodding, so I distract her with some games of Twenty Questions and I'm Going on a Picnic. I haven't played either since my brothers and I were kids. It's surprisingly entertaining for both of us, and it passes the hour or so until the doctor returns, declaring her lungs okay and confirming that she'll need to stay the night.

The real trouble starts about an hour after that when, in the middle of our third game of hangman, a nurse pops in looking harassed.

"Ms. Lewis, a woman who says she's your daughter is here to see you, along with her husband. Shall I let them in?"

"Bossy little thing with curly brown hair?" Dorothy asks.

The nurse presses her lips together, clearly trying not to laugh. Dorothy waves a hand vaguely.

"Yes, yes, let them in."

"Do you want me to go?" I ask.

She shakes her head. "You can stay if you want. Though you may not want to in a minute."

I give her a quizzical look but am stopped short of asking when a tall, middle-aged woman with dark, curly brown hair comes barreling in, pulling an average-looking middle-aged man along behind her.

"Oh good, you're okay," are the first words the woman says.

"Hello, Linda. Yes, I'm fine, thank you for asking." She nods at the man. "Mark." She looks back to her daughter. "How did you even know I was here?"

Linda plops onto the hospital bed near Dorothy's legs.

"I'm your emergency contact, Ma. They called me after you checked in."

Dorothy looks at me questioningly. "Why would they do that if I was awake and you were here?"

Linda and Mark notice me for the first time. Linda sits up straighter and turns the full intensity of her gaze onto me. I can almost feel it searing my skin. Geez, this one is something.

I shrug, and turn my eyes to Dorothy. "Standard procedure?" I guess. "I'm not a family member. And sometimes they're not exactly …" I try to think of a nice way to explain discrimination against the elderly in hospitals.

"They thought I might not have all my marbles," Dorothy deduces wryly. "Great."

"I'm sorry, you are …?" Linda asks.

Dorothy turns back to her daughter. "This is Nate Edwards. He's a friend, and he brought me in today." She gestures between us. "Nate, this is my daughter, Linda, and her husband, Mark."

I nod curtly to them both. "Pleasure to meet you."

Mark steps forward, extending a hand. I rise to take his, shaking it. "Thanks for looking out for her," he says. "But you needn't stay any longer."

I look toward Dorothy. Her eyes plead with me not to leave her with these two.

And I haven't seen anything yet to assure me she'd be in better hands than mine, so I have no plans to go anywhere.

"I know," I reply, sinking back into the chair on the opposite side of the bed without another word.

Linda gives me a dirty look that makes me smile widely in return. She lets out a low but clearly disgusted noise and turns back to her mother.

"So if you feel okay, why'd they call? What's going on?"

Dorothy shrugs. "They don't really know. They haven't found anything yet, I just have a bit of a fever."

There's silence in the room for a beat, save the intermittent beeping of the monitor. This time, I don't interject. It's Dorothy's business how much she wants her family to know.

"Well that's just great. What a cracking medical team they've got here." Linda leans forward and grabs the bed remote, hammering the nurse call button.

A few moments later, the nurse returns. "What can I do for you?"

"I'd like to speak with my mother's doctor," she insists.

Dorothy rolls her eyes, but that raises my hackles. I lean into Dorothy, talking lowly in her ear. But not too lowly. "Don't worry, he can't talk to her about anything if you don't give permission."

The nurse smirks and Linda's head snaps toward me. "I heard that."

I lean back into my chair and smile. "I meant for you to."

"I'll just go get Dr. Jacobson," the nurse says, ducking out the door.

We sit in stony silence until he enters. Well, Linda does. The rest of us tolerate it.

Dr. Jacobson enters soon after, looking a bit confused. "Did you have a question?"

I lay a hand on Dorothy's arm, looking pointedly at her daughter as a reminder that she doesn't need to let her stay for this part. Dorothy's other hand snakes over mine, squeezing it.

"Linda, Mark, would you two be dears and go get me some ice water?" Dorothy asks in a tone that makes it very clear she's trying to get rid of them.

Linda's mouth opens and closes, then opens again. "Why does he get to stay?" Her chin jerks toward me, and I swear she sounds more like a four-year-old than a woman in her fifties.

"Nate is a friend *and* a doctor," Dorothy says firmly. "I'd like his counsel."

I try not to look smug, I really do. But when Linda throws me one last glance before rising, I can't help give her a self-satisfied smile. I'm not usually so petty, but some people just bring that out, I guess.

Finally, once they've left, Dorothy asks why they were called. With no good answer, I pipe in for her.

"Is there any reason she'll need family around?"

Dr. Jacobson looks between us. "We drew blood, but we won't have full results until tomorrow. In any case, since the fever hasn't come down despite treatment over the last few hours, I'm thinking we'll want to continue her on it for a few days and see how she responds. But she won't be able to drive and it would be best if someone stayed with her to make sure she doesn't overexert herself or have any ill effects from the drugs, as she may be pretty woozy."

"Woozy? Is that a technical term?" Dorothy asks with a chuckle, clearly using humor to deflect her discomfort at the thought of having to rely so much on anyone.

Dr. Jacobson smiles.

I put my hand on Dorothy's arm again. "I'm happy to stay with you. Just so you know you have options."

Her hand finds mine again. "Thank you, Nate." She tilts her head back toward Dr. Jacobson. "And thank you, Doctor."

He gives a brisk nod and, sensing the dismissal, leaves. Almost immediately, Linda and Mark reenter. With no ice water.

"Well, I hope you had a nice little chat," Linda says sharply, clearly still pouting. It strikes me suddenly how quiet Mark is every time his wife throws her little hissy fits. And how unlike Dorothy Linda is.

"We did," Dorothy replies sweetly. "Long story short, I'll be here overnight, then Nate will watch over me the next few days while I take a course of medicine that should handle the fever. So you needn't stay, honey."

Mark nudges his wife, who gives him a resigned and very disgruntled look.

"Nonsense, Dorothy," Mark says. "With all due respect to Nate, we'd feel much better if you were taken care of by family."

Dorothy's expression softens. "I would love that," she says softly.

Linda beams. "Then it's settled. We'll call Mia and get her here before you're discharged tomorrow."

Dorothy's expression changes in an instant. And even though I've got nearly a foot in height and more than a hundred pounds of pure muscle on her, the expression on her face scares even me.

"You will do no such thing," she says in a stern voice I've never heard come out of her mouth.

"Be reasonable, Ma," Linda says, suddenly all soft and sweet. "You love Mia, and Mark and I both have jobs we can't just walk away from for a few days. And Carrie's got her studies, after all."

"Of course I love Mia," she snaps. "I think the better question is, do *you*?" She looks sternly between the two of them.

"What kind of question is that?" Mark says, looking all butt-hurt.

It's all I can do not to roll my eyes. But I don't. I'm a fly on the wall right now. Or, I'm trying to be. This is some family drama I have zero intention of getting in the middle of.

"A highly valid one. That girl needs a break, and I have someone who will take perfectly good care of me."

Dorothy's blood pressure monitor beeps loudly.

I lay a hand on her arm. "Let's just talk about this later, okay?" I suggest calmly. "Nothing needs to be decided right now."

"Nate is right, Ma," Linda says flippantly, rising from the bed. "It's almost dinner time. We'll go check into a hotel nearby, we can all have some dinner. Then we'll be back in the morning to take care of you. Don't worry about anything, okay?"

Dorothy looks at her skeptically.

"All right, then."

Linda leans in and kisses her mother on the forehead. "We love you. You'll be all better soon, you'll see."

With a small wave from Mark, they both disappear out the door.

"Well, that was fun. Shall we follow that raging party with some hospital food?" I tease.

Dorothy huffs a dry laugh. "I guarantee you it's going to be a lot easier to swallow than those two."

I laugh too. At least she's still got her sense of humor. Clearly, she's going to need it.

CHAPTER THREE

MIA

"Holy. Fucking. Shit."

I can't help when the words tumble out of my mouth as we hit the full expanse of Waikiki beach. It's stunning. Light sand, water that's a crystalline blue color I've never seen outside of a pool, and scantily clad sunbathers dotted all over the beach in both directions.

"Welcome to paradise," Joanie says with a grin. "Now let's get our sun, sand, and fun on, bitch."

I laugh, finally feeling carefree after the stress of traveling. Finally feeling like the fun really can begin. Trying not to feel like all this humidity is going to give me scary hair.

Joanie pulls us down the beach for longer than makes sense, until she finally settles on a spot a little closer to the water than I'd think is wise.

"Uh, Jo?" I ask, pointing back at a shady spot under some palm trees, farther back on the beach. "Why don't we lie there? Unless you *want* to look like a lobster later."

She gives me a look and jerks her chin toward the waves. I look up and see two guys on surfboards paddling out. All I can see from here is that have nice asses. I'm sure that's all Joanie needs to know.

"If we're back there, we'll be too far for them to see when they come in," she explains as if talking to a child. She spreads out her rainbow-colored towel and proceeds to plop on it, starting to spread sunblock all over her slender body. "Help me with my back?" She holds up the bottle, and with a sigh, I drop my bag on the sand next to her towel and take it.

Once we're both slathered up, we lie down on our towels and soak in the sun for a while.

"Now all we need is the piña coladas," I murmur.

"Ah," Joanie says, rising to a sitting position. She roots through her tote and pulls out what looks like a small, insulated bag. From it emerge two stainless steel tumblers with lids, which she replaces with straw tops. She hands me one with a grin. "I've got you covered."

I take it reluctantly. "Are we allowed to have alcohol on the beach?" I ask tentatively.

Joanie rolls her eyes. "It's nonalcoholic, Mom," she assures me. "We'll get the real thing when we have dinner. Clearly you're going to need some booze to lighten up."

"Oh, I'm light," I assure her, about to drop the bomb I haven't yet been able to, as we'd taken separate flights. "In fact, when we get back, I'm going to tell my dad I'm done living the life he picked for me. I'm going to quit my job."

Joanie chokes on the sip she was taking. "I'm sorry, did I just hear you correctly? Daddy's little girl is going to tell him where he can shove his ridiculous expectations?"

I throw my hands up. "Why did nobody tell me they thought he was out of line?"

"Gran?" she asks with a sly grin.

"Yes," I grumble.

Joanie chuckles. "Because we both know you're stubborn as hell, Mia. You wouldn't have listened anyway."

I pull a face. "I fucking hate it when you're right."

"Thank you for supporting my case, counselor. That's exactly why you had to figure this out yourself." She purses her lips and gives me an *I told you so* expression. "So, what next?"

I take a deep sip of my drink that, despite being delicious, I suddenly wish had lots and lots of alcohol in it. This is the part where, even though I've decided I want a different life, I haven't exactly figured out what that life will look like. Like, at all.

"I don't know," I admit nervously. "And that's what scares me most. I just know my dad is going to shit all over me if I don't have some solid reason, a real plan for why I'm doing this, what I'm going to get out of it."

"Ugh," she groans, reaching over and smacking me on the arm. "Wake up! This is the same shit that got you here. You don't owe him an explanation. You don't have to have a plan. You've finally realized you're a hamster on a wheel, and you want to roam free. How can you possibly be expected to know where you want to go, what you want to do, when your captors have kept you safely confined in their little hamster house?"

I look at her in horror. "For the love of god, Jo, please don't ever compare me to a hamster again." I know everyone else thinks they're cute, but I hate them. They bite and they pee all over everything.

She waves a hand, brushing me off. "You know what I mean."

I shake my head. "Yes. Yes, I do," I admit begrudgingly. "I guess it's going to be a shitshow either way."

"Well, let me know when you're going to do it and I'll be ready for however you need to recover from the ordeal. I'm thinking Vegas, strippers, and —"

I throw up a hand, really not wanting to hear the end of that sentence.

"Let's just enjoy Hawaii first, shall we?" I suggest.

"Oh, we shall," she agrees. "We've got dinner reservations for four at Roy's tonight."

"Four?" I ask, though I should know better. Because before she can respond, the two surfers who have been catching waves in front of us emerge from the water, dripping, sexy as hell, and making eyes at us. Joanie is good.

They stick their boards in the sand between us and the water and approach with grins on their faces. The closer they get, the more my stomach churns. I am so not good at flirting. Thank god Joanie is here.

"Hey ladies, lookin' good," the shorter one calls as they approach.

Joanie props herself up on her elbows, adjusting her bright yellow bikini top, and looks at him over her sunglasses.

"And you guys looked pretty good out there," she replies back in what I know is her sultry voice.

Both guys have rich, glowing brown skin, killer smiles, short, wavy brown hair, and gorgeous Polynesian features. Well-muscled but not over-the-top ripped, they're pretty damn nice to look at.

"Yeah? You wanna learn how to surf?" he asks her, plopping down on the sand next to her.

"I don't know, you gonna teach me?" she asks coyly.

One of his dark brows lifts. "Oh, I could teach you a thing or two," he agrees, licking his lips.

Joanie titters and starts to introduce herself, but I'm distracted by a buzzing in my bag.

I fish out my cellphone and see my mom's profile pic flashing on the screen. I roll my eyes and mumble something along the lines of "be right back" before rising and loping down the beach. So I can put a stop to whatever tactic she's trying to pull to get me to work on my vacation. I was expecting it, so my resolve is strong.

When I'm far enough away to avoid being overheard by Joanie and her new friends, I answer.

"If Dad asked you to try to get me to do work while I'm on vacation, the answer is no," I say right out of the gate.

"That's not why I'm calling," my mother says tersely, and something about the tone of her voice unnerves me. "My mother's in the hospital, Mia. I'm sorry to ruin your vacation, but you need to come home immediately."

My heart drops into my stomach and a lump forms in my throat. "I'm on my way."

⚜

Joanie was, naturally, just as concerned as I was, so she gave me zero shit for having to bail on the very first day of vacation. It's almost five o'clock by the time I get to the airport after racing back to the hotel room, cleaning up, and checking out, then heading back to the airport I just came into this morning. There's a flight out at six, which I just make after getting through security and finding the gate at the far end of the terminal.

As we take off, I calculate the path in my head. We'll land in Seattle just after two a.m. It'll take me at least thirty minutes to get out of the airport. Another fifteen to get to the lot my car is parked in and hit the road. Two hours to Ellensburg. So I should be there around five a.m. tomorrow.

I'm sick with worry the whole flight, unable to eat or sleep. Mom gave no details, and I didn't waste time asking for them. Gran has always been as healthy as a horse, save a knee injury a few years back, but she is getting up there in years. I can only hope that whatever it is, she's going to be okay.

When I finally get into Seattle and make it to my car, I'm tempted to call my parents. But it's basically the middle of the night, so I text them that I've arrived, am on the way to the hospital, and will call them when I get there. They're both usually up by then anyway.

And then I drive. I try not to think about the fact that I've been up for almost twenty-four hours at this point. Gran is in the hospital, and I need to get there. That's all that matters.

I crack the windows to let the cool early morning air wake me. I sip on the dregs of the now-cold extra-large coffee I picked up at a drive-through on my way out of the city. It's just enough, and I make it to the hospital a little after five-fifteen.

I call my mom first and she answers right away.

"Oh good, you're finally here," she says without preamble.

Part of me is irritated that she thinks I could get here any faster, but I have bigger concerns right now.

"I'm at the hospital. Where are you?" I ask.

"Your father and I are at a hotel just down the road. We'll leave in a few minutes and meet you in the parking lot," she explains.

"Is Carrie here?"

"No, dear, she's got finals to study for," my mother says impatiently, as if that should be obvious.

Something bothers me about that, beyond the obvious, but I shake my head, simply trying to stay awake at this point. "Okay, fine, whatever, just get here soon, okay?"

"I just said we were leaving," my mother replies impatiently.

My jaw tightens. "See you soon then." And I hang up. Because I just can't take anymore. My mother and I have always had a difficult relationship, which is part of the reason I've always been such a daddy's girl, but you'd think a family emergency would bring people closer together. Guess not.

I lean my head back against the head rest and let my eyes slide closed.

I must've drifted off, because a sharp rap on my window startles me awake. A glance at the dashboard clock tells me it was only a few minutes though. I look up to see my mom staring in at me, so I get out.

"How could you possibly be sleeping right now?" she asks, shaking her head.

"Because I've been awake for more than a day?" I snap back.

My dad comes around her and hugs me. "Hi, pumpkin. Thanks for coming."

"Of course," I reply, squeezing him back. "Can we see her now please? I'm kind of freaking out here."

"Don't worry, she's going to be okay," Dad says earnestly, leading us in through the sliding door entrance.

"What happened?" I ask.

"She was feeling sick yesterday and had a friend in town take her into the hospital," he explains.

We get to the information counter and Mom signs in. The person behind the counter buzzes us through the locked doors, and Mom opens them so Dad and I can walk through.

"So do they know what it is?" I ask, ready to implode.

Dad shakes his head. "It sounds like they've ruled out anything life-threatening," he says. "They wanted to keep her overnight for observation, but she can go home today."

I stop in my tracks.

"Wait. So … I'm confused. She can go home? Does that mean it's not that serious?"

This time, Mom answers. "They're not sure. They're going to give her some medication to help keep the fever down, but she'll need to be watched for the next few days."

She gestures to the door we've stopped at.

And it suddenly clicks why it bothered me that Carrie isn't here. Because on some level I think I realized that meant Gran is okay, more or less. That it's not that serious, or they'd have told her to come too. And after what Mom just said, my stomach drops for a whole other reason as I realize why I'm here.

"You want me to stay with Gran."

Dad pats me on the shoulder. "I knew you'd understand. Her friend offered, but it should really be family, don't you think?"

My jaw drops. "You called me back from vacation for this? Why couldn't one of you do it?" I wave toward Mom. "She's your mother, after all. Don't you want to make sure she's okay?"

My mom shakes her head like my suggestion is obviously ridiculous. "I have a business to run, and so does your father," she says in a chastising tone. "You were lying on a beach, Mia. Just do this, for Gran."

I grind my teeth as I realize they not only pulled me away from the only vacation I've had in eight years — well, would've had — but also clearly purposely made it seem like the situation was more dire than it was. And now they're not even asking for my help, they simply expect that I'll do what they tell me to.

But then, why wouldn't they? I always have.

I'm about to drastically shift their reality when the door to Gran's room open and a man steps out. We all turn to look at him.

My parents don't seem surprised to see him. I, however, am both surprised and distracted. He's tall, well over six feet, and looks like a bodybuilder. With shaggy, light-brown hair and hazel eyes, he's dressed in sweats and a T-shirt that clings in places I'm not ready to deal with in my current state of mind. The sudden appearance of this smoking hot stranger has drawn my anger toward him.

"Who the hell are you?" I ask sharply.

He raises an eyebrow. "Sorry to interrupt, I heard voices." He extends a hand toward me. "I'm Nate Edwards. I brought your grandmother in yesterday. You must be Mia."

I look at my mother, then at my father. This is Gran's friend. And they've obviously already told him I'd be arriving, and probably that I'd be Gran's new babysitter. I take a subtle deep breath and calm myself down by remembering that this isn't his fault. That he helped Gran.

I slip my hand in his. "Thank you for helping my grandmother," I reply. I can't help the tension in my voice. I'm just so angry, but it's at my parents. I can only hope he doesn't think it's about him. His facial expression is unreadable.

He lets go and nods to my parents in greeting. Obviously, he's a man of few words.

My dad turns to me and kisses me on the forehead. "Well, now that you're here, we should get back to Seattle. Let us know if you need anything, okay?" But he's already walking off, and if I know my father, he's just being polite and assumes I'll happily take care of everything.

My mom doesn't say anything, she just turns to leave.

"Bye, Mom," I say with an edge to my voice.

She turns and gives a faint smile. "Goodbye, dear. We'll be in touch to see how she's doing." And then she follows Dad out of the sliding doors. Just like that.

My parents, ladies and gentlemen.

Nate is silent beside me. I turn to him, beyond exhausted.

"How's she doing?" I ask.

"Still sleeping. You look like you could use some sleep too."

I give a faint smile. "Understatement."

He hooks a thumb over his shoulder, gesturing down the long hallway. "There's a crash room. Number eighteen, end of the hall, just around the corner. I'll come get you when she wakes up."

I contemplate that for a moment. But Gran's usually an early riser and I want to be there when she wakes up.

"Thanks, but I'll be fine."

The corner of Nate's mouth lifts and he looks like he wants to say something, but then thinks better of it. "If you're sure. Dorothy's got my number if you need anything."

I nod. "I'm sure. Thanks again. It was nice to meet you, Nate."

"Mia." He dips his head in parting and leaves. Almost as abruptly as my parents.

What is with that? Do I exude some sort of pheromone that leaves people with the impression that I'm so capable of handling whatever it is that needs handling that they barely need to say two words to me about it? I guess some girls get the pheromones that would actually attract a guy that hot. And I get the ones that send him packing. Awesome.

I squeeze my fists, close my eyes, and take a deep breath in through the nose, then let it out through my mouth. Gran needs someone right now. And even though my parents are perfectly capable of rearranging their schedules, clearly she is not their priority. Thankfully she is mine, though. And that's all that matters at the moment.

Not the anger I feel toward my parents for assuming I'll do their bidding. Nor the frustration I feel for losing what was promising to be a very exciting vacation. Or the embarrassment I feel meeting Nate, a total — very attractive — stranger, who just got a window into the worst version of myself, equal parts uncaring jerk and doormat. Because as soon as I open the door, I can see and feel that it's paper thin and hollow, so I'm sure he heard everything. Fantastic.

What I also observe is Gran, hooked up to a bunch of machines and clothed in a hospital gown, lying under a blanket. In the giant mechanical bed, under the dim lighting, she looks every single day of her eighty-two years, and my heart swells with concern.

But I don't wake her. Instead, I sink into the chair next to her bed and surrender to the overwhelming exhaustion.

CHAPTER FOUR

NATE

I stop on my way out of Ellensburg and get the biggest, blackest coffee the drive-through shack next to the freeway offers. I'm too damn old to have slept in a hard chair all night, but here we are. Time to head home, work out, and get on with my day.

I roll the windows all the way down as I hit the freeway, even though it feels like it's in the forties and I'm only wearing a T-shirt. But I'm both that tired and that worked up. Am I angry at Linda and Mark? Not really. They behaved pretty much like I expected them to this morning.

But Mia. Goddamn, Mia. She's what's got me unhinged.

Dorothy has talked a lot about her granddaughter. I'd even call Mia her favorite, though Dorothy would never admit that. But when what you're told is skewed by the grandma lens, there's no knowing what reality is. And I honestly never planned on meeting the woman. Despite Dorothy's intentions, I don't date. I'm retired. From everything.

Hearing her in that hallway, arguing with her parents, I couldn't tell if she was a spoiled brat or if that was simply her dynamic with her parents. Either or both would make sense based on my own experience with them the night before.

But as soon as her eyes locked on mine, as soon as I saw the intelligence, the fire in them as she demanded to know *who the hell I was*, I knew she was no pushover. I knew she was no spoiled princess. This was a woman who has been denying her fire and it was starting to burn her alive from the inside out.

I know, because I've been there.

It was more than that, though. I felt ... protective of her. Between their conversation with Dorothy and what I heard this morning, they're clearly used to bossing her around and having her take it.

Does that make her a pushover? Maybe in some people's books. But that's something I have experienced: the desire to please others that runs so deep and dark that it dims the light of your own soul, your own desires. And something in me wanted to save her from that.

On some level I understand that need stemmed from wanting to do for her what I couldn't do for myself until it was too late. And maybe I'm projecting a little bit.

Though my problem was never with my parents. They were, and are to this day, a stable source of loving support. Would that I could say the same for the rest of the world.

Mia, though. With a few sentences, my world shifted. Something inside of me shifted. Maybe it was recognizing the demons I've faced in her eyes. Or maybe it was just those bright ocean-blue eyes, that long wavy chocolate hair, and that ridiculously curvy body that should come with a warning label.

Yes, that had to be it. I'm still a man, after all. I may have retired from life, but apparently my dick didn't get the memo.

CHAPTER FIVE

MIA

I'm woken by Gran's doctor entering the room. But as soon as I open my eyes, I can see that she's been awake for some time. And she looks disappointed. As if she heard the exchange in the hallway too. Or perhaps my mere presence is enough.

The doctor checks her over and explains that they're still waiting for the rest of her blood test results. Since it was a Sunday night, and her vitals looked good despite the fever, which has since come down, they didn't expedite them all. He gives me the okay to take her home and explains the routine for the pills she needs to take, assuring me that we should hear back later today on the remaining tests so they know who to schedule her follow-up with and for when.

As soon as he's gone, I turn to apologize, but she holds up a hand.

"Why don't you go wait for me in the hall? I'll get dressed and we can go. I don't think we should discuss anything right now. Not yet. Not here."

I nod, blinking back tears, terrified that I've upset her during an already difficult time. "Okay," I say softly.

I stand in the hallway like I'm being punished at school. And when Gran joins me, we walk silently out of the hospital. Into the car. Back on the road to Alpine Ridge. I wonder for a bit if she's going to be silent the whole half hour it'll take to get her home. I don't have to wonder long.

"What are you doing here, honey?" she asks after a few minutes.

I shoot her a bemused glance before returning my eyes to the road.

"I'm here to help you," I reply. "I'm guessing that means you *didn't* hear me talking to Mom and Dad in the hall outside your room this morning?"

"Oh, so they actually stayed all the way until this morning, did they?" she asks drolly.

Relieved that she didn't hear me and think I didn't want to be here, I let out a laugh. "Yes, well, that's how long it took me to get here from Hawaii. They seemed pretty put out that I wasn't magically able to make airplanes go faster."

Gran lays a hand on my knee. "I'm so sorry they put this on you. You don't have to stay. Nate will take care of me."

I shake my head. "I'm here, I might as well stay. I *want* to stay, okay?"

I watch Gran run her hands over her face out of the corner of my eye.

"If you're sure," she finally says. "You know I'm always happy to see you. I just don't want this to derail your new plan. Except it already has." She presses her lips together and releases a sigh out of her nose.

I don't respond. I don't know what to say. She's not wrong. But I'm trying not to focus on missing out on Hawaii. If I really do go through with my new plan, I can go ahead and quit anytime now. The plan was to quit when I got back. And now I'm back. But I don't want to add to Gran's stress. Clearly she's got enough on her plate, because she didn't even ask for a progress report on my homework. The thought makes me smile, because it reminds me how much she really cares.

I reach out and give her hand a brief squeeze.

"Don't worry about me," I assure her. "Let's just focus on you right now, okay? I'm not going anywhere until I know you'll be all right."

"I'll be fine. I have plenty of people here who can help me if I need it, you know. Even if your parents are too busy to be here, I'll manage," she replies, and I can practically hear her rolling her eyes.

"First of all, I don't have anything to do that's more important than being with you right now," I assure her. "Second of all, I'm going to need to know more about this 'friend' Nate you've got. How'd you meet? Is he your boyfriend?"

She smacks me on the arm and I laugh.

"Heavens, no, Mia, what on earth are you thinking? The man is half my age," she chastises me. "He helped me rehab my knee after my injury, if you must know."

Well, if he's a physical therapist or something along those lines, that might explain why she called him for a medical issue. I guess.

Alpine Ridge is a town of less than ten thousand people, so there's no hospital or even a clinic that I'm aware of. I'm sure an ambulance would've come for her, but Gran is made of tough stuff, and I have no doubt that she'd find an ambulance overkill.

"Hey, I wouldn't judge if he were," I tease. "Either way, I'm glad you had someone to help you. But I promise. I want to be here. So please, let me be here. Okay, Gran?"

I reach out an open hand, and she takes it.

"Okay. But only if you make more cinnamon buns."

I chuckle. "Deal."

We hear back that afternoon on Gran's blood tests. They're a bit concerned about some of her levels, so they schedule her to come back in in two days' time for a full exam and more tests. I spend the rest of the day cooking and baking before getting Gran her evening meds and tucking her in for the night. Simba quickly curls up next to her, and I give him a scratch behind the ears before I leave.

Then I settle in myself with a book and read until I fall asleep.

It's a pattern that repeats the following day, then Wednesday after breakfast we head into Ellensburg again for Gran's appointment. I don't go in with her, and she doesn't talk much about it afterward.

Not even on the car ride back when I ask.

"So have you heard from your parents?" she asks in a clear bid to take the attention off herself.

"What do you think?" I ask, the *no* implied by my tone.

"And you're not going to call them?"

"They said they'd be in touch. If they can't be fussed, I have no reason to call them until we have something definitive to share." I glance over at her. "Do you have anything you want me to share with them?"

She gives me a stern look. "Well played, Mia, but if there was something I wanted to share, you'd be the first to hear about it."

I grin at her use of my first name. She almost always calls me "honey." I must've really annoyed her.

"Seriously, though," I continue. "I'm supposed to be back at work on Monday. So I'll call on Friday if I haven't heard from them."

Gran's head snaps toward me. "Oh, really? To say what?"

I smile and roll my eyes. "To quit, Gran. I hadn't planned on going back, and that was *before* their recent epic demonstration of selfishness."

"Bravo, darling," she says, her voice bursting with pride. "Bravo."

We make small talk the rest of the ride back, but when we get to her house, there's a vehicle in the dirt driveway. A truck. A big one.

We climb out and I see Nate on the porch, looking much like he did at the hospital. Sweats and T-shirts must be his uniform.

"Nate," Gran calls joyfully. "So nice of you to drop by. I do hope you haven't been waiting long."

He smiles and I swear it's like I'm looking at a different person. Suddenly he looks younger, and a lot more attractive. I mean, he was attractive to start but … *That's enough, Mia*, I chastise myself. God, even my internal dialogue can't handle itself today.

"Just wanted to see how you are," he replies. His tone is lighter, too, making him seem much more approachable.

"You're such a dear," Gran croons as she climbs the steps and stands next to him. "You've met Mia." She gestures toward me and I give a small self-conscious wave.

He nods curtly, "Mia." And the Nate I met is back.

"Do come in and visit," Gran encourages him.

"I'd love to," he says, looking at her once more. They both go in ahead of me, and I follow, feeling a bit like a tagalong.

She leads us into the living room, gesturing for him to have a seat.

"Would you like a chocolate muffin? Mia made them just this morning."

"Thanks, but you know I don't eat wheat," he responds.

"They're gluten free," I tell him. He opens his mouth. "And dairy free," I add, anticipating his next objection. He gives me an odd look. Is he really that surprised?

I'm not an idiot. I know you don't get a body like his by eating junk food. And though I'll never be nearly as in shape as he is, I do try. Sometimes.

"Are they really?" Gran asks, looking scandalized.

I chuckle. "Yes, Gran, I've been sneaking you health food. You caught me."

"Well, they sure taste like the real thing," she says, wandering into the kitchen and adding a few small plates with napkins to the tray the muffins are on before bringing it into the living room. "Now I guess you *have* to try one."

She winks at Nate. Gran is a winker, so I'm not surprised. I am, however, surprised as shit when he winks back. He certainly has a way with the old ladies.

"Guess so," he agrees.

I wait nervously as he takes a bite. I'm not sure why. I know I'm a good baker; I don't need his approval. But when his eyes meet mine, I see it in his expression. And it makes me more satisfied than I'd like to admit.

"This is *really* good," he says with a note of awe in his voice.

"Thank you," I reply demurely, even though I want to give him crap for sounding so surprised.

Gran rises from the couch. "If you two will excuse me for a few minutes, I need to freshen up after our trip."

We both nod and she heads to her room. The thought crosses my mind that she's simply trying to leave us alone together. Oh, lord. Did she tell him to be here when we got back? Is she trying to set me up?

"Did you really just come to check on her, or did she ask you to be here?" I blurt out.

Nate sets his now-empty plate down and smirks. "I really did just come to check on her. How is she?"

I eye him skeptically for a moment longer before responding. "She seems okay, if a bit tired," I finally reply. "We just went back for an exam and more tests, so I guess we'll see."

"It's kind of you to look after her," he responds.

I bristle. "Look, I know what you heard in the hall on Monday, but you should know —"

Nate holds up a hand. "You don't need to explain yourself to me."

I open my mouth to protest before realizing he's right. I don't. Not really.

"I know," I admit. "But you're friends with my grandmother. And you deserve to know that I'm not looking after her because I'm kind — well, I mean, I can be kind, but ... anyway, that's not the point. I'm not here because my parents basically demanded it. I'm a grown woman, after all. I'm here because I love her and I *want* to be here for her. There are just some ... issues with my parents that I've been avoiding until recently. That's what that was about."

I clamp my mouth shut suddenly, berating myself for talking about it with this guy. Why do I care what he thinks? And why can't I shut up?

Nate studies me for a minute, and I feel the heat creeping up my neck. Something about him totally unseats me and turns me into a self-conscious ball of blathering goo.

"I met your parents on Sunday night," he finally replies. "I wasn't the least bit surprised at anything they said on Monday."

My brow furrows as I process that. Sooo … he gets that they're selfish jerks and he wasn't surprised that they dumped the responsibility on me? Okay. Great. And funny how that fact seemed to be obvious to everyone but me until now. Though I don't miss he didn't say a word about his assessment of me.

"I'm not going to apologize for them being assholes," I respond. "But I will apologize for sounding less than enthused about taking care of Gran. I was just … well, there's no excuse. But I'm not that person. I promise. You don't have to worry about her while I'm here. That's all."

He does that assessing glance thing again and I want to shrink inside myself. How can I be faced with judges, irate spouses, and overbearing attorneys on a daily basis and not flinch, but one look from this guy and I feel like he can see everything I am and am not? Quiet people. It's a gift I've never had.

"Good to know."

Good to know? That's it? But I stop the thought in my head, determined not to go back to verbal diarrhea mode.

Thankfully, Gran returns, but she pauses between where he's sitting on the couch and where I'm standing across the coffee table and looks between us both. I'm sure there's a weird vibe in the room that she's picking up on.

"I'm going to go clean up too and let you guys catch up now," I offer, doing my best not to show my embarrassment. And to avoid Gran's knowing gaze.

Before either of them can say a word, I duck into the hall and take a deep breath, trying to stop the shakes from coming.

Well, that was nerve-racking.

My plan really was to shower, but when I put my phone on the dresser I see a missed call. I forgot to take it off silent after we left the hospital. The call is from my father, and only a couple of minutes ago.

So I step into lawyer mode and call him back. I'm going to need professional me to keep my shit together.

"Hey, pumpkin," he answers. "How's your Gran doing?"

"Hey, Dad. She seems mostly okay so far. We just got back from a follow-up exam. They're doing some more blood tests. We should have the results in a day or two," I explain.

"Good, great," he responds like he didn't hear a word I said. "I was actually calling to talk to you about a new case. There's a —"

"Stop," I interrupt. "I'm sorry. I didn't want to do this over the phone, but I won't be talking about a new case. I quit." The words rush out, unplanned and with no finesse before I can stop them. I feel horror-struck that I said them. But so, so relieved that it's out there.

Dead silence greets my declaration.

Then, "You can't quit, Mia."

I almost laugh, but stop myself. I'm feeling lighter than I have in, well, years. But I know how difficult letting me go is going to be for my father, and derision won't help matters any.

"I just did," I reply simply.

"There's no reason —"

"There's *every* reason," I interrupt. "I became a lawyer because you wanted me to. I tried it. It's not for me. I'm miserable, Dad. I work *all the time*. I haven't done any of the things I've wanted to do in my life."

"So this is my fault?" he bellows indignantly. It startles me, as he's usually so mild-mannered. Mom is the yeller. Clearly, he's just as upset as I thought he'd be.

But mostly, I realize … I quit and he makes it about him. How could I not see before that it's *always* been about him? I force myself back into lawyer mode, desperately hoping to defuse the situation.

"I'm not assigning blame. Nor does it matter. The fact is, I no longer wish to work as an attorney. I know my decision will be difficult for you to accept, but I'm tendering my resignation as of today. You and Janice will have an email officially documenting the details in your inboxes as soon as our call is over."

"I'm certain your employment contract won't allow you to quit with no notice," he says in a threatening tone. "You can't quit. Who will run the company when I retire, Mia? Do you have any idea how selfish you're being?"

Tears fill my eyes and rage fills my heart. *I'm* being selfish? It's a level of hypocrisy I can't stand. But still, I know rising to the bait and arguing isn't going to help. He argues for a living. And he's been doing it a hell of a lot longer than I have.

"Yes, Dad, I'm completely aware that I'm making a decision that's in my best interest. I'm sorry you're having difficulty accepting that. We can discuss how you're feeling later, but I need to go."

"Mia —"

I end the call before it gets any worse. And before the tears overtake me, I open my email and hit send on the message that's been in my drafts folder since the day I flew to Hawaii. The relief I feel once it's sent tells me I've made the right choice. No matter how much it hurt. Or how much trouble it's about to cause.

CHAPTER SIX

NATE

As soon as Mia leaves the room, I lean back into the couch and level a look at Dorothy.

"That was quite an act you put on," I tell her, knowing everything since her enthusiastic greeting was all a show for Mia. "So, how are you, really?"

"What makes you think it was an act?" she asks with a smile, sinking into the couch herself, finally letting herself look as tired as she clearly is.

"Come on, Dorothy," I chide her. "You know I can read your body language even when you try to hide behind that pretty smile of yours." I give her a wink and she chuckles.

"Charmer," she says accusingly. "I hope you turned some of that on my granddaughter. She could use it."

"I think Mia has enough on her plate," I reply carefully.

"Yes, I suppose she does. Still, she's going to get pretty bored around here, just looking after me. She could use a friend."

"I'm sure she could. I'll mention it to Rae next time I see her. With the baking and all, I'm sure they'd be fast friends."

"I hadn't thought of that," Dorothy replies. "But you're right, I suppose they would."

"What'd the doctor say?"

Dorothy's eyes meet mine. "I have a lump under my arm, Nate. I didn't think anything of it. He thinks it's lymphoma." Her eyes fill with tears, but she brushes them away quickly.

"Hey," I protest, scooting closer and wrapping my hand around hers. "You don't have to pretend with me. It's okay to be upset and afraid. I'd be worried if you weren't. But if that's really what it is, there are worse diagnoses."

"Yeah? Because I hear chemo's a real party," Dorothy says sarcastically. But she lets the tears out, not wiping them away this time.

The corner of my mouth lifts. "If it's not too advanced, they may not even need to do that," I point out. "But if it's what they recommend, it'll be because it gives you the best chance of beating this disease. And, more likely than not, you can."

Dorothy's other hand wraps over mine. "Good. Because I want to see my great-grandbabies someday." She looks at me pointedly.

I laugh. "Oh, Dorothy, you know you're like a grandmother to me. But you're barking up the wrong tree."

"And you're like family to me too, Nate. You've been here for me in a way I've never relied on anyone but my husband before. I know I've asked a lot of you, but I have one more favor I need from you."

My brows pull together. I don't like where she's going with this kind of talk.

"Don't get me wrong, there's pretty much nothing I wouldn't do for you. But it sounds like you're giving up before you even know for sure what you're fighting."

Dorothy smiles grimly. "I'll fight until the end, whenever that may be. But just in case it's sooner than I'd like, I need one more favor."

I blow out a breath, not sure I'm ready for this heavy of a conversation. But I'm not about to let her down either.

"Okay, go ahead."

"This isn't me trying to set you two up again. But Mia's in a difficult place right now. If anything happens to me, promise me you'll look out for her."

A tight feeling spreads in my chest that takes me a minute to name. *Sorrow*. I've heard people talk like this before, when something inside of them recognizes that the end is near. I swallow hard against the lump that's formed in my throat.

"I promise," I finally reply. "As much as she'll let me, anyway."

Dorothy chuckles. "You really have been paying attention, haven't you?" She tilts her head and gives me that look. The one that says she knows every thought I've had around Mia.

But even Dorothy doesn't know why I came to Alpine Ridge. Why I retired. Why I have no plans to be anything but alone. Her request doesn't change that, even though I know she hopes it will.

"You don't have to pay very close attention to know that Mia has a mind of her own," I reply carefully. "But I'll do what I can."

"Thank you," she says, mercifully not pushing the topic any further. Because I know she's noticed how little I talk around Mia.

We say our goodbyes and I leave Dorothy to get some rest. Then I spend the afternoon wondering what it is about Mia that makes me clam up so badly. I don't normally have a problem talking to women. Not even ones as beautiful as her, even if it has been a while.

It finally hits me after my afternoon lifting session. Once I'm too tired to hide behind bullshit excuses. I like her, despite myself. And I'm closing up in a subconscious response to the part of me that wants to open up, to reach for her in every fucking way possible.

Sure, she's gorgeous, but I think it's her unique mix of strength and vulnerability that does it to me. The scared look in her eyes when she climbed out of her car today. Then her rambling explanation of something she never needed to say in the first place. I never thought for a minute she didn't want to be there for her grandmother. But her openness about her issues with her parents surprised me. Most people don't surprise me. In fact, I can't remember the last time anyone did.

Because most people want to pretend everything is okay. They have an innate need to convince everyone else that they're awesome, that they've got everything under control.

Nothing about Mia's explanation displayed that kind of fakeness. Her realness oozes out of every damn pore. Every word rang with the conflict she's facing and the conviction that she's doing her best. Finally naming it helps me realize why I felt protective of her before. Why I feel so pulled to her.

It's not just because I've been there. It's something deeper. On the one hand I understand why Dorothy puts on a front for her. It's love. She doesn't want to worry Mia or make her suffer any more than she has to. But anyone with eyes can see that Mia carries her heart on her sleeve for her grandmother. That she'd do anything for her.

Maybe that's what draws me to her the most. And another reason I need to figure out how to get over my attraction. I'm drawn to her for all selfish reasons. And as I said to Dorothy, Mia has enough on her plate. She doesn't need another selfish person in her life. The best choice I can make for her is to stay away.

CHAPTER SEVEN

MIA

I don't tell Gran that I quit. At least, not right away. I figure I can do it when it comes up naturally. I just don't want to have to go through what Dad and I said to each other yet. Or ever.

But when we get her test results on Thursday, it gets shoved on the back burner. Gran is napping when the doctor's office calls, but since she authorized me on her forms, they tell me that, as suspected, she has levels indicative of lymphoma. I have to go along with the "as suspected" part like I already knew, since Gran hadn't actually filled me in on the doctor's suspicions. I make another appointment for the next day, Friday, for more tests.

As soon as Gran is up from her nap, I make sure I'm in the kitchen waiting.

One look at my face and she turns right around to head back to her room.

"Oh, no, you don't," I call after her.

With a sigh, she stops and turns to face me. "I'm guessing the doctor called?" she asks, heading resignedly into the living room.

"Yes, Gran. And your blood tests point to lymphoma. *Lymphoma*," I stress. "When were you going to tell me?"

Gran sinks onto the couch, crosses her legs, and rests her head on the arm she has propped on the back of the couch. I take a seat at the opposite end, leaning toward her with my hands in my lap.

"I was hoping I wouldn't have to," she admits. "The doctor felt a lump in my armpit. It was either lymphoma, breast cancer, or, less likely, a benign tumor of some sort. But with the placement, fatigue, and fevers, he was leaning lymphoma. I suppose that means we'll be going back soon?"

"Tomorrow," I confirm. "For a biopsy and scans."

"It's really not that big of a deal, honey," Gran says. "Apparently lymphoma responds well to treatment."

"You could've told me," I grumble like a sullen teenager.

She smiles at me. "I didn't want to add to your plate for no reason. Really, I'm not worried, so you shouldn't be either. You have enough to worry about."

I can't help the guilty blush that steals over my cheeks. Because I realize I just got mad at her for hiding something, even though I was too.

"Speaking of which," I respond. "I quit yesterday."

That gets her attention. She smiles sadly, clearly knowing how that probably went down.

"How'd your father take it?"

"Not well."

She nods. "I take it you haven't heard from your mother?"

I shake my head.

"No, you wouldn't have, would you?" she murmurs, seemingly more to herself than anything. Her hand reaches down and traces the pink-stitched rose pattern on the cream couch. "She wasn't always this way. I'm sure you remember how much sweeter she was when you were a child."

"I can't say that I do," I admit. "She's always had high expectations and low sympathy. At least, as far back as I can remember."

"It's a control issue," Gran explains. "She feels better when her life is going according to plan. You can thank your Gramps for that. The older she got, the more he asked of her. I suspect your mother drives a lot of your father's expectations from you. Or they're just cut from the same cloth. The result is the same, in any case. I'm sorry it had to come to this, honey."

"Thanks, Gran. I'll be okay. We'll both be okay." I reach out for her hand and she meets me in the middle, running her thumb over my knuckles.

"We absolutely will, my dear." Her gaze follows her thumb as it continues to stroke the back of my hand. Finally, she looks up. "I was going to tell you, really. But I'd rather not tell your parents. Not until there's something they really need to know."

I open my mouth to reply when my phone starts buzzing in my pocket, so I disentangle my hand to pull it out.

"It's Joanie," I tell Gran.

"Of course, go, talk to your friend," she says, shooing me away.

I smile. "Thanks. I'll go take this in my room."

I walk down the hall and into my bedroom, closing the door behind me.

"Hey, Jo," I answer. "How's Hawaii?"

"Mia! It misses you! I miss you!" She's so loud I have to pull the phone away from my ear.

"Geez, are you drunk?"

There's a clattering. "Noooo." Joanie sounds closer and much quieter now. "Sorry, had you on speaker."

"All righty then. How'd you make out with the hot surfers?" Right now I honestly don't care, but I need a distraction from my own bullshit.

"Oh, Mia, do you really want to know?" she asks coyly.

"You had sex with them both, didn't you?" I return drily.

"Not saying I did, not saying I didn't," she replies, bursting into laughter. "Seriously though, how's your Gran doing? Everything okay?"

I sigh heavily and it all comes pouring out. The awful reception by my parents. Repeatedly embarrassing myself in front of Nate. Gran's potential diagnosis. And finally, quitting my job.

"Damn, I should've called sooner," she says.

"No, it's okay, I'm glad you're having fun," I reply. "And I'm sorry to spoil it. It'll all be okay, I know it will. It's just a lot right now."

"Clearly. How about I come visit next weekend once I'm back?" she offers.

"I'd appreciate that," I admit. "There's not exactly a lot to do here, and only Gran to talk to. I could use a shoulder to cry on."

"Girl, sounds like this Nate guy has some other good stuff you could cry on," she suggests lasciviously.

"That didn't even make sense," I reply with a chuckle.

"You know what I mean," she insists. "I'll make you a deal. I'll visit, you can cry on my shoulder, and *I'll* handle Nate's good stuff."

I roll my eyes and laugh. "Whatever gets you here, Jo." Leave it to Joanie to focus on the hot guy part of this equation.

"Hey, I've got to meet the boys for dinner soon. But I'll call when I'm back, all right? Love you so much, babe, text me if you need to."

"Sure thing. Love you too, Jo. Have fun. Be safe."

"Always am." And then she's gone.

I should feel better. She always makes me feel better.

But not today. Today, my parents are upset with me, my beloved grandmother may have a serious illness, and I have no idea what comes next for any of us.

Friday is even harder. They cut a whole lymph node out of Gran's underarm. They used a local anesthetic, but as it wears off on the ride home, I can tell she's uncomfortable, even if she is trying to be her normal spry self. But just like she sees through my act, I see through hers. Unfortunately, she can't take the pain meds they sent with us until she's had some food.

"I'm sorry, Gran, we should've picked up something to eat on our way out. We can turn back. It's closer right now, and I hate to see you suffer."

Gran huffs. "Don't be silly, I'll be fine," she responds.

And then she proceeds to not say another word for the rest of the ride. It's not like her, which means she must be in more pain than she's letting on. A little ball of helplessness starts to churn in my chest. A tight, sick feeling that this may just be the beginning of being able to do nothing but watch Gran struggle.

I try to push the thought out. Gran is right. We don't know anything for sure yet, so there's no point in worrying.

Especially since her biopsy results won't be back until next week. The scans showed potential issues at multiple lymph nodes that have the doctor concerned, but again it wasn't definitive enough for a diagnosis. He took yet more blood to check specific levels that would help figure out what type of lymphoma she has, how widespread and advanced it is, and all of that, which will also be next week. So until then, I decide I'm going to stay positive.

But first things first, and when we get back to the house, I focus on getting her fed.

"What can I make you for dinner? Roast beef with au jus? A veggie panini?" I ask in the most upbeat voice I can manage. Though I kind of feel like calling it dinner at five p.m. only just qualifies, and I feel anything but upbeat.

Gran shrugs and sinks onto the couch. "I don't feel like much. Just toast, please," she replies.

I prop a hand on my hip and tap my fingers against my jeans, deciding whether I want to push her to eat something more. But she's stubborn, and I know arguing will just make her discomfort worse.

"Fine," I finally reply. "Coming right up."

I make her toast but top it with a layer of peanut butter, thin slices of banana, and a drizzle of honey.

She raises an eyebrow when I hand her the plate but simply says, "Thank you, honey."

With a shake of my head, I head back into the kitchen. After a bit of poking around and planning, I throw together a grocery list for everything I'll need to pull her out of her funk with food this weekend.

"I'm going to the grocery store, need anything?" I ask as I slip a light jacket and shoes on.

That gets Gran's attention. "Now? Whatever for? Did you already run through all of the flour and sugar in the house?" She smirks at me. Well, at least she seems to be feeling better.

I stick my tongue out at her. "As a matter of fact, I may have. And if you want more goodies, I'm going to need to do some shopping. So, I take it there's nothing you need then?"

"There's a list on the side of the fridge," she tells me as she sinks her teeth into the second piece of toast.

I give a triumphant little smile at watching her start in on that second piece before retrieving her list and putting it with my own in my purse. I wave on my way out.

"Have fun," she calls after me.

I snort at her comment, but I doubt she heard me. I haven't been to the grocery store here in years, but if it's anything like I remember, "fun" isn't a word I'd associate with shopping there. Depressing, maybe. All I remember is it being dark, dilapidated, and dreary. Not to mention seriously lacking in selection.

When I pull up about ten minutes later, it's the same lackluster squat, shabby dark wood building complete with wagon wheels at regular intervals all the way around the small structure. The former gold mining/pioneer camp vibe is strong in all of the town's main buildings. I used to think it was fun as a kid.

As I enter, the stock seems as lacking in variety as it always was, so I look skeptically between the lists in my hand and the store. I'm probably going to have to make some concessions. The crystallized ginger for the overnight stuffed French toast may have to be swapped for powdered ginger. If they even have that. And I'll be lucky to find *any* rum, much less the spiced rum I would normally use to make Gran's favorite rum cake.

"Well, hello," a man's voice says, dripping with innuendo.

My head snaps up and my eyes lock on the only person who could've said it. The skeeviest-looking dude I've ever seen stands behind the single register, his eyes roaming freely over every inch of me. It makes my skin crawl instantly.

Probably a few years younger than me, he's thin and short with greasy black hair and beady eyes. I'm too far away to read his name badge, and there's no way in hell I'm getting closer until I have to.

I look around nervously, suddenly realizing the store is almost completely empty. There's one person on the other side, far enough away that I can't tell if it's a man or a woman. Great.

"Hi," I say meekly, grabbing a cart and trying to hurry away.

"Haven't seen you around before," he calls after me. "Just passin' through?"

I hesitate, turning just enough to respond while trying to make it obvious I'm not interested in talking. Or anything when it comes to him.

"No, I'm staying with relatives. Who are expecting me back soon, so I should …" I trail off, gesturing toward the store. I give him a tight smile and quickly hustle into the first aisle.

I make it through three aisles before the hairs on the back of my neck stand up.

"Oh, you don't want that stuff." It's unmistakably the cashier's voice, and I whip around, instinctively drawing my hands up to protect myself.

His eyes drop to the chicken stock I'm holding. Or maybe my boobs. Probably the boobs.

"Why not?" I ask, my eyes darting up and down the aisle, assessing the best way out.

He creeps closer and I step back, but my bottom hits the shelf.

"That organic crap is just a marketing gimmick," he says, taking another step forward, leering at me. He's so close I can smell his rancid breath. He leans in. My heart races as my flight instincts kick in. "Here, let me show you —"

"Mia, there you are."

Cashier dude looks over my shoulder and takes a giant step back. I'm not surprised. I'm pretty sure I recognized the voice. And if I were skeevy cashier dude, I'd take a step back too.

A glance behind me confirms it. Nate. His long legs eating up the floor space between us as he approaches, wearing his usual sweats and T-shirt, this time with a baseball cap over his unruly light-brown hair. I can't remember the last time I was so happy to see someone besides Gran or Joanie. Normally, I'd find the murderous look he's giving the cashier totally over the top, but right now? He's my knight in shining armor.

CHAPTER EIGHT

NATE

When Dorothy called to tell me Mia was on her way to the local grocery store, I don't think I've ever gotten out the door so fast in my life. For the first time, living farther out was a hindrance, as I raced the backroads, desperate to get to Mia before the sleazy bastard who works afternoons could lay his disgusting hands on her.

How could Dorothy not warn her? Or better question, what the fuck is wrong with the owners? Despite continuous complaints, "he's harmless" seems to be their only response. Fucking nepotism.

I'm throwing every bit of my anger toward them and him into my expression as I advance on the bastard. I barely register Mia standing there, every fiber of my being bent on intimidating this little fucker out of ever even thinking about her again.

"Yep, here I am," Mia says, drawing my gaze to her. It takes me a second to remember I'd just spoken. The words bypassed my brain while I was thinking about tearing Ned apart.

Her smile is so relieved I can practically feel it. I reach down, lightly placing my hand on her back. Politely, but possessively enough to send a message.

"You didn't think I'd leave you to do all the shopping on your own, did you?" I ask, hoping she'll play along.

She looks up at me and her cheeks flush a bright red.

"Um, no?" she replies.

She's clearly flustered, which just makes me more pissed off. I break eye contact, shifting my gaze back to the douchebag.

"I think we've got it from here, Ned." My glare is a finely honed weapon, sending him skittering back to his station at the front of the store.

I can feel the tension in Mia's back unwind.

"Thank you," she says in a low, shaky voice. "I don't know what I would've done if you hadn't shown up."

She sets the box she was holding onto for dear life in the cart, then wrings her hands together. I suddenly realize she's shaking.

"Hey," I say, lifting her chin with a finger so she looks up at me. "Deep breaths, okay?"

She nods and sucks in air like her life depends on it. I slip my hands around hers, gently kneading them. I breathe with her, slow and long, through a few breaths until the shaking stops.

"Sorry, I'm not usually such a baby," she murmurs self-consciously.

Before I can think about what I'm doing, my hands shift to her shoulders and gently skim her upper arms. "It's not you. It's Ned. Every woman in town knows not to shop after two p.m."

"Guess I missed that memo."

I look down into her eyes and something twists inside of me. I stop rubbing her arms and take a step back.

I clear my throat. "I'll just stick close, okay?" I offer.

She considers my offer, but clearly realizes without me she's either going to have to leave or deal with Ned.

"I appreciate that," she finally responds.

The relief I feel is deep. "So what are we shopping for?" I ask genially as we continue down the aisle.

She takes a deep breath. "All of Gran's favorite foods. She had some tests today, and I can tell she's in pain and a little run-down. I thought it would be nice to make her favorite dishes this weekend."

My brow lifts. Goddamn, she's thoughtful. Knowing Dorothy, that'll be exactly what she needs right now.

"So what kind of food are we talking, here?"

"What, you don't want to know what her tests were?" she teases.

"If Dorothy wants me to know, she'll tell me," I reply simply, not letting on than I know a lot more than she thinks I do.

She pauses at the alcohol display and pulls off a bottle of rum, holding it up for me to see.

"For the rum cake. Which will, of course, be chock-full of wheat and dairy." She gives me a wink. "I'm also going to make prime rib, mashed potatoes, and green bean casserole for dinner tomorrow. Then overnight stuffed French toast for Sunday brunch."

My whole mouth fills with saliva, even though it's mostly stuff I would never eat. But damn.

"Good lord, that sounds …"

"Delicious?" she offers. "Oh, it will be. You should come for dinner." Then, she blushes hard like she didn't mean to say it.

And as tempting as her offer is, it definitely doesn't fall under "staying away from her." Not that that's what I'm doing right now. But I'm only here because Dorothy asked me to be. That's my story, and I'm sticking to it.

"I doubt I could actually eat any of that," I respond dismissively.

"Meat. Potatoes. I can make a batch with no dairy. And some roasted green beans, sans casserole. Come on, it's the least I can do to thank you for looking out for me. And Gran."

God, she makes it difficult to say no. I watch her eyes drift away and lock on Ned at the cash register.

My eyes flick over and meet his for a brief instant before he turns around, pretending to be busy with something. I hear Mia chuckle.

It's a sound I want to hear from her more. I decide I can control myself enough for dinner.

"I guess that sounds better than a frozen dinner and beer at home."

"Can you even get gluten-free beer here?" she asks with a mocking tone.

"You always this sassy?" I parry back. But damn do I like it. Feisty is way better than sad or upset.

"Yep. You always this quiet?"

Oh, if only she knew. But I can't help myself, responding with a simple shrug. After a beat, we both bust up laughing.

"Touché," she says. "All right, I've got everything."

I step in and take the handles of the cart. "Go on out to your car, I'll check out and bring everything to you."

"Um, okay," she says, scrambling with her purse, but I shake my head and start pushing toward the front of the store.

"Don't worry about it," I say, already halfway to the register.

"O-kay…" she says from behind me.

Like I was going to make her deal with Ned again. I enjoy the frightened rabbit look on his face as I approach. And I try to pretend like I'm not following Mia's progress out of the store. I start unloading the groceries silently onto the counter. That is, until the sliding doors have closed behind her.

"I'll be making sure my girl doesn't have to come in here while you're working again," I say nonchalantly as I unload the last item. I straighten up and look down at Ned. "But if I hear you so much as looked at her here or anywhere else, you'll be answering to me. Got that?"

Thankfully, he's not a complete idiot, because he just nods. He's obviously too scared to say a word. Good. He better be fucking scared.

I've had words with him before. Polite warnings. But I've never had cause to threaten him before. I don't feel bad about calling her my girl, either. He needs to know she has my protection. Even if she's not really mine.

But mine or not, if he ever goes near Mia again, I will happily make a Ned-pretzel out of his skinny ass. As he hands me my receipt, I smile at that thought. He shrinks back, and I realize how sinister it must have come off.

The thought makes me chuckle as I heft the bags into my arms and head out the door.

Mia's leaning against the back of her car, with the trunk open. She turns when she hears me approach.

I lean down and slide the bags into the trunk. She closes the lid and offers a smile.

"Thank you again," she says. "I'm lucky you happened along."

"Oh, I didn't happen along. Dorothy called me. Said she forgot to warn you about Ned."

"Ah. I see," she murmurs. She fiddles with her keys for a second before looking back up at me curiously. "So … why does Gran call you for help all the time?"

"I like helping her. I'm also one of the few guys in town who's young enough to help her when she needs it yet old enough to have a driver's license."

"So, what you're saying is, you're somewhere between sixteen and sixty and have nothing better to do?"

"That about sums it up."

"Don't you have a job?" she teases.

The smile that was on my face disappears and I'm immediately defensive.

"Don't you?" I counter.

And then I suddenly feel like an ass as I watch her eyes tighten and her shoulders droop. I obviously hit a sore spot.

"Sorry," I follow up. "I just … anyway, you're welcome. Glad I could help. Just stick to shopping in the mornings in the future, okay?"

I don't mention that I normally do her grandmother's shopping, since I doubt Dorothy would want her to know.

"Yeah, of course," she replies with a vague smile.

"Enjoy the rest of your evening, Mia."

I start walking toward my truck, which is parked a couple of spaces away.

"Dinner's at six tomorrow," she calls as I open the driver's side door.

I climb in and look over at her. She arches an eyebrow at me in that sassy way of hers. *Do* I have enough control to spend a whole night with her? Because just that look is enough to rile me up in ways it shouldn't.

Still, it's a tough invitation to turn down. I dip my head in agreement, then close the door before I can say something that will get me in trouble. I realize that's another reason I don't say much with her. Because I'm actually tempted to *flirt*.

I start the engine and let the rumbling settle my nerves. Besides the harmless banter I have with Dorothy and Rae, I haven't flirted with any women in four fucking years. The fact I even want to is unnerving. Mia is waking up urges I thought I'd long ago killed off. I don't know whether that makes me more scared or thrilled.

CHAPTER NINE

MIA

"I 'm back," I call to Gran as I carry the first two bags into the house.

Gran appears from the kitchen, wiping her hands.

"You weren't cleaning up, were you?" I ask sharply as I hustle to get the bags in. "Because I was going to do that."

Gran waves me off. "It's fine, honey."

I roll my eyes. "There are two more bags, I'll be right back." I turn away and hear rustling, so I whip back around and throw up a finger. "No peeking." She gives me a guilty look that makes me laugh. I give her a wink and head back to the car.

As I heft the heavy load into the house, I'm impressed with Nate's strength that he managed to carry all four at the same time. But then, I am pretty ridiculously out of shape. My previous life didn't exactly leave much time for exercise. At least I have something to add to my plans.

Gran leans against the sink, watching me as I'm about to start unpacking the bags.

"I'm going to be here while you're cooking whatever it is you've got planned, so you might as well show me your cards now," she says with a smirk.

I chuckle and shake my head. "You just can't stand surprises, can you, Gran?" I tease. "Fine, have it your way."

I pick through the bags slowly, unpacking her groceries and the nondescript items like flour, sugar, yeast, and eggs. The fried onions are the first obvious item I pull out, and Gran straightens up. So I fish out the three-rib prime roast next and wiggle it in the air with a smile.

"You didn't," Gran gasps, clapping her hands together. "Prime rib, green bean casserole, and —"

"Mashed potatoes. Yes, Gran," I reply with a grin. "And ..." I pull the rum out.

"Oh, Mia, rum cake. That's my favorite. I swear, you're going to spoil me."

I give her a kiss on the cheek as I take an armload to the pantry. "You deserve it."

"I take it since you made it back unscathed that Nate found you?" she calls after me.

I emerge from the pantry with a frown. I know that tone. That too-casual "I'm not up to anything" note she gets in her voice when she is, in fact, up to something.

"You didn't forget to tell me about Ned, did you?" I accuse her.

She smiles and widens her eyes innocently. "I have no idea what you're talking about."

I roll my eyes at the obvious setup. Which totally worked. Dammit.

"Uh-huh. So since you're *not* trying to get Nate and I together, you won't mind me telling you I have no intention of dating him. This is a pitstop, Gran. I'm not staying forever, so there's no point."

Gran shrugs. "May as well have some fun while you're here."

"Nate seems … okay and all, but I wouldn't exactly call him fun," I point out. Smoking hot, yes. A towering, intense hunk of man I can imagine having fun between the sheets with, absolutely. But not in my Gran's house. And in another life where I was the type of person to have casual sex. One where I also wasn't in a tailspin.

She waves a hand airily. "You have to get to know him. Trust me, he's plenty fun."

I cock an eyebrow at her. "I still think it's you who has the hots for this guy, Gran," I tease her.

She blushes just enough to confirm that's true.

"You'll be glad to know I invited him for dinner tomorrow, then," I follow up.

Her smile turns full-on grandma smug. "That was nice of you."

With the groceries put away, I wash my hands and turn back to Gran.

"How about we play Scrabble?" I suggest, purposely and obviously changing the subject.

Thankfully, she either takes the bait or lets me off the hook, because she says yes and we spend the rest of the evening at it. Knowing Gran, she let me off the hook. For now.

As soon as we're done with breakfast on Saturday and Gran has settled onto the couch with a book and Simba next to her, I get started on the rum cake, happy to return to the sanctuary that is baking.

Once the cake is in the oven, I go ahead and make the French bread I'll need for the overnight stuffed French toast. The recipe makes two loaves, which means we'll have some to go with dinner too.

Then I get to work on the dessert I purposely didn't mention to Nate, because I didn't want to give him a chance to object. The avocado-based dairy-free chocolate mousse comes together in a flash, and I separate it into four ramekins to chill.

I've just scored the bread loaves and set them for their final rise when the cake is ready to come out of the oven. And I'm ready for some lunch.

I pause my cookathon to throw together a couple of veggie paninis with kettle chips.

I go to deliver Gran's only to find her dozing, an open book resting on her chest.

It stops me in my tracks. The sight both warms my heart, reminding me of all the times we'd curl up on the couch together and nap when I was little, and it also sends a bolt of concern shooting through my chest. Gran may have pretended to nap when I was little, but I've never known her to actually need a midday rest. I can only hope it's not a bad sign.

But then, I remind myself that I'm a pro at worrying and it's probably nothing. She is an octogenarian after all. And I don't want her to worry either.

"Well," I say loudly, continuing forward. Gran snaps awake and I try not to smile. "Cake's cooling and there's bread rising. I think it's time for a well-earned lunch." I offer her a plate. "Panini?"

Gran rights herself and sets her book down, accepting the plate with a smile. "Thanks, honey."

I sink into the love seat across from her and take a bite of my sandwich. It's perfectly crunchy on the outside, and the warm, gooey mozzarella oozes around bites of grilled zucchini and bell pepper. How on earth do people live without wheat and dairy?

We both munch in silence for a while before Gran offers, "I'm happy to help if you need anything this afternoon."

"I've got it under control, but I appreciate the offer," I assure her.

Gran carefully doesn't look at me, examining her sandwich instead. "Just be sure to leave enough time to get yourself ready too, honey."

I snort a laugh around the bite I just took. "I'll be perfectly presentable, don't worry." I shake my head lightly. I'm not wearing a dress, even though I know that's what she means. But she should know better. It's never been my style. With my sandwich now finished, I put down the plate. "So why are you so intent on me impressing this guy?"

"Why are you so against getting to know him?" she returns.

I throw my hands up. "You two went to the same damn school of answer-a-question-with-a-question. I'm not against it, Gran. I'm the one who invited him to dinner, after all."

"Okay, true," Gran allows. "But you're clearly closed off to the possibility of getting to know him as a suitor —"

"Gran," I interrupt, laughing. "It's the 2020s, not the 1920s. We call them boyfriends now. And I'm not *closed off*. I'm just not … interested." My volume dies on the last word, because as I say it I realize it's not true. I am interested. Sexually, for sure. But the guy is also a pile of contradictions I wouldn't mind deciphering … in another life, perhaps. In the one I'm living right now? I may still be interested, but the thought of going there is somehow mentally overwhelming. My life is mentally overwhelming. I don't have space for complications.

I think Gran sees my internal battle playing out over my face, because she doesn't keep pushing, instead saying, "Suit yourself. I'm sure we'll all have a lovely time, in any case."

Before I can reply, the rise timer goes off in the kitchen. "Duty calls," I say mock-apologetically. I stand, collecting both of our plates and returning to the kitchen.

As the bread bakes and I glaze the cake, I can't help thinking about Gran's choice of words: closed off.

It bothers me, because the whole point of quitting my job, my old life, was to open myself up to all of the possibilities in front of me.

But what I hadn't factored in is my dire need for a plan. And right now I feel … planless. That's the problem. I feel like I can't move forward on anything because it's not part of a plan. So I need to make a plan, even if it's not elaborate or long term. And then I make a new one when I need to.

Feeling better now that I have a plan for a plan at least, I prep the rib rack to rest in the oven until a timer turns it on, put together the green bean casserole and a tray of plain green beans and stow them in the fridge, and scrub and chop the potatoes, putting them in water and into the fridge. The rest will take mere minutes here and there throughout the afternoon.

Now free to do as I please, I decide Gran is right. Maybe a little primping is in order. But not for Nate, for me. Time to put myself together again.

I take a long, hot bath and think about what I want. What if my plan *is* to just stay here for as long as Gran needs me? I must have resisted acknowledging it consciously because it would mean I could be here from days to weeks to months. I don't do well with open timelines.

But I know I'm not going anywhere until Gran's okay, which is most important. So I have a plan: I'm staying here as long as Gran needs me. Financially, it's not a problem at least. I have the luxury of not needing to work right now. I lived on a mere fraction of my salary before, and I don't see my expenses changing much while I'm here. I could probably not work for a while if I really wanted. Though I can't imagine not working at all. I know myself, and sooner or later — most likely sooner — I'm going to need to feel like I'm doing something useful and productive.

Which means, while I'm here, I'm going to have to work on figuring out what I want to do next. So. I'll be here for Gran and figure out what makes me happy.

I get dressed in black skinny jeans and a red and black flannel shirt, taking the time to tame my thick, dark hair so it hangs sleek and straight down to my mid-back. I put a hair tie around my wrist so I can pull it back while I finish cooking, then head out of my room back to the kitchen.

As soon as I open my door, the smell of roasting meat hits me and my mouth instantly waters. I pull the green bean casserole and tray of plain beans out of the fridge and go to pop them in the oven. Opening the oven door sends an intense wave of the tantalizing aroma straight into my face as I snug the other dishes onto the shelf below it.

"Good lord, Mia, if that tastes as good as it smells, I'm in trouble," Gran says, coming into the kitchen.

I close the oven door and turn to her with a smile. "Oh, it will," I assure her. I pull the potatoes out of the fridge and set them to boil while I line up finishing ingredients on two sides of a hot pad on the island.

"What's all that for?" Gran asks, gesturing toward the two bowls and sets of items around them.

"One side for regular mashed potatoes, the other for dairy-free," I say, as if it should be obvious. "Nate's not going to eat potatoes with a pound of butter and cream in them."

"If I ate the dairy-free ones, would I be able to tell the difference?" Gran asks.

I tilt my head. "Well, they don't taste exactly the same. I use coconut milk in the dairy-free ones instead of milk and butter. So they're definitely still creamy, they just have a bit of a different kick. Though once I add the roasted garlic and chives, it's harder to tell."

"Why don't you make the whole batch dairy-free then?" she offers. "The green bean casserole will be dairy enough."

"Are you sure?" I ask skeptically. Gran usually loves her dairy.

"Absolutely. I don't want to make him uncomfortable by serving him all different food," she scoffs.

"That's sweet of you, Gran," I reply drily. I'm sure as long as it tastes good, Nate won't care. But if Gran does, then all dairy-free potatoes it is. I start putting away the items on the dairy side and glance up at the clock. "Speaking of Nate, he should be here any minute."

The thought makes me fidget, so I go to the oven to remove the roast to rest to give myself something to do with my hands.

Gran watches me with those sharp eyes of hers, but I'm saved her commenting by the doorbell. I tent aluminum foil around the roast and move to grab the plates and utensils to set the table with. I can hear them talking, but I can't quite hear what they're saying with the wall between us.

I'm laying the forks and knives down on napkins when they enter. My insides jump, and it forces me to admit to myself exactly how nervous I am. And when my eyes flick up and meet Nate's, my stomach clenches. Shit. It was one thing when I felt this way when he rescued me at the store. But feeling it now …

"Hey, Mia," he greets me sheepishly. It's only when my eyes skim down to his navy-blue Henley and jeans that I notice he's holding out flowers. "These are for you."

"Hey, Nate," I greet him, stepping around the table. I take the bouquet, admiring the pink and white alstroemerias. "Thank you, they're beautiful." I resist the urge to tease him about being out of uniform. Seeing as he's being so nice with the flowers.

"He brought me some too," Gran croons, coming up from behind him holding her own bouquet of yellow lilies.

I step back into the kitchen and fish two vases out of the cabinet. "That was very nice of you," I say to him. "They'll definitely help dress up the table since I'm not so much with the fancy table settings," I give him an apologetic smile.

"Works for me, I'm not really a fancy guy," he replies.

I'm frozen, holding the lilies I'd meant to put in the second vase, as our eyes lock. I see Gran looking between us out of the corner of my eye, but I can't seem to stop. And neither can he. Like it or not, this is turning out to have been a loaded invitation.

Gran finally clears her throat and we break our gaze to both look to her.

"Oh good, glad you know I'm still here," Gran teases.

I blush bright red and Nate gives a faint smile.

"Nate, how are you with carving?" I ask, attempting to change the subject.

"Just point me at it," he says. I pull out the carving knife and a fork and step aside for him to work while I mash the potatoes.

"Gran, why don't you slice the bread?" I offer, pointing at a cutting board, bread knife, and plate on the counter nearest her.

With all three of us working, it definitely mellows out the vibe in the room.

I finish the potatoes, then pull out the casserole and plain beans and line them up on the island. Gran starts to take the bread plate to the table.

"Let's just put everything here," I suggest, gesturing to the island. "That way I won't be tempted to eat it all because it's sitting right in front of me."

Nate looks up and our eyes lock again. Before Gran takes notice, I turn away abruptly, though I know he probably saw the heat in my cheeks. I'm not sure why, but the vibe between us has definitely shifted.

"All right, everyone, go ahead and get a plate. Nate, we have water, club soda, red wine, and beer. What would you like?" I ask.

He smirks at me. "Do you ladies always have beer in the house?"

And I may or may not turn bright red, having gotten that beer just for him. Which he should know, since he paid for it.

"Club soda sounds great," he follows up, a hint of laughter in his voice.

"For me as well," Gran says as she loads her plate.

I pour three club sodas and add slices of lemon and lime, depositing them on the table before going to load up my own plate.

Nate is still at the island, with everything but potatoes on his plate. He points down at them questioningly.

"Dairy-free," I assure him with a smile.

He raises an eyebrow but doesn't comment, simply loading up his plate. And damn is his plate loaded. To the point where I wonder if he can actually eat it all. And where he puts all those calories. The man may be large, but there's barely an ounce of fat on him.

Once all of our plates are filled and we've sat down at the small table, I realize there wouldn't have been room for the food anyway. At a table meant for four, Nate takes up about a third of it with his bulk, and our plates take up a good amount of room too.

It's actually heartwarming to be eating with more than just Gran in a way I haven't felt in a while. Our family hasn't really gotten together in so long that I didn't realize how much I missed communal meals.

And as she always has, Gran insists on praying before letting us dive in. But once we do, we all dive in like starving people. Everyone goes for the meat first, and we all make noises at our first bites.

"Oh, Mia, darling, you've outdone yourself," Gran says.

"I'm with her. This is the best prime rib I think I've ever had," Nate agrees.

"Not to toot my own horn, but this *is* phenomenal," I reply, letting my eyes roll back into my head.

There are similar reactions over the potatoes, even from Gran, who swears she'd never know they didn't have dairy. And I clearly underestimated Nate, as he demolishes every scrap of food in record time.

Gran and I finish not long after. It was a rare holiday-style meal that's hard not to devour. Lots of eating, little talk, though I'm sure there will be time for that later.

"Well, I don't think there's much topping that," Gran says, rubbing her belly contentedly.

"I don't know, there's still dessert," I say with a wink. "Why don't you two go into the living room and I'll clean up in here?"

"Dorothy, why don't you go on? I'll help Mia," Nate offers.

Gran grins like the cat who got the cream, and I can't help smiling and shaking my head.

"That's so sweet of you," she says. "I think I'll do just that." And with a smug smile, she leaves us alone.

"You really don't have to," I assure him as I start to collect the empty plates. But he swipes them before I'm able to get any but my own.

"I'll do dishes. You put away the food. Deal?"

I press my lips together to suppress a smile. "Deal."

As he starts to scrape plates, rinses everything, and loads the dishwasher, I sneakily load up a container with as much meat, potatoes, and beans as he'd eaten tonight to slip it in the fridge along with the rest that we'll be snacking off of the next few days. I make a mental note to remember to give him the container when he leaves.

"So where'd you learn how to cook like that?" Nate asks.

I glance up guiltily from the container I'm filling for him, but he's not looking at me.

"Gran," I reply simply as I pop the container into the fridge and start to package up the rest.

He looks up curiously. "Not your parents?"

"Nope," I reply matter-of-factly. "My dad runs a law firm, has since before I was born. Mom started her own small accounting business once my sister and I were in school. Neither had much time for us. Though my sister never really cared about cooking either, come to think of it."

"Carrie," Nate says, surprising me.

"Yeah, how'd you know that?"

Nate closes the dishwasher and turns to me as I seal up the last of the food. His smirk almost says everything I need to know. "Dorothy talks about you both a lot."

Yep, there it is. Crap. Reading between the lines: She's been trying to set one or both of us up with him. Probably for as long as she's known him. Awesome.

"Yes, well, she pretty much raised us," I reply with a shrug, popping the last of the containers in the fridge. "Thanks for your help. You can go join her while I get dessert together if you want."

He pushes up from where he'd been leaning against the sink, putting him almost in my space.

"And if I want to stay?"

My insides tighten at his words. I stand there, speechless, for just a moment before forcing myself to gather my wits.

"Then you'll ruin the surprise," I say sternly, arching an eyebrow.

Both of his eyebrows jump. "Guess I wouldn't want that."

His eyes stay connected with mine for an instant longer before he brushes past me to join Gran in the living room.

I take a deep, steadying breath that calms me enough so I feel like I can safely handle a knife. I slice off a generous helping of the golden rum cake for Gran, then pull out two portions of the chocolate mousse. I carve of a small chunk of cake, chop it up, and sprinkle it over one of the portions. Because that's how I roll.

I put all three confections on a tray, add utensils and napkins, and take it into the living room.

"I come bearing sugar," I tease.

They both look up from their conversation, clearly interested in whatever I'm serving. I feel something like a swell of pride as I palm the tray on my left hand like a waitress, handing Gran her slice of rum cake.

"Rum cake for the lady."

I hand her a fork and napkin to go with it, then pass Nate the plain chocolate mousse, followed by a spoon and napkin.

"It's chocolate mousse," I explain, without qualifying the "dairy-free" part. Because I think I've demonstrated I get that that's how *he* rolls.

I set the tray on the coffee table and grab my own dish, sinking down onto the love seat across from Nate and Gran.

Nate cranes his neck to look at what I've got. I tilt it toward him.

"Best of both worlds," I explain with a grin.

Gran doesn't hesitate, she sinks right into her dessert. When the first bite hits her tongue, she closes her eyes and hums in appreciation.

"This tastes like the holidays," she sighs appreciatively.

I eye Nate, who still hasn't taken a bite. I get a large spoonful of my own dessert and pointedly down it. It's even better than I thought it'd be. The sugary-boozy softness of the cake is an unexpectedly perfect complement to the rich, silky mousse that I'd never in a million years guess had avocado in it.

"You don't have to eat it if you don't want to," I tell Nate around my first bite. Perhaps not the most ladylike thing to do, but he honestly looks like he doesn't know whether to eat it or not.

He considers me for a moment, then without any indication he was going to, takes a *huge* bite. His eyes go wide almost instantly. His spoon immediately dips back into the ramekin and he shovels another bite into his mouth. And another. It doesn't take long before it's completely gone. Clearly, once he decides to eat something he absolutely demolishes it.

"Holy crap, what was in that?" he asks once he's done.

I smile around the spoon I just put in my mouth and actually swallow this time before I talk.

"Avocados, cacao powder, almond milk, vanilla, salt, and just a little bit of maple syrup," I tell him.

He shakes his head. "Damn, I wish I hadn't asked."

That makes me laugh. "Why not?"

He carefully sets his dish down on the coffee table and looks up at me. "Because now I'm going to want to eat it all the time."

"Then I guess I shouldn't tell you it's actually really easy to make?" I tease.

Nate groans, and I'd be lying if I said the noise didn't instantly turn me on. Damn hormones. Yep, that's all it is. Hormones.

"You're killing me," he says.

"I promise I won't give you the recipe if you don't want it."

He smirks. "Why do I need the recipe when I have you around?"

I can't help it, my eyes go wide. And Gran looks a little too pleased.

"Speaking of which," Gran segues. "Since you're going to be around, Mia, didn't you say you were looking to get back in shape?"

My head snaps back at the abrupt subject change. "Excuse me?"

"Last night, when we were playing Scrabble. Your arms were hurting from carrying the grocery bags, and you told me you knew you needed to start working out again. I just thought, since you'll be around anyway, Nate's the perfect person to help you."

Ah, so that's her game. More shoving Mia and Nate together. Lord have mercy.

"Yeah, I guess I did, Gran, but I don't need to bother Nate."

"Nonsense," she insists. "He's the one everyone around here goes to for help in the gym. Right, Nate?"

"Well, if everyone is going to him, I especially don't want to take up more of his time," I say before he can answer.

"Dorothy's exaggerating," Nate himself finally interjects. "I've trained a few people. Helped Dorothy and a couple others with rehab. Nothing major. But if you want help, I'm at the gym every day anyway." Of course he is.

Gran gives me her best *Go on, honey* look. One I know well from all the silent encouragement — read commands — she's given me over the years. My gut reaction is to shut her suggestion down. I'm embarrassingly out of shape. Which is the reason, Gran's pressure and expectations aside, someone to help motivate me is probably exactly what I need. Because I'm not sure I would have any clue where to start. I've never been athletic. And clearly the man knows his way around a gym.

It would even give me a socially acceptable, non-dating reason to learn more about him and see what he's all about. Because I am curious.

"Okay," I blurt out. "I mean, if it's no trouble."

"None at all," Nate assures me.

I don't think I've seen Gran this pleased with herself in a very long time. If it weren't at the expense of her getting me to do exactly her bidding, I'd be happier about it. Though I know I should be happy. Having someone help me get in shape could be good. Really.

"So, when do we start?"

CHAPTER TEN

NATE

"Okay, so, when you said you were at the gym every day, I guess I assumed that meant we'd be doing this *at* the gym." Mia puts her hands on her hips, flattening the baggy long-sleeved pink T-shirt she's wearing over fitted black leggings.

I lift a finger and point behind her.

"There's the gym."

She rolls her eyes and rubs her hands over her forearms. I probably should've warned her to bring a jacket.

"We'll get there, don't worry," I assure her. "Come on, let's get started."

I lead her around the back, where there's a fitness station before the trailhead.

She eyes the freestanding pole, waist-height bar, and overhead bar with more than a little trepidation.

"All right," she says, rubbing her hands together and blowing in them. "Let the torture begin."

I huff a short laugh and shake my head. "Don't worry, princess, we're just going to warm up. Easy stuff."

She narrows her eyes at me, obviously disliking being called princess. "Bring it on, Hulk."

I smirk at her revenge nickname. Both fair and appropriate. "Just do what I do."

I start doing arm circles, and she follows, clearly feeling a little silly.

"So what landed you in Alpine Ridge of all places, training the locals and rehabbing the elderly?" she asks.

I switch the direction of my arm circles while I contemplate how to answer. "I retired," I reply, sticking to the simplest truth.

"You don't look that old."

"Who says you have to be old to retire?"

"Fine. Why'd you retire?" she shoots back.

I stop doing circles and place a hand on the far end of the waist-height horizontal bar, swinging one leg back and forth.

"Because I was ready to," I reply evasively. "Why aren't you working?"

She assesses me for a minute like she's not sure she should answer. Or maybe because I'm not being very forthcoming.

"I was working for my dad and realized it wasn't what I wanted to do with my life," she finally responds. "So I quit."

I switch to swinging the other leg as I absorb that.

"You're a lawyer?" I ask skeptically. I would've guessed if she took after any parent, accounting would seem more up her alley. Though I'm not sure why.

She tilts her head. "I was," she corrects. "Now? I don't know what I am."

I'm silent as we finish our warm-up. Just as I thought, she's in the in-between. After breaking out of the expectations the world placed on her, she has no clue what she expects of herself. A place I know very, very well. A place where everything feels uncertain and temporary. Not a place where lasting relationships start.

"Now what?" she asks, breaking into my thoughts.

I look up at her and I can see the uncertainty in her stance.

"You really need to know the plan, don't you?" I tease.

She scrunches her face at me. "As a matter of fact, I do."

A smile pulls at the corner of my mouth. "Now, we walk."

"That's it?"

"Yep. We'll warm up, walk, and stretch every day this week."

"Oh. Well, that sounds easy enough."

I gesture toward the trail and we head out. It's level and well marked, and quite pleasant as the midafternoon sun starts to warm the air up a bit. Eventually, my curiosity gets the better of me and I want to know more about exactly where she's at.

"So, is that why you were in Hawaii? Because you were going to travel around the world in an *Eat Pray Love*-style bid to find meaning in life?" I ask.

Her eyebrows jump. "Oh my god," she says, bursting out laughing. "How do you even know what that is?"

"I saw the movie," I say defensively, kicking at a rock on the trail.

She gives me a disbelieving look. "Really? Into chick flicks, are we?"

"It was on a date," I reply with a shrug.

She shakes her head, still smiling. "To answer your question, no, that's not exactly what I was doing," she replies. "Though it was the first time I'd traveled in years, and I'd like to do more. But I don't expect to suddenly find my purpose in life on some epic journey of self-discovery."

"Good, because in my experience, aha moments are rare. It's pain that changes you, shapes you."

She looks up at me, her mouth agape.

"What pain changed you?"

Now I'm the one who's shocked, and it must show on my face, because she backpedals instantly.

"I'm sorry, I shouldn't have asked that. You just … it sounded like you were speaking from experience. I'm too nosy for my own good sometimes."

I shrug, trying to seem nonchalant but unnerved how much she picked up from the little I said. "It's okay. It was just … life," I respond vaguely, trying to discourage her from pushing for more.

"Life will do it," she murmurs pensively. She watches her feet as she walks, clearly thinking about her own situation.

"So I imagine your dad was none too pleased," I offer.

Her eyes snap up to meet mine. "Dude, are you reading my mind?"

I chuckle. "Not really. We were just talking about the fact that you quit. And based on the little experience I've had with your dad, he doesn't seem like the type to take news like that well."

Her jaw drops. "You really are observant. No, he didn't take it well. At all."

We're both silent for a minute as the elevation increases and Mia's breath comes heavier as she works to climb a winding path.

We're rewarded at the top when the trail pushes through trees into a clearing filled with tall grass and a rainbow of wildflowers. It's one of my favorite places in all of Alpine Ridge.

"Wow, it's really pretty back here," she murmurs.

I nod, quietly pleased that she likes it too, and I steer her to another fitness area just off the path. I sit down on the bench there, one leg propped up.

She makes to imitate me, and I laugh. "I'm just sitting, Mia. Take a break."

She smiles self-consciously and pulls both legs up, wrapping her arms around them.

"How are you feeling?" I ask.

She takes a deep breath and tilts her face toward the sun. "Pretty good, actually. Guess all I needed was some fresh air and a little exercise."

I tip my head back to look up at the sun too, though that wasn't exactly what I'd meant. "You'd be surprised how many ills that can cure," I agree. I gaze back down at her. "It's okay to keep it simple. Life has a way of showing you what you need when you're ready for it."

She turns away from the sun to meet my gaze. She stares into my eyes for a moment like she's trying to figure me out before her eyes drop to my lips. Then they dart away, and she turns her head. And I swear I saw a blush on her cheeks.

"Mia," I say quietly.

She turns her head slowly and we lock eyes again. And her cheeks are still red. I almost laugh, but now isn't the time for teasing.

"You don't have to hide from me," I assure her.

"What makes you think I'm hiding?" she challenges, jutting out her chin stubbornly.

It's too fucking cute. But she clearly had a moment where she thought about my lips. Which almost certainly means she thought about kissing me. So she's attracted to me too. It's totally natural. I'm not going to admit to feeling the same way, as much as a part of me wants to. That won't help. Nothing is worth making this part of her life harder, and she needs to know she can trust me.

"Because you've been doing it so long, it's all you know right now. But I'm here to help you, no matter what. Okay?"

She meets my gaze again, and while I don't see trust there, I do see acceptance. And that's about all I can expect. We're still getting to know each other, and I can see what Dorothy meant. Mia needs someone to lean on.

I rise to my feet, offering her a hand. She accepts, and we continue on the rest of the walk in comfortable silence.

CHAPTER ELEVEN

MIA

I'm getting ready to meet Nate on Tuesday when the doctor's office calls. Gran is awake, so I can only watch as they tell her something that makes her stop pacing and sit down abruptly on the couch.

"Oh, I see," is all she says before listening more. "And when would that begin? … No, I understand the risks, I've already discussed it with Dr. Sanchez. … Yes, let's do that. … Okay, we'll see you then."

Gran sets down the phone. She looks up at me, her face filled with resolve.

"Come sit, honey," she says firmly, patting the couch cushion next to her.

With my heart in my throat, I quickly cross the room and perch on the edge of the cushion.

"What'd they say?" I ask, even though I already have an idea.

Gran slips a hand over mine. "It's non-Hodgkin lymphoma. Stage four. That means it's spread, and the next step is chemo."

Tears fill my eyes. "What's the … what are the chances …" I'm at a loss for how to ask my grandmother what the chances are of her making it. It's too much.

"They've had good results treating this type of cancer, honey. My odds aren't bad, really. A bit better than fifty-fifty. And at my age, pretty much every day comes with those kinds of odds." She smiles ruefully, and I can't handle her brave face, even though I'm trying desperately to keep my own.

"Oh, Gran," I say on a shaky sigh. "So you're going through with the treatment?"

She nods. "I already talked alternatives with the doctor based on his preliminary diagnosis. This isn't a surprise, and I've had plenty of time to think about it. I want to fight, Mia. I've had worse odds in my life."

I squeeze her hand and swallow hard. "Then I'm here to fight with you."

And for the first time, Gran tears up, but she smiles wide. She squeezes back, and her gratitude radiates through the simple touch.

"Good, because I start chemo on Monday. The first course will be six treatments, once a week. And if it helps, they'll do a second course of six treatments biweekly."

We look at each other, knowing exactly what that means. Gramps had colon cancer. He made it through chemo successfully, though the cancer came back a couple of years later. He died before they could do anything about it. While the chemo wasn't the worst of his suffering, it wasn't pretty either.

It also sinks in that that means I'll be here for another four or five months.

"Looks like I'm moving in for real, then," I declare. "I'll let Mom and Dad know I need to collect the rest of my belongings."

Gran withdraws her hand. "Why don't you give me a bit to process this, honey? We'll call them tomorrow, together. They should know why. It'll make it easier for you."

The lump in my throat thickens, and I blink back against the tears pricking my eyes. Even through a cancer diagnosis Gran is more worried about me.

"Whatever you want," I tell her.

Gran reaches up and strokes my face. "I want you to keep your chin up and go see that young man now. I can already tell he's helping you."

I laugh the through tears swimming in my eyes and reach up to brush them away. "He's an odd one, but you're right," I agree. "I think he's going to help me feel better."

"Good," Gran says firmly, rising from the couch. "Get out of here. I'm going to read and rest. I'll see you for dinner, honey."

I nod and watch her head to her room. Part of me wants to stay, just in case she needs me. But I also know that would drive her nuts, so even though it's a battle, I force myself into the car and drive to meet Nate.

As I get out of the car, I can tell it's slightly warmer today, so I leave the jacket I'd brought in the backseat.

Nate is at the same spot as yesterday, and when he sees me he actually *smiles*. Like a wide, *I'm so happy to see you* grin. And I don't know why, but it breaks me. I start sobbing uncontrollably in a way I can't remember doing since I was a teenager.

I bury my face in my hands, trying to hide, but it's useless. A moment later I feel Nate's arms wrap around me and he pulls me against the hard plane of his chest. I don't even try to resist. I lean into him, bawling like a baby. He holds me against him with one arm while the other rubs soothing circles over my back.

After a few minutes, the tears stop, and I press myself away. But Nate's not having it, his hands holding me gently by my upper arms as he looks down into my eyes, his expression full of concern.

"Hey," I say lamely, wiping my mess of a face.

He gives a half-smile. "Hey," he returns. "Want to talk about it?"

"I ..." I do. But I don't know if it's a betrayal of Gran's trust or not. Though somehow I know inherently that I can trust Nate to keep it to himself regardless. "Gran's got lymphoma. Stage four. We just found out."

Nate's lips drop into a frown. "I'm so sorry, Mia." He hesitates. "You really didn't have to come today. I would've understood."

I nod. "I know. But Gran wanted to be alone. And I guess I needed to break down a little about it. I'm glad I came, because I wouldn't want to do that in front of her. She's already going through enough." I shake my head, remembering how quickly she tried to protect me from dealing with my parents, even in light of the news.

The thought sends another wave of tears washing down my face, thankfully this time without the hysterics.

Nate reaches up and swipes his thumb across my cheek. "Let's just walk. It'll help, I promise."

With a sigh, I pull back. "Yeah, okay." I don't add that there's nothing else to do anyway. Nothing that will make me feel any better, that is. So I follow him onto the trail, trying to enjoy the near-spring weather.

We walk in silence to the fitness area near the field of wildflowers. Nate leads me to the bench, and once I've sat down it all starts pouring out.

How my mother called while I was in Hawaii, saying Gran was in the hospital and I needed to come home right away. My realization of the fullness of their selfishness that day at the hospital when I found out it was something they could've — and should've — handled. Finding out Gran might have cancer. Quitting my job, and my parents not speaking to me since. Then finding out Gran actually has cancer, and remembering when this happened to Gramps. In talking about it, I realize part of my anguish is remembering how awful that was.

"You're afraid your grandmother is going to suffer just as badly," Nate interjects, voicing the thought forming on my tongue. "That she's going to die."

"Yes, I think that's it exactly," I agree, sniffing. I lift a hand to my cheek and feel wetness there. Apparently I started crying again. Or maybe I never stopped.

Nate puts one leg up on the bench and turns toward me. "I hate to say this, but she will die eventually," he says hesitantly. "Hopefully not for a long time, but either way, I've gotten to know Dorothy pretty well. She does things on her terms. And she's a tough lady. I think your decision to simply be here for her during this is the best. And the hardest. Because I don't think she'll let you do something you don't want to do. But even if what you want is to stay, I don't think she's going to let you help her more than she needs."

He certainly does know her. I close my eyes, wondering if there's another option. If I just started traveling now instead of watching Gran battle cancer. Is that want I want? Even if it is, I couldn't. But no, it's not what I want.

I open my eyes and look back at Nate. "Then for once I guess I've chosen the difficult path because I know it's what's right for me. I'll never regret that, no matter how hard it gets. She's been there for me my whole life. And I don't just want to do this because I owe it to her. I want to do it to bring her whatever comfort I can. But you're right. It's going to be hard."

Nate lays his hand over mine. My heart races and the waterworks flow afresh at all of the emotions I'm feeling, what his comfort adds to that.

"You won't be alone," he murmurs.

I smile through the tears. Even my own family couldn't pull their heads out of their asses long enough to offer real support. "You have no idea how much I appreciate that."

"It's the least I can do for Dorothy," he says, pulling back. "I don't make friends easily, in case that wasn't obvious, but she was relentless."

I laugh. "That's Gran."

"I also don't give up on people I care about," he continues. "So you're both stuck with me now."

I wipe my face and laugh. "I'll take it. I could obviously use a friend right now."

Nate rises and holds out his hand. "Come on. I know exactly what you need."

I take his hand and let him pull me to my feet, then we proceed along the rest of the trail loop back to the gym.

When we get to the parking lot, he gestures to his truck.

"Hop in. I'll drop you back here when we're done."

I hesitate for a moment, but when he opens the passenger door and holds out a hand, I figure what the hell. So I take his hand and let him help me into the truck. Even with his assistance, it's still a trick. The damn truck is huge.

He climbs into the driver's side and we head out. I don't even have time to question him as to where he's taking me before he pulls off the main highway running through town at a sign that says *Alpine Ridge Tavern.*

A square building with the usual town motif sits there with barely a couple of cars in the lot.

"Day drinking? Really?" I ask as he pulls into a parking spot.

"Nope. I mean, not unless you really want to."

I give him a funny look and climb out of the truck. Getting out is definitely easier than getting in. I meet him on the walkway and follow him in, still wondering what else there is to do at a bar besides drink.

"Hey, Rae," Nate calls as we enter.

A middle-aged woman with sandy blond hair who's standing behind the bar looks up and grins.

"Well, Nate Edwards, I do declare," she teases. "Long time no see. Here for the good stuff, I presume?" Her eyes flick to me in interest.

Nate climbs onto a barstool. "Yep. Two, please."

"Well, all right then," Rae replies, leaving the bar and disappearing into a door at the back of the room.

I climb onto the stool next to him. "I'm guessing you're a regular here?" I ask.

"Not really. But it's a small town. Everyone knows everyone." He shrugs.

I'm distracted out of pressing him further by Rae returning through the door with two plates, one in each hand.

She goes back behind the bar and approaches, setting one plate in front of each of us.

"Pie?" I ask incredulously, turning to Nate. "*You* eat *pie?*"

Rae chuckles.

"I eat *this* pie," he affirms. "Rae, this is Mia Anderson. Dorothy's granddaughter."

At Gran's name, Rae lights up. "Nice to meet you, Mia," she replies, extending a hand. I shake it, still a little confused as to what's going on here. "Haven't seen Dorothy in an age either. How's she been?"

Unsure of how to answer the question, my eyes dart toward Nate.

"Never mind all that," Nate says. "Tell her about the pie."

Rae rolls her eyes, but she smiles. "It's my great-grandmother's recipe. Wild huckleberry pie. Award winning, yadda, yadda, yadda." She blushes a little.

Nate takes a monster bite that includes both the whipped cream on top and the crust, and I can't help it, my eyebrows shoot up to my hairline.

"If Nate's eating it, it must be amazing," I allow.

"Well, go on then," Rae says, going back to what she'd been doing when we arrived. But I can see her watching me out of the corner of her eye.

When I take a bite, I know exactly why Nate brought me here.

"Holy freaking hell," I exclaim. "This is incredible."

Rae is still pretending to ignore us, but I see her satisfied smile. She should be satisfied. Somehow both tart and sweet, the filling is in perfect balance. The crust is likewise perfection, soft and flakey and buttery. And I'm almost positive the whipped cream is homemade too. It's not just delicious, it somehow tastes like childhood. But no offense to Gran, her huckleberry pies never tasted like *this*.

I'm silent as I demolish my slice, just as fast as Nate does this time. And decorum be damned, I lick the plate clean, causing Nate to laugh.

"I'm guessing you liked it?" he teases. He reaches up and his thumb brushes the side of my mouth. I blush, realizing I probably have it all over my face, so I grab my napkin and wipe at my lips self-consciously.

"I *loved* it. And you were right. It was just what I needed." I turn to Rae. "That was phenomenal, really, thank you."

"Glad you liked it," she replies humbly. "Come by any time for more."

Nate puts some bills up on the counter and stands. "Well, now that I've thoroughly ruined your dinner, I'll get you back to your car."

"Totally worth it," I assure him.

"Oh good. I know huckleberries aren't everyone's favorite, but I took a shot," he replies, opening the door for me.

"I've eaten them since I was a little kid," I assure him. "And don't tell Gran, but that's hands down the best huckleberry pie I've ever had."

Nate laughs. "Your secret is safe with me."

As we ride the few minutes in companionable silence, I glance over at his profile. I'm not sure if I can be just friends with a man that holds me while I cry, listens when I babble, and then buys me pie. Oh, and the fact that he's both insanely hot and clearly intelligent.

But I need to try. My life is already complicated enough. Besides, I'm sure he's not interested in me like that. He referred to me as a friend, after all. And it's probably best it stays that way. Even if Gran clearly wants us to be more.

"Mia," Nate says gently.

I shake myself and look up, realizing we're parked next to my car. I blush hard.

"Sorry, lost in thought," I admit.

"Of course you are," Nate says understandingly. "Go home, spend some time with your grandmother. I'll see you again tomorrow."

"Yes, see you tomorrow," I agree, popping the door open.

"Oh, and Mia?"

I turn to find Nate looking at me intently. "I'm going to make you pay for that pie tomorrow." And then he winks at me.

Oh, brother. I should've known. "Uh-huh. I'll be ready," I assure him with a roll of the eyes. Then I drop onto the pavement and close the door behind me.

As he pulls away, I can't help smiling. If nothing else, Nate is a good distraction. I try not to think about the fact that leaving him is quickly becoming one of the hardest parts of my day.

CHAPTER TWELVE

MIA

Wednesday evening finds me with my butt whupped from Nate's grueling "walk" today. And by walk, I mean hike. Nearly vertically at times. Apparently our regular trail branches out, and Nate hinted at even tougher loops to come. Clearly he went very easy on me yesterday due to my mental state.

Still, I'd call it the good kind of tired. Though as I'm now sitting reluctantly at the dining table with Gran, ready to call my parents, I wonder if I have enough energy left to deal with them.

But Gran is already dialing, the phone on speaker, so ready or not, here we go.

"Hi, Ma," my mother answers.

"Hello, Linda," Gran replies. *Oooh, burn.* She didn't call her "honey" like she normally does for all of us. Gran must be angrier with her than she's let on. "How are you?"

"Busy, as usual. Any news from the doctor?" Mom asks, cutting to the chase. Always cutting to the chase.

Gran rolls her eyes. "Yes, there is. And there's no nice way to say this," she hedges. "I have advanced lymphoma and I start chemo on Monday."

There's silence on the other end of the phone and Gran gives me a smug look. I press my lips together, trying to keep from laughing. This situation should be anything but funny, yet somehow Gran still manages to crack me up. God, I love this woman.

"Well, I wasn't expecting that," Mom finally says.

"Me neither," Gran replies drily. "But here we are."

Another beat of silence, followed by, "Is Mia still there?"

Anger flares through me, but Gran puts a hand on mine, indicating I should keep quiet.

"Of course she is," Gran replies. "She would never leave me at a time like this."

My anger melts and I have to put a hand over my mouth to stop the laughter. She is *good*.

"We didn't leave you, Mother, don't be dramatic," Mom replies, instantly picking up on the innuendo. "We have businesses to run and Carrie had finals. It's why we left Mia there, after all. What else did you expect us to do? Anyway, now Carrie wants to come for spring break, so I think this is the perfect excuse for us all to visit."

"You know you're always welcome," Gran replies. I look at her incredulously and she shrugs. "Oh, and since you're all coming, I'd like you to bring the rest of Mia's effects along from the guest house. Seeing as she'll be staying here a while."

My mother sighs heavily. "I'm not sure we'll have room," she protests.

Really? They won't have room in their giant SUV? More like they can't be bothered to finish packing up the few clothes, toiletries, and personal effects I hadn't already left with in the first place.

"I'm not sure I can spare her for a whole day while she goes all the way back there just to bring a few boxes all the way back here. Since you'll already be heading this way, I'm sure you can figure it out," Gran replies.

"I can't make any promises, but I'll see what I can do."

"You do that, dear," Gran replies.

"Well, I guess we'll see you Saturday late morning. Love you, Ma."

"Didn't you want to talk to Mia?" Gran asks.

"I think it's best if I don't," Mom says tersely.

Ouch. Seriously?

"Really, Linda? She's your daughter."

"When she starts *acting* like my daughter, I'll start *treating* her like my daughter."

"Oh, grow up," Gran snaps. "Do you really have so little respect for her choices?"

Mom snorts. "She didn't exactly have any respect for her father with the choice she made, so no, not particularly. Look, I really don't want to get into this. We'll come see you, I'm sure we'll all play nice as long as we have to. But I don't have to like it. End of story. Bye, Ma." And she hangs up.

Gran sighs. "I'm sorry you had to hear that, honey. She'll come to her senses. You'll see."

I shake my head. "Mom? Back down? Doubtful." My stomach roils with anger, but I push it down. No need to blow up in front of Gran.

"You don't have to be here this weekend," Gran points out.

"And leave you to the wolves?" I reply. "I would never."

She waves a hand at me. "I can handle them. And I may even be able to put them in their place a little better if you weren't here."

"All right, if you're sure. I'll check with Joanie. She was going to come here this weekend anyway, so maybe I can meet her somewhere for a girls weekend."

Gran pats my hand reassuringly. "Sounds perfect, honey. Now, I think I've had quite enough excitement for one day. I'm going to go get ready for bed."

I throw her a vague smile as she gets up and leaves. Since I know Joanie's probably still working to catch up from vacation, I text her.

Unfortunately, a few texts back and forth outs that she's not only catching up, she committed to work travel through next week. So our weekend get-together is postponed, and now I'm worried I may have to make good on my promise not to leave Gran to the wolves.

CHAPTER THIRTEEN

NATE

"Cancer is an excuse to visit? Seriously?" I look at Mia incredulously.

"I wish I were kidding."

Even though I'm standing still, Mia continues the warm-up exercises. I'm just having trouble processing the extent of her family's issues.

"Well, good luck with that. Sounds like a blast," I finally say sarcastically.

"And that's exactly why Gran wants me to stay away while they're here."

My glower deepens. "I agree with her. No sense hanging around just to be treated like dirt."

"You both have a point. Maybe I'll go back to Seattle for the weekend. Play tourist. Not like I did much of that these last ten years."

Mia finishes warming up and heads down the trail. I'm so thrown by a thought her last comment sparked that it takes me a minute to catch up. I'd planned on heading up to Lake Wenatchee this weekend. That's sufficiently non-date-ish, right?

"Or you could come camping with me," I suggest as casually as possible.

"Isn't it a little early in the season for camping?" she asks.

I shrug. "Figured I'd head up to the lake. Do some fishing. Might be a little cold, but it'll be all right."

Mia snorts. "You do know it's spring break, right? The lake is going to be packed with kids renting party cabins and stumbling around drunk all day and night."

I pull a face. "Damn. Guess that blows my weekend plans out of the water."

"So come to Seattle with me instead," she suggests.

I try not to let my surprise show on my face. That *definitely* doesn't sound platonic. In fact, it sounds romantic, and definitely not in the realm I'm struggling to keep our relationship.

"No, ma'am," I reply emphatically. "You just talked me out of traveling. Just come stay at my place. We'll figure out something to do." The words are out of my mouth before I'm able to stop them. My subconscious just gave our non-relationship a hard shove in the opposite direction. But the selfish part of me hopes she'll say yes.

"Did you just *ma'am* me?" she asks. "I'm not quite thirty yet, good sir."

That surprises me. I had her pegged for early thirties, easy. "Really? Because you seem older — uh, more mature … than most twenty-nine-year-olds."

She laughs. "Nice save," she says sarcastically.

I can feel the heat rising in my neck out of embarrassment. "Sorry. Been a while since I've, you know …"

"Talked to a woman?" she suggests with a smile.

The blush spreads over my face.

"Maybe," I reply hesitantly.

"You talk to Gran," she points out playfully.

I give her a sharp look. "You know what I mean."

"Well, we're just friends, so you don't have to worry. You're not going to offend me. Probably."

I chuckle and wipe my brow comically, demonstrating my relief. Except I'm still nervous as hell, because it sounds like she might actually be considering it.

"So when's the big day?" I ask, referring to her thirtieth birthday. Except after I say it, I realize it sounds like I'm asking when she's getting married. And I've officially turned into a blathering idiot. I know it's the thought of having her alone at night, in a place where I can't walk away from how she makes me feel.

Mia grimaces. "You're not going to try to surprise me or something, are you? Because I'm not a fan of surprises."

I shake my head and laugh. "No, but if you tell me there might be huckleberry pie in it for you."

"April second," she immediately offers up. "Pie?" She holds out a hand like I'm magically going to produce a pie out of thin air.

"I meant on your birthday. You haven't earned more pie yet."

"Nate. I'm a grown woman. If I want pie, I'm going to eat pie."

"If you want to feel better, maybe you choose not to."

"Treading on thin ice there, Edwards. You're old enough to know better than to tell a woman what to eat."

"Hey, you asked for my help getting in shape, right? It's all about balance. There's a time and place for pie, don't worry. But we literally just had pie two days ago. Bit soon."

"Damn, was that really only two days ago?" she asks incredulously.

"Yes, it was. And by the way, I was serious about you staying at my place this weekend," I reiterate.

"Yeah, I caught that, funny enough," she replies drily. "What's it going to cost me?"

"Avocado chocolate mousse?" I suggest playfully as we hook around the final loop of the trail.

"If I don't get pie, you don't get mousse," she grouses jokingly. She stops at our stretching station. "Awww, you took it easy on me today."

"All part of the plan," I assure her, throwing up a leg onto the bar to stretch out my hamstrings.

"And you say you don't know how to talk to a woman." She gives me a wink as she bends into her own stretch. When she stands back up, she looks me levelly in the eye. "Okay, if you're sure it's not too much trouble, I'll come hang out with you this weekend."

"No trouble at all," I assure her with a wink.

She turns so red she shifts her next stretch so she's facing away. Obviously I affect her too. Maybe exploring that a little wouldn't be the worst idea. Or I could be reading her wrong and it could completely blow up in my face. One way or another, this is going to be a very interesting weekend.

CHAPTER FOURTEEN

MIA

I'm pretty sure when I told Gran I'd be staying at Nate's she started planning our wedding. Why am I so sure? Because it's Saturday morning, we're saying our goodbyes, and she's bursting with excitement. And I *know* that's not because my family is coming to visit.

"Call me if you need me to come back," I remind her for the thousandth time. "I won't be far away."

"Oh, I won't interrupt your weekend, honey, don't you worry about me." Her grin widens to face-splitting proportions.

"There won't be anything to interrupt," I assure her, again for the thousandth time. "Just two friends, hanging out. That's all." I'm going to keep repeating it until we both believe it. Because I can't deny I've had some very not-friend-appropriate feelings around Nate lately.

"Whatever you say," she trills.

I roll my eyes, sick of trying to convince Gran there's nothing going on between Nate and me, despite her best efforts. Despite that, every time I see him, I have to remind myself now isn't the time to start a relationship. He deserves better than my mess.

I give her a kiss on the cheek and grab my pack from next to the couch.

"See you tomorrow." And with that, I leave.

I stop at the grocery store first, getting the fresh ingredients I'll need to make the avocado chocolate mousse as well as lunch. I may have given Nate a hard time, but it's the least I can do in exchange for an escape from family drama.

Then I plug in the address Nate gave me and start toward his place. I end up going on roads I didn't know existed, winding further up the mountain than I knew Alpine Ridge even went. Though technically it's all unincorporated Kittitas County, so I doubt they're picky about town boundaries out here.

Eventually I round a turn that ends on a dirt road. Presumably Nate's driveaway.

This place is a good twenty minutes outside of town proper. On top of being a bachelor pad, I don't have high expectations. But as the tree-lined drive opens to the clearing where the house is, I'm floored.

The modern structure is stunning. Nestled into the slope of the mountain, it has three stories that stagger along the terrain. The entire frame is a silvery metal that glints in the sun, but almost all of the walls are glass, all the way around the house. I imagine from the inside it almost feels like you're *in* the forest. Though from what I can see of the inside, it looks pretty swank.

I pull up in front of a two-car garage to the side of the imposing structure. It's the only part of the building with non-glass walls.

I climb out of the car, hard-pressed to take my eyes off of it. I grab the groceries and my pack, head to the front door, and press the doorbell button. My neck cranes as I take in the streamlined cream bench and smoke-gray cabinet just inside, which I can see through the glass door. The combinations of light and dark are perfection, making the entrance look like shadows in the trees.

Finally, the door pops open. I tear my eyes away and they land on Nate. Shirtless. In those damn grey sweats he wears all the time. And he's covered in a sheen of sweat that highlights every dip and line in his well-muscled chest and stomach. Good. Lord. It was one thing imagining it, but this … holy. Fucking. Shit.

"Mia," he says breathlessly. "I thought you weren't coming until after lunch."

"I'm … I …" I stutter, trying to compose myself. I will my eyes to meet his. "No, the fam was due to show up before lunch. Sorry, if I'm disturbing you, I can come back later." My eyes drop back down to his glistening torso like they have a mind of their own.

"God, no, it's fine," he assures me, reaching out for the grocery bags in my hands. "Let me help you with those."

I hand them over and he steps back, inviting me in. I step under the archway and the shadow effect expands and unfolds before my eyes, thankfully drawing my eyes away from Nate's body.

"This house is … wow," I say.

"Wow … good?" he asks warily.

I nod and look back at him. "Very good. Very unexpected."

That gets a smirk out of him. "What did you expect?"

"Honestly? Pretty much the opposite of this."

He huffs a laugh. "Are these groceries?" he asks, looking down at the bags in his hands.

"Yes, I brought stuff to make lunch. If that's okay with you?"

"That's great, actually. I was just lifting. I'll show you to the kitchen then get cleaned up while you do your thing, if that's cool." He starts walking and I follow mindlessly.

"Very cool," I murmur, my eyes traveling over his toned back. The tiny muscles in his lower back flex as he carries the bags. Forcing my attention off his body, I remind myself that I'm surrounded by some of the most gorgeous architecture I've ever seen.

So I let my gaze travel over the house instead as he leads me down the hall, past a spacious living area, and into a sleek, beautifully appointed kitchen with cream marble countertops and flat-front white cabinets.

Even in here the windows peek under the cabinets, and from across the room where the dining table sits, lush greenery and light are visible every direction you look.

"I'll be back. Make yourself at home." And with that, Nate disappears.

Not that I mind. I spend a few minutes exploring the kitchen, finding all the tools I'll need. I make the mousse first, since it's quick, then cover it and put it in the back of the fridge. Though as I start to prepare the chicken salad, it takes all of my focus not to stare out the window the whole time. Probably not a great idea with a knife in your hand.

I've only just finished when Nate returns, his light brown locks darkened from the shower he obviously just took, and he's fully clothed this time in black jeans and a black T-shirt. But even the presence of clothing makes me remember its absence — and the sparkling droplets all over his upper body when I arrived. I close my eyes and force myself to stop ogling him. Friends don't do that.

I open my eyes and plaster a smile on my face. "Good timing," I tell him, gesturing at the makeshift buffet I've set up. "I didn't know what you like, so I got a bit of everything. Spinach, kale, chickpeas, black beans, corn, tomatoes, carrots, broccoli, cucumber, bell pepper, red onion, beets, avocado, sliced almonds, dried cranberries, and sunflower seeds." I point to each as I name them. "Oh, and chicken." I hold up the bowl of diced chicken breast I just finished chopping.

He lets out a low whistle. "What, no salad dressing?"

I smirk. "There's olive oil and balsamic vinegar. The store here was fresh out of non-dairy dressing alternatives. Shocking, I know."

"I'm just kidding, Mia, the food looks fantastic. And I'm starving, so let's eat."

Nate grabs a plate and starts heaping a bit of everything into a pile. I watch in awe as he balances a small mountain of chicken on the giant mound of produce he manages to create. By the time he's done, there's only a bit of each left. Probably enough for a version a quarter the size of his. Which, thankfully, is still way more than enough food for me.

"Has anyone ever told you that you eat like a teenaged boy?" I ask as I make my own salad.

He looks up from dousing his food in oil and raises an eyebrow. "Do I look like a teenaged boy?" he retorts.

I blush instantly. As much as I'd love to ignore the fact, he's all man. Tall, strapping, well-muscled … *focus, Mia, focus.*

I don't respond, instead paying attention to assembling my own plate and taking it to the dining room table.

Nate takes a seat across from me.

"You know, I'm not sure I've ever eaten here," he says, pointing down at the table with his fork before spearing a huge bite of chicken and veggies.

"Then why do you have it?" I ask before taking my own bite.

Nate smiles. "Came with the house." He winks at me and I have to laugh.

"Seriously?" I can't help asking.

He scoffs. "No, Mia. I had the house built four years ago and the interior designer helped me pick it."

"Oh," I reply sheepishly. "Wait. You built this place?" My mouth pops open in surprise.

Nate lifts a shoulder. "A construction company built it and an architect designed it. But yes, I requested something that felt like you were outdoors even when you were indoors. I'd say they rose to the challenge pretty well."

"Pretty well? This place is insane," I murmur as I take another bite of my food. "So why do you like the outdoors so much?"

His eyes stay on his plate, laser-focused on the beans he's stabbing onto his fork. "Nature heals. Guess I felt like I needed a lot of that."

I huff a breath out of my nose. "I know how you feel. God, I hope my parents aren't being too bitchy to Gran."

Nate finally looks up. "If I know anything about Dorothy, it's that she can handle herself. Don't worry."

I shrug noncommittally. "I'm not worried, exactly. Curious, maybe. Why my sister even wanted to come here for spring break is beyond me. We haven't done that since we were kids."

"Everyone wants to feel like a kid again sometimes," he suggests.

I process that, finishing the last of my meal. Suddenly wishing I was having a glass of wine with it to take the edge off this strange day. Maybe later though.

"So what do you want to do this afternoon?" I ask. Anything to change the subject.

"Well, it's a little late in the day for fishing, but there's a big pond a bit down the hill that's a great spot."

I wrinkle my nose. "While I appreciate your letting me hang out here, I'm not really into fishing. We may be friends, but fishing buddies?" I shake my head. "Sorry, dude, not gonna happen."

He laughs and tosses his napkin on his now-empty plate. "Fair enough. Do you have an alternative?"

A mischievous smile spreads across my face.

"How are you at Scrabble?"

Nate gives me a look. "It's been a long time since I've played."

I tilt my head. "Then maybe not. I don't want to bruise your ego by kicking your ass."

"I think I'm man enough to deal with a little ass-kicking," he assures me. "But I don't have it here."

"Oh, I brought it with me," I assure him, jumping out of my chair and grabbing his plate. I take it with mine back to the kitchen and give them both a quick rinse before popping them in the dishwasher. I gesture to the remains of the salad bar. "You deal with this, I'll go get it out of my bag."

As Nate tidies, I set the game up at the dining room table. He joins me not long after, dropping back into his chair heavily.

"All right, let's do this," he says in a resigned tone.

"Don't sound so happy about it," I reply sarcastically. I pull seven tiles out of the velvet bag and hand it over to him. "You get seven."

He levels another undecipherable look at me. "I'm familiar with the rules."

"Hey, you're the one who said you hadn't played in a while," I remind him. "I'll even let you go first."

Nate narrows his eyes at me like he doesn't trust the generosity. "No, ladies first, I insist."

I shrug and try not to let loose the predatory grin I feel pulling at my lips. "Suit yourself."

And we play.

For three hours. Three hours in which I realize I've been completely duped.

As he demolishes me for the third time in a row, I throw my hands up.

"That's it, it's official. You're a Scrabble shark. What the fuck does 'quotidian' even mean?" I ask, gesturing toward the one-hundred-and-eight-point word he just creamed me with.

"It's a medical term for something that's a daily occurrence," he explains, trying and failing to hide his triumphant smile.

"Know a lot of medical terms, do you?" I ask sarcastically.

His eyes lift to meet mine. "Kind of comes with the medical degree."

Well, that gets my attention.

"I'm sorry, did you just casually drop that you're a doctor?"

Nate leans back in his chair. "*Was.* I was a doctor. Like you were a lawyer."

"And you haven't mentioned this until now because ..." I look at him questioningly, still not sure if he's pulling my leg. He doesn't exactly give off a doctor vibe.

"It's not something I like talking about."

"So why'd you bring it up, then?"

"I didn't. You asked how I knew a lot of medical terms. I answered. I may not like talking about it, but I'm not going to lie either."

"Wow," I say, totally shocked. "Are there any other major revelations about you that I'm not going to learn until I ask a specific enough question?"

Nate laughs. "Guess you'll just have to find out."

"You're a bastard, Nate."

"Nope. My parents were married when I was born. Still are."

I start to roll my eyes when I realize it's not a snappy comeback. Well, not *just* a snappy comeback.

It's like a lightbulb goes off over my head. What if this is how Nate opens up? So, instead of giving him a ration of shit back, I lean forward on the table.

"Yeah? Where do they live?" I ask.

"Portland."

"Any brothers or sisters?"

"Two younger brothers. One's an actor in L.A., one's a musician. He travels a lot."

"That's an artistic family you've got there."

He shrugs. "I dunno. That gene skipped me."

"Me too," I admit. "Though Carrie's a political science major, so it skipped our whole family, it would seem."

"Oh, I disagree with that. You're the best baker I know. That takes a lot of creativity. I definitely think it's an art form."

"It's only a hobby," I reply, brushing him off.

"If you say so."

I give him a sharp look. "Quit talking about baking or you're going to make me hungry again."

Nate chuckles. "Speaking of which, we've been at this a while, and I'd planned on grilling some steaks for dinner. Sound good?"

If the amount of saliva that fills my mouth is a measure, then the answer is yes. "Sounds amazing."

"All right, then." Nate rises and heads back into the kitchen.

I start putting the Scrabble tiles back in their bag as I watch him take out two foil-wrapped platters.

"What's the other one?" I ask curiously.

"Corn," he replies without looking up. "And don't think I didn't notice the dessert in there."

"Consider it a thank you," I reply.

That gets his attention and his eyes lift to meet mine. "For what?"

A swell of emotion hits me, but I don't waver. "For being a good friend. I don't have many of those these days."

Nate stares at me for long enough to where I start to wonder if I said something wrong. "You don't have to thank me for that," he finally replies.

"Then consider it a perk of our friendship."

One of his genuine, full smiles crosses his face, and it melts me a little. Nate has a way of pushing through my natural defensiveness. Just like him, I've never connected with people easily. But something about how we relate to each other when we both set aside our resistances … well, it just feels good. Easy.

CHAPTER FIFTEEN

NATE

As I make dinner, Mia sits on the padded wicker couch on the back patio and watches the sun set while drinking a glass of the red wine I brought out to go with our meal. And I watch her, looking for any signs that will tell me what is going on in her head.

This afternoon has been unprecedented for me in a lot of ways. I can't remember the last time I actually shared parts of myself, of my life, with anyone, much less an attractive woman. One I get along with, which is remarkable in and of itself. I mean, this afternoon was really … *fun*.

There was also all the staring she did at my chest when she showed up. Though I'll take the blame for that. I probably should've put on a shirt before answering the door. But it did make me wonder. There have been moments between us before where I could feel the connection, and I knew she could too. But the staring was the first time I thought she might actually find me as attractive as I find her.

And the fact that she very pointedly referred to us as friends at least a dozen times smacked of her trying to remind herself of that. I mean, there's the slight possibility that she was trying to remind *me* of that fact. But since I've been a perfect gentleman, not even having stared at her chest, ass, or anything else — at least not when she could possibly catch me — I'm not sure why she'd need to drive that point home for my benefit.

That pits me against myself. Do I remember where she's at and enforce the friendship angle? Or do I test the waters?

As if she senses my thoughts, she turns back toward me and hits me with a smile that rips right through me. I'm not sure I've ever seen her smile like that. A feeling equal parts joy and longing twists in my chest.

"Enjoying yourself?" I ask.

"It's gorgeous here, Nate. So peaceful. I didn't realize how much I needed this kind of peace."

I pull the steaks and corn off the grill and bring them to the table, setting the tray down next to the salad bowl.

I meant to sit in the wicker chair to her left, next to the empty space on the couch, leaving as much distance as possible between us. But my subconscious betrays me and I find myself beside her before I realize what I've done.

"I'm glad," I say, looking into her eyes. "That's what I needed too. A sanctuary."

"That's a good word for this place," she murmurs, looking around.

I unwrap the corn and dish out portions, and we eat while the sun sets, finishing the bottle of wine and breaking out another.

Surprisingly, I'm the one who ends up doing most of the talking. Finally, it seems like we've settled into a place where my tongue cooperates around her. I'd say it's the wine, but she's had more than I have. In any case, I tell her about all the details that went into the house, such as using the trees that were cleared as flooring and landscaping that was designed to protect water quality.

And she tells me about all the places she wants to travel someday, languages she wants to learn, and all the other things she feels like she didn't get to do while living a life she let someone else choose for her. I don't tell her that I've been there. This part of the conversation isn't about me. It's about her understanding where she's been, so she can figure out where she needs to go. It's a good reminder that she's still very upset and confused about everything right now. And that's even without Dorothy's illness, which we don't talk about but I know weighs on her too.

By the time she's done talking, the food is long gone and the remnants put away, the wine is almost gone too, and stars are dotting the evening sky. We're sitting silently when Mia folds her legs beneath her and leans into me. And like a reflex, I wrap my arm around her shoulders.

I hold my breath for a moment, expecting there to be tension. But there's not. It just feels right. Comfortable. We watch stars fill the sky like that for a bit.

"Do you ever get lonely out here?" she asks out of the blue.

"No," I reply honestly. What I don't say is that I never have. But now that she's been here with me, I'm fairly certain that I'll never be able to sit on this porch again and watch the sunset without missing her.

And I realize in that moment that I'm falling for her.

I don't bother wondering when that started happening. Because I know. I've been fighting it since I met her.

It hurts my heart, since I can't ask her to start something right now. Even if she wanted to, as deep down I'd know how it would end if we do that before she's figured herself out.

"Nate?" she whispers.

I turn my head and look down at her. Her face is framed in moonlight and starlight, and she's so fucking beautiful it hurts.

She shifts so she's upright, then wraps her fists in my T-shirt. My heart beats faster.

"I need to know something," she says, her voice filled with emotion, but which one I'm not sure.

I swallow hard. "What's that?"

She pulls herself toward me, or maybe she meant to pull me, but the effect is the same: Her face inches from mine. Her mouth close to my mouth as she leans her forehead against mine. So close I can smell the wine on her breath.

"I need to know what it's like to kiss you," she whispers.

My chest tightens with longing, but I press her away far enough to look into her eyes. "Mia, you've had a lot to drink, and —"

"No, I think I've had just enough," she interrupts, and then she breaks free of my hold and kisses me.

I'm so startled I don't react until her arms are around the back of my neck and she slides into my lap.

Her lips are hot and supple, and she definitely tastes like the wine. But I can only fight it so much when she's warm and willing and sitting on top of me, and I wrap my arms around her. I open my mouth and slide my tongue over her bottom lip to allow myself a real taste.

It nearly undoes me as she accepts it, as our tongues tangle while her hands wind into my hair. I slide my hands to her face, tilting her head to give me better access to her delicious mouth.

It's heaven and hell at the same time, as all the fantasies I didn't even let myself have come to life. Fantasies I knew I shouldn't want. Couldn't want. But right now, I don't care.

I've kissed a lot of women in my day, but it's never been so good. I'm burning with desire on every possible level. The fire I've seen in her eyes has become a raging passion between us that continues to build to an inferno as she grinds into me, as I slip a hand under her shirt, the soft skin under my fingertips causing me to moan into her mouth.

She inhales sharply and tilts her head up, and my lips finds the soft skin of her neck, licking, sucking, and biting as she makes the most erotic noises. It makes me want to strip her bare, slip inside of her, and see what other noises I can get her to make. My cock swells at the thought and she clearly feels it, grinding harder toward the spot where it meets her thigh.

It's been too long since I've let myself go, and as she tugs at my shirt, my good sense rallies a cry from underneath the mind-numbing need Mia just drew out of me.

"Stop," I breathe out, gathering myself and pressing her back. "We can't do this."

She looks at me, clearly bewildered. "I think your erection disagrees with you," she sasses me.

I can't help but laugh a little. "I didn't say I didn't *want* to," I point out. "But we can't, Mia. That's not why I asked you to come here tonight. That's not ... it's not what I expected." I briefly consider tossing in the "friends don't kiss" line, but after that kiss there's no way I can ever be just friends with this woman again. I don't even want to use that word around her anymore.

"God, you're such a gentleman," she says, shaking her head. And just as unexpectedly as when she pounced on me the first time, in a move I would never have seen coming in a million years she pulls off her top and bra in one swift move. "Tell me you don't want me, Nate."

I'm speechless. And not just because it's so unlike her to be this forward. Her tits are fucking perfect. Huge and teardrop-shaped, with dark, full nipples I just want to explore with my tongue. I work to master myself but it's just been so damn long.

I force my eyes to hers, looking at least for one last reassurance that I'm not taking advantage of her.

"I want you more than you could possibly know, Mia," I assure her. "But I don't want you to do something you'll regret tomorrow."

She grabs my hand, bringing it to her breast, forcing it to press into the ridiculously silky flesh. Without thought, my thumb runs over her puckered nipple, and I feel it harden further under my touch. My cock twitches in my pants and she moans.

"I need this," she assures me, sounding perfectly clearheaded. "More than *you* could possibly know."

My hands still, and I look into her eyes. I see the turmoil there. A feeling I remember well. A part of me realizes she's trying to fuck her problems away. To replace the hurt and confusion with something else. Something our connection today obviously sparked, as she's never behaved like this with me before.

I realize suddenly that it's my own selfish desire to be with her — really *be* with her — that's holding me back. The hope for something more. But really, what would a woman like this want with a man like me for the long haul? I'm so broken I've resigned the rest of my life to small-town mountain life. This woman is meant for so much more.

My delusion of falling in love with her evaporates. That's never going to happen, I see that. So if I can't have all of her, I'll take what I can get.

In one swift movement, I rise with her in my arms. She squeals in surprise, locking her legs around my waist and wrapping her arms tightly around my neck.

I use the opportunity to suck the spot below her ear that makes her pant as I carry her upstairs to the guest bedroom.

I lay her out on the bed, intending to take my shirt off, but the sight of her topless and waiting for me is too much. I climb on top of her, long-suppressed need turning me into an animal.

I grind into her core as I claim her with my mouth. In a clash of teeth and tongues and groans, all of the little flirtations and touches and moments I dismissed as nothing explode between us.

She rips my shirt off. I pull her jeans off. Her shoes go with them when they get in the way. She tugs at my jeans, but I shake my head, knowing I'm going to come hard and fast when we get there.

So instead of pounding her like I want, I decide to take the frantic need I have for her out on her with my mouth. I drop my head between her legs and she gasps in surprise. And when my tongue hits her, she gasps for other reasons. Her panting gasps quickly escalate to writhing moans as I lap furiously at her.

Her fingers twist and pull at my hair, sending signals straight to my dick. Equal parts frustrated and on fire, I add two fingers to the mix, thrusting unrepentantly into her.

"Oh fuck, Mia, you're so goddamn tight," I grind out through clenched teeth.

She bucks and moans and fucks my fingers. I can't help watching her chase her orgasm. It's such a turn on that I'm in danger of blowing my load right now.

But I push through, twisting and flicking my fingers inside of her until she clenches and screams "Holy fucking shit!" over and over.

The chant trails off to a whisper as her body unfurls and slumps back down to the bed languidly. It's then that I remember I don't have any condoms.

"Fuck." The angry curse slips out before I can stop it.

She lifts her head from the bed and gives me a questioning look.

I shake my head in response. Maybe I can just distract her with more orgasms.

She sits up, pulls me toward her. "Fuck me, Nate. Please." She kisses down my neck, one of her hands dipping down to stroke me over my jeans.

Well, there goes that plan.

"I don't have condoms."

Her hand dives into my waistband, gripping me so tightly I moan.

"I don't care," she says before pulling my pants down and leaning forward to slip the tip of my dick in her mouth.

Her tongue swirls around it as her hands continue to push the fabric down my legs. She presses me over onto my back and pulls my bottoms completely off, then goes back to work on my cock.

My brain goes fuzzy with pleasure, and when her hand starts working with her mouth, I've regressed to a full primal state where all I know is I need to be inside this woman.

Like she read my mind, she climbs up and sinks onto me.

"Oh fuck," I cry out, so close to coming I have to disconnect my brain completely not to focus on the fact that she's started to ride me like a fucking cowgirl. That her breasts are bouncing on my chest as her core slides over my length repeatedly. "God, Mia, you're gonna make me come."

The warning comes in a voice I don't even recognize. It's throaty and husky, and I feel like I'm floating outside of my own body for a moment listening to it.

"Good," she says breathlessly. She reels back up into a full sitting position, pressing down into me and swirling in circles with me buried fully in her slick grip. It's another level of amazing, but breaks the rhythm enough to stave off the explosion.

That is, until she leans back and starts bouncing in a way that makes the tip of my cock slam into a spot inside her. The one that makes her start screaming. The one that makes her come on my cock, squeezing me hard. And I lose all sense, jerking up, fucking her as she loses the ability to control her thrusts, sending me to my own peak. My orgasm rips out of me in head-spinning bursts. On the last surge, I push hard and deep into her, spending the last moment with her quaking around me.

She tumbles forward onto my chest, her mouth meeting mine. I kiss her fervently, breaking off only when I need to catch my breath.

It's not long before I realize things are getting very slippery between us. I shift and roll her onto the bed next to me.

"Be right back," I promise, heading to the guest bathroom. I use a towel clean myself up before heading back to her with a wet washcloth.

"Mmm, what's that for?" she asks sleepily as she looks up at me.

"You," I tell her, dipping it between her legs and gently wiping the mess away.

She bites into her bottom lip. "Is it weird that that feels really nice?" she asks with a giggle.

It makes me smile to see her so relaxed.

I lean over and give her a kiss. "I'm going to go get us some water from the kitchen. Be back in a few."

She nods dismissively and closes her eyes. I stare at her for a moment. All dark, wild hair, flushed cheeks, and curves that are even more devastatingly stunning now that she's bare before me. I'm usually the aggressive one, sexually, but having her take control like she did tonight was one of the biggest turn-ons of my life.

Once downstairs, I drop the washcloth in the laundry room hamper before heading into the kitchen. I notice the two wine bottles are still on the kitchen counter, so I turn to put them in the recycling bin. Only to look down in puzzlement at the bottle already in there. Because I'm not a wine drinker, and I only had a couple of glasses tonight. I didn't think much of Mia having more, since I know she drinks it regularly and it was over the course of the evening.

Which would've been great if it was just a bottle and a half. But it wasn't.

My heart drops into my stomach when I realize how much she really drank.

How, regardless of seeming sober, she has to be off-her-ass drunk.

And that I just completely took advantage of her.

"Goddamn it," I curse.

I grab a couple of bottles of water and go back to the laundry room, where I grab a pair of sweats and a shirt from the dryer. I can't go back up there naked.

Once dressed, I bound up the stairs, taking them three at a time. But when I get back in the room, Mia is in the same position I left her, eyes still closed.

"Mia?" I say softly.

She doesn't move a muscle.

I drop the water bottles on the end of the bed and crawl toward her, suddenly concerned.

"Mia," I try again, this time resting a hand gently on her arm.

Still nothing. I put a finger under her nose and confirm she's still breathing. With a relieved sigh, I sit back on the other side of the bed and watch her for a minute.

How could I not have realized? How could I have let this happen? Will she remember it? Is it better if she doesn't?

No, I decide. It's better if she remembers, even if she regrets it. Because if she doesn't remember, she's definitely going to figure it out given how hard we fucked. And I can't even imagine how violated she'd feel.

At the thought, I bury my face in my hands in shame. God, I'm a world-class prick. I scrub my hands over my eyes and shake myself out of it.

Rising, I put a water bottle on her side of the bed and shimmy the comforter out from under her so I can cover her naked body. Then I fold her clothes neatly onto the dresser and grab my own discarded ones. I put them in the laundry room downstairs and grab some ibuprofen, which I bring back into the guest room and quietly set next to the bottle of water. And then I head to my room.

I'm not sure if it's because I don't want to scare her by being there unexpectedly in the morning if she doesn't remember or if I'm just a coward. It's both, I know. I can't lie next to her knowing what I've done. I only hope we can talk about it tomorrow.

CHAPTER SIXTEEN

MIA

I wake up feeling cotton-mouthed and fuzzy-headed in an unfamiliar bed. It takes me a minute to remember that I'm at Nate's. It takes me another minute to remember that I'm at Nate's because I'm avoiding my family. The tired, sick feeling must be from booze, and lots of it. I don't remember getting drunk, but I know that that's what this feeling is from. I don't get this level of hungover often — in fact, I can probably count the number of times on one hand — but it's a feeling you don't soon forget.

I lift my head and search for a clock. I turn to look over my shoulder and the world suddenly tilts, the contents of my stomach tilting with it.

I jump out of bed, only briefly registering that I'm completely naked as I desperately scan the room. There's a door in the corner and I can see a sink. Thank god.

I bolt inside and dive at the toilet just in time to empty my stomach into the porcelain bowl.

When the hell finally stops, I sink onto the blessedly cool tile floor and lean back against a tub. By the taste in my mouth, it was wine. Lots and lots of wine. And maybe ... beef?

I try hard to remember yesterday. There was lunch. I definitely remember lunch. But that was chicken salad. And then Scrabble. Then I think there was dinner ... yes, that's where the beef came from. I remember now, we had steak. And yes, wine ... but that's where everything starts to blur around the edges and disappear.

When I finally stop sweating and the room stops spinning, I rise, now on a mission to find my clothes. *Why am I not wearing clothes?* I wonder. As I push myself to a standing position, certain parts of me complain loudly. Ones between my legs.

Holy.

Fucking.

Shit.

No. "No, no, no, no, no," I moan out loud, heading back into the bedroom. I scan the room for signs of Nate. But there aren't any, unless you count the bottle of water and pills on the nightstand and my clothes, folded into a neat pile, sitting on the dresser.

Nate touched my clothes. Nate almost certainly tucked me into bed, and left water and medicine knowing I would need it. Nate knew I was drunk. Nate and I had sex, even though he knew I was drunk.

A fury like I've never known unfurls in my chest. How *dare* he? I trusted him. I came here because I needed to get away from all the hurt and confusion that is my family. And he exploited my emotional, drunk state.

I start to crumble, tears pouring down my face. And a million questions fly through my head. Did we use protection? What if I get something? What if I get pregnant? How could he do this?

I take a deep breath, realizing I need to pull my shit together and get the hell out of here. I look at the clock on the nightstand I noticed in my search for evidence of Nate. It's just before five o'clock. The sun won't even be up for a couple more hours. And I hope Nate won't either.

It won't be easy to make my way back to Gran's while it's dark, but I don't care. I dress quickly and poke my head out of the bedroom door.

The house is dark and quiet. I move quickly and quietly, keeping alert for any signs of Nate. But I make it all the way downstairs without any. I find my things where I'd left them last night, and head to the front door. Here's hoping he doesn't have a burglar alarm.

I pop open the front door … and nothing. With a sigh of relief, I slip out into the cold, black morning. I get in my car as quietly as I can, knowing starting the car will be my biggest risk. I take a deep breath and turn the key. I have it in drive before it even fully starts and coast down Nate's driveway.

I watch the rearview, but there's nothing. No lights, no signs he heard.

I sigh with relief as I hit the main paved road again and focus on not driving off the side of the mountain.

It takes twice as long to get down into town as it did to get to Nate's, and the faintest signs of sunlight have started to turn the sky around me a barely lighter blue with a tiny bit of pink on the horizon.

As I pass through the main drag on the way back to Gran's, I remember that what I'm going back to isn't a lot better than what I just left. Because if my parents and sister are still there, it'll just be a different kind of awful.

Once I realize that, I pull over into the first parking lot I see. And I slump forward on the steering wheel, letting the tears flow. How did my life become such a mess?

Before I can start freaking out too badly, I decide to call Joanie. I don't care if it's early. She's the most real person I know, and my best friend, and I need her.

She answers on the third ring. "You're lucky I'm on the East Coast right now."

"I think I had sex with Nate last night," I blurt out.

"You *think*?"

"Well, judging by my battered va-jay-jay and massive hangover, I guess I'm comfortable saying I *know* I did."

"I take it you don't remember said sexual intercourse?" she asks, sounding every inch a lawyer.

"I don't," I admit, my voice thick with the tears streaming down my face.

"Well, that's a shame," she murmurs.

"Or it's sexual assault," I spit back angrily.

"Are you saying you *do* remember? Or did he … wait," she says. "It's like six a.m. there. Did you just leave his place?"

"Yes."

"Was he aware of this?"

"Not exactly."

"So you haven't talked to him about it?"

"Jo, there was a bottle of water and two ibuprofen on the nightstand when I woke up. And no Nate. It's pretty safe to say he realized I was drunk and had sex with me anyway. My attorney brain wants to call that sexual assault."

"Oh god. I get it. Though he didn't sound like that kind of guy with the taking care of your grandma and all that jazz. Maybe he was drunk too? Or maybe … he didn't figure out you weren't sober until you were doing the deed."

"What does *that* mean?" I ask angrily.

"Well, you *are* the soberest drunk ever. You know that."

"Well, sure, after I've had a few. But this was blackout drunk, Jo. I can't remember anything after dinner."

"I've seen you literally black out while drunk, Mia. The first time it happened I was so terrified I almost called an ambulance until I figured out that you'd just passed out. You seemed totally normal right up until you weren't conscious anymore."

"Really?" I ask in disbelief.

"Yes, really. Maybe he knew you'd had a few and was just being courteous with the water and the pills."

"Why are you defending him? You think it was okay that he took advantage of me like that? I didn't call you so you could tell me I was overreacting —"

"Hey, deep breaths. I'm in your corner. If you say Nate raped you, I believe you, but in that case you should be talking to the police right now instead of me. Because if he did, you know as well as I do that time is of the essence."

Her words are like a bucket of ice water dumped over my head. Because, no, I don't really think Nate raped me. Deep down, I know he wouldn't hurt me on purpose. I'm just in shock.

"I don't think he raped me," I admit. "But I feel … upset. I'm going through enough right now. I didn't need this too."

Joanie *laughs*. "Oh, Mia. I'm sorry, I shouldn't laugh. Look, I'm glad you don't think it was assault. Like I said, that definitely didn't jibe with what you've told me about this guy. But based on what you *have* told me, it's just a damn shame you don't remember it. Because a good roll in the sack with a hot guy is exactly what you need right now to take your mind off of all the bullshit you're dealing with. Just do it without the booze next time, okay? Because you're right, you do have enough to worry about. Sober, casual sex. Got it?"

"That would be great if I was a casual sex kind of girl," I reply. "But you know I'm not. I'm just not wired that way."

"Well, your wiring is all screwed up right now anyway," she points out. "Now is the time to do things you wouldn't normally do. Though that ship might have sailed with our pal Nate if you just bailed on him. He's probably shitting himself right now."

I close my eyes and shake my head. God, she's right. "I keep making messes, Jo. How do I get off this ride?"

"You face the music, my dear. And then you move on and start living your life."

"We're not talking about Nate anymore, are we?"

"Can't get anything past you. The Nate thing is a bump. The real life-shaker is this shit with your family. Until you face it, you're going to be stuck in a mindfuck. You're taking out your frustration on Nate. At worst, he slept with you knowing you weren't totally sober and are in a bad place in your life. Give the guy a break. You *are* pretty irresistible."

That gets a laugh out of me. "Well, my parents are at Gran's right now," I tell her. "Guess I should go rip that band-aid off, huh?"

"Wow, um, yeah, that's … if you're ready, go for it, babe," she replies.

"Maybe I'm too emotional. I wouldn't want to say something —"

"That you really mean?" she teases. "There's never going to be a perfect time."

I inhale slowly. Then exhale slowly. "You're right. Thank you, Jo. I miss you."

"Well, you're going to see me on Saturday, okay? And you know you can call me anytime."

"I know. Same. Talk soon?"

"You know it."

I set my phone down in my lap and dry my face with my hands. I flip the rearview mirror down and check my reflection.

"You can do this," I tell myself with a stern look. I nod to myself and get back on the road.

A sense of determination settles over me as I drive the last couple of miles to Gran's. I'm going to say what I need to say. And they can say whatever they want. But once it's done, my life is mine again. End of story. And then I'll figure out how to fix this mess with Nate.

But when I pull up to Gran's there's a conspicuous lack of any cars except Gran's tiny silver coupe that's parked on the side of the house since it never gets driven anymore.

I get out and unload, looking and listening suspiciously as I walk up the steps.

When I step inside, I'm hit with the smell of coffee.

"Mia," Gran says in surprise, emerging from the kitchen. "You're back early."

I shoot a look around the living room. "Where is everybody?"

Gran smiles and takes a sip from the cup in her hand. "They left yesterday afternoon."

I drop my bag next to the couch. "Are you serious?" I ask angrily. Both because they've just taken the wind out of my sails on getting closure and, if I had known, I could have come back yesterday and avoided the whole Nate debacle. "Why didn't you call me and tell me that?"

That would-be innocent look spreads over her features. "Oh, I figured you'd have more fun at Nate's than spending time watching me nap on the couch. Besides, I'm sure Nate gets lonely up there."

Her words jar something in my memory. *"Don't you get lonely up here?"* Me, asking Nate ... while snuggled against him? And stars. I remember stars. But mostly, I remember feeling safe.

My throat tightens with regret, but I push it back. "Why'd they leave?" I ask, heading into the kitchen for my own cup of coffee.

"Well, your sister apparently only stopped in for lunch. After that, she went to meet some friends at the lake," Gran explains, taking a seat at the dining table. I can tell by her tone that she's not impressed with Carrie at the moment. "And your mother didn't want to stay overnight without your father."

"Dad didn't come?" I ask, joining her at the table.

"No, he didn't." That's all she says, but it speaks volumes.

"He didn't want to see me," I deduce.

"It would seem not," Gran says softly. "But it's his loss." She pats my hand.

I take a deep drink of java and sigh heavily. "So did you have a nice visit with Mom, at least?"

"Actually, I did. The best we've had in a while. I think she's more herself without your father around."

I raise an eyebrow. "Really? That's interesting."

Gran shrugs. "Or maybe it's just easier for us to fall back into patterns of better times when it's just us two. I tried to use the opportunity to talk to her about you, but she insisted we didn't, so I didn't force the issue. She did bring your belongings, at least. So that's something. In any case, I don't expect we'll see any of them again for a while."

I take another deep drink. "That's unfortunate. I'd just worked myself up for us all to get everything out on the table. I think I need to so I can make it clear where I'm at, so they understand."

"Oh, honey," Gran says, pity in her voice. "You don't need to explain yourself to anyone. Least of all your parents. After the way they've behaved, you really don't owe them that."

"I know," I agree. "But I need to do it for me. I need to set the boundary so I can stop thinking about their reaction and how I'll navigate whatever comes next."

"Well, that's a horse of a different color," she agrees. "You can go to them whenever you'd like, you know. I can get someone here to take me to chemo tomorrow."

I put my mug down instantly and wrap my hand over Gran's. "No," I say more forcefully than I'd intend. "I mean, please don't worry about that. I want to take you. I'll talk to Nate this week about being with you for the day while I talk to Mom and Dad."

Gran's eyes sparkle at the mention of Nate. "That sounds lovely, honey."

I wish I could say I was as enthused.

Guess this means I need to get my head straight about what I'm going to say to Nate first. Then my parents. All on top of Gran's first round of chemo. Awesome.

I return my cup to the kitchen sink then take my bag into my room. I shower before I do anything else, hoping it will help clear my head.

It doesn't. And checking my phone after I'm dressed doesn't help either. There's a missed call and a text from Nate.

I take a deep breath and open the text.

NATE

Can we talk about last night?

My heart races, even though it's exactly what I intended to do. Just … maybe not right now.

I'm busy today and Gran has chemo tomorrow. Walk Tuesday?

I set the phone down and walk away, unwilling to torture myself by waiting for his response. I actually do get busy cleaning the house and doing some baking, to the point where I don't think to check my phone again until after lunch.

When I do, I find his short response:

NATE

Okay.

I spend the rest of the day trying not to think about it. Or what could've possibly happened. But while Gran is napping, I leave a note and head into Ellensburg. While I'm on birth control, I'm not taking any chances, so I head to the Fred Meyer pharmacy and get Plan B. I also make a mental note to make an appointment to get tested. Just in case.

CHAPTER SEVENTEEN

NATE

"Christ, Nate, you need to give the free weights a fucking break." Greg, the community fitness center coordinator, gives me a judgmental frown from the treadmill he's repairing to my left.

"What do you care?" I snap back. "It's a Tuesday morning. There's nobody else here."

I look back to the mirror, watching my form as I do a fourth set of bicep curls. The muscles in my arms and torso are straining, and a sheen of sweat covers my entire body. Maybe I have been pushing it a little too hard. I lower the weights to the floor and sit down on the bench, dropping my head and toweling the back of my neck, then moving to my shoulders and chest.

I hear Greg approach and return the dumbbells to the rack. I feel the bench shift as he sits on the other end.

"I don't give a shit about whoever shows up. I'm worried about you, man. You were pushing it all day yesterday too. You wanna talk about it?"

Do I want to talk about the fact that I woke up on Sunday morning and Mia had disappeared? That clearly she bolted, which means she was upset? And that I was terrified to push her to talk sooner, so I didn't call her or show up to find out where her head's at, even though I've been dying a little more every minute since I saw that wine bottle in the recycling bin?

"No," I say firmly. Greg's a good guy, but I wouldn't say we're close enough friends for that kind of discussion. Then again, there's nobody I'm that close with anymore. By design.

"Suit yourself," Greg mutters, going back to what he was doing.

I glance up at the mirror to check the time on the clock behind me. Time to shower anyway. Then meet Mia. I'm equal parts dreading it and needing time to move faster so I can make sure she's okay. That we're okay.

While I'm showering, without the physical distraction of pumping iron, I have to focus to keep my thoughts off our night together. It's why I've barely stopped moving since I woke up to find her gone. I can't think of it, of her that way, without the immense guilt that follows.

As I exit the gym a few minutes later, I have the brief thought that she may not even show. But that's quickly dispelled as I see her already waiting in our usual spot.

Her arms are folded over her chest and she's faced toward the back of the building, toward the trail. Her long, dark hair is pulled back by a hairband at the nape of her neck. She's not wearing her usual workout clothes. But the jeans and long-sleeved light blue pullover are still perfectly appropriate for a walk on a cool day.

I shuffle my feet on the dirt path as I approach her from behind, so as not to startle her. She turns immediately, and my heart drops into my shoes. Her face is pale, sad, and drawn. She looks so tired.

I stop in front of her and she looks up at me without a word. Like neither of us knows what to say.

"How'd Dorothy's chemo go?" I ask.

She smiles tightly, and it doesn't reach her eyes. Her arms hug tighter around her. "It was nerve-racking for us both," she admits. "But they gave her a pile of pills to manage any side effects, so I guess we'll see how she handles it."

"I wanted to come by yesterday and check on her."

She nods. "I figured."

I want to ask about Saturday, but I don't want to do it here, so I start walking and she follows. Even though we didn't do our usual warm-up. But there's not going to be anything usual about our visit today.

When we're out of earshot of the gym, I take a deep breath. "So, do you remember what happened Saturday night?"

She doesn't look at me. "When did you figure out I was drunk?" she returns without answering my question.

I'm almost positive that means she doesn't. I already assumed even if she didn't, she'd figured it out. There's no other explanation for her disappearing act.

"After." I get in front of her and stop. "I swear, Mia, you seemed one hundred percent sober. I even asked you more than once and watched you. I had no idea until I went downstairs to get us some water and saw the extra wine bottle. I would have never gone there if I'd known."

"I know. It took me a bit to calm down after I'd left to realize that. And then I figured out what really bothered me was that even if you didn't know I was drunk, you knew what I was going through." She finally looks up at me, tears swimming in her eyes.

And it fucking guts me. Because I've been beating myself up for exactly that. I did know. And even in the moment, I knew I was taking advantage of her.

"I know, and I'm so sorry, you have no idea. And I don't mean to make excuses, but you were … uh, pretty persuasive." I feel heat spread over my face as I remember her, on my lap, removing her shirt and bra and exposing herself to me. I look away and breathe deeply, trying to control my reaction to the memory.

"Oh god," she says, covering her face. "I hadn't even thought about what I might've done. Was it awful?"

I look back at her and tug her hands away from her face. "God, no," I assure her. "If you'd have been sober I'd be remembering it as one of the best nights of my life. But you weren't, so I pretty much feel like the biggest asshole on the planet."

"Did we, umm … did we use protection?" She looks away, blushing furiously.

My mouth sets in a firm line. "I didn't have any, so no. But if it helps, I haven't been with anyone else in four years, and I've tested clean every year since."

She looks back at me, jaw dropped. "*Four years?*"

I shrug, trying not to look as embarrassed as I feel. "It wasn't for lack of opportunity," I reply defensively.

Her brows scrunch together. "So why me? God, I didn't rape you, did I?" She looks horror-struck at the thought.

"No, damn, of course you didn't," I assure her. "I was a very willing participant. I just … haven't. I don't know."

I continue down the path, hoping moving will calm the anxiety that's tightening my chest.

"Well, it's been more than a year for me, and I'm clean too, for what it's worth," she tells me. "And I'm on birth control, but I took a Plan B on Sunday afternoon just in case."

My stomach clenches. It takes me a minute to recognize the feeling as disappointment. Because while I hadn't been in any frame of mind to consider the possibility of getting her pregnant, apparently my subconscious wasn't opposed to the idea.

Fuck, this woman really appeals to my caveman side. I've *never* wanted to get a woman pregnant. And here I am, saddened at the thought that I didn't knock up a woman who doesn't even remember having sex with me. Goddamn, I'm a headcase.

I'm so tied up in my thoughts that I don't realize for a moment that we've reached the meadow until Mia gives a quick tug on the hem of my T-shirt. I turn and watch her heading to our usual bench, then scramble to catch up.

She sits with both legs up and wraps her arms around them.

I sit next to her, crooking one leg up so I can face her. "So what now? We pretend like it never happened and go back to being friends?" I ask.

She studies me for a minute, and I can practically see the wheels turning behind her bright blue eyes.

"Can you do that?" she asks shrewdly, as if she sees right through me.

It hurts a little that she didn't protest, didn't suggest we see where this goes. But I didn't really expect that, even if I hoped for it. Either way, though, I will never want to be just friends with this woman ever again. I'm done ignoring how drawn to her I am. How much her fire, her strength, and her struggles make me want to be with her, protect her, even though I know she's perfectly capable of protecting herself. But because I'm a complete masochist, I'll pretend if she's willing. Just to be near her.

"Yes," I reply simply.

She blows out a breath, sending a stray strand of hair fluttering back over her head. "God, I don't even remember it and I'm not sure I can," she admits.

The tightness in my chest ratchets up a notch when I realize having given in to her may cause me to lose her completely.

I'm not sure what to say in response, so I don't say anything. I know what I want to say. I want to tell her that even before the sex, I'd finally admitted to myself that she'd gotten under my skin. That she captivated me. That I want a repeat with her while she's sober so she can see how insanely good we are together. That we're good together even out of bed, and I want a chance to prove that.

But I say none of it, not wanting to put more pressure on her. Not wanting to ask anything after what I took. Not wanting to scare her away.

Besides, I've already gotten more of her than I deserve. This is my penance.

She continues to stare out over the field. "I'm not sure if I can. I need some time," she finally says. She lets her legs drop down and looks over at me. "To that end, I also need to go back to Seattle on Friday. Can you hang out with Gran while I'm gone?"

"Of course," I assure her. "How long?"

"Just the day, I hope. I have a friend coming here on Saturday, so I have to be back by Friday night regardless."

She rises from the bench, and I do the same. We make the walk back in silence. When we get to the end of the path, we look at each other. Her eyes are shining with tears. I stare at her for a moment, resisting the urge to pull her into my arms.

"If you need to talk, I'm here," I say instead.

She blinks hard and sniffs. "I know. Thank you. I'll see you Friday morning?"

I nod. "Tell Dorothy I've got a new puzzle for her."

Mia smiles. "She'll like that."

She gives me a look filled with so much warmth that under any other circumstances I'd be encouraged by. But as it is, it just hurts my heart.

"I know. Bye, Mia." Out of self-preservation, I give a small wave, and I walk away.

CHAPTER EIGHTEEN

MIA

"Oh, Mia, it's so good to see you. I've missed you so much." Janice jumps up and rushes around the reception desk to envelop me in a huge hug.

At least someone around here missed me.

"It's good to see you too, Janice," I reply, squeezing her back.

She lets me go finally. "So, to what do we owe the pleasure?"

I smile dimly. "I'm here to see Dad. I know I don't have an appointment, but I also know he always keeps his eleven to twelve on Fridays open for long lunches."

Janice looks at me over her glasses. "That was before you left. He's been so busy he barely ever has open slots on his calendar anymore."

I press my lips together, realizing an unannounced visit may not have been the best. "So he's not here?"

"Oh, he's here all right, in his office working his behind off. He just might not be all that happy to see you."

I take a deep breath. "I kind of figured. But we need to talk, and I don't think there's ever going to be a good time."

Janice pats me on the hand and goes back to her chair. "You do what you need to, dear. I'll hold his calls."

"Thanks, Janice." I take a deep breath and march through the office, turning quite a few heads as I do. It's mostly glares, but I do get the occasional friendly smile and wave, which I return without stopping until I'm at my dad's office door. I knock sharply twice, but I don't give him time to respond.

I open the door and poke my head in to find him surrounded by piles of paper, scrutinizing something in front of him through his reading glasses.

"Hi," I say tentatively, slipping inside and closing the door behind me. He looks up, obviously shocked to see me. "I'm sorry to drop in like this, but we need to talk."

He composes himself quickly. "I'm busy," he says curtly, going back to perusing his document. "No thanks to you."

I shake my head. So stubborn. I slide into the chair in front of his desk. "Then I won't keep you long," I promise, resisting the urge to point out that losing a single employee wouldn't be so disruptive if he didn't overbook and overwork them all so much.

He looks at me with anger written all over his face, still gripping the report in his hands. We stare each other down for a minute before he resignedly drops the papers and takes off his glasses, tossing them on top of the discarded pile.

"Fine. Say whatever it is you came here to say."

I don't hesitate, launching into the speech I practiced in the car on the way here.

"I know you're upset. And I'm sorry I quit so abruptly. But I need to find my own path. I hope someday you can come to understand that and stop shutting me out. Because I'd like us to have a relationship. But I just couldn't keep going the way I was. It was draining me, Daddy." I blink hard against the tears burning at the backs of my eyes. "I ignored it for a long time, because I wanted to make you happy. To make you proud. But in the end, I need to think about my future."

He flexes his hands agitatedly. "And what future, exactly, is that? Because it seems to me you threw away a very promising one and abandoned your commitments in the process. You've really put me in a bad spot, and I can't say that's something I'll easily forget. That's not the behavior of a person who cares about their relationship with someone. You'll never be successful if you don't see your commitments through."

I tilt my head. "I suppose that's because my definition of success is different from yours. And I understand if you can't forget how hard my decision has made work for you, but I do hope you can forgive me someday."

He throws his hands up, some real emotion finally breaking through. "Bring back *my* daughter and I could forgive just about anything. But you are not my daughter. My daughter wouldn't just walk away from her responsibilities." His tone is stern.

"I'm still your daughter. I know it's hard for you to understand, but I had to leave. I was so focused on trying to be the daughter you wanted me to be I lost sight of what *I* wanted."

"Was it so bad?" he asks, the hurt showing in his eyes. "Couldn't you just come back? I'm sure we could find a way to give you a little more time off."

I shake my head vehemently. "You haven't been listening. It's not just the hours, it's the work. I don't want to be a lawyer. Just because I was good at it doesn't mean it's what I want to do for the rest of my life. It just took me a while to realize that. And I'm sorry for the ways it's hurting you."

"Then show me you're sorry," he insists. "By making it right and coming back. Honestly. You have no idea what you've done, Mia. I've lost clients. Everyone is working overtime to keep our commitments. How can I forgive you if you don't seem to care about the mess you've made?"

"I do care," I reply tightly, trying not to yell or rant at him about his role in my decision. "Why would I be here if I didn't? I need you to understand I didn't make this decision lightly. My life is a mess because of everything I've given here. It was too much. You've asked too much."

"Why is everything my fault?" he barks back. "If you want to play the victim, you won't get any sympathy here." His face is red and his hands are clenched tightly.

And I see I'm not going to get anywhere.

"That's not how I see this situation at all," I reply calmly.

"Oh, then how *do* you see it, Mia? I'm dying to know," he says sarcastically.

"I see it as making the choice I needed to make for myself. And I came here hoping you could accept my decision, as my father, even if you weren't happy about it, so we could get back some semblance of our relationship." I rise. "I hope someday we can. Because no matter what, I love you, Daddy."

I don't wait for his response, because I know it's not going to be nice. So I leave, having said what I needed to say.

I thank Janice on my way out and tell her I'll keep in touch.

I keep my emotions in check until I'm back in the car.

Sitting behind the wheel, finally alone again, I expect to burst into tears from all of the heightened emotion. But instead, I burst into laughter. And the fact that I'm laughing is so funny, it only makes me laugh harder, until I *am* crying, but they're tears of laughter.

As I calm down, I realize what I'm really feeling is relief. And pride. In myself, for insisting on my path. For not caving. For trying to regain the pieces of my relationship with my father that matter to me. Even though he's not there, it's okay. I can't control his reactions.

While I drive back to Alpine Ridge, I also think about my mother. I didn't bother calling or trying to see her. Our relationship was never very good, and I don't find myself in a place where I particularly care to try to salvage it. Maybe I will, someday. The damage I did to my relationship with my father, the uncertainty of whether he'd accepted my choice, that was what's been holding me back, mentally at least.

But now, I feel free. Even if nothing has changed, everything has changed. Because I've made it clear that this choice is mine, and I don't need his understanding or acceptance. It was a mental shift I needed to make, regardless of whether it did anything at all to repair our relationship.

And now, in this moment, I feel like I could fly.

I call Joanie, even though she's at work. Thankfully, she takes a short break and lets me gush about what I did today and my newfound feeling of freedom. She congratulates me on cutting the apron strings, which normally I'd find annoying, but right now I feel like nothing can bring me down.

That feeling lasts until I'm pulling up to Gran's to find Nate sitting on the porch swing, looking gloomy. My heart sinks in my chest as I get out and approach him.

I haven't seen him since Tuesday, keeping our brief exchanges to texts about his being with Gran today. And, like a coward, when he texted that he was on his way this morning, I left before he got here.

I climb the stairs and stop in front of him.

"You look nice," I comment, gesturing to his tan slacks and short-sleeved black polo shirt. His hair is even styled nicely. He cleans up well, which is saying something because his everyday look is uncomfortably attractive as it is.

"Thanks," he says, rising when I don't join him on the swing. "I have somewhere to be later and I didn't know when you'd be back, so I didn't count on being able to go home and change."

"Ah," I say quietly, wondering if he's got a date or something. For some reason hoping it's something else, even though I shouldn't care. "Where's Gran?"

"Napping," he replies, shoving his hands in his pockets. "How long has the vomiting been going on?"

I look up into his hazel eyes and I see deep concern there. "I haven't noticed any at all," I say honestly. "She's just been more tired than usual. Going to the bathroom a lot. Which, you know, since they told her to drink a ton of water, didn't surprise me."

"So you haven't heard her throwing up?" he asks, surprised. "Because she looks like she's already lost a little more weight, so I assume it's been going on for a few days."

"She mostly uses the bathroom in her bedroom, so no," I explain, beating myself up for not paying closer attention. "But I guess I should've."

"And I should've warned you she'd probably try to hide her symptoms from you," he says with a sigh. "She's been doing it for months, after all."

My eyebrows shoot up. "Excuse me?"

He gives me a grim look. "I didn't want to break her confidence, but she's been having issues for a while, Mia. So don't let her trick you into thinking she's okay. Make sure she keeps drinking a lot of water so she doesn't get dehydrated, and keep a close eye on her, all right? I left supplies in the medicine bin in the pantry so you can take her vitals. Temperature, blood pressure, oxygen levels, pulse, and pain levels. Write them down once a day. And when you go with her to chemo, don't let her go in alone so you can give the information to her doctor."

I heard everything he said, but my brain is stuck on the very first words that came out of his mouth. *She's been having issues for a while, Mia.*

The breath leaves my body and I sidestep Nate to sink onto the porch swing.

Gran's been hiding her pain from me for months.

Gran's been sick for months.

Gran's more sick now than she's letting on.

I feel the swing shift as Nate settles next to me.

"How do I do this?" I ask, looking up at him and blinking back tears. "How do I help her if she won't tell me what's going on?" I feel powerless and more scared than I'm willing to acknowledge.

His eyes search my face and his expression is just as lost as I feel right now.

"You're helping her by just being here," he replies. "Her behavior isn't uncommon, you know. Most people don't want to admit how sick they are. Not to themselves or to other people."

My stomach clenches. He basically just admitted that Gran is even worse than I thought she was.

I slump back, totally drained. Nate leans back and wraps his arm around me and, as if on reflex, I lean into him. Just for a moment, when the memory of stars and wine and feeling safe washes through me.

I jump up as if I've been burned.

"I'm sorry, I shouldn't have —"

"No," I say, stopping him. "I'm just upset. You didn't do anything wrong. I need to … I need to …" I sink back down onto the edge of the swing, burying my face in my hands. "I don't know what I need. I'm sorry."

This time Nate doesn't reach out to comfort me. Part of me is relieved, part of me is sad. But I don't want him to think this is something it's not. *I* don't want to think it's something it's not.

"Why don't I show you how to use the pulse oximeter and the blood pressure cuff?" he offers.

I drop my hands and nod. "Thanks."

He stands and I follow, going with him back into the house.

As he patiently explains how to use the simple electronics, I realize he's not just trying to show me how they work. He's giving me something to focus on. Something to do. I can't lie, it does make me feel slightly more in control.

Which is ridiculous, I know, because it's a small, relatively insignificant way to help in the grand scheme. It's not going to make Gran any better. But it might make me feel better to have some way to keep an eye on her. Information that may help her doctors take better care of her.

And as Nate leaves, I watch him go through the sheer curtains. An ache and confusion totally unrelated to Gran pulls at my gut. It's exactly why I've been avoiding him. Why I'll probably continue to avoid him. Because I can't deny he does things to me. He's so kind to Gran, and so supportive. And even though I can't remember our night together, I think my body does, because the effect he has on me has been amplified. It's made everything harder. And that's the last thing I need right now.

"God, Mia, I'm so sorry about your Gran," Joanie whispers.

"She's on the other side of the house sleeping. You don't have to whisper, Jo," I tell her. "She's going to be fine."

"Is she? Because it's seven-thirty in the evening and she's asleep. And I don't remember her being so small, or so quiet. Is she in a lot of pain?" Joanie persists.

"She's had chemo. That doesn't exactly make you feel great," I point out. "But I have to admit, she keeps saying she doesn't feel that bad. Nate warned me she'd do that."

"Oh? When was that? Before or after you scurried out of here yesterday morning so you didn't have to face him?"

I make a sour face. "I never should've called you." Then with a sigh, "After."

"So what is this thing between you two?" she asks, tilting her head and giving me an analytical look. "Because I don't care how drunk you were, I can't see you sleeping with just anyone."

"He cares about Gran. He's nice to me. We're friends."

"Really? That's it? Because according to you he's also got a body that won't quit, is a smarty pants to boot, *and* cooked for you the night you can't remember. He sounds like a catch."

"He is," I agree. "Just not for me."

I don't admit that's not all I remember. And that's not all I feel for him. But it doesn't matter. I can't trust my feelings right now.

"I take it I won't be meeting him while I'm here then?"

I look at her pointedly. "I hadn't planned on it. Inviting him over for a nightcap would ruin all the avoiding him I've been doing," I reply drily.

"Boy, this guy really scares the shit out of you, doesn't he?" she asks.

My breath catches in my throat. Because she's named what I couldn't. "Yes," I admit on a sigh. "And I have enough to be scared of at the moment."

Joanie's brows scrunch together. "Like what?"

"Like … will Gran be okay? Will my dad ever forgive me? What the hell am I going to do with my life now? Isn't that enough?"

She taps her fingers on her thigh. "Did you ever consider it might help to have someone to lean on?" she replies.

"I *can* lean on him," I protest. "But if we dated and it went bad, that would be hard for Gran. And I don't want that."

"And if it didn't?"

"Then what, I stay in Alpine Ridge forever? That's more of a commitment than I'm willing to make right now."

"Oh, and nobody has ever moved in their life," she scoffs. "Is he even from here? Is anyone actually *from* here?"

I pick up the throw pillow I'm leaning on and chuck it at her face. "Stop making sense. I'm having an existential crisis over here and I don't need you *or* Nate fucking up my pity party."

Joanie laughs and tosses the pillow back toward me. "Fine, be in denial of your feelings all you want. As long as I reserve the right to say 'I told you so' later, it's your choice. Now. Speaking of parties. We're supposed to be celebrating your birthday. Is it too much to hope that there's a club or a bar in this backwater town?"

"There's a bar. But I've got plenty of booze here."

"Aww, what fun is that?" she shoots back. "Come on, get pretty. Let's go have a drink."

"Nate's not going to be there, if that's what you're hoping," I inform her.

She shoots me a grimace that makes it obvious that was exactly what she was hoping. "Where would he be then?"

I snort. "Probably at home. Drinking gluten-free beer." I rise from the couch and head to the kitchen.

She stands and follows. "Well, he sounds like just as much of a bore as you are," she replies teasingly. "So, whatcha got?"

I emerge from rummaging in the pantry and plunk down the barely touched bottle of rum I used for Gran's cake and a bottle of cognac that's probably older than I am. Then I fish the untouched six pack of beer I also bought for the night Nate came to dinner out of the fridge.

"That's all I've got. But it looks like a party to me," I deadpan.

Joanie laughs. "What, no cake?"

With a grin, I open the fridge again and pull out ... a cake. "Are you kidding me? What the fuck kind of party would this be without cake? Honestly, what do you take me for?" I plop it down on the island between us.

We both laugh this time, and then we dive in to the chocolate frosted chocolate cake with gusto. No plates. Just a fork each and complete indulgence. And it turns out rum and chocolate cake go pretty well together. Not terribly surprising since almost everything goes well with chocolate cake. Ditto for rum.

All in all, it turns out to be exactly the almost-thirty birthday celebration I needed. If it weren't for the rum, though, it would be pretty much identical to my sweet sixteen. My bestie sleeping over, lots of sugar, and staying up all night to talk about boys.

I learn way more about threesomes and Hawaiian guys than I ever wanted to know, but connecting with Joanie again is just the carefree break I need.

We even have cake for breakfast the next morning before Joanie leaves, which perks Gran up considerably. All in all, it's a necessary reset so I can get through the week.

CHAPTER NINETEEN

NATE

"Oh, Dorothy."

Her face tightens. And I know it's not the words, it's the sadness in my tone and probably on my face. But I can't help it. For the first time, Dorothy Lewis, the force of nature that I've come to know and love, is a mere shadow of what she was even just a month ago. For the first time, she really looks as sick as she clearly is.

"Now, none of that," she cautions, stepping back to let me in. "That's not why I asked you here."

I enter the house, my eyes already searching for Mia. "Then why did you?" I ask bluntly.

"She's gone grocery shopping," Dorothy says, ignoring the question I asked and answering the one I'm thinking.

She heads into the living room and settles onto the couch. Based on the pile of books on the coffee table, the cup of tea next to it, and the blanket scrunched next to her, I'd wager she's been spending a lot of time in that spot.

"Well, that's a shame, because I brought her a birthday present," I say, holding up a plain gift bag as I settle onto the love seat opposite her.

"That was very thoughtful of you."

"It's nothing, really," I deflect.

She huffs as she examines me with those sharp eyes of hers. Probably one of the only qualities about her that hasn't changed.

"I hoped for a bit there that it wasn't nothing," she finally says. "That is, whatever happened between you two that night she stayed with you."

I'm silent for a beat wondering if Mia talked to her about it. Something tells me she didn't, but Dorothy isn't stupid.

"But?"

"But it seems my granddaughter is in denial. About everything, these days."

Our eyes lock as I try to figure out how much she knows about how I feel. No … fuck that. How much does she know about what *Mia* feels? Because I sure as hell can't figure that one out.

"I'm not sure what she is, if we're being honest. But she's a smart woman. She'll figure herself out." I don't ask what she knows. Or what she thinks she knows. It won't make Mia stop avoiding me.

"I was hoping she'd do it sooner rather than later," Dorothy admits. "But I'm afraid any hope of seeing my great-grandbabies is a lost cause at this point."

My brow furrows, wondering if she really means Mia is a lost cause. But then, her real meaning hits me and my chest tightens.

"Why am I here, Dorothy?" I ask, but the ice in my veins tells me I already know why.

"Because I don't have much longer, Nate. So my time for beating around the bush is over."

"You shouldn't say things like that," I protest. "Staying positive is important to overcoming illness."

She shakes her head sadly. "I'm afraid I haven't been entirely up front with you. It's taken getting, well —" she gestures to herself grimly "— like this for me to even admit it to myself. The chemo is a last-ditch effort. The lymphoma was already very advanced when they diagnosed it."

The ice crawls from my veins into my heart. "How advanced?"

"I believe the phrase the doctor used was 'severely metastasized,'" she replies.

I swallow hard, unwilling to accept that she's been handed a death sentence. "I don't understand. Why would he recommend chemo if he didn't think it would help?"

She smiles sorrowfully. "Because without it, I had weeks at best. With it, he said it could be more. How much, he couldn't say, because there was every chance it would do the opposite. That it would deplete what little fight my body had left and allow the cancer to win. But I thought it was worth the risk." She pauses, closing her eyes. "I was wrong."

"You're dying." The words catch against the sob in my throat and come out choked.

"Yes," she replies, opening her eyes and her arms.

Without hesitation, I move to the couch next to her and wrap my arms around her. A tear escapes the corner of my eye and rolls down my cheek as I hold her frail body against me. Her embrace is so weak, her body so thin and delicate, it's all I can do to keep it together.

"I'm so sorry, Dorothy. What can I do? Are you in a lot of pain?"

She gives me a squeeze before letting go and looking up at me. She places one delicate, wrinkled hand on my cheek.

"No, I'm not. Dr. Sanchez was kind enough to give me all the pain medication I need. But there is something you can do for me. Stop hiding from life, Nathan," she urges. "I've never asked why, and I don't need to know. But it's time you started living again."

I laugh through the tears that keep leaking out of my eyes. "No more beating around the bush, indeed."

She smiles up at me, patting my cheek before withdrawing her hand. "Sometimes we all need a little tough love. Just promise me you'll try."

I sniff deeply. "I'll try."

"And don't forget that you promised to look after Mia," she reminds me.

"I'm not sure she wants me to," I say, leaning back into the couch.

"Yes, well, we don't always want what's good for us, do we?" she muses. "I trust you'll manage."

"I'm going to go out on a limb here and assume you haven't told Mia any of this yet?"

She shoots me an irritated look. "No, and I'm not going to. I haven't tried to shelter her by any means, but there are a lot of truths she's just not ready to hear."

"Maybe. But it's harder to accept a truth you weren't given the chance to understand, either." I discreetly wipe the tears that have finally stopped flowing from my cheeks.

"I'll consider that," she replies after a moment. "But she's only just settled the disagreement with her father, finally. At least, to the degree she needed to. I had to let her breathe a little after that."

"I'm sure whatever you decide won't make Mia love you any less," I assure her.

She gives me a tired smile. "I hope not."

I watch her sag a little, from all the emotion or her illness, I'm not sure which.

"I should go and let you rest," I say. "But thank you for telling me. And for the tough love. You know you're like a grandmother to me too, Dorothy. I love you."

I blink hard to keep the tears in check this time. I shouldn't have cried before; she's got enough going on. Now is the time to be strong. For Dorothy. For myself. And for Mia, if she'll let me.

"And you know I love you like a grandson," she replies fondly. "Take care of yourself, Nathan."

Hearing her talk like we won't see each other again is too much. It's all suddenly too much.

"I'll come by again tomorrow, okay?" I assure her. "And every day after that as long as you'll put up with me."

She pats me on the hand. "I'm always happy to see you."

"All right," I say, rising. "Tomorrow, then."

She rises too. "I'll walk you out."

"No need," I assure her. And Dorothy and I aren't usually so affectionate, but I can't help giving her another hug and a kiss on the top of her head. "See you soon."

"Goodbye," she says, sinking back onto the couch.

Unable to shake the foreboding feeling her words have left with me, I don't look back as I leave. It would feel too final.

CHAPTER TWENTY

MIA

"I'm back. With my own birthday dinner fixings and everything," I joke as I walk in the door.

My eyes land on Gran, asleep on the couch. It's not even lunchtime yet, so I can't help but be concerned.

I quietly put the groceries away, then go back to the living room to clear up. I put the blanket over her and pick up her cold, half-drank tea. When I look up, I notice a plain white gift bag on the love seat.

I set the tea back down and retrieve it. At the top of the bag, on a mess of white tissue paper is a card with my name on it in handwriting I don't recognize.

I open the envelope and pull out a card featuring Monet's *The Water Lily Pond* on the front. I open it curiously.

There's no better place to find yourself than Paris. And if nothing else, you'd enjoy the pastries. Happy Birthday, Mia. –Nate

My eyebrows jump. Nate was here. And he left me a birthday present. Still a little mystified by the card, I pull the contents from the bag and unwrap them from the gads of white tissue paper.

Two books emerge from the fluff. One, a guide to the French language for travelers. The other, a walking guide of Paris.

I sink onto the love seat cushion, overwhelmed by his thoughtfulness. I barely remember telling him about wanting to travel. But clearly *he* remembered.

"Mia." Gran's soft voice startles me out of my thoughts. I look up and she's scooting into a seated position. "Goodness, I must've dozed off."

I give her a perfunctory smile. "Nate was here?" I ask, holding up the bag.

"Yes. You found his birthday present. What is it?" she asks, picking up the cold tea and drinking it even though it's hours old.

"A French language guide and a book with a bunch of walking tours of Paris."

"Ah, Paris," she says with a sigh. "Your grandfather and I went there before your mother was born."

"How funny. I can't see Gramps in Paris," I reply with a smirk. He was always more of a camping and fishing kind of vacationer when we were little.

"I made him take me. You can't do those kinds of trips for very long. Once you get married and start a family, there's just not time and money for that kind of thing," she explains.

I resist the urge to roll my eyes. "Well, I would love to go someday. We'll see." I pop the books and card in the bag, wadding up all the paper to recycle. "How about I get you some fresh tea and lunch?"

Gran sets the cup back on its saucer. "That sounds lovely, honey, thank you."

I pick up the dish with my free hand and kiss Gran on the forehead. "Coming right up."

I make our lunch, which we enjoy together while she tells me about their Paris trip and several other vacations they had as newlyweds. It's all so romantic and nostalgic, but then I think it was so long ago that time has only left the good and erased everything else.

Gran reads and rests for the afternoon, Simba by her side as always, while I make a lemon- and herb-roasted chicken over root vegetables for dinner later. And of course, there's baking. I know I already made a cake for my birthday celebration with Joanie last week, but I can't resist making a New York-style cheesecake to celebrate today. Since it is my actual birthday and all.

It's just Gran and I for a quiet dinner and celebration. But honestly? I wouldn't have it any other way. I've always loved spending time with Gran, but it's taken on a new tenor. It's both more comfortable than it ever has been and more precious.

I don't miss that she seems so much more frail and tired, or that she doesn't eat nearly as much as she used to. But I'm too scared to ask if it's the chemo or if it's a sign of something worse. They won't check for tumor changes until after next week's treatment, so it's not like we know anything yet anyway.

Once Gran is in bed for the night, I sit in the living room with a glass of wine, flipping through the walking tour book. It's packed with daylong meanderings through different routes of Paris. Some well-traveled touristy types, some more local, low-key hidden gems. All have at least two coffee and pastry stops, sometimes three.

Between the pictures and the descriptions, I couldn't be more sold. After I've gone through the whole book at least twice, I chuck it onto the coffee table. I realize I feel frustrated.

I also feel like a prize asshole as soon as I admit that to myself. Because I would love to go to Paris. But I can't. Even if Gran weren't sick, I'm not sure I'd have the courage to travel by myself. Just like I don't have the courage to act on my feelings for Nate. Which is also something I hadn't acknowledged until now.

I want Nate. I'd love to find out what it's like to touch that flawless, sculpted body of his while completely sober. But I'm not a fling kind of girl, and I can't imagine taking on anything more than that right now.

So my conclusion of the night: Nate frustrates me because he's fucking perfect. Gorgeous and clearly capable of respecting that I'm not interested in starting anything serious right now. Nate's gift frustrates me because it reminds me of the life I want but don't know how to go after.

I realize the redundancy immediately and it makes me laugh. Short version? I'm a total chickenshit. Well, not completely. I did quit my job and burn bridges with my parents in a spectacular fashion. But I'm having trouble finding that kind of nerve again. Once bitten, a million times shy, I guess?

I go to bed slightly tipsy and with no solution to any of my problems. Something to deal with another day, I suppose.

I wake up late on Saturday morning with a slight headache and the sudden realization that I'm now thirty. And that I'm barely any better off than I was at twenty-nine. In fact, I may be worse off, as now I have no job and I'm living with my grandmother.

By the time I get showered and dressed, it's pretty much lunchtime. I head into the kitchen to find Gran drinking coffee at the dining table.

"Morning, sleepyhead," she greets me with a feeble smile.

"Hey," I reply. "Sorry, I guess you need more sleep when you're old."

Gran chuckles. "Now you're starting to understand why I sleep so much."

"Well, I hope that's all it is," I say. "Now, let's get you fed. What sounds good for lunch?"

"Oh, I'm not hungry, honey," she replies, shaking her head. "I had some of that cheesecake before my coffee."

"You rebel, you," I tease her. "I may just take a page out of your book. Though, I gotta say, for some weird reason, the cheesecake made me want pie."

Gran raises an eyebrow. "Goodness, Mia, I can barely keep up with you and your sugar cravings."

"Don't worry, I won't actually make a whole pie. I'll just go to the tavern and get a piece after lunch," I promise.

"You don't need to eat lunch first on my account," Gran teases. "I'm going to go take a nap anyway. Do as you please."

She rises with effort and scoots out of the kitchen, planting a kiss on my cheek as she passes. I give her one back.

"You know, I think I will go now. Thanks, Gran."

Gran looks up at me with shining eyes. "Of course. I love you, honey."

"Love you too, Gran. Have a nice nap."

Gran shuffles off and I grab my keys and purse. As soon as I'm outside, I note that the deceptive spring has passed and it's back to dreary, cloudy, and cool. The depressing weather convinces me there's even more reason to eat pie now.

I crank the music on my way, determined to start my thirties as happy as I can be. Recognizing that the world is my oyster. I can do anything and everything. Blah, blah, blah.

Clearly I'm not great at convincing myself, but as I pull into the tavern, I'm hoping the pie will go a long way toward improving my mood.

"Mia," Rae greets me from behind the bar. "Good to see you."

"Hey, Rae," I reply, sliding onto a barstool. "I'm here for the good stuff."

Rae grins. "Coming right up."

She disappears and is back in a flash with what looks like an extra-large slice of pie topped with a mountain of whipped cream.

"Ohhhh, Rae, I knew I liked you," I tease as she sets it in front of me.

"Well, I hear you had a birthday, so consider it a belated present," she responds with a wink.

I freeze, a loaded forkful of pie and cream halfway to my mouth. "Who told you that?"

She cocks one eyebrow. "Nate. He was in here earlier this week. Don't be mad, I asked him what you'd been up to."

I shove the bite in my mouth and chew somewhat angrily to keep myself from saying something telling.

But Rae chuckles, clearly not needing my response. "Aww, come on, Mia, Nate's a good guy. Don't get mad at him just because he's sweet on you."

"He's not sweet on me," I protest after swallowing the every-bit-as-delicious-as-I-remember bite of pie. "It's just ... complicated."

She smirks at me. "Always is, darlin'. But that's none of my business."

"Well, thanks for the pie, anyway. You have no idea how much I needed this."

She leans forward and folds her arms on the counter.

"Yeah? You wanna talk about it?"

I grimace and take another bite. "Not if it slows down my sugar high," I joke.

"Fair enough," she says with a knowing smile. "Offer's always open."

"Thanks," I reply. "And thanks for the pie. It's seriously amazing. You said it was your great-grandmother's recipe, right?"

"Sure was," she agrees, righting herself, picking up a glass from the drip tray next to her, and starting to dry it with a rag. "She owned the bakery here in town ages ago. I've never met anyone who can bake like my Great Grams."

Well, *that's* interesting. "There was a bakery in Alpine Ridge?"

"Yes, ma'am. Just down the road behind the grocery store. It's been shuttered since my mother mismanaged it into the ground when I was in high school. I used to work there every day after school, though. Unfortunately, this pie recipe is the only one I remember."

"That's a shame," I reply, still eating the pie and not particularly caring about talking with my mouth full. "Surely she left her recipes somewhere?"

Rae shrugs. "Maybe. My mom passed a few years back and we didn't find them in her house or the bakery. It's for the best, though. I never could make them the way Great Grams did after she passed. Even this pie isn't quite the same."

"This pie is phenomenal. I can't imagine how it could be better."

"You're too sweet," she replies. "Who knows? Maybe I just remember it tasting better because it was better times. Memories are powerful."

"Funny you should say that, because it's part of why I like it so much. It reminds me of childhood." I don't say it also reminds me of the pies Gran used to make, only better. It feels disrespectful to Gran. Maybe the shiny parts of my memories with her are, well, about her.

Coupled with Rae's fond memories of her Great Grams, my own happy memories of Gran, and the fact that I'm done with my pie make me realize it's time to get back home. I'm not wasting one second away from her while I have it.

I thank Rae for the pie and promise to come back again soon, then hop back in the car. I keep the radio on low this time, lost in memories. The good ones really do stick with you. All those summers playing at the lake, making s'mores by the campfire at night, playing games as a family.

I may be at odds with my parents right now. I may always be, who knows. But I'll always have the good memories to hold onto. Even they can't take that away from me.

I go back in the house with a smile on my face. Gran is still asleep in her room, so I spend some time tidying up.

When she still hasn't emerged by late afternoon and my stomach is starting to protest only having eaten pie today, I decide I should see if she wants some food too. I knock lightly at her door but don't get a response.

"Gran?" I call, knocking a bit louder. When she still doesn't respond, I quietly open the door in case she's still really sleeping.

And she is still in bed, tucked under the covers with her eyes closed. I frown deeply, concerned at how much she's slept today.

"Gran, you still sleeping?" I ask, approaching the bed. When she doesn't respond, I put my hand to her forehead to see if she has a fever.

Only to find it ice cold.

My chest constricts.

"Gran," I say firmly.

My hand slips to her neck, looking for a pulse.

But I can't find one.

"Gran," I cry, leaning in to listen for breathing, placing one hand on her chest.

Nothing.

"No, Gran, *no*," I screech.

I scramble in my pocket for my cellphone, my hands shaking with adrenaline.

"911 what's your emergency?" a pleasant female voice asks.

"Please — please send an ambulance," I beg in a shaky, stuttering voice. "My — my grandmother isn't breathing and I — I can't find a pulse. I — I think she — she's dead."

CHAPTER TWENTY-ONE

NATE

As the clock rolls to five, I scroll through my phone's address book, hovering over Dorothy's name. Wondering if I should wait just a bit longer.

This morning she said she'd call me when she was up from her afternoon nap, but she didn't say when that would be. Maybe I'm paranoid, but I can't help worrying that it's too late for her to still be napping. That something's wrong.

I set the phone down and rise, pacing to the wall of windows facing west. I'm only anxious because of what she said yesterday. She's sick. Naturally she needs a lot of sleep right now. I lean against the window and look at the sun hovering over the trees as it makes its descent in the sky.

Still, I can't shake the feeling. So when my phone rings, I bolt back across the space and snatch it off the couch where I'd left it.

But it's not Dorothy. It's Mia. She must've gotten her birthday present.

"Hey," I answer.

I'm greeted by a choked sob. My chest tightens and my stomach drops.

"She's — she's gone, Nate," Mia cries.

With the confirmation that the very happening I feared has come to life, it takes me a minute to get ahold of myself. I can deal with it later.

"Fuck. What can I do?"

"I don't know. I don't know. I'm — I don't even know what I'm supposed to do now." The despair in her voice is killing me, but I don't give in to my own.

"Where are you?" I ask in a barely controlled voice.

"The hospital in Ellensburg. They — they just brought her here by — by ambulance. Please help, Nate. I don't — I don't know what to do."

I close my eyes, choking back the pain. "I'm on my way."

"Thank you," she whispers.

I end the call before I hear anymore. And I shut my emotions down. Now is not the time to mourn. Right now, Mia needs me.

I use every ounce of my strength to make it to her as quickly as possible.

Forty harried minutes later, I burst through the emergency entrance, and I see her.

Sitting in a chair in the corner of the waiting room, she has her head in her hands and is rocking back and forth. It's not until I'm right in front of her that I hear her labored breathing.

"Mia." It comes out as broken as my heart is right now.

She looks up at me. Her face is surprisingly dry, though her eyes are red. She rises without hesitation, throwing her arms around me. I pull her into my embrace, holding her close, burying my face in her hair.

We hold each other like that for a long time, saying nothing. Eventually she sniffs loudly and presses away, stepping out of my arms.

"She was napping too long. I went in to wake her, and she was just gone. I called for an ambulance and they brought her here. Guess they needed a doctor to confirm it. But it's done, and they spoke with her oncologist. She had already made all the arrangements. The funeral home will come get her on Monday."

I look down at her, battling against my own need to comfort her. I compromise by reaching out and cupping her cheek.

"Tell me what you need."

She closes her eyes. "Just get me out of here. Please." A single tear drifts down her cheek.

I catch it with a stroke of my thumb.

"Let's go." I drop my hand to hers, tugging gently to let her know it's okay to follow. That I'll take care of her.

She lets me lead her out of the hospital and into the truck. She wraps her arms around herself and goes into her own self-protective cocoon. A reaction I understand well.

Through the whole silent drive back, I want to hold her hand, to tell her everything is going to be okay. But I don't because I know that's not what she wants right now. That she's not ready for it yet.

When we pull up to the house, I chance my first real look at her.

"Are you going to be okay here by yourself?"

She turns to me. With sorrow-filled eyes, she shakes her head. "I'm not going to be okay anywhere."

I bite back all the thoughts I want to say. That Dorothy knew, and she was brave. That she loved Mia so fucking much she couldn't bear to make her suffer any more than she already had. That she wouldn't want her to suffer now. That I don't want her to suffer.

But suffering is part of life. I know that better than anyone. And Mia was still figuring out hers only to be hit with the death of her grandmother in the middle of it all. Anything I say right now will just overwhelm her.

So despite my fierce need to fix this for her, I surrender to the fact that I can't. It's even harder than I thought it would be.

"Call me if you need anything at all, okay?"

She looks away and nods, cracking the door open.

"Nate?" She turns back to me. I think for a moment she's going to let me in. But I see it in her eyes when she decides against it. "Thank you."

She slides out of the truck before I can respond. And instead of jumping out and going after her, I watch her walk away. And a part of me feels like I may have lost her too.

It's the day of Dorothy's funeral. One week since she passed away. One week since I've seen or spoken to Mia, save her single response to multiple texts I'd sent her over the days after Dorothy's death. *I need to be alone.*

One week of pure fucking hell, mourning the loss of a woman who carved herself a place in my heart. Tenaciously. Relentlessly. And now she's indelibly a part of me.

I've shed more tears this week than I care to admit. My anxiety has reared back to levels it hasn't been at in years. Not over Dorothy, no. Dorothy is beyond the reach of the pain and suffering that took her from this world. But Mia isn't.

Despite Mia wanting space, I still drove by the house every day. Her car was always there. But there were no signs of life inside, despite watching for longer than I should've.

So now, as I dress in a black suit I haven't worn in years, the knots in my stomach are equal parts fear of losing it when faced with remembering Dorothy's life so publicly and of facing Mia, knowing she doesn't need me. Not like I've come to need her. I can live with that, though, so long as I can see that she's all right. That she'll be all right. Even if she won't let me in. Won't let me help. Won't let me fulfill my promise to Dorothy.

But then, I suppose I only ever promised to do my best.

I stretch out my arms, grimacing against the tight fit of the jacket. I wasn't so bulky the last time I wore it. Guess that's what happens when you spend all your time weightlifting to avoid life. But it will do.

I climb in my truck and begin the half-hour trip to the cemetery in west Ellensburg where Dorothy will be buried next to her husband. Where I'll see Mia.

I spend the whole trip trying to think of what I can say that will possibly convey how sorry I am. I don't think the words exist, and I've never been the best at expressing myself as it is.

When I pull into the small lot at the main building, I can see the mourners already assembled in the field beyond. A lump forms in my throat, and I realize I may not be able to form the words at all.

I climb out of the truck and start walking toward the site. Not knowing what to do with my hands, I shove them in my pockets, suddenly wishing I hadn't sent flowers ahead. It would've given me something hold. Something tangible to offer when I got there to show how much I care. As if flowers could really say how much I'm going to miss that woman.

I make it to the chairs lined around the double gravestone just in time to hear the officiant ask everyone to take a seat. I'm not focused on the grim sight of the

114

closed black coffin poised over the open grave where Dorothy's body will rest. I'm scanning the seats as I take the one closest, in the back row on the side of Dorothy's husband's headstone.

On the opposite side are Mia's parents, closest to Dorothy's headstone. Next to them sits a girl who looks an awful lot like Mia, but younger. It's undoubtedly Carrie.

I spot Rae on the other side but don't see Mia until I crane my neck to get a look at the seats in the front row of the section I'm in on the opposite side. All I catch is her dark waves tumbling down her back, but it's enough. I'd know them anywhere.

The tightness in my chest unwinds a fraction, knowing she's okay. Well, physically at least. I didn't realize until this moment how much not being able to lay eyes on her has worried me.

The funeral itself is short and to the point. Apparently Dorothy asked that it be simple. That nobody be asked to stand up and speak, that everyone be allowed to grieve in their own way. At the end, the officiant announces that there will be no formal gathering afterward, but that people can lay flowers in the grave and say their goodbyes privately if they wish.

As he steps back and the coffin is lowered, I scan the faces in the crowd. So many tears. So much love. The love is what Dorothy has left behind. And I know I will never forget it, or her.

Once the casket has been placed, everyone stands, some heading back to their cars, a fair few staying to pay their respects. Mia stays. While I have no need to speak to the body Dorothy has left behind as we already said what mattered on our last visit, I stay and wait for Mia. I need to look in her eyes. I need to look past the barriers she has around herself and try to see what she really needs right now.

So I head to the front row where she'd been sitting and watch her toss a white rose into the grave. She doesn't speak aloud, but I can practically hear the love and loss screaming from her heart. When she turns around and our eyes meet, I can see just how poorly she's been doing this past week.

She's thinner, with deep, dark circles under her eyes. Her whole posture is defeated and desolate. Without thinking, I step toward her as she does the same, opening my arms and pulling her against me. Surprisingly, she melts into my embrace, her hands clutching my lapels as she cries soundlessly into my chest. I stroke her hair, comforting her in silence.

After a spell, she looks up at me. "Thank you for being here," she says quietly.

I shake my head in disbelief, knowing she doesn't mean here, at the funeral. But here, for her.

"I'll always be here for you," I reply.

She turns away and wipes at her cheeks. "Don't say that."

I grab her by the shoulders and turn her to look at me. "I will *always* be here for you," I repeat firmly.

She blinks hard, then her eyes scan my face. She rests her hands on my chest, and I feel her press closer and hold my breath.

"Nate, I —"

"Mia?" We both turn to see Carrie standing there.

"Carrie," Mia says, surprise lacing her tone. She turns from me toward her sister.

"Oh, Mia, I can't believe it," Carrie sobs, launching herself at Mia. "I can't believe she's gone."

Mia wraps her arms around her sister. "Me neither, Care-bear, me neither," she murmurs.

Carrie smiles sadly through her tears and squeezes Mia tighter. "You haven't called me that since we were kids."

"Guess I haven't," Mia replies. "I've missed you."

Carrie finally lets go. "I've missed you too. I wanted to come see you sooner, but …"

Mia nods. "Mom and Dad. I know. It's okay."

Mia's sister frowns. "It's really not. Life's too short for this bull—"

"Carrie," a snappish voice cuts in. We all three turn to see Linda stalking toward us, her husband in tow as usual. They are both glaring at Mia. Oh boy. Here we go.

Carrie pulls a face but takes a step back from Mia and me. Guess Mia wasn't the only daughter under Mommy and Daddy Dearest's thumbs.

Their parents stop next to Carrie. Linda rests a possessive hand on her younger daughter's shoulder.

"We're leaving now," she says to Carrie. Then she turns her glare and her vitriol back to Mia. "Mia."

"Mother," Mia responds, crossing her arms over her chest protectively. She looks sadly at her father. "Hi, Daddy."

Her dad raises his chin and looks away, and I can see the hurt written all over Mia's face.

"Now that my mother is gone, no thanks to you, you have no right to be in her house anymore. Give me back the key, please."

My first reaction? I can't believe she said please. But the rest … well, how shitty can you get?

Naturally, Mia's mouth pops open in utter shock and horror. "I … you …" Her voice shakes as she tries to find words to defend herself.

I step forward, doing my best to control my rage. "Since you haven't been here to do a damn thing for your own mother, you have no idea how wrong you are. Dorothy knew she had terminal cancer. She only kept going *for Mia.* And Mia took amazing care of her. Dorothy passed knowing how much she was loved because *Mia* showed her. And even though she's gone, I can say with absolute certainty that Dorothy wouldn't want Mia to leave. Besides, you have absolutely no right to kick her out of that house."

Linda sniffs haughtily. "I have every right. She was *my* mother, and Mia is only here because I made it so. Now I'm unmaking it. Besides, we'll be going there after dinner to collect a few items that are rightfully mine." She looks sharply at Mia. "If the key isn't on the kitchen counter by the time we get there, we'll be having the locks changed."

She turns and faces her startled-looking husband. Seems like even he thinks she's gone too far this time, but he still doesn't say a word.

She starts marching away and he follows, like the spineless dickwad he is. Carrie, however, lingers.

"I'm so sorry, Mia," she whispers. And then she follows her parents.

I stand there, clenching and unclenching my fists for a moment, resisting the urge to do something I know I'll regret.

Mia lays a hand on my arm. "Don't," she cautions, clearly knowing exactly what I'm thinking.

I turn to her. "I'm sorry you have to deal with this, today of all days," I tell her through gritted teeth.

But as soon as I see that her eyes are swimming with tears, the anger fades. I open my arms, and this time I don't have to pull her in. She wraps herself around me. I can only tell she's crying when a wet sensation trickles through my shirt.

"Hey, it's going to be okay," I assure her.

She shakes her head. "It's not. It's really not. This is the last straw. I've been spiraling since Gran died, and this is just ... I just ... I can't anymore." She buries her face in her hands and my heart breaks.

I've failed. I was supposed to look out for her. Supposed to help her. To keep her from being alone. The one thing Dorothy asked of me, and I couldn't even do it.

I take the only path left now. I decide to do whatever I can to fix the situation Mia is in. If it's even fixable.

"Did you drive here?" I ask.

She shakes her head against my chest. "I came with Rae."

"Good. I'm taking you to Dorothy's. We'll get your belongings and Simba, and then you'll come with me to my place." I use my hand to lift her face so she's looking at me. "If that's okay with you."

She stares at me, conflicting emotions in her eyes, but she doesn't pull away. "It's okay. I can stay at a hotel. I would go back to Seattle and stay at Joanie's, but she's traveling on business. I just don't want to complicate my life right now."

I let her go, realizing her hesitation is *me*. Maybe I was always doomed to fail. I internalize a sigh. "Okay. At least let me help you get out of the house. In case everything doesn't fit in your car. And I might still need to take Simba if you can't find a hotel that allows pets."

"Shit, I hadn't thought about that," she admits.

Sorrow fills my heart for this beautiful woman. She shouldn't have to be thinking about leaving her home or finding a hotel that takes pets or anything else right now. I should've been there to protect her from all of this from the start.

"I meant it when I said I'll always be here for you," I tell her quietly. "In whatever way you need. Without complications."

She chews on her bottom lip. "All right," she finally replies. "I'll come stay at your place until I can figure out my next move. Thank you."

"You're welcome, Mia. Always. Now let's go so we can get you out before your parents show up at the house. Because I really don't know if I'd be able to restrain myself if they keep up this behavior."

Mia huffs a breath out of her nose. "Maybe we should take our time then. Because it was awesome watching you put my mother in her place."

She gives me the tiniest smile and the tightness in my chest unravels just a bit more. I look down at her with a mixture of awe for her resiliency and ... well, all the other feelings I have for her. Regret. Desire. Failure. Love. She looks back up at me with just enough heat that I can't help hoping that someday, when she's not going through so much bullshit, we might be able to untangle this mess I've made to see what these feelings between us really mean.

CHAPTER TWENTY-TWO

MIA

Turns out all of my worldly possessions *almost* fit in my car but not quite. And definitely not with a yowling Simba in his carrier. Still, as I follow Nate up his driveway, I have to admit clearing out of the house was a good physical outlet to channel the negative emotions I have toward my parents right now.

I didn't take anything else. It doesn't matter what Mom is after, it's all just stuff. Without Gran there, it doesn't feel quite as much like home anyway. And while I left a copy of the key on the counter, it was the spare Gran always kept around. So I still have mine. Take that, Mom.

Nate offers to start transferring my boxes to the guest bedroom while I set Simba up in the laundry room. Letting him loose in the huge house would no doubt be overwhelming for him, so I spend a bit of time snuggling him on the floor and feeding him treats. Once he's stopped yowling, I go to help Nate finish bringing everything in.

Except he's already finished. So instead, I make him dinner. To avoid talking about my parents, we trade stories about Gran. It's our own personal wake, and by later that night I'm feeling much more at peace, and beyond tired.

As Nate walks upstairs behind me, it occurs to me I have no idea where his room is.

"Is your room on this floor?" I ask as I stop at the guest room door.

He leans against the doorframe, looking down at me in that way that makes it hard to deny how attractive I find him.

"No, the entire third floor is the master suite."

"Wow. The whole floor? That must be something," I murmur, suddenly feeling awkward at all this talk about bedrooms. I look down into my hands, trying to fight a surge of … something I'd rather not be feeling.

"Hey, you okay?" Nate asks.

My eyes lift to meet his. "Yeah. Just ... long day, I guess."

He studies me for a moment before saying anything. "Long week, I'd imagine."

I close my eyes for a moment before looking back up at him. "Yeah. It was. I don't think I did myself any favors by wallowing for so long."

It's an understatement. Most days I barely got out of bed. I spent my time crying or staring forlornly at the ceiling. Sometimes both. Gran's death pushed me over the edge for a bit, and the depression has been real. But Nate woke me up today.

He looks at me like he knows exactly what I was going through. Maybe he was going through it too.

"Are *you* okay?" I ask him.

"It's been a long week for me too," he admits. "But I know it won't always be this hard."

I nod in agreement. And yet, I can still feel the desolation, the anger trying to pull me back under.

"Well, guess I'll see you tomorrow," I say.

"Yeah. See you tomorrow." He heads back to the stairs, quickly disappearing with those long, quick strides of his.

I head into the room and change into a camisole and loose pajama pants, brush my teeth, and wash my face. I settle onto the bed and plug my phone in to charge. The exhaustion hits full force, so I slide under the covers and turn out the light.

But even though I feel like I could sleep for a week, it eludes me, and I end up tossing and turning for the better part of an hour. Thinking about Gran's death. About my parents not even calling after I'd left them messages. About dodging Nate. Feeling guilty about all of it. I'm just about to give it up and go downstairs for a drink when there's a light knock on the door.

"Come in," I call into the darkness, scooting to a sitting position.

The door opens and I can just make out Nate, wearing a T-shirt and plaid lounge pants.

"I hope I didn't wake you."

"You didn't. I'm tired, but I can't seem to get to sleep."

He stalks to the end of the bed. "Me neither." He sits down. "I can't stop wishing that I'd tried harder to be there for you this week."

I give him a sad smile. "I wish I'd let you," I admit. "It's been nice, talking to someone who misses her too."

"Same." He falls silent, but I can feel him staring at me in the dark. "Why don't you lie down, and I'll tell you about the time she told off the town council when they tried to charge her quilting group for meeting in the community center."

I chuckle softly and lie back into the pillows.

Nate lies down next to me on top of the covers and props his head on his arm on the other pillow.

"Did Dorothy ever tell you about Betty McDonald?"

"Is she that awful old bat who wanted everyone to paint their houses and decorate with wagon wheels to match the town theme?"

"That's the one."

"Oh, lord. This is going to be good."

I listen to Nate talk about their epic brawl over the quilting club. Or, at least I start to. Lulled by the memory of my feisty grandmother, I drift off in the middle of the story.

I wake up to daylight just starting to stream through the window wall across from me. Feeling better rested than I have in more than a week, I languidly stretch my legs and arms.

As I lift my arm, though, it brushes something. Or, someone. I look over to see Nate, asleep on the other side of the bed. It takes me a moment to get past a surge of panic to remember why he's here. We must've both fallen asleep reminiscing about Gran.

I'm suddenly self-conscious about getting out of bed when he might see me in a top that leaves pretty much nothing to the imagination. Even though I know he doesn't need to use his imagination because he's seen me completely naked. The thought makes me cringe even harder.

"Nate," I hiss, poking him while still keeping the covers pulled tightly up to my neck.

A protesting groan rumbles through him at being woken. "What?" he croaks, cracking an eye open.

"You fell asleep here."

Both of his eyes open and fix on me. "I know. I couldn't leave you to go through this alone. Not anymore." He pulls himself to a sitting position and scrubs his hands over his face, then looks back down at me with his arms resting on his knees. "Hope that's okay."

A swell of gratitude washes over me. "That's … yes, that's okay," I reply softly, sitting up but with the covers still pulled up over my chest.

"Good," he says with a smile. "Because that was the best sleep I've had in a long time."

"Me too," I admit.

We stare at each other for a moment before Nate rises. "I'll go make us some breakfast. Ham and eggs okay with you?"

"Sounds great," I agree.

With a nod, he heads toward the door.

"Hey, Nate?" I call after him. He turns and gives me a questioning look. "Thank you." And I hope he knows that I don't mean for breakfast. Well, not *just* for breakfast, anyway.

"Anytime, Mia." He leaves, closing the door behind him.

I sit there for a bit, trying to figure out what I'm feeling. It's the first time since Gran died that I feel like someone cared enough to really be there for me. It's bittersweet, since I would've hoped it would have been my parents. Or, at the very least, my sister.

But it was Nate. A man whom I've known only a month. A virtual stranger. Life is weird sometimes.

When the smell of ham wafts in despite the closed door, I'm forced to get out of bed and make myself decent enough to go downstairs.

I spend the day settling Simba in, finding places for my belongings, and doing some baking.

That night, Nate visits again after bedtime. And there are no stories this time. We simply fall asleep quietly, side by side, to wake the next morning to another unusually restful night's sleep.

I hear from Gran's attorney on Monday. He'd like to meet on Thursday to go over Gran's will. I briefly panic that my mother will be there, but he tells me she's asked to receive a copy after the fact as she won't be able to attend. Oddly, Nate also receives a call asking him to be there.

We spend some time speculating why but give up quickly. Gran is still full of surprises, even from beyond the grave. We do, however, pick back up our warm-up, walk, and stretch routine with small hikes around Nate's place. For some reason we have an unspoken agreement not to go into town proper for a few days. It's nice, actually, being in our own little bubble away from reality.

The combination of nature and talking to someone who loved Gran and obviously cares for me too has me feeling practically normal again. And every night spent sleeping next to each other makes me remember how safe I feel with him. The feeling that was interrupted by my stupid blackout drunk mistake.

I think about that night increasingly as every morning when I wake to Nate sleeping on the bed next to me, I remember Joanie's words about a good, sober roll in the sack with a hot guy being exactly what I need to take my mind off of everything I'm dealing with. It's something that gets harder to ignore the closer we get. He's exactly what he promised to be — there for me in a totally uncomplicated way. And ironically, it's giving me some very complicated feelings.

I know I'll be here for the will reading. But after that? Well, my plan never was to stay here. It was to see the world. Explore. Find my path. A plan that's tugging at me with increasing fervor every day I start to feel more like myself. Except that I'm only getting back to that place because of Nate. It's a duality that's impossible to reconcile. So I don't try. There's no point. Not yet, anyway.

On Thursday we make the drive into Ellensburg for our afternoon meeting with the attorney. When we're shown into his office, it's comforting to find it's just him, Nate, and me.

He's younger than I would've expected and asks us to call him by his first name — Tony. Definitely not how I'm used to doing business, but okay.

"So usually we simply notify the beneficiaries of their inheritance, but I wanted to give everyone the opportunity to come here today in case there were any questions or issues," he explains from behind his large mahogany desk.

Nate looks at me questioningly. But I know exactly what he means. "You're worried my mother is going to contest something in the will," I say plainly.

Tony smiles. "That's exactly what I'm worried about. The latest will revision was so close to her death that your mother could claim she was unduly influenced or lacked the necessary mental capacity to make such changes. But fortunately, we were able to make other arrangements that may remove much of the debate. Most of what you both stand to inherit has been placed in living trusts."

I don't even bother asking how she made all these preparations over the past weeks. She mastered her sneaky ways well before I was born.

"I take it then that you're the executor of my grandmother's estate?"

He dips his head in agreement. "She thought it would be best to take the burden off of her family and to avoid potential disputes in the disposition of assets."

"I'm sorry, I'm not sure exactly what's going on here," Nate admits.

Tony looks between us. "Dorothy left the bulk of her estate to Mia, save a small financial sum and a few personal effects to her daughter, Linda, and her other granddaughter, Carrie. She also left assets to you, Nate. The trusts mean those assets will automatically be transferred to you. Effectively, the only issue still up for debate is her personal effects."

"Well, as far as I'm concerned my mother can take all or none of it. But she's not going to be happy about the asset distribution."

"I haven't even told you what it is yet," Tony replies, bemused.

I shake my head. "It doesn't matter. She's not going to be happy about it if I'm getting *anything*."

"Well, you can't contest a living trust," Nate objects. "Right?"

"No, a trust doesn't have to go through probate. But it can be challenged in court," I explain.

Tony raises an eyebrow. "You're a lawyer, aren't you?"

I sigh heavily. "I was, yes. And so is my father. So be prepared for settling this estate to get very ugly."

"Well. Dorothy forgot to mention that little tidbit," he murmurs. "But she did empower me to handle any issues that might arise. So let me worry about that, okay?"

It goes against everything in my nature, but after a knowing look from Nate, I nod. "Okay, thank you. So, what exactly is in the trusts?"

Tony hands us each a bound report. "Mia, your trust contains Dorothy's primary residence and a sizeable sum of money. In addition, there's a note that she's asked me to give you. Once you've read it, we should meet again." He turns to Nate. "Nate, yours also contains property and a monetary sum, with a note accompanying it as well."

"Do we need to meet after I've read that too?" he asks, opening his folder. He withdraws a large, thick envelope with his name on it, eyeing it curiously.

"No, everything you need should be there."

I scan the documents in my report, looking for the transfer dates.

"It's all done," I say in surprise. The amounts are also surprising. Gran wasn't rich, but she was frugal, and she and Gramps were savvy investors over the years. So I guess I shouldn't be so shocked.

"Yes," Tony agrees, folding his hands in front of him. "She wanted to make sure the transfers happened quickly. Understanding now that there may be some familial issues going on, I can see why. It will, as you probably know, make it harder for your mother to take something back than it would to stop something from happening."

I nod, running a hand over the deed to Gran's house.

"This means I can change the locks," I realize out loud.

Tony suppresses a smile. "Yes. Yes, you can."

Nate chuckles beside me. "Guess we're stopping at the hardware store."

I shoot him a grateful smile. Because lord knows I wouldn't begin to know how to do that on my own.

"That's all I have for you today," Tony says. "But look everything over and let me know if you have any questions. And Mia, just let me know when you're ready to meet again."

"Is there a deadline?" I ask curiously.

He smiles. "Read the note when you feel up to it. I know it can be hard so soon. There's no rush, okay?"

I nod gratefully. "Thank you."

Tony rises, offering his hand. "It was my pleasure. And again, my deepest condolences to you both. Dorothy was a wonderful woman."

Nate rises and takes his hand, thanking him. We leave, reports and notes in hand. I don't notice the tears in my eyes until we're out of the office and everything looks blurry. I blink hard and peer up at Nate. He slides his hand into mine and squeezes.

"Come on. Let's go lock those bastards out of your house."

I laugh and nod, letting the tears fall. I'm ready to start taking back my life.

The afternoon flies quickly, as Nate insists on changing the locks straightaway, swearing it won't take long. And it doesn't. After, I feel an amazing sense of empowerment.

We head back to Nate's to feed Simba, then Nate makes us dinner. After that, I decide I don't want to wait any longer to read Gran's note. For better or worse, I want to rip the band-aid off.

I don't even tell Nate I'm going to. I just head up to the guest room and sink onto the bed. With a deep breath, I slide open the envelope and pull out the letter.

My dearest Mia,

If you're reading this letter, it means you've learned that my illness was much worse than I let on. Forgive me for keeping it from you, but you already had so much to worry about I couldn't bear to add to your troubles.

You've been my heart, my darling girl, since you opened those beautiful blue eyes. It's been my gift to get so much time with you, to guide you, to love you. And while it's been difficult watching you go through everything you've been dealing with recently, I wouldn't take this pain away from you for the world.

Because I hope someday you realize that you needed to go through this painful time to shape who you will become. And I have complete faith that you will use this opportunity to do wonderful things.

But you know me. I can't resist a bit of tough love. So here's your "homework," honey. I want you to pursue your love of baking. I've seen the joy it brings you and others, and even if you decide it's not your calling, I have a feeling it's a good place to start. So open a home-based baking business, go to culinary school, open a full-on bakery, I don't care. Just pick a direction and give it a go. Not just for me, but for yourself. Once you do, let Tony know what you decide.

But don't let anyone tell you what the right thing to do is for your life. Not even me. Being true to yourself and not letting anyone get in your way is the toughest love there is — self love.

I've also given you the house in hopes that someday your grandchildren will visit you there. But if it doesn't serve you, let it go. As with all things.

With all my love,

Your Gran

By the time I'm done reading, tears are pouring down my face. But I'm smiling. Only Gran could get me so thoroughly. I read it several more times, imagining her voice, feeling her presence all around me.

"Hey, you okay?"

Nate's voice jars me back to reality. And when he sees my face, he walks fully into the room, settling on the bed next to me in his usual spot. It's only then that I realize he's already in his pajamas. A glance at the clock tells me why. It's way later than I thought it was.

"You read her letter, didn't you?" he asks, looking down at the paper.

"Yes. She wants me to do something with my baking." I sniff deeply and wipe the tears away.

"She always was wise. You have a gift there, Mia." He looks at me sadly.

"I always thought of it more as a hobby. It sounds fun, but I'm not sure I have what it takes to make it a whole career."

"You have what it takes to do whatever you put your mind to. Don't ever think anything different." Nate's eyes burn with an intensity that makes me blush.

"Thank you. Have you read your letter yet?"

The intensity in his eyes turns to anxiety.

"No."

I tilt my head. "Are you afraid to?"

"I don't know what I am. But I'm not ready to read it yet."

I slide my hand over his. "I understand. But you don't have to be afraid, Nate. Gran loved you."

I don't know why I said it. She never told me that. But I know it's true.

"I know," he agrees. "I loved her too."

Gran loved Nate. Nate loved Gran. Nate … well, I'm not sure exactly what Nate feels for me. But I'm pretty sure I feel something for him. He's been so good to me. Maybe the night I drank too much, I did it at least partially to find the courage to act on the attraction between us. As much I try to deny it, it's there. At least, I think it is.

So maybe Joanie is right. Maybe I need to explore that while sober. Maybe I need to give into whatever is between Nate and I. Maybe it's just what I need.

"I need to get out of these clothes." The words pop out of my mouth before I even realize I formed them.

He raises an eyebrow. "I'll leave you to it then," he replies, going to leave. But I grab his wrist.

"Or … don't?" I chew my bottom lip anxiously. I am quite possibly the worst seductress ever.

But Nate sinks back down onto the bed, and I'm pretty sure I have his full attention. "Are you saying what I think you're saying?" he asks in a low, rough voice.

"Yes?" It comes out a squeak. I clear my throat and try again. "I'm sorry, I'm horrible at this. Well, sober anyway. I mean —"

Nate puts his finger over my mouth.

"Just tell me what you want. I need to hear you say it." His eyes are guarded but intense.

And I get it. Last time we were in this position I was very drunk while seeming perfectly sober. I know that didn't work out very well for him.

"You know I haven't had anything to drink. And you can check my room for empty bottles if you want."

He smirks. "I know you haven't. Say it, Mia."

I look down, blushing harder than I can ever remember. "I want you, Nate. And I want to remember it this time."

He chuckles softly and lifts my chin with his finger. His thumb slides over my lips. In a moment of wanton brazenness, I capture it as it goes by, pulling it into my mouth. I suck on it hard and his eyes go wide.

The small act feeds my confidence, so I drop his thumb and move toward him. But he's already ahead of me, and his mouth is on mine before I know what's happening, his teeth pulling at my bottom lip, his tongue sliding into my mouth. His hands follow, caressing my neck, my shoulders, down my back.

I climb into his lap, desperate for more. I forgot how alive being touched by a man can make you feel. And Nate's hands on my skin are like electricity, lighting me up from the inside out.

I run my fingers through his hair, relishing the silky strands as our tongues dance, as his palms skate over my breasts, lightly teasing my nipples. Tingles dance across my skin.

I push into him, needing to feel that everywhere at once. I grind hungrily on his lap, my core searching for him. He groans into my mouth and tips me back on the bed, pressing his hips into me, giving me what I want. I gasp as I feel his hard length press into me, my hands gripping his hair.

"Tell me what you want," he repeats, his mouth at my ear as his cock grinds against me. It's enough to drive a girl out of her senses.

"Skin." It's gasped out as my breath races. It's all I can manage as my heart pounds in my chest. As my body burns with a fire I haven't felt in too long. Well, that I can remember. I'm too turned on to be embarrassed that we've been together before. I need him. Joanie was so, so right.

Nate stops touching me long enough to take off his own shirt first. I flash back to the first time I saw him shirtless, at his front door. If possible, it's even better than I remember. Because this time, I can touch it. And I do just that. My hands run over his impossibly smooth, hard muscles. I graze his nipples in payback. He clenches his jaw but doesn't react otherwise.

"More," I beg.

He presses back in response, taking off his sweats this time.

Holy fucking shit, he wasn't wearing underwear, I realize. The sight of his cock makes my whole body tense in anticipation. But when he fishes a condom out of the pocket before discarding them, I narrow my eyes.

"Don't give me that look," he teases. "I didn't have any expectations. I just wasn't going to be taken by surprise again."

Fair enough. Though I still can't form the words.

Nate returns to me, his naked body pinning me to the bed. The very act of it has me so worked up I can barely think. Nate is naked on top of me. I couldn't have even imagined how amazing he'd look completely naked. How good his weight would feel on top of me. How right. How am I even here right now?

When his hands slide under my shirt, I forget everything else and nod eagerly, raising my arms. He chuckles again, the sound reverberating through me. He doesn't take my bra with it, so I reach behind me and do away with it. Desperate to be joined to him, I pull at my pants and underwear, scrambling out of them awkwardly but quickly.

His mouth drops to my nipples as he presses a leg between my thighs. His tongue stimulates me while his leg rubs me into a frenzy. All I can do is writhe and moan, grabbing desperately at him, pushing into him, needing this. Needing him. I had no idea how much I needed him.

His mouth breaks away from my chest and he brings his forehead up to touch mine. His fingers play with my breasts as he covers me with his body.

"Is this what you want?" he asks breathlessly.

I nod, catching his eye. "What do you want?" I ask.

His mouth covers mine, demanding for just an instant before pulling away. "You, Mia. Just you."

"Then take me," I beg.

Nate's jaw clenches. I can see him battling with himself. But need wins, and he grabs the condom, roughly opening it and sheathing himself. And before the wrapper even hits the floor, he's buried inside me in a stroke so smooth and fast I only register it as my head hits the headboard and a feeling of fullness spreads between my legs.

"Holy fucking shit," I gasp.

"Too much?" he grinds out, clearly working to not move more.

"Not enough." I give him a look that tells him I want so much more. I *need* so much more.

A look of relief crosses over his face right before he unleashes. The fire that had been building blazes into an inferno as he takes me, as his thrusts slam me into the headboard. He obviously knows just how I wanted to be fucked, as he holds nothing back. Or maybe he's been holding back all this time and is finally getting to let go. Either way, it's bliss. Every thrust pushes me closer to orgasm. Every time the muscles of his back tighten under my hand and his cock buries to the hilt, our hips touching, I climb higher.

In minutes I'm there, at the edge. My hips and legs tighten around him. It was a cue he was obviously waiting for, as he rears up and squeezes one of my legs with his hand to give himself leverage to take me harder, faster. The other hand drifts between us, his thumb sliding just as hard and fast over my clit in a move that makes a galaxy of stars explode around us.

I cry out, arching into the celestial explosion, still constantly aware of our bodies moving together as I come apart. Nate groans deep in his chest and pushes hard into me in jerking, stuttering thrusts that soon die off.

When he collapses on top of me, we are both breathing heavily and covered in sweat. And completely, utterly, totally one. I feel connected to him on a level so deep that my exhausted body can't contain the gravity of this moment. I'm floating in space with only Nate to tether me to reality. But something in my tired brain trusts him, so I simply enjoy the feeling, tracing my hands over his back as he kisses my neck.

The moment is timeless, so I have no idea how long it has been when he rolls to the side, now next to me on the bed. With effort, I turn and curl myself into his side, like on some level I can't bear not to touch him.

"Dare I ask how that compares to the first time?" My words are barely audible over our heavy breathing.

Nate chuckles, clearly having heard me. "I didn't think it could possibly be better." He props himself up to look down at me. "I was wrong." He leans down and kisses me deeply before pushing up off the bed to head to the bathroom.

I'm too spent to move, so I simply watch until he returns and settles next to me. We lie together for an age. I keep thinking sleep will find me, but it doesn't. I'm too wrapped up in enjoying how being with him feels.

And I realize something else is bothering me. "Nate?"

"Hm?" His chest rumbles and he lifts his head to look at me.

"Why are you nervous about reading your letter?"

He sighs heavily and props an arm under his head so he can maintain eye contact. "I don't know."

I raise an eyebrow. "You don't know or you don't want to tell me?"

He raises *both* eyebrows, so I'm pretty sure I've hit the nail on the head.

"All right, then," he allows, this time sitting all the way up, forcing me to as well. "I failed her. I feel like I don't deserve anything she left me or anything good she has to say."

"How did you fail her?" I ask. Knowing my Gran, there's nothing she couldn't forgive. Surely he knows that?

His eyes glitter intensely. "She asked me to look out for you and I didn't. Not when you needed me the most. I've been trying to fix that ever since, but I'm afraid I've still failed her. There's no way to make it up to either of you the despair you felt when I left you on your own after she died."

The intense relaxation I'd been feeling a few minutes ago is abruptly replaced by indignant shock.

"I'm sorry, are you saying you've only been spending time with me out of *obligation*?"

"No, I'm saying I *didn't* spend time with you when I should've because of my promise to her," he replies.

"Same difference," I scoff.

Looking back on our relationship, I realize I can't even call it that. He saw me throw a tantrum with my parents. Then Gran forced us together on multiple occasions. Then I threw myself at him and made him out to be the bad guy when I didn't remember having sex with him the next day. And now I've thrown myself at him again. Remembering it this time doesn't make me any less disgusted with myself. Because now I know he's only spent time with me because of a promise to Gran.

Suddenly the best sex of my life viewed through that lens has now become one of my biggest embarrassments. Come to think of it, many of my top ten humiliating moments have been with Nate. What is it about this guy that makes me so stupid? So blind?

"Mia, don't," he pleads.

I turn to glare at him when I catch myself. My stupidity isn't his fault. It's mine. I think the agreement was pretty clear: no obligations. And isn't that what Joanie suggested? Casual sex? I'm only upset because I'd fooled myself into thinking it could be more. That whatever it was between Nate and me might be something more.

Which is ridiculous, because it's not what I wanted at the start. I wanted to keep my options open. To not start something because I'm not a casual sex kind of girl. Except I basically drew him into it under that premise. God, I'm so stupid. I assumed he changed his mind because I changed my mind. I assumed he felt what I felt. Fuck. I feel something for Nate. That's undeniable. Which means whatever it is needs to stop right fucking now so my humiliation doesn't get any worse.

"You're right," I agree. "Thanks for looking after me, Nate. And thanks for the fuck. You can go back to your own bed now."

Nate blanches. "Why are you being so aloof all of a sudden?"

I climb out of bed and pull some pajamas out of the dresser. "This was the agreement, right? No obligations." I pull the clothes on, sliding under the blanket. I give him a pointed look. Play time is over.

He crosses his arms over his chest, not budging. "So what, you regret being with me now?"

"Nope. But we both got what we wanted, right? Why pretend it's something it's not?"

I say it hoping to hurt him. I didn't actually expect it to, so the wounded expression on his face cuts me just as badly as I cut him.

"Fine. Goodnight, then," he replies tightly. And before I can stop him, he's gone.

I realize that's exactly what I want to do too. Maybe it's time to get the hell out of dodge.

CHAPTER TWENTY-THREE

NATE

I wake up so late on Friday the midday sun streams through the windows. I'm not surprised, given that I was up until the wee hours of the morning trying to figure out where it all went to hell with Mia.

I climb out of bed with a sigh. Sleeping without her sucks. I need to find a way to make this right today. Maybe I should've told her that I'm in love with her. But I was afraid that would just scare her. Because it's nuts. I'm nuts.

I head downstairs, sure I'll run into Mia somewhere. But her bedroom door is wide open with no sign of her, and I don't see her once I'm downstairs in the kitchen. I do a quick tour of the bottom floor, but no Mia. Simba brushes my legs as I head to the front door.

"Not right now, cutie," I mumble.

As I round the corner into the foyer I can see clearly into the driveway. Mia's car is gone. My chest tightens.

"Fuck," I curse aloud.

I head back into the kitchen to the side counter where I charge my phone. But on top of it is a note.

Thanks for everything. For what it's worth, you looked after me more than anyone has in a long time. Gone to find myself in Paris. Hope you don't mind looking after Simba. -Mia

I read the note three times before I can make heads or tails of it. Anxiety swirls inside me as I run up the stairs, my feet carrying me with a mind of their own.

Once I'm in her room, the suspicion is confirmed. All of her belongings are gone. Mia is gone. For good, it would seem.

I go back downstairs and pour myself a generous glass of whiskey. I swallow it without a thought. Then I pour another. But as I raise it to my lips, I know it's not really the answer to my problems. So I put it in the sink, then drop my head to the cool countertop.

"Where did I go wrong, Dorothy?" I ask into the void.

The thought of Dorothy has me upright and headed for the table in the foyer, where I dropped everything on our way back in yesterday. Ready to do probably the worst possible thing, given my already crappy state of mind.

I find her note and rip it open as I walk to the couch. This might make me feel even worse, but I'm taking a gamble that it might contain some of Dorothy's trademark wisdom. And I could use that right about now. So I sit down and read.

Nate,

I bet you're wondering what more I can ask of you from beyond the grave. You've already done so much for me, my friend, and so much for my granddaughter. Thank you. For that and so much more. Between the two of us, I think we may have shown Mia that there's enough love in this world to overcome the selfishness.

Don't expect her to ever admit that or thank you for it, though. She's stubborn, that one. But maybe, if you're lucky, and very, very patient, she'll figure it out. If she does, there's something else in the envelope for you.

Either way, I'm sure you've read your trust documents by now and know I've left you the building in the same business park as the grocery and bakery. I want you to turn it into a health practice. I don't care what kind. Help old farts like me with rehabilitation. Take people on walks to help them find themselves. Or maybe actually go back to practicing medicine if you can find peace with that part of yourself.

But live, Nate. Because one of us should.

Always,

Dorothy

I don't cry. God, I want to. But I've done so much more crying lately than I ever thought possible that the tears simply won't come.

Wearily, I upend the envelope to see what else is in there. A tiny envelope falls out. I rip the seal and pull out a small, padded bubble pouch. I don't even need to open it to see what it is. I flex the little envelope and, sure enough, there's a slip of paper folded inside. Unfolding it reveals a simple message.

This was my wedding ring. Give it to Mia, one way or another.

I absorb that. And then I burst into maniacal laughter. That's my Dorothy.

Hopeful until the last. But Mia doesn't love me. I was a crutch for her. Someone to vent to. Someone to lean on when she needed it. Fuck when she needed it. And you know what? I was okay with all of that. Because I do love her.

I'm in love with Mia. And Mia is gone. She's off traveling. In Paris, where I suggested she go. She'll probably even do one of the walking tours of Paris in the book I gave her. Meet a French guy. Fall in love. Move to France. Live happily ever after.

And me? I'll still be hiding in Alpine Ridge, in love with a woman I never had a chance with. It's time to wake up. It's time to get out of this town and back to reality.

CHAPTER TWENTY-FOUR

MIA

It took two weeks in Paris and enough pastries to open my own bakery later for me to realize that's exactly what I want to do. Nate wasn't wrong: There's no better place to find yourself than Paris. It's a beautiful city. I saw more of the world than I have in my entire adult life. That in itself was transformative.

But for the first time I was also away from everything and everyone who had pulled my attention in every direction but where I needed it: me. I had all my attention. It was tough at first. But after a few days of talking to hardly anyone, especially given my dismal attempts at French, the silence reconnected me to my inner voice. The part of me that knows what I want.

And I want to take a risk while I can. While it's just me and a bunch of money burning a hole in my pocket. I'm not totally sure it will be enough, but it's a start. And to hell with culinary school. Nate was right: I have a gift for baking. There's practically no pastry I haven't attempted, if not mastered, at this point, including all the various dietary-restricted variations. I can do this. I want to do this.

Now that I've made the decision, my next stop will be to see Gran's attorney. Then I'll tie off my life in Alpine Ridge, collect my belongings, and return to Seattle. Because lord knows Seattleites love pastries. And maybe this time I can actually enjoy living in the Emerald City. I've always loved its beauty but never really got to enjoy it the way I would've liked to.

I get back into Alpine Ridge on Sunday afternoon. On Monday morning, I call Tony's office. And he actually answers his own phone.

"Hi, Tony, this is Mia Anderson."

"Mia, so glad to hear from you. What can I do for you?"

"Well, first, I wanted to check to see if there was any response from my mother on the will."

"She did call to discuss it, yes," he admits. "But they haven't challenged anything yet."

"I see. Remind me, is there a time limit on that?"

"Sixty days," he replies.

Oh boy. So, that leaves them another month.

"But Mia," he pipes back up when I don't respond, "I highly doubt they'd win if they challenged. She left medical documentation of her fitness to make her own decisions. And everything was properly notarized and filed. Not liking her choices is not grounds for revoking the trust. I don't think you have anything to worry about."

"You're right. Thank you for saying that," I reply. "I also wanted to tell you I've read Gran's letter. She wanted me to do something with my baking. So I've decided to open a bakery."

"Ah, I see," Tony says. "Did you know there used to be a bakery right there in Alpine Ridge?"

"I did know that. Though I've never actually seen it."

"Oh? It's a great little spot behind the grocery store on the main road. I used to go there as a kid, and I have a lot of fond memories of that place. You should go check it out. From what I understand it's still got all the original equipment."

"I guess it couldn't hurt, but I hadn't really envisioned starting a business in Alpine Ridge. It's a little ..."

"Yeah, I know, it seems off the beaten path. But you'd be surprised how many people drive through there. Anyway, it was just a suggestion."

"All right, well, is there anything else I need to do?"

"Just a couple of forms to sign to finish up the paperwork. Come by my office anytime."

"Will do, thanks, Tony."

"No problem. See you soon, Mia."

When I end the call, I sit there for a minute, trying to decide whether to even bother looking at the bakery. But curiosity gets the better of me, and I find myself in the car before I even know what I'm doing.

I make the drive into the main part of town, trying to enjoy the beauty around me for what could be the last time. It's peaceful here in a way the city never will be, that's for sure.

I pull into the grocery store driveway, looping around to the other side of the business park. I've never been on this side, but there are two storefronts. I park and get out, and it doesn't take long to figure out which is the bakery, even though the sign has long since been taken down.

I can see the shiny glass cases through the window. They're in surprisingly good shape. A lot of the equipment still sits behind the counter, untouched and totally seventies, but seemingly unbroken. The décor is all horrible though, with the gross oranges and pinks and browns of the era, but that's easily fixed.

No, Mia. What the hell? You're not fixing anything. You're just looking. Still ... it's a great size and, like Tony said, on the main road. And it's surprisingly untouched by vandals or thieves given that. Maybe because it's not directly visible from the street? But with a few signs and some marketing ... god, I'm insane for even entertaining the thought.

I'm just excited about opening a bakery. I'm letting my imagination run away with me. My eyes flick up one last time and scan the length of the store. A circular sign with a picture of huckleberry pie catches my attention.

That's what I need. I need pie. Not a shabby bakery in the middle of nowhere. Pie. For lunch. Because I'm a grownup and I can eat pie for lunch if I want to. Pie will make everything better. Clearer.

With a self-satisfied smirk, I hop back in my car and head for the tavern down the road.

I'm already salivating at the thought of pie by the time I get there, so I'm happy to see Rae behind the bar as I walk in.

"Mia," she calls in delight. "Get on over here, darlin'."

She leans over the bar and pulls me into a hug. I can't help laughing at her enthusiasm. "Hey, Rae, long time no see."

"I bet you're here for the good stuff," she says with a wink, and I nod. "Be right back." She pops out of the bar and to the back, returning swiftly with the prized pie.

She plunks it down in front of me.

"Thank you, Rae, you have no idea how much I need this right now." I take a huge bite, hoping it will erase thoughts of starting a bakery in a town I both love and can't stand to be in anymore.

"Ah, it's nothing. I expected you to come in after Dorothy died to drown your sorrows, one way or the other."

I look up at her and smile around the mouthful of pie.

She chuckles. "Well, good to see you anyway. Where've you been hiding?"

I finally swallow the bite. "I was in Paris for a couple of weeks."

"Lord, girl, and you came back here to eat my pie? I would've just stayed there and lived off pain au chocolat," she exclaims.

"Oh, believe me, I was tempted," I admit. "Though I didn't come back *just* for your pie. I have to wrap up Gran's estate."

"Ah," she says knowingly. "Yeah, that stuff's always a big mess. But I hope you'll be around for a bit. It's nice to see you."

I shrug noncommittally and take another bite of pie while I debate whether to bring up the bakery. Curiosity once again wins.

"Rae, why didn't you ever reopen the bakery?" I ask. "I just went by, and it's in surprisingly good shape."

That gets an eyebrow raise. "Been poking around, have you?" she teases. "Well, like I said, I'm only good at the pie, and frankly I still don't think it's as good as the original, no matter what flattery you throw at me. Plus, I've got no head for business. It's why I work in a bar instead of owning one."

"So there's nothing wrong with the place?" I press.

She stops what she's doing and gives me a suspicious look. "You're not thinking of buying it, are you?"

"If I were, who would I buy it from?" I ask before I can stop myself. And there it is. Proof that my attachment to this place might just be stronger than all of the difficulties I experienced here these last months.

Now she really looks surprised. "Holy hell, you *are*. Well, to answer your first question, no, there ain't nothing wrong with it. My momma may have sucked at business as bad as I do, but she took pride in keeping that place shipshape. As to who owns it, she sold it off. Don't know to who. I was seventeen. Didn't really care. Not sure who owns it now."

I tap my fingers on the bar next to my empty plate. Now that I've opened the floodgates, I can't get the idea out of my head. Only …

"I'm not sure whether I'm seriously considering it. I think it would be too hard to stay here. As much as I love your pie."

Rae smiles. "Well, can't say I blame you. Not much going on in Alpine Ridge these days. Even if it was a bigger deal a while back."

"Oh, no, I actually love it here," I admit. "I just … I kind of messed something up. And sticking around would be … awkward."

I blush bright red, and she looks at me as if she sees right into my soul. "This is about Nate, isn't it?" she asks bluntly, hands on hips.

"Maybe," I mumble.

"Well, then you don't need to worry about that. He took off 'bout the same time you did."

"He what?"

"He left," she says again. "Stopped in to say goodbye."

My heart drops. "Did he say where he was going?"

She shrugs. "Said he needed to get back to his life. I asked him if he'd be back, got a shrug. That's Nate."

As I process the information, I realize I'm sad. Which is so, so stupid. I was only an obligation and an easy fuck to him. Obviously, I wasn't that important, because he's gone and didn't even tell me.

But now that I know he's not here anymore, I realize there's no good reason to leave Alpine Ridge. In fact, I can't think of anywhere else that's ever felt more like home than here. Between my childhood memories and spending so much time with Gran recently, it kind of feels like my only home now. Sure, it was hard to think of staying when I might run into Nate. But now … maybe I could see a life here. I'll just buy some mace so I can shop at the grocery store after two p.m. and everything will be great. The thought almost makes me laugh out loud.

"Rae, would you be okay with me buying the bakery?" The second the question is out in the ether, a feeling of rightness settle over me and tears spring to my eyes.

My question is greeted with a huge grin. "If you do, can I come work for you?"

I laugh, blink back my tears, and hold up my hand for a high-five. "It's a deal."

"Well, all right then," Rae says, enthusiastically slapping my hand.

I reach for my wallet, but she shakes her head. "Thank you," I tell her. "I'm going to go see the attorney to close Gran's estate. And then have him help me figure out who owns the bakery. I'll be back."

"You better be," she calls after me as I head out. I hear her whoop behind me and I laugh. Maybe reopening the bakery here is going to be a good idea after all. Maybe Alpine Ridge is exactly where I'm supposed to be.

The drive to Ellensburg is surprisingly pleasant. Though on the way it occurs to me that Nate had Simba. At the very least, I'm going to need to figure out what became of him and get him back if I can.

When I get to the law firm, the receptionist shows me into Tony's office.

"Well, that was quick," he remarks, standing to greet me.

We shake hands and I take a seat. "I guess you don't need a lot of time when you figure out what you want."

He looks confused. "I'm sorry, but I'm not sure what that means."

I smile tolerantly. "I went and looked at the bakery. You're right. It's perfect. And I talked to Rae, whose family used to own it, and she confirmed that it was well kept until it closed and hasn't been touched since. So I have a location and a first employee. Now I just have to figure out who owns the bakery. Think you can help me with that?"

Tony smiles widely. "Oh, Mia. I can do more than that." He fishes a folder out of the pile on his desk. "This is the paperwork for an additional trust your grandmother created in the event that you decided to start your own baking business."

I take the folder with wide eyes and a racing heart. *Oh, Gran.* Tears well in my eyes as I open it. And after I've skimmed the first page, I start laughing, tears spilling everywhere. I close the folder to keep from destroying the paper.

"Gran owned the damn bakery," I say through the laughter. Talk about meant to be. That seals it. The feeling of rightness has bloomed to full-on destiny.

"And now you do," Tony adds. "Plus a sizeable sum to get it back into shape. Congratulations, Mia. You own a bakery."

I shake my head, tears still spilling from the corners of my eyes. Gran may have been all about tough love, but it was the "love" part that she always excelled at. Her love keeps following me, even now.

"You may want to wait until you get home," Tony hedges. "But there's another note in there for you."

I nod to show I understand, then we wrap up the paperwork. And I head back to Gran's house. *My* house. I'll need to redecorate, I decide as I walk through the living room and into the kitchen. If I'm going to stay here, I might as well make the house my own.

I sit down at the dining table in my usual chair, imaging Gran in hers as I open her note. It's shorter than her last.

Bravo, darling, bravo. You've made your choice. Now give it your all so you don't ever have to do anything again just because you think you should.

All my love,
Your Gran

CHAPTER TWENTY-FIVE

NATE

It took three weeks away for me to realize Alpine Ridge *is* my reality. So now it's back to the reality I chose.

My old life, the one I thought I could go back to, *that* was my fake life. But then, Los Angeles is one of the fakest places I've ever lived. On the plus side, it was nice to spend time with my brother again. But I figured out quickly that I could find my way back into the same circles I used to travel in there, and just as quickly I realized I didn't want to. I'm not sure I ever wanted to. I knew that on some level, though I also felt like I needed to stop hiding.

That's what I thought I was doing here: hiding. And, at first, I was. After all, I purposely picked the remotest town I could find in the Cascades still within driving distance of Seattle, where I'd gone to medical school and done my first residency. Where I still knew people, but nobody with expectations of me. It seemed like the perfect place to both escape and stay distantly connected to my old life.

But something shifted. Somewhere between befriending Dorothy all those years ago and meeting Mia, I became the small-town guy who helps his neighbors. Rehabbing Dorothy's knee. Helping Greg petition for a gym and get it set up. Okay, that one might have been kind of selfish too. But still, it became a place where I got to know a lot of other people and help them too. And it was the place I took Mia to start the journey back to herself. A journey that changed me as much as it changed her.

So I'm back to do what I didn't think I could when I read Dorothy's note. What scared me to even think about. Until now. But now I'm here to go all in on Alpine Ridge, this time because it's where I want to be. It's home. I've found more peace here in four years than I did in nearly twenty years of pursuing all the wrong relationships, career paths, and life goals.

To that end, trying to get my medical license back would be a long and arduous journey that, in the end, I realize isn't what I want anyway. Ironic, considering how hard I worked for it. But it was for all the wrong reasons. Someone else's reasons.

Now, I'm here to do exactly what Dorothy, in her infinite wisdom, suggested I do in the first place. I'm going to open a wellness center in the retail space she left me.

As soon as I get home, I retrieve Simba from my closest neighbor down the hill who was looking after him, then I head back into town to get a look at my new office and do some planning.

As I pull around the grocery store to the back side of the retail center, I realize the first change this place could use is a driveaway on the empty side. That'll be a fun battle with the slow-as-molasses town council.

But as I pull up to the dual storefront, I'm surprised to find workers going in and out of the old bakery.

I climb out of my truck and have a look. Most of the old fixtures are still in place, but the furniture, linoleum, and pretty much everything else that was nailed down has been removed. Someone is renovating the bakery.

I catch a guy in a tool belt walking by. "Hey, man, what's going on here?"

"We're starting a ballet," he replies sarcastically. "What's it look like we're doing?"

"Yeah, okay, smartass. *Who* are you doing this for? Is Rae Donovan reopening this place?"

The guy shrugs. "Don't know, don't care. My boss tells me what to do, I do it."

I shake my head and give up. I'll go ask Rae myself when I'm done here. But I'm sure as shit not hiring whatever jackasses are running this show to fix up the other half of the building. Not that I wouldn't have done it myself anyway.

I fish out the key that was given to me with the paperwork and head into my new space. Well, new to me. As soon as I step inside, I realize the place needs a *lot* of work. But there's a large, open room in the front, a smaller room that could serve as an office in the back, a bathroom, and a storage room. All in all, it could work. I take a few measurements, make a few notes, spend some time getting a feel for the space. Picturing what it will look like when I'm done with it.

When I'm finished, I lock up and flip off the joker from before getting back in my truck. The bastard actually laughs.

I shake my head and start down the road to the tavern, deciding I'm going to have some damn pie to celebrate my new beginning.

When I enter the bar, it's surprisingly busy for a Monday afternoon. I sit down and actually have to wait a minute before Rae comes over.

"Nate, holy hell, you're back," she exclaims, reaching out to squeeze my hand.

"Never said I was gone for good," I reply, squeezing back. "Why's it so busy today?"

Rae grins. "Lots of buzz around the bakery being redone, even though it won't reopen for a couple months. But it's got the locals all in a tizzy. Been lots of folks in and out all week, getting excited that this might mean that old Alpine Ridge is coming back to life."

"Yeah, I saw the guys working on it. I didn't think you owned it anymore."

Rae waves a hand. "Oh, I don't. Hey, did you want a drink or something?"

I decide an explanation can wait another few minutes. "Pie, if you have any left. And a glass of water, please."

"Sure thing," she says with a wink, then darts out of the bar. I notice Jerry, the owner, actually serving drinks. Damn, business must be hopping if that old codger is deigning to work in his own establishment.

The thought makes me smirk, but I'm interrupted by a slice of heaven landing in front of me.

"Once the bakery opens, you'll have to get your fix there," Rae says.

That gets my attention. "Did you sell the recipe to the new owner?" I ask, surprise lacing my tone. Rae is notoriously protective of her Great Grams' pie recipe.

"Well, not exactly," she says. "I agreed to work there once it opens. But turns out she would've gotten it anyway. We found my Grams' recipes buried under some old equipment in the office before the renovations started." Jerry calls for Rae from the other end of the bar, and she gives me an apologetic smile. "Be back."

I nod, mulling over what she says while I eat my pie. Until it hits me. Rae said *she*. The new owner is a woman. And what other woman in Alpine Ridge could open a goddamn bakery? Whose grandmother specifically encouraged her to do that in her last wishes? I set my fork down, my appetite suddenly gone.

Mia is back. And she's opening the bakery. The business next to mine. Fuck. I should've known instantly since Dorothy owned the office she gave me, she *must* own both. Which means she must've left the bakery to Mia.

Rae approaches, a look of concern on her face. "Something wrong with the pie?"

I shake my head. "Where's Mia, Rae?"

Rae appraises me matter-of-factly. "Well, that didn't take you long, did it?" she says with a teasing note to her voice. "She's up at her house, doing some work there. She comes down every evening to check on the bakery's progress, though. Should be there in about an hour."

I toss a twenty on the bar. "I can't wait that long. Thanks, Rae."

"Go get her, Nate."

I meet Rae's eyes. Obviously, she noticed how much I liked Mia or she wouldn't have said that. But it makes me wonder what Mia has said to her. I dismiss it quickly. I both doubt she'd tell me, and I've got a sudden fire lit under my ass. So I head out without replying.

Because I can't start a business next to a woman who may want nothing to do with me. And there are unresolved issues between us, at least from where I stand. So it's time to lay everything out on the table and let the chips fall where they may.

CHAPTER TWENTY-SIX

MIA

"Goddamn it," I curse, dropping the hammer and clutching my hand to my chest. I look down reticently at my throbbing thumb. But it's only red. I didn't damage it badly enough to crack the nail, much less draw blood.

With a sigh I stand up and head into the kitchen to run it under some cold water. No more attempting to nail in new living room baseboards for me. I've barely been on this whole home improvement kick for a week and I'm already so over it.

Unfortunately, as I nurse my injury with a cold cloth after the rinse, I survey my work so far and find it lacking. I managed to strip everything out, but that's about it. The baseboards were my first attempt at putting it back together. And that's going about as well as the rest of it has. Translated: This shit is hard. Maybe I'll pay someone to do this part too.

But then, what would I do with myself for the next six weeks until the bakery is ready?

I sigh heavily, determined to get back to it, when there's a knock on the door.

I scowl, hoping it's not another wrong-date delivery. I've already got a bunch of rolls of carpet clogging up my bedroom that I can't use yet.

Cranky and hungry even though I've got another half hour before I'd planned to check in on the bakery before getting some dinner, I answer the door.

Only to see the last person I expected.

"What are you doing here?" I sound every bit as stunned as I am.

"Well, hello to you too," Nate replies. His eyes travel down my sweaty and dirty clothes. "Is this a bad time?"

My eyes travel down his white button-front shirt and grey slacks before snapping back up to his suspiciously. "It's as good or bad a time as any. Why are you dressed like that?"

"Why are *you* dressed like *that*?" he shoots back. But I can tell he's teasing. "It's just what I've been wearing these past few weeks. Guess I got used to it."

"Oh," I say, stepping back. "Well, come in then. I'm dressed like this because I'm redoing the living room, so just go straight through to the dining room."

He crosses the threshold but stops and looks down at me for a beat, like he's going to say something. My eyes lock with his and nervous energy shoots through me. After a moment, he thinks better of whatever he was going to say and keeps going.

As he settles at the dining table, I try not to stare at him. He looks … happier? I'm not sure that's quite the right word.

"Can I get you something to drink?" I offer, getting myself a glass of ice water from the fridge dispensers.

"Water's good," he replies. And then, "I went by the bakery."

I level a look at him as I set his glass down and take a seat across from him. "Just happened by, did you?"

He takes a sip from his glass and stares at me over the rim. "No," he says as he sets it back down. "Dorothy left me the other shop. I was there to have a look at it."

My eyebrows shoot up, though I realize I should've known Gran would pull something like this. She's still trying to shove us together, even from beyond the grave. Yeesh.

"You're not really going to use it, are you?" I ask nervously. God. Nate back in town. Nate opening a shop next to mine. My worst fears about awkward and embarrassing run-ins are coming to life.

"Not if you don't want me to," he assures me. "But there's a lot I need to say before you make up your mind one way or the other."

I equal parts want to crawl into a hole and die of embarrassment and laugh out loud at the ridiculous turn this conversation has taken.

Instead, I decide to put my big girl panties on.

"You don't need to say anything. We're both adults. Open a shop there if you want to, Nate. I'll live with the utter embarrassment of the way I behaved, don't worry."

Nate's brow furrows. "What the hell are you talking about? I thought you were mad at me."

"Oh, I was, at first," I admit. "But I realized pretty quickly that I wasn't really mad at you. I was mad at myself for thinking you could possibly see me as anything but Dorothy's granddaughter. I made some stupid assumptions, and I was just humiliated when I realized the truth, and then I didn't behave very nicely. But that's not your fault. I appreciate everything you did for Gran, and by extension, for me. Really."

Nate leans back in his chair, thinks about that for a moment, then bursts out laughing. And I want to curl into a tiny ball and disappear.

"I'm sorry," he finally sputters as he regains control. "I'm just … I can't believe that's how you think I think of you."

I fold my arms over my chest crossly. "Well, what else is there to think? You said it yourself: You were only looking out for me like Gran asked."

"Oh, Mia," Nate says with a sigh. He leans forward on the table, looking me in the eye. "I was doing that, yes. But I've also been falling for you since the moment we met."

My eyes go wide and I freeze in place as my heart races at his words. "You … were falling for me?" I ask in a hushed voice.

"You really had no idea? God, I thought I was so transparent."

I shake my head slowly. "But … how? I embarrassed myself around you more times than I can count. I threw myself at you twice. And you never said a word about wanting anything more."

"I tried not to. I knew I shouldn't with everything you were going through. That's why I never pushed. At least, that's what I told myself. But I realize now that was all complete bullshit. I was hiding behind excuses." His eyebrows pull together. "Wait, how did you embarrass yourself?"

I snort. "Just caught that, did you?" I shake my head and rub the back of my neck. "Well, there was the whole incident at the hospital when we met —"

"Which I've already told you I understood," he points out.

"Yes, well, there was also Gran continually throwing me at you. Like when she made you help me exercise."

"I hate to break this to you, but she'd long been trying to get us together. Hell, I'm pretty sure she's *still* trying to do that. But I know that's not your doing."

"Well, jumping you drunk was," I point out drily. "Then jumping you sober." I put my hands over my face in humiliation.

"Okay, I'll give you that the drunk version was embarrassing — but for me. You have no idea how awful I felt." He leans closer. "But the other one? Hottest fucking thing ever."

The knots in my stomach catch fire under his gaze. I swallow hard. "So you're telling me you weren't just with me because Gran made you. You actually wanted to be? I … I can't wrap my head around that."

"Why not?" he asks, leaning back in his chair, looking troubled.

"Because I've been nothing but a goddamn mess since the moment we met." I gesture to my current disheveled self to demonstrate my point. "I've had no idea what I really wanted, where my life was going, or how to handle any of the shit that was happening to me. Even now, Nate. I just committed to opening a bakery in fucking Alpine Ridge. I must be crazy. But most of all?" I take a deep breath against the knots that tie back together inside me as I realize what my real problem is. "I can't possibly fathom a universe where I deserve you."

Tears well in my eyes as the admission hits home. I was embarrassed by my actions because I wanted Nate, even if I didn't know how he fit into my mess of a life. And deep down, my real problem is knowing he's too good for me, even on my best days.

"Oh, Mia," he replies, leaning forward, his hand shooting out to grab mine. "I can't even begin to tell you how much we're the same. You don't even know."

"What don't I know?" I plead. Begging to hear something that makes me feel less unworthy. Less like I've just laid my heart out on the table for a man I already know is the most patient, caring, intelligent, and downright sexy man I have ever and will ever know.

"I was hiding from that same truth. I don't feel like I deserve to be with you. Because I'm a fucking coward. I've been hiding from the whole world just hoping to forget that, to find peace."

I stay quiet, watching him, hoping he'll say more. He looks like he wants to. "Did you?"

His eyes meet mine. "I thought I had, but you blew that façade to pieces. I didn't find peace. I found avoidance." He sighs heavily. "I've hinted before that I know what it's like to live a life someone else chose for you. But the difference is my cowardice had serious consequences."

"No," I protest. "You're a lot of things, Nate. Quiet. Stubborn. Not so great with communication sometimes. But a coward? That's not the man I know."

He huffs. "Well, maybe you've made me a better man. Because it's who I was, for so long." He shifts uncomfortably in his chair. "I was a partner in a medical practice. I had a girlfriend, a woman I'd been with since college. I thought I had it pretty good, that I shouldn't complain. But my specialization was in reconstructive surgery for burn victims, and somehow I found myself part owner of a cosmetic surgery practice. It was little nudges over the years from my girlfriend. *There's more money in it, Nate. You only have to do it when you don't have real plastic surgery to do. Don't you want to make me happy, Nate?*" He snorts.

"So you let her talk you into doing work you hated?" I surmise.

He nods slowly, looking down at his laced fingers. "I could have said no. But I did want to make her happy. I figured it was easier not to argue. That I didn't mind the work. I only went to medical school in the first place because she pushed me to. But I was good at it, and in a sense, I figured she was right. All of the procedures were helping people, one way or another. The more I told myself that, the more complacent I became. But I didn't give her everything she asked for. She wanted houses, cars, and a lifestyle that just wasn't me. I let her buy clothes, and lord if that wasn't something she did to excess. But I convinced myself she deserved it for being as supportive and loyal as she'd been over the years. Turns out I'm not very good at reading people either."

"She left you?" I guess.

"If only it was that simple," he murmurs, then looks up at me. "No. I came back early from lunch one day to find her fucking my partner in his office. Turns out *he* had the kind of money and lifestyle she was after. Unfortunately, so did his wife, and she wasn't exactly keen on giving that up when he tried to divorce her to marry my ex."

"Oh my god, you were still working with this guy after that?" There is so much more I want to say about his story, but that's the only question I couldn't help interrupting him to ask.

"No. I ended the relationship with my girlfriend and told him I needed a break. Time to think about what I wanted to do next. I was going to let him buy me out. But he was killed a few days later. His wife went away for his murder, and since I was a partner in the business, it all went to me because apparently he'd siloed his business and marital funds. But I didn't want any part of any of it anymore. So I sold it off. And here I am, living off the proceeds of a business I helped build. Off of a life I hated."

He shakes his head, silent once again. It might be the most I've ever heard him talk before. And the first time I've heard anything substantial about his past.

"Why are you telling me this?" I ask, twisting my fingers together, not knowing what I'm supposed to do with all the sorrow he's giving off right now. Should I wrap my arms around him like I want to? Or should I keep my distance?

He turns back toward me, capturing my hands in his, looking deeply into my eyes. "I'm telling you this so you know that I know what it's like to live a life that wasn't entirely of your choosing. But the difference is, you took your own life back before it was too late. That's what made me fall for you. You are so fucking brave, Mia. And even though your parents are complete assholes, you still tried to treat them with respect and compassion despite their being incapable of either. I've never met anyone like you. I'm telling you this so you understand that I may have told myself to keep our relationship platonic so I didn't make this part of your life harder, but in truth I didn't think I deserved you either."

I take a shaky breath, trying not to be overwhelmed by his words.

"What changed? Why are you fighting now?" I ask, all the hurt I feel in my voice. It may be petty, but why couldn't he have realized this sooner, before I felt like a complete embarrassment who only had the guy because he was doing a favor to my grandmother?

"I got some tough love from a good friend," he replies quietly. "It just took me a little while to realize she was always right. About everything."

I feel tears spill over my cheeks, hot and wet, and I start laughing. "Gran?"

Nate nods. "I wanted to ignore it. I even tried to go back to my life before Alpine Ridge. Figure out how to make it work. But I didn't get very far before I realized it wasn't what I really wanted." He slides out of his chair and comes to kneel before me. "What I really want is you. Please, start over with me, Mia. Give me a shot. I promise, I won't let you down this time."

His words melt me. He's right. We're so much alike. I tried to ignore how much he affected me, what that meant. But no more.

"You never let me down. I let myself down." I reach out and stroke a hand down his cheek. "I told myself that casual sex was the most I could expect, but it was a lie to keep me from admitting that I felt something for you too, because it scared me."

He turns his head and kisses my palm. "Are you still scared?" His kisses travel up my arm.

"Yes," I admit. "But in a good way this time."

He stands, pulling me by the hands so I'm standing in front of him.

"Good. Because you need someone around to teach you paint first, then carpet, *then* baseboards."

I burst out laughing but am abruptly cut off by Nate's lips on mine. It's a kiss unlike any we've had before. It's full of passion and promise. It's terrifying and thrilling and everything I want.

But I pull back after a moment, suddenly self-conscious of how gross I am right now. Covered in paint and reeking of chemicals is definitely not how I would've chosen to look or smell at this moment.

"I really need a shower," I explain at his confused look. A sly smile spreads over his face. "*Alone.* I don't have the kind of time for whatever it is you're thinking. I was supposed to leave ten minutes ago to check on the progress at the bakery."

"Yeah, about that," he says, looking down at me with a frown. "Do you really trust those asshats?"

I give him a sharp look. "Should I not?"

"I can't comment on their quality, but the guy I talked to today's attitude sucked."

"So come with me. Talk to the contractor I hired. Tell me what you think."

"You sure?"

"I'm sure," I confirm. "I value your opinion."

"Well, all right then. Now go get showered and I'll rip those baseboards out while I pretend you're not naked within grabbing distance."

I smile and leave the room, because if I don't I may cave to the temptation. One thing's for sure. Being with Nate will never be boring.

CHAPTER TWENTY-SEVEN

NATE

Being wrong feels good. Never thought I'd say that, but these past eight weeks have given me everything I've ever wanted, despite firmly believing I was doomed to a life of misery.

Mia fired her contractor and I took care of the work for her in half the time they quoted, and for a mere fraction of the cost. She's spent the last two weeks finalizing the menu, testing the ovens, and decorating. But today's the day.

My girl is opening her bakery. Yeah, that's another thing I never thought I'd have. Mia. I was worried that our connection was so based in the tragedy of Dorothy's illness and passing, on top of Mia's huge life shift, that the we'd both fallen for something that wouldn't exist anymore.

That couldn't be farther from the truth. Sure, we're both in different places now. Mia is constantly full of nervous energy, flitting from anxiously planning every last detail of her bakery's debut to fretting over paint colors for the bathrooms in her house. Honestly? It's fucking adorable.

I've found a lot of satisfaction in helping her with both while doing work on my own office space. I'm still in the planning stages, but my wellness center is coming together.

We've both found paths that utilize the best parts of us. And together? Well, I can't speak for Mia, but she's given me life and a sense of peace that I have no doubt will last. I never thought I could be this happy.

"Are you just going to stand there and watch?" she asks impatiently from behind the counter.

I snap out of it and look up to find her, hands on hips, smirking at me. Her brown waves are twisted into a knot at the back of her head, and she's wearing a blue polka dot fifties-style dress that gives me all kinds of fantasies.

"I was just enjoying the view," I tease. "What can I do to help?"

"The bunting in the corner fell down," she says, pointing.

"I'm on it," I promise.

Rae comes out of the back and walks by me with a tray of crullers that smell heavenly. She starts putting them on a stand next to the register while I grab the step ladder and fix the drooping decorations.

"Well, I think we've done good," Rae says, dusting the sugar off of her hands. "Are we ready to get this party started?"

I step down and turn toward Mia. She scans the shop again with a critical eye.

"Babe, there's a line around the block. Let's put these people out of their misery."

Mia gives me stink eye and looks at the clock. "All right, fine. We're done early anyway." She and Rae go back behind the counter and she gives me the signal.

I open the door and go to greet everyone, but I'm overtaken by the surge of people pouring in the door. I laugh as probably half the town attempts to stream into the shop.

I end up going back behind the counter and into the back room when it gets too packed, not wanting to get in the way of the throngs of sugar seekers.

I run refills as needed, make sure Mia and Rae get breaks when lunch rolls around, and even keep the peace when two old ladies almost throw down over the last old-fashioned donut.

They end up closing almost three hours early, having run out of pretty much everything. I help them clean up, then Mia puts a sign on the door stating they'll be back tomorrow.

She follows silently into the truck and I start the drive home. Well, to my home, where she stays most of the time these days anyway.

"How are you feeling?" I ask gently.

She rolls her head toward me. "How do you think? I've been up since three. I'm exhausted."

"And?"

She smiles widely. "So happy, Nate. It went really well. Didn't it?"

I chuckle quietly. "It went perfect. You're perfect. I'm so fucking proud of you, Mia."

She continues to smile to herself the rest of the drive home. But once she steps out of the truck, I run around to scoop her up.

"Time for you to relax, princess," I tease her.

"Oh god, Nate, I'm disgusting. Put me down," she squeals.

"No way," I protest. "I've been dying to peel this dress off of you all day."

She smiles. "Joanie will be happy to hear it. It was her 'good luck' present for me today since she couldn't be here."

"Well, remind me to thank her later," I murmur as I carry her into the house and up to the third floor. I set her down next to the giant jetted tub in the master suite and flip on the water. "Now don't worry about a thing." I run my hand around to her back and find the zipper on her dress. "Just relax." I slide the zipper down and she leans into me, her head hitting my shoulder.

"Mmm, I can definitely do that," she mumbles.

With her dress fully unzipped, I slide it over her shoulders and she lets me push it down her arms. A shimmy of her hips later and it's fallen to the floor.

As she removes her undergarments, I undress and sink into the tub, flicking off the tap as I do. Once fully disrobed, she climbs in and settles in front of me. We begin what's become a well-practiced routine of me gently washing her. It's not just great foreplay, it's also a Zen moment between us of relaxation and complete trust.

"I couldn't have done it without you today, you know," she says as I soap her long, shapely legs.

"Oh, you could've, and you will," I tease her. "Every day going forward."

She laughs. "God, I'm already thinking about hiring more staff so I don't have to do this every damn day. But one day at a time, I suppose."

"One day at a time," I agree.

She turns and hooks her legs around me. "Seriously, though. Thank you, for everything."

I brush a thumb over her cheek. "You're welcome. You know I've always got your back." I look deeply into her eyes, dying to say the words. I haven't yet. We've taken this slow, emotionally anyway. Between recovering from her grandmother's death, dealing with her parents challenging the trusts and failing, and pioneering this whole new life for herself, we've just kept our relationship comfortable and easy. It's been fantastic in its own way. But I already know I want so much more.

"I know," she whispers as she leans forward to kiss me.

I accept her mouth hungrily, having barely restrained myself from suggesting we have sex in the bakery after everyone was gone. I'll never get enough of this woman.

I slide my hands over her wet skin and pull her close to me.

She reaches between us and with a flick of her wrist, we're one. I sink deep into her, sighing in pleasure as we begin the familiar dance of our hips, the trace of tongues on skin, the tips of our fingers stimulating all the most sensitive spots.

I pull her nipple into my mouth just to hear her moan, to feel her clench around me. I buck hard into her, knowing what it does to her. She gyrates her hips, knowing what it does to me. Desire and heat and tension build between us as we move together toward ecstasy. I press my hands into her hips, tilting them down so her clit will rub into me harder. She accepts the friction, moving into it, her cheeks flushing, her eyes closing. Her mouth opens as her breathing accelerates. Her breasts tighten in my hands. Even just her near-orgasm cues are enough to drive me wild. Watching her climax is my favorite part of the day.

I languish in it, holding back just enough to draw it out until her eyebrows pinch together in the way they do when she starts to get frustrated with the chase. And then I give her everything. Fast and hard, tilting so I rub her clit while my fingers pull at her nipples until she's screaming and bucking her release. She tightens so hard around me, I explode with her.

I pull her against me, my mouth licking and kissing at her chest as we come down from the high. Her hands grasp my face, tilting it to look at her.

The intensity in her deep blue eyes is like a brand on my heart. The words dance behind my lips, begging to be free. And I see no reason to hold them back anymore.

"I love you, Mia."

A burst of air from her lips is following by a tired laugh. Her hips tilt, teasing my sensitive cock.

"Took you long enough to say it," she says on a breath, wrapping her arms around my neck and claiming my lips with hers. Once she's thoroughly taken what she wanted, she pulls away. "I love you too, Nate."

I rest my forehead against hers, relieved that I don't have to wonder anymore. I'd long since stopped fearing the worst. Mia has a way of calming my anxieties. Still, it was a question in my mind. Because I know what I want with Mia. Forever. And now that I know she loves me, forever is that much closer.

EPILOGUE

MIA

I stare at the headline for so long, at some point I start to think I'm hallucinating it. *Alpine Ridge Bakery Named Hidden Gem by Seattle Magazine.*

"If you keep staring at that, you'll go blind," Nate teases from across the bedroom.

"I'm just in shock," I admit. "The bakery's only been open eight months. I never expected an honor like this so soon."

I look up to find him smirking at me, dumbbells hanging from his hands, his toned chest and abs on full display over his usual grey sweats. I put down the newspaper and lick my lips.

He flicks an eyebrow like he knows exactly what I'm thinking. "I'm just teasing you. I get it. You should be happy. You've earned it."

"I have. I think I've also earned you putting those weights down and showing me how proud you are of me," I tease back.

He sets the weights down and puts his hands on his hips. "What, you don't want me to shower first?"

"Nope," I insist, making exaggerated grabby hands.

He laughs. "You sure? You could help me." He grins and takes off his sweats and makes to head toward the bathroom.

I hop off the bed and grab him around the wrist. "You know I'm just going to get you all sweaty again," I murmur, pulling him toward the bed.

Just by the fact that it works, I know he was only playing hard to get. If the man wanted to shower, he'd already be in there. No, he was putting on a show to get my attention away from that article. It definitely worked, even if it did take a minute.

We spend a good while getting each other sweatier until, exhausted and very satisfied, we call it a night and rinse off in the shower together before settling back into bed.

Lying down and looking through the skylight is always one of my favorite parts of the night.

"I'm happy," I say aloud.

Nate squeezes my hand. "Me too. Even if the wellness center hasn't been named a hidden gem by Seattle Magazine."

I turn and prop myself up on my elbow, looking down at him with concern. "You're not upset, are you?"

"God, no, babe. I was just joking. Seriously. The wellness center is exactly what I wanted it to be. Besides, with all the guilty gluttons that come out of the bakery, the exercise and nutrition classes are booked through the end of the year." He winks at me. "I'd say we're both doing pretty damn good."

"Life has been pretty great. Guess I should've cut my parents out of my life years ago." I give him a rueful smile.

"They cut themselves out. You know if they wanted to act like grownups, you'd forgive them," he corrects me.

"I've already forgiven them. But hey, at least Carrie's come around, right? Though she probably just wanted free pastries and a place to crash for spring break." I smile to show I'm not really serious.

"Family is important," Nate murmurs. "Speaking of which, my parents keep asking when they'll get to meet you."

"You know I'd love to. Whenever you're ready."

"Okay. We'll see what works," he replies noncommittally.

He's brought visiting his folks up before, and each time it's made me wonder. Why haven't I met them yet? He's talked about them enough. He even went to see them in the fall without me. But then, I couldn't exactly leave the bakery at that point since it was still just me and Rae. But I hired two new employees before the holidays, so a trip isn't out of the question.

That was four months ago. I thought maybe we'd go for Christmas. And when we didn't … well, it made me wonder. We tell each other "I love you" all the time. But we don't talk much about the future. I can't help but think maybe that means he doesn't want one with me. That being with me is fine for now but that's as far as he's thought about it. Or that maybe he did at one point but has changed his mind.

But for me? Nate is it. He makes me better. He fills life with lightheartedness, serenity, and love. And, of course, orgasms. What more could a girl ask for? Except there's an obvious answer to that question that I never thought I'd personally experience. Marriage and babies. I thought I'd been scared off of at least marriage forever. But Nate is different. We're different.

Or, maybe we're not, if we've been together this long without talking about the future.

"Hey, everything okay?" Nate asks, rolling onto his side to face me.

I shrug. "Yeah, fine." I place a perfunctory kiss on his lips and roll over onto my side, trying to fight back the anxious tears that have sprung into my eyes. "'Nite."

"Nuh-uh," he protests, hauling me back over. "It's Saturday night. I get you until at least ten." I see the moment he notices the tears. "Babe, what's wrong?"

I shake my head, angrily wiping the tears away. "It's nothing. I'm just tired."

He hooks a finger under my chin, forcing me to face him. "Talk to me."

I sniff angrily. "Fine. Why haven't I met your parents yet?"

His eyebrows jump. "That's not the question you really want to ask, is it?" His tone is hard. And when he scoots to a sitting position, my stomach plummets. I already don't like the direction this conversation is going.

I sit up too, anger jumping to the surface in defense. "No, it's not. What are we even doing, Nate? You're forty-three. Do you *ever* see yourself getting married? Having kids? Because we never talk about any of that. And I've been terrified to bring it up because I'm pretty sure you don't."

"God, you're really going to make me do this?" he asks tiredly.

My stomach twists. I jump out of bed. "No. I get it. You don't need to say anything else."

Nate jumps up after me, his long legs giving him an advantage that allows him to close the door in my face before I can escape.

"Don't move," he demands tightly.

I hug my arms around myself, suddenly unsure what to do, how to salvage this. Nate walks over to the dresser and fishes around in his sock drawer. He comes back and holds up a tiny envelope.

"Hold out your hand."

Terrified, I lift my hand and lay it flat. He turns the envelope upside down and something heavy tumbles into my hand. I look down to see a ring. And not just any ring.

"Is that ..."

"Your grandmother's ring? Yes. I've been trying to think of a way to propose to you with it. But I guess my time is up." He puts his hands on his hips and gives me a displeased look.

I look down at the ring and back up at him.

"I'm sorry," I whisper, my eyes filling with tears. "I'm so stupid, I —"

Nate shushes me. "Let me do this right, at least." He takes the ring from my hand and drops down to one knee. My hands go over my mouth and my breath catches in my throat.

"Mia Anderson, I've known for the better part of a year that I want to spend the rest of my life with you. If I haven't made it perfectly clear how much you've set my world on fire, how much joy you bring me every day, how much I love you, then I'm truly sorry. If you can forgive me, I'd love nothing more than to be your husband, make beautiful babies with you, grow old with you, to love you for the rest of our lives. Will you marry me?"

Tears start to spill over my cheeks and hands. I can't even speak, so I just nod.

"Yes?" he asks.

I nod more.

"Come on, Mia, say it," he goads me with a grin.

I drop my hands. "Yes." It comes out a croaked whisper.

"Well, all right then," Nate says, his eyes softening. He slides the ring onto my finger and rises. "I love you, Mia. I'll love you forever."

"I love you too, Nate. Forever."

His lips find mine, and it's all I need for the silly spell of self-doubt to break. Because the answers have always been in his arms. And now, so will I.

RECKLESSLY IN LOVE

A STEAMY SMALL-TOWN FORCED PROXIMITY ROMANCE

CONTENT WARNING

Recklessly in Love is a small-town forced proximity romance novel that includes elements that might not be suitable for some readers, including the use of profanity, open-door sex scenes, and other potentially sensitive topics. Visit https://melanieasmithauthor.com/rilcw.html for a full list (warning: may include spoilers).

CHAPTER ONE

JOANIE

"You got fired for having sex with one of the junior partners in the copy room?" Mia gasps, parroting back the words I'd just used in the form of a question.

I grin, getting the exact amount of shock value I hoped for.

"During business hours," I add. "If it'd been after hours, it would've just been a slap on the wrist." I don't bother mentioning that's probably because they'd have to fire everyone if that were the rule.

"Where do I even start with that?" Mia says with a sigh. "At work, Jo? Really? While anyone could walk in?"

I snort. "That's part of what made it such a thrill," I respond. "Unfortunately, as hot as he was, the sex was awful."

"So, you got fired for having bad sex. At work."

"That about sums it up."

"And what about him?" she asks, a note of suspicion in her voice.

"Oh, don't worry, he was fired too. No sexist double standards there, at least."

"Well, that's … good? I have to say, you don't sound upset about losing your job," Mia points out.

I shrug, even though she can't see me over the phone. "I knew it was a possibility. Again, that's kind of what made it stimulating."

"Why do I get the feeling you hoped it would happen?" Mia asks.

I can't help my shit-eating grin. "Ah, Mia, darling, you know me so well."

It's precisely what I'd been banking on when I seduced the poor bastard into fucking me not just in the copy room but on the copy machine itself. Maximum noise. Maximum evidence. Too bad it didn't live up to the fantasy of during-work sex. And photocopying a dick isn't nearly as entertaining as I thought it would be, either. Still, the encounter served its purpose.

"Well, that's one way to get the holidays off work," she replies drily. "Were you that desperate for a break? Because you know you could've just taken an actual vacation. It's been almost two years since we went to Hawaii. You certainly deserve one. But like this?"

I snort. "I'm not you, Mia. I wasn't *overwhelmed* by my job; I was *done* with it. The same stupid cases over and over. Defending corporations facing criminal charges for their shady business practices was getting tiresome. I want something different. Something that's a challenge. But now that you mention it, a vacation sounds divine."

My mind drifts back to that week in Hawaii and the two hot local surfers I'd spent it with. The original intent was for Mia and I to each have one guy to keep us company that week, but when she had to leave suddenly to take care of her Gran — on day one of our vacation, no less — they both seemed interested in sticking around. And there was lots and lots of sticking around if you know what I mean. That was a first, even for me. One that still features prominently in my fantasies. Maybe a few new "firsts" wouldn't be such a bad idea. And since Mia found hunky Nate in her Gran's tiny mountain town — and herself while she was at it — it ended up working out well for us both.

"That reminds me. We're reviving the Alpine Ridge Winter Festival. With the bakery doing pretty well and Nate's practice getting off the ground, it'll be a good opportunity to capitalize on the seasonal traffic to Leavenworth. You should come to stay with us and join in," Mia offers.

I wrinkle my nose. "Snowy mountain town wholesome goodness isn't exactly my idea of a fun vacation," I reply hesitantly.

"Come on, Jo, you've only visited *once* since the bakery opened, and that was only for a day. I miss you," Mia pleads.

"It's not like you haven't seen me at all. You've come here to Seattle a couple of times, too. Hell, we could go on vacation together. Let's do something crazy. How does Thailand sound?" I counteroffer.

"I may be able to take off a day or two here and there, but I can't leave the bakery for weeks while traipsing off to a foreign country," Mia points out. "Trust me, it'll be fun. Just for starters, I'm making cocoa and gingerbread macarons to go with Rae's hot mulled wine and apple cider, plus there will be all sorts of fun activities like ice skating, snow sculptures, concerts —"

"All right, all right, you had me at gingerbread macarons," I agree with a sigh, even though the rest sounds like it's straight out of a Hallmark Christmas movie, which is definitely not my scene. "Will there at least be some hot guys?"

"There are some single guys in town," Mia hedges.

I quirk an eyebrow at the lack of qualifying their attractiveness. "Well, that's a start. Are any under fifty? Because you know I cap it at fifteen years older than me. Any more than that, and it treads into 'daddy' territory." I shudder at the thought. I may be wild at times, but that's one kink that's a hard no for me.

"I mean, sure, there are, but ..." Mia trails off, and I roll my eyes.

"What, am I too worldly for your small-town boys? Are you worried about your harlot friend tainting your perfect mountain paradise?" I tease, reading between the lines.

"Honestly? Yes. A little," Mia says with a chuckle. "I'm not sure the guys here are ready for Hurricane Joanie."

"That sounds an awful lot like a challenge," I reply.

Mia groans, and I laugh.

"Nate is going to be furious with me for talking you into this," she jokes.

"I guess we're both going to be on the naughty list this year," I joke back. "Welcome, Mia. It's so much more fun than the nice list."

The following weekend and a two-plus-hour drive finds me bundled up against chilly air and piles of snow, yet still freezing my ass off, while I stand next to a radiant Mia and her smoking hot fiancé Nate, staring at a tree.

Yep. A tree.

Those gingerbread macarons better be damn good.

Granted, the tree is humongous and right in the center of what I suppose qualifies as "downtown" Alpine Ridge. Mia's bakery is just down the road behind us, next to Nate's shop and the grocery store. And I see a sign for a bar and restaurant across the main drag. There's also an unmarked building behind the tree, plus a couple of other buildings further up the road from where we stand. All done up in the same rustic wood with wagon wheels style. Quaint, if not a little trite. But that's about it. Alpine Ridge is a small town.

"So, this is where all the fun will be?" I ask drily, shooting an equally dry look at Mia.

She responds with a dramatic eye roll. "This is where the tree lighting ceremony will be. But many of the activities will be inside —" she points at the unmarked building "—at the community center."

I smirk. "A community center, huh?" I tease. "I wouldn't have thought the town was big enough to have one."

Mia slips her arm into mine and starts to lead me toward the building. "Real funny. Maybe keep those kinds of comments to yourself around the locals, hm?" Mia hums.

I look pointedly between her and Nate. "I guess that means you don't consider yourself locals?"

Nate snorts. "By the usual definition, sure. I mean, we live here full-time. But by Alpine Ridge definitions? Not even close. If you weren't born here, you're not local."

I raise an eyebrow. "Is there even a hospital here where you can give birth?"

Mia suppresses a smile. "Not yet. But you know what he means; many people in town have lived here their whole lives." She pushes the heavy door to the building open, and we head inside.

The small entry alcove has a desk to one side and opens to a larger room behind it. A hallway leads off to the right behind the desk.

My head swings around, trying to take in the massive amounts of knotty pine. Paneling. Beams. Even the damn desk is made of it.

"Well. This is … rustic," I mumble, following Mia into the larger room. Long tables are arranged against the walls. And then my eyes land on a bent figure in the corner. And the spectacular ass pointed in my direction.

"Hey, Greg," Nate calls toward the ass. I mean, the guy. Because there is obviously a guy attached to that splendid backside. A fact that becomes startlingly clear when he rises and turns toward me. Because the guy is just as spectacular as the ass.

At about Mia's height, short for a dude but perfect for my tiny self, he's all lean muscle, rugged five o'clock shadow, and full lips on a mountain man face. The face of a man who can rough it or rough you up in bed — in the best way possible, of course.

"Nate," he returns, heading over and slapping Nate on the shoulder in greeting. "Perfect timing. Know anything about rewiring wall heaters?"

Nate follows him over to the corner to work on his heater issue. And I turn to Mia, shooting her a meaningful look.

"Girl, you were holding out on me," I accuse her in a low voice.

Mia's brows scrunch together. "Greg? Really?" she whispers back.

I raise my eyebrows incredulously. "Yes, *Greg*," I snap back. "Holy hotness, Mia. What's his deal? Is he married?" I curse myself for being too tangled up in fantasies of that scruff scraping along the insides of my thighs to notice whether he was wearing a ring.

Mia shrugs. "Nope. He runs this place. He and Nate work out together a few times a week, and he also helps at the wellness center sometimes. He's a good guy. Quiet. I wouldn't have thought he was your type."

I huff a breath out of my nose. "Hot isn't my type? Yeah, okay, Mia."

A faint smile plays over Mia's lips. "I've got Nate. I don't even think about whether other guys are hot anymore. I mean … look at him." She sighs wistfully as she eyes her man. And it's not like I'm going to deny that the towering hunk of muscle matched with the brains of a former doctor isn't fucking hot. At least to myself. To my best friend about her fiancé? That's a no.

"Eh. You don't think about other guys; I don't think about guys who are taken." I shrug — such a lie. I'd totally do a threesome with them — just sex, of course. I'm not into polyamory by any means. Just a good time. But I know even suggesting anything like that would probably make Mia's head explode.

She graces me with a smirk that says she knows anyway. "Well, you'll see a lot of him while we're here. Just … don't break him, okay?"

I snort. "No promises."

And with a flip of my long, dark hair over my shoulder, I tug Mia toward the boys. Scratch that — men. Definitely men. So sayeth my tingling girlie parts.

"Greg, this is my friend, Joanie," Mia offers as we stop beside them. "She lives in Seattle but will join us for the festivities."

Greg's gaze turns to me, and his cornflower blue irises meet my ice blues. And I never knew it was possible to be jealous of the shade of a man's eyes.

"Nice to meet you," he says, offering a hand.

I slip mine into his, shaking it firmly. He's noticeably surprised.

"Joanie is a lawyer too," Mia offers as if in explanation. I'm a little surprised at the "too" since she's not technically a lawyer now that she's given that life up to run a bakery in the middle of nowhere. But that's neither here nor there.

I look back at Greg to find an "aha" look on his face, and I fight the urge to roll my eyes. Yes, tiny girls can have firm handshakes — and law degrees.

"Well, that's impressive," Greg says with a smile that may have just melted my panties off.

I can't tell if he's sincere, so I smile sweetly. "Thank you. And it's nice to meet you too, Greg," I say, pointedly giving Mia the stink eye. But then, if he's the kind of guy who is easily intimidated by a strong, intelligent woman, I guess I wouldn't be interested anyway.

"Feel free to put us both to work," Mia offers with a nod in my direction. "I know there's a lot to do before the festival opens next week."

Greg smiles that devastating smile again. "Be careful; I may just take you up on that. It's a lot of dirty work."

I purse my lips. "Well, good thing I'm always up for getting dirty," I reply in as suggestive a tone as I can manage. And in case he doesn't get it, I wink at him for good measure.

Greg looks mildly shocked, and I can't help grinning. Nate shakes his head and laughs, and Mia rolls her eyes. "And that's why you're on the naughty list, Jo," Mia says.

My grin grows to Cheshire-cat proportions, and Nate facepalms. He walks past Mia and mumbles just lowly enough for only Mia and me to hear, "Well, if he wasn't interested before, he is now."

Hours later, I'm fluffing a fake, silvery Christmas tree in the entry alcove when Greg finally approaches me. Mia has been doing her best to keep me decorating so I wouldn't have time to pounce on him immediately. The joke's on her because I always give them a few hours minimum to get a look at the goods first. And I've caught him checking out my ass more than a couple of times this afternoon.

"You're a pro at that," he says, leaning against the knotty pine desk. Once again checking out my ass.

I turn and bat my eyelashes at him. "I'm a woman of many talents," I assure him.

He laughs, and his dimpled grin sets Bev aflutter. Yes, Bev. My beaver. My lady parts. What? Guys name their dicks, so I figured I should name my pussy.

"I'll just bet you are," he murmurs, his eyes sweeping over my frame. "So, how are you liking Alpine Ridge, Joanie?"

I step off the stool I'd been standing on and turn toward him. "It's fine," I reply succinctly. "But let's just cut to the chase, shall we?"

He raises an eyebrow, looking intrigued.

"I do like a good chase," he responds in a low voice.

I bite into my bottom lip to keep from grinning too widely. Now we're talking.

"Mmm," I murmur noncommittally, reaching up and running my hand down his chest — and holy shit. The muscle tone I feel under his dark plaid work shirt is no joke. "But the catching part is much more fun, isn't it?" I look up at him from under my eyelashes, giving him a coy smile.

He chuckles, low and deep. Damn, I just want to eat this man for Christmas dinner. Yum.

"It can be," he allows. "But —" he leans in, his hot breath tickling the shell of my ear "— anticipation can be pretty fucking hot too." His nose grazes my lobe, sending tingles shivering down my entire left side. He straightens up and, with a wink, is gone.

I'd turn to watch his ass as he walks away, but I find that I've lost control of myself. My whole body has turned to Jell-O from the husky, dirty promise in his words.

Well, this vacation just took a turn for the better.

I'm pulled from dreams of all the ways I want Greg's wicked tongue teasing me by something big and soft landing on my head. I blink my eyes open against the light shining through a crack in the guest bedroom's door to find half of my head covered by a pillow.

"Good morning, sunshine," Mia calls from the doorway.

I pull myself into a sitting position. "I knew I should've stayed at the B&B," I grumble. But it used to be Mia's Gran's house, and now that she's gone, that would be a different type of torture. So pillows in the head at an ungodly hour it is.

Mia laughs. "And that's why I threw the pillow from here. So pleasant in the morning, aren't you?" she asks wryly.

"What the fuck time is it?" I ask, scrabbling for my phone on the nightstand.

"It's almost six. Normally, I'd have been at the bakery for hours by now, but I let you sleep in." Mia strides into the room and sets something down on the nightstand in the spot just vacated by my phone.

Notes of coffee and hazelnut hit my nose, and I inhale deeply. "Your offering of caffeine is accepted. But baked goods better be next."

"Don't worry. Rae and Penny are at the bakery, so I'm sure there are fresh donuts by now. Up."

I mock grumble as I get out of bed, and she leaves, but she had me at hazelnut-flavored coffee. Though there isn't much I wouldn't do for fresh donuts, too.

When I make it downstairs, it's to a shirtless Nate fondling my best friend in the kitchen. Said best friend's tongue looks like it's getting very familiar with his tonsils.

"You two are disgustingly cute," I grumble.

Nate tries to pull away, but Mia won't let him, flipping me off while she finishes mauling her man. When she finally pulls away, I get one of the rare glimpses I've had of Nate's torso, and I can't say I blame her for being hot for him even after a year and a half of coupledom. The man has the definition *and* the bulk. Plus, he has a penchant for grey sweatpants that leave nothing to the imagination about the ginormous dick he's packing. On top of already knowing — only from prying it out of Mia — that he's a beast in the sack and that he adores her, I have to admit she's hit the jackpot. You know, if committing yourself to one dick for the rest of your life is your thing. The jury's still out for me. It'd have to be one spectacular dick.

"So, what's on the agenda besides eating my weight in baked goods?" I ask as I drain my coffee mug and set it in the sink.

"Well, after we get a head start on macarons, cookies, and pies, we're going to help Rae bottle her wine and cider," Mia responds.

Nate makes to walk past me out of the room. "What about you, muscles?" I ask, poking him in his ridonculous bicep. "Are you baking with us babes?"

"Nope. I'm helping Greg set up the snowshoe obstacle course." And with that, he leaves the room, presumably to find a shirt and pants that'll keep that lovely dick from freezing off.

"All right, let's do this thing," I say resignedly.

Mia's eyes flick to the door.

"Don't worry, we'll be bringing the guys lunch later," she says with a smirk, her eyes flicking back to mine. "It won't be all girl time."

I don't even try to pretend like I'm not relieved while we pack up and head out. Because hanging with the ladies is great and all, but Bev is as hungry for cock as I am for donuts right about now.

CHAPTER TWO

GREG

Nate groans as we lay the last humongous tire in place for the final leg of the obstacle course in the field behind the community center.

"All right there, old man?" I joke as we straighten up.

He shoots me a look. "Just ready for lunch." He jerks his chin toward something over my shoulder, and I look back to see an SUV that's appeared next to his truck in the parking lot back by the building. "Looks like the girls are here."

I nod casually, trying not to show too much interest. Because I think I may have overplayed my hand with that Joanie chick already. But fuck if she isn't hot. And I'm not just talking about the body I couldn't stop staring at to save my life. It was how *forward* she was that threw me for a loop. I've never found that attractive before. But with Joanie ... well, it was *such* a turn-on that I'm afraid some long unused parts of me took over my brain. But this time, I'm determined to play it cool until I figure out if going after her would be a good thing or a bad thing.

After all, we are on my territory, so if things go south, that'd be hard to escape, especially since I don't know how long she'll be around. There's a reason I don't date girls in town. I like it here, and small-town plus breakup equals bad news for everyone, including Joanie's Alpine Ridge resident best friend. The last thing I want to do is create friction between Mia and me because of a hookup with her best friend that has gone wrong. Something that didn't occur to me until after my dick ran my mouth when we met.

Bringing myself back to the present, I focus on keeping calm as we trudge back through the deep snow, though it's just far enough to keep the sweat coming under my thick jacket and gloves ... yeah, the nervous excitement has nothing to do with it. That's what I'm telling myself, though I know it's bullshit.

When we get to the building, we knock the snow and mud off our boots and pants before heading indoors. It's nice and toasty inside, but as I strip off my jacket, gloves, and hat, goosebumps spread over my skin.

At first, I think it's just the air hitting my sweat-soaked T-shirt, but then my eyes flick up and meet Joanie's ice-blue stare. Just like the first time, I feel her sharp gaze X-raying me. I can't help the grin that pulls at my lips. I swear my body has a fucking mind of its own when it comes to this chick. Because it's sure as hell not listening to my decision to stay cool around her.

Now done stripping out of his snow gear, Nate doesn't seem bothered by his sweaty shirt. Or the sexual tension that's suddenly thickened the air. He starts heading toward the girls but gives me a look when I don't follow.

I only see it out of my periphery as I don't actually look at him, unable to look away from Joanie despite my determination to be cool. "I'm going to change my shirt in the office," I say in Nate's direction. It takes all my willpower to tear my gaze away and head down the hallway.

I half hope she'll follow, then kick myself at the thought. That definitely wouldn't be feeling her out first. Well, there'd be feeling something, but ... I mentally slap myself as my mind starts to picture feeling Joanie up. Jesus fucking Christ.

Changing my shirt cools me down but does nothing for the thoughts racing through my head. So, when I return to the room, keeping my eyes to myself is way more difficult than it should be. I look only long enough to notice Mia and Nate seated on one side of the table, with Joanie standing near Mia, chatting.

Food, Greg. Focus on the food. You're hungry, right? As my eyes settle on the spread of sandwiches, sides, and desserts, it does help divert my focus a little as my stomach rumbles in anticipation. Between the meatball subs dripping with marinara and melted cheese and the array of clearly fresh-baked sweets, it smells fantastic in here. Way better than stale air and sweat, which is what it usually smells like.

But my focus is abruptly broken since I'd been standing there admiring the food a hair too long as Joanie saunters between me and the table. Her tight little ass nearly grazes the front of my jeans as she picks up a plate and starts loading it with sweets before settling in one of the chairs on the other side of the table.

"You know, I made meatball subs just for you," Mia grumbles to her friend.

Joanie pops a jam tart in her mouth and grins around it. "Sorry," she mumbles, making an exaggerated yum face. Except it looks pretty much like an O face, so there goes my determination to focus on the food. Though, I may still be drooling, for different reasons now. Not helped at all by Joanie licking her lips and blowing me a kiss.

The little vixen knows exactly what she's doing.

I smirk and shake my head at her, grabbing a plate for myself and loading it up with a bit of everything before sitting down in the chair next to her, across from Nate.

Food.

Focus. On. The. Fucking. Food.

"I'm on vacation. I'm allowed to eat dessert first," Joanie declares.

I look over at her without thought, and her eyes move from Mia to meet mine. I hold her gaze as I continue eating. She grins.

"And you did just lose your job. If I were you, I'd eat whatever I wanted, too," Nate agrees. My eyes flick over to him. She just lost her job? Well, that's interesting. Then he adds with a thoughtful face, "Actually, I'm pretty sure that's exactly what I did when I moved here after quitting my job." He looks at Joanie with concern. "Just … uh … don't do it for as long as I did."

Joanie laughs. "What, did your body fat get above ten percent for the first time, hot stuff?" she teases.

Nate blushes, and I hold back a laugh. He was a little softer around the middle back then. Like she heard my thoughts, Joanie's attention shifts back to me.

"So, Greg," she says, leaning toward me and wrapping her lips around a cookie. I watch, mesmerized as she licks the crumbs off her lips before continuing. "Tell me all about your mountain man life. Lots of chopping down trees? Skinning animals to sell their fur? Swimming naked in remote lakes?" She bats her eyelashes.

I set down the sub I was working on and wipe my mouth, trying to hold back the smirk. "Yeah, exactly," I reply. "Just like I'm sure you spent your days lying to defend remorseless criminals and getting paid exorbitant amounts of money to play the justice system." I meant to point out that she was applying ridiculous stereotypes to me, just like I'm sure people do to her. But as soon as the words are out of my mouth, I realize they may have come off as harsh and judgmental.

To my surprise, she grins and points her fork at me. "That is actually pretty accurate." Then she takes a bite of the cheesecake on her plate, licking the fork clean. Of course. My eyes track the movement despite trying to pry them away. If she wants to turn me on … well, I'd be lying if I said it wasn't working. Honestly, I'm just relieved I didn't offend her.

"All right then," I concede. "No, I don't skin animals to sell their fur." I raise an eyebrow, then add with a shrug, "But the rest?" I smirk, leaving her to imagine me chopping down trees and swimming naked in remote lakes.

Just by the look on her face, I know she is. Just like I was imagining feeling up those perky little tits earlier. I shift in my seat, trying to give my dick some relief from the pressure it's suddenly under.

"Well," she says, a bit breathlessly. "I hope tree chopping and naked swimming are part of this whole winter festival crap. Because if they are, I may be warming up to the idea."

Before I can peel an acceptable response from the dirty ones floating through my brain, Mia offers, "There is the Freeze Your Buns Run." I suspect she's mostly just trying to move on from talk of naked swimming. I should be grateful. It's not a great time of year for that. But if it was *Joanie* swimming naked … I shake myself. You'd think I was eighteen again instead of thirty-eight with all these horny little fantasies.

"Oh?" Joanie asks with interest. "Does that require nudity as well?"

I almost choke on a chip. This woman is going to be the death of me. I cough and take a swig of beer before answering her. "Almost, but not quite. It's an undies run. In the snow." I decide to screw with her just a little to get back at her, so I wink at her. "Think you can handle that, city girl?"

She gives me a challenging look. "I can, if you can, mountain man." She lifts her chin, pink staining her cheeks, presumably in embarrassment at the rhyme.

Nate busts up laughing, but I try my hardest not to since a laugh at her expense seems like a bad idea. Mia looks at Joanie sympathetically, and suddenly, Joanie laughs, too. Relieved, I stop holding back my laughter.

"Good," I respond. "Because it's next weekend. Better start practicing." I finish my food, drink what's left of my beer, and then give her a wink.

She raises a brow in answer. "Better ease up on the meatball subs and beer if you want to be light enough on your feet to beat me."

I raise a brow in return, leaning back and lifting my shirt, patting my flat stomach. "Oh, I think I'll be fine."

I don't miss for one second the hungry look in her eyes as she looks at my abs. So, when her gaze rises to meet mine, I give her another wink. She purses her lips. And though I wasn't lying to her before — I usually like the chase — the anticipation is already killing me.

I don't catch more than a few glimpses of Joanie throughout the week. I'm busy organizing the Freeze Your Buns Run, checking the ice-skating pond, and building a platform for the musicians playing Christmas music for the tree lighting ceremony and other events throughout the festival. Nate switches between helping me and going with the girls to post signs, managing decorating the tree, and carving paths in the snow between the events.

But Friday is tree lighting day. And I'm over letting the anticipation build. It's worse that Joanie hasn't been around, which is weird because usually, for me, out of sight is out of mind. But I can't stop thinking about her.

So as twilight descends, I do rounds of the town square, checking the strands of white lights strung between lamp posts, making sure Rae's cider stand is adequately covered from the elements, and watching as the townsfolk start to show, gazing up at the massive tree in anticipation.

It looks damn good, even unlit. The towering, fifty-foot monstrosity looms darkly in the square, light from the street lamps and Christmas lights glinting off the hundreds of massive baubles strung around its not inconsiderable girth. Staring up at the neat rows of decorations, nostalgia spreads through me. Alpine Ridge hasn't seen a winter festival in almost thirty years. It brings me back to simpler times.

I shake off the good and bad memories that start to push through. It's almost showtime. The crowd is now thick, and the line for hot cider winds around half the square.

I see Mia setting a tray of something down on Rae's table. And next to her is Joanie.

Since she's not looking at me, I take the opportunity to soak her in. Her tight-fitting fur-lined jacket and snug fleece pants cover her completely, yet she still looks like a wet dream. Sexy as fucking hell. Her dark hair spills around her, and her little bow lips are pursed and a natural peachy color. Her cheeks and nose are red from the cold. An urge to warm her up almost overwhelms me.

Still, I approach casually.

"Hey, city girl."

She turns, and I grin, self-consciously running a hand through my hair. Which I never do. It's that X-ray vision of hers, making me feel turned inside out.

Her brows bunch together, and she tips her head to the side, giving me a confused look.

"Oh, yeah, hey, Gary," she replies evenly.

The smile melts off my face, and I cock an eyebrow. "It's Greg," I correct her.

She gives me the fakest smile I think I've ever seen. "Ah, yes. Sorry, my mistake." She bats her eyelashes and returns to the booth, helping Mia and Rae serve drinks and cinnamon twists. "See you around, Gary."

Rae glances over at Joanie, bemused, just as my douchebag cousin, Ned, steps up to get a drink. And I know Ned. Even without the leering look he's giving Joanie, I knew he'd go straight for her the second I saw him. And he does.

He slicks back his inky hair, which looks like it's been dipped in cooking oil, and gives Joanie a sleazy grin as if she's this year's Christmas treat. "Hello there, beautiful." He sounds just as shady as he looks. And then he leans in and *winks* at her.

Oh, hell no.

But before I can intercede, Joanie does the exact last thing I'd expect, as always.

She leans toward him with an answering wink. "Well, hello," she says huskily. "Cider?"

He slaps a five on the table. "I don't know. Do I get a little sugar with that?"

My fists ball at my sides, but Joanie seems unfazed, throwing her head back and laughing. "I don't know, this might be too much sugar for you to handle, big boy," she teases with a coy smile. "But the cinnamon twists are good, too."

When I almost lose it at her response, it clicks — she's doing it all on purpose: pretending to forget me, calling me Gary, and flirting with Ned.

She's screwing with me.

"Oh, I can handle it. But maybe we can take this someplace more … private?" he asks, not even bothering to keep his voice down.

And that's it. That's my limit. Before I can stop myself, I close the distance and grab Joanie gently yet firmly by the elbow. But my glare is all for Ned.

"Get lost, Edweird," I grind out, using the nickname he earned when we were kids.

Thankfully, he's smart enough to look terrified and scamper away without a word, forgetting to take the food he paid for. I think I see a glint of amusement in Joanie's eyes as she watches him go, but her face is all indignation when she whirls on me.

"Excuse me, but we were talking," she says haughtily.

I snort and lead her by the elbow out of the booth toward the community center.

"I'm not stupid, Joanie."

My long strides have her scrambling to keep up as I pull her by the arm. I push open the heavy door and haul her inside. I'm all reaction now. Logic is out the window. I need to make a few things clear to her.

Darkness envelops us as the door closes behind us. With a flick of my wrist, I turn her and push her up against the back of the door, my arms caging her in.

"I never said you were," she finally replies. Even in the near darkness, I can see her outline, the stubborn set of her jaw, the tension in her body. My head dips down as my eyes take her in. "But I'm also not your property, and I don't appreciate being dragged in here like I am."

"If you think I was going to let my piece of shit cousin lay one disgusting finger on you —"

"That guy is your cousin?" she barks out with a laugh.

"Yes," I reply. "And whatever angle you're working, don't work it with him."

As my eyes adjust to the dimness, our gazes lock. I see fire in her eyes.

"Let me go," she demands, pushing against my chest.

"Not until you admit you were flirting with him to get on my nerves. Just like you pretended to forget my name."

She rolls her eyes. "Someone has a big ego. Maybe I did just forget."

I lean in, my lips parting. "Doubtful. I bet if I fucked you hard against this door, you'd remember whose name to scream when you came all over my dick." The words shock even me. Not because they're not true; they most definitely are. But because I've never spoken to a woman like that. And because they came from such a primal place of need, I can feel them in every inch of my skin. Just as much as I want to own every inch of hers.

Joanie's eyes flash. "Maybe you should —"

But I don't get to hear what she thinks I should do. My mouth claims hers without any forethought. It's pure need on a level so deeply physical I have no control over it. My tongue invades her mouth. My body crushes hers against the doors. My hips press against her, making the erection I didn't even realize I had plain to us both.

And she kisses me back with an intensity that matches mine. Our breaths mingle as we gasp for air between each crush of our mouths, as the palpable heat and need build with every stroke of our tongues. She grinds against my cock, but the lust ruling my body isn't enough to stop me from making her work for it just a little more.

I pull my mouth from hers, keeping her pinned with my hips, my forehead pressed against hers.

"Say my name, Joanie," I demand.

She bites into her lip to suppress a grin. "Gar —"

I growl and twist my hips in an attempt to crush her defiance with my need for her. Her teeth sink deeper into her bottom lip, but her gaze is insolent.

"Say it, city girl," I prompt huskily, more softly this time.

"Make me scream it," she counters. "Like you promised, mountain man."

My balls tighten in answer, and I open my mouth to spew all the filthy things I want to do to her that will make us both scream, but I'm stopped by an attempted shove at the other side of the door that rattles us both, physically and otherwise.

"What the hell?" Nate's voice comes through the door, muffled.

I pull Joanie into the room, dropping my arms to my sides as the door opens and Nate and Mia appear, framed in light from the nearly full moon and the faint lights around the square behind them.

An awkward silence descends for a few very long moments.

"Uh, it's almost time for the ceremony," Nate finally offers.

I nod and brush past Joanie. "We were just heading out."

Nate snorts. "Sure you were."

I shoulder-check him with a smirk but say nothing as we look back at the girls expectantly.

Mia looks at Joanie, also saying nothing. Well, not with words, anyway. Her knowing look, however, speaks volumes.

"What?" Joanie asks innocently, looping her arm through Mia's.

Mia shakes her head and laughs. "Nothing. Never mind."

Nate and I let the ladies walk out ahead of us, arm in arm. As I make to follow, Nate stops me with a hand on the chest and gives me a hard look.

"Watch yourself with that one," he warns me.

My insides tighten for a different reason this time. It doesn't take me but an instant to recognize the feeling: fear.

"What do you mean?" I ask, playing dumb.

He glances furtively towards the girls. "I know she's Mia's best friend, and I don't want to say anything bad about her. She's just —"

"Nate?" Mia calls, looking back. "Come on, you're going to miss it!"

His eyes dart back to me guiltily. "Never mind, let's just go."

This time, I'm the one to stop him with a hand to the chest. "Short version then," I insist.

"Short version?" he parrots with a sigh. "What's the female version of a player?"

I snort. "You're worried she's going to play me?"

He shrugs. "From what you've told me, you're a relationship kind of guy. I just didn't want you to expect that from her."

I shake my head and laugh. "I mean, sure, I've had a couple of long-term relationships," I allow. "But it's not like I've never had hookups, dude. And here I was worried that she was clingy or crazy."

Nate huffs a laugh. "Clingy? I don't think so. Crazy? Well … if you're okay with kink, probably not in a way that's a deal breaker."

Well, shit, that's got my attention. "I appreciate your looking out for me, man, but you told me what I wanted to know about her."

Nate nods knowingly. "Just … suit up, all right, man? Be safe and all that."

That gets a full belly laugh out of me. "All right, pops," I tease him with a wink. I like to rib him like he's an old man, even though he's only five or six years older than me. But right now, I'm in a pretty good fucking mood. He's acting like a concerned older brother, and I dig that. But what I dig more is that Joanie may be exactly what I've been looking for.

CHAPTER THREE

JOANIE

Unfortunately, there were no screaming orgasms to be had Friday night after the tree-lighting ceremony. Lots of cider? Yes. Eating my weight in cinnamon twists that must have been laced with crack, they were so addictive? Absolutely. But the rest of the night was exactly as Hallmark as I'd pegged this whole event to be. Listening to a quartet that played holiday music. Oohing and aahing over the pretty tree.

Okay, to be fair, the tree was stunning. Then again, I helped decorate it, so naturally, it was beautiful. But at the end of the night, there were no advances. No invitations. And it all broke up so quickly that I didn't have time to make my own before I was in Nate's truck, heading back up the mountain to Mia and Nate's glass palace in the trees.

So, lying in bed on Saturday morning, I decide that today will be different. Starting with a self-provided orgasm. All I have to do is remember how Greg pushed me up against that door, how his woodsy scent alone had me wet. Then there was the kiss. Shit, that was a fantastic kiss. I rub circles over my clit as I think of it. My back arches remembering his taste. How hard his cock was against my stomach. What it might look like. What it might feel like to lick around the crown while he watched, those bright blue eyes challenging me to take it all. The thought starts the low tingle in my core. I remember his breath against my ear as he demanded I say his name. The tingling spreads, and my nipples peak beneath my nightshirt. A few more swirls and presses, and I let myself remember his promise to fuck me against the door until I screamed his name while coming … and then I am. I keep quiet, which intensifies the orgasm, until I slump back down onto the mattress, only partially satisfied.

I try not to think of Nate and Mia in the bedroom upstairs, who I can hear frequently getting much more fully satisfied. I may have even used it as fuel for my own satisfaction once or twice. They do it constantly; I may as well reap the benefits of their ridiculously hot soundtrack. But now? Thoughts of my mountain man are all I need. Gary the Mountain Man. The thought makes me giggle. I really *do* belong on the naughty list.

Once Mia returns from the bakery, we have lunch and head out to the snowshoe obstacle course competition that afternoon. There was fresh snow last night, so the whole town is glistening prettily. And I must admit that small though the town is, it's undeniably beautiful.

As we park near the community center and walk around the building, I notice the ice-skating pond as we head toward the obstacle course. With the rustic building as a backdrop, the whole thing has a very Thomas Kinkade feel.

A feeling that doesn't stop there, permeating practically every corner of the untouched drifts of snow covering every flat space. Well, except for the obstacle course, which looks like it has been dutifully re-dug out of the fresh piles of snow. Greg's work, no doubt. Too bad I wasn't around to watch him. That would've been excellent foreplay.

A staked rope separates the shoveled walkway from the course itself. I can see a crowd gathered at the far end, presumably waiting to start. As we walk the length of the field, the "obstacles" get increasingly weird. The first thing I notice is a group of massive, mismatched tires. All right then. That seems like it would belong on an obstacle course. Then there are a bunch of lengths of rope that I quickly figure out are jump ropes. Normally, I could see that. But in snowshoes? How the hell do they expect people to do that? Since I'm not participating, though, it doesn't worry me. But the bunch of sleds packed with outrageously dressed snowmen gets my attention. The punk rocker snowman with a mohawk, pierced carrot nose, and earphones is good. The police officer snowman with a donut in one hand and a Starbucks cup in the other is pretty funny — because, really, is there even a Starbucks within an hour of here? But it's the snowman dressed in a Hawaiian shirt, lei, sunglasses, and strapped to what looks like a small surfboard that makes me stop in my tracks.

I pull on Mia's arm, stopping her with me as Nate continues toward Greg, who is standing on the other side of the sleds, presumably at the starting line as the crowd is gathered behind him.

"What?" she asks, giving me a curious look.

I gesture with my chin toward the surfer snowman. "Is that a coincidence, or did you tell Greg about Hawaii?" I ask plainly.

Mia's brows bunch together before a look of horrified understanding crosses her face. "Oh God, no, I didn't," she rushes to reassure me. "I swear I didn't say a word."

"Say a word about what?" Nate asks, appearing behind Mia.

I make to brush it off, but my eyes flick guiltily to the snowman. Nate follows my gaze, then looks back at me with a smirk.

Figures he'd know.

Greg steps up next to Nate.

"Something wrong?" he asks.

The smirk slides off Nate's face, and he claps Greg on the shoulder. "Nope. Are we ready to do this?"

I breathe a sigh of relief at Nate's discretion, and Mia gives me a funny look. I try not to give her a guilty one back. For some reason, I don't want Greg to know about my surfer ménage. When did I start giving a shit what anyone thinks of me? The thought is like a poke on the shoulder that there's something I need to acknowledge here. Instead, I brush it off and follow the guys toward the waiting crowd.

Greg quiets everyone down and explains the drill: The eighteen people signed up will go in six groups of three. Each person must pull a snowman-laden sled — which he assures them are very heavy — from the start to the jump ropes fifty feet away, jump rope ten times, high step through the tires, and sprint approximately two hundred feet to the finish. Nothing *too* crazy, but eyeing the assembled crowd's varying ages and general apparent lack of fitness, that's probably for the best.

Greg explains that the winners of the first three groups will face off, and then the same with the second. The two finalists will then compete to determine the winner.

Greg positions himself at the start, and Nate heads down the field and stands between the ropes and the tires.

"Mia, can you man the finish line?" Greg asks.

"I think you mean *woman* the finish line," I cut in.

The corner of Greg's mouth tips up, but before he can respond, Mia shakes her head and says, "Sorry, can't. I have to meet Rae inside to set up the food for after." She turns to me. "Looks like it's up to you, *woman*." She gives me a wink and walks away, not even waiting for a response.

Greg smiles at me so wide his eyes crinkle at the corners. "You up for it, city girl?"

I contemplate him coolly for a moment. "What the hell, why not?" I reply.

He steps toward me and leans in, his mouth brushing my earlobe, sending chills down the entire side of my body. "There are two red flags that mark the finish line. Just make sure they're still visible over the snow so you can see who crosses first." He straightens up and walks backward the few feet to the green starting flags.

Refusing to let him see how much he affects me, I head to the opposite end of the field purposefully but without rushing like I'm trying to escape the fact that I'd rather stay there and let him whisper all sorts of other, dirtier, things in my ear.

It's not long before Greg has lined up the first set, and they begin. Right out of the gate, they all struggle with the sleds. I almost laugh, realizing that must mean they formed the snowmen with rocks or something equally heavy because even the biggest dude in the bunch is red and straining the whole way. Alas, that's the funniest part of the course, as the jump ropes, tires, and sprint are all boring to watch. Even in snowshoes, it all looks almost too easy.

And I quickly start to get cold. Thankfully, Mia comes out with a travel mug after the first three batches.

"Thought you might need this," she says, offering me the cup as we watch the next set line up.

"I hope it has booze. Because this will be much more fun if it does," I grumble.

She wraps an arm around me and rubs my shoulder. "Nope. But don't worry, there will be booze later."

I take a deep drink. It's just cocoa. But I'm cold, and it tastes good, so I don't complain. "There better be." I watch as the latest group starts to hit the jump ropes. "Aren't Nate and Greg going to do this? *That* might be fun to watch. Especially if they did it shirtless." The thought perks me up, and I smile into my mug.

"I'm sure they've already done it to test everything, but Nate said it wouldn't be fair if they competed," she replies with a shrug.

I let out a shriek of laughter as the first competitor of the bunch — a much older man — *trips* the second guy, who is half his age, to get into the tires first. But Nate is right. I haven't seen a single participant who could compete with either him or Greg.

It's not long before the old man is barreling toward me, and Mia takes that as her cue to leave. I try to pay more attention to the race than my cocoa. It's tough. The cocoa is much more interesting, even without the booze.

What feels like a lifetime later, the older man is crowned the overall winner — since all the dirty tricks he pulled to get there somehow weren't against the rules — and is awarded his gift basket, which was no doubt put together by Mia or Rae as it's stuffed with bottled cider, baked goodies, and what appear to be a few gift certificates. Once that's done, the crowd starts to disperse.

Greg starts to head toward Nate, but Nate shouts something, and Greg returns to the starting line. Nate jogs toward me until he's close enough to shout, "We're racing."

I throw up my hands in a gesture of "whatever." And I may be cold and tired, but I'm lying; I'm not "whatever" about watching these two go at it. I glance guiltily back toward the community center behind me, wondering if I'm betraying Mia by even thinking of ogling her fiancé. But fuck that. I've earned a little show after two-plus hours out here.

As they start, I only wish they were closer. Because while I can see them pulling the sleds, I'm not close enough to see any muscles rippling. It's a travesty. But the jump roping, I can see. Except that they're both so fucking good at it that it's over in *seconds*. And then they're playfully shoving each other as they jockey for position ahead of the tires. Nate wins by sheer bulk and goes barreling through them, with Greg not far behind. But Nate's bulk works against him as Greg emerges from the tires, hot on his heels and much lighter and faster across the snow. While it took the fastest of the earlier competitors a good thirty seconds to cross the distance, I have less than half that before I realize Greg is about to run right into me.

I step out of the way just in time to yell angrily at his passing back, "Watch where you're going!"

He slows to a jog as Nate streaks by me, then slows with him. Laughing, he pats Nate on the back. "Good try, old man."

Nate shakes his head. "At least I can still outlift you." Nate removes the snowshoes and hands them to Greg before heading toward the community center.

I make to follow, but Greg catches my arm.

"Nuh-uh," he protests, still breathing heavily and holding the snowshoes up. "Let's see what you've got, city girl."

"Oh please, those would never fit me," I scoff.

Yeah. Because that's what's stopping me.

"I've got ones that'll fit you at the starting line," he promises with a sly grin.

I cross my arms over my chest. "I'm freezing. I've been standing out here all afternoon. There's no way I'm doing an obstacle course after that."

He smirks. "You're just afraid I'll kick your ass."

My competitive side yearns to shove his smug mug into a pile of snow. "Of course you'll kick my ass. You're way stronger than I am. Not that I've tried myself, but I just watched a bunch of grown men struggle to pull those sleds. It'd take me as long to move one ten feet as it would for you to do the whole course."

"Then we'll start at the jump ropes," he says with a shrug. "Come on. It'll warm you up."

I shift nervously. I hate admitting I can't do something, especially to a hot guy. But I'm not sure I have a choice.

"I've never worn snowshoes," I confess, looking away from him pointedly.

Greg tips his head back and laughs. I scrunch my face at his enjoyment of my discomfort, but he steps toward me, slipping a gloved hand under my chin and forcing me to look at him.

"Then let me help you. We'll just do it for fun. Promise." He smiles winningly, and it's hard to say no.

I roll my eyes. "Yeah, sounds like a blast." But secretly, I can't help thinking that for someone with serious alpha male vibes, he's awfully considerate.

He steps forward, his thick jacket now touching mine. Just close enough to command my full attention. "When's the last time you did something out of your comfort zone?"

I keep my face a mask, unwilling to smirk at that question and give any indication that I have no problem being out of my comfort zone.

But then I realize that that's only true sexually. When *was* the last time I did something non-sexual that pushed my limits?

"What do I get if I do?" I ask, just to push back a little.

"How about a kiss?" he teases.

"How about an orgasm?" I counter.

His answering laugh warms the air between us and is so rich and full that I have to smile in return.

"Do I get one too?" he asks teasingly.

I bite into my lip. "I think that can be arranged."

His grin mellows into a small, sexy smile. "Let's just start with a kiss, and we'll see where things go from there, shall we?" He sees the protest forming on my lips because he throws up a hand. "I'm not saying no orgasms. Just trust me. You won't walk away from this unhappy, I promise."

His warm eyes search mine, and while I'd normally balk at not being in control, he's hard to say no to.

"Okay." It slips out more easily than I'd have expected.

So, I let him lead me down the field. I let him pick a pair of snowshoes and help me into them. I follow him to the jump ropes. And he counts us down.

The rest is pure comedy. I stumble through it like ... well, like a lawyer in snowshoes. I'm as awful at it as I feared I would be, and it's way harder than Greg, Nate, and the others made it look. Then again, living in the snowy Cascades, they all probably use snowshoes regularly.

Still, by the time we reach the finish line, we're both laughing uncontrollably, holding on to each other to remain upright. I tip onto my bottom right at the finish line, and he flops beside me.

Only then do I notice that the afternoon has faded into evening. The sun is setting over the mountains, with bright oranges blending toward the deep pink of the horizon, and it's beautiful.

I groan and flop backward, tired but much warmer, as he'd promised.

"What? What's wrong?"

I put my cold, gloved hands to my face. "I've become the Hallmark movie," I moan.

Greg laughs and rolls on top of me, prying my hands away from my face. "If it makes you feel better, I'm having some very un-Hallmark thoughts right now," he says huskily.

I wriggle my hips under him. "Go on."

He grins and touches his lips lightly to mine, making good on his promise. But it's only light at first. Then, like before, he devastates me with his mouth, his teeth pulling at the sensitive skin of my lower lip, followed by his tongue pushing its way between my lips.

A groan breaks through our kiss, and I'm so gone I'm not sure which one of us it came from until Greg says, "God, I can't wait until you make that noise because I'm between your legs."

I arch against him, and his mouth drops to my neck. "With your mouth or your dick?" I ask.

His teeth graze my skin, and his hips dig against me. In any other circumstances, I'd wish I wasn't wearing snow pants so I could feel him.

"With my dick," he promises against my skin. "As much as I want to taste you, I want to fuck you more."

"Then do it," I beg, not really wanting that to happen right here, right now. But I wouldn't say no to the closest warm, dry spot.

His mouth covers mine in a searing kiss that's interrupted by Mia calling from the building behind us.

"I know you guys aren't going to fuck in the snow, so you might as well come in and have dinner," she taunts.

Greg buries his laugh in my neck before he shoves himself off me and stands, offering me a hand. "To be continued," he promises.

I narrow my eyes and take his hand. "Soon?"

He grins. "Very soon."

CHAPTER FOUR

GREG

It takes everything I've got to walk away from Joanie on Saturday night. Am I an asshole because "soon" wasn't that same night? Maybe. But something is telling me to wait. To make *her* wait. That it'll be worth it. And frankly, I'm kind of just enjoying her company.

Nate texts me that morning to let me know he and the girls will be at the skating pond after breakfast. I'm not sure what to make of him informing me of their whereabouts after his warning me off Mia's best friend, but I'll take the help.

I finish off a steaming mug of black coffee as I stare down my snowy driveway, and anxiety settles over me. Not because of skating. That part I'm looking forward to. It's what comes after that.

Yakima. The Tyler clan. And my holiday visit-slash-annual report-in with my parents. Where I get to tell them all about what's happening in Alpine Ridge, and they get to tell me how I'm wasting my life staying here. Good times.

As I throw my suitcase in the backseat of my truck and head out, I realize "soon" will probably have to wait even more. I can't fuck and run with Joanie. Something tells me that I won't want to stop for a while once we start. And I will seriously need my head in the game to survive this week.

I park in my usual spot at the community center, though a few other vehicles dot the small parking lot on the skating pond side of the building, Nate's truck included. I go inside the building and grab my skates from the office.

As I head to the pond, the cold air does a much better job waking me up than the coffee, and I can hear laughter floating in the air. It breaks through the gloomy cloud hanging over my head, and as I get close, I can see that besides Nate and the girls, there isn't anyone else out at the pond yet. It's still early, I guess.

As I get closer, I can see Mia and Joanie spinning in circles, their hands clasped between them as they whirl around, heads tipped back while they laugh. The innocent joy on their faces is something to behold. It probably explains why Nate is stopped, watching them with a grin. Something like I'm doing right now.

I watch the girls break apart, Mia tumbling onto the ice with her momentum, still laughing, while Joanie catapults herself in a wide, graceful arc. She turns, then executes a perfect toe loop jump. And then, with confidence radiating out of her, she follows it with a *double*-toe loop jump.

I grin widely and advance to the pond's edge while clapping, and she skids to a stop, startled at the sight of me.

"Where'd you learn to skate like that?" I say by way of greeting, sitting on one of the nearby benches as I change into my skates.

She glides across the ice and hobbles over the small strip of snowy grass to settle beside me.

"I've had lessons since I was six," she explains, crossing her legs toward me. "So, I'm not shit at *all* winter sports."

I lace up with a smirk. "Just snowshoeing, then?"

She narrows her eyes. "We can't all be good at everything. Surely there's something *you're* bad at."

I finish lacing the other skate, stand, and extend my hand. "I'm sure there is," I agree. She takes my hand and lets me lead her onto the ice. I drop her hand and skate a quick, tight circle around her. "I'll let you know when I figure out what that is."

She rolls her eyes, and I skate away backward, saying hi to Nate as I pass him. Mia rolls her eyes as I glide by her, causing my grin to widen. Okay, so maybe I'm showing off a bit too much. I turn and stop right in front of Joanie.

"Cute," she says. "But can you do any jumps?"

"No," I admit. "I played hockey for years. I can skate, and I can handle a stick."

"I'm not even going to rise to that bait, mountain man," she says with a tilt of her eyebrow.

I tip my head back and laugh. "Then how about a spin around the ice instead?" I offer, holding out my gloved hand once more.

She takes it and lets me lead her around the pond. We do a few laps in perfect, silent sync, and I can't help spinning her into a twirl as we go for our third lap. She laughs as we disconnect and then spins out, using the momentum to execute a loop jump.

I resist teasing her for being a showoff. I'm not exactly one to talk, especially around her. I can't help it; something about this girl makes me want to impress her.

I notice that Nate and Mia have stepped off the skating pond and are putting on their boots.

"Where are you lovebirds off to?" I ask, skating to a stop nearby.

"Oh, noticed we were still here, did you?" Mia replies.

Nate shakes his head with a smile. "We're going to go pick up some lunch. Want us to bring you anything back?"

"What, we're not invited?" I joke.

Nate looks at me and says quietly enough that Joanie, still showing off her skills on the ice, doesn't hear, "I figured we'd give you two some time alone."

"Ah." I nod. Nate knows I'm headed out this afternoon since he'll be covering for me this week at the festival. "Thanks, man."

Mia starts back toward the parking lot, and Nate nods in return. "We'll be back in an hour. Maybe more." He gives me a subtle wink as he follows his woman.

I watch them walk away, climb in the car, and drive off before I return to Joanie. Only to find she's at the bench across the pond, changing back into her boots.

"Going somewhere?" I call across the sheet of ice as I sit back down to change into my own boots.

She smirks and strolls around the edge until she stops before me.

"*We*," she stresses, "are going in there." She tips her head toward the community center. "I'm cold. Want to warm me up?" She looks at me seductively.

I smile at her, then rise, offering my hand again. She takes it, and I lead her through the snow toward the building.

"So, this is your main gig, huh?" she asks, gesturing around her. "Running this place?"

I raise an eyebrow. "The community center? Yeah, something like that."

She peers out over the pond as we make to round the corner. "There are worse jobs," she says, then flashes me a smile to let me know she's not being critical.

"Alpine Ridge growing on you, city girl?" I tease, also realizing I hope it is. I wouldn't mind if she visited more. But I'm getting ahead of myself, I know.

She shrugs, but I can tell it's feigned indifference. "It's all right. So, are you one of the famed locals? Born and raised here?"

I laugh. "God, no. Though my family has had property here for decades," I explain. "But I came back a few years ago and just kind of stuck around."

"Fell in love, huh?" she pokes. Not quite teasing, more ... looking for information?

"Not just with the town. I have a lot of good memories of this place, and it's peaceful here," I explain freely. "No pressure. No expectations. I can just ... *be* here. Do what I want when I want."

We get to the building, and I push the door open, holding it for her to walk through. I follow her in and let the heavy door close behind us. The sound of it shutting heralds the first time we've been completely alone in private, nobody waiting outside to bust in and bother us. At least not for a while yet.

"What did you do before?" she asks.

I lead her down the hall to the office, the only room with a comfortable seat for us both, while I contemplate how to answer her question without spilling my entire life story.

I open the door into the small room and gesture to the old, maroon loveseat under the window next to the small desk and bookshelves that fill the other side of the room.

She folds herself onto one half and drops her coat, hat, gloves, and skates to the side. I toss mine back in the pile on the other side of the desk before joining her on the couch.

"I was a middle school PE teacher in Ellensburg," I finally admit. "I was 'made redundant' and decided that was as good an excuse as any to focus on something else for a while."

"Did you like it?"

I'm a bit taken aback by her question. "I loved it, actually. I've always had a passion for fitness, and it was great getting kids excited about it, too."

Joanie's expression softens. "That's sweet," she admits. Then she gives me a wicked smile. "God, I can't imagine if I'd had a PE teacher who looked like you. I bet all those little preteen girls *loved* you."

I chuckle. "Unfortunately, yes, that came with the territory."

"Unfortunately?" she asks shrewdly.

I gaze fixedly into her ice-blue, cutting eyes. I'll never get used to the effect they have on me. Like I want to tell her everything. I'm not sure if it comes with the law degree or if it's just *her*.

"I was dating another teacher. She didn't love it."

Joanie barks a sharp laugh. "Well, good that that's over then. What kind of woman is jealous of a bunch of twelve-year-olds?"

I hesitate, not wanting to badmouth my ex. Or even talk about her right now, not with Joanie.

"We were together a while. I don't think it was a big deal in and of itself, but when you have to deal with that day in and day out for years …" I shrug.

"How many years?"

"Six." The word drops into the silence like a stone in a still pond. The ripples of emotion on her face come and go, and I give her a minute. "Not one for long-term relationships?"

She tips her head back and forth. "I guess I haven't met someone I wanted to be with for that long."

"How about someone you want to be with for right now?" I tease, reaching out and running my thumb over her cheek.

She tilts her head into the touch, her long, dark hair spilling over her shoulder. Fuck if I don't want to run my hands through those waves. Gather them in my fist. Pull them hard while I take her from behind.

I shift as my dick rises at the thought. She misinterprets my shift as a move to kiss her, and her mouth meets mine.

Which I can't be mad about at all, as her soft lips open to me, and our tongues meet. I slide my hand to her neck, tilting her head so I can kiss her more deeply, my tongue exploring her mouth. She groans deep in her chest and then moves into my lap.

She straddles me as her face descends on mine, her teeth grazing my lip, the sensation traveling straight to my already too-hard dick. I lock my hands onto her waist, but she beats me to the next move, grinding her hips over mine, her core rubbing across my length through our jeans.

A groan escapes my lips, and she smiles down at me.

"You gonna show me that cock, mountain man? Make me scream with it?" she whispers, circling her hips over me. Electricity zaps down my spine, coiling in my balls. Fucking hell.

"All in good time," I promise, kissing her lightly on the lips. Deceptively.

Because my next move is to upend her on her back, which I do in one quick movement, pinning her onto the couch with my hips between her thighs, my dick rubbing her warm center through our clothes. "But I bet I can make you come without ever whipping it out."

She bites into her bottom lip, but it doesn't stop the grin that breaks over her face. "How do you make *not* sticking your dick in me sound so good?" she asks breathily.

"You haven't heard anything yet," I promise, descending on her. I run my lips up her neck, sucking the place where it meets her shoulder, then up the sensitive column to drag my tongue along the shell of her ear. She shudders under me. "I'm going to lick and suck you all over until you're begging for more, city girl."

She nods and turns her head so the other side of her neck is exposed to me. I grin and kiss it gently while simultaneously reaching down and twisting one of her nipples mercilessly. She gasps in surprise and arches into me. I twist it again, and she moans. When I twist it a third time, I bite her neck and suck just as mercilessly. She bucks against me as the pleasure goes through her.

I growl against her skin, the need to dominate, take, pleasure, fuck, own tearing through my veins. I use both hands to squeeze her breasts while my tongue returns to plundering her mouth. She grabs at my ass, desperately grinding against me. I tilt my hips into her, relenting on everything else, letting her focus on the one sensation. I twist and roll circles around her wet heat until her eyes flutter closed, and she stills. Her brows pinch together, and her breathing accelerates. I'd be smug knowing how close I have her already, but the sight is going to make me nut in my undershorts if I'm not careful. So, I slow it down. And her eyes flutter open.

I run my hands down her chest, landing on her hips and pinning her as I lower my mouth to her. As I bite her nipple through her shirt. She fists a hand in my hair in approval. So, I move to the other. She nods and gasps. I move between her breasts slowly, repeating the process as I gradually start to flex my covered cock against her.

I increase my speed leisurely, moving my mouth from her breasts to her neck, then to her mouth, letting my hand tweak her nipple as I speed up. The combined assault has her so worked up that her body undulates to the rhythm I'm squeezing her nipple, which I match to the thrust of my tongue in her hot mouth, the tilt of my hard, denim-covered dick against her warm, damp core, until I can tell she's on the edge.

Drawing my mouth from hers, I lean up and knead both of her breasts with my full hands. Her eyes pop open and stare at me, glazed with lust.

"You like that?" I ask, tilting my hips into her.

She nods.

"Tell me," I push.

"I like it," she breathes. "I need more."

"Like this?" I push myself against her hard, and she groans and nods. I squeeze her nipples hard in tandem, drawing them upward as I push our fully clothed centers together. God, the friction is killing me. I'm not sure I won't come too. But that's not what this is about. "This is just a taste, city girl." I lean in, working her nipples harder, faster as I dry fuck her toward orgasm. "Just a small preview. When

I have the time to get you naked…" I thrust hard, and one of her legs clamps around my backside while the other shudders — a good sign. I hold back my smug grin. "God, Joanie, I'm going to fuck you so good. So fucking hard. For so long your pussy is going to —"

"Oh shit, Greg, fuck, fuck, fuck," Joanie screams, coming apart under me, her hands clamping on my forearms.

I slow the tilt of my hips and the pressure on her nipples as she comes down from her climax. I lean into her, my mouth skating over hers, feeling her sharp, hot bursts of breath on my lips. I place one soft, sweet kiss on her mouth, high on hearing her call out my name in orgasm and so wanting to rub it in her face. But I hold back. I wait.

Eventually, her eyes open lazily, filled with satisfaction. A matching smile spreads over her lips.

"So, when will you get me naked? Because if that was just a preview…"

I laugh and kiss her before hauling us both upright. "All in good time," I repeat in promise. "But I'm glad it didn't disappoint."

Joanie levels me with a look so heated my cock almost finishes what our dry fuck started.

"While it was the best tease I've ever had, I'm going to need you to fuck me. And soon," she says huskily, not breaking eye contact.

Her tone, her gaze, the wet spots on her shirt over her tight nipples make me lose track of everything; whatever I was about to promise, whatever I'm supposed to be doing today — the beast in my pants wants to do exactly as she demands and fuck her seventeen ways from Sunday.

But just as I'm about to lose control, Nate's voice barks down the hall, "Lunch is here."

Joanie scoots up and pulls her legs out from between my thighs with a grin. She leans in, her breath hot on my ear. "To be continued. Soon, mountain man." And then she licks my earlobe.

I suck in a sharp breath and watch her sashay to the door, flipping her hair over a shoulder and giving me an expectant look.

"I'll be there in a minute," I promise.

She shrugs and waltzes through the opening. I rise to close it behind her. And I waste no time unzipping and gripping my dick hard, stroking it once, twice, and a third time — that's all it takes, and I quietly finish into my waiting palm.

As I tip my head back against the door, breathing hard, I let out a choked laugh. I have a feeling I'm going to be jerking off like a fucking teenager this week because of that woman.

CHAPTER FIVE

JOANIE

While I expected Greg to be an entertaining distraction, what I did not expect was for him to get me off with nothing but some over-the-clothes action. And then I further didn't expect him to disappear completely, leaving me salivating for more. I'm usually the one pulling that move.

I'd be furious with the bastard for flipping the script, but he had a reasonable excuse — it is the week before Christmas, and he'd committed to spend this week with his family out of town. But Bev needs cock. And not just any cock. Mountain man's cock. She's salivating for it. Literally.

Because while there's plenty to do at Mia's bakery, at the daily winter festival events, and just hanging out with Mia and Nate, thoughts of our tryst in that little room on that godawful couch have me wet and distracted all week. I've been masturbating like I haven't since I got my first vibrator.

Not even training for the Freeze Your Buns Run has been enough to cool my libido. I tried to convince Mia to train in underwear since that's what we'll be running in, and it's the only thing I haven't tried to calm Bev the fuck down, but Mia wasn't having it. It's a shame, as she's got a cute little body, and I know Nate wouldn't have minded watching us run the laps in the field behind the community center. I enjoyed watching him run them in only basketball shorts and sneakers. Sue me.

But alas, it was no substitute for what I really wanted. Greg's trouser snake. His cooch cork. His skin flute. His jolly stick. Love plunger. Man meat. Pocket rocket. Third leg. Uterus unicorn. One-eyed snake. Pink torpedo. Taco hammer.

Do I have too many names for a man's dick? Perhaps. But call it what you will, it's not just any dick I want. It is, in fact, his and his alone. The man got my — and Bev's — attention, and I won't be satisfied until I've had the full experience.

So, on Friday afternoon, when I head with Mia and Nate to the community center for the race, I'm full of nervous energy. And not about the race. I may be short, but I'm all legs, and I ran track in college, so I could win this shit in my sleep.

No, my nerves are because Bev and I know Greg is back since he called Nate right before we headed out to ask him to bring some supplies.

Nate parks in his usual spot and unloads the stack of plastic bins Greg requested, crunching behind us in the snow as we head toward the field. I can see people milling about the starting line and that the track has been widened with fresh gravel added to the packed snow, which runs between the drifts that are bound to keep my nipples hard as rocks for the entire four-lap mile-long run.

Just a mile, you say? No big deal, you say? Yeah, you try running a mile in thin air and cold-as-fuck temperatures. And I've only done it clothed so far.

At some point, Nate overtakes us, gets to Greg first, and they line the bins up. It immediately becomes apparent what they're for as a dozen or so men start stripping and putting their clothes in the bins. I shoot Mia a grin, and she rolls her eyes.

"Well, *now* we're talking," I murmur. "Finally, some NSFW, non-Hallmark-y action." I waggle my eyebrows toward the crowd.

Mia snorts. "I'll bet Rae's enjoying this as much as you are," she agrees, jerking her chin toward the starting line flag where Rae stands, overseeing the operation with a grin.

I laugh. "She's been busting her ass these last couple of weeks. I'd say she's earned it."

Mia lifts a shoulder, then heads toward the crowd of remaining men and women in the spectator area while I attempt to follow as my eyes search the sea of skin. Unfortunately, it's not all goodness, as there are plenty of old saggy asses and round, hairy bellies to be had. But what I'm searching for will be worth the mild trauma.

My eyes skip over Nate, as it's nothing I haven't seen practically daily at this point. Nice, but not what I'm after.

And then there it is. Greg's thick, dark hair catches my eye first. I'd know those waves anywhere. His back is to me, but I remember the feel of those broad shoulders and those strong arms, which are even thicker and more sculpted than I'd expected. And that back ... holy shit. Defined and strong, leading to tight muscles above his perfect globed ass-cheeks, covered only by the dark blue cloth that clings to his beautiful backside. His thick, muscled thighs support his frame, leading to strong calves. I lick my lips, silently begging him to turn around.

But someone fires the starting gun, and he disappears in a sea of moving flesh.

Thankfully, he, Nate, and a third guy pull out of the pack before the first lap is done, and I catch a glimpse of Greg's glorious front as he whips past the crowd. Alas, his perfect ass is gone too quickly to watch for long.

As it comes down to the wire and Greg is clearly in the lead, with Nate not too far behind, I realize I haven't taken my eyes off the race once. Haven't stopped looking for him once. And something about that worries me because I know it's not just wanting to catch glimpses of that body. I'm *rooting* for him. I fucking *care*. Am I getting attached to this sexy, sweet former PE teacher?

I think I am.

Crap.

Finally, he crosses the finish line, arms raised triumphantly to Rae's and everyone else's cheering. He deserved it after stepping aside in all the other events this week. Mia pulls me along to where Greg, now joined by Nate, is fishing around for his clothes. Both men are panting and sweaty. And naturally, I find it insanely hot. I raise my eyebrows and give Mia a look.

"Whatever you're thinking, stop," she remarks drily.

I give her a knowing smile, but she's already on to congratulating her man for making second place.

"Congratulations," I say, stepping into Greg's eye-line as he pulls his sweater on.

He looks up with a smile that doesn't reach his eyes. And it's the first time we've been face-to-face since Sunday. And despite his win, he looks *defeated*.

"Thanks," he murmurs.

I open my mouth to ask him what's up, but Rae calls for the women to get ready to take their marks. In the moments it took me to glance her way and back at Greg, he's disappeared. And now I'm sure something's up.

But whatever it is will have to wait until after I've kicked all these bitches' asses.

I do a few quick stretches before claiming an empty bin and stripping. When I get to the line, I realize there are half as many women as there were men, most of them much older. You've got to respect the grannies out here in their underpants. Hell, I hope that's me someday.

I chuckle at the thought as Rae fires the starting gun … and promptly get elbowed hard just as my left sneaker hits a rock-less, icy patch. My core muscles engage as my body flails, but it's hopeless. My legs fly from under me as I fall backward behind the pack of hos that pay no attention to my plight. Pain registers as the back of my skull meets ice and rock and snow. And everything goes black.

CHAPTER SIX

GREG

I'm standing between the runners and the building, debating whether I should help Rae monitor the race or hide in my office when I hear the collective, horrified gasp of the crowd that can mean nothing good. Thankfully my instincts override my shit mood, and I run the few hundred feet back to the race.

I find Nate, his back to me, dragging someone just off the race's path. Shit.

"Someone get her a blanket," he calls to the unmoving spectators as he kneels to assess the person.

I see Ned spring toward the pile of supplies Rae had on hand, digging for a blanket. But I move faster, removing my coat. Ned is not touching a nearly naked woman on my watch.

But as I skid to a halt, dropping to my knees next to him, my heart drops.

Joanie.

Pale and still, and somehow even more beautiful than ever. I wiggle my coat under her with Nate's help and button it around her just as Ned arrives with a blanket. I shoot him dagger-eyes and take the blanket for her legs. Thankfully he fucks off right quick.

"What happened?" I ask as Nate delicately examines her head.

"Slipped," he grunts. Then, he fishes a car key out of his pocket with one hand. "Black bag, behind the driver's seat."

I nod and run for the parking lot, trying not to worry myself into a panic.

In the few minutes it takes me to get back, the race has been stopped, and the runners are either crowded around Joanie with the rest of the town or pulling on clothes. As I drop Nate's bag next to him, I note Mia still in her underwear, kneeling on the snow beside her friend, tears spilling down her cheeks.

I shake my head and make for the bins, locating Mia and Joanie's clothes with Rae's help. By the time I get back with them, Joanie's eyes are open, and Nate is asking her questions in a gentle voice. I nudge Mia, then again before she finally looks at me, and I silently hand her the pile of clothes. She nods her thanks and returns her attention to her friend, simply clutching the garments to her chest.

"She's okay," Nate finally declares in a clear, raised voice. Then looks at Mia, "Put your clothes on, babe, so you can help me get her dressed, okay?"

Mia sniffs deeply and nods, fumbling through the pile. With a sigh, I crouch beside her and extract the pieces she needs, handing them to her one at a time until she's dressed. Just as she's zipping her coat, Joanie starts to sit up with Nate's help. He watches her like a hawk as she settles into a seated position.

"Doing okay?" he asks.

"I mean, not really. I feel like I got hit by a truck," she mumbles and glances down at herself. "What the fuck am I wearing?"

Mia lets out a choked laugh. "You're swearing. That's a good sign."

"It's my coat and a blanket," I offer, still crouched near her feet. "But we've got your clothes if you're ready to put them on."

Joanie's eyes meet mine. Her gaze is undecipherable, and I try to give her one in return that reassures her that we're here, that we've got her.

She finally tears her eyes away and looks at the clothes in Mia's arms. "Anything to get off this ice and onto something softer. And warmer."

"I can move her to the couch in the office," I offer to Nate.

"Probably for the best," he agrees, stepping back and deferring to me.

I rise, then position myself back in a crouch next to her. "I'm going to bring you inside, okay, city girl?"

She grimaces and nods faintly — no exuberant agreement to me carrying her while she's mostly naked and only covered by my coat. My eyes flick up to Nate's momentarily, communicating that observation. He dips his chin in acknowledgment.

I slide my arms under her and pull her to me as I rise, cradling her as gently as I can against my chest. Mia performs a few tucks of the coat and blanket dangling around her, and we head away from the dispersing crowd. Nate stays beside us, and Mia gets in front to open the community center door.

I bring Joanie through, and we repeat the process with the office door before I carefully set her down on the small couch.

Rae pokes her head in. "I've got Penny wrapping up the event. I'll find Miss Joanie something hot to drink."

Nate nods. "And something to eat, too, I think, Rae. Thank you."

"Sure thing, Nate." Rae disappears just as quickly as she appeared, and Mia sinks to the floor next to the couch, clasping Joanie's hands in hers.

"Well, that wasn't exactly how I wanted to steal the show," Joanie jokes in a much quieter tone than usual.

Mia huffs a laugh. "I'm just glad you're awake. You freaked me out there, Jo."

Joanie cringes. I'm not sure if it's pain or embarrassment. "How long was I out?"

"Just a few minutes," Nate says. "But you're lucid, the bump isn't big, and you don't have radiating pain, so it's probably a concussion at most. Though given the fact that you were unconscious at all, and you did hit your head, I think it's best if we take you into the emergency room just in case."

Joanie grimaces again. "What, no ambulance?" she remarks drily.

Nate's eyebrows jump up, and he holds up a hand with three fingers raised. "How many fingers?" he asks abruptly.

Joanie rolls her eyes. "Three. And it was sarcasm. I'm fine."

Nate continues to eye her skeptically. "First of all, you don't fuck around with head injuries. Second, it'll be far quicker if we take you. I'm not sure emergency services will come here unless someone needs to be airlifted."

"That's barbaric," Joanie scoffs.

Mia nods in agreement. "I know. When I started the bakery, I tried to push to incorporate the town so we'd get basic services out here. No dice."

Well, that's news. I've attempted it myself, but now isn't the time or place to swap stories.

"We can discuss town politics another time," I inject pointedly. "Joanie should get to the hospital as soon as possible."

Nate nods his agreement and gestures for Mia to grab Joanie's clothes.

I move next to Nate. "Let me know how it goes, okay?" I say in a low voice.

But apparently, it was not low enough because Joanie turns her gaze from Mia, who is starting to help dress her, and gives me the biggest puppy dog eyes I've ever seen. "You're not coming?"

If the look didn't do it, the soft, sad tone does. I hesitate for only a heartbeat.

"Of course I am, city girl."

Nearly five hours later, we arrive at the community center parking lot so Nate can drop me off at my truck before heading back up the mountain. Thankfully, the doctor's exam came to the exact conclusion as Nate had: just a concussion and a mild one at that.

Joanie is leaning into me, my arm around her. The thought of leaving her is giving me a pit in my stomach.

She looks up at me with a vulnerability I've never seen her display, and the knot in my gut tightens.

"Come home with me," I murmur. "Let me take care of you."

She goes to respond, but Nate turns his head toward us. "I don't think that's the best idea."

I raise my eyebrows, looking around at the dark sky and deep snow. "Why not? She's tired. She's already been dragged all over hell and back, and my place is five minutes away. In these conditions, it'll take you guys another forty minutes to get up the mountain. Plus, it's not like I have anything else to do."

Mia turns fully around in her seat. "She's my best friend. There's nothing more important I have to do than take care of her," she insists sharply.

Joanie sits up, ramrod straight. "Um, hi, hey," she cuts in, waving a hand between us. "Adult here. I'm not dead. Just a bump on the head. Pretty sure I get to decide for myself."

Nate frowns. "I'm glad you're okay, Joanie," he says, then turns and looks at me. "But I'm going to say this flat out. Can you tell me if you take her home, you won't fool around? Because sexual activity is off the table —" Joanie opens her mouth to interject "—sexual activity of *any kind*," he stresses, and she sinks back with a grimace, deflated, "for at least twenty-four hours. Ideally, more. She needs to rest. Physical stuff aside, even getting too worked up isn't good right now."

I huff a wry laugh. "Believe it or not, I am capable of putting her needs before mine, or I wouldn't have offered," I respond matter-of-factly.

Mia arches a brow. "You may be, but her —" she tips her chin at Joanie "— I'm not so sure about."

Joanie rolls her eyes. "I'd rather stay with him and keep it Hallmark than go home and listen to you two fucking," she retorts. "So going with you is practically a guarantee that I'll get all hot and bothered with that soundtrack playing all night."

Nate turns bright red, and I hold back a laugh. "City girl has a point. She might get more rest with me since your ... nightly activities won't keep her up."

"First of all, I had no idea you could hear us —" Mia starts, clearly mortified.

Joanie cuts her off with a sharp laugh. "Mia, you're both so loud in bed, even *I* know the exact noises you both make right before you —"

"Okay, okay, we get it," Nate interjects. "But I think Mia's 'second of all' was going to be that we can ... not do that while you rest — no big deal. Then I'll be around if you need medical care. I'd feel better that way."

"And you'd do what?" I counter. "It's not like there's much you could do that I couldn't. I'm first-aid and CPR certified. Plus, if she needed a hospital, she'd get to one much faster from my place. And I won't be in another room not fucking my fiancée."

Nate presses his lips together as he realizes I'm right. Confirmed when he gives Mia a look. She throws her hands up. "Fine. But text me regularly."

Joanie scoffs. "Okay, Mom. Jesus Christ, why do I feel like a teenage girl whose parents don't want her to be alone with her first boyfriend instead of a grown-ass woman who can do what and who she pleases? I promise I'll be good." She shakes her head and gives me a small nudge. "Let's go."

Mia follows us out of the truck, and the girls embrace despite their tension, murmuring words that I can only assume mean they're making peace. Then I help Joanie get into the passenger side of my truck.

As I climb into the driver's seat and close the door, she sighs in relief. "Their kids are going to be so fucking neurotic."

I laugh. "But well-loved," I point out.

She shrugs, but I can see a small smile on her lips. And exhaustion written all over her face.

"Come on, city girl. Let's get you to bed." I give her a wink.

CHAPTER SEVEN

JOANIE

Greg's bed, as it turns out, is the stuff of legend, humongous and the exact right balance between soft and firm, with silken pillowcases that make me feel like I've died and gone to heaven, and the highest thread count sheets I've ever felt outside of a hotel.

And between his sheets is exactly where I am now, wearing only one of his shirts and panties as he puts together some food in the kitchen. The gorgeous kitchen of his modestly sized yet beautifully appointed home just outside of "downtown" Alpine Ridge. Nothing about it says "bachelor" from the stylish yet functional furniture to the Pottery-Barn-esque décor.

"Dinner for the lady," Greg announces as he walks in, carrying a laden tray.

"What, you're not going to eat with me?" I tease as he sets it down in front of me.

"Oh, I am," he assures me with a wink. "I'll be back with my tray."

When he turns and leaves, I look at the spread before me. And I burst out laughing. I'm still laughing a minute later when he returns.

"What?" he asks, clearly a little affronted as he settles beside me. "You don't like it?"

I wipe the tears of laughter from my eyes. "No, I love it," I declare. "Really. Tomato soup with grilled cheese sandwiches takes me right back to third grade."

He shrugs. "It's what my mom always made me when I wasn't feeling well. It's my go-to comfort meal."

I tilt my head, an unfamiliar sensation washing through me. "Greg, I'm … touched," I say, naming the feeling. "You wanted to comfort me."

He blushes and takes a bite of his grilled cheese with another shrug but says nothing. So, I go ahead and start eating. And it tastes every bit as nostalgic as I'd expected it would.

We eat in companionable silence until another unfamiliar feeling starts gnawing at me, and I stop eating.

"Is something wrong with the soup?" he asks. I look up to find him gazing at me in concern.

"Not at all. I was just ... thinking," I respond.

"About?"

I push the tray away, agitated in a way I'm ashamed to admit. "Nobody has ever cooked for me before. I mean, my mom has. And lord knows Mia has, but ..."

"Ah," he says, pushing away his own now-empty tray. "You've never had a *man* cook for you before."

I press my lips together and shake my head. "Can't say I have."

Greg reaches up and brushes his thumb over my cheek. "I'm honored to be your first," he teases, leaning in and placing a chaste, grilled-cheese-flavored kiss on my lips.

I scrunch my nose and make a face at him. "Well, I'm willing to bet I'm not the first girl you've fed in this bed. No man chooses sheets this nice by himself." I try not to think too hard about the fact that I care about being another notch on his seriously luxurious bedpost.

"Well, that's presumptuous," he scoffs.

I raise an eyebrow. "You're telling me you picked these out?" I ask, running a hand over the luxuriously thick and smooth material.

He rises and carefully sets the trays on the dresser opposite the bed before climbing back in until he's right in my face. "No. I'm telling you that you're the first girl I've fed in this bed." And then his mouth is on mine, gentle but firm. Unbidden relief washes over me, and I open my lips to welcome him in, but he pulls back. "And that's all we're doing in this bed tonight, city girl. No taking advantage of me." He winks and pulls me back on the pillows, cradling me against his chest.

"So, a woman did pick out these sheets," I say, but since it's against the hard plane of his pecs, it comes out garbled. He laughs, the sound rumbling through where my lips and cheek meet his shirt. And it makes me smile.

"Yes, but it was my Aunt Margaret, so you have nothing to worry about. I haven't fucked anyone in this bed."

I pull my head back to look at him. Hating that I'm not up for all the things I want to do to him after that declaration. "Yet," I reply, batting my eyelashes.

He smirks and shakes his head. "I'm glad you like the sheets."

"And I liked the dinner." Greg gives me a deeply skeptical look. "Really. Thank you," I add, running my hand down his chest, once again struck by this softer side to him.

"You're welcome," he replies. And then, as if out of nowhere, "What are you still doing here, Joanie? I didn't expect you to stay in Alpine Ridge this long."

I'm a little startled, but it's a fair question. "I didn't either," I admit with a small shrug. Then, with a sly grin, "Maybe there's just been enough worth sticking around for."

Now he looks surprised. "Me?" he asks incredulously.

"Full of yourself much? I was talking about the macarons. And the spectacular array of winter sports. Concussions and all."

He narrows his eyes at me, my humor fooling nobody.

"You like me." It almost sounds like an accusation.

I roll my eyes, playing it off. He's not wrong, though admitting things like that out loud isn't my style. "I'd like your cock in me, but since that's not an option, I'm happy to lay here and feel you up."

Greg grasps my chin and looks into my eyes. "Well, I like you, Joanie — a lot. You're smart, honest, and sarcastic. Oh, and way too sexy for your own good. Especially tonight."

I lick my lips. How does this man always know the right things to say? And how can he turn me on so much while barely touching me?

"You know, maybe we could just …" I slide my hand lower, down his tight abdomen, but don't get far before he laces his fingers with mine.

"Is intimacy without sex that terrifying for you?" he asks bluntly.

A sarcastic remark hangs on the tip of my tongue, but something about his expression seals it behind my lips. His pupils are dilated, his expression open and searching.

I take a deep breath. In through my nose. Out through my mouth.

"Yes. If a guy isn't looking to just fuck me, he's looking to get something by fucking me. Ergo, I don't do real intimacy. It's asking for trouble. I like my life how it is. I don't need intimacy, just sex. Relationships complicate things."

He shakes his head sadly. "Are you telling me there's not a single man who has successfully broken through your bullshit?"

"Excuse me? My bullshit?"

"Yes, Joanie. Your bullshit. Your 'I don't need men for anything but sex' attitude. Are you telling me you honestly don't want more? A life partner?"

"Not a priority for me," I reply flippantly.

"Maybe not, but isn't everyone looking for someone who gets them? Who wants to be with them for who they are? For more than just sex?" he presses.

I close my eyes and realize I'm too tired for this shit. And the pain is creeping back out from under the drugs they gave me at the hospital.

"If you're looking to uncover some trauma that's made me afraid to love, you're wasting your time," I say flatly, then open my eyes and stare hard into his. "I guess I just haven't found anyone worth sharing … *more* with. Which is fine by me. I like my independence." I scooch up into a sitting position, and he scrambles to follow. "Can we just … not talk about this anymore? I need more acetaminophen and some rest."

His eyes search mine for a long moment. "Yeah, okay, of course," he finally accedes, rising from the bed. He stacks the contents of both trays onto one and takes them out of the room with him. He returns a few minutes later with a glass of water and two pills. "Here."

I take them without looking at him, swallowing the pills and chugging the water. "Thanks."

Greg draws the blackout curtains, sealing the room in semi-darkness, the only light from the lamp on my side of the bed.

I slip under the covers and lay on my back, watching Greg round the bed to his side. He kicks off his slippers and removes his sweatpants, revealing boxers underneath. Despite the tension of our conversation, I'm disappointed when he leaves his T-shirt on and climbs into bed.

After all, he is ridiculously attractive. But then, I've been with plenty of attractive men. With Greg, though, it's … more than that. I mean, the physical attraction is clearly strong for both of us, but he's the first guy possibly ever to want to stick around when sex was off the table. On top of that, he's taken care of me. And even though he doesn't seem to get that I don't need a man to feel complete, he respectfully dropped the subject when I asked him to.

I think he's what most women would call a keeper.

Shit, do I want to keep him?

I realize … maybe.

Maybe I do.

The realization makes emotions drum quietly but steadily against my insides. So, against my better judgment, I decide to let him in. Just a little. Just enough to reassure him that I'm not *totally* opposed to the idea. That I've just never trusted someone enough for things to get even close to needing them. That maybe I've just been looking in the wrong places all this time. Places that weren't here.

"When a man wants to focus on his career to the exclusion of an intimate relationship, he's seen as ambitious and hard-working. But when a woman does it, she's closed off and frigid and clearly messed up somehow," I begin. I feel rather than see Greg stiffen beside me. "I love being a lawyer. I loved the challenge of getting ahead at my firm. Even though I don't work there anymore, I still need that kind of challenge. And I intend to find it again." I turn, and we lock eyes. "What I didn't intend was you."

Greg considers that before sitting up and stroking a hand down my back. "I'm not trying to distract you from getting your career back on track. I did a shit job of saying it, but what I was trying to tell you is that … well, I don't just want you for sex, Joanie. If you want more, I'm up for it. That's all."

A smile pulls at the corners of my lips. There he goes, saying exactly the right thing again. "And if I just want sex?"

Greg's eyes darken, and he goes still. "Christ, I wish you didn't have a concussion right now."

A laugh slips through my lips, and he chuckles. "I'll take that as you're up for that, too," I tease.

Greg closes his eyes briefly, shakes his head, then reaches for my hand and places it over his boxers. Letting me feel the hard length of him underneath. "Definitely." My breath catches, and I look up to find his eyes open again and fixed on my face. "But I'm not going anywhere, city girl," he says in a deep, warm voice that washes through me like a balm.

I take a subtle deep breath. I'm too tired and in too much pain to deal with what I'm feeling and how that fits in the picture I had for my life. I'm not sure what excuse I'll have once I'm feeling better, but one problem at a time.

"Good. Because tonight we're going to have to settle for spooning," I tease, trying to lighten the mood as I slip down so my ass is right over his hard cock.

He groans and rests his forehead on my back. "You're killing me here."

I laugh and pull his arm around me. "Well, if you're not up for the challenge …" I wiggle my ass, and he laughs, thrusting his hardness into me.

"I am if you are," he says huskily in my ear.

I bite into my bottom lip, even though I know he couldn't see me if I did smile. Well, when he puts it like that …

"Weren't you listening? I'm always up for a challenge."

CHAPTER EIGHT

GREG

I wake on Saturday morning with Joanie's sweet ass still planted firmly over my hard dick. It makes me wonder if it ever calmed down. But feeling her in my arms right now? Worth a hundred cases of blue balls.

I also realize that since her fall, I haven't thought about the fiasco that was the visit to see my family this past week. Not that I'm glad she was hurt, but it has distracted me from my pity party. But then, Joanie has been the distraction I didn't know I needed from the moment we met.

I love Alpine Ridge. I didn't come here to hide like Nate. I came here out of duty. Though like Nate, I stayed because I found peace here. But Joanie has blown that all apart. Because now? I want to be wherever she is. Maybe it's just infatuation, but it's certainly something I want to explore. Though to do that, I need her to see this as more than just sex.

Having to delay fucking until she's recovered will help. Today, we'll spend all kinds of non-sex time together, cookie decorating, sampling at the chili cookoff, and watching the orchestral Christmas Eve show. All low-key enough that they've been Nate-approved during Joanie's recovery. And I will use every minute to convince her there's something here. It's a feeling that burrows deeper the more I'm around her, and I know she feels something, too. Or she would if she'd let herself.

Today's mission: Give Joanie enough space and opportunity to connect with those feelings. With no pressure.

Easier said than done. Thankfully, I've already realized I'll take whatever she's willing to give.

⤙⥽

"Are you sure you're up for the show?" Mia asks Joanie for the third time in as many minutes. "You've already done so much today."

197

Joanie rolls her eyes. "I ate my weight in cookies and chili, Mia, I didn't run a freaking marathon. A little Christmas music will probably just put me to sleep."

Mia looks pleadingly at Nate, but he shrugs. "I was worried last night, but she's fine. Just let her enjoy the show, babe." Mia grimaces but finally seems to accept it as we take our seats: Nate, then Mia, then Joanie, then me.

Joanie leans toward me and whispers, "On second thought, if Nate thinks I'm good as new, maybe we leave now and go back to your place." She gives me a meaningful look.

And I'm so fucking tempted.

"No can do, city girl. Trust me; you'll want to stick around for this." I nod toward the stage where a jazz quartet has taken the low stage, along with Rae. Joanie quirks a brow at Rae's appearance and gives me a look. I simply gesture to the stage with a smile as the musicians tune their instruments.

And then the show begins. Alpine Ridge may be a small town, but the people who own homes here are as cultured and varied as you'll find anywhere. Three of the four were professional musicians at some point. And Rae …

"*Oh my God,*" Joanie gasps as Rae sings the first few notes of *Let it Snow*. She looks over at me with wide eyes, and I shrug. It surprises everyone when sweet, unassuming Rae busts out her sultry, smooth singing voice.

As Joanie watches the performance, I watch her. Her pure, simple joy. She's been like this all day. Icing cookies like it wasn't something mostly kids were doing. Tasting the various chilis like they were all gourmet. Experiencing everything in an un-sarcastic or cynical manner. Enjoying all the things that I enjoy about this small but tight-knit community. I'm not sure if it was the bump on the head or what, but she seems happier.

When the final notes of the last song fade, she looks over at me, her eyes filled with emotion. But then her brows bunch together.

"Why are you looking at me like that?" she asks.

I laugh. "I'm just in awe. What's gotten into you today?"

She shrugs and rises from her chair. "I don't know what you mean."

I purse my lips but keep my thoughts to myself. Either she knows she's bald-faced lying and doesn't want to talk about it, or she doesn't and nothing good will come from me pointing it out.

"All right guys, we're headed to Portland early tomorrow for Christmas morning with Nate's parents," Mia declares, opening her arms to Joanie.

"Better get home so you can fuck *and* sleep before then," Joanie teases, hugging her friend. "I'll see you guys for dinner tomorrow."

We finish a round of goodbyes, and I look to Joanie. "So, I guess that means you're coming home with me?"

She smirks, the first sign of the naughty girl I've seen all day. "Was that ever even a question?" She bats her eyelashes at me, and I laugh.

"Guess not. What if I had plans for Christmas?"

She cocks her head. "Do you?"

"Nope. Got enough of my family last week. You're not spending Christmas with yours?"

Joanie shrugs and loops her arm through mine as we return to my truck. "Mia *is* family. But no, my parents are in Australia. Christmas tradition. They despise the cold."

"And they're fine leaving their only child alone at the holidays?"

"Oh, they used to offer to bring me out there to join them. But I've always worked through the holidays, so at some point, they just stopped asking."

I frown. "Do they know you lost your job?" I ask curiously.

She gives me a sharp look. "Not yet, no," she responds, her tone as sharp as her gaze.

I nod, reading between the lines that it's not something she wants to discuss.

She stops so abruptly that I end up a few steps ahead of her before I can react. I turn back, and she's frowning.

"Do you *want* me to come home with you?" she asks, seemingly equally irritated and disappointed.

I quickly close the gap between us, choosing the language she speaks best to answer first. My mouth is on hers, my tongue pushing between her lips, and my arms pulling her to me. I'm afraid at first when she doesn't respond, but after a few long moments, she opens her mouth for me.

When we finally break apart, I rest my forehead against hers. "More than anything," I swear. "I want you more than anything."

I lace my fingers with hers, and we silently walk the rest of the distance. We finish the short ride to my place in silence. We make it to the bedroom in silence.

Joanie sits on the edge of the bed, patting the spot next to her seductively. Rather than take it, I drop to my knees before her, looking up into her ice-blue eyes. Her gaze is filled with heat and lust. But all I see is her.

"Time to make me scream, mountain man," she purrs.

I shake my head. "Another time. Tonight, I'm going to worship you." We stare at each other for a moment. I'm waiting for her to protest at the intimacy of that request. She's … well, I can't tell if she's more confused or excited. I hope she's both. I want to turn everything she thinks she knows about me on its head.

I start by slowly slipping off her shoes and socks. She watches, allowing it, somewhat amused by the process. When I'm done, I lift her sweater up and over her head, revealing a red, lacy bra through which I can see her peaked nipples.

"Fuck, city girl," I breathe, leaning in and closing my mouth over her left nipple. I suck at it through the fabric, and she winds her fingers into my hair, tugging with approval, so I do it to her other nipple, too. Then I move to her mouth, using a kiss to press her back onto the bed.

I pull away, unbuttoning her jeans and shimmying them over her pert ass and down her long legs. Unsurprisingly, her panties match the bra perfectly, and dark curls are visible underneath, into which I promptly bury my face and inhale. The scent of her arousal has me hard in an instant.

"You smell like heaven," I murmur. She giggles, presumably at the sensation of my voice reverberating through her core.

But we can't have laughing. Not while I'm between her legs. So, I move aside her panties and plunge my tongue into her, lifting her knees to widen her slit, diving deeper. She groans and arches and squirms, so I press a hand on her hips, stilling her for my mouth.

"Look at me, Joanie," I demand.

She presses onto her elbows, drawing her head up until our eyes meet. I flick my tongue from ass to clit and she hisses in a breath but maintains eye contact.

Next, I use a thumb to press into her, slowly fucking her. Her breaths come heavier. So, I use the other thumb to circle her nub. Her eyes drop closed as she moans. So, I stop. And her eyes spring open. It takes a couple of rounds of that for her to realize she has to watch for me to keep going.

Her eyes on me, as I pleasure her, have me so wound up, it's all I can do not to pounce on her. But I don't. I keep fucking her with my thumb, fingers, tongue. Alternating each at various speeds and forces. Until I find what makes her grip the comforter, pant, groan, and struggle to keep watching. And I do that faster, harder, until her pussy convulses around my hand. I reach in deep and twist, throwing her higher, so high that she falls back, grabbing at her tits, tweaking her nipples to keep it going. It's so fucking sexy I have to stop before I come on the spot.

My absence goes unnoticed until she rides the wave down. I'm still gritting my teeth against the image of her coming when I hear, "Greg?"

I suck a breath in sharply. God, I need to hear her say that when she orgasms with me inside of her.

I climb onto the bed, over her, and hold myself above her. "I'm here." I give her my mouth and let her taste her juices on me. She moans as our tongues tangle.

"I need more," she demands.

I lick up the column of her neck, stopping with my mouth at her ear. "Tell me what you need."

"I need you inside me. On top of me. Behind me. In my mouth. I need you everywhere."

I shiver hard and let my hips fall between her legs, my hardness rubbing into her slick cunt. "You need that?"

She nods, and I push harder. The front of my jeans will be soaked, but I don't care. I use the friction to tease her, grinding in circles until she can't take it anymore.

"Jeans off," she demands. "Now."

I rise, unzipping and pulling my dick out while I head to the nightstand drawer, where I fish out a condom. She turns her head and licks her lips at the sight of my engorged cock.

"You like that?" I ask.

She nods.

"You want to suck my dick, Joanie?"

She bites into her lower lip and nods again.

I grin, kicking the jeans off. Then I rip the foil and roll the condom down my dick, climbing over her and settling between her legs. "Another time, beautiful." And without warning, I bury myself in her in one smooth stroke.

It was stupid. It's been too long since I've been with anyone, much less someone who turned me on as much as Joanie does. My dick has swelled to epic proportions. And she's so tight and wet from her first orgasm. The hot clench of her pussy makes me see stars.

I lean over her onto my arms, catching my breath and mastering myself before I nut in one.

"Fuck," I groan, sliding back out. Joanie shivers under me. And then I plunge back into the abyss. Over and over. Slowly. Deliberately. Until my body cooperates with my need to keep it together. So I can feel her for as long as possible. Watch her arch under me for as long as possible. Make her come harder than she thought possible.

I lean up, hauling her hips into my lap as I continue to pump into her. She's almost a rag doll, clearly surrendered to the pleasure. I hold her in place with one hand and use the other to knead her covered breast. God, I should've taken her underthings off, too. Because frankly the friction of her panties on the side of my cock may ruin my plans.

I pull out and rip them off. Then I roll her over and undo her bra before hauling her hips up and plunging back in. She groans into the bed. But I can't hear it like I want to. So I pull out again and roll her onto her side, positioning myself behind her.

Lifting her leg, I slide back in. And fuck, she's tight from this angle. It also allows me to hear her moan as I take her. Still slow and steady. I'm a little surprised she hasn't demanded fast and hard. She seems like the kind to want it rough.

"You like that?" I ask as I flex my hips and bury myself deep in her.

"God, yes," she moans.

"You know what I'd like?" I ask, kissing her neck. "I'd like you on top of me. So I can kiss you." I kiss her neck again. "Suck on those gorgeous tits." I squeeze one for effect. "Watch my dick going in and out of your beautiful pussy." Her back arches, and she nods.

I pull out, leaning back into the pillows. I expect it'll take her a minute to gather herself, so I'm more than a little surprised when she immediately climbs on top of me, and her mouth devours mine as her wet cunt devours my cock. I groan into her mouth now, helpless against her as she controls the speed and depth.

She leans back, bracing herself with her hands, using the arch of her back to fuck me. Watching her is hands-down the hottest thing I've ever witnessed. I grip her thighs, watching as my dick repeatedly disappears into her dark, wet curls. As her peaked nipples point to the ceiling. Her mouth goes slack while her legs tremble, and her pace stutters.

I take the cue and thrust up into her, dropping a thumb to circle her clit. She falls backward, which would've separated us if I weren't ready for it. I switch my grip to her hips and pull her toward me so I can keep thrusting up into her. So I can watch her shatter.

"You are so sexy, Joanie," I groan as I pick up my pace, feeling her walls start to clench harder. "Come for me, baby. Say my name."

And I unleash. Hard and fast. Pounding her pussy until she clenches so tightly it's all I can do to keep fucking her through her orgasm.

"Oh … oh … oh," Joanie cries. "Yes, God, yes, Greg, oh my God, yes!"

When my name falls from her lips, I'm done. My cock explodes, release whipping through me like a firebrand as I empty into the condom. As she quivers around me. As my world shifts.

I may have gotten her to scream my name. I may have owned her orgasm. But the truth is, Joanie Morris owns me.

CHAPTER NINE

JOANIE

Even though I've never been big on holidays, Christmas morning holds the echoes of the joy of all my childhood Christmases. But this Christmas morning holds the echoes of the joy of all my orgasms of the past twelve hours. And there have been a lot.

With that thought, I wake fully, suppressing my giggle in case Greg's not up yet. Because there's one thing we *didn't* do last night that I will make sure we do this morning.

Unfortunately, the blackout curtains make the room so dark that all I can see is his outline. I listen quietly and hear only his deep breaths. He's still asleep. But not for long.

With a sly grin, I slip under the covers. And then I close my lips over his cock. Already semi-hard with morning wood, he nearly fills my mouth. And a few good sucks leave me with not much more than a crown and Greg groaning.

"Shit, Joanie," he says. "That's ..." More groans.

I slip my hand around him, grinning and pumping his shaft as I emerge to find he's turned on the lamp. The low light casts a golden glow over his gorgeous face.

His head is thrown back, his eyes closed as his muscles tighten against the sensation of me working him.

"Look at me, Greg," I demand, just like he did when he went down on me yesterday. And I intend to make this every bit as epic as what he did to me, if that's possible. It was the best oral I've ever received, after all, but I'm confident I can give it as good as I got.

His eyes are dark and filled with need, but he watches. And I watch back as I lick around the tip of him, the fantasies of doing this to him coming to life even better than I'd imagined. He grits his teeth, and I smirk, pumping him with sure, wet strokes before closing my mouth over him again, opening my throat, and releasing my hand. One of the few ways I'll surrender to a man.

With a sharp groan of approval that shows he understood the invitation, Greg pumps into my mouth, bracing himself against the bed to get as deep as he can. Moisture streams from my eyes and down my cheeks as I take it all, sucking around his thrusts as he fucks my mouth until my clit is throbbing, my nipples are hard, and my throat is raw. With a roar, he spills down my throat. I smile around his cock, then lick gently to clean him as he withdraws. But then his dick is replaced by his lips as he pulls me in for a claiming kiss, his tongue plundering my mouth.

Once he lets me go, he drops back to the bed, panting. "Fucking hell, Joanie," he groans. "Give me a minute and then I'm going to make you come so hard you —"

The sound of a door closing outside the bedroom makes us both sit up abruptly.

"Gregory?" a man's voice calls.

I look over at Greg, wide-eyed. His expression is sour.

"Fucking hell," he mutters. "It's my father." He rises and goes to the door, sticking his head around the gap where it was open. "I'll be out in a minute." His tone is terse, unfriendly. I don't miss that there's no "*Merry Christmas, Dad*" or "*Hey, Dad, what a nice surprise.*"

Greg closes the door, then walks to the window and opens the drapes, presumably so he can see better. He pulls on his jeans and a sweater before ducking out of the room and pulling the door almost closed behind him … but not quite all the way closed. And seeing as how I have no shame, I slink out of bed and retrieve my sweater from where it'd landed on the floor last night, slipping it on. Since it hits below my ass, it covers everything that matters in case I get caught, so I don't bother with anything else. Instead, I creep to the door to listen.

"—and I told you that your mother and I expected you to come home. We've had enough, son."

"First; I'm a fucking adult, and you may not like that I decided your plans to turn Alpine Ridge into the next tourist trap in the Cascades would destroy everything I love about this place —"

"It's not your decision to make," Greg's father interrupts, his voice icy.

"Not *just* mine, maybe. But I came here to look after our investments this side of the mountains. I was happy to do that until you wanted to change what that meant. I never agreed —"

"I thought you'd care more about what's in the family's best interests, Gregory. But since you don't, you have no right —"

"I have *every* right. Your father left me half of that land, plus *all* of the property you're standing on. Clearly, you didn't get that Grandpa Tyler was trying to get us to learn how to work together, Dad. But it's all about what you want, isn't it?" The harsh, commanding note in Greg's voice sends shivers down my spine.

Greg's dad scoffs. "So, what, you want to waste your life with no career, no wife, no *family*, and now without thought for the real estate empire you've been part of since birth? You're abandoning your duties to yourself and your mother and me. If you won't see sense, at least come home for your mother. You have no idea how devastated she is by your behavior."

Now it's Greg's turn to scoff. "You're peas in a pod. Do you care at all that being here is what makes me happy? That I'd rather leave *no* legacy than one built on greed?" My heart clenches at the plea in his words, the obvious desire for his father's approval. While my own parents weren't the most hands on, all they've ever wanted was my happiness. It hurts knowing Greg's clearly never had that, and I find my anger rising against his father.

"Those are interesting words, considering you've lived large on the legacy that your grandfather and his brother started. That your trust fund has allowed you luxuries that —"

Greg's laughter cuts off his father. "Shows what you know. I haven't touched a fucking dime of that money. I've lived only off the fruits of my own labor." My eyebrows fly up at the information spilling out of this argument.

"From being a *PE teacher*?" His father practically spits the words. "You truly expect me to believe that?"

"Just because I haven't sold or developed our joint land doesn't mean I haven't done anything, *Dad*," Greg throws the last word back at him with as much disdain as his dad had with his former title. "You need me because, unlike you, I learned from Grandpa Tyler. And I've made my own money with other investments. So, I have absolutely nothing to gain from destroying this place so you can make money. And using Christmas and Mom to guilt me into coming home and being a good boy? That's low, even for you." I bite my lip, pride and respect flowing through me that Greg isn't taking a lick of shit from this tyrant.

"Fine," his dad seethes. "Stay here. Miserable and alone."

And I can't help it, my anger boils over. I didn't even grow up with this dickwad and I've had enough. I swing open the door and sashay out, delighting in the surprise on both men's faces as I tuck myself against Greg's side. He wraps his arm around me reflexively, but I don't meet the questioning gaze I know is pointed my way.

No, my eyes are on Papa Tyler right now.

"Oh, he won't be alone," I greet him with my favorite intimidate-the-prosecutor glare.

Papa Tyler's eyes narrow on me. "Great, now you're bringing prostitutes home?" His eyes flick to his son's.

Greg steps forward menacingly, tucking me behind him. The gesture makes my heart race and I place a hand on his back in solidarity.

"You're going to apologize for that remark, and then you're going to leave," Greg says in a calm, dangerous voice.

"Or what? You'll make me?" his dad asks flippantly.

Tense silence hangs in the air. Knowing nothing good will happen if things don't calm the fuck down, I step forward, placing myself in front of Greg, resting my hands on his chest. "Don't rise to the bait, darling," I purr. "He's not worth it." And then I turn to face the old man. "For the record, I'm a lawyer, though I guess some might say that isn't much better than a prostitute. But I sure as fuck know how to make your son a whole lot happier than you seem to be able to. So, I highly suggest you take your self-righteous bullshit and shove it up your guilt-tripping, delusional ass."

His father's mouth opens and closes in shock. And when the vein on his forehead starts pulsing, I almost laugh.

"I won't be spoken to like that by some gold-digging trollop who —"

"Oh, I'm most definitely a trollop and proud of it. But I had no idea Greg came from money or even had any of his own to speak of. Not that I would care because, as it happens, I'm also a trust fund baby who doesn't need her family's money since I'm more than capable of making piles of my own. And if you don't like how we talk to you, you know where the door is. That you dared to walk through it in the first place is beyond me. In case it wasn't clear: whatever power you think you had here? You don't. Now run along like a good boy, and please, don't have a Merry Christmas. Because you're a fucking asshole who doesn't deserve it." I turn back to Greg, who is grinning from ear to ear. "Now. Ready to make me come like you promised, baby?"

Greg shakes his head and laughs. Then, he looks up at his father.

"Well. I couldn't have put it better myself. You know where the door is. Bye, Dad."

His father starts spluttering threats, but Greg ignores him and lifts me up. The near-joyful look on his face sends warm tingles through my whole body. I wrap my legs around his waist, and he turns his back to his dad as he carries me to the bedroom, clearly paying him no attention.

He kicks the bedroom door closed behind us and tosses me on the bed.

I watch him carefully as he stalks the length of the bed until he's hovered over me.

"I hope I didn't go too overboard out there. I couldn't listen to his bullshit anymore," I offer. Even though I'm not sorry, I know if I emasculated Greg, the whole orgasm promise might be out the window.

"Are you kidding?" he asks, looking down at me with dark eyes. "That was the hottest fucking thing I've ever seen." He grinds his pelvis into mine, demonstrating his excitement.

I make to return the sentiment, but out in the main room, the front door slams. We give each other a triumphant grin.

"So, you're rich, huh?" I raise an eyebrow.

He smirks. "Guess the cat's out of the bag. I wasn't trying to hide it or anything." He shrugs lightly.

"I meant what I said. I honestly don't care if you had nothing. But …"

"But?" he asks, his brows jumping.

"It did make me realize that there's a lot I don't know about you," I reply.

Now his brows bunch together. "There's *nothing* I'm trying to hide. I swear to you; you don't have anything to worry about from me."

I chew my lip. "I know. It's not that. I just … it also made me realize …"

I cover my face with my hands, unsure I can admit this to myself. I feel his weight settle and his fingers close around my wrists, pulling my hands from my face.

"Talk to me, city girl." The look he gives me is all lust and longing. And it makes me realize that's what I'm feeling. Longing. For more.

"I want to know you," I admit in a whisper. "I want more than sex, too, Greg."

He goes perfectly still, and I worry that he'd changed his mind about wanting that, too, based on my little performance with his dad. I guess even I get insecure putting myself out there.

It's weird that I'm waiting for his answer with bated breath. But … good weird. I think. Though just when I think I may not be cut out for going beyond sex, that he may have truly realized I am as bat-shit crazy as … well, I am, his lips are on mine. His hand freeing his cock. His tip nudging me for permission to enter bare.

I don't even have to think about it. I use my heels to pull him in, joining my mouth to his as he slides in deep. I groan into his mouth when I feel the silky hardness of him thrusting into me.

It feels *so* good. And a man who answers my vulnerability with his dick? I'm so screwed in every way.

"I take it," I say, panting, "that means you're okay with that?" I give him a teasing smile as he rears back, continuing to slide in and out of me.

He smiles back, running his hands down my tits to my hips, holding tight. "More than okay," he agrees, then leans forward. "Because all I wanted for Christmas was you."

I tilt my hips to meet his thrusts. "Oh, but I'm on the naughty list. I'm nobody's present, baby."

He slams into me, and my head drops back. "Fuck, Joanie. Keep calling me that, and I'll show you just how much it pays to be naughty."

"Calling you what?" I ask innocently, wiggling my hips against him. "Baby?"

His jaw tightens, and he unleashes, pounding into me. "Fuck yes," he agrees in a husky, gritty whisper in my ear as his thrusts turn frenzied. "Scream it for me, naughty girl."

I tip my head back, surrendering to how much he owns me. How much I want him to own me. No man has ever brought that feeling out of me during sex, much less outside of it.

"Make me yours, mountain man," I groan in agreement.

Even though deep down, I'm pretty sure he already has.

CHAPTER TEN

JOANIE

By the time Greg and I arrive at Mia and Nate's Christmas evening, Bev's insatiable appetite has been quelled many times over, but my stomach is rumbling and ready for the feast I know Mia's likely whipped up, even with having traveled hours to and from Portland.

As Mia opens the door, the wall of heavenly aromas that hits me confirms my assumption.

"Hey guys," Mia greets us, her eyes falling on our linked hands. She quirks an eyebrow and smirks at me.

"Merry Christmas," I respond, holding up my other hand with the bottle of wine Greg thoughtfully suggested we bring.

"Merry Christmas, indeed." She grins and takes the bottle, stepping back to allow us over the threshold, and I'm stunned by the complete lack of decoration inside. Especially considering how much Mia loves Christmas.

Mia rolls her eyes, interpreting my shock as Greg shrugs out of his jacket. "It's been busy. We didn't have time to decorate," she explains with a shrug.

"Well, as long as you had time to cook, you know I'm a happy camper," I respond.

Greg helps me out of my coat, his fingers skating over my collarbone, sending pleasant shivers down my arm. I give him a suggestive grin, which he returns. Mia narrows her eyes at the exchange but says nothing.

I'm distracted by a brush against my legs, and I look down to see Simba, Mia's cat, once her Gran's, begging for pets. I reach down and scratch him between the ears as he purrs against my palm.

"Aw, did you miss me, buddy?" I croon.

Apparently, not that much because he quickly abandons my affections to explore Greg's legs. Much to my surprise, Greg picks him up, and Simba nuzzles Greg's chin.

"Okay, he'll tolerate me petting him, but he never lets me do *that*," I grouse.

Greg smiles at me beatifically. "Stick around a while, and he will, city girl." He leans in and gently kisses my lips, then winks and heads down the hall.

Mia's eyebrows rise so high that they're threatening to merge with her hairline. I purse my lips and push her down the hall toward the dining room.

We enter the room to find Nate pouring drinks — red wine for us ladies and whisky for the guys, apparently. Nate looks at Mia expectantly.

"Dinner will be ready soon," Mia assures him. "Joanie, want to help me in the kitchen for a minute?"

I raise an eyebrow since we both know I'm not the help in the kitchen type, but I nod, following her out of the dining room. As soon as we're out of earshot, Mia turns on me.

"Okay, spill. What is going on with you two? You've obviously had sex already. But why do I get the feeling there's more going on here?" she demands.

I shrug nonchalantly. "You're right. We're together."

Mia's brows jump to her hairline. "Together? Like *together* together?" I shrug again but can't contain my grin. "Jo! This is huge! I assumed you'd have fucked him out of your system by now, given your history. But *together* ... like for real? I never would've predicted that."

I can't help my goofy grin. "It's new, so we haven't exactly labeled anything. But it's good, Mia. Really good. Like ... not just the sex," I admit. Then I close my eyes briefly and shudder, remembering exactly how good the sex is. And how much it means to admit that it's more.

She takes me by the shoulders and looks me dead in the eye. "This is a big deal for you, I know."

I inhale, slow and deep. "It is. But I'm happy. So fucking happy, Mia. It's crazy, right?"

She shakes her head slowly. "Like I can't even process it, crazy. Yes."

I laugh. "Well, process it, sister. Because I may be sticking around for a while to see where things go."

Mia's eyes fill with tears, and she puts a hand to her mouth. "My little girl's all grown up," she teases. I scoff and shove her shoulder playfully. "Well, he better treat you right. Ooh, do I need to give him the best friend talk?" she adds sternly.

I laugh. "Stand down, tiger mama. I'm a big girl. I can handle myself. And him. *All* of him." I wink salaciously.

Mia grimaces playfully. "Ugh. Forget I asked."

"Forget you asked what?" Nate asks, popping his head into the kitchen.

"Nothing," we reply in unison.

Nate looks between us skeptically and shakes his head. "Ooookay then. Well, the table is set if dinner is ready ..."

"Five more minutes," Mia tells him.

He nods and disappears.

"I mean it, Jo," Mia says quietly, leaning in close. "I know how much you've avoided relationships. I just want to make sure you're ready for this and that Greg is on the same page. I don't want you to get hurt."

I clasp Mia's hands in mine. "I promise. We're both grownups, and we both want this. The rest … well, it will be what it will be. You don't need to worry. But thank you. I'm glad I have you in my corner."

Mia smiles gently. "Always, bitch."

We laugh and turn to finish getting dinner on the table.

As we all sit down to eat Mia's famous prime rib feast, Greg rests his hand on my thigh under the table, his thumb rubbing possessive circles close to my core. I shoot him a heated look as the warmth of his touch seeps through my leggings and my resolve to act like I wouldn't have rather stayed in bed with him all night. Thankfully, with all that sex, Bev needs a break anyway, so I manage to overcome the urge to tear his clothes off right here.

"Well, Merry Christmas, everyone. And since it's Christmas, Alpine Ridge's first winter festival in years is over. And it seems like it was a huge success," Nate says, raising his glass. "Here's to doing it all again next year."

We clink glasses and drink deeply. Mia makes an insanely good prime rib, and the wine Nate picked pairs with it perfectly. However, I wouldn't say no to a glass of whisky later.

"I'll say," Mia agrees. "The bakery has never been busier. I'll need to hire more staff next year to keep up if it's like that again. My property manager said the B&B was full all week for the first time since we converted it. Gran would be pleased that so many people are staying in her house and learning to love this town."

"I know you remodeled, but I haven't had a chance to see it," I remind her. "It was pretty dated. I bet you had to use a good chunk of the cash Gran left to convert it."

Mia nods. "Yes, but not nearly all of it. Though the rest will probably go into maintenance and the bakery. Business isn't always so good, after all."

Mia smiles in a way I know she thinks is reassuring, but I'm her best friend. And I see the exhaustion under that smile.

As if reading my thoughts, Greg says, "I know I've been here for it all, but I never thought about how hard it must've been this past year converting your grandmother's house into a bed and breakfast while starting up your bakery at the same time. How are you doing with all this, Mia?"

Mia smiles sadly. "Honestly? I miss Gran every single day. Sometimes, I swear I can feel her around me. But I think she'd be happy with the changes, and business is better than I expected, in no small part thanks to her." She lifts her glass again. "To Gran."

"To Dorothy," Nate and Greg chime in as I echo Mia's words, swallowing around the lump in my throat. She was like a grandma to me, too, after all. I shake myself. All this emotion lately is a lot.

"What about you, mountain man?" I ask lightly, turning to Greg. "How's business at the community center?" The seemingly superficial question is a disguise for my curiosity over what his official day job is really like.

Greg gives me a quizzical look. "How'd you know I own it?"

I raise a brow. "I didn't; Mia just told me you ran the place. Though I guess I know now. Except, aren't community centers usually public property?"

"Alpine Ridge is unincorporated," Greg reminds me. "The only public property is owned by the county, which doesn't include any actual buildings. Just land, some utility access points, main roads, that sort of thing."

"Huh," I reply, wheels turning.

"Anyway, I definitely saw a lot more activity during the festival. Some of our residents live pretty far out, so it was good visibility for the center. I'm hoping we got enough traffic to make an impression so more folks will use the facilities regularly now that they know what's there."

I nod and turn to Nate, now curious about how this tiny town works. "And the wellness center? I bet you all are regular business moguls by now with all the festival traffic."

Nate huffs a laugh. "I wish. I mean, it definitely drives more people looking to get fit after gorging themselves on sweets —" he cuts a playful glance at Mia, who feigns indignation in response, "— but I'm getting more and more folks with actual medical problems that I'm not equipped to deal with."

I frown. "What do you mean?"

He sighs. "I have people coming in with undiagnosed conditions looking for help since the nearest medical facility is anywhere from half an hour to an hour away, depending on where in town they live, and as you know, there's no urgent care here. Or medical care of any kind, as it were. It kills me to turn them away, knowing I probably *could* help with my medical background, but I can't risk the liability, and I sure don't have everything I'd need to treat patients."

I'm confused. "But you helped me when I fell during the race. What was different about that?"

Nate shakes his head. "I didn't do anything any other bystander with first aid training wouldn't do. I checked you out, then got you to a hospital for scans since you'd lost consciousness. I wasn't diagnosing or treating you in any formal capacity."

"Okay, I guess that makes sense," I allow. "But surely, with the older population base, the town council would prioritize having emergency medical services available? There have to be hundreds of people who live here."

Mia sighs heavily. "You'd think. And it's actually a few thousand. But we're unincorporated, so there's no established tax base for that kind of thing. No local ambulances, police, fire department, or any other municipal services. It's crazy. And not helping the town any."

"Didn't you say you tried to get the town incorporated?" I ask, recalling an earlier conversation.

Mia nods. "Yep. I went to the town council and everything. They shot me down immediately. They said it would drive up costs, that people choose to live here precisely to avoid those things."

"Same thing happened to me when I tried," Greg commiserates.

"Sounds like the town council needs some new blood," I muse.

Greg shakes his head. "They'll never go for it, Joanie. We've tried everything."

"If you say so," I murmur, ideas already taking root.

The conversation moves on as Nate asks Greg about equipment sharing between the wellness practice and the community center, but I don't miss Mia giving me an assessing look. Like she knows what I'm thinking about doing.

I give her an innocent smile even though I know it won't fool her. It doesn't matter. Either way, the town council won't see me coming. Because if I'm going to stick around and see where things go with my mountain man, I might as well make myself useful. And what better way than to help my friends out? With that thought, I decide that making Alpine Ridge an official town, with all the bells and whistles, just became my new mission.

Thankfully, the conversation soon turns to other topics I can engage in so nobody else catches on to my scheming. For example, Nate and Mia's wedding plans, when Greg jokingly asks if they wouldn't rather elope than deal with the hot mess that is the situation with Mia's parents.

"How do you even know about that?" Mia asks sharply, casting a suspicious gaze at Nate.

"Oh, don't blame him; this town *talks*," Greg responds. "You probably didn't notice, but there were a good number of townies at Dorothy's funeral."

Mia's face falls. "Ah."

Ugh. I wasn't able to go to Gran's funeral due to work commitments, but Mia told me about the epic bout of awfulness that was her parents that day. I reach over the table and cover her hand with mine.

"Still nothing on that front?" I ask gently.

Mia shakes her head but sniffs briefly and collects herself. "Nope. But Carrie and I are talking a lot more these days. She graduates this summer. She's making noise about trying to break away from them. I'm trying to be as supportive as I can without saying anything bad about our parents."

I snort. "Because they're giving you the same courtesy, I'm sure," I reply sarcastically, shaking my head. "You're a better person than I would be in your shoes."

Mia gives me a shaky smile. "Honestly, I could probably use your take-no-shit attitude when it comes to them. I may yet have to. Weddings bring out the worst, it seems."

"Hey," I protest. "Not yours. Yours will be the fucking *best*. Even if I have to fight some bitches."

Mia laughs heartily and wipes away her tears. Greg chimes in that he's ready to throw down for her and Nate, too. Soon, Mia's happy again, and we're back to joking and laughing.

As we all tease and chatter over the remnants of a fantastic meal, I realize how seamlessly we fit together. And for a moment, I can see life as part of a couple. Life in this town, with close friends, good food, and beautiful vistas. And even though I'd never admit it? Well, it makes my heart swell a little.

Under the table, I lace my fingers with Greg's where they still rest on my leg. He looks at me with such open affection that I lose my breath for a moment. Whatever is happening between us, I know Mia is right — it's a big deal for me. I hope I'm ready for it. But as Greg squeezes my hand, I know one thing: I'm willing to try.

CHAPTER ELEVEN

GREG

The crisp mountain air fills my lungs as Joanie and I hike the trail to my favorite lake. I've wanted to share this place with her, and today seemed like the perfect opportunity.

"Ugh, why did I agree to hike to a fucking lake in the mountains the day after Christmas? I'm going to be picking ice out of my ass for a week," Joanie grumbles from behind me as she picks herself up from her third slip.

I snicker and shoot her a look over my shoulder. "Can't handle a little snow, city girl?" I tease.

She stops and plants her pole-filled hands on her hips. "Last I checked, two feet of snow is not a little."

"I guess that depends on where you're talking about. Though last I checked, Seattle gets its fair share of snow from time to time," I respond. "And it's not like you aren't wearing snowshoes and using poles."

"I'm a runner, mountain man, not a snowshoer, remember? I live in one of the hilliest neighborhoods in north Seattle, but I do not go gallivanting about in these conditions. These are stay inside and fuck conditions."

"We'll get there, but you've got to earn it first," I tease her. She shoots me a deeply unsatisfied look, and I can't help but laugh. "All right, fine. Climb on." I shift my pack to my front and crouch down for her to get on my back.

"Seriously?" she asks incredulously.

I smirk at her over my shoulder. "Seriously, city girl. Come on, I'll carry you. Part of the mountain man boyfriend privileges."

The small rosy circles on her cheeks expand, presumably due to the B-word. I had to try it out to see how she'd react. When she climbs on my back, I decide she must've liked it.

"You know I could whisper all sorts of dirty things in your ear right now," she murmurs, her hot breath fanning over my ear and cheek.

I smile but don't respond. Well, at least not in words. My hardening dick sure has an opinion. She must've *really* liked my using the B-word.

I push forward, and as we crest the final hill, the lake comes into view, its still surface reflecting the surrounding snow-capped evergreens like a mirror. The flat expanse of the serene water is surrounded by snowy rocks, dense white-flocked evergreen forest, and dramatically tall, snow-covered mountains against a clear blue sky. I hear and feel Joanie's small gasp, an excited puff of hot air on my neck. I turn my head to see her jaw drop and her eyes widen.

"It's beautiful," she murmurs.

I slide her gently back to the ground and slip my arm around her waist, pulling her close. "Not as beautiful as you."

She rolls her eyes but leans into me. "Cheesy much?"

I chuckle and press a kiss to her temple. "Only for you, baby," I murmur in her ear. I feel her shiver, and I smile against her cheek. "Remember what you asked me about my mountain man life?"

I see the moment she remembers as she slowly turns her head and looks at me like I'm crazy. "We are not swimming in *that* naked. It's freezing!"

A mischievous grin spreads across my face. "Just for a minute. I dare you."

Her eyes spark with challenge. "How about we have sex on that rock instead?" She gestures with her chin toward a large, flat rock that's bare of snow. Presumably, that melted off under the midday sunlight that's hitting it. "That'll warm us up."

I raise an eyebrow. "I thought you said it was too cold?"

She shrugs, already pulling off her pink gloves. "In the water, sure. And skinny dipping is so cliché. I bet you've never fucked by a lake, mountain man."

"And you have, city girl?" I taunt back.

She reaches down and feels the front of my dark blue snow pants. "Not yet. Worried someone will catch us?"

A thrill shoots through me at the idea of someone happening along while I've got this woman panting under me, screaming my name. "Nope. Just worried I can't get my dick out of my pants fast enough."

She grins and pulls me along before unbuttoning her snow pants and pulling them down with her leggings. With both around her ankles, she bends over, planting her hands firmly on the rock, her sex glistening in the sunlight like the gates to heaven.

I drop my pack, and I've never pulled my pants down faster. Within seconds I've shoved my now rock-hard cock into her soft, slick waiting flesh. The way she's bent causes me to slide all the way home with no effort at all, and her wet heat around me sends a surge of blood to my dick that nearly knocks me unconscious.

She groans at our joining, and the sound brings me back to earth. And then she starts to move, and my senses snap into focus as I watch my cock disappear into her pussy over and over.

Fuck, this woman.

I stand there for another moment longer while she fucks me before I grab her by the hips and take control.

I slam into her hard, pounding and fucking and taking until she's limp in my arms, until I'm holding her up by her hips as I unleash myself on her, driving into her over and over as indecipherable noises tumble out of her mouth, as my balls tighten and heat spreads through me.

I feel her walls flutter around my dick, and I sink in deep, wrapping an arm around her to tease her clit while I tilt my hips over her to rub her deep inner wall. It triggers her climax, and her inner muscles strangle my cock, wringing my orgasm out of me all at once as I empty into her, hot and hard.

As she convulses in my arms, as I come inside her, I walk through the gates to heaven, and the feeling of bliss spreads through every cell in my body.

Our knees give way simultaneously, pitching us into a crouched heap on the ice-cold rock. The frigid surface is a welcome contrast to the heat radiating from our still-joined bodies.

"I think they call this position 'make a child pose'," Joanie jokes from under me in a sultry, sex-saturated voice.

I stroke a hand down her side and laugh because she's not wrong. With her head resting on the rock and her arms splayed in front of her while I'm still buried in her from behind … it's like the bastard Kama Sutra-Yoga baby of doggy style and child's pose.

And when Joanie lets her chest sink down, her ass tilts up ever so slightly, causing my slippery cock to slide in deeper.

"Fuck," I grunt at the unexpected friction. "That's … holy shit."

Joanie giggles and flexes her hips. And holy. Fucking. Shit. My flagging cock starts to harden again.

"You like that?" she asks sensually. But I know she can feel me getting hard again, so I don't answer.

Instead, I press my chest into her back, letting my dick slide through her folds, teasing her sensitive labia. She groans under me. "As much as you like that," I finally murmur in her ear. "God, I love fucking you, Joanie." She trembles beneath me, and it eggs me on. "I love feeling you surrender that pussy to me." Her breaths turn short and sharp, and she tilts her pelvis frantically. "You want me to keep fucking that beautiful, tight pussy?"

"Fuck yes," she breathes. "Fuck it, baby."

A bolt of lust shoots through me, and I'm fully hard once more. So I do exactly as she asks, fucking her with sharp, shallow tilts of my hips that I know are hitting her G-spot based on her rapid breathing and hungry cunt that sucks me in with every thrust. Something about the position, about her clear surrender, undoes me on a level more primal than I've ever felt.

And I unleash. Hard then deep, soft then shallow, fast then slow; I lose myself to how she feels, how my body responds to hers, to the dirty words she inspires me to growl in her ear as our bodies realign on a level I didn't even know existed until all that I am is hers, and all that she is is mine. Until my world shrinks to one woman, this woman, and my heart expands with the understanding that she has offered herself to me in a way I don't think she's ever offered herself to anyone; a way beyond sex, even though it's the language our bodies seem to understand each other best.

So I say everything I'm feeling by worshipping her with pleasure. I offer myself as a partner who can speak the language she understands. The language of her body.

Of our bodies, entwined. And as she convulses underneath me, gasping my name over and over, as I explode once more inside her, I know when all the pieces of me come back together, they'll be rearranged.

And they will all be hers.

They all are hers.

I'm hers.

The thought has gravity, and it settles deep in my chest as we both come down from orgasm.

I pull away slowly, retrieving a towel from my discarded pack and using it to gently clean Joanie and myself. She rolls over on the rock and lifts her hips to shimmy back into her pants while I put my own to rights.

I've caught my breath by the time I sink down beside her. Mostly. I lose it a little again when I look at her. Her alabaster skin is flushed, her ice-blue eyes bright, and her dark hair spilled out from under her cap and splayed over her shoulders and neck. She's just-fucked beautiful, and with the snow-covered trees and mountains behind her, she's this mountain man's dream girl.

That feeling in my chest burrows deep, and words escape me. At least all the ones that mean anything. I know she doesn't usually do deep, and the last thing I want to do is scare her off so soon.

So I settle for asking, "Hungry?"

She grins, and her face lighting up outshines the bright winter sun above us. "Starving."

I unpack the lunch I brought, and we settle on the rock, side by side.

Joanie lifts her sandwich with a laugh. "First grilled cheese, now PB&J? You sure you weren't a mother hen in another life?" she teases, taking a big bite of her sandwich.

"Hey, I'm no Mia, but I'll have you know I make a mean PB&J," I tease back.

She chews, a thoughtful expression on her face before finally giving a slow nod. "That you do." She looks like she wants to say something else. Eventually, she asks about my work at the community center.

Even though I'm pretty sure that's not what she wanted to say, I go with it.

"It's rewarding," I tell her. "I get to help people, whether it's seniors staying active or kids learning new skills. Plus, it gives me plenty of time for my own hobbies, like fishing and hiking."

She nods. "Sounds idyllic. Very different from my old life."

"What kind of law did you practice?" I ask, realizing I don't know much about her career.

She sighs. "I was a corporate defense attorney. Basically, I helped big companies get away with shady shit." She shakes her head. "And the higher-ups never took me seriously no matter how good I was. I was too 'aggressive', apparently. A man with my style would've made partner years ago."

I frown. "That's bullshit."

"Tell me about it." She takes another bite of her sandwich. "Anyway, enough about my past. Tell me more about this town. Who runs what around here?"

I'm surprised by how little she wants to discuss herself, but I don't push it. So, I give her the rundown.

"My Uncle Henry owns the grocery store where he handles the second half of business hours, with my cousin Ned, who you've met —" Joanie smirks "— handling the first half of the day. My Uncle's wife, Margaret, runs a small mail shop with the world's tiniest post office inside. My father and uncle co-own the gas station and convenience store-slash-tackle shop. Jerry owns the tavern and the sad excuse for a coffee stand. Then, of course, there are Nate and Mia's businesses. And as you know, I own the community center, though I also own the land with the pond, my house, and a good amount of acreage besides. Oh, and I co-own a shit ton of land in and around the town with my father."

"Hm," she murmurs. "So what's with the whole Old West vibe? The wagon wheels and stuff?"

I explain the town's gold rush history and the shuttered museum.

Joanie mulls on that for a minute before asking, "Who owns the museum?"

I stop, realizing I'd never thought about that. "I don't know," I admit.

"So no one in your family then?" she presses.

I shrug. "Guess not. Anyway, my dad had all these grand plans to turn Alpine Ridge into a Wild West tourist trap, which sounds great, in theory, since that's the town's roots. But all of his ideas were so over the top that they'd make a mockery of it. Themed campgrounds, boardwalks, the works. He even wanted to put in an amusement park. But he couldn't get approval for any of it, thank fuck."

Her eyes narrow. "So he's not on the town council?"

I laugh. "God, no. He only inherited land here a few years ago. He hasn't spent much time in Alpine Ridge, but he's sure got opinions on what to do with it." I shake my head. "His pushiness has made things harder for me with the council. They're all old-timers who resist change, and now they don't trust me much either." I pause, debating whether to ask her something.

"What's that look?" she asks, furrowing her brow.

"I'm just not sure why you'd care about any of this," I say, not technically asking while asking.

The corner of her mouth lifts in a half-smile. "I guess I just wanted to know more about this town. Because it's important to people I care about. Including you."

I reach over and tuck a strand of hair behind her ear. "I care about you too, Joanie," I say, my voice thick with more emotion than I've felt in a long time.

We stare into each other's eyes, a thread of understanding weaving between us. Her eyes soften, and she leans in to kiss me deeply.

When she pulls back, there's a glint in her eye that I'm coming to recognize. "Take me home, mountain man. I'm not done with you yet."

I grin and start packing up. "Yes, ma'am."

Later, as Joanie sleeps curled against my chest, I think about what she said to me. She's right — Alpine Ridge is important to me. And the idea that Joanie might be warming to it makes me feel even more protective of it. And of her.

My last thought before drifting off is that maybe, just maybe, I've finally found a place worth fighting for ... and someone worth fighting for.

CHAPTER TWELVE

JOANIE

I've been in Alpine Ridge for about three weeks now, and the more I learn about this town with its character and unique beauty, the more I realize how much potential it has and how much the people here, especially my beautiful best friend, are missing out on because the town has not been incorporated.

With only a few thousand residents, there isn't enough traffic to sustain her business long-term, even alongside the folks ambling through from Ellensburg looking to head to Wenatchee or Leavenworth. Or any of the businesses. And then there's the other thing my research turned up: Alpine Ridge's population is aging *and* dwindling. In short, the town needs fresh blood if it's even going to survive, much less thrive.

So, given my new mission to breathe official township life into this place, armed with more knowledge thanks to Mia and Greg, I do what any good lawyer would do and spend the day researching. And what I find is pretty damn shocking.

It turns out, by definition, that there shouldn't even *be* a town council in an unincorporated town. Which means this supposed "council" that denied Greg and Mia's requests to incorporate? They had no right.

Since Mia isn't around to hold my earrings while I make to throw down, I do the only logical thing I can: I go find her. Greg took off way too fucking early this morning, so that leaves me to drive in my car, which Mia thoughtfully drove down the hill yesterday while Greg and I were hiking. Thankfully, my Subaru has all-wheel drive, and it's not that far.

Still, with ice and an uneven road, it takes way longer than I expected to get here, with a good heap more sliding around and nearly losing control of the car than I was prepared for. By the time I arrive, it feels like it's been ages since I made myself a light lunch, so I'm less ready to fight some old farts and more ready for a hot cup of coffee and some pastries.

"Jo," Mia greets me with surprise. "I wasn't expecting to see you emerge from the sex cocoon anytime soon."

I shoot her a mock dirty look, and she smirks.

"Coffee," I grunt jokingly, collapsing into a chair across from the pastry display case. "Sugar," I add. Mia crosses her arms over her chest and gives me an expectant look. "Please?"

She grins. "You got it. And you're lucky because Rae just pulled a fresh huckleberry pie out of the oven a few minutes ago."

"Ooh, I haven't tried the famous huckleberry pie yet," I say excitedly. To hear Nate and Mia talk it's life-changing, but Mia and Rae have been so focused on holiday treats lately.

A couple of minutes later, Mia sets a large, steaming cup of Joe down on the table in front of me, then a delicate round plate decorated with pink flowers and topped with a huge slice of gooey purple-blue filled pie crust covered in an artfully swirled pile of whipped cream. And my whole mouth fills with saliva.

As Mia sits across from me, I don't even pretend to have manners; I grab the fork and shovel a scoop of the warm, fragrant sugary goodness into my mouth. The sweet, tart taste of the filling spreads over my tongue, and I'm a goner.

"Ohmygawd," I mumble around the pie. "Dish is uhmashing."

Mia shakes her head and laughs. "Oh, I know. But geez, Jo, for the love of God, swallow before you speak."

I shrug, then down another huge bite, causing Mia to chuckle as she sips her coffee. After that bite, I take a drink from my cup and sigh contentedly.

"Rae, you're fucking awesome," I call to the back of the bakery.

"Glad you like the pie," she calls back.

I smile at Mia. "You're never going to believe what I just figured out." I take another bite of pie as I watch her eyes light up with curiosity.

"Well?" she demands after I don't cough up the info immediately.

I take another sip of coffee and slowly set my cup down before leaning forward on my elbows. "The town council?" She nods encouragingly. "Total bullshit. Unincorporated towns don't have town councils, Mia. Those old fuckers are frauds."

Mia gasps. "No way!"

"Way," I respond before eating more pie.

Mia slams a fist on the table. "Assholes! Holy fucking shit!"

I can't help but laugh a little. She must be *really* pissed. She rarely curses this much.

Rae steps out of the back, drying her hands on a dishtowel. "Is everything okay out here?" she asks, her brows bunched together in concern.

"No," Mia says vehemently. "Did you know the supposed town council isn't legitimate?"

Rae's brow furrows farther in confusion. "I don't understand," she replies.

"Alpine Ridge isn't technically a town, right?" I offer, babystepping her through the information. Rae nods, though she still looks confused. "If it's not a town, it can't have a council."

Rae's mouth pops open. "Well fuck me sideways," she murmurs. "I never thought about that." She shakes her head slowly as her features pinch together in anger. "Those old bastards sure have some explaining to do."

I nod smugly. "They sure do. Any idea where we can find them?" I look between Mia and Rae.

Rae lifts her chin. "Now that I'm working for Mia, Jerry has to handle my old afternoon shift at the tavern. He's been lording his town council member status over everyone for as long as I can remember. How about we close up a bit early and go have a little chat with him?"

Mia and I exchange a look. "Let's do it," Mia agrees.

After a quick clean-up, Mia shepherds us out, flips the sign on the door to "closed," and locks up. Mia peeks into the wellness center but comes back shaking her head.

"Nate's working with someone. We'll tell him later," she says.

"I'll drive," Rae offers, gesturing to a well-kept older Bronco.

We pile in, and Rae guns the engine a little more than is necessary.

"Easy there," I tease. "Maybe we should pick one of us to take point so we don't all rip his throat out at once."

"I vote for you, Jo," Mia says immediately. "Not only did you make this discovery, but I've seen you go after someone on the witness stand."

I smirk but wait for Rae's response. She nods in confirmation. "If I open my mouth, nothing good will come out of it," she mutters.

She navigates down the road and into the tavern's parking lot, pulling smoothly into a spot and cutting the engine.

"All right, let's do this," Mia says darkly.

The three of us march into the tavern, and Rae jerks her chin toward an old guy behind the bar. Jerry.

I zero in on him, prowling forward with Mia and Rae flanking me.

He looks to be in his mid-sixties, with dark grey hair neatly clipped short. He's wearing a faded blue and grey plaid shirt tucked into old Wranglers. His light brown eyes scan me from head to toe as I approach, but not in a skeevy way—more like assessing. Given my company and manner of approach, I can tell he senses something is up, not to mention the fact that I wore a starched blue button-up blouse and black slacks to at least look like I meant business.

"Hello, Rae," he says, addressing her first. Then he looks at Mia and dips his chin. "Mia." His eyes flick back over me. "Who's your friend?"

I slide a business card out of my pocket and deposit it on the bar. "I'm Joanie Morris, a corporate law attorney. I have some questions for you about the town council," I begin, not bothering with small talk.

He shifts uncomfortably. "What about it?"

"Is it true that you and your fellow 'council members' —" I throw heavy sarcasm into the words and add air quotes to give a nice, bitchy edge to it "— have been purporting to legally represent Alpine Ridge?"

Jerry's neck turns red, and he stops toweling off the beer mug he'd been drying. "Well, I ... that is to say ..." he splutters.

"I'll take that as a yes," I press on with a dangerous smile. Aware that the tavern has quieted around us, I raise my voice and continue, "I presume you're aware that since Alpine Ridge is, in fact, an unincorporated area of Kittitas County, it is not legally recognized as a town and, as such, there is also no legally recognized town council or governing body of any kind?"

"Listen here —" Jerry starts, seeming to find his voice.

I don't let him finish. "And given that, you had no right to deny Gregory Tyler and Mia Anderson's requests to pursue incorporation for the town, likewise denying necessary services, including emergency responders, utilities, infrastructure, and more to the residents of this area?"

"You've got this all wrong, we just —"

"And surely you know that misrepresenting yourself as legally capable of denying such requests is a violation of county and state ordinances —"

"Now, wait just a minute!" Jerry bellows.

The silence that follows his outburst is deep. I fight back my smirk, knowing everyone in the place is waiting for Jerry to dig himself out of or deeper into this hole.

Jerry, for his part, is breathing hard, his eyes angry and wild. "The people here needed someone to look to for help, for answers. They like it quiet and simple, but sometimes someone has to make decisions to keep everything from going off the rails."

"So you and your friends —" I pull a sheet of paper from my pocket and read the short list of names while Jerry becomes increasingly pale at the depth of my knowledge "— decided it was your job to take that on? Even knowing you had no legal right to do so? And denying residents and business owners of the area the resources they need?"

"Nobody here wants to pay more taxes so some stupid bakery can keep making cookies," Jerry says bitterly. Mia scoffs, and Jerry's eyes narrow on her, delivering his next words as if only for her. "It died years ago for a reason, and it should've stayed dead."

Mia pushes forward angrily, but I lift an arm to stop her.

"What about this tavern, then? And the grocery store? The gas station? There are necessary services here that are dying too, and you're putting the nails in their coffin all in the name of your property taxes not increasing a few dollars a year," I point out calmly. "Awfully short-sighted considering that statistically incorporation causes a boost in property values and business revenue that *vastly* outweighs property tax increases." I pause, tilting my head and returning the assessing look he gave me when I entered.

"Did you consider that, or simply your own wishes for things not to change, despite the steady decline in population in this area over the last thirty years? By my calculations, based on those rates, your businesses here will all die within ten years, with your population dropping to nearly zero within another ten years. Were you banking on not living long enough for that to be your problem?"

Rae chuckles beside me, and Mia's hand squeezes mine, communicating her approval.

But the real success comes with Jerry's silence, which stretches long enough for one of the guys in the tavern to stand up and ask in a demanding voice, "Jerry, is this all true?"

Jerry splutters, the redness having crept from his neck to his face, and he's unable to form a coherent response.

I finally allow Mia to step forward. "She's right. The bed and breakfast, the bakery, and the wellness center aren't doing as well as they could be, and they won't last more than another few years with the way things are. I pushed for incorporation to give the town the resources to draw more people in, which would be good for *all* of the businesses in town." She turns to face the room. "My Gran lived here for decades, and I spent a lot of time here over the years, even before I became a permanent resident. Through her love for this town, I came to love it too. And I can't watch it die. Not when we have the power to do something about it."

Jerry's face turns an alarming shade of purple. "You're all ungrateful," he spits out. "You're going to ruin what makes this town worth living in."

The crowd, whose faces had shone with empathy after Mia's speech, turns angry. But it's Rae who scoffs and says, "Jerry, your own wife died because an ambulance couldn't get to her in time. Is that what you want for everyone else?"

The tavern erupts in murmurs.

Rae continues, undeterred. "Joanie's research is right. The town is shrinking. I knew that without research and numbers. We need new families if we want Alpine Ridge to survive. And how will we attract them when we have no schools? When residents have to drive nearly an hour to get to the dump, and at best, have to live with satellite internet and TV service that only work half the time? Not to mention all the other services Miss Joanie listed."

Her speech is met with vocal agreement from most of the patrons. Outnumbered and outmatched, Jerry angrily throws his towel down and stomps through the swinging door behind the bar.

The patrons continue talking, though, sharing stories about how great the town used to be and the audacity of Jerry and his cronies to pretend like they ran the place.

As the ideas we planted catch fire, Mia pulls me aside. "This was your plan all along. To publicly humiliate Jerry and get the town talking?"

"Damn straight. But this was just the beginning. Let them stew on it for the week. We can't do anything until after the New Year anyway."

"And then?" Rae prompts.

I wink at them both. "Then we start working with the county on incorporation documents. Because we don't need anyone's fucking permission."

Mia and Rae exchange an excited glance.

"I should go back and tell Nate what's going on," Mia responds. "Plus, he'll expect to head home for dinner soon."

I nod, and we follow Rae back out to the Bronco.

Once she drops us off, Mia keeps me from heading into the wellness center.

"Have you told Greg yet?" she asks.

I shake my head. "He's at the community center today, so I came straight to you. Besides, I figured once we tracked down one of the council members, I'd have more to share anyway, so I wanted to wait until I had more to tell."

Mia nods distractedly, and I can tell her mind is racing through what this means for her and Nate.

"Hey," I say softly. "Is this okay? I'm mostly doing it for you. But if this causes too many waves, I don't have to go all Hurricane Joanie on Alpine Ridge."

Mia huffs a laugh. "It's more than okay. If I had the time and energy, I'd be going after this too. Which has been tearing me up because I knew if it didn't happen, all the time and energy I'm using on the bakery instead would be a waste."

"Honestly, you're right, it would be. While I haven't seen your financials, even my generous calculations for the businesses here weren't pretty," I admit. "I don't want to see you put your heart into this only to have it die, babe. The world deserves your pastries, after all." I wink at her playfully, trying to lighten the heaviness of the conversation.

"Is that all this is?" she asks.

My brows dip together. "What do you mean?"

"I mean … are you maybe doing this because you can see yourself spending more time here with a certain mountain man?" she clarifies with a mischievous smile.

I press my lips together. "Okay, maybe a little?" I admit cautiously. Mia gets a look on her face, and I hold up a hand. "Let's not make it a thing, okay?"

"I mean, I'm not, I just …" she trails off, chewing her lip nervously.

I sigh heavily and cross my arms. "Okay, fine. Get whatever it is you need to say off your chest," I say, gesturing for her to continue.

She rolls her eyes. "You know you'd give me the talk, too," she points out. I nod resignedly and gesture again for her to continue. "Just ... don't move too fast with Greg, okay? Keep your options open. Maybe even start looking for jobs back in Seattle?"

I narrow my eyes at her. "Are you trying to get rid of me?"

"No, of course not," she rushes to assure me. "I just can't see you being happy staying in a small town long-term. And it won't hurt to keep your options open," she reiterates.

I take a deep breath and try to focus on where I know this is coming from. "I hear you. I know you're trying to look out for me. And that's good advice."

"But?"

I let out a breath and laugh. "God, you know me a little too well, Mia." I shake my head. "But I don't know any other way than all in," I say with a shrug.

Mia steps forward and wraps her arms around me. "I know. It's one of the things I love most about you."

I hear her unspoken concern that it's also the thing that might get me burned.

I want to dismiss it from my thoughts as easily as I did in our conversation, but her words niggle at the back of my mind as we say our goodbyes and I head back to Greg's.

Will I be happy here? I'd been so caught up in my budding relationship with Greg and the thrill of taking on the town council that I hadn't thought too hard about the future.

Maybe she's right. Maybe I'm not cut out for small-town life. Maybe I'm not cut out for a relationship and the thrill of being with Greg will wear off. Hell, maybe Greg will get sick of me.

That thought makes me laugh. Because based on my history, I'm far more likely to get sick of him first. And he seems like a relationship kind of guy.

When he returns from the community center, I'm still stewing on it an hour later, curled up on his couch that faces the expanse of forest behind the house.

"There's my girl," he says with a smirk, settling beside me.

"Hey," I reply. And then I look closer at his face. "What's with the smirk?"

"A little birdie told me you and the girls visited the tavern this afternoon."

I huff a laugh. "Jesus H. Fucking Christ, news travels fast in this town," I grumble. And then, to cover my ass, "I was going to tell you."

He grins and nods. "I know. I'm not mad. In fact ..." he leans forward and hauls my legs up so I'm lying flat on the couch under him. "I think you deserve something for what was evidently a fantastic performance."

I bite into my lip. "Yeah? Like what?"

He smiles and dips down to run his nose down my neck and between my breasts, stopping to place a kiss on my now-exposed navel. "I don't know, what do you want?"

I take a deep breath. And I let the dirty thoughts pass through my head because those are fleeting desires.

"I want to know what we're doing here," I say honestly.

He sits up, brows raised. "Seriously?"

I scoot back up to a sitting position, wrapping my arms around my legs. While I'm not usually self-conscious, I've never had a conversation like this. With anyone. Ever.

"Seriously," I confirm with a trace of irritation. "Obviously, we're enjoying ourselves, but what is this? I know we said it's more than sex. But how much more?"

"How much more do you want it to be?" he parries.

I flinch at his response. "I don't know," I reply honestly. "I mean, I have a condo in Seattle. I could go back there and start looking for a job."

"Or?" he asks, sensing the implied choice.

"Or I could stay here for a while and use my time to pursue making Alpine Ridge official and handling all the legalities that come with that. From my preliminary research, that's no small task, and it would require someone with my knowledge and contacts to pull it off."

"Are we going to pretend like that's not exactly what you're planning to do?" he asks with a smirk.

I scrunch my nose and press my lips together to keep from smiling. Shit, he already knows me too well. "No. But even if I do, that doesn't mean I have to keep staying with you. I mean, this is your sacred space. It occurred to me that I might already be intruding on that."

"Occurred to you, or Mia told you we're going too fast?" he asks bluntly.

Fuck, he clearly also knows Mia too well.

When I don't answer, he slides close to me and takes my face in his hands. "You don't have to stay with me if you don't want to, Joanie, but I fucking love having you in my bed. In my life. And I loved coming home to you today. I don't see that changing anytime soon. I'm not saying I want you to live here permanently yet ...

but I also don't want you to go. Beyond that?" He strokes his thumb over my cheek and looks deeply into my eyes. "While I've never cared much about getting married, I'll admit that I want someone to share this life with."

His eyes continue to search mine, and I feel the words he's not saying. *I want to share this life with you.*

A knot forms in my throat. I can't tell if it's fear or love. This is new territory for me, but I realize I'm falling for Greg. And he's clearly falling for me.

I should find it comforting that we both seem to have a healthy fear of it because love isn't something to be taken lightly. Nor is commitment. I've never been good at either. But with Greg, I want to try.

I nod softly and let him make love to me on the couch. Everything feels so much ... *more*. By the time we curl up in bed that night, Greg's warm body wrapped around mine, I'm no less concerned about whether this is the life for me or a pitstop.

But as Greg pulls me closer in his sleep, I can't ignore how my heart clenches at the thought of leaving him.

Shit. When did this get so complicated?

I close my eyes, pushing the doubts away. I'll figure it out. I always do.

But for now, I'm exactly where I want to be.

CHAPTER THIRTEEN

JOANIE

The community center is a flurry of activity as we all pitch in to decorate for the New Year's Eve party Greg decided to have earlier this week. Mia, Nate, Rae, and I have been here for hours, hanging streamers, setting up tables, and generally helping Greg make the place look festive.

Since I didn't think there would be any time to change, I did it all in my halter-necked champagne sequined bodycon dress. But if I can litigate in four-inch heels, I can sure as hell decorate in a tight outfit. I also got to watch Greg working in his own tailored black dress shirt and tight black pants. It was worth it.

Looking around, I'm pretty satisfied with what we've accomplished. Nate made a trip to Costco, and you can tell by looking at the two joined long, loaded buffet tables. We're not lacking food or alcohol. And with Mia around, we're never lacking for sweet treats. Positioned at one end of the tables are cupcakes with sparklers waiting to be lit; at the other end, round sugar cookies decorated to look like clocks striking midnight, and toward the middle, a large tray with two types of macarons, white chocolate ones arranged in the new year's numbers and dark pink raspberry ones arranged around the numbers to make them pop.

Small bar-height tables with pairs of matched chairs dot the edge of the room, their plain black utilitarian look disguised by sparkly slip-on covers.

As I arrange a centerpiece with white flowers in a tall, blinged-out vase for the main tables, I hear the door open and turn to see Mia's sister, Carrie, walking in. It was a pleasant surprise to hear that Mia invited her. I thought it meant both women were working past the bullshit their parents thrust upon them.

But instead of the excited smile I expected, her face is pinched. The obvious trauma on her features starkly contrasts the playful beaded blue sweetheart-neckline dress with a flared skirt she's wearing, which offsets the long, wavy brown hair and blue eyes that run in the family. But as she approaches, I see those dark blues are red-rimmed.

Mia notices Carrie's distress too and rushes over to her sister, enveloping her in a hug, careful not to snag the fringe of her silver sheath dress on the beads of her sister's. "Oh no, Care-bear, what's wrong?"

Carrie sniffs and wipes at her eyes. "When I told Mom and Dad I was coming here for New Year's, they tried to guilt me into staying home. They said I was choosing you over them."

Mia's face hardens. "That's not fair. Seeing me doesn't mean you're choosing sides."

Carrie nods. "I know. Still. I hate being in the middle of this." She gives Mia an apologetic smile. "Not that I'm blaming you."

Rae and I exchange a look and move to join them.

"They're just being assholes," I offer by way of greeting, rubbing Carrie's back. "Trust me, we've had our share of drama this week with the old farts in town."

Carrie looks up, her curiosity obviously piqued. "Really? Drama in sleepy little Alpine Ridge? I've got to hear about this."

So we fill her in on our confrontation with Jerry and the whole town council debacle. By the end, she's laughing.

"Serves them right," she says with a grin. "I can't believe they thought they could get away with pretending to be in charge."

"Yes, well, there are certainly enough power players in this town to be getting on with. Turns out my new boyfriend's family owns most of it, and they're as wackadoo as your parents," I offer.

Carrie gives me a sympathetic smile.

"Hey, not all the landowners here are assholes," Mia interjects.

I smirk. "Of course not. You, Nate, and Greg are all gems. And I'm sure whoever owns the old gold-mining museum is sane because they don't seem to be making a fuss," I add thoughtfully.

Rae's eyebrows jump in surprise. "You didn't know?" she asks.

Mia's brow furrows in confusion. "Know what?"

Rae looks between us almost guiltily. "I own it. Well, now I do. It was passed down through my daddy's family. He used to run it when I was a kid. But when he left my mom ... well, you get the idea." She shrugs sheepishly.

My jaw drops. "Seriously? Well, I guess it *used* to be owned by an asshole, anyway. Yeesh. I'm so sorry, Rae." I pause, wondering if I should even ask my next question. But then again, why start holding back now? "Why haven't you done anything with it?"

Rae shrugs. "Never had the time or money. But maybe now, with the town incorporating, we can figure out how it fits into the new Alpine Ridge."

The wheels start turning in my head, but people arrive for the party before I can voice my ideas. Rae rushes off to change out of the T-shirt and jeans she'd showed up in and returns in a gorgeous mint-colored wrap dress that sets off her short, golden blond locks and brings out the green in her hazel eyes. I give her a thumbs up, and she grins at me across the room.

Nate also reappears, looking like hot business in grey slacks that look painted on his huge, muscled legs and a starched white button-front shirt.

Still, he's got nothing on Greg, I decide as I watch the two men talk. Greg's back is turned to me, and his gorgeous backside is calling my name.

But the community center begins to fill quickly with what seems like half the town before I can make it to him. However, it doesn't take long before Greg weaves through the crowd to me, grinning from ear to ear.

"It looks like the festival got people excited about community events after all," I comment as he approaches.

He slips an arm around my waist and pulls me close. "Seems that way. I'm glad we're keeping the momentum going. Save me a dance?"

I nod, and he kisses me before disappearing into the crowd, presumably to ensure everything is running smoothly. I watch him flit around the room before sampling the food and getting myself a drink.

As the party kicks into high gear, the music is loud enough to dance to but soft enough to hold a conversation, and I lose track of Greg completely. I'm chatting with Mia and Rae when I spot Carrie across the room, looking uncomfortable as Greg's cousin Ned corners her.

I remember the first time he approached me. He's as sketchy-looking now as he was then. Wrung out, greasy, and sporting a leer that would make a prostitute turn tail and run in the opposite direction. The guy is bad news. And Carrie looks like she wants to bolt, but he's got her trapped near the drinks. And I know Carrie. She's too polite for her own good.

I'm about to intervene when I see Ned turn away and slip something into a cup, then try to hand it to her. He's not subtle about it, but I can tell it was just out of Carrie's eye-line, and the crowd around them is thick enough that she likely didn't notice. But before I can react, Nate is there, snatching the drink away and grabbing Ned by the collar.

Mia catches the look on my face. "What is it?" she asks, turning toward where I'm looking just in time to see Nate drag Ned toward the door, fury etched on every line of his face.

"Oh shit," Mia curses.

Rae's eyes finally catch up, and she puts a hand to her mouth. Having lived here longer than us, I'm sure she's more than familiar with Ned and his way of creeping on the ladies.

We watch as Nate tosses Ned out the door, pulling it closed behind him. Greg appears and, after a tense conversation with Nate, storms outside after Ned.

"I'm going to go check on Carrie," Mia tells us.

"I'm coming with you," I insist, following her through the crowd.

When we get to Carrie, she looks beyond confused.

"Are you okay?" Mia asks, checking her over like she's looking for injuries.

Carrie nods, looking shaken. "I think so. What the hell was that?"

"Nate saw Ned put something in your drink," I explain.

Both Carrie and Mia's eyes widen. "He tried to drug me?" Carrie asks incredulously.

"He tried to drug her?!" Mia echoes, outraged.

Nate joins us, still seething and clearly having heard Mia. "Yes, but I took the drink before he could hand it to her. Fuck, I hope Greg is beating the shit out of that psychopath." My eyes widen at how hard he grinds his teeth in anger. "Fucking hell. We don't even have a damn police force to report it to."

We all stew momentarily, the gravity of the situation sinking in. Then, raised voices draw our attention outside. Yes, from outside. That's how loud they are. Murmurs start to ripple through the crowd, so Mia and I follow Nate to the door to help get things back under control so the whole town doesn't know about this in the next two minutes. As we pass Rae, I ask her to go look after Carrie. She nods, and we continue.

Once outside, we find Greg in a heated argument with an older couple.

"... refused to believe all the other reports of his bad behavior, and now this!" Greg is shouting.

"He's a good boy; he wouldn't do something like that," the woman insists. Ah. This must be his aunt and uncle.

Greg laughs harshly. "A good boy? He's a predator. But you two are so far up Dad's ass, you can't see what's right in front of you."

"How dare you speak to us like that!" his uncle bellows. "You're a disgrace to this family, turning your back on us, on the business. You're nothing but a disappointment. Our Ned is twice the man you'll ever be."

I scoff loudly, but they've already turned and stormed off. Greg stands there, chest heaving, hands clenched into fists.

We all let out a collective breath. I'm relieved it seems to be over, but I'm worried about Greg.

I start to go to him, but Mia catches my arm. "Give Nate a minute," she murmurs as her fiancé heads over to him.

We watch as Nate says something to Greg that is too low for us to hear. Greg nods, and they head back inside together.

Mia turns to me with a rueful smile. "Well, this isn't quite how I expected to ring in the new year."

I snort. "At least it's not boring. Remember our last New Year's together?"

"God, don't remind me. My apartment. That sad little cake and cheap champagne ..."

"And the kiss at midnight since neither of us had anyone else," I finish with a smile.

Mia chuckles. "We've come a long way since then, haven't we? I mean, even with all this drama tonight, look at us. Look at where we are."

I pause, unsure I want to unpack that with Mia right now. "Where we are is outside of the party. Let's go back in, shall we?" I deflect.

She nods and leads the way, but as we head back inside, I privately consider her words.

She's right. Two years ago, Mia was miserable at her job, and I was burning the candle at both ends and trying to find fulfillment in all the wrong places. And by places, I mean dicks.

And now? Mia is engaged to the love of her life, running a successful business she's passionate about. She's happier than I've ever seen her, even if she's not exactly more relaxed these days. But that's Mia. Like me, she needs a challenge, and now she's got one that she actually enjoys.

As for me, I walked away from a going-nowhere career which gave me the opportunity to take a chance on something that matters. This incorporation project has meaning. Purpose. And in Greg, I may have found a partner who will support me and give me room to do my thing. That's always been my biggest reason for not getting into relationships: losing myself. And on some level, I know that if this relationship goes the distance, that won't happen with Greg.

The realization hits me like a freight train. I want that. I want him. Not just for now but for ... no, I can't think the F-word. I may have come far, but there are still things I'm not ready for, and forever is definitely on that list. Only time will prove whether we work together on that level.

As if summoned by my thoughts, Greg appears at my side. "Hey," he says softly. "Sorry about all that."

I shake my head and lean into him. "Don't apologize. You were standing up for what's right. I'm just pissed that that little weasel of a cousin of yours isn't going to face any consequences for trying to drug Carrie."

He presses a kiss to my temple. "He'll get his, don't worry. But I'm sorry because that is not how I wanted this night to go."

"It's not your fault," I assure him. "And it's totally last year, baby. Let's start the new year how we want it to be." I give him a suggestive grin as I slide my hand up his chest and sink my fingers into his dark curls.

As if on cue, the crowd around us starts chanting. "Ten, nine, eight..."

Greg smiles slyly and pulls me against him, his hands wrapping around my backside possessively.

"Seven, six, five..."

I run my nose along his.

"Four, three, two, one ... Happy New Year!"

As cheers erupt around us, Greg lowers his mouth to mine. He nibbles gently at my bottom lip, then swipes his tongue over it. I open to him, and he slips inside, meeting me in gentle strokes that get harder as his cock does against my stomach. His hands pull me tighter, sliding up my back and tugging at my hair. Still, he's gentle and thorough, clearly devoted to making me feel the passion behind the kiss. But given the timing, it also feels like a promise for the coming year of the passion waiting for me. For us.

When we break apart, he rests his forehead against mine. "Is it too soon to tell you I love you?" he whispers.

My heart races in my chest at his question-slash-confession. "It's never too soon to tell someone how you feel," I reply honestly. "But I'm not sure I can say it back yet."

He pulls back slightly, disappointment flickering in his eyes before it's replaced with understanding. "That's okay. I can wait."

I smirk at his clear confidence that I will say it back when I'm not even sure I will. But then, as he pulls me back into his arms, I breathe him in, feeling the rightness of this, of us, settle into my bones.

I may not be ready to say the words, but I know, without a doubt, that I'm falling head over heels for this man.

And I'm not running from it for the first time in my life. So maybe he's right after all, and I will say it someday. Perhaps even someday soon.

"Is it too late to tell you I want to be fucked thoroughly in your office for New Year's?" I tease, deflecting the seriousness of the moment.

His pupils dilate as his cock twitches against me, and I bite my lip.

"It's never too late for that," he replies before his mouth crushes mine. But only briefly before he breaks off and pulls me through the room and to his office, where we ring in the new year properly. Twice. And if the crazy hot sex shoved up against his door is any indication, it's going to be a good year.

CHAPTER FOURTEEN

GREG

I wake up on New Year's Day with Joanie curled against my side, her soft breaths tickling my chest. Last night was incredible, both the party and the private celebration with Joanie afterward. I should be feeling great and ready to start the year strong.

Instead, my mind is consumed with thoughts of Ned and the stunt he tried to pull with Carrie. I spin through all the times he's crossed the line by propositioning women who come through his checkout. And that's not even the worst of it. I knew it had escalated lately, hearing through the town's grapevine that he'd recently put his hands on at least two women. Unfortunately, he's always careful to stay in line when Nate or I are around, even if he does mutter insults under his breath that he thinks we can't hear. That shit is nothing. But groping ... I should've realized it was a progression toward something even worse.

I'm sick to my stomach, not just over his behavior, but that I haven't found a way to put a stop to it sooner. Based on the discussion Nate and I had last night, he feels the same way. Surely, between us, we should've seen this coming and been able to stop it before he got as far as he did.

And yet, we weren't. My biggest fear is that he'll succeed sooner rather than later because one of us won't always be there to stop him.

Restless and agitated, I slip out of bed, careful not to wake Joanie, pulling the bedroom door closed behind me. I walk through the living room and head to the kitchen to make coffee. I'll think better with caffeine, though I feel pretty fucking defeated on the idea front right now.

I suddenly wish I'd thought to put socks on. The tiled floors are cold, and though I'd gone with all the bells and whistles for my bachelor pad, the heated floors take longer than I've got to start working their magic.

With a sigh, I drag the coffee maker across the granite countertop and pull the supplies out for my usual brew. The rich aroma fills the air, soothing me a bit. I lean against the counter and rub a hand over my face as I stare out the living room window at the quiet, snow-covered forest surrounding the house.

Despite the calmness I'd purposely designed for myself here, this whole thing with Ned has me shaking and doubting myself in other ways, too.

Really, how can I be of any use to Joanie with the town's incorporation when I can't even keep my own family in check? What kind of person does that make me?

And then there's the reaction from my aunt and uncle. Their blind defense of Ned, their anger at me for calling out his behavior — it's disheartening. They've always been my dad's little soldiers, but this? This is a new low.

I pour myself a cup of coffee and wander to the living room, sinking onto the soft, brown leather couch. The worst part is that I know this will get back to my father. And that's sure to stir up even more drama. As evidenced by his Christmas morning tirade, he's never approved of my "abandonment" of the family business, and this will be one more thing for him to hold against me.

I'm so lost in my thoughts that I don't hear Joanie approach until she's beside me, with a concerned look, wearing only one of my T-shirts. It just goes to show how pissed off I am that it barely stirs me to see so much of her creamy skin on display and the outline of her soft, perky tits through the thin fabric.

"Hey," she says softly, sitting down next to me. "I was surprised to wake up alone. You okay?"

I force a smile. "Yeah, just thinking about everything that needs to be done at the community center," I lie.

She studies me for a moment, clearly not buying it, but for the first time possibly ever, she doesn't push. I'm partly relieved and partly disappointed.

"Okay. Um. Are you going in today, then?" she asks tentatively.

Something's off about her tone, but I'm too distracted by my bullshit to pull at the thread of whatever hers might be.

I shrug, rising from the couch. "Yeah, actually. I should put everything back so the center's ready for tomorrow."

"All right ... well, I'll dive into more research today. Don't forget, Mia's making dinner tonight," she replies.

I grunt my understanding and dump the dregs of my coffee in the sink before heading upstairs for a shower. I'm just not capable of talking about this right now, which I know is making me an asshole. Which, in turn, makes me feel like even more of a failure. Definitely not how I saw the new year starting.

It only gets worse over the next few days. I spend every day at the community center, thankful for New Year's resolutions and the influx of people who want to get fit. It's exactly the distraction I need.

Joanie buries herself in her work and doesn't even stop when I get home. She's always polite and asks how my day was, but there's a wall between us that wasn't there before. As the week rolls by, she becomes more and more distant.

It's not until the end of the week, when I'm showering at the center before heading home, that the massive erection I get soaping myself makes me realize we haven't had sex since New Year's Eve.

Every night, I've been going to sleep early, physically exhausted from the day, assuming she'd wake me up when she came to bed. But she never did. By morning, my dreams had chased me from sleep and dragged me deeper into my pit of self-flagellation.

How could I be so distracted not to realize we'd drifted so far? And why hasn't she said anything?

I resist the urge to jerk off, intent on fixing this between us. Whatever it is that needs fixing.

And then, as I'm dressing, it hits me like a sledgehammer why Joanie wouldn't seek me out for sex, why she'd be burying herself in research and not demanding to know what the hell my problem was this week.

She thinks I'm pulling away because she didn't say "I love you" back. And like an idiot, I didn't even realize it.

I hurry through the rest of my tasks for the day and am just about to head out when there's a knock on the community center door.

Confused, I open it to find a stern-faced man in a suit.

"Gregory Tyler?" he asks.

"Yes?" I reply suspiciously.

He thrusts a packet of papers at me. "You've been served. Have a nice day."

Well, shit. This can't be anything good.

My heart sinks as I close the door and look down at the documents in my hand. As I read, my confusion turns to anger and disbelief.

It's a lawsuit from my father to start a partition action on the property we co-own. On the surface, it's baffling because I thought a partition action was when one property co-owner doesn't want to sell, and the other does. While my father has asked me to agree to development, he's never said a word about selling the property. But clearly, I don't understand all the ins and outs of partition actions because this paperwork flat out says that the motherfucker is claiming rights to *all* the land, citing mishandling of the original trust from my grandfather.

While I know fuck all about the legalities of trusts and how someone could challenge one this long after the fact, or what that has anything to do with a partition action, luckily, I know someone who almost certainly does.

With shaking hands, I pull out my phone and call my second cousin, Sera. She inherited my grandfather's brother's investments and owns a real estate business in Seattle. If anyone can make sense of this, it's her.

"Greg!" she answers warmly. "It's been a while. To what do I owe the pleasure?"

"Hey, Sera. I wish I were calling under better circumstances. Unfortunately, I just got served with some papers from my dad, and I could use your help figuring out if what he's trying to do is even legal and, if it is, how I can stop him. He's trying to claim full ownership of the properties we co-inherited from my grandfather."

There's a pause on the other end of the line. "Shit, Greg, I'm sorry. Your dad's a real piece of work, isn't he? My mother was talking about doing something similar when my grandfather died. Luckily for you, that means I'm pretty familiar with this kind of scenario. Send me the paperwork. I'll take a look and see what your options are, okay?"

I let out a massive sigh of relief. "Thanks, Sera. You have no idea how much I appreciate it. Or, actually, maybe you do," I reply.

She chuckles empathetically. "Family legacies, eh?"

"Indeed," I murmur, realizing that Sera, on top of being smart as a whip, has gone through a lot in the last few years and probably understands where I'm at better than anyone. "Maybe we can meet for lunch to talk when you've got something?"

"I'd love that," she replies sincerely.

"Great. Talk to you soon, then."

We say our goodbyes, and I hang up, feeling marginally better. At least I have someone in my corner who knows their shit. Now it's time to head home and make things right with Joanie.

I find Joanie hunched over her laptop in my home office, which I'd encouraged her to use. She looks up as I enter, her expression guarded. Her long, dark brown hair is piled haphazardly on her head, and she's wearing another one of my T-shirts. I resist smiling at her adorably disheveled appearance. She's obviously buried herself in her task to the exclusion of all else.

My throat constricts, knowing it's because she's avoiding me.

"Can we talk?" I ask.

Her wary, ice-blue eyes thaw a bit, and she nods, closing her laptop. "Of course. What's up?" She pulls her legs up to her chest and wraps her arms around them.

The move is so defensive it makes my chest hurt.

I settle on the loveseat next to the window on the opposite wall from the desk and gesture for her to join me.

It takes her a minute, but she eventually unwraps herself and rises, revealing pink plaid lounge pants and purple fuzzy slippers that make her look even more adorable. She settles tentatively on the other seat but still draws her legs up in front of her, though her hands rest on the cushion.

I reach out and offer a hand. She slips hers in it, and the tightness in my chest eases a bit.

"First of all, I'm sorry. I know I've been distant this week, and I didn't realize until today that you probably think it was because of what happened on New Year's. What you didn't say, I mean. But that's not it at all."

Her expression softens. "It's not?" she asks so tentatively that I want to punch myself in the fucking face for not realizing it and reassuring her sooner.

"No," I reply adamantly. "The truth is, I've been stressed about Ned. And about what he might do next. I'm frustrated that my family can't see him for what he is. That I haven't been able to stop his escalating behavior somehow."

Joanie shocks me by climbing onto my lap and cupping my face in her hands. "Well, now I feel like the asshole for assuming it had anything to do with me. I can see why it would bother you, but listen to me," she says, gripping my face tighter and looking deep into my eyes. "It's not your fault that your piece-of-shit cousin is a walking felony waiting to happen. It is, however, my fault for letting you deal with this alone. I should've asked what was happening with you instead of conceitedly assuming it was all about me." She tips her head back and groans.

"Okay, fine, we're both assholes," I murmur teasingly. Still, I can only be mildly amused because I haven't told her the worst part. I want to kiss her so badly, but I don't want to get distracted from the rest of the conversation we need to have. I sigh heavily and lean my forehead against hers. "There's more. My aunt and uncle clearly ran and tattled on me because my dad just served me with papers. He's trying to claim full ownership of the property we inherited."

She pulls back abruptly, shock written all over her face. "Are you fucking kidding me? Can he even do that?"

I huff out a breath and shake my head. "I don't know. I've got my cousin Sera looking into it. She's in real estate and has dealt with this kind of thing before, so hopefully, she can help me figure out my next steps."

Joanie chews on her lower lip. "How can I help?" she asks softly.

I look up into her eyes. Concern and something more is written there. To me? It looks like love. It's not the first time she's looked at me this way, and it's why I was so confident she'd say "I love you" back. But the rawness I'm feeling right now makes her obvious feelings hit differently. I want to beg her to say it. But I know I can't. She needs to say it when she's ready.

"Just knowing you're not upset anymore is all I need," I promise.

She gives me a faint smile. "I'm not. I was never upset with you. I was upset with myself, which was silly. And so not me," she says with a shake of her head.

I tug on an escaped lock of her hair. "I wasn't exactly myself this week either," I offer. "But I'm glad we finally talked. Forgive me?"

She smirks. "I'd say there's nothing to forgive, but you were pretty moody all week. And apparently extremely oblivious to how that came off," she teases, poking me in the stomach.

I wrap my hand around her finger and lift it to my mouth, placing a gentle kiss on the tip. "How can I make it up to you?"

Her smirk turns into a salacious grin. "Oh, I can think of many, many ways," she murmurs, giving me a searing look as her hands trace my chest.

"So can I, city girl," I murmur, running a finger down her cheek. "Starting with eating that pussy while you ride my face."

Her pupils dilate, and a small, breathy gasp slips between her lips.

"Dirty boy," she says mock-accusingly.

I can't help but unleash a predatory smile. "Are you going to punish me?" I reply teasingly.

In answer, she lifts her shirt and tosses it aside. Her creamy breasts are a sight for sore eyes, and her nipples are tight. She brushes a hand down her chest, over one rosy peak invitingly.

"No, I'm going to reward you, silly. So. Do you want me to fuck you here or in bed, mountain man?" she asks sultrily.

My balls tighten in anticipation. "There's not enough room here for you to ride me like I want, baby."

Her back arches, and she inhales sharply, and I can tell she feels those words down to her core — a core I want wrapped around me as soon as possible.

I shift her off my lap and turn her toward the door with a playful smack on the ass.

And as she leads me to the bedroom, stripping off her pants as she goes, giving me a gorgeous view of her perfect ass, I feel a weight lift off my shoulders.

Yes, there are challenges ahead. But if we can end a week this epically awful with understanding and amazing sex? Well, it makes me realize that I can face anything with Joanie by my side.

I also realize she probably needs this as much as I do, though in a different way. So, I will also focus on reassuring her of how much she means to me and that it doesn't matter if she's not ready to leap. But that when she is, I'm here to catch her. With lots and lots of orgasms. And killer grilled cheese sandwiches, of course. What woman could resist that combo?

CHAPTER FIFTEEN

JOANIE

Sunday, two days after Greg's bombshell about his father's legal action, I gather him, Nate, Mia, and Rae at Greg's house for a strategy session. I've done enough research. It's time to get this incorporation ball rolling. And maybe it'll be a good distraction for Greg.

"Okay, folks," I begin, spreading a stack of papers on the coffee table. "I've reviewed the codes and procedures for incorporating a town in Washington state and consulted with some lawyer friends who specialize in this area. Here's what we're looking at."

I look up to make sure everyone's with me. Greg slides his hand over my thigh encouragingly, and I look at Mia and Nate on the other corner of the sectional, then at Rae, who is sitting on a floor pillow by the window. They all nod that they're listening, so I begin by outlining the key steps.

"All right. We have to propose town boundaries and then determine the population within those boundaries, which I can do using census data since it doesn't have to be precise; that'll come later.

"We also have to decide whether Alpine Ridge will have a mayor, which is an elected position, or a town manager, which is similar in function but is appointed by the town council members.

"Once we have those, we can file the incorporation proposal. I'll handle the paperwork portion since it's mostly legalese," I assure them. "But we'll need a surveyor or someone like that to help with the boundary map. Does anyone know someone?"

Nate raises his hand. "I've got one that did my property before we built. I know he's worked with the county plenty, so I'll call him and see if he can do that."

I nod. "Great. Now. Should we ask the town for input on the mayor versus manager question or pick an option ourselves?"

Rae leans forward. "I think we should involve the community as much as possible. Builds trust and buy-in."

"I agree," Mia chimes in. "What if we go even further and hold a series of meetings? Give people a chance to learn about the options and voice their opinions?"

We all agree it's a good idea, so we plan to hold three meetings next weekend at the community center: one Saturday morning, another that afternoon, and a final one Sunday afternoon. Not Sunday morning, less due to potential church conflicts, and more because Saturday night is apparently a big night for folks to hit the tavern.

In any case, Nate offers to make a flyer, which Mia will take to the mail shop post office to distribute to every resident of the area. Finally, Rae will post the flyers in all the local businesses she can. Though we all agree Jerry probably won't let her put them up at the tavern or coffee stand.

"Hopefully, this will help generate some early support," Greg muses after we draft the flyer's wording. "We're going to need it."

I nod my head in agreement. "Especially since after the initial filing, the county's boundary review board will hold a meeting to give everyone a chance to say their piece for or against the incorporation. Best to have as many people behind us as possible by then."

"When will that happen?" Mia asks.

"Code says within thirty days, but I did some preliminary poking around, and it seems like Kittitas County is pretty good at getting things done quickly," I respond. "But we'll see. I'll let you know as soon as I know. Either way, that's just a bitch fest, and I doubt it's going to sway anyone one way or another. The biggest hurdle comes after that. We'll have about six months to get signatures from at least ten percent of the population, which will mean a lot of answering questions and hand-holding. I'm hoping to get that done as quickly as possible to get it over with. And, the sooner, the better anyway."

Mia's eyes light up. "What if we throw a big St. Patrick's Day event? Food, drinks, games, and a petition signing booth. We could get a huge chunk of signatures in one fell swoop while people are in a good mood and a little liquored up."

Rae snickers, though we all agree it's actually a brilliant idea. The timing is perfect, and we've already established that the folks here can't resist pastries, drinks, and holiday-themed events.

"All right. Good plan, guys," I say encouragingly. "After that, we file the paperwork, and the county auditor reviews — and hopefully approves   the petition in about a month. Then, there's one final boundary review board meeting to formally approve the incorporation plan. Which is, incidentally, where my role in this hootenanny ends."

Mia's brow furrows. "That's it, then Alpine Ridge is a town?"

I huff a laugh. "Um. No. Not even close. After that is the voting phase. First, a vote of the affected residents to approve the incorporation. Assuming a forty percent or higher approval, it goes on to a vote to nominate town officials. Then, finally, a vote to elect those officials. Those'll all be pretty spread out. And even once that's done, it's up to the new town council and mayor or manager to finish the incorporation and start setting up town services. Which could take years."

"Shit," Nate mutters.

"Yup. We're just getting started here, kiddos. Strap in for a long, hard ride. And probably not the fun kind," I tease.

Greg laces his fingers through mine, and I glance over at him. "You said 'we'," he murmurs. I suppress a smile, but I do lean in and kiss him. Because he's not wrong. I'm already thinking of myself as part of this kooky town. When the hell did that happen?

I look up to find everyone watching us with doe eyes, and I roll my own. "All right, back to business," I snip jokingly. "So, as I was saying, the actual election process will need to be handled by someone else, alongside the county. You'll need someone who understands the electoral system, or can at least figure it out, and can support and organize the candidates."

Mia perks up. "Carrie's getting her master's in political science in June. Maybe she could take that on?"

Rae hesitates. "The townsfolk might not take kindly to an outsider running things, even if she is your sister. We should look for volunteers locally first."

Mia concedes the point, and we agree to start recruiting election volunteers once the incorporation is approved. There's no rush, considering that it will be anywhere from four to six months from now.

With the plan laid out, a sense of excitement and purpose settles over the room. We're really doing this.

As the conversation shifts to more casual topics, I turn to Rae. "Hey, have you thought about what you want to do with the museum?"

She leans back against the wall, considering. "It's a great space with a lot of history. Maybe we could turn it into a community center annex? Offer classes, workshops, events that Greg can't accommodate?"

Greg nods thoughtfully. "That could work. Or what about keeping it a tourist attraction, at least partly? Play up the gold rush angle and give people a reason to stop and spend money in town. Keeping it low-key, of course, nothing too flashy, so it's in keeping with the feel of the town."

We discuss a few more ideas but agree to decide later — one step at a time.

But as I think we're wrapping up, Nate's expression turns serious. "Guys, what will we do about Ned in the meantime? It could be a year or more before we have a police force."

A heavy silence falls over the room. And it may be just that I'm more tuned into him, but I can feel Greg's unease. Yet Rae is the first to speak.

"We can't just let him keep preying on women," she says firmly, her usual friendly smile notably absent. "But we also can't take the law into our own hands."

"What if we encourage anyone who's had a run-in with him to file a complaint with the county sheriff?" Mia suggests quietly, twisting her fingers together. "Establish a pattern of behavior, even if they can't act on it immediately."

"That's a good start," I agree. "And we should spread the word for women to be cautious around him and report anything immediately."

Nate snorts. "Oh, believe me, everyone here knows. It's outsiders I'm most worried about. Like Carrie." He grimaces and slips his hand around Mia's.

Mia nods her head in solemn agreement. "Especially if this whole plan to draw more people to town works. But what can we do?"

Greg runs a hand through his hair, his frustration boiling over. "I hate feeling so powerless. Not that I want him to do something so awful again, but I wish there were a way to catch him red-handed if and when he does, so there'd be no question of his guilt."

"Except, we kind of already did," I point out. "I saw him put something in Carrie's drink."

"So did I," Nate agrees, his tone laced with anger and frustration.

Mia nods again, slowly, sadly. "I'll talk to Carrie about filing a report. If she doesn't, maybe you two still can?"

Nate squeezes her hand, and I nod somberly. Carrie's something of a little sister to me, too, after all these years. I don't know why I didn't think of it sooner.

A dangerous idea starts to form in my mind, but I keep quiet. I know they'd never agree to me putting myself at risk, no matter how noble the cause. But if we can't catch him red-handed accidentally ... maybe we can on purpose. There's a fine legal line to walk there, though, and I'd have to be smart about it, so they can't call it entrapment.

Still, someone needs to do something about this guy before he gets away with something horrible when we're not there to do anything about it. The exact scenario I know Greg is tearing himself up over these days.

As everyone starts to leave, I watch Greg as I hug Mia and Rae goodbye. He's talking lowly with Nate, looking defeated again. It makes me want to wrap myself around him, and not even in a sexy way, which is big. My chest aches for his obvious struggle, and I wish we hadn't ended on such a sad note.

I sigh internally as the door closes behind our friends, and Greg turns to me.

"Thank you for doing all this," he says softly, slipping his arms around my waist and burying his face in my hair. My arms circle his neck almost automatically. "I know it's a lot of work, but it means the world to me. To all of us."

"That's just how I am. Point me at a problem, and I'll fix it," I murmur, still struggling with how to fix Greg's feelings of failure. Even though I know that's not my burden. It's his. Still, I don't want him to carry it alone.

God, I feel *protective* of him, I realize. That's a first for me with a man.

I pull back a bit and look into his bright blue eyes. And in another first, I feel *those* three words catch in my throat. No, not "fuck me now." The serious ones that show how far gone I am for this man. I shake my head, refusing even to think them. It still feels too soon, like we haven't been together long enough, gotten to know each other well enough, for the urge to say those words to be coming from a real place. It could be just lust and the intensity of it all.

"I know," he replies. "It's one of the many things I love about you." He leans in and presses a tender kiss to my temple. Between his words and his actions, I melt inside. The backs of my eyes prickle with tears.

Despite myself, I feel so much I can barely stand it.

I just need time. We need time.

And orgasms. Lots of orgasms. Yes, that's always the answer.

So I push up and cover his lips with mine. He groans into my mouth as he responds, his hands sliding over my ass.

"Let's go to bed, and I'll remind you of everything else you love about me, mountain man," I murmur against his lips.

I feel his grin on my mouth and his hardness on my stomach. "Fuck yeah, city girl."

Greg lifts me, and I wrap my legs around him as he carries me to his room.

Greg's dad? Ned? They'll get theirs. I'll make damn sure of it. But right now, all I care about is getting mine. And Greg damn well gives it to me all night.

When we finally come together, when he whispers dirty sweet words in the dark, I realize I can't fuck my feelings away. Because it's all I can do to swallow *those* three words down when they climb from my throat to the tip of my tongue as he holds me while we drift to sleep.

CHAPTER SIXTEEN

JOANIE

The week leading up to the town meetings is a whirlwind of activity and not the fun, sexy kind. No, it's me helping Greg plan the agenda and pull out what feels like a million chairs from storage while he constructs a new podium since the old one had apparently bit the dust. Definitely not sexy … well, unless you count watching Greg work with his hands.

But I'm neck deep in my own world, thinking through how this will go, and as we're setting up the great room, I eye the sea of metal folding chairs skeptically. "Is two hundred chairs going to be enough?" I ask.

Greg shrugs. "There will still be room for people to stand. And we've done this kind of thing before — at best, a quarter of the town will show up total."

I'm unsure if that's encouraging, but I trust his judgment. He knows this town better than I do. Still, doing that math in my head, assuming a few thousand residents, we're likely to be over capacity for all three sessions.

Unfortunately, at this point, it is what it is.

On the bright side, while we're working, Nate drops by with a progress update. "So good news and bad news," he hedges, arms crossed over his massive chest.

I raise a brow. "Well, out with it, muscles."

Nate smirks. "The bad news is that my surveyor doesn't handle town level boundary definition. The good news is he put me in touch with someone in Seattle who's handled multiple cases like that in the Pacific Northwest. He books up quickly, but he just had a cancellation for next week. Unfortunately, I don't have time to meet with him, and I didn't want to volunteer your time without checking with you first." He hands me a small square of paper with a name and phone number scribbled on it. "I'd advise you to call him ASAP."

"Thanks, Nate. I'll reach out to him," I promise, taking the slip.

He nods, then turns to go but stops short. "One more thing. I tried to talk Mia out of it, but she's insisting on making cookies for the meetings. Like thousands of cookies. And she plans to set up a coffee and water station."

I laugh. "That's Mia for you. Always trying to feed everyone."

"We'll put some tables in the entryway," Greg assures him. "Fuck knows I'll need plenty of coffee and a cookie or ten by the time this is all done. Let her know I'll pay her for it too."

Nate huffs a laugh. "You know she won't let you do that. At least I convinced her not to do pastries, hot chocolate, or anything else too fancy."

"Cookies are fancy enough, in my book," Greg returns. "Tell her thanks."

I hold up the slip of paper Nate gave me. "And thanks for this, hot stuff." I give him a wink as he heads back out, and he waves as he goes.

I turn to find Greg giving me a look.

My brows pinch together. "What?"

He cocks an eyebrow and approaches slowly, slinging the hammer he's holding through his belt loop before putting his hands on my hips and drawing me close.

"Do I have something to worry about?" he murmurs, looking down at me.

My brow furrows deeper until I realize he means me calling Nate "muscles" and "hot stuff," and I burst out laughing. "Of course not. Nate just has a habit of being shirtless around the house. The nicknames came from me teasing him about it." I leave off how much I enjoyed the sight and Nate's reactions to my taunting. What can I say? I love making a grown man blush.

Greg looks understandably skeptical. "Yeah, I've seen him without a shirt plenty of times," he says drily.

"Oh, baby, are you *jealous*?" I tease, running my hands down his dusty shirt. I lean in and lightly touch my lips to his. "I hope not because he's got *nothing* on my mountain man."

Greg narrows his eyes, but a grin pulls at his lips. "Still. I think I might need to find a way to wipe that image from your mind forever," he murmurs, teasing his lips along the shell of my ear, sending shivers down that entire side of my body.

"Mmmm, you definitely need to do that," I groan, my hand slipping over the front of his pants before I press him away. "Tonight. Because right now, I need to call the boundary definition guy."

I step back and pull out my cell phone, waving teasingly at Greg as I head outside to make the call. He shakes his head and laughs before heading back to podium construction.

Chuckling, I place the call. A few minutes later, I've scheduled an in-person meeting for the following week, which is one more item checked off the to-do list.

By Saturday morning, the great room is stuffed with chairs, an elevated podium sits at the front, and the foyer is set up with Mia's promised refreshments. Greg and I are ready to take the stage, with Rae, Mia, and Nate on hand to help field questions. It's go time.

And before I know it, the first session is in swing. I'm not sure if it's because it's the first or due to the early hour, but it's nowhere close to full, with only about a hundred and fifty people in attendance. There are very few questions, which I'm unsure whether to be grateful for or nervous about. It's hard to get a feel for whether they'll support the incorporation if they don't speak up. And just as I feared, when we ask for a show of hands on the mayor versus manager issue, only a smattering of people vote, all for mayor.

But then, as we're about to wind down, an older woman with a short grey bob and a purple pantsuit stands up. She identifies herself as Betty McDonald, then asks, "Why are we even bothering with this? Nobody here wants to pay more taxes to make a few small business owners feel important when the town was just fine before they showed up." She lifts her chin, and her too-familiar words have me seeing red. And I know, based on Nate throwing a hand up to hold Mia back, that I'm not the only one.

Greg shoots me a sympathetic look that still clearly tells me to stand down. He's far more diplomatic than I would've been as he calmly reiterates the benefits of incorporation: improved infrastructure, essential services, increased property values, protection for local businesses, etc.

And the more Betty parrots what are obviously Jerry's words, the more advantages Greg is able to highlight. It's annoying that Jerry has influenced some of the other townspeople. But by the end, the rest of the attendees seem more convinced of our position, given the questions they finally start to ask. There's more curiousness and openness than there was at the beginning of the session, that's for damn sure. And when Betty finally retakes her seat with a "harumph," I can feel the smugness rolling off my bestie. Me? I'm ready to rip Greg's clothes off right here. His calm and masterful handling of the situation was *hot*.

"Ever thought about being a lawyer?" I murmur to him as the crowd breaks up.

He turns to face me with a smirk. "Not really."

I slide up to him and lean in, lowering my voice so only he can hear what I'm about to say. "You'd make a good one. You owned this room, baby. And later, I'm going to own that dick." I reach around and squeeze his ass for effect.

"I'd say get a room, but we only have an hour for lunch," Nate points out drolly from behind me, herding us toward the hallway. I smile up at him innocently, but before I can respond, Mia interjects.

"Thank you for handling that so well," Mia says to Greg as we pass the last of the folks leaving. I don't miss Mia watching Betty McDonald snatch three cookies from the table before scampering out. Mia shakes her head. "Gran hated that bitch, and I'm starting to see why."

My eyebrows jump. "Dorothy Lewis, the sweetest and most patient woman to ever grace this earth, *hated* someone? Wow. Betty McDonald must be a bigger pain in the ass than I realized."

Nate grimaces. "Unfortunately, Alpine Ridge isn't short on gossipy, controlling busybodies. She was the first disruption, but I guarantee she won't be the last."

I shrug lightly. "Honestly, I'm just surprised there was someone Gran couldn't melt. But I think Betty speaking up turned the tide. Before she said anything, everyone seemed really …" I tap my lips, trying to think of the word.

"Unsure," Rae offers. "They don't know what to think at this point." She pauses. "They were waiting for someone to speak up and lead them one way or another."

"I wish it were someone other than Betty McDonald. Even if we managed to convince them otherwise, if she keeps that up outside this room where we can't refute her, she's bound to sway them back," Mia grumbles.

Rae smiles patiently and shakes her head as we sit down at a table Mia set up in another room with our lunch. "Oh, honey, don't you worry. I didn't mean Batty Betty. I meant Greg."

Surprise flashes across Greg's face, stopping him with a half-filled plate in hand. "Me? They can't possibly look to me as a leader. I've only lived here a few years."

Rae shrugs as she loads up her own plate with a sandwich and chips. "I think they might. You've given yourself a lot of positive visibility lately between the winter festival and New Year's Eve. You reminded them that you built someplace for them to come together. And those who have come to you for help over the years will likely vouch for you as this all plays out. I think you're in just about the best position of all of us to make them see sense."

Greg blows out what I think is a nervous breath. I look at him appraisingly. Hoping he's up for it. Because Rae is right, people are sheep. Better one of us takes the reins in leading them than someone like Batty Betty. I snag a pre-packed chicken salad and a bag of chips and sit beside Greg.

"While I agree that Greg is a great person to lead this charge," Nate interjects from across the table, speaking to Rae. "Why not you? You've lived here the longest."

Rae's eyes go wide as saucers, and she tips her head back and laughs. "I have, but that means I've got history with this town and its people. Unfortunately, to them, I'll always be Chet's little girl who was just as much trouble as her daddy." She shakes her head. "Besides, I'm no leader. But you, Greg? You're a natural."

The tips of Greg's ears turn pink as he eats, and he is pointedly staying silent.

"Well, here's hoping for an even better turnout this afternoon. And maybe another Betty McDonald or two to give my man room to shine," I tease, nudging Greg with my elbow.

Greg glances at me skeptically, then gives Nate a long-suffering look. Both Nate and Mia bust up laughing. Mia lifts her styrofoam cup of coffee.

"Here's to round two with the old busybodies of Alpine Ridge," she teases.

I hoped for a better turnout, and boy, do we get it. The afternoon meeting is standing room only, with nearly three hundred people crammed into the space. Like word has gotten around about all the questions asked at the first session, the questions in the afternoon session build on them, coming fast and furious, mostly about timelines and money.

When will incorporation be complete? How soon can we get trash service? How high will taxes go? We answer most of the queries, though not always to the asker's satisfaction. But the fact that almost every question assumes the incorporation is going forward makes me want to run a victory lap around the town.

Even more interestingly, almost everyone votes when asked, and nearly all for mayor as well.

The final session on Sunday is full but not quite as packed. The discussion flows more smoothly and less contentiously than yesterday, with more fundamental questions about what it means to incorporate and what will be expected of them through the process. I can see that Greg is worried, presumably because it means that people are talking about the incorporation with each other. And that it might not all be positive. I try to reassure him with my presence and a few subtle touches that their engagement is a good sign. The vote, once again, goes for mayor.

Greg concludes the meeting, and people rise from their seats, talking in small clusters and grabbing what's left of the cookies and coffee.

"I like how not even one of them asked what a town manager is," Mia says quietly.

I snort.

"I doubt anyone wanted to look stupid by asking," Rae comments in a low voice.

"So they all voted for a mayor to save face?" Nate asks, screwing his lips to the side.

"It's as stupid and plausible as it sounds," I murmur. Greg snickers. I shoot him a look. "We all agreed you should lead this charge, remember? What are you waiting for? Go mingle and win over the doubters." I shove him jokingly toward the crowds.

He swoops in and kisses me. "Yes, ma'am," he replies, trotting off to do what I suggested like the good boy he is. I giggle to myself at the fantasies that thought brings to mind.

"We should all probably do that," Mia points out. I nod my agreement and pretend like I wasn't imagining role-play kink while the rest of our group breaks up to work the room. Still, my eyes follow Greg for a few moments as I watch him settle into a conversation with a group of older ladies who look a hell of a lot nicer than Betty McDonald.

Then my gaze drifts toward the foyer, and I notice Ned lurking by the snack table. My inner sneak lifts her head. I watch him stand there awkwardly for a few minutes until his gaze meets mine. And like I'd cast a fishing line and started reeling him in, he moves toward me. I can't help the satisfied grin that settles over my face.

Instead of seeing the cunning behind it, he takes it as encouragement, his leering grin answering mine.

"Looking good today, Joanie," he says, his beady dark eyes scanning me from tits to ass before landing on the former. "Can I get you a drink?"

I paste on a flirty smile. "Oh, I'd just love that. I'm so thirsty after that long meeting." I lay my hand on his arm and bat my eyelashes at him invitingly. "Thank you, Ned, you're so thoughtful."

Ned dutifully scampers off, and I watch him approach the table. But his back is facing me, I hope strategically, as he prepares my drink. He returns a few minutes later, handing me a styrofoam cup of black coffee.

I carefully accept it with my fingertips holding the rim, but I don't take a sip.

"Thank you," I purr.

"I hope you like your coffee black," he responds. "I love the taste of straight-up coffee, don't you?"

I nod agreeably. "Oh, absolutely. I like my men *and* my coffee tall, dark, and delicious," I say, pointedly scanning him from head to toe.

He misses the innuendo, his eyes flicking between me and the cup, and I work to school my expression — time to distract him from the fact that I'm not drinking it.

"So tell me more about yourself, Ned." I run my free hand down his arm. "What do you do for fun?" I give him a meaningful look from under my eyelashes.

His grin stretches even wider. "I could tell you," he says in what I'm sure he thinks is a sexy voice. He leans in, and it's all I can do not to wince at the foul odor of his rancid breath. "Or I could show you."

"Oh Ned, you're so funny," I titter, stepping back. Not getting the hint at all, he presses forward.

"And you're —" I don't get to find out what I am because a growl rips through the air between us, and suddenly Greg is there.

All I see is thick, dark hair, broad shoulders, and a tapered waist as he shoves in front of me. He pushes Ned, and though Ned's a touch taller, his skinny ass stumbles back several feet.

"Touch her, and you die," Greg snarls.

The hair on the back of my neck stands up, and a unique mixture of fear and arousal courses through me. Ned, for his part, scurries away like the rat he is.

And Greg whirls in place to face me, fury written all over his face. "Come with me." His hand closes over mine, pulling me through the thinning crowd and into his office. I struggle to keep the coffee from spilling as he slams the door behind us.

"What the hell was that?" Greg demands, barely containing his anger.

I sigh and shake my head, pulling a folded plastic zipper bag from my back pocket. I set the cup on Greg's desk, open the bag, slip it in, and carefully seal it shut. Greg's eyes track every movement as his chest heaves. With that done, I step into him, placing my hands gently on his chest. But I can see in his eyes he already has a pretty damn good idea of what I just did. And that it was, at least in part, premeditated.

"Tell me you didn't bait him into trying to drug you." Greg's tone is as hard as his expression. His hands are clenched into fists, and his eyes are wild.

I can't help it; my hands find my hips as I glare back at him. "I didn't bait him to do anything. He offered me a drink, and I accepted, but I didn't drink it. That's all."

"That's all?" Greg explodes. "You had a fucking evidence bag ready, Joanie! Even if you were just waiting for him to make a move, he could have tried to lure you away, or injected you with something when Plan A failed, or —"

"We were in public. And I can take care of myself," I cut in calmly.

He scoffs. "Oh really? So if he grabbed you, you'd be fine?"

I raise an eyebrow. "You think I couldn't handle that?" I challenge. "I'd like to see you try to grab me against my will."

Greg smirks, but it quickly fades at my stony expression.

"Don't mess around, Joanie," he replies, irritated.

"I'm not messing around. Go ahead. Try to grab me," I grit out through my teeth.

His brow furrows. "I'm a lot stronger than you. I don't want to hurt you, even by accident."

I roll my eyes. "Quit treating me like a china doll and fucking grab me, wimp," I goad him.

Greg gives me the "Oh no, you didn't" look, and I almost laugh. Almost.

"Fine," he says in a clipped tone. And then he lunges.

In a flash, I have Greg pinned to the ground, my knee at his throat. He tries to shove my knee off, but I twist, cutting off his air. His face turns red, and he taps out.

"Third-degree black belt in taekwondo," I explain, releasing him. "I'm not as helpless as I look." I bat my eyelashes at him in the most menacing way I can manage.

"Holy shit." He sits up, gasping and rubbing at his neck. As he climbs to his feet, I see a mix of emotions on his face: surprise, relief, and ... arousal? "Still ... what you did was reckless," he says, but his voice has lost its edge, and he won't meet my eyes now. "You shouldn't take unnecessary risks. I couldn't handle it if anything happened to you."

And now I feel like a complete asshole. Greg wasn't saying he didn't think I could handle myself. He was saying he couldn't handle knowing I'd have to. I soften, touched by his concern. "I'm sorry. If I knew you'd be this upset ..." I trail off, chewing at my bottom lip.

He huffs a dry laugh. "You would've what? Not done it?" He shakes his head. "I think we both know that's not true."

I scrunch my nose and reach out, lacing my fingers through his. "Still. I am sorry."

He nods and pulls me into his arms. "I know," he murmurs into my hair. "And it helps that you're even more capable of handling yourself than I knew. But that doesn't stop me from wanting to tear Ned's head off at the thought of him even looking at you wrong. So maybe just ... be more careful? Please?"

I melt into his embrace at the earnestness in his voice. And even though I despise being told what to do, especially by a man ... well, I'm finding I can't deny Greg anything. And the idea that I mean enough for him to threaten his own family member like he did ... it makes those three little words dance on my lips again.

But I bite them back. Though I do say, "I will, I promise." I blink hard as the feelings Greg stirs in me bring tears to my eyes. It's still all too much. So I do the only thing I know how to do to distract myself with a man. "And to show you I'm sorry, and I mean it ..."

I press him away and unbuckle his belt, dropping to my knees.

Greg's eyes darken. "You don't have to do that, Joanie." He makes to tug me up, but I can't handle looking him in the eyes right now because my name on his lips sends a fresh wave of things I'm not ready to feel coursing through my body.

So instead, I withdraw his cock from his boxers and shove it down my throat. His head tips back, and I let those three words melt back into my mouth as he does. I let his moans fill the space in my head where my swirling emotions were. I let his gentle touch on the back of my head soothe the turmoil inside me. But nothing, not the taste or smell of him, the way he feels thrusting in and out of my mouth, or the hot spill of his seed down my throat can distract me from the realization that my heart is his.

Or the knowledge that this visit, this project has become more than a pitstop between what was and whatever comes next. Deep down, I know it's now my path. And ready or not, I'm walking it with this man. He's what comes next — no pun intended, for once.

I'm shaken out of my thoughts by Greg hauling me to my feet and kissing me with such passion that it nearly knocks me back off them. When he stops, he's breathing hard, our foreheads pressed together. "Goddamnit, you drive me so fucking crazy," he groans against my lips. And I know by his tone and body language that he doesn't mean sexually. He means that a stellar blowjob wasn't enough to distract him from what I did and how that made him feel.

"I know," I murmur back. "I'm sorry for making you worry today."

He nods, his nose grazing mine with the motion. "I know. But if anything happened to you …" He pulls back to look into my eyes, and I see fear at the idea in them. He shakes his head, and his hand reaches up to cup the back of my neck. His thumb swipes tenderly over my cheek. "I love you, Joanie."

My heart nearly stops in my chest at his words. I reach for something, anything to say. Except "I know." Because I'm not going to Han Solo him after that heartfelt confession, after what I did today.

Instead, I nod. "I'm …" I swallow hard. His thumb swipes over my cheek again, making my thoughts go haywire.

"I know you're not ready to say it yet."

I look up into his dark eyes with surprise. But I shouldn't be. He gets me like no one has in a very long time. Possibly ever. And again, the knowledge that he will never ask me to be anyone but who I am nudges me toward giving in.

And yet, I can't. Not yet.

"I'm not," I agree. "But take me home, mountain man, and I'll show you how I feel about that." I bite into my bottom lip, willing my arousal to show through more than my feelings. Though I'm pretty sure he gets the message: I may not be ready to say it, but that doesn't mean I don't feel it.

CHAPTER SEVENTEEN

GREG

As much as I've enjoyed burying myself in Joanie in every way possible these last few days, I'm glad to be driving out of Alpine Ridge and into Seattle to meet with Sera while Joanie meets with the boundary map expert.

After talking to my lawyer, I better understand what my father can and can't do. However, he's also waiting for me to speak with Sera before responding to my father's suit. Since she left a voicemail letting me know she'd finished her research, I suggested we meet for lunch to discuss it and catch up.

The two-hour drive out of the mountains and through the Eastside is like descending into a different world. Busier. More packed. Businesses, homes, roads, people — more of them than even the last time I was here a few months ago — and the hundred miles feels like light years from the quiet isolation of Alpine Ridge.

Despite the gorgeous drive past Lake Sammamish, over Lake Washington, and toward the striking downtown Seattle skyline, I'm not excited to be back. I'm a small-town guy through and through, and this is all … well, a lot. Or maybe I'm already on edge from the looming conflict with my father.

Given that, as I park and walk to the café where I'm meeting Sera in Belltown, I'm not surprised that I find the amount of traffic and noise overwhelming. Then again, it could just be from growing up in Yakima, a small city in the middle of Washington state, far from the bustle of Seattle, and then having moved to an even smaller one, even though Ellensburg barely counts as a city with just under twenty thousand residents. And then again to an even smaller town … well, *almost* a town. In any case, I'm just not equipped to be in the city anymore.

I sigh in relief as I spot Sera at a small table in the back corner. I wave and head over. She stands to greet me, her long and wavy light brown hair shifting with the movement. She's wearing a long-sleeved purple shirtdress that's somewhere between business and casual. She hasn't changed a bit since I last saw her, save the happy grin she's giving me. I remember her being more serious. It's a good change, and I smile at her as I approach.

"Hey, you," I greet her, pulling her in for a hug.

She squeezes me hard. "Hey, hermit, long time no see," she teases.

I release her and shake my head, laughing. "Don't knock the hermit life. It's pretty nice. I don't know how you live in all this chaos," I respond as I sit across from her. "Though I gotta say, you look pretty happy."

Her grin widens. "I am. And I'm sorry we're not getting together under better circumstances," she responds, her smile fading.

I nod and grab a menu from between the napkin holder and the ketchup bottle. "We'll get to that. First, food. What's good here?"

She makes some suggestions, and we order. "So, shall we get the worst of it over with?" she asks bluntly.

I give her a wry smile. "Let's." It's one of the things I love about Sera and why she's one of the only family members on my dad's side, or at all for that matter, that I get along with. Well, that, and she doesn't get along with most of our family either. Neither of us suffers fools or sugarcoats things. Two traits that have always kept my circle small.

She folds her hands together and leans on the table. "All right. I imagine it will come as no surprise that the window to challenge your grandfather's will has been closed for a long time. So he's got no legal basis for challenging your ownership from that angle," she begins.

"But?" I ask suspiciously.

"But he's clearly up to something. However, I can't figure out what. A partition action can only do one of three things: force a partition in kind, which is a physical partition of the property that divides the land equally and assigns you each a wholly-owned parcel; a partition by sale, which is exactly what it sounds like — the property is sold, and the proceeds are split equally between you; or a partition by appraisal, where, in this case, your father buys you out by paying you your share of the appraised value of the land. So the only way he could claim complete ownership is the partition by appraisal."

"But he'd have to buy me out to do that?" I clarify.

Sera nods. "Yes. By bringing in the trust, I believe he's trying to prove he shouldn't *have* to buy you out. But no judge in Washington state is going to buy that. Trust laws are clear on challenge periods, and you're well past those."

"So why try? Why not just offer to buy me out?"

Sera's eyebrows raise. "He hasn't?"

I shake my head. "Not once. He's always only pressured me to go ahead with development I didn't support."

A look of understanding passes over Sera's face. "Have you considered that your father may not have the money to buy you out?"

My jaw drops. "No, I haven't." But I kick myself because I should've. "But I think you might be onto something."

"It would explain his attempts to drive you out without a payout. And his grasping at legal straws," she muses.

"It's also consistent with his complete inability to have ever run Grandpa's empire to begin with," I murmur, my mind spinning on the possibility that my parents might be that broke.

Our waiter delivers our food right then, and we eat silently while I process this. After a few minutes, Sera gently says, "If it's true, you hold all the cards, you know."

I set my burger down and wipe my mouth. "How so?"

"If he doesn't have the cash to buy you out, he sure as hell doesn't have enough to go forward with development."

"And?"

Sera smirks. "He must be planning to finance it. Which he's obviously figured out he can't do without your approval."

"Fuck."

Sera smiles wryly. "Precisely," she replies, going back to her sandwich. After she chews and swallows a bite, she adds, "But unless you get really lucky with a judge who's willing to dismiss the case, you're likely to be offered the choice between the three options."

"You mean I'd be *forced* to choose."

"That's exactly what I mean. If one owner initiates a partition action, most judges will require the other owner to choose between the three options unless there's a procedural or other issue that stops them from doing so. So you need to ask yourself which you think *he'll* want and which is most advantageous for *you.*"

My appetite is gone; I think about that as she eats. If it's the first option, he'll own his part of the land and can finance development. But at least it would be limited, and perhaps there's a way to control how much development and what he can do. If we both have to sell ... well, who the hell knows what the next owner would want to do with the land? It could be worse than what my father has planned. And we've already established that he doesn't have the money for the last option.

The kernel of an idea forms in my mind.

"So, how are things going at Sutton Developments, by the way?" I ask, referring to the company that bought out the real estate business she'd built.

Sera narrows her eyes at me. "Things are great. The owner, who is my boss and mentor, plans to retire in another five years, at which point I'll take over." She tilts her head. "You have that look Grandpa Tyler used to get."

I can't help the grin that escapes me because I know exactly what she means. My Grandpa Tyler, her grandfather's brother, got the same look when he smelled a good deal.

"How would Sutton Developments like to get in on the ground floor of a newly forming town in the Cascades? One that can be a rustic yet luxury second-home location for hikers, skiers, and other outdoor enthusiasts?"

"You're going to turn Alpine Ridge into a destination vacation home spot for the rich and snobby?" Sera asks drily.

I press my lips together. "Okay, I just came up with the idea. Because my dad wants to turn it into the next Leavenworth, and I've been fighting that pretty much since we inherited the land. But if we turn it into something else ... something that preserves what makes it special ..."

"Then you could cut him off at the knees and kick him out of your hidey-hole,"

Sera surmises. She huffs a laugh. Then she levels me with a look. "This is a stretch, you know that."

I nod. "I know. If you have a better idea, I'm all ears."

Sera stares at me evenly for a minute. "My husband runs a corporate security firm. Are you sure you don't want me to have him see what he can dig up on your father?"

I bark a laugh. "You want me to *blackmail* Everett Tyler?" I scoff.

She shrugs lightly. "You said it, not me," she responds with a twinkle in her eye. "Couldn't hurt to try it."

I shake my head, still chuckling. "Even the thought of having to talk to him enough to pull that off has me 'noping' out of that one. But I admire your boldness." I take a deep breath and let it out slowly. "I'll do my own research, run some numbers, and get you a proposal. Either way, I think pushing for an outright sale is the best path. I don't want this to end with any of that land solely in my father's hands. And I want him out of Alpine Ridge." And my life. But I don't add that out loud, even though I'm pretty sure she picks up on it. "Thanks for looking into this for me. I appreciate your help."

Sera smiles and nods. "What's family for?" she replies.

We both pause and look at each other before we burst out laughing. Because our families? Yeah, no. They're for driving us crazy, apparently. But it's nice that we still have each other anyway.

We finish our lunch and chat for a few more minutes before saying our goodbyes. As I walk out of the café, my mind is already churning on this new idea and how we could pull it off. But first, research. Lots and lots of research.

No, actually, first, I need to check on my house in North Queen Anne before I head back to Alpine Ridge. It's another property I inherited from Grandpa Tyler, and it's where I usually stay when I'm in Seattle for more than a day. I've got a property manager who generally looks after it for me, but I like to see it for myself occasionally.

Since it's only about fifteen minutes north, I make it through the packed streets to the 1920s remodeled craftsman that's one of the only things I love about this town. The inside has wood detailing, and the back has a huge outdoor porch and sprawling views going down the hill to the ship canal into Lake Union. It's about as nature-oriented as it gets in Seattle, but it's enough to make me feel a little less caged in when I visit.

I park in the narrow driveaway and note that the maple tree branches, still bare for the winter, have grown over the walkway to the porch. I tilt my head, realizing I haven't been here in longer than I thought … probably closer to a year.

I shake my head and let myself into the house, noting that the blue paint on the front door could use touching up. I make a mental note to tell the property manager. Per our agreement, a stack of whatever mail comes to the house is on the table inside the foyer. I toss my keys next to it, deciding to do a lap through the house before I go through what is likely all junk mail.

Three bedrooms, three bathrooms, and all two thousand square feet later, and I'm satisfied that the place has been well cared for. It has the musty smell of dust, but the sheer curtains let enough light in to keep the house from looking too dark and disused.

Satisfied, I grab the stack of mail and take it through the entryway, past the stairs, the kitchen, and out onto the back patio. I brush some old, dried-out leaves off one of the wicker patio chairs and settle on it, flipping through the envelopes and glossy advertisements. Halfway through, I find a folded piece of paper.

I open it to find a handwritten note. My heart stops in my chest at handwriting I remember all too well.

> Greg,
> I know this seems out of the blue, but I've just moved to Fremont and thought I'd look you up since I knew you had a house here, though I don't know how often you get out this way. I hope that's not too creepy. But since you've seen me naked more times than I can count, I figured it might be okay, and I have something I'd like to tell you. Call me?
> Hailey

I sigh heavily, debating whether to ignore it. Then I debate whether to call my property manager and ask if he remembers when and where he found this note because it was clearly not mailed. I nix that idea since, ultimately, it doesn't matter anyway.

Unfortunately, I know myself. And if I don't call, I'll always wonder why the woman who dumped me after six years together suddenly wants to talk to me. It could be as simple as her wanting to get together for old times' sake. But it could also be a secret child she's been hiding from me. Doubtful, since we were way more careful than I've been with Joanie, which should tell me how I felt about Hailey all along. Still, the possibilities are endless.

So, in the end, my curiosity gets the better of me, and I dial her number.

"Hello?" Her voice stirs the dusty corners of my mind, and not so much in a good way.

"Hey, Hailey, it's Greg," I say awkwardly. "I just found your note."

"Greg, oh my God, hi," Hailey replies, sounding surprised and pleased. "Thanks for calling."

"Yeah, no problem," I respond, trying to keep my tone neutral. "What's up?"

"I was hoping we could talk in person. I have something important I want to discuss with you. Are you in Seattle?"

"I am, but I'm heading out in a bit," I respond.

"Oh. I see. I mean … I can come over now if you have a few minutes?"

I hesitate; I'm not sure I want to open that can of worms. But I find myself agreeing anyway. Curiosity and all. "Sure, I guess that'd be okay."

"Awesome. I'll head over now. See you soon."

I barely have time to register what the fuck I just agreed to before Hailey is knocking on the door less than fifteen minutes later.

I open it expecting to feel something. But even though her blond hair is the same cascade of golden waves, and she wears the same tight T-shirt, a light blue this time, and jeans she's always favored that show off her huge chest and tiny waist, all I feel is wary.

"Hey," I greet her.

She grins and launches herself at me, wrapping her arms around my neck and squeezing me tight. "I missed you," she breathes against my ear. Her heavily perfumed smell wraps around me, and I shake off all the sense memories that go with that as I gently press her away.

"Why don't you come in and tell me what's up," I offer, stepping back and gesturing toward the living room.

She nods and heads in, sitting on one end of the light grey three-seater couch. She looks up at me earnestly as I settle on the other end.

"I'm just going to cut right to the chase because seeing you makes me feel even more like no time has passed, and I know you need to get going soon," she begins, then takes a deep breath. "Letting you go was a mistake. I want us to get back together."

I blink in surprise; this is a huge shock. "Wow, that's ... unexpected. But we haven't spoken in years, Hailey. We can't just ... get back together," I reply slowly. "I'm not who I was back then. And I have no idea who you are now or where you're at." I take a deep breath, gentling my voice. "But most importantly, I'm with someone else now. I've moved on. Haven't you?"

"I've tried. But I can't stop thinking about you," she admits, twisting her fingers in the long strands of hair that flow over her shoulder.

I shake my head. "I can't say the same. I'm sorry."

"But ... we were together for six years, Greg." She slides closer, dropping her hand on my knee. "And we were so good together. Don't you remember?"

I wrap my fingers over hers and gently remove them from my leg. "I remember. I also remember you leaving me."

"I know. And I'm so sorry. You have no idea how sorry. Surely that means something to you?"

I close my eyes and take a deep breath. "It does," I admit. "I'm glad you realize it was a mistake, at least." I don't say it, but it hurt me a lot more than I wanted to admit for a long time that I was so easy to leave after giving her all those years. After thinking we might be headed toward marriage. "But that doesn't change anything."

Hailey grabs my retreating hand and squeezes. "But it does. It changes everything. How long have you been seeing the person you're with?"

I shrug lightly, not sure I like where she's going with this. And then I pause, realizing with a start that it's only been about a month with Joanie. Given the depth of my feelings for her, it feels like so much longer.

"Not long. Just about a month," I admit. "But that doesn't change anything. We're over, Hailey."

She leans forward, placing her hand on my knee. "See, but I've had the same problem. I can only date someone for a few months before I realize they're just not *you*. It hasn't been the same for you? Surely all our years together mean more than a month with this woman?"

I pull back and stand up. This is nuts. Why now? And I can't help but blurt that out.

"Why now? Why like this?"

"I get that this seems abrupt. But it's been *months* since I left that note, Greg. And when you called, I was thinking about you. That means something, I know it."

I shake my head, overwhelmed by the sudden strange turn to the day. My phone buzzes in my pocket, and I withdraw it only to see Joanie's name. And the time. Shit. She's probably wondering why I haven't let her know I was headed back already.

"I've got to take this," I murmur, answering the call.

Hailey stands up, clearly agitated, and just as I hear Joanie say "Hello?" in my ear, Hailey says, "Is it her? Does she really mean more to you than me? You wanted to *marry* me, Greg."

And then Joanie hangs up. I pull the phone from my ear and confirm that the call ended.

"Fuck," I curse. I look up at Hailey, trying not to let my anger get the best of me. "I don't know where this desperation is coming from, but you do not come into my house, *my life*, and make demands of me like this. The woman I love now probably thinks I'm cheating on her, thanks to you. Get out, Hailey. And move on, like I did."

Hailey draws in a breath. "If she thinks you'd cheat, she obviously doesn't know you," she pushes. "Not like I do."

I throw up my hands in disgust. "You have got to be fucking kidding me." I press my lips together and take a deep breath, so I don't go nuclear. "*You* dumped *me. Years* ago. You don't know jack shit about me. If *you'd* ever known me, you wouldn't have been worried about a bunch of pre-teen girls' crushes. But you know what? You haven't changed. You still need to grow the fuck up and stop living in a fantasy. Get out, Hailey. And don't ever contact me again." Hailey opens her mouth, and I can feel the protest coming before she utters a word. "Now," I growl in the harshest tone I can manage, cutting her off before she can start up again.

And thank God she finally has the sense to look worried. She scampers out the door and is gone. And the whole episode has given me whiplash and one big fucking headache. A headache that I know has only just begun.

I immediately try to call Joanie back, but she doesn't answer. Worry gnaws at my gut as I hop in my truck and drive back to Alpine Ridge. Hoping I can get there before Joanie decides to take off. Because I know my city girl, she's been afraid of committing this whole time. Afraid of telling me that she loves me too, of what that means for her future. And I'd bet every penny I have that this is the excuse she's been looking for to turn tail and run from her feelings.

I make record time getting back to my place, but it still doesn't feel fast enough.

And when I walk inside, Joanie sits on the couch with her packed bag at her feet. My heart sinks.

"Joanie, please, let me explain," I plead.

She looks at me, her blue eyes guarded. But she nods. So I launch into the whole story: how Hailey left a note, how I stupidly agreed to let her come over, how she wanted to get back together, but I turned her down unequivocally.

"I'm so sorry, baby. It was nothing, I swear," I finish, reaching for her hand.

She allows the contact and a fraction of the tightness in my chest eases.

"I know," she admits. And I swear my shoulders drop a foot. A small, sad smile pulls at her lips. "But it made me realize that there's *still* a lot I don't know about you. And that this —" she gestures between us "— is going *so* fast."

I let my head drop into her lap with a sigh. "Maybe, but every relationship goes at its own pace," I reply. I look back up into her eyes. "Tell me you're not falling as fast as I am, Joanie, and I'll give you all the space you need."

Her eyes shine in the dimming afternoon light. "I am. And honestly, I was trying not to freak out about it *before* I heard that you were planning to marry your ex once upon a time." She tilts her head back, blinking hard.

"That wasn't me," I explain. "That was all my parents. Or what I thought I was supposed to be doing to make them happy, anyway. When she broke up with me, I was just as relieved as I was upset, even though it took me a long time to realize it was because I *didn't* want to marry her. And I never felt about her the way I feel about you."

Joanie's head tips forward, and a manic laugh escapes her lips. "That. That right there is what I'm trying not to freak out about."

My brows slam together. "So you're not upset that it sounded like I was spending time with my ex behind your back but that I'm more in love with you than I ever was with her?"

She snaps her fingers and points at me. "Bingo." A single tear escapes her shimmering eyes and skitters down her cheek. "I don't know how to do this. I don't know if I *want* to do this or if I'm just caught up in how good it feels to be with you."

I pull back, stung by her words, but she grabs my hands before I can withdraw.

"That's not about you, Greg." She so rarely uses my name outside of orgasming. The few times she has, it's gone straight to my heart. But this time, it's like a knife.

"I know," I say thickly.

"Do you?" she asks earnestly, leaning forward. "I'm not sure I understood how much I prized my independence until you made me want to give it up."

I shake my head. "I would never ask that of you."

She shakes her head, and a few more tears skitter out. "*I know.* I wouldn't have even wanted to if you were the type of man who would. But it's because you are …" She trails off, closing her eyes, pushing more tears down her cheeks. I reach up and wipe them away.

When she opens her eyes, I can see her resolve to leave. But I've listened, too. And I know she's closer than ever to giving in to this. I just need to push through this with her. However, she needs that to happen.

"Don't go too far for too long, city girl," I murmur, leaning forward and kissing away the last tears that fell.

She cups my face in her hand, leans in, and places the most tender kiss on my lips. It's so unlike her that it sends chills through me, both good and bad. One kiss that is somehow both comfort and fear. Love and loss. Fight and surrender. But that's Joanie and me. A contradiction that shouldn't make sense, yet somehow does. I hope.

"I'll see you soon," she promises, rising and picking up her bag.

I want to beg her to stay, but I force myself to nod instead. "I understand. I'll be here whenever you're ready."

She gives me a long look, then walks out the door. I sink onto the couch, my head in my hands.

How did things go sideways so fast? I can only hope Joanie will work through this and come back to me. Because the thought of losing her … it's unbearable.

I've never been one to run from a challenge. And I'm sure as hell not starting now. I'll give Joanie the space she needs. But I'm not letting her go. Not without a fight.

CHAPTER EIGHTEEN

JOANIE

As I drive away from Greg's place, my heart feels like it's being squeezed in a vice. I know I'm doing the right thing for myself by taking some space, but it doesn't make it any easier. The look on his face … well, it was all I could do to leave.

With shaking hands, I pull out my phone and call Mia.

"Hey, Jo. What's up?" Mia answers cheerfully.

I take a deep breath. "I need a place to stay for a bit. Can I get a room at the B&B?"

There's a pause. "Of course. But why? Did something happen with Greg?"

I sigh heavily. "Things are just moving really fast, Mia. I need some time to figure out what I want."

"Ah. Well, there's definitely a room there for you, but on one condition. I meet you there for a girl's night," Mia replies.

Gratitude swells in my chest. "You know I'll never turn down that deal," I respond. "Thanks, babe. I'll see you soon."

I make it to Gran's old place a few minutes later and wait in my car for Mia. It takes her nearly half an hour to make it down the mountain.

As soon as I step out of the car, she rushes over, wrapping me in a hug.

"God, Joanie, you look —"

"Don't you dare finish that sentence," I say threateningly.

She chuckles and leads me inside. "The place is all ours until tomorrow," she says, gesturing around.

Gran's former house mostly looks the same, but with newer furniture arranged in a more lobby-style sitting area instead of the old living room with its overstuffed couch and TV. A podium by the door has a logbook and a pile of brochures. A peek into the dining room gives me the same impression — newer, stuffier, and, well, more like a B&B. The kitchen, though, has been walled in completely with actual doors put in place. It makes sense, but it's still super weird.

"You don't do check-ins, cooking, and cleaning, do you?" I ask curiously, settling onto the closer of the two linen settees. It's decidedly less comfortable than Gran's old couch was.

Mia waves a hand and settles on the other one across from me. "Lord no. There's a property manager out of Ellensburg who comes as needed and a local who does the daily cooking, cleaning, and such. Though the bakery does supply pastries for breakfast."

I perk up a little at that. "Ah, so there's food here?"

Mia smirks. "There's food here, but I didn't bring any goodies. There is, however, always wine. And chocolates for the pillows, but I see no harm in plundering that stash." She rises and enters the kitchen, emerging shortly with a tray bearing a bottle of wine, corkscrew, two glasses, and a good-sized cardboard box of what I can only assume is chocolates.

I raise a brow at her. "Those look mass-produced," I accuse her in a teasing tone.

Mia rolls her eyes and sets the tray between us on the long, narrow wooden coffee table. "Since they're for the pillows, we need to keep a bunch of them on hand. Besides, candy-making isn't my thing. Candy eating, though, I'm here for." She winks at me and pops open the box, tossing me a chocolate while she unwraps one for herself. "Okay, now that we have provisions, spill," she demands as she pours us each a generous glass of red.

She hands me one, and I take a fortifying sip before launching into the story about Greg's ex showing up and my subsequent freak-out.

Mia listens intently, her brow furrowed. "Wow. That's a lot to process. But it sounds like Greg handled it well. He was clear with her that he's with you now."

I nod. "He did. And he was." I take a deep breath. "But hearing another woman trying to convince him to take her back because they'd once planned on getting married?" I shake my head.

Mia clears her throat. "I can't even begin to imagine what I'd think if something like that happened to me. And not to sound too much like a therapist, Jo, but … how did that make you feel?"

I bark a sharp laugh and drain the rest of my wine. "Like I wanted to claw her eyes out. Which scared me so much that I hung up. Because I've never thought of myself as the type to fight a bitch over a man."

"It wouldn't be a fight, and you know it. You'd crush her." Mia nudges me with her foot, and I laugh.

"Well, it sure wouldn't be a *fair* fight anyway," I agree. "But that was just my gut reaction. I wouldn't have done it. I think. Maybe." Mia gives me a skeptical look. "Okay, fine, there might have been some hair-pulling or something. Seriously, though, the fact that I reacted so strongly freaked me out. Because I had no idea they were talking about marriage. That he even wanted that. And here I am, falling for him, not having had those kinds of conversations. It just made me realize how fast we're moving. I mean, I was ready to tell him I love him."

Mia chokes on the chocolate she'd just popped in her mouth. "Excuse me?" she says around the mouthful. "You were going to do what now?"

I wrinkle my nose. "Did I forget to mention that part?"

Mia swallows and wipes the chocolate off her lips with a napkin. "Um, *yeah*," she replies. Her eyes soften. "You really love him?"

I draw in a slow breath before nodding. Tears prick at the backs of my eyes. "Yeah. I think I do." I tip my head back and blink them away. "Which is nuts, right? Who falls in love with someone they've only known a month?"

Mia snorts. "You, apparently, and I'm not the least bit surprised. I knew it'd happen fast once you found the right guy."

I raise an eyebrow and give her a skeptical look. "Oh please, you did not."

Mia lifts her chin. "I did. You may be impulsive and reckless, but you know what you want and go after it. What made you think falling in love would be any different?"

I tip my head to the side and give her a look. "Oh, I don't know, maybe because once you do, it's not just you anymore? Having to consider another person in my plans for the future is huge. No more doing what I want, when I want. It's not just *me* anymore; it's *us.* How do you just … make that switch?"

Mia reaches over and squeezes my hand. "I get it. Falling in love is a huge adjustment, which is scary. But you're looking at it backward. It can also be wonderful. You have someone there to do all the awesome things you want to do with. Someone to cheer you up after a shitty day. Someone to support you through the good and the bad. Doing everything alone may seem like freedom, but it can also be a burden. I won't tell you the transition is easy, but it's worth it."

"But what if —"

"It works out, and you get more than you ever dreamed of having?" Mia interrupts with a smirk.

"That's not what I was going to say at all," I reply drily.

She rolls her eyes at me. "Don't let fear rob you of something great, Jo."

I swallow hard. "I know. And I thought I was ready to make that leap. I left because I needed some time to wrap my head around it. To make sure I'm ready."

Mia nods understandingly and refills my wine glass. We sit in companionable silence, sipping our wine and eating chocolate.

"So, have you talked to Carrie about whether she's willing to file a report over the incident with Ned?" I ask, changing the subject.

Mia shakes her head sadly. "She said she didn't even know that was happening, and she's already overwhelmed between finishing her degree and dealing with our parents. But I'm pretty sure Nate is planning to."

"Good. That asshole needs to be stopped," I mutter darkly. I sigh heavily, unsure why I brought up another depressing topic. I rack my brain for good news, then remember my meeting earlier. "Oh, I met with the boundary definition expert today. He said he should have something preliminary for us in about a week. The boundary review committee will make changes anyway, but it's a start."

Mia smiles. "That's great news. Thanks for handling all of that, Jo. I know it's a lot of work."

I shrug. "It's what I'm good at. And I want to help." I don't deny that it isn't just for Nate and Mia's sake; Greg was a big part of my decision to take this on. My thoughts run in circles, so I decide distraction would be a better tactic.

"Is there still a place we can watch movies in this joint?" I ask.

Mia nods. "Your room has a TV with satellite cable. Come on. Let's go watch something that'll have us peeing laughing."

I pull a face and laugh. "As long as there's more wine and chocolate."

"What do you take me for? Of course there is," Mia assures me.

So we spend the rest of the evening watching old-school Jim Carrey movies and polishing off the wine and chocolate. And I know I gave her shit, but it's the exact combination of nostalgia, comfort, and easy companionship that I needed.

The next day, I wake up alone, Mia having ducked out at likely an ungodly hour to head into the bakery. I'm grateful because now that I'm rested and calm, I have the headspace to reflect on yesterday's events.

My conclusion? I'm a fucking moron.

I love Greg. I want to be with him. And yes, I'll be giving something up to do that. But Mia is right; I could gain so much more. If anyone is worth the risk, it's my mountain man. Even through what could've been a horrible, relationship-ending misunderstanding, he was nothing but apologetic, concerned, and considerate. And the man knows how to destroy my pussy in the best way possible. A combination I thought impossible, yet here we are.

Could this all blow up in my face? Sure. But anything worth having is also worth the risk. And if anyone is worth that risk, Greg is.

Funny how a little distance and perspective can make you see through all of your bullshit.

Mia was also right that when I know what I want, I go after it. So I get my ass out of bed, throw on some tight jeans and a blouse that makes my small tits look luscious, and head out to drop in on Greg at the community center.

Though the late January midday temperature is a nipple-freezing cold — not literally thanks to a thick jacket — I'm once again bowled over by how gorgeous this place is. A light snow must've fallen earlier this morning; everything glitters as the sun reflects off the fast-melting crystals. I drive slowly because Greg's nickname for me is apt: I'm a city girl through and through, and driving in snow and ice is not my favorite.

Still, I'm nearly vibrating with anticipation and excitement when I get there, though the building is quiet as I enter. I peek my head in Greg's partially closed office door to find him at his desk, hunched over some paperwork. His chin is leaned on one strong forearm, a wayward curl gracing his forehead. His strong jaw is clenched, and I wonder if it's the paperwork or the tough conversation from yesterday evening.

"Hey," I say softly.

His eyes snap up, surprise evident on his face. He scans me from head to toe, and I suppress a shiver under his gaze. "Joanie. Hey. I wasn't expecting to see you today."

I step inside, closing the door behind me. "Do you have a minute to talk?"

"For you? Always," he says, gesturing for me to sit. I perch on the edge of the chair opposite his desk. "How was your night?"

I huff a small laugh. "Better than I expected it to be. Mia and I had a girls' night. Wine, chocolate, and Jim Carrey. It was great, actually. You?"

He pushes out a breath. "Honestly? Rough."

I grimace. "I'm sorry."

He waves a hand dismissively. "It's not your fault. It wasn't just what went down between us, anyway. This thing with my dad … I guess it's affecting me more than I thought it would," he admits.

My mouth forms a small "O" of surprise. I don't know why I hadn't remembered that he had gone to Seattle in the first place to talk to his cousin about the lawsuit. And I didn't even ask. But then, the sudden reappearance of his ex forcing me to face my feelings was a little distracting.

"God, Greg, I forgot. Do you want to talk about it?" I ask.

He leans forward, steepling his hands under his nose. "Maybe later. What was it that you wanted to talk about?"

"Oh," I say, uncharacteristically sheepish. "Yeah. That." I take a subtle deep breath. "If you still want to, I'd like to keep seeing you. I feared committing to this would mean giving up parts of myself that I considered vital. But … you're more vital to me." I shake my head, annoyed that I still can't seem to say those three words. I look up into his eyes. "This is just new territory for me. But I want to be here. With you."

He leans forward, his blue eyes earnest, and opens his mouth to respond, but he's interrupted by a sharp knock on the door. We both turn toward it to see an older gentleman looking in expectantly. "I'm sorry to interrupt. I'm here for my training appointment," he says.

Greg rises. "Of course, Bob, I'll be right out."

I stand up and step toward the door. "I'm sorry, I should've realized you'd be busy. I'll go."

Greg gently pulls me toward him as if waiting for me to protest. When I don't, he holds my hands and looks down into my eyes. "I am, but we can continue this later. If you want."

"This evening?" I offer.

"I'd like that."

"All right. Meet me at the B&B at six. I'll make dinner."

His eyebrows jump. "I thought you didn't cook."

I shrug lightly. "I said I don't cook, not that I can't."

Greg chuckles. "You never stop surprising me, city girl."

I bite into my bottom lip. "See you at six?"

"Wouldn't miss it for the world." His eyes drop to my lips, and my breath catches in my throat. But instead of kissing me, he pulls me into his embrace. The feeling I get with his strong arms encircling me is almost harder to resist than his lips on mine. "If I kiss you, I'm afraid I won't want to stop," he murmurs in my ear.

I nod against his chest before pulling away. "Later," I promise.

He dips his chin in response, and I turn to leave.

Once I get in the car, I let out a sigh of relief. I've taken the first step. And I'll take the next one tonight. I can do this.

Focusing back on the task at hand, I glance at the clock and realize it's just after one. If I wait until two, I can avoid Ned at the grocery store. But if I want to do the braised beef I'm thinking of, I'd need to get it going as soon as possible. Since it's the only thing I know how to cook that's both easy and impressive, I don't have another alternative short of asking Mia to cook something for me. But that would defeat the point. Cooking for him is a big deal for me. I don't cook for anyone, not even myself. And I want to show him that he's special.

That aside, I also refuse to let one creep deter me from my plans.

Mind made up, I start the car and head toward the grocery store.

A few minutes later, I park and step out, squaring my shoulders as I march into the store. I pass the register but don't see anyone in the store, not even another shopper. Ned must be in the back, and it seems it's not only the women of Alpine Ridge avoiding him these days.

With a smirk, I head to the refrigerated meat section at the back of the store.

I'm examining the few available chuck roasts when I feel a presence behind me.

"Well, hello there, beautiful." There's no mistaking Ned's lecherous voice. And now that I know exactly what kind of predator he is, I'm not playing games anymore.

I whirl around to face him. "If it isn't the disgusting creep who tried to drug me and my friend."

Ned's eyes widen, and he lets out a nervous laugh. "I would never do anything like that to a beautiful lady like you." He steps closer, backing me up against the beef case. "I thought we had a connection."

"We definitely do not, and if you don't get away from me, you will regret it."

An unsettling, leering grin splits his wide mouth. "Oh, come on, baby, you don't have to play hard to get. I've got what you want right here."

He grabs my wrists, wrenching them down toward his crotch. His grip is so tight it hurts. The thought of being forced to touch his dick, even over his pants, almost makes me vomit on the spot.

I attempt to pull away, but he's stronger than I'd expected. While he may have strength, I have smarts. And training. So before he can force my hands where he wants them, I jerk upward just enough to duck under his arms, swinging my knee up as I move to his side. I aim for his crotch, but he bends forward, and I end up landing the blow to his stomach.

Even better.

It knocks the air out of him, and he releases me in surprise.

The thing is, taekwondo isn't about attacking. They train you to escape a dangerous situation first, whenever possible. But this guy? He needs to be taught a lesson. And he's about to be taught one by someone he assumed was too small and weak to fight back.

It's all to ensure he can't do me more harm.

Really.

Because, in fact, my wrists are throbbing so badly from being wrenched around that I decide in the few seconds it takes him to get upright and whirl on me that a roundhouse kick to the chest is the only way to make sure he doesn't get back up next time.

As soon as my booted foot lands in the center of his chest, the "Oh shit, what the hell did I get myself into" look flashes across Ned's face. Well, for the split second he has before he goes flying backward, landing on the shelves behind him. The display crashes under his weight, sending dozens of wrapped cuts of meat tumbling over him as he, the shelves, and the broken stand collapse.

With Ned howling in pain and down for the count, I don't stick around to savor the moment. I race out of the store, adrenaline pumping through my veins.

As soon as I'm back in my car and on the road, I can see the angry welts and marks on my wrists that I know from experience are only going to get worse over the next few minutes. I take a few deep breaths before driving straight to the hospital in Ellensburg.

When I get there just over thirty minutes later, the intake nurse takes one look at my wrists and face, where there's a bruise I hadn't noticed — probably a glancing blow I didn't feel when I jerked Ned's arms up — and tells me that they'll get someone from the sheriff's office to come by after I'm treated.

Still, given the volume of higher-priority cases, it takes a few hours before they can get to me. Once they've assessed and photographed my bruises, I have to wait another hour for the sheriff to show up so that I can give an official statement. I make sure to tell him about today and seeing Ned try to drug Carrie on New Year's Eve. I even mention the coffee cup with his prints that I never drank from. I'd intended to find a way to get it tested, but I'm betting that's about to be taken care of.

"All right, ma'am. I'll get this report filed this evening, and someone should be up to collect the evidence you mentioned tomorrow. I assume you'd like to press charges?" He gives me a look that clearly says, "You'd better press charges."

"Absolutely," I say firmly.

He nods his approval, his lips pressed into a thin line that tells me exactly how he feels about men who abuse women. "With any luck, what you've given us will allow us to nail this bastard."

Once he leaves, I'm given my discharge papers. As I head back to the car, exhausted and realizing that making dinner for Greg is out, I check my phone to see if there's time to pick up something on my way back.

I find that it's after six, when I was supposed to meet Greg, and I have a few missed texts, one call, and a voicemail. All from Greg.

I contemplate calling, but this is a conversation I want to have in person, so I send him a text instead, letting him know that I'm okay and that I'll be there in a half hour or so to explain everything.

When I return to the B&B, Greg is pacing the sitting room. He takes one look at me and stops in his tracks. The anger on his face makes me take a step back.

"Who did this to you?" he demands. I can practically hear his teeth grinding together from here.

"Ned. But I'm betting he looks worse," I offer. The veins on Greg's forehead visibly flex, and I hold up my hands. "Let me explain. I'm fine, I promise."

The door opens, and a couple I've never seen walk in. They give us a friendly, though curious smile as they make their way through the sitting room and up the stairs, presumably to their room.

"Let's go to my room," I say, sliding my hand into Greg's and pulling him down the hall.

When we get inside, I find the bed made up and my things folded onto the armchair in the corner. I settle on the end of the bed and pull Greg down next to me. Then I tell him what happened at the grocery store. Greg grows even quieter as I talk, his jaw clenching and his hands curling into fists.

When I finish, he looks like he's ready to blow a fuse. "I'm going to fucking kill him," he grits out.

I close my eyes briefly and shake my head. "Don't you see? You don't need to do a damn thing. He's finally going to get his."

Greg's jaw grinds. "I fucking hope so." His unfocused eyes finally zone in on me. "Why'd you go there, Joanie? You promised me you'd be more careful."

My brow furrows. "That's what you're focusing on in all of this?"

He shakes his head. "I'm glad you're safe. But I hate that you put yourself in harm's way like that. *Again*."

I bristle at his tone. "I can take care of myself, Greg. You know that."

He runs a hand through his hair. "I know. But I feel like you have this need to prove it. And promises mean something to me, Joanie."

I reel back like he slapped me. "So I'm just supposed to not go places I might run into someone unsavory because you're afraid for me? Even when I'm not?"

Greg's nostrils flare. "Maybe you should be a little more afraid. There's such a thing as being *too* fearless."

An ironic laugh escapes me. Given that I'd planned to use this evening to show him that I wasn't letting my fear of commitment stop me from being with him, I find this twist particularly infuriating. I was prepared to accept him for who he is and what we could be to each other. But maybe he's not ready to do the same. Maybe I had him all wrong.

"I think you should go," I tell him, standing abruptly and pointing at the door.

"I think we should talk about this," he insists, rising and putting himself in front of me.

"Talk about what, how you want me to become your cooperative little woman? Newsflash: I'm your city girl, mountain man. I come with self-defense training that I'm not afraid to use. I don't let creepy jerks who think they can get away with threatening women keep me from living my life. And I also don't let misogynistic assholes who think they can change me do it either."

"You know that's not who I am or what I'm saying," he responds.

I look at him like he's nuts. "Sounds like it to me."

"Then, obviously, we need to start over. I —"

I hold up a hand. "Don't bother. If you won't leave, I will." I grab my bag from the closet and shove the clothes from the chair into it.

And then I walk out without looking back.

One sleepless night later, I get a call from the sheriff's office asking to collect the coffee cup evidence. I arrange to meet them at the bakery. Since I hadn't felt like talking about it last night, I need to fill Mia in this morning before the town gossips do. Even though I still don't feel like reliving that awful, strange turn our relationship just took. Or former relationship? Either way, our fight in my room wasn't quiet, and apparently, all the other rooms were full. And if I've learned anything about Alpine Ridge, it's that news travels fast.

I meet the deputy outside the bakery, though as soon as I walk in, I can see the questions all over Mia's face. Rae at least has the good manners to pretend she wasn't watching.

I instantly put Mia out of her misery, telling her everything that had happened since I last saw her: talking to Greg, planning to make him dinner, my run-in with Ned, the subsequent hospital visit, filing charges, and handing off the evidence to the sheriff's deputy just now. I leave out all the relationship stuff and our fight last night. I can fill Mia in on that later when it's just her and me.

To that end, since I need some distance from Greg to clear my head, literally and metaphorically, I decide to spend the weekend at Mia and Nate's. It gives me time to tell Mia everything that went on with Greg. However, I don't wallow in it or let her dissect it endlessly. I try not to think much about it at all. It's still too raw. And I still have no idea how to feel or what to do next.

On Saturday evening, Nate pulls me aside.

"Mia told me what Ned did," he says, his normally warm eyes hard. "I'm going down to the sheriff's office first thing Monday to give my statement about what I saw at the New Year's Eve party."

I give him the most grateful look I can muster, given everything that's going on in my head right now. "Thanks, Nate. Every bit helps."

Despite Nate and Mia's support, the week is torture. They work every day. I spend my days mostly with Simba, looking for jobs in Seattle. Something I've been putting off to see how things panned out here, but it's time to at least start thinking about my options again. Unfortunately, January isn't a great time to be unemployed, apparently, so that's a dead end for now.

Thankfully, at the end of the week, I get the proposed boundary definition from my contact. I immediately head to the county clerk's office and file the petition, a thrill running through me for the first time in a while. We're one step closer to helping Mia and Nate and to me taking a break from Alpine Ridge. I should have a few weeks until I need to be here for the initial boundary review meeting, so I think I might head back to Seattle. Hopefully being home and on my own for a bit will help me get my head back on straight so I can refocus on what I really want my path forward to look like.

I must not have had good reception as I drove as I notice a voicemail when I return from the county clerk's office. It's from the sheriff. The coffee cup had Ned's prints, and the coffee was spiked with ketamine. They're waiting on a warrant but plan to arrest him formally as soon as they get it. They also request that I remain available to testify when it goes before a judge.

I sit down heavily on the guest room bed, relief and anger and a million other emotions swirling inside me. Ned will face consequences for his actions. But my personal life is still a mess, and it looks like I'll be here for a bit longer. So no escaping to get back in touch with myself. For now, anyway.

In any case, I also realize that Greg should know that the coffee cup stunt worked. Not that I expect that to convince him the risk was worth it, but because it's his cousin, and there's bound to be more blowback once he's arrested. I may not be sure what is going on between Greg and me anymore, but I can't let this blindside him.

I shake my head, laughing at myself when I realize how much I must really care about him to look out for him even when I'm angry.

Which makes me reflect on that anger a little more. Even though he made me feel like he doesn't accept me as I am, I know I probably overreacted. And because I've never been prone to overreacting or extreme emotions, that's when I know. I'm truly in love with Greg. Because only love is that irrational.

CHAPTER NINETEEN

GREG

I'm at the community center, trying to focus on paperwork, but my mind keeps drifting back to the fight with Joanie. The look of hurt and anger on her face when she told me to leave is seared into my brain.

I know I reacted badly. I was just so scared when I saw her injuries, knowing she'd been attacked. But she's right. She can take care of herself. Maybe I should trust her judgment, even though her actions scare me sometimes.

I'm jolted out of my thoughts by my phone ringing. And like my thoughts conjured her, it's Joanie. My heart leaps into my throat as I answer.

"Joanie, hi," I say, trying to keep my voice steady.

"I have some news," she replies, bypassing pleasantries. "The cup of coffee I gave to the sheriff? It turns out it was spiked with ketamine. And since it had Ned's prints, it was enough for them to request a warrant for his arrest. They're working on getting that as we speak."

I'm stunned into silence for a moment. Then I find my voice. "That's great news. I mean, I'm pissed that he's just as dangerous as I feared, but it's great that there's evidence."

"Yeah," she agrees. "I just thought you should know."

"Thanks," I reply. "And Joanie ... I'm sorry about our fight. You were right to get that evidence. I was being a jerk, telling you that you weren't being careful. Clearly, you know what you can handle and when taking a risk is necessary. I just worry because I care about you so fucking much."

There's a pause, and I hear her take a deep breath. "I know you do. And I'm sorry, too. I shouldn't have blown up at you like that. The truth is, before Ned attacked me, I was planning to make you dinner, as you know. What you don't know is that I was also going to tell you that I love you."

My breath catches in my throat. "You love me?" It's so Joanie to tell me that for the first time over the phone. I almost laugh. But my heart is too full right now to do anything but revel in hearing her say it.

"Yeah," she says softly. "I do. But then, when you got so upset about me going to the store, I started questioning if I could be with someone who didn't accept that sometimes I might seem reckless when I'm doing what I think needs to be done."

"Joanie, no," I rush to assure her. "It's not that I don't accept you. I love all of you, even the parts that sometimes scare me. I was just upset that you got hurt."

"I realized that," she says. "And I also realized that I keep finding reasons not to commit to this, to us fully. But I don't want to do that anymore. Because despite what I said, I know who you are. And I do love you, Greg. I want to be with you."

I close my eyes, emotion welling up in my chest. "I want that too. More than anything. Where are you right now?"

"I'm at Mia and Nate's because the B&B is fully booked this weekend. Why?"

"Because I need to see you," I tell her honestly. Her answering silence unnerves me. "That is, assuming you want to see me."

A breathy laugh escapes her. "Of course I do. I was just trying to figure out if I could get to you faster than you could get here."

I grin. "Well, that's easy. I'm on my way."

I make it up the hill in record time. When Joanie opens the door, the sight of her takes my breath away. And it's not even her long, dark hair up in a messy bun that shows her slender neck or the tiny shorts and tank top she's wearing. It's her inner beauty radiating through the stunning exterior. She may drive me crazy, but it's also what makes us work. She smiles at me like she knows, and I sweep her into my arms and hold her tight.

"Hey, baby," I murmur into her hair.

She pulls back to look at me, her blue eyes shining. "I missed you."

I lean down and kiss her, pouring all my love into it, showing her how much I missed her too. She responds with equal enthusiasm, her hands fisting in my shirt as she pulls me inside and upstairs to the second-floor guest room.

We stumble inside, shedding clothes as we go. Her top goes first so that I can lick those pert little nipples. While I do that, she unbuckles my belt. As soon as her fingertips graze my cock, I growl and shove her back onto the bed, ripping the tiny shorts off of her. I likewise tear off my shirt.

Looking down at her naked and gorgeous, I wish I had the patience to worship every inch of her body slowly. But something about our reunion, even after such a short time, has me desperate for her.

"Fuck me, Greg," Joanie demands, obviously right there with me.

Her words travel through me, making me impossibly hard for her. So much so that I can't be bothered to finish undressing. Instead, I shove inside her, hard and fast. I lean in so I can take her mouth as I take her pussy.

"I love you," I tell her as I move inside her. "God, I love you so fucking much."

"I love you too," she gasps, arching into me. She scrapes her fingernails down my back, and my cock pulses.

"Fuck," I groan. She grins and does it again. Something about the sharp pain contrasted against her tight heat wrapped around my cock has me ready to explode. "If you keep doing that, I'm going to come inside you, baby." A small gasp escapes her, and her pupils dilate. I raise an eyebrow. "You want that?" She nods desperately. "You want me to come in your tight little pussy?" Joanie groans and spasms around me as her orgasm crashes into her impossibly fast. I barely have time to mentally take note that the dirty talk makes her squeeze my cock harder than ever before I'm doing exactly what I promised.

Joanie's final moan in my ear is another "I love you." My vision blurs as we come apart together and are forever remade with pieces of each other.

We lay tangled together, basking in the afterglow, our newly declared feelings, and the fantastic sex that went with it.

"Shit," I curse, panting into her neck. I place a gentle kiss on her clavicle. "That was different."

Joanie tilts her pelvis into me, and my cock twitches in response. "It was," she agrees with a giggle. "I'm going to need more of that seriously sexy dirty talk."

"Yeah? Like how? You want me to tell you what a good girl you are?" I tease, pumping gently, setting her shivering under me.

"God, no," she groans, wiggling her hips. "I want you to tell me I'm your naughty girl. Your dirty, naughty little whore."

My balls tighten, and my cock thickens. "Fuck, Joanie, you're making me hard again already," I warn her.

She flicks her hips. "Good. Fuck that cum into me harder then," she challenges.

My breath catches, and arousal shoots through me like fire. I haven't gotten hard this fast again so often since I was a teenager. But this woman …

I work my hips, giving her a small taste. "Like that?" She nods. "You want me to fuck you with both of our cum all over us?" She groans and tips her head back. "You want me to get harder and harder and fuck your dirty little cunt until it's covered in me, baby?"

"Oh fuck, yes, God, yes," she groans, arching so her tits push up. I hitch back to free my hands and grab both nipples, tweaking hard so she gasps and bucks on my cock, bringing me back to full mast. Our centers are still joined but slippery with cum and her fresh arousal. It's next-level hot.

"Then brace yourself, baby." I grab her hips hard. "Because I'm going to fuck you like the dirty little slut you are. My dirty little slut."

I've never spoken to a woman this way during sex — or ever — but somehow, it's the biggest turn-on of my life. And as I pound her beneath me, the keening moans coming out of her tell me it's working for her, too. I continue to pour out a filthy stream of encouragement until I'm coming so hard I can barely stay upright, until Joanie's moans take a sharp turn into "dear God, someone's murdering her in there," and she comes so hard on my cock that I see stars as I empty into her once more.

"Jesus fucking Christ, Greg," Joanie screams as she convulses under me. "God, baby, yes, fuck, yes."

I cover her body with mine, the pace of our bodies colliding slowing as our orgasms fade. Sticky, sweaty, messy, and unbelievably sated, I cover her lips with mine as she wraps her legs around me.

"I love you, Joanie," I say softly onto her lips. "I'm crazy, recklessly in love with you."

Joanie giggles and presses a gentle kiss to my lips. "I love you too, Gary."

I pull my head back to give her a look of incredulity, but I can't maintain it, and we both burst out laughing.

"Oh good, you're done fucking," Mia's voice calls from downstairs. "Next time, close the damn door."

The admonition makes us pause for a split second before we laugh again.

"Payback's a bitch!" Joanie calls loudly to Mia.

Unfortunately, she yelled so loud it took ab muscles, so it pushed my cock, and everything else, out of her. I look down between us and back up at her with a smirk.

"Shower for my dirty girl?" I ask teasingly.

She grins and nods. "Definitely in order. But maybe after that, we can go to your place," she suggests.

My eyes darken at the idea of having her back in my bed. "A quick shower, then."

After a night filled with more dirty talk and dirty sex than I've ever had in my entire life, I, unfortunately, have to go into the community center for some scheduled training sessions. But I can't bear the thought of being far from Joanie, so I ask her to come with me.

But when my aunt and uncle barge in between appointments, I realize that was a huge mistake.

"You bitch!" my aunt screams, pointing at Joanie. "Our baby is in *jail* because of your lies! We're going to have you arrested for filing a false report!"

"And after you're done serving your time, we'll be suing you for defamation!" my uncle adds, his face purple with rage. "How *dare* you?"

Before I can even react, my aunt is in front of Joanie, shoving her. Joanie stumbles back, shock on her face.

And just like that, I see red, which snaps me out of my shock. I step between them, forcibly moving my aunt away. "Are you fucking kidding me? Get the hell out of here," I snarl. "Before I call the cops on *you* for assault." I advance on them, forcing them back toward the door as they continue to hurl insults at Joanie.

"This isn't over," my uncle threatens as I push the door closed behind them. "You'll pay for this!"

I turn to Joanie, and in a few long strides, I'm cupping her face in my hands, my eyes searching her for any physical damage. "Are you okay?"

She nods, but I can see she's shaken. I am, too, honestly. That all happened so fast. "I'm fine," she assures me. "I just … I'm a little blindsided."

"Me too," I admit. "On the bright side, it sounds like Ned was arrested, so there's that. Still, let's report this."

Joanie's shoulders rise as she steels herself, and her shaking stops. "I agree. Let's go down to the sheriff's office. And then I guess it's back to the County Clerk's office on Monday." She presses her lips together grimly.

My brow furrows in confusion. "Why?"

"To file an order of protection against Ned *and* his parents." She squeezes my hand. "Just to be careful."

My chest aches in both a good and bad way. Bad because this whole thing with Ned just took an even more fucked-up turn. Good because somehow she's managing to show me that even in a shitty situation, she wants to reassure me that she heard me, that she's trying.

I pull her into my arms and stroke her hair. "Thank you," I murmur. She wraps her arms around me and rests her head on my chest. For a brief moment, the world stops, and there is no Ned, no bullshit with my father, nothing standing between Joanie and me. It's just us. It feels so fucking good that I never want to let go.

Still, I have to, so we close the center and head to the sheriff's office, where we give our statements. Joanie mentions the orders of protection. Given their history, I mention that I doubt they'll care about a piece of paper. The officer assures us it's a good idea to have everything on record.

When we return to Alpine Ridge, we stop at the bakery so Joanie can tell Mia what's happening if she hasn't already heard.

But as soon as we walk in, I know she has. Mia removes her apron and darts around the counter to envelop Joanie in a hug.

"Are you guys okay? We heard Ned was arrested last night. And that his parents were seen outside the community center this morning."

Joanie rolls her eyes, presumably at the speed and accuracy of the rumor mill around here.

"We're fine. His mom just had some choice words for me. And a good, hard shove."

Mia pales. "Oh no. Did you shove back?"

Joanie smirks. "I would've if I weren't so fucking surprised to see them. We didn't even know Ned had been officially arrested."

Mia smirks in return. "Maybe if you guys hadn't been so *busy* ..."

From behind the counter, Rae coughs to cover her laugh.

A small blond woman sitting at one of the small tables on the other side of the bakery hesitantly approaches.

"Excuse me, are you the one who reported Ned Tyler for assault?" she asks.

Joanie nods. "Yes, that's me."

The woman takes a deep breath. "I just wanted to say thank you. And that ... he assaulted me, too. A few months ago. I was too scared to say anything then, but hearing about what he did to you ... I filed a report this morning."

Joanie's eyes widen. "I'm so sorry that happened to you. But thank you for coming forward now."

The woman gives a small smile. "Of course. Everyone knows his parents always get him off the hook, and I don't want to see that happen this time. I hope he gets what he deserves and isn't allowed to hurt anyone else."

"I hope that too. I'm Joanie, by the way," she offers, holding out a hand.

"Meg," the other woman responds shyly, shaking it. "Guess I'll see you around?"

Joanie nods, and Meg waves goodbye to Rae before heading out.

Once she's gone, Rae clears her throat. "She's not the only one," she says quietly. "Lots of other women have come to me, telling me Ned assaulted or harassed them too. I encouraged them all to file reports."

We're all silent for a moment, processing the enormity of the situation. The phrase "lots of other women" loops through my mind, and my stomach churns with anger and disgust.

"At least they're speaking up now," Mia finally says. "With more victims coming forward, there's no way Ned's getting out of this."

"He better not," I say through gritted teeth. The thought of what he's done to Joanie and so many others makes me want to bring a world of hurt down on his shoulders. But Joanie is right again; I need to let the law handle this. And trust that justice will be served. And if it's not, then I'm sure Nate can help me find a suitable place to bury his body where no one will ever find it.

That idea shouldn't give me so much satisfaction.

I wrap my arm around Joanie, holding her close. "You're amazing, you know that?" I murmur. "Your bravery, your strength in all this ... I'm in awe of you."

She leans into me. "I couldn't do it without you," she says softly, then looks around. "Any of you. Knowing you've all got my back —"

"We've got each other's backs," Nate corrects from the doorway, where apparently he'd been leaning. "I came in when Meg went out, so I caught the gist," he adds with a wink. Mia goes to him, and he wraps her in his arms.

I press a kiss to Joanie's temple. "Come on, guys," I say, trying to inject a lighter energy into the room. "It's Saturday night. Let's go blow off some steam."

"But I made a roast back at the house," Mia objects, looking stricken.

Nate and Joanie laugh. "Sounds like a party to me," Joanie responds.

"Ooh, and we can play Scrabble," Mia adds excitedly.

"I'm not playing Scrabble with this guy," I say, gesturing at Nate. "He's a fucking doctor. He knows way too many big words."

Nate's answering grin makes me chuckle, but Joanie pipes up. "Um, lawyers," she says, pointing between her and Mia. "I think we can take him."

Mia shakes her head. "Trust me, we can't."

Rae folds up her apron and walks around the counter. "I'm willing to give it a shot."

All four of us turn to her with raised eyebrows. Joanie gives her an appraising look. "My money's on Rae. That voice of hers came out of nowhere for me, too, so I'm betting she's got some other mad skills she's hiding."

Now it's Rae's turn to wink, and we all laugh.

"Bring it on," Nate says, rubbing his hands together. "You bringing some pastries home, babe?"

Mia rolls her eyes and trudges into the back.

"We'll meet you guys there, okay?" I pipe up. Nate nods, and we wave goodbye.

When we get out into the cold, fading afternoon, I press Joanie up against the passenger side of my truck.

"I meant what I said in there. You amaze me, city girl."

She grins up at me, trailing a finger down my chest. "You haven't seen anything yet."

I shake my head and smile down at her. "I love you, Joanie. Exactly as you are. And I'm so damn proud to be yours."

She tilts her face up to mine. "I love you too, mountain man. More than I ever thought possible."

I lean in and kiss her, not holding back. Our tongues meet, and I groan into her mouth. And as I lose myself in her kiss, I know that whatever comes next, we'll face it together. Through all this, I realize she's not just my love; she's so much more. For the first time, I'm picturing what it would be like to share my life with someone. To grow old together.

Despite all this drama, I want to be with this woman. To protect her. To take care of her. Despite all the obstacles that have been thrown our way. Because a love like this? It's worth fighting for.

⚔

I'm there for Joanie when she tackles the next obstacle first thing Monday morning at the County Clerk's office. She files the protection order and is informed that she'll be on the docket this afternoon. When she comments on how quickly she'll get in, the clerk shares that Ned's arraignment will immediately follow her appointment in a courtroom across the hall. In case we're interested in attending that as well.

Obviously, we are.

Given that information, I'm much less surprised when neither Ned nor his parents personally appear at the protection order hearing and instead are represented by an attorney. Probably not even their main attorney, as Joanie speculates they'll be helping Ned prepare for his arraignment.

But the protection orders are a slam dunk either way. With the evidence and our statements, Joanie is granted temporary protection orders against Ned and my aunt, given that they both assaulted her, even though Joanie has declined to press charges against my aunt. Since my uncle didn't touch her and didn't make direct threats of bodily harm, that order is denied. The temporary orders will be in place until a hearing they schedule for next Wednesday to make the orders permanent.

It goes so quickly that we have to wait a few minutes before entering the courtroom across the hall.

When we're allowed in, Joanie sits toward the back to avoid notice, and I sit beside her, wrapping an arm around her protectively.

"Why didn't they tell you the arraignment was today?" I ask in a hushed tone.

She shakes her head. "They'd only bring me in if they needed me for the pre-trial hearing. Given the mounting evidence against him, I doubt they will."

I open my mouth to ask another question, but the judge calls the matter to order.

276

My eyes scan the front and land on Ned's greasy head next to an older gentleman, who I presume is his lawyer, with my aunt and uncle seated behind him.

"Are you supposed to be in the same room with them, given the protection orders?" I can't help asking quietly.

Joanie smirks at me and points to the heavily armed bailiff. "I think we're good," she murmurs.

We listen as the judge reads the list of charges against Ned. It's a whole fuckload longer than I thought it would be and is filled with legal jargon, not all of which I understand. But I catch "sexual assault," and I'm floored when the judge lists crimes against minors. One look at Joanie's face tells me there's more going on here than just the charges she filed. When the judge is done, he asks Ned to enter an official plea.

His lawyer stands. "My client pleads not guilty, your honor."

My mouth opens to protest, but Joanie immediately shuts me down with a look. "That's standard procedure," she says soothingly. "Don't worry."

They move on to reviewing bail, and I'm pleasantly surprised when the judge denies Ned bail. But again, looking at Joanie's deep frown, I know there's something else I'm missing here. Once they set the pre-trial hearing for this Thursday, Joanie grabs me and quietly pulls me out of the courtroom.

"Based on the look on your face, I'm going to guess Ned is in some deep shit?" I hazard as we head back to the car.

"Deep, *deep* shit," she confirms. "The good news is, he's likely to go away until he's a very old man. Going after women was bad enough. But Federal charges for involvement in the sexual exploitation and assault of minors ... that's one of the deepest levels of shit there is."

My jaw drops. "I'm sorry, he did what now?" Minors. The words rattle through my head, and my stomach turns. Not even knowing exactly what she means by that, I'm already disgusted by the thought that I could ever be related to someone who would hurt kids.

Joanie stops at the car and turns to face me. "On top of drugging and raping both adult and minor females, they're accusing him of being involved with criminals that sell kids for sex." My jaw drops even further, and she holds up a hand. "I doubt he's *that* dumb. Or that far gone, as it were. But who knows? Anyway, my guess is he used their services, and, in turn, the legal system is using him to flush out the people behind that operation."

Fuck. Holy fuck. Holy fucking shit fuck. I take a long, deep breath as I process that. The depth of his depravity is ... astounding. That his parents have denied and covered up his behavior all these years has clearly only fed his sick nature. This is exactly the kind of thing I've been worried might have been going on. Still, now that he's been caught, there's an end in sight. And I'll focus on that so I don't beat myself up over what I should've done sooner. As the shock passes, Joanie's words sink in.

"They're trying to scare him into taking a deal," I realize out loud.

"Bingo," Joanie confirms. "Even if he's not involved with organizing it, for them to find evidence that fast that he was involved ..." Her face takes on an uncharacteristically furious look. "However that went down, he deserves whatever he's got coming to him."

"Well, now I'm doubly glad they denied him bail," I murmur angrily.

She shakes her head grimly. "Can't have him alerting anyone. Or assaulting anyone else." We share a heavy look.

"Come on," I say, opening the passenger door for her. "Let's go home."

One side of her lips tips up ever so slightly, but I can tell it will be a while until the clouds that have formed over her break up — probably not until at least after the pretrial hearing in three days. It's a feeling I understand. I've long felt responsible for him knowing he was a creep — even if I didn't know exactly how much of one — and not being able to do a damn thing about it.

Unfortunately, when Joanie contacts the court for the exact time and location, she's told it's a closed hearing. Which means we won't know what goes down until after the fact. Joanie doesn't seem surprised. I guess I shouldn't have been either, given her suspicions. There are some serious stakes here, and I can see how sensitive information might come out that they'd want to keep a lid on.

But we don't talk about it. We don't talk about much. Joanie seems withdrawn, and God knows I've got enough on my mind between keeping momentum at the community center and surreptitiously researching my luxury town idea. It's slow going, with intrusive thoughts of Ned getting off the hook breaking through constantly.

I can tell Joanie is anxious, though. And God knows I am, too. Everyone wants to see Ned go away for a long time so he can't continue terrorizing the women of Alpine Ridge. He likely will, though the waiting and anticipation leave plenty of room for doubt.

Finally, Thursday, the pre-trial hearing day, arrives. If the past three days have felt long, it's nothing on waiting out the day for news. But we don't hear anything. Well, not until Friday anyway, when someone from the sheriff's office calls.

Joanie answers and listens intently for a few minutes, asking very few questions that don't reveal anything. Her face is blank when she hangs up.

Her shoulders sag with either relief or despair.

"Ned has accepted a plea bargain. He'll be held at the county jail until he's transferred to federal prison in a few weeks. And that he'll be in for a minimum of twenty-five years." She huffs a wry laugh as tears start to spill down her cheeks.

It was relief. Definitely relief. She climbs into my lap and wraps herself around me. I hold her tight.

"Thank God," I murmur, squeezing her against me. "Thank fucking God."

CHAPTER TWENTY

JOANIE

As news of Ned's sentencing spreads through Alpine Ridge, a collective sigh of relief seems to wash over the town. The dark cloud over us all dissipates, and life feels normal again. Better than usual, even.

I'm further bolstered by the finalization of the protective orders against Ned and Greg's aunt and the news that the initial boundary review meeting for the incorporation will be held at the end of the month. Things are moving forward on all fronts, and I can't help but feel a sense of excitement and possibility.

My relationship with Greg is blossoming, too. Today, Valentine's Day, he surprised me by taking the day off and suggesting we hike back to our special lake. The weather is still brisk, but the sun shines, and the snow sparkles like diamonds as we make our way through the pristine wilderness.

When we arrive at the lake, Greg pulls out a picnic basket he'd stashed in his backpack. He spreads a blanket, and we settle down, enjoying the sandwiches, fruit, and chocolates he packed.

I can't help but reflect on how we got here as we eat. And there's still a question I haven't had the courage to ask until now.

"So, about that whole thing where you were planning to marry your ex," I say, trying to sound casual.

Greg smirks. "What about it?"

I shrug nonchalantly. "Is that something you want? Marriage, I mean?"

Greg takes a moment to consider. "Honestly, I've never felt strongly about it one way or the other. I'm not against the idea, but it's never been a driving force for me. I think I only discussed it with Hailey because I knew she wanted it, and my parents were all for it. What about you?"

I lean back on my elbows, looking out over the serene water. "I never thought I'd find someone I wanted to marry," I admit. "I always figured I'd be the perpetual bachelorette, married to my career. That was the plan, anyway."

Greg's eyes meet mine, a hint of a smile playing at his lips. "And now?"

I bite my lip, feeling suddenly shy. "Now ... I can see myself being swayed toward it. If the timing was right."

His smile widens, but he doesn't press further. Instead, he asks, "Since we're on heavier topics, what about having kids? Is that something you've ever considered?"

"I'm open to it," I reply slowly. "But again, it's not something I've yearned for. I guess I've always been a bit ambivalent about the whole motherhood thing."

"I get that. It's a big deal," Greg says. "And it's funny that even though I've never cared much about marriage, I've always known I want kids someday. "

I let his words roll around in my mind for a few minutes. "I don't think deciding to have kids is something you should do to please someone else," I finally say. "If I had them, it would be because I wanted them too. Would it be a deal breaker if I never felt that way?"

Greg licks his lips and leans back. "That's a good question," he replies, his eyes scanning the towering evergreens on the opposite side of the lake. "I honestly don't know." He pauses before meeting my eyes. "When you asked me that just now, all I could picture was a little girl with your face. Your sass. And how much she'd have me wrapped around her little finger."

Oh fuck me, my uterus just did a little somersault. Who knew that was a thing? But picturing Greg as daddy to a little girl ... holy shit, I'm so screwed. He'd be a fantastic father, of course.

Then, the idea of a little boy with Greg's curls and bright blue eyes pops into my head. I nearly faint at the thought of contending with two beautiful men who take my breath away. Albeit in very different ways, of course.

"Fucking, hell, mountain man, don't say things like that," I reply in a husky voice I don't recognize.

Greg grins mischievously in response. "Sorry?"

I fan myself. "You should be. It's all I can do not to jump you so we can start making beautiful babies right now."

Greg tips his head back and laughs. "So obviously, you could be convinced. Noted." His tone is so smug and *male*. It should make me angry, but it makes me even more soaking wet.

Down, Bev. Down. Since we're neck deep into the heavy stuff, as he said, I have one more for him before I get to tearing off his clothes.

"There's something else we should probably talk about," I venture, picking at the edge of the blanket. "I'm a city girl, Greg. And you love the mountains. How do we make that work long-term?"

Greg reaches over and takes my hand, lacing his fingers through mine. "I've thought about that," he says. "And the way I see it, we have homes in both places. We can split our time and travel back and forth. Oh, and speaking of travel, I've always wished I had done more of that. I'd love to explore the world with you, Joanie."

Jesus H. Roosevelt Fucking Christ. If he gets any more perfect, I might lose my mind.

"I love to travel," I tell him, even though it's something I'm pretty sure he already knows. "There are so many places I want to go. And so many places I've been that I'd love to show you."

"I could deal with that. I think I play it a bit too safe most of the time. I could use a dose of patented Joanie recklessness to liven things up," he says with a chuckle.

I raise an eyebrow at him. "Oh yeah?" I rise to my feet, taking off my jacket. "I think I can bring some of that to you right here, right now. Didn't you say something about skinny dipping here?" I lift my sweater off and toss it at his feet.

"Are you serious?" Greg asks, laughing.

I unclasp my bra and throw it on top of my sweater. "Does that answer your question?" I tease, starting to shimmy out of my fleece-lined leggings, turning so he gets a view of my bare ass. "Come on, mountain man. Live a little."

I look back to see him stripping and grin. "Let's do this, baby," he agrees, racing past me. Hot on his heels, I follow him in.

We both yelp as we plunge into the icy water, but the exhilaration is worth it. The cold makes me feel alive in a way I've never experienced before.

Greg ducks under the water, and I follow. My lungs seize from the cold, and I come back up spluttering. Nope. I was wrong. The cold is going to kill me.

"Okay, okay, this was a horrible idea!" I shriek, laughing as I race back to the shore.

Greg follows, cackling at my sudden change of heart. Dripping wet and shivering, he pulls another blanket out of his pack and wraps us in it, and we settle back onto the picnic blanket.

His hands rub up and down my arms. "Skin to skin, baby, that'll warm you right back up," he murmurs. His hot breath on my neck and the shell of my ear sends a different sort of shiver through me.

My hands skate down his back as I wrap my legs around him. My core grazes his cock, and Bev weeps with happiness.

"Fuck, city girl, how are you so hot and wet after that?" he groans.

I grind against him. "What can I say? Bev loves you."

Greg's head pulls back, and he gives me a bemused look. "Bev?"

I raise an eyebrow. "My beaver?" I say with a very "duh" tone.

Greg's head tips back as he lets out a deep, loud laugh so full of joy and amusement that I'm soon laughing with him. The shaking does interesting things to Bev *and* his cock. Soon, our laughs dissolve into kisses. And as the heat builds between us, Greg slips inside me. I'm so wet that he slides in to the hilt before I realize, stretching me pleasurably.

"God, yes," I breathe.

Greg's lips trail up my neck, and he takes my mouth with his as he tilts his hips to drive in and out of me gently. "That good, baby?"

I swirl my hips with him, the soft strokes stimulating in a way I've never experienced before. The press of his chest against mine, our hearts beating in tandem, is almost overwhelming. "So good," I agree.

His lips gently pry mine open, his tongue stroking against mine. Greg runs his fingers down my back as his cock slides deeply and firmly inside me. The tight fit of him against me has my clit rubbing the base of his cock with every push. My orgasm builds inch by inch as our bodies stay locked together. I can't help the low moans that slip out of me.

"Damn, Joanie, how is making love to you just as good as fucking you senseless?" Greg whispers in my ear.

My core tightens, and I arch into him, pushing him deeper inside. It takes him a fraction of a second to realize he should keep talking.

"Your pussy feels so good around me, baby," he continues. "So wet for me. So beautiful. You're beautiful." He kisses under my ear as he gradually ramps up his pace. "Hearing how much pleasure I give you? Such a fucking turn-on." He pumps harder, and I groan.

"Yes, just like that. I want to hear you come on my cock. I want to love you until you come apart and squeeze me, baby. Ride me, Joanie. You own this dick. You own me."

I buck my hips hard at his sweet, dirty words. I look into his eyes as I chase my orgasm. The love and lust in them nearly undoes me. "You're mine," I tell him.

He nods and bites my bottom lip, sweeping his tongue into my mouth. "Ride me like I'm yours. Because I am. Every fucking inch of that cock is yours." He reaches a hand down and squeezes my breast gently, flicking his thumb over my nipple. "Every inch of my body is yours. Take it, Joanie." He tilts his hips faster to meet mine. My breaths turn shallow and rapid, and I feel myself hanging on the edge. "I love you, Joanie Morris. You're all mine." He punctuates his words with thrusts, and I'm a goner, tumbling into ecstasy. And he tumbles with me, moaning and biting my shoulder gently as he comes apart with me.

Afterward, as we lay tangled together, Greg strokes my hair and says softly, "I meant every word, you know. I can't imagine my future without you in it. I love you more than I've ever loved anyone."

Tears prick at my eyes, and I bury my face in his chest. "I love you too, Greg. So much it scares me sometimes." I look up into his eyes, deciding to let him see the love and fear in mine. "But you know that never stops me."

He chuckles and kisses my forehead tenderly. "Good. Because I want you to move in with me," he says. "I know you have to go back to Seattle at some point, and I understand that. But I want my home to be yours whenever you're in Alpine Ridge. It feels empty now when you're not there." He strokes a thumb over my cheek as he looks into my eyes.

I swallow hard, emotion clogging my throat as I envision nights spent fucking this man in every way possible. Mornings in his arms. And so much more in between.

"Okay," I agree. "Yes. I want that, too."

Greg's answering grin crinkles the corners of his eyes, and we seal it with a kiss. Amazingly, I'm not even a little bit afraid. Instead, I feel a sense of rightness settle over me. I'm not running from commitment for the first time in my life. I'm running toward a future with this incredible man by my side. It's like winning a big court case, Christmas morning, and a dozen orgasms all rolled up into one amazing feeling.

The high of it lasts the whole hike back. The time is filled with laughter and stolen kisses, our hearts light and full of love. And as we make our way down the trail, hand in hand, I can't help but marvel at how much has changed in such a short time.

When I first came to Alpine Ridge, I was adrift — wondering what was next after escaping the confines of my crappy job, unsure of my next steps. But now? Now I have a purpose, a passion project in helping to incorporate the town. I have friends who have become like family. Most importantly, I have Greg.

My mountain man. My partner in every sense of the word. That idea would've had me running for the hills just months ago.

But now?

Together, we're building something beautiful. A life that blends both of our worlds, celebrates our differences, and strengthens us both. And damn if that doesn't feel like hope.

As we return to his truck, I squeeze Greg's hand and smile at him. "Thank you," I say softly.

"For what?" he asks, cocking his head.

"For being you. For loving me. For showing me what it means to truly belong somewhere."

He pulls me into his arms. "You never have to thank me for that, Joanie. You deserve it and so much more."

I bury my face in his chest, breathing him in. And for once, I don't feel the urge to run or push him away. For once, I'm exactly where I'm meant to be.

I know there will be challenges. The incorporation process will be long and complicated. I'll have to figure out how to balance my time between Alpine Ridge and Seattle since there isn't a permanent, full-time job for me here, and my condo and parents are there. Greg and I will undoubtedly have our share of ups and downs as we navigate this new phase of our relationship. Because let's face it, even though I'm in this, I still come with heaps of drama.

But I'm not afraid anymore. Because I know that whatever comes our way, we'll face it together.

Alpine Ridge is more than just a quaint mountain town to me now. It's where I found myself and learned to open my heart and take a chance on love.

It's the place that finally feels like home.

God, Mia is going to flip. The thought makes me laugh, and Greg looks at me as we climb into the truck.

"What?" he asks curiously.

I shake my head as he starts the engine and navigates back onto the road home. "I was just thinking about Mia."

Greg cocks an eyebrow. "And?"

"She's not going to believe that I, of all people, fell in love with this place too."

His hand reaches over and wraps around mine. "Why not?"

I run my thumb over the back of his hand. "Oh sweet, innocent, Greg," I tease. "I've spent years jumping around, doing whatever and whoever struck my fancy." He frowns jokingly, and I laugh. "I agreed to spend the holidays in a tiny mountain town, assuming I'd have a sexy romp in the snow with the hottest man I could find before going back to my selfish little world. And here I am, planning a future with said hottest man in said town." I shake my head. "You came out of nowhere and turned my world upside down, mountain man."

A grin spreads slowly over Greg's face. "You know you love it, though."

I tip my head back and laugh, squeezing his hand.

"Yes, I do. Take me home, Greg."

This time, when he turns to look at me, there's no teasing. His face is serious, his eyes brimming with heat. "Say it again."

I grin. "Take me back to our home, mountain man, and make love to me all night long," I croon teasingly.

Greg gives an exaggerated shiver. "With pleasure."

CHAPTER TWENTY-ONE

GREG

The news that Ned has officially reported to prison brings a sense of closure, and I find myself breathing a little easier. With one major hurdle behind us, Joanie and I focus on the next challenge: the initial boundary review meeting.

The meeting is held at the Central Washington University student union in Ellensburg, and as we walk in, I can't help grumbling. "They could've handled this at the community center. We only have a few hundred people here."

I'm sure the large ballroom is great for functions, but the rows upon rows of chairs aren't close to filled.

Joanie gives me a wry look. "The county has to account for a certain percentage of the town being able to attend, even if they don't show up."

I huff out a breath and nod, conceding her point. As we take our seats, I scan the room, and my gaze lands on my father. He's sitting quietly, not speaking to anyone. My chest tightens, knowing he can't be up to anything good.

The meeting itself goes smoothly. The county official presents the proposed boundaries, fields questions, and opens the floor for public comments. Surprisingly, very few people speak up, and we wrap up in under an hour. I should've known it went too smoothly because as everyone files out, my father approaches me. "Gregory, may I have a word in private?"

I exchange a glance with Joanie before nodding reluctantly. "Fine," I say tersely to my father. And then to Joanie, "I'll meet you outside in a minute, baby."

She gives me a supportive wink and squeeze of the ass before leaving. I chuckle as I watch her go before turning back to my father. Who looks like he just sucked on a lemon.

And with no preamble whatsoever, my father hands me a thick envelope. "I think you should take a look at this. It's about your ... *girlfriend*."

Frowning, I ignore the disdain in his voice when referring to Joanie and open the envelope, perusing its contents. My stomach drops as I do. It's evidence that

Joanie had an affair with one of her former law firm's managing partners and was using it to blackmail him for a promotion and other perks. Text message conversations, emails, performance reviews, and even a few photographs of Joanie looking flirty and touching an older, albeit not unattractive, man.

"Where did you get this?" I ask, my voice tight.

"Since your girlfriend made such an … interesting impression at our first meeting, once I heard she was spearheading the town's incorporation and that you two have been seen about town looking rather cozy, I took it upon myself to learn a bit more about the woman my son was getting into bed with. Literally and figuratively, as it were. Luckily, my attorney knows one of the other managing partners at the firm she worked for," he explains. "Listen carefully, Gregory. If you do not end this relationship with her and relinquish your interest in our joint property, her former firm and I will release this information to every law firm in Washington. She'll never work in law in this state again. I will not have you prancing about with a harlot while doing everything in your power to sink this family's legacy."

Anger surges through me, but I force myself to stay calm. "I'll look at the evidence and think about it," I say evenly, but even that amount of deference chafes against my pride. Still, I know my father, and he doesn't make idle threats.

My father nods, a smug smile on his face. He thinks he's won. But I know playing this card means he expects to lose his lawsuit against me. He's getting desperate. Still, if what he says is true, Joanie's career is now in my hands. As soon as my father walks away, I allow myself a moment to feel the despair that's already tearing me apart. But I pull it back together. I need to walk out of these doors and pretend everything is fine in front of Joanie until I can decide what I'll do next.

Back at home, I pour over the documents alone, searching for chinks in the story that's laid out in front of me, my mind racing. I'm upset, but I need to talk to Joanie about this. I don't want to believe it, but it's all laid out in black and white.

When I call her into the room, I can see that she wonders why I've been locked away in here. But when her eyes land on the documents spread over the desk, her face pales.

"Is that what was in the envelope your father gave you?" she asks gravely.

I nod. "Yes," I reply simply.

Her eyes turn glassy, and her shoulders rise with the deep breath she takes as she settles into the chair across from me. "I can explain."

"Please do," I say, gesturing for her to go ahead while trying to keep my voice neutral. "Because I don't want to believe this, but it's hard to ignore."

She takes another deep breath, but I can see her hands shaking. It hits me right in the gut. Even knowing she may have done these horrible things, my heart still reaches for her.

"When one of the managing partner's sons was promoted to junior partner, even though I'd been promised the position, I threatened to sue for gender discrimination. I'd been building a case against them for years, noticing patterns in their promotions. In response, they fabricated this story and evidence to discredit me if I ever proceeded with a lawsuit. They asked for my resignation."

I lean forward, listening intently as she continues. "Their story wouldn't stop the lawsuit, but it would ruin my reputation and prevent me from getting a job at any law firm in Western Washington. So I decided I didn't want to work there anymore. But instead of quietly resigning, I chose to have sex with the recently promoted son and get us both fired. A final 'fuck you' to the partners." She blinks her eyes and barks a harsh laugh. "The joke was on me because even though I've tried to pretend it never happened, it's been difficult to move on from. "

My brows jump. "How so?"

She rubs at her forehead. "I don't like to focus on the negative. I'm all about what's next, what I can do, not what I can't do. It takes a lot to keep me down, but after years of dealing with their shit … it just wore me out. And then they made up all this —" she gestures at the documents "— and I knew even if I could prove it wasn't true, the damage would be done by the time I could get anyone to listen. It made me hate the industry. Because this is how it is. Lies and fabrications and mind fuckery. They sure don't tell you about all that in law school, and it's why I was having such a hard time deciding what to do next with my life." She shakes her head like it doesn't matter, but I can see her breaking from here.

I gesture for her to come to me. With a sniff, she rises and rounds the desk. I pull her into my lap and wrap my arms around her. She rests her head on mine, and I kiss her neck where it meets her shoulder.

"I'm so sorry, Joanie. I'm sorry they mistreated you. I'm sorry they made up a pack of lies to keep you quiet. But I'm mostly sorry that I didn't instantly see this for the complete bullshit that it is," I apologize. I tilt my head up and look her in her ice-blue eyes. "And I'm sorry my father has gotten his hands on this information."

Joanie snorts. "Hey, I'm the one who called him powerless. I was practically baiting him to do something like this." She shakes her head, anger written in the tight lines around her mouth and eyes.

"This isn't your fault," I assure her. "But the fact remains that my father could destroy your career over this. So I think … as much as I hate to let him think he's won even for a moment, I think we should at least appear to break up for now. Just until I figure out what to do."

Joanie's eyes flash with hurt, but she nods. "You're probably right. Except about one thing."

I give her a half-hearted smirk. "What's that?"

She nuzzles into me and places a gentle kiss on my lips. "Until we figure out what to do."

I don't contradict her that this is my father, my battle to fight. Instead, I run my hands up and down her arms. "You need to be here for the incorporation. I have some ideas that I can look into in Seattle. I'll keep you in the loop as much as I can."

Joanie cups my face in her hands, looking deep into my eyes. "I'll go stay with Mia and Nate for a while."

"You can stay here while I'm gone if you want to," I assure her.

She shakes her head. "It'd make me miss you too much."

Overwhelmed with affection at her words, I lean in for another kiss, soaking her in, knowing that no matter what, I'm going to miss her like crazy.

"I'll spend the rest of the afternoon clearing my calendar for the next few weeks. And then I want to have you for dinner," I growl into her ear.

She arches against me, stroking a hand down the back of my head. I bury my face in her breasts and sigh.

"When will you leave?" she asks quietly.

I kiss her clavicle. "Tomorrow morning." Her chin rests on my head, and I wrap my arms around her. "This is just a bump in the road, baby. We'll get through this."

She slides off my lap and heads toward the door. She turns back from the doorway and smiles sadly. "I know." Her gaze drops to the desk. "Thanks for believing me."

I shake my head, angry at the idea that someone believing her is something to be grateful for like the alternative is even remotely acceptable. And again, I'm angry at myself for the small window of doubt my father's delivering this package instilled in me. I'm an asshole.

"You deserve all the faith in the world, Joanie. Believe that."

Once she's gone, I clear my schedule and put the documents back in their envelope to take to Seattle. Somehow, I'll figure this out. I just hope I do it before my father gets tired of waiting for my complete submission.

After making love to Joanie twice the next morning, it takes everything I've got to walk out the door, bag packed for fuck knows how long away from her. With a heavy heart, I start the trek, letting my mind sift through everything as I drive.

By the time I get to the house in Queen Anne, I don't have any brilliant ideas—save calling Sera and asking her advice. At the very least, she asked for updates on the property stuff, and it would be good to talk to someone about this.

I call her, and we arrange to meet for lunch near her office the next day. That done, I make up a bed and head to the grocery store. If I'm going to be here a while, I may as well get settled in.

The restaurant Sera wants to meet at near her office is in the heart of downtown Seattle, and it hasn't been long enough since my last trip for the stress of the city to leech entirely out of me. So it's even more overwhelming this time. It probably doesn't help that I'm already on high alert, given everything that's going on.

Once I step into the burger joint, the noise level falls considerably, and my shoulders drop from around my ears. The inside is done in the 1950s diner style, with bright colors and period-appropriate posters. It's cute, if not a little kitschy. And I'm a bit early, so I wait in the entryway until Sera breezes in a few minutes later, looking pretty in a khaki shirtdress.

"Hey, you," I greet her, going in for a hug.

She squeezes me briefly before putting me back at arm's length. "You look even more stressed out than before," she comments drily.

I give her a wry smile. "Thanks?"

A hostess leads us to a small booth, and we settle in.

"So, what's daddy dearest up to now?" Sera asks as she flips through her menu.

I snort. "I'm going to need beer for this conversation," I joke. Thankfully, the waiter shows up and takes our drink orders, bustling back with them before I can so much as take another breath.

"Well?" Sera asks after he takes our orders and rushes off again.

"He dug up some dirt on my girlfriend, Joanie, and threatened to kill her career with it if I don't stop seeing her and sign over my share of the property," I summarize succinctly, knowing Sera's fondness for getting to the point.

"Shit," she says. "What an asshole."

I chuckle. "Yep. Speaking of assholes, how's your mom doing?" I tease.

She rolls her eyes. "Don't even get me started," she grouses jokingly. She taps the table. "I did have an idea after our last meeting, though. I was going to hold onto it until the right time, and this seems like it."

I raise an eyebrow. "This I've got to hear."

"I'd like to buy you out of your interest in the property you own with your father," she replies.

Not that I had any idea what I expected her to say, but I'm still shocked by her suggestion. "Sera, I can't ask you to take that on. And I'm not even sure it would work that way ... legally, I mean."

She smiles. "I looked at your draft proposal and I've done my research. Your type of ownership allows you to sell your interest. I'll buy in and use cash to build facilities for the city, which I'll then lease to them. Once the initial city planning is done, I'll use the remaining land to build luxury retail and residential spaces to promote town growth. Your father won't see a penny, and if he's smart, he'll let me buy him out, too, which will be hard for him to turn down as I plan to make him a very generous offer. You won't have to fight him anymore, and the town wins."

"Sera ... I appreciate the thought, but I think I'm just going to give in and let him have the property. It's not worth fighting over, and I don't need to drag you into it."

"It's cute that you think that'll stop his reign of terror," she comments lightly. "You don't think he'll use full ownership of prime real estate in your new hometown to lord every little decision he makes over you? To terrorize you into doing exactly what he wants?"

I let out a frustrated growl because she's right. "Okay, fine, you may have a point."

Sera laughs. "Sorry. I understand wanting to fix things on your own. But you can lean on me, Greg. That's not weakness. That's what family *should* be for."

"Damn. I forgot what that's like," I say, breathing a sigh of relief. "Thank you, Sera. You're brilliant and amazing, and I'm forever in your debt. Yes, let's do it."

She beams at me. "Excellent. I'll start the paperwork. Full disclosure: I plan to clean up on that investment as Alpine Ridge grows, so don't worry, I win, too."

I shake my head and laugh. "I would hope so. It's an amazing plan and one only you could pull off. If you're sure, I'm in. Though I still don't know how I'm going to deal with what my dad's got on Joanie."

Sera tips her head to the side as our burgers arrive. "Tell me about it."

I take a huge bite of my bacon cheeseburger as I consider how to frame it. Then I remember who I'm talking to, and I just tell her about the firm's fabricated evidence to stop Joanie's discrimination lawsuit.

"Wow, they've got some seriously big balls," she says, irritation lacing her tone, her nose wrinkled in disgust. "But I have an idea on that too."

I huff a laugh and finish off my beer. "Well, aren't you a jack of all trades?"

She shakes her head before popping a ketchup-laden fry into her mouth. "Oh no, my idea is to point you at someone who will have real ideas." She swallows and takes a sip of water. "Remember I told you my husband owns a corporate security firm?"

My eyebrows pull together, but I nod. "Yeah, I remember."

She looks at me with a glint in her eye. "Trust me. Bryce will know exactly what to do." She whips out her phone and starts composing a text.

"Really?" I ask skeptically. "I thought his company protected other companies from spies and hackers, like he did for you."

She nods as she sends the message, setting her phone down and looking back up at me. "He does that. But they handle threats of all kinds, too. I'll put you in touch with his assistant so you can get the packet your dad gave you to him. He'll let you know if he needs anything from there."

I push out a breath. "I don't know what I did to deserve all this help, but you have no idea how much I appreciate it," I assure her.

Sera nods sagely. "Been there. And I wouldn't be here to help you if I hadn't had help, too. So just say thank you and take it, Tyler," she teases.

I laugh unreservedly. "Thanks, Sera. You're the best."

She winks at me. "I know. Now, that was a good burger, but how do you feel about coconut cream pie?"

I spend the next couple of weeks waiting for Sera's husband to do his thing. But thanks to Sera, I walk to the Dahlia Bakery daily for a coconut cream pie. Because damn, those things are good. She offers to take me on a chocolate walking tour that's offered downtown, but I decline. It's bad enough that I don't have access to the community center gym right now. I have to be extra purposeful about cardio and strength training, and even then, I'm getting creative since I don't have any equipment with me.

Joanie and I talked every night for the first few nights, but it started to get difficult to be so far from her and with nothing new to report, so we talked less frequently as the days passed.

The only day this week we've talked was Monday after Sera had me sign the ownership transfer paperwork. The relief I felt was real, and Joanie and I had some seriously hot phone sex that night. But right after, she asked me to come home. And I had to tell her I couldn't. I could tell she was upset, but there wasn't much to be done about it. So, I promised to call again when there was something to share. It's been radio silence from us both since. Me, because I didn't have anything to report. Her … well, she's probably busy, but I also know it's probably mostly because she's upset. Hopefully less at me and more just at the situation, but it still leaves me on edge.

Finally, Bryce's assistant calls asking me to come in the next day. I was starting to get antsy given that St. Patrick's Day is two days away, and last I spoke to Joanie, they were full steam ahead on organizing an event as a cover to get signatures for the incorporation petition. I've used that to convince myself she's been too busy to call. Either way, I miss her like crazy, and I was hoping I could be there.

So I'm glad to finally get moving again on solving this last sticky issue. I'm taken aback as I walk into Sera's husband's office. Bryce, with his height and muscles, reminds me so much of Nate, save Bryce's hair, which is short and chestnut brown instead of tawny, and his eyes, which are blue, not hazel. But they both have that intimidating air. And suddenly, strangely, I miss Nate too.

Though to be fair, dressed in crisp khakis and a light blue button-front shirt, Bryce is much better dressed than Nate usually is. I fight a smirk at the thought and extend my hand.

"You must be Greg," he greets me. "Nice to meet you."

"Nice to meet you, too, Bryce. Sera has told me a lot of good things about you," I say.

"She's my biggest fan," he jokes. "And obviously, she's told me things about you. Including the threats your father's made against your girlfriend."

I huff a sharp sigh and shake my head. "Yes, unfortunately. I'm sure she's also told you it was part of his bid to regain complete control of the family property. Thankfully, your amazing wife was able to help me with that."

"Sera's good at what she does," he replies with a glint in his eye. "And luckily, so am I."

My brows raise. "You've got something? Already?"

"Oh, I've got what we need," he assures me. "And while sharing the details with you would be unethical, let's just say it didn't take much digging to find evidence of serious misconduct by Joanie's former employers that is related to the evidence they fabricated. And that releasing said fabricated evidence would also end up revealing their indiscretions."

I choke down a laugh. "You're going to blackmail them right back?" I ask incredulously.

Bryce contemplates that for a moment. "Strictly speaking, it isn't blackmail. I'm simply pointing out to them that if they choose to disseminate false information about former employees, they will inadvertently be drawing attention to other information that *isn't* false. You'd have to look closely, but it's not hard to find. Thankfully, I'm under no legal obligation to report what I noticed, nor am I in any way guaranteeing it will never be revealed. Just not by me." He smirks.

And there's no better word for it: I'm gobsmacked. If Sera is a real estate whiz, this guy is her security counterpart. If what he's saying is true, it sounds like he knows the exact line he shouldn't cross and uses it fully to his advantage.

"Well, I'm glad you're on my side," I finally reply. "So what happens now?"

"The next step would be to approach the law firm."

I ruminate on that, but I'm still unsure since I don't know what information he has or if what he says is true; that this is all on the up and up.

"You're sure there's nothing illegal about this?"

Bryce leans back in his chair and crosses his legs. "I'm sure. I wouldn't risk my company, you, or Joanie," he assures me. Despite hardly knowing him, he's got a very confident, reassuring air about him, and it's hard not to trust him. Still …

"What would you do if you were in my shoes?" I ask.

"If it was Sera in this situation, there's nothing I wouldn't do to protect her," Bryce says without hesitation.

His words remind me that he's done exactly that in the past and that he's the reason my cousin is alive today. Moreover, he's right. There's nothing I wouldn't do to protect Joanie. So I nod resolutely. "Do it."

Bryce smiles sheepishly. "Would you be mad if I told you I already did?"

I can't help it; I burst out laughing. "Hell, no," I assure him. "Are you serious?"

He shrugs, grinning now. "It was time-sensitive, so I had to act fast."

"Damn," I say, shaking my head and laughing. "I'm guessing it went well then?"

Bryce dips his chin in agreement. "They've agreed to destroy all the false evidence against Joanie. The partner who gave the information to your father's attorney has warned him that if it ever gets out, they'll ruin him — their words. And just to be safe," Bryce adds, "I had the firm issue a public statement disclaiming any erroneous information about former employees that may have been leaked."

I lean back in my chair, scrubbing my hands over my face. "Holy shit," I say with a laugh. "I can't even begin to thank you enough, Bryce."

"I'm glad I was able to help," he replies sincerely.

"I'm just having trouble wrapping my head around this. It's over? Just like that?"

The corner of Bryce's mouth tips into a smile. "Well, there was some posturing and threatening, but … yes, pretty much just like that," he replies. "We take care of our clients, Greg. Especially ones that are related to my wife."

I chuckle. "Well, I'm grateful for that, but you haven't asked me to pay you anything yet, so am I really a client?" I point out.

Bryce grins. "Buy me a drink, and we're even."

"Right now?"

Bryce cocks his head to the side. "You know what? Yes. Right now. You game?"

I spread my arms and stand up. "Absolutely," I reply. How can I turn him down after that?

Over whisky, Bryce gets me talking about Joanie and encourages me to return to her as soon as possible.

"I'm afraid she's too mad at me," I confess. "She asked me to come back a few days ago, but I said I couldn't. I haven't heard from her since."

Bryce clasps my shoulder. "Life is short, Greg. Never let your woman forget how much you love her."

He's right. I've been an idiot. I've been aching to get back to Joanie; I just wasn't expecting things to wrap up so quickly here. But I'm more than ready to go back. I resolve to head back to Alpine Ridge first thing in the morning. I'll miss the St. Patrick's Day event, but Joanie will be busy anyway. Better to show up after and grovel for forgiveness.

As I settle into bed that night, my heart feels lighter than in weeks. The obstacles ahead don't seem so daunting anymore. I have a plan, allies, and, most importantly, Joanie.

I just hope she can forgive me for pushing her away, even if it was to protect her. I drift off to sleep, dreaming of her smile, her sass, and the feel of her in my arms.

Tomorrow, I'll make things right. Tomorrow, I'll remind her that she's my everything. My partner, my love, my future.

And come what may, I'll never let her doubt that again.

CHAPTER TWENTY-TWO

JOANIE

As Mia and I get ready to head to the town square for the St. Patrick's Day event, she's practically vibrating with excitement. At first, I assume it's just because of the event, but then she turns to me with a huge grin.

"Nate and I finally set a date for the wedding," she announces. "We're getting married on September twenty-third!"

I squeal and pull her into a tight hug. "Oh my God, Mia, that's amazing! I'm so happy for you both."

And I am. Truly. But as we pull apart and I see the pure joy on her face, I can't help the pang in my chest. It makes me miss Greg even more, seeing Mia and Nate blissfully in love and planning their future.

I push down the feeling and focus on the day ahead. We've got a lot to do, and I need to be on my A-game.

When we arrive at the town square, there is a flurry of activity. Mia heads to the pastry booth, where she sets out a mouth-watering array of shamrock cookies, Irish apple cakes, and soda bread. I'm running the costume contest with a gift basket for the best-dressed leprechaun. It's silly, but people seem to be getting into the spirit of things.

Ever the peacemaker, Nate has convinced Jerry to set up a booth serving green beer and limeade. I'm not sure how he managed that feat, but I'm impressed. Nate oversees the shamrock scavenger hunt in the field behind the community center, with kids and adults alike racing around, laughing and shouting.

And then there's Rae manning the all-important petition-signing booth. Beyond festivity, the whole point of this event is to gather those crucial signatures for the incorporation.

As the day goes on, I get swept up in the fun. There's something about the camaraderie, the laughter, the sense of community that warms me from the inside out. For a few hours, I almost forget the ache of missing Greg.

Toward the end of the event, Rae comes running over to us with a huge smile. "We did it!" she exclaims. "We have more than enough signatures!"

Mia, Nate, and I erupt in cheers and hi-fives. With the event winding down, it was just in time. It's a major victory, and everything feels right in the world for a moment.

But the joy is short-lived. As we're cleaning up, Rae comes rushing back, her face stricken. "The signatures," she pants. "Someone stole them when my back was turned."

My stomach drops. "What? How?"

She shakes her head, looking distraught. "I don't know. I just turned around for a second to put the clipboards in a bin, and when I looked back ... they were gone. I'm so sorry, you guys. This is all my fault. I should've been keeping a closer eye on them."

Mia immediately pulls Rae into a comforting hug. "Hey, it's okay. It's not your fault. That could've happened to any of us. We'll figure this out. If we can't find out who did it, we'll get the signatures again. It's not the end of the world."

Mia's right. It's not the end of the world. But after weeks of missing Greg, of waiting to know if my career is out of my hands, if Greg's father is going to ruin both of our lives, Mia and Nate's wedding plans reminding me of what I don't have, and now this... I'm at my limit. My chest tightens as all the stress I've been suppressing rushes to the surface. And even though we're outside, I feel like I just can't breathe.

I pull Mia aside while Nate continues to reassure Rae.

"Mia, I'm sorry, but I need to leave," I tell her.

She puts a hand on my shoulder and smiles reassuringly. "Of course. I'll catch up with you later?"

I huff out a breath and shake my head. "No, I mean, I need to go *home*," I say, my voice cracking. "I've been trying to stay strong and act normally, but I just ... can't. I feel like I don't know which end up is anymore. All this waiting and worrying ... I think I just need to get out of Alpine Ridge for a little while."

A look of understanding dawns on Mia's face. "I was wondering when this would all hit you. But you seemed to be doing so well. God, I should've known you were faking it," she says, frustration evident in her voice.

"Hey, this is on me. I should've spoken up sooner. Before I started having a mental breakdown," I joke.

Mia's eyes go wide. "Are you really having a mental breakdown?"

I open my mouth to deny it, but ... "Yeah, kind of?" I admit. "For a while, everything seemed too perfect to be true. But when Greg's father showed up with those documents ... well, it all just unraveled, and I've been going downhill since." Mia reaches out and squeezes my hand. When I'd finally told her about why I'd really lost my job, she was furious on my behalf. Even with her and Greg's support, I'm only now realizing how much it affected me. "I feel like ... Fuck, I don't know how to feel anymore. And I can't wait around forever for Greg to fix things for me. Who knows if he can or how long he'll be gone."

"He hasn't said when he'll be back?" she asks, pressing her lips together in concern.

"Nope. I even asked him to come home," I admit in a small voice.

"Oh, Jo. He said no?" she asks incredulously.

I close my eyes and nod. "I tried not to see it as a rejection. I really did. I know he's doing what he can. But that doesn't mean it'll work. And I feel like I'm hanging over the edge of a cliff right now, and I need to do something to pull myself back. Does any of this make sense?"

Mia sighs and nods. "Actually, yes," she admits. "If I were you, I'd be going out of my mind."

I give her a small smile. "I think I just need to reconnect with my real life. Since Greg is off doing his thing, maybe I should be too."

Mia's brow furrows, and I know what she's thinking. She thought Alpine Ridge and Greg had become my real life. I'd thought so, too. Now, everything seems like a mess that I don't know how or have the energy to fix.

Still, ever supportive, Mia steps forward and hugs me tightly. "Okay," she murmurs. "I understand. We'll look into the signatures issue and take care of everything here. You focus on taking care of yourself, okay?"

I nod against her shoulder, grateful for her support even as I feel like I'm abandoning her, abandoning all of them.

But I can't think about that now. I need to go, breathe, and clear my head. So I give Mia one last squeeze, wave goodbye to Nate and Rae, and head for my car. I stop by Mia and Nate's house only long enough to get my things, and then I'm back on the road.

Driving out of Alpine Ridge, I feel a sense of déjà vu. It wasn't that long ago that I was fleeing Seattle, running away from my old life and all its problems, if only for a little while. And now, here I am, running back to it.

The difference is that I'm not sure what I'm running toward this time. Seattle doesn't feel like home anymore, but neither does Alpine Ridge without Greg.

Greg. Just thinking his name makes my heart clench. I know he's been busy trying to fix this mess with his dad and protect me, but the silence this past week after not seeing him for so long on top of it has been torture. I miss him so much it's like a physical ache.

But I can't think about that now either because Greg was clear about why we needed to be apart. So, all I can do is focus on myself and what I should do now.

I let out a harsh laugh. Who am I kidding? I have no idea what I should do. But I have to do *something*.

As the snowy peaks of Alpine Ridge fade in my rearview mirror, I feel a sense of loss. But also, strangely, a flicker of hope. Maybe this really is what I need. A chance to regroup and gain some perspective.

Maybe it's time to remember who Joanie Morris is, separate from this town and these people I've come to love. It's time to rediscover my strength and figure out what I really want.

Again, who am I kidding with this? Because what I really want is a certain mountain man with eyes like the summer sky and a heart as big as the Cascades.

I know that sooner or later, we'll figure things out. I'd hoped for sooner, but clearly, that's not meant to be. It's a good opportunity to focus on myself for now, anyway.

Seattle isn't quite how I left it; it's somehow busier. Fuller. As I drive through the rain-soaked city, a sea of umbrellas skim the sidewalks.

When I let myself in, the condo feels impersonal. The quiet is deafening. I drop my bag on the floor, and it echoes through the small space.

After I've unpacked a bit, I flop onto the couch with a sigh. Funny how a place I once loved can seem so different now.

Maybe I should try harder. Maybe getting back to work would make me feel more like myself. I can still handle the incorporation project from afar, and Greg and I agreed we'd split time between Seattle and Alpine Ridge. It could work.

My eyes slide to my laptop on the dining room table, but I'm too restless to look at job listings right now. Maybe later.

I decide to finish unpacking first, methodically putting away my clothes. But as I do, I realize my wardrobe no longer feels like me. It's all sharp angles and power suits, remnants of a life that no longer fits.

On impulse, I start pulling things out and making a pile for donation: skirts I can't imagine ever wearing again, blouses that feel too constricting, towering heels that now seem impractical. It's cathartic, shedding these layers of my old self.

When I'm done, my closet looks bare. But somehow, I feel lighter.

Next, I wander into the kitchen, opening cupboards and the fridge. They're all depressingly empty, so I decide to brave the rain and do some grocery shopping. Hopefully, the normalcy will help snap me back to myself.

But as I walk the store's aisles, I miss Alpine Ridge — the friendly faces that were becoming familiar. Here, everyone avoids eye contact, and I feel lost and faceless in the crowd of shoppers.

I shake off the melancholy and focus on the task at hand. I grab some essentials — coffee, eggs, bread, butter, and cheese — to get me through the next few days until I can figure out a plan.

Back at the condo, I put away the groceries and make myself a grilled cheese sandwich. I purposely wanted to feel closer to Greg by remembering when he made me one, but all it does is make me miss him more. I eat at the counter, staring out the window at the grey Seattle skyline — a far cry from the snow-capped forest and majestic mountains of Alpine Ridge.

As I do the dishes, my mind starts to wander. What am I doing here? Running away from my problems? From the best thing that's ever happened to me? The thought makes me pause, sudsy water dripping from my hands.

Am I really going to let Greg's father dictate my life? Let my former employer's threats push me away from the man I love, the friends who have become family, and the town that's started to feel like home? What is there for me here, really? Coming home to no one from a job in an industry that now chafes? It's not like I spend much time with my parents either. Even before they retired to travel the world, we were never close, all three of us being uber career-focused. And I don't have true friends here anymore, either, merely a professional network of barely-acquaintances.

I think of Mia and her unwavering faith in love, Nate and his quiet strength, Rae and her resilience, and Greg, who loves me for exactly who I am, flaws and all.

They're worth fighting for, and this life I've started to build with them is worth fighting for because it's so much better than anything I ever had here. Fuck the law firm. And fuck Everett Tyler.

I finish the dishes, my mind spinning. I need to talk to Greg. I should've called him before I left Alpine Ridge, before I freaked out and ran. Again.

Which makes me remember … he's here in Seattle.

How did I not think of that until now?

I reach for my phone, my heart in my throat. But when I place the call, it goes straight to voicemail. Shit. Shit, shit, shit. I'd never even asked him where he was staying, either. I mean, I know he has a house here, but where, I have no clue.

So now I'm back in Seattle, wishing I was with a man I met a hundred miles from here, who is also somewhere in this city. I just can't win today.

CHAPTER TWENTY-THREE

GREG

As I drive back to Alpine Ridge from Seattle, my heart feels lighter than it has in weeks. The weight of my father's threats, the worry about Joanie's career, the uncertainty of our future together—it's all been lifted from my shoulders. I can't wait to share the good news with Joanie, to take her in my arms and tell her everything will be okay.

When I arrive at my house, the first thing I do is call Joanie, but it goes straight to voicemail. A knot forms in my stomach. It's not like Joanie to be unreachable.

I wait a while, unpacking and making a cup of coffee before trying again, only to get her voicemail once more. And now I have a feeling in the pit of my stomach that something's not right, so I call Nate.

"Hey, man," he answers. "What's up?"

"Is Joanie with you guys?" I ask, trying to keep the anxiety out of my voice.

There's a pause. "No, she's not. She, uh... she went back to Seattle, Greg."

My heart sinks. "What? When?"

"Right after the event. Apparently, she needed some space. She told Mia she needed to reconnect with her real life."

I close my eyes, a mixture of confusion and hurt washing over me. Why would she leave without telling me? Then again, it's not exactly like I told her I was coming back, either. I shake my head at my idiocy.

"Thanks for letting me know," I manage to say. "Hey, can Mia give me Joanie's address?"

"Going after her, huh?"

"That's the idea," I confirm.

"All right, hold on a sec."

I hear muffled voices in the background; then Mia comes on the line. "So what's your plan, hot shot?"

I can't help but laugh despite my nerves being on edge right now. "I'm going to apologize for not being able to come back sooner, beg her forgiveness, then spend the rest of my life making her feel like a fucking queen if she'll let me. Good enough?"

"It'll do," she replies primly. "I'll have Nate text you the address."

"Thanks, Mia."

"Don't make me regret it." And with that, she hangs up.

I can't even be mad at her for protecting Joanie because it's what I've been trying to do, too.

As soon as I have the address, I'm back in my truck, heading for Seattle once again. My mind races the whole drive, trying to decide what to say. It's hard because I'm just guessing what's going on with her. Is she angry with me for being gone so long? Hurt that I didn't come back when she asked? Or is it something else entirely?

When I finally arrive at her condo, my nerves are completely shot. I take a deep breath and knock on her door.

It swings open, revealing a surprised Joanie. She looks tired, her usually bright eyes shadowed. But she's still the most beautiful thing I've ever seen, and I want to wrap her in my arms. I hold back, though, to see where she's at first.

"Greg," she breathes. "I just tried to call you. Why didn't you answer?" She steps back, and I cross the threshold with a sigh of relief as she closes the door behind me.

"I was driving back from Alpine Ridge. I went back because the thing with my father is over, Joanie. You know Sera bought out my ownership in the property, but her husband also worked a fucking miracle and got both your old law firm and my dad to destroy the fabricated evidence and issue a public retraction in case it went any further. I went back as soon as I could to tell you, but you were gone."

Her brow furrows. "He did what? How? But wait … you're not mad at me?"

I laugh at the backward question. "Why would *I* be mad?" I ask.

"I bailed on Alpine Ridge, on *you*. I knew you'd be back eventually. I just … God, I can't believe it, but I freaked out and ran away from everything. The waiting and wondering was just … I couldn't handle it anymore. So I thought I'd come home and just … breathe, I guess." She buries her face in her hands. I gently pull them away and wrap my arms around her. She slides into my embrace.

I shake my head. "I could never be mad at you for needing space. I'm just sorry you felt like you had to leave in the first place." I take her hands in mine. "Are you still upset with me?"

Joanie's eyes fill with tears. "I was never upset with you. Your dad and my former bosses? Hell yes. But mostly, I just missed you so much. Phone calls weren't enough anymore. And then Mia and Nate set a wedding date, and the petition signatures were stolen —"

"Holy shit," I exclaim. I feel my anger rising, but I try to push it down. That can wait. First, I need to make sure Joanie and I are okay because that's much more important. I shake my head, shaking it off. "That's awful, but we can deal with it." I cradle her face in my hands and look deep into her eyes. "What matters most is that

I missed you like crazy, too. I don't ever want to have to be away from you like that again."

Joanie's top teeth sink into her bottom lip. "Then don't," she replies. "I think I'm done here, Greg. I came back thinking I could get a handle on my emotions by plugging back into who I was. But I'm not the woman I was when I left. And I don't want a job in Seattle, though it's good to know I don't have to worry about those bastards potentially sabotaging me. Either way, this isn't who I am anymore. This isn't where I want to be."

My breath catches as I stare at her in disbelief. "You're ... are you serious?"

She looks at me with pleading eyes. "Yes. I left because Alpine Ridge didn't feel right without you, but it turns out neither does Seattle. Actually, I think it really turns out that I don't do so well being away from you. Who knew so much could change in a few months? But it has. I want to be with you, in the place you love ... like, permanently. But if that's too much, then I can —"

I cut her off with my lips on hers. Because like hell am I going to let her think I want it any other way.

I back her against the door and plunge my hands into her silky hair, tugging her head to the side so I can deepen the kiss. Her hands skate down my back to my ass, squeezing me closer. My cock swells as she rubs her hips against me.

I break away, panting. "It's not too much. I want you to come live with me, too, Joanie. You're sure? Really sure?" I have to ask because I just can't believe it.

She nods. "That's all I want."

I can see the truth in her clear blue eyes. So many emotions swirl through me. I shake my head and let out a disbelieving laugh. This is really happening. "Guess I can't call you 'city girl' anymore, then," I murmur.

Joanie rubs me through my jeans. "Just call me yours, Greg. Only yours."

My heart sings, and I need this woman. Now. I push into her hand, and she takes the cue, unbuttoning my jeans to free my cock. She makes to drop to her knees, but I grasp her by the arms and turn her around, roughly yanking her leggings to her knees before bending her forward until she's pressed against the door, and I enter her from behind.

We fuck hard and fast and possessive. Her hand reaches back for mine. I hold on while we both work our hips together. Until she's convulsing with bliss, and I'm spilling inside her. I lean onto her back, kissing her neck.

"I missed that too," she says, breathing hard, her cheeks rosy.

I chuckle and straighten up, smacking her ass cheek. She yelps in surprise and grins at me. "Like that?" I tease as I pull out of her.

"Mhm," she murmurs. "We can explore that later. First, shower."

Once we've thoroughly cleaned ourselves, gotten dirty again under the water, and cleaned ourselves again, we get dressed and head back to the living room.

We settle onto the couch, and Joanie puts her legs in my lap. I stroke them gently, glad she's relaxed and more herself again.

"So it's really over?" she asks, presumably referring to the mess with my father and her former employer.

I take a steadying breath. "For the most part. I imagine my father will throw a tantrum now that he has no way to control me anymore. But that's nothing new." I look up at her. "Either way, your career is safe now. You can do whatever you want without fear of retaliation."

"Whatever I want, huh?" she asks in a sultry tone, running a finger down my arm.

"Whatever you want," I reply huskily.

Joanie smirks. "Well, after I'm done having my way with you here and we go back to Alpine Ridge, I want to see this incorporation through and figure out if there's a way I can keep helping the town. That's what I want."

I smile and squeeze her calf. "Well, considering that a lot of running a town involves legal matters, that seems like a viable option. But is that enough for you?"

Joanie shrugs but has a thoughtful look on her face. "I could always start my own practice and take on private clients if I need more," she muses, then meets my gaze. "But if you're asking whether *you're* enough ... yes, Greg. You're more than enough. While I never saw myself living in a small town in the mountains with a man who swims naked in ice-cold lakes, I apparently didn't dream big enough. I'd be insane to turn down that life."

I lean in and kiss her softly. "If I get to keep you, I'll swim naked wherever you want, Joanie."

She tips her head back and laughs. "This just keeps getting better and better."

I cover her lips with mine and give her a real kiss. One that leaves her — and me — a little breathless. "That. That right there is my new life goal. To make you say that every damn day."

Joanie's expression softens, and she puts a hand on my chest. "I love you, Greg. Being with you, the life we can have, it's more than I ever thought to dream of. All you need to do is love me, and I'm there. For as long as you'll have me," she says. The uncharacteristic seriousness pierces me right in the heart, in a good way.

"Forever okay with you?" I ask softly.

Joanie smirks at me. "I could be convinced," she says nonchalantly.

I chuckle. "Shall I attempt to convince you right here, or would your bedroom be better?" I tease.

Her pupils dilate, and she grins. "Yes to both," she teases back. "And you can keep convincing me every day, in our bed, in our home. Deal?"

I extend my hand for her to shake. "Deal. But for the record? My home is wherever you are."

She nods in agreement. "And my bed is our bed now. Care to get started?"

Instead of answering with words, I scoop her up and take her to the bedroom. To show her I mean it.

Because she is my home. My heart. My everything.

And I'm never letting her go again.

EPILOGUE

JOANIE

As I stand in the wildflower field behind the community center, getting ready to watch my best friend marry the love of her life, I can't help but reflect on the whirlwind of the past six months.

After Greg and I reunited in Seattle, everything quickly fell into place, surprising even me. I moved in with him in Alpine Ridge, and a few months later, I sold my condo in the city. Though we still use Greg's Queen Anne house for our Seattle getaways, my heart is firmly rooted in the mountains.

The incorporation efforts hit a snag when the petition signatures were stolen, but Rae, ever the determined force, took it upon herself to collect them again. Within a couple of weeks, we were back on track. The final boundary meeting in June went smoothly, and now we're just six weeks away from the election that will officially make Alpine Ridge a town.

Mia's sister, Carrie, has been another surprising but welcome addition to our little family. After graduating and having a massive falling out with their parents, she moved in with Mia and Nate in July. She's been doing remote work for Western Washington politicians as we enter election season, and she's also agreed to spearhead our upcoming elections since while a few folks in town were willing to help, none were willing to run the show. It's a win for everyone; I won't have to handle something I know nothing about, Carrie's resume will be even more impressive afterward, and the town will benefit, too.

Greg's father did try to stir up trouble at the 4th of July celebration, but the town made it clear he wasn't welcome. He hasn't been heard from since. To my knowledge, he's also still holding out on Sera's buyout offer.

Ned's parents have likewise found Alpine Ridge less than hospitable now that the truth about their son's crimes and their cover-ups has spread. They recently put their grocery store up for sale, and Sera pounced on the opportunity. She has grand plans to turn it into something reminiscent of a Trader Joe's, much to everyone's delight.

But today is all about celebrating Mia and Nate. The setting couldn't be more perfect — a sea of purple fireweed, white asters, and lingering yellow buttercups, framed by trees just beginning to don their autumn colors. Mia looks ethereal in her flowy white gown and aster crown, like a fairy bride straight out of a storybook. And Nate, dashing in his light grey slacks and crisp white shirt, can't take his eyes off her.

The guest list is small but meaningful. Greg and I, of course, along with Rae and Carrie. Nate's parents and brothers. Everyone is surprised to discover that Nate's youngest brother is the famous Evan Edwards, one of the hottest action stars in Hollywood. Carrie seems particularly mesmerized by him, and the feeling seems mutual from how he's flirting. And a handful of our closest friends from town round out the group. Mia's decision not to invite her parents was difficult, but seeing the pure joy radiating from her and Nate, I know she made the right call.

Nate's other brother, Dylan, officiates. He's a musician, but apparently, anyone can become an officiant. When he calls the ceremony to order, Mia gives me a joyful but nervous smile. I squeeze her hand and push her toward the front of the crowd.

"Thank you all for coming today to share in uniting Nathan Edwards and Mia Anderson in marriage," he begins.

Everyone quiets down, and Nate and Mia join hands in front of Dylan, eyes locked on each other, grins on both of their faces.

"Now, the bride and groom have elected to do their own additional vows privately after the ceremony, so everyone pay attention because this is going to go fast. Which is good because there's Chantilly crème chiffon cake waiting for us," he jokes. My mouth fills with saliva at the thought of one of Mia's best cakes, so I don't chuckle with everyone for fear of drooling all over my new lilac-colored tulle gown.

Dylan turns to Nate. "Do you, Nathan Edwards, take this woman to be your lawfully wedded wife, to live together in matrimony, to love her, comfort her, honor and keep her, in sickness and in health, in sorrow and joy, to have and to hold, from this day forward, as long as you both shall live?"

"I do," Nate says thickly.

Mia choke-sobs, and I hold a hand up to my mouth to stifle a similar noise. They've both already been through so much between Gran's death, struggles with Mia's parents, and opening their businesses. Not to mention all the recent drama.

Nate smiles down at her, but I can tell he's about to lose it, too.

Now Dylan turns to Mia, and just the look on her face has me blinking back tears. Even as a sobbing mess, she's beautiful and radiating joy. "Do you, Mia Anderson, take this man to be your lawfully wedded husband, to live together in matrimony, to love him, comfort him, honor and keep him, in sickness and in health, in sorrow and joy, to have and to hold, from this day forward, as long as you both shall live?"

Mia nods for a moment as she swallows another happy sob. "Yes." Dylan looks at her with raised eyebrows. She's only confused for a moment before she laughs and chokes out, "I do" around giggles.

I facepalm and shake my head, laughing. Only Mia would forget the *one line* she's supposed to nail. Thankfully, Nate is chuckling, too.

Dylan smirks. "Nate and Mia will now exchange the rings they've chosen for each other as a symbol of their unending love." He turns to Nate, who fishes a ring from his pants pocket. "As you place this ring on Mia's finger, please repeat after me." Mia offers her hand, which Nate takes, carefully sliding the simple band onto her finger next to her blindingly huge engagement ring. "With this ring, I thee wed and pledge you my love now and forever."

And that's the line that does Nate in. Tears pouring down his face, he manages in a thick, joy-filled voice, "With this ring, I thee wed and pledge you my love now and forever."

Tears are pouring down Mia's face, too, as her hand shakes in his. And I wish I'd brought a towel to mop these two up afterward. I brush away a few of my own tears, realizing I probably also need one. An elbow gently nudges me from the side, and Nate's mom slips me a tissue. I gratefully accept it, hoping she has more of those on hand.

"You ready, Mia, or do you guys need a minute?" Dylan teases.

Mia laughs and shakes her head. "I'm so ready." She takes Nate's hand and reveals the ring she'd had tucked in her palm.

Dylan smiles patiently and prompts her, "With this ring, I thee wed and pledge you my love now and forever."

Mia takes a shaky, deep breath and slides the ring onto Nate's finger, looking lovingly up into his face. "With this ring, I thee wed and pledge you my love now and forever." And I think the worst of the tears have passed for her because she's far steadier than Nate was. Nate, however, continues to cry unabashedly.

I'm not usually one for emotional displays, but seeing Nate, a steady rock of a man, cry like this is getting to me. Almost as much as Mia's tears are. I can feel Greg's eyes on me, but I don't look. If I do, I know I'll see his love and concern there, and then I'll lose it, too. We can't have the *whole* wedding party be a blubbering mess.

Dylan grins at the happy couple and spreads his arms out. "By the authority vested in me by the State of Washington … I now pronounce you husband and wife!"

The small crowd, myself included, claps, hoots, and cheers as Nate leans in and kisses Mia sweetly. And I can't help it; I lean into Greg and whisper in his ear. "You can bet your gorgeous ass if that were us, there'd be a whole lot more tongue."

Greg chuckles and leans toward me. "And probably some groping." He winks at me.

I grin and give him a "guilty as charged" shrug because we both know he means me.

Nate and Mia turn to us all and are passed around for hugs before Rae leads us back to the community center, where the reception is held. It's full of laughter, love, and more pastries than even I can handle. The cake is out of this world, and I'm pretty sure I'm going to be ordering this on the regular just because it's practically orgasmic. Light, fluffy, and buttery, the cake itself is bliss even without the decadent vanilla-flavored whipped heaven. But watching Mia and Nate's joy is the cherry on top. It's the perfect day for my best friend, and my heart is so full of happiness for her and Nate.

As the happy couple departs for their Hawaiian honeymoon – a nod to the trip Mia was forced to abandon, ultimately allowing them to meet in the first place – Greg pulls me aside. We walk hand in hand to the pond on one side of the community center, settling on a bench overlooking the tranquil water.

I smile to myself remembering ice skating last winter when Greg and I showed off for each other before our first real heavy-petting session in his office.

"Well, it seems like that went off without a hitch. That might be the first event here that has," Greg teases, running his hand through the layers of tulle of my skirt.

I turn toward him with a smirk. "I'm glad. They deserved it. Though I half expected her parents to show up and start some shit."

"God, I hadn't even thought of that," he admits. "I hope my parents don't do that when we get married."

A laugh spills out of me. "When we get married?" I tease. "I don't remember you even asking."

Greg smirks and looks down. I follow his gaze. And in his hand is a small velvet box. My heart stutters as he opens it to reveal what appears to be a stunning diamond ring that's the same shade of blue as my eyes.

"Joanie," he begins, his eyes shining with emotion. "You came out of nowhere and made me feel alive. Being with you has made me a better man, one who wants everything out of this life with you by my side. As your husband, if you'll have me. Joanie Morris, will you marry me?"

"You know," I muse, looking away so he doesn't see the sheen of tears in my eyes, "I always pictured you proposing during sex."

Greg tips his head back and laughs loudly. Then he leans in and kisses me. "Then let's go home, and I'll try this again."

I shrug lightly and gesture for him to give me the ring. He shakes his head, chuckling as he withdraws the ring and slides it onto my finger. I hold my hand out, examining the gorgeous jewelry exaggeratedly as I pretend to contemplate it and his question.

"Wait …" he says before I can say anything else. "You just said you've pictured me proposing."

I give him a sly smile. "Maybe."

He grins. "And did you see yourself saying yes to that proposal?"

My grin widens. "Maaaaybe."

Greg laughs. "Joanie?"

And I can't keep it up anymore. I laugh and grab him by the shirt, pulling him toward me. "Yes. Make me Mrs. Mountain Man, stud."

Greg laughs against my lips, pulling me into his lap. And I don't give a shit that I'm wearing a dress; I wrap my legs around him. He runs his hands up my bare thighs and groans into my mouth.

"I might get to propose again sooner than I thought," he murmurs, pulling my core against his hard length.

"Public sex?" I gasp in a scandalized tone. "For shame."

Greg sucks hard at the spot under my ear, and I moan. "You know you love it, dirty girl," he teases.

I lean back and put my hands on his face. "I know I love you," I reply sincerely. No snark, no teasing. "And I'd be honored to be your wife, Gregory Tyler." And I seal it with a tender kiss so there's no question that my "yes" is for real.

When his mouth breaks away, he rests his forehead against mine. "Ready to go home, fiancée?"

I nod, my heart soaring at the new title. At the idea of being his forever. Because he's most definitely mine.

As we walk back to the community center, hand in hand, I can't stop smiling. The future stretches out before us, filled with promise and possibility.

It's wild that I've finally found my home. My happy ever after. I never imagined that path would lead me here, to this incredible man, to this life that feels like a dream come true.

But that's the beauty of life, isn't it? The unexpected detours, the surprises that catch us off guard and change everything.

Alpine Ridge brought me a better life than I'd had planned. It gave me love, purpose, and a sense of belonging. And now, it will be the setting for the next chapter of my story. Our story.

And I can't wait to see what adventures await us. Mountain man and (former) city girl. Ready to take on the world. Together. Forever.

UNSCRIPTED LOVE

A STEAMY SMALL-TOWN CELEBRITY ROMANCE

CONTENT WARNING

Unscripted Love is a small-town celebrity romance novel that includes elements that might not be suitable for some readers, including the use of profanity, open-door sex scenes, and other potentially sensitive topics. Visit https://melanieasmithauthor.com/ulcw.html for a full list (warning: may include spoilers).

CHAPTER ONE

EVAN

"Cut! For fuck's sake, just stop." John, one of the most patient directors in the movie industry, pinches the bridge of his nose and lets out a long-suffering sigh before looking up at Kaitlyn and me. "Evan. You're leaving her behind to go bust up a fucking drug cartel. A mission from which you likely won't return. And you're kissing her like I kiss my goddamn Aunt Ethel."

My brows shoot up, but I bite back a sarcastic retort. Because he's not wrong. Kaitlyn and I have practically zip in the chemistry department. Don't get me wrong, she's cute. But she's fifteen years younger than me and doesn't have much going on upstairs or great acting chops. Unfortunately, she was clearly hired to be set dressing. Trying to talk scene blocking and motivation with her has been pointless, as has attempting to drum up a nonexistent attraction. Even John McKennon, the best action director I've worked with in my sixteen-year career, isn't good enough to direct us out of this awfulness.

"Okay," I reply diplomatically instead of suggesting we find a replacement with only two weeks left to shoot. Given that we only started shooting her scenes yesterday, I wonder if the timing wasn't intended to ensure we had no choice but to go with her. My bet's on nepotism. It wouldn't be the first time. "What would you like us to do differently?"

John blows out a breath so hard his cheeks puff up. "Give me more *passion*."

Translation: he's just as clueless as I am about how to fix this.

"So, what, like, more tongue?" Kaitlyn asks, twirling a piece of her long blond hair around her finger.

I shoot John a look that says, "You see what I'm working with?"

He waves a hand dismissively at my unspoken comment. Or maybe at Kaitlyn's question. Who knows. At least we've been nailing the rest of the non-Kaitlyn shots. But this one? This one has taken all damn day. Or it feels like it, anyway.

"Just … do something different," he grumbles. He signals to the makeup person to touch us up. A few pats and swipes later, he calls action.

I deliver my lines, which are at least convincing, and then go in for the kiss. I've tried a dozen different methods so far. Save one. As I close my eyes, I feel like Harry Potter trying to conjure my first patronus. Clearly, I will have to pull my absolute sexiest memory to make magic here. I don't like to resort to this since it usually gives me a hard-on. But desperate times and all.

So, as our lips meet, I let my mind slip back to last summer in Bali. The hottest model of the moment, naked under me in the sand, beautiful huge tits bouncing as I fucked her under the stars. The things that woman could do with her mouth. She gave the most amazing blow job ever, had this way of flicking her tongue over my nipples that could get me hard in an instant, and — most importantly for this moment — she was the *best* kisser. So, I imagine it's her as I press myself against Kaitlyn and devastate her with my mouth.

I'm so absorbed in my little fantasy that I almost don't hear John when he says, "Cut." Followed by, "That'll do, kids. And we're done for the day. *Finally.*"

I pull back with a sigh of relief to find Kaitlyn looking at me like a hungry wolf.

Shit. That's the other potential negative side effect of that technique.

Kaitlyn leans close, batting her eyelashes. "That was totally hot," she breathes. "Wanna go fuck in my trailer? It's closer than yours."

I huff a short laugh under my breath. "Thanks, but I'm going to shower and head out," I reply shortly. "I've got places to be."

She reaches out and gropes my still semi-hard dick over my pants. "Really? You can't tell me *that* doesn't say you want me."

I jump back, throwing my hands up to bypass the urge to push her away. "Whoa, hey, not cool," I growl. "You wouldn't like it if someone touched your crotch, would you?"

Her smile turns feline. "You can touch me all you want. Come on, I know your rep. You don't have to play hard to get."

I step back, noting that everyone else has left the set. Great. They probably all cleared out thinking we'd be fucking right here. Awesome. Clearly, they all know my reputation, too — Evan Edwards, playboy action star extraordinaire.

"I'm not playing, and I'm not interested." I run a hand through my shaggy light brown hair, shake my head, and walk away.

"If you change your mind, you know where to find me," she calls to my retreating back.

"Not gonna happen," I mutter.

When I get to my trailer, I take the quickest shower known to man in case Kaitlyn has designs on catching me naked. It gets most of the stage makeup off, anyway. Once I'm dressed, I breathe a sigh of relief and grab my phone.

I note that I missed a call from my brother, Nate. It's been a while since we've spoken, and it's not like him to call. We usually just catch up at Mom and Dad's at the holidays, and I just saw him at Christmas a few months ago.

"Hello?" Nate answers.

"Hey, bro, what's up?"

"Evan. Wow. I wasn't expecting you to call back so fast." My big bro is usually pretty stoic, but right now, he sounds happy, which piques my interest.

"Yeah, we just wrapped up for the day, and I saw you called. You never call."

"Hey, you're not the only one keeping busy," he replies jokingly. "And obviously, I call when I have something to say. Mia and I set a date. September twenty-third. Can you make it?"

I collapse onto the overstuffed loveseat in the trailer's tiny living room. "Damn. So, this is for real. You're getting hitched." They've been engaged so long I was starting to wonder. But then again, they both own their own businesses, even if they are in a sleepy little town in Washington's Cascade Mountains. Still, I imagine they've been busy enough without wedding planning.

"It's for real," Nate confirms. "And while I know it's a long shot, I'd love to have you there."

I let out a sigh. "You know I'd love to come."

"But?"

I huff a sharp laugh. "But I don't want to take away from your big day."

Nate's quiet for a moment, presumably considering that. It wouldn't be the first time I stole his limelight.

"I really want you there, Ev, so I'll deal with whatever else comes with that," he finally says. "It's going to be a small, casual wedding anyway. Just family and a few friends."

I nod slowly. I'd love to be there. And it would be damn good to get the hell out of L.A. for a bit. "I'll check with my assistant and let you know."

"Sounds good," Nate agrees.

A soft knock comes at the rickety trailer door. "Hey, hold on just a second," I tell him.

I get up and open the door. Only to see Kaitlyn on the step. She opens a long jacket to reveal her naked body. Lithe and supple and totally inappropriate in the bright March Southern California evening, out where anyone could see.

"Shit. I gotta go, Nate. I'll call you back, okay?"

I don't even wait for his response; I hang up and reach out, wrenching Kaitlyn's jacket closed.

"Are you insane?" I ask bluntly.

She tries to push past me into the trailer, but I don't budge. "Oh, come on, Evan. You know you want it," she says coyly, opening her jacket again.

I glare down at her and shake my head firmly. "No means no, Kaitlyn. I don't sleep with costars during production. Period." That much is true anyway. Maybe the non-personal rejection will do the trick. Doubtful, but worth a shot anyway.

She angrily ties the closure of her jacket and folds her arms over her chest. "Fine. But I'm going to tell everyone I fucked you anyway, so I figured you might as well get something out of it."

Oh lord. Here we go.

Again.

I take a calm, deep breath before pointing at the camera mounted on the corner of the trailer. "You can try, but that —" I jerk my chin at the camera for emphasis "— has high-resolution video and audio. It'd be a shame for this little episode to become public knowledge. Might ruin what could be a promising start to a career." She isn't the first wanna-be starlet to try to fuck her way onto the A-list via my cock, and I'm sure she won't be the last.

Kaitlyn's eyes narrow, and her nostrils flare. I can practically hear the rusty wheels in her head turning.

"Fine," she eventually snaps. "Your loss, then." And then, thank God, she turns on her heel and leaves.

Sighing, I collect my things before heading to my car. I'll call Nate back later when I'm in a better headspace.

As I drive home, even with the top down on a beautiful evening, I feel bone-deep exhaustion. The shit that went down today with Kaitlyn is the kind of thing that just wears on me. I've learned to fight back against the users over the years. I've had to, if for no other reason than to save what little is left of my reputation. One false accusation, one wrong decision, and I know I could become persona non grata in the industry. It's why my contract rider includes not being left alone with female costars. Something I'll have words with John about later. But mostly? I'm damn sick of having to worry about this kind of crap.

You'd think my success would've earned me more respect, more privileges, and less bullshit. And in some ways, I suppose it has. Dibs on scripts. My pick of projects. Choosing what directors I work with and, to an extent, which co-stars. But the total loss of privacy and control of my personal life ... that hole just keeps getting deeper. Some days, it's worth it. When a movie gets a great response, or I really connect with the fans, or a particularly exciting script comes my way.

But some days ... besides blatant sexual harassment, the industry has just changed. Appearances are *everything*. Even when I'm not on a shoot, I feel like I'm play-acting my entire life to project a certain image that keeps me hot, current, and in demand.

Or maybe I wasn't clued into this part of the gig early on. But boy, do I miss anonymity. Being able to go to the grocery store. Or out for a run without paps chasing me down. Or dating someone without internet trolls tearing apart her entire life for their own entertainment.

And there's no escaping it. I have houses in New York City, Miami, and Honolulu, but none provide anonymity. If anything, they're worse than L.A. because most people are used to seeing celebrities here. If only there were somewhere I could go that nobody cared about that shit. Somewhere where I could just be myself.

As I pull into my multi-million-dollar estate in the Hollywood Hills, I have to laugh at myself — poor rich and famous me. I know I'm an ungrateful asshole. I'm living the life everyone else wants.

So why aren't I happy?

CHAPTER TWO

CARRIE

Spring break. To anyone else, those two words conjure up images of sunny beaches, exotic locales, and wild parties. But not for me. No, instead of living it up, I'm stuck running errands for my overbearing parents, dog sitting — for free, like the chump I am — for a friend of a friend, and trying (and failing) to progress on my master's capstone project. Some break this is turning out to be.

I sigh as I clip the leash onto Rufus, a loveably energetic golden retriever. He wags his tail excitedly, his pink tongue lolling out. At least someone's happy.

"All right, buddy, let's go," I murmur, leading him out the door. The early Seattle spring air still holds a chill, and I zip my jacket up higher, burying my chin in the fleece collar.

We make it about halfway around the block when my phone buzzes in my pocket. Glancing at the screen, I see it's my older sister, Mia. A smile tugs at my lips. We haven't talked in a while, as both of us have been wrapped up in our lives.

Okay, that's not totally true. I mean, I have been wrapped up with school. But I've also been avoiding her after the epic fight with my parents that followed visiting their other, "traitorous" daughter on New Year's Eve. I shake my head, shaking off the memory, wishing everyone could just get along.

"Hey, Mia, what's up?" I answer, trying to infuse some cheer into my voice.

"Carrie! I have big news," Mia gushes, her excitement palpable even through the phone. "Nate and I finally set a date. We're getting married on September twenty-third!"

"Oh wow, Mia, that's great," I reply, genuinely happy for her. Mia deserves this after everything she's been through, especially with our parents. She may have quit her job at our dad's law firm, but normal parents would've understood how miserable she'd been there and would be happy that she's doing so much better now. "I'm so excited for you!"

There's a beat of silence.

And I know what's coming next.

"I'd love to have you there. Do you think you can make it?" Mia asks gently, an undercurrent of tension in her voice. She knows as well as I do how complicated that request is.

I hesitate, biting my lip. I can't tell her that our parents are still furious about the New Year's Eve party and have all but said they'll disown me if I keep seeing her. That's not her fault, as much as my parents want to put the blame on her.

"I mean, I want to, of course," I hedge. "It's just, you know, I haven't lined up a job yet after graduation, so I'm not sure where I'll be ..."

It's a flimsy excuse, and we both know it. But I can't bring myself to admit the real reason for my reluctance — that I'm terrified of upsetting our parents further. They are paying for my education, after all, which Mia knows. But she doesn't know that after months of pressure, I finally caved and agreed to work for Dad's company after graduation. How could I not? I know he'd be miserable if I didn't, even if it's not what I want to do. But who knows? Maybe I'll end up loving it. Despite my parents' temperaments, they've always made sure we wanted for nothing. Well, nothing material, at least. So, it's hard to say no to them. If only I had Mia's courage.

"Oh. I see." Mia's disappointment is evident, and my heart clenches. "Well, if you can make it, we'd love to have you there. But if you can't, I totally understand."

My eyes burn with tears at the thought of letting down my big sister. My parents are already upset with me — or *still* are, as it were, but I'm sure I can find a way to go without them knowing. Mia is my sister, and now that Gran's gone, she's the only family member left who doesn't pressure me to do things I don't want to do. My parents know I just want to make everyone happy, and they use that to their full advantage.

"No, you know what? I'll be there," I promise impulsively. "I wouldn't miss your big day for anything. I'll figure out the details later."

"Really?" Mia brightens. "Thank you, Carrie. It means so much to me. I can't imagine getting married without my little sister there."

I press my lips together and wipe away a tear as Rufus pulls me down the sidewalk. "And I can't imagine not being there. Love you, big sis."

Mia tells me what they've planned so far, and then we say our goodbyes, and I hang up. My chest is tight with excitement for my sister and dread of hiding this from my parents. It irks me that I have to. I'm twenty-six years old, for crying out loud. But this is my life.

Lost in thought, I don't notice Rufus lunging after a squirrel until it's too late. His leash flies out of my hand as he takes off, barking excitedly.

"Rufus, no! Come back!" I yell, jolting into action.

But he's already halfway down the street, his fluffy golden tail disappearing around the corner.

Panic rises in my throat as I sprint after him, my mind spiraling. I can't even handle dog sitting. How am I supposed to juggle my family drama, finish my degree, and start a job I'm not even sure I want?

Tears prick at my eyes, making it difficult to see where I'm going as I bolt after the overgrown puppy. A frustrated scream builds in my chest. Everything is spinning out of control, and I feel powerless to stop it.

Rounding the corner, I scan the street frantically for any sign of Rufus. But he's nowhere to be seen. Defeated, I slump against a lamppost, burying my face in my hands.

Some spring break this is turning out to be, indeed. I need to get my life together fast. But right now, I'll settle for finding that damn dog.

With a heavy sigh, I push off the post and trudge down the sidewalk to continue my search, the weight of my future pressing down on my shoulders with every step.

CHAPTER THREE

CARRIE

TWO MONTHS LATER

I stare at my laptop screen, the email cursor blinking mockingly. I've been agonizing over this invitation for days, but I can't put it off any longer. Graduation is only two weeks away, and I need to make a decision.

I want Mia there. No, I *need* her there. Just like she couldn't imagine getting married without me, I can't picture walking across that stage without my big sister cheering me on. She's been a constant source of support, even from afar, as I've poured my heart and soul into finishing my master's degree in political science.

But I know inviting her will cause a shit storm with our parents. Even if I ask Mia to sit separately, Mom and Dad will view it as a betrayal even if they never see each other.

I'm starting to understand why Mia didn't invite them to her wedding. The constant walking on eggshells, the fear of setting off their hair-trigger tempers — it's exhausting, even soul-crushing.

I take a deep breath, steeling myself. Despite my people-pleasing tendencies, I have to talk to my parents about this. I can't let their bitterness rob me of sharing this milestone with Mia.

Hands shaking slightly, I rise and go downstairs, where my parents are sitting, watching the nightly news as usual.

"Mom? Dad? Can I talk to you guys for a minute?" I ask meekly.

Dad looks up from his place in the armchair across the living room, a greying dark-brown lock of hair curling onto his forehead, his square-rimmed glasses framing the dark blue eyes he passed on to Mia and me. Technically, we also got his wavy hair, but ours is just dark brown. Though I may wind up with a few grey hairs after this conversation. Mom's shoulder-length, curly brown hair bobs as she swings her gaze toward me from the end of the couch closest to Dad.

"Is everything all right?" she asks with an undercurrent of suspicion. I never interrupt their evening ritual.

"Everything's fine, Mom. I just ... I need to talk to you and Dad about something. About graduation." I settle uneasily on the opposite end of the couch from my mom.

"What's this about?" Dad asks gruffly, clearly irritated at the interruption.

I swallow hard. It's now or never.

"I've been thinking a lot about graduation and how much I want my whole family there to celebrate with me. I know things are difficult between you and Mia, but —"

"Absolutely not." Dad cuts me off; his tone is as sharp as a knife. "After what she did, abandoning her family, her responsibilities? No. She's not welcome."

"You wouldn't even have to see her," I plead, hating how small my voice sounds. "She could sit separately and —"

"And what? Pretend she's not there? Pretend she didn't choose her little bakery over her own flesh and blood?" Mom's voice is suddenly shrill, and I flinch. "Carrie, I can't believe you'd even suggest such a thing. Are you choosing her over us?"

Tears prick at my eyes, frustration and hurt welling in my chest at this old refrain. "That's not it at all! I appreciate everything you've done for me, and I'm not choosing sides. I just want my sister there for one of the biggest days of my life."

"If she goes, we won't," Dad declares flatly. "That's final."

A sob catches in my throat, and I crumple, all my carefully practiced arguments dissolving like mist. Mia will understand that I can't graduate without my parents there.

"Okay. I just thought you might understand, just this once. But I won't invite her. I'm sorry I brought it up."

"No, you know what? I don't believe you," Mom snaps. "You're just telling us what we want to hear, but you'll probably sneak behind our backs. Just like Mia."

"That's not true! I wouldn't —"

"I think," Dad cuts in, his voice cold as ice, "that if you're so eager to side with Mia, perhaps you should stay with *her*. Since you clearly don't appreciate everything *we've* provided for you."

"What?" I gasp, my stomach plummeting. "Dad, no, I —"

"As a matter of fact, you can find your own place to live *and* your own job," Dad growls. "Consider this a lesson, Carrie. Betrayal and ungratefulness will not be rewarded in this family. You can stay the night, but tomorrow, go find someone else to take for granted."

I stare at them in shock, tears streaming down my face. This can't be happening.

I rise on shaky legs, a maelstrom of emotions spinning inside me. I raise my chin. "Fine. If you don't believe me, I won't *burden* you anymore. I'll leave tonight."

I flee the room, not wanting to hear their response or see the expressions on their faces. I have no doubt it would only make me feel worse.

In a daze, I return to my room and pack my things, cramming clothes and books haphazardly into bags and suitcases. My mind races as I load up my car while my parents stare at the television, pretending I'm not even there.

Where will I go? What will I do? My whole life plan, the security of my parents' support and their love, gone in an instant.

It takes me less than an hour. One hour to erase my presence like I was never here. One hour to remove any trace of twenty-six years of life. I realize as I make my last trek downstairs that there isn't so much as a picture of me displayed anywhere.

Pride has always been a weapon to be wielded against us, Mia and I, never displayed freely and openly. Maybe I'm not losing out on as much as it feels like I am, after all. Unfortunately, the thought brings me little solace as I leave my key on the small table by the front door.

Still, they don't look up. I hold back another sob as the door clicks shut behind me.

I walk mechanically to my car, open the door, and slide into the driver's seat. As soon as I do, everything that just happened crashes over me like a wave, and my throat clogs with tears as I attempt to hold back the floodgates.

Knowing I can't drive like this, I let go and sob uncontrollably for a few minutes. Only the darkening sky brings me to my senses enough to think about my next steps.

I text my grad school friend group, desperately hoping for a lifeline. While I haven't told them everything, they know enough about my parents to know how they are.

Epic fight with the parents tonight, and I'm officially homeless. Can I come crash with one of you until I figure out what I'm going to do? A day or two, maybe? I'll cook and clean!

SAVANNAH

I'd say yes, but my roommate would never be okay with that. You know how she is!

CELESTE

I wish I could help, but my new BF just moved in, and we really need our privacy, if you know what I mean.

IMOGEN

Ugh, I'm drowning in my capstone project. I can't handle any distractions right now. Sorry!

Each reply twists the knife deeper. These girls, who I've poured so much time and energy into over the last two years, can't even offer me a couch to crash on? A shoulder to cry on? A single word of sympathy?

With painful clarity, I realize these friendships have been a one-way street. I've always been there for them, but they scatter like leaves in the wind when I need support.

With shaking hands, I hold back a fresh wave of tears and dial the one person I know I can always count on. Mia.

She answers immediately, concern coloring her voice as I pour out the whole awful story, hiccupping and sobbing.

"Oh, Carrie ... I'm so sorry. This is all my fault," she murmurs, and I can hear the pain in her voice.

"No, Mia, it's not. They're the ones who can't let go of their anger. You were right to get away." The realization hits me like a freight train.

"Listen, let me make a few calls. I'll get back to you in a few minutes, okay? Everything will be all right, I promise."

Even though she can't see me, I nod and whisper a thank you before hanging up.

True to her word, Mia calls back shortly. "I spoke to Joanie. She says you're welcome to stay at her condo in Fremont. She's living here with Greg now, so it's empty, though it's still furnished. The building super will meet you to give you the key."

Fresh tears spring to my eyes, this time from overwhelming gratitude. "Mia ... I don't know what to say. Thank you. And thank Joanie for me, please."

"Of course," Mia says, her voice thick with concern. "Just take care of yourself, Care-bear, okay? And call me tomorrow to let me know you're settled in."

"Will do. Thanks again, Mia. I love you."

"Love you too, kiddo."

As soon as I hang up, Mia texts me the address.

As I navigate the Seattle streets, the streetlights glinting off the windshields of passing cars, a strange sense of calm settles over me. Yes, my life has just been upended. Yes, I'm terrified of what comes next.

But I'm not alone. I have my sister and her friends. People who love and support her, and by extension, me, unconditionally. They demonstrated that on New Year's Eve, when I showed up crying, thanks to more awfulness from my parents. They reassured me, listened, and even cheered me up. And then the whole thing with that Ned creep who apparently tried to spike my drink. I didn't even know it had happened before Nate, Mia's fiancé, swooped in and handled it. And now they're making sure I'm housed and cared for. I tear up again, this time for very different reasons.

As I pull up to Joanie's building to see the super waiting with a kind smile and a shiny new key, I feel the first flicker of hope.

Maybe, just maybe, everything really will be okay.

CHAPTER FOUR

EVAN

"So, Evan, tell us about your favorite scene to film in *Rogue Agent*," the interviewer asks, her smile a bit too wide, her eyes too hungry for a scoop.

I lean back in my chair, painting on my patented charming grin. "Oh, definitely the rooftop chase scene. Lots of stunts, very physical. It was a blast to shoot."

"Any funny behind-the-scenes moments you can share?"

I chuckle and launch into a rehearsed anecdote about a prank my costar and I pulled on the director. The interviewer laughs on cue, but her eyes are glazed over. She's not interested in movie talk.

"Now, Evan," she segues, leaning forward conspiratorially, "what do you like to do when you're not busy being an action hero?"

I shrug, keeping my smile easy. "The usual. Hang out with friends, work out, catch up on sleep."

"No special someone to spend your downtime with?" She arches a perfectly plucked brow.

And there it is. The question I've been fielding for years, the one that never fails to set my teeth on edge.

"I like to keep my personal life private," I deflect, my standard response rolling off my tongue. "But I'm sure you'd rather hear about the incredible special effects in *Rogue Agent*, right?"

But she's not having it. "Come on, Evan. Inquiring minds want to know. Do you ever see yourself settling down? Leaving your playboy days behind?"

I force a laugh, even as irritation prickles under my skin. "Never say never, but I'm focused on my career right now."

The rest of the interview crawls by, a tug-of-war between her probing personal questions and my increasingly strained attempts to steer the conversation back to the movie.

It's a relief when it's over, but short-lived. I'm shuffled to the next interview, then the next, each one a carbon copy of the last: the same inane questions, the same thinly veiled obsession with my personal life.

One interview includes the whole cast, and Kaitlyn is all over me, touching my arm and laughing a bit too loudly at my jokes. She drops hints about our "connection" but never outright says we're dating. It's infuriating.

I try to physically distance myself, scooting my chair away, but she leans closer. By the end, I'm practically hugging the armrest, my jaw clenched so tight I'm surprised my teeth don't crack.

When the press junket finally wraps, I'm exhausted and irritable. I plaster on a smile for the fans outside, sign a few autographs, and then make a beeline for my car.

As I navigate the L.A. traffic, my mind drifts. There was a time when all of this — the interviews, the attention, the adoring fans — was exhilarating. A high I chased relentlessly. But now? Now, it just feels like a never-ending headache.

I realize, with startling clarity, that I need a break. A chance to breathe, to just be Evan for a while, not Evan Edwards, Movie Star.

But my promotional duties are just ramping up. *Rogue Agent* premieres in a month, and then it's off to Europe and Asia for more press tours. I won't have a moment to myself for weeks.

Except for Nate's wedding. A small smile tugs at my lips at the thought. Maybe I could extend my visit and take some real time off.

I pull into my driveway and head inside as I place the call.

"Hey, bro," he answers, sounding surprised but pleased. "What's up?"

"I was thinking about your wedding," I begin, kicking off my shoes and flopping onto the couch. "How would you feel about me sticking around for a bit? I could really use a breather from all the Hollywood insanity."

There's a pause, and I can practically hear Nate's thoughtful frown. "We'll be pretty swamped leading up to the big day," he says slowly. "Then Mia and I are taking off for a week for our honeymoon ..."

"I was hoping to stay for a few weeks total. Maybe through mid-October? I can entertain myself while you're gone, then we can catch up when you're back."

"Yeah, okay," Nate agrees, warmth seeping into his voice. "That sounds great. It's been too long since we've had some quality brother time."

Relief washes over me. "Thanks, man. I'm really looking forward to it."

We chat for a few more minutes, then say our goodbyes. As I hang up, I feel lighter than I have in weeks. Having something to look forward to, a light at the end of the endless press tour tunnel, makes everything seem more bearable.

The feeling lasts approximately four days.

"Evan, darling," my agent greets me over the phone, his tone a mix of forced joviality and underlying tension. "A little birdie told me you're planning quite the extended vacation this fall."

I sigh, pinching the bridge of my nose. "It's not a vacation, Rick. It's my brother's wedding and some much-needed R&R."

"Right, right. But here's the thing. You haven't been getting as many scripts lately. After the *Rogue Agent* press tour wraps, I plan to line up some new genre auditions for you. Expand your audience and keep your career fresh. Can't do that if you're MIA for a month."

My stomach drops. "New genres? Like what?"

"Rom-coms, for starters. Big money right now, and you're a charming, good-looking guy, Evan. You could totally pull off the leading man in a romantic comedy."

I barely suppress a snort. "Flattery will get you nowhere, Rick. I'm not interested in rom-coms."

"Just think about it," he wheedles. "It could be great for your career."

"My career is fine," I snap, but doubt niggles at the back of my mind. Am I not getting as many offers? Have I been so wrapped up in the *Rogue Agent* hype that I haven't noticed?

"At least consider reading a few scripts when you're back," Rick presses.

"I'll think about it," I concede grudgingly. "But the break is non-negotiable. I need this, Rick."

He sighs heavily. "Okay, okay. Go, recharge. But don't stay away too long. This industry has a short memory."

We wrap up the call, but his words linger, echoing in my head long after I've hung up.

Is my career on a downswing? Will I have to start branching out, taking roles outside my wheelhouse, just to stay relevant?

The thought unsettles me more than I care to admit. I've worked hard to get where I am and make a name for myself in action films. The idea of starting over, of having to prove myself all over again ...

I shake my head, pushing the thoughts away. I can't deal with this now. All I can do is focus on the present, on getting through the next few months.

And then, finally, I can escape to Alpine Ridge. To Nate's wedding, to a semblance of normalcy, even if it's just for a little while.

But as I stare out at the glittering expanse of the L.A. skyline, I can't help but wonder if I'm running towards something better ... or just running away from a future I'm not sure I'm ready to face.

CHAPTER FIVE

CARRIE

I stand in front of the mirror, adjusting my cap and gown for the hundredth time. The black fabric feels heavy on my shoulders, weighted with the significance of the day, though the peacock blue hood gives it a pop of brightness that hints at its joy, too.

Graduation. The culmination of years of hard work, late nights, and endless cups of coffee. I should be ecstatic, and part of me is. But there's also a hollow ache in my chest, a pain I can't quite ignore.

My eyes drift to my phone, silent and dark on the dresser. There have been no calls or texts, not from my so-called friends or parents. I checked with the university this morning, and they never even picked up their tickets.

I swallow hard, blinking back the tears that threaten to spill over. I won't let them ruin this day for me. I won't.

A knock at the door startles me out of my melancholy.

"Carrie? You ready?" Mia calls, her voice warm and excited.

I take a deep breath, smoothing my gown one last time. "Yeah, I'm coming."

Mia beams at me as I step out, her eyes suspiciously shiny. "Oh, Care-bear. You look amazing. I'm so proud of you."

Her words wrap around me like a hug, and I feel some of the tightness in my chest ease. At least I have her.

We wind through the busy Seattle streets to the University of Washington's main campus, parting ways for Mia to find her seat while I get in line with the other master's graduates.

There's not much time to be nervous as they begin while I find my place in line. The ceremony passes in a blur of speeches and applause. When my name is called, I walk across the stage with my head held high, focusing on Mia's whoops and cheers, letting them drown out intrusive thoughts of the empty seats where my parents should be.

Afterward, it takes me a bit to find Mia in the sea of bodies. She pulls me into a fierce hug, her smile so wide it must hurt. "Congratulations, graduate! How does it feel?"

"Surreal," I admit, laughing a little. "Like, is this really happening? Am I actually done?"

"You're done," she confirms, grinning. "And we're going to celebrate. Dinner, my treat."

She takes me to Rossi's, a nice Italian place, and as we sip wine and twirl pasta, she asks the question I've been dreading.

"So, what's next for you? I'm sure you've got job offers lined up around the block."

I bite my lip, suddenly fascinated by the remnants of my carbonara. "Actually ... I don't have anything lined up. Not really."

Mia's brow furrows. "What? But you're brilliant, and you've worked so hard. I thought —"

"I was able to snag some last-minute research work for a local election campaign," I interrupt, forcing a smile. "It's just part-time, but it's something."

Mia sets down her fork, her gaze sharpening like her inner lawyer just sniffed out a lie on the witness stand. She may own a bakery now but clearly hasn't lost her edge. "Carrie. What's going on? You know you can tell me anything."

I sigh, the words I've held back for weeks rising in my throat. "It's Mom and Dad," I confess, my voice barely above a whisper. "I ... kind of agreed to work for Dad after graduation. At least, that was the plan. But when they kicked me out —"

"They took back the job offer," Mia finishes, realization dawning on her face. "Oh, Carrie. I'm so sorry."

"No, *I'm* sorry. I should have told you sooner," I mumble, shame burning my cheeks. "I just ... I didn't want to admit how bad it was or that I'd let him talk me into it even after everything you went through with them."

Mia reaches across the table, gripping my hand tightly. "You have nothing to be sorry for. They're the ones who should be ashamed, not you."

Her fierce protectiveness and the anger simmering beneath her words hit me hard. Tears sting my eyes, and I let them fall, too tired to hold them back.

Mia moves to my side of the booth, wrapping her arm around me as I cry. She doesn't say anything, just holds me, letting me purge the pain and disappointment.

When my sobs finally subside, she hands me a napkin, her own eyes red-rimmed. "Okay," she says, her voice steady and determined. "Here's what we're going to do. That research position, can you do it remotely?"

I nod, wiping my nose. "I think so. Why?"

"Because I want you to stay with me and Nate in Alpine Ridge. Honestly, we could really use your help with the town elections, but I didn't ask before because I figured you'd be on to bigger and better things. While we have a few volunteers, none really know the process's ins and outs. Not like you do."

I stare at her, hope blooming in my chest. "Really? You'd want me to do that?"

"Of course!" Mia exclaims. "It would be perfect. You could use your skills, build your resume, and have a place to stay while you figure out your next move.

And the town wins, too. Plus," she adds, smiling softly, "I'd get to have my little sister around for a while."

I throw my arms around her, fresh tears falling, but this time from relief and gratitude. "Thank you," I whisper. "Thank you so much."

"Is that a yes?" she teases.

I smile through the tears and nod. She hugs me back tightly. "Good. And you're welcome. Because that's what family is for," she murmurs. "*Real* family, anyway."

We finish our meal, and the conversation turns to lighter things — Mia's wedding plans, funny stories from my grad school days, fond memories from our childhood. But in the back of my mind, I'm already thinking ahead to Alpine Ridge, to the opportunity waiting for me there.

It's not the path I'd planned, not by a long shot. But maybe, just maybe, it's the path I'm meant to be on. A chance to start fresh, to prove to myself and everyone else what I'm capable of, away from the unreasonable demands of so-called family and fake friends.

As we leave the restaurant, Mia's arm linked through mine, I feel excitement amid the uncertainty. I don't know what the future holds, but for the first time in a long time, I'm eager to find out.

CHAPTER SIX

CARRIE

Who knew so much could change in a few short months? I was skeptical it would work out when Mia asked me to move in with her and Nate. Yet, here I am, still in Alpine Ridge. Though I'd visited here so often as a child, it's long since felt like a second home. But when Gran died, I'll admit I avoided it for a long time. Or maybe that had to do with Gran's passing coinciding with Mia's change in direction and the subsequent fallout with our parents. That sure didn't help.

Fortunately, I've finally re-found the peace I once had here. Something about the fresh mountain air and beautiful surroundings makes it impossible to hold on to a past that doesn't want to hold on to you anymore. I see why Mia and the rest of our found family decided to make Alpine Ridge their refuge. Mia's soon-to-be-husband Nate, their friend Greg, heck, even Mia's sassy, cynical best friend from law school, Joanie, seems happy here. And I'm starting to be too.

I at least have a purpose now and people who don't demand things from me but give me room to be myself. It's allowed me to shed the sheltered, spoiled version of me that was a result of being raised by shitty parents. I'm happy with myself in a way I've never been before. Though right now, that might be because I'm sitting in Greg and Joanie's living room, surrounded by friends and painting my toenails a bride-approved shade of hot pink.

In fact, the smell of nail polish fills the air as we all lounge around the living room, our hands and feet in various drying stages. It's the night before Mia's wedding, and we decided a little pampering was in order. Mia, Joanie, Rae, who works at the bakery with Mia, and even their bakery assistant, Penny. Just us girls.

"All right," Joanie announces, hobbling in from the kitchen with champagne flutes on a tray. "Time for a toast." She hands us each a glass in turn.

"God, Joanie, be careful you don't trip," Mia says anxiously.

Joanie shoots her a look. "Mia. You know my five-foot-nothing self is used to litigating in sky-high heels. I think I can handle doling out a few drinks while heel walking so I don't smudge Rae's beautiful work."

Rae chuckles and accepts her flute. "I'll go first," she says, diverting the attention back to why we're here. She lifts her glass. "To Mia and Nate, who I watched fall in love. And tomorrow, I'll get to watch them become husband and wife. Here's to watching them make some beautiful babies next." She winks, and Mia good-naturedly rolls her eyes.

"Ooh, yes, make pretty babies I can spoil!" Joanie agrees, raising her flute. "Oh, and to the bride and groom, of course. Here's to hopefully never leaving your hotel room in Hawaii." She winks suggestively at Mia. Mia rolls her eyes for real this time, but she laughs at her audacious best friend.

"To my big sister," I offer, raising my glass. "Who taught me about boys, driving stick, and how to sneak out of my bedroom window —"

"Bet those all came in handy on the same night," Joanie murmurs, and we all laugh.

I shake my head, having lost my train of thought but not minding. "Anyway … to Mia. You deserve all the happiness in the world, and I'm so glad you've found someone like Nate."

Joanie purses her lips and nods emphatically. "Have you seen him with his shirt off? She's a *very* lucky woman."

Penny, who has said very little this whole time, turns bright red. Mia gestures toward her while glaring at Joanie. "You're scaring Penny, Jo."

Penny blushes harder and shakes her head. "He is pretty hot," she offers in a small voice. Joanie sits up with a triumphant grin.

Mia bursts out laughing. "Can we not talk about how hot my fiancé is? In fact, no more wedding talk. Let's just have fun, okay?"

"Oh, come on," Joanie protests. "I haven't even inspected your honeymoon lingerie. Surely —"

"So, I can't believe the vote to make Alpine Ridge an official town is finally happening in November," Rae says in an obvious bid to change the subject while admiring her freshly painted toes.

Mia gives her a grateful look, which Rae responds to with a smile. "Right? It seems like it's all happened so fast," Mia agrees. "I hope it goes through."

"It will," I assure her, reaching over and squeezing her hand. "I've been talking to people around town. Almost everyone is on board and looking forward to all the benefits of the incorporation. It's a foregone conclusion in everyone's minds at this point."

"And my work here is done." Joanie dusts off her shoulders jokingly. She's not wrong, though. She was the one who listened to everyone's wish for it and made it happen.

Mia smiles tolerantly at her. "Yes, thank you, Joanie, master of the universe and all things lawyerly," she teases. "Seriously, though, it's exactly what I'd hoped for. And the bakery is already getting busier. I had to hire more help, especially since I'll be gone for a week." She grins, clearly giddy at the thought of her impending honeymoon.

"And we're all ready to chip in, so you don't have to worry about a thing," Rae assures her. "Penny, Riley, and I will hold down the fort while you're gone. So, you just focus on enjoying yourself."

Joanie opens her mouth, and Mia holds up a hand and says, "Nope, I'm not going there."

We all laugh.

"Oh please, that was too easy anyway. I was going to say that since we're off wedding topics … I've been talking to some law firms in Ellensburg," she shares. "Seeing if they'd be interested in having an Alpine Ridge-based partner to expand their client base. Now that my part in the incorporation is done, I've got time on my hands. I could help with their cases in my areas of expertise, and they could help with mine. I've got some promising leads."

"That's great, Joanie," I gush. I've known Joanie for years through Mia, and I've never seen her at anything but full tilt. She's clearly happy here with Greg but I'm glad to hear she's still pursuing her own passions too. "So, I guess Greg's going to have to get used to flying solo at the community center again, huh?"

Joanie smirks. "Yes, well, I suspect he'll be fine. I'm not sure he's noticed all the organizing I've been doing, though it's kept me busy enough."

Mia lays a hand on Joanie's arm. "He notices more than you think. The other day, he told Nate that you discovered a stash of tools and equipment he'd forgotten about that allowed him to fix up a few of the broken machines. Some of which Nate can use at the wellness center, too."

"Oh good, because lord knows they don't have enough exercise equipment already," Joanie jokes drily.

Rae smirks at the pair of them, then turns to Penny. "How about you, sugar? What's new in your life these days?" It's just like Rae to pull everyone into the conversation. She's such a sweetheart.

Penny blushes. "I'm thinking of transferring to the University of Washington once I finish my lower division classes at Yakima Valley College," she replies bashfully. "But I'm not sure. It's a big change."

"Oh, you should. U-dub is a great school," Mia says warmly. "Carrie, Joanie, and I all loved it there. You should go for it."

"I want to. It's just … it's so *big*," she explains. "I'm afraid I'd be overwhelmed by it all."

"Well, you know yourself best," I offer. "But they have a couple of smaller campuses in Tacoma and Bothell. Both are great and could offer you a more low-key experience."

Penny brightens visibly. "I hadn't thought of that. Thanks."

I smile warmly at her, remembering how overwhelming it was for me, even having lived in Seattle my whole life. I feel a sudden swell of affection for Penny and all these women as we listen to and encourage each other.

"What about you, Carrie?" Joanie asks. "How's the election prep going?"

I sit up a little straighter, excitement bubbling in my chest. "It's going well. I've been doing a lot of research, preparing to guide the candidates through the mayoral and town council elections. And like I mentioned, I've even started talking to people, just listening to their hopes and dreams for Alpine Ridge. It's been eye-opening."

"I bet," Mia says, pride in her eyes. "You're going to rock this."

I duck my head, feeling a blush creep up my neck. "Thanks, Mia. I'm just so excited to get started."

"And how's living with Rae?" Joanie asks, a teasing glint in her eye.

I laugh. "It's been great. It was kind of a goal for me to live apart from my family. Not that I don't love you, Mia, and while I wanted to give you and Nate space once you were married, honestly, I mostly just wanted to start living my own life. And Rae's a great roommate. I mean, she always brings home extra goodies from the bakery," I joke to take the focus off the seriousness of my confession. I didn't mention that my part-time research job doesn't cover the rent, so the inheritance Gran left me has been a safety net and a godsend. I hope overseeing the town's elections will give me the experience to land a full-time job after this.

Rae laughs, bringing me back to the conversation. "What can I say? Leftovers are one of my favorite perks of the job."

We all giggle, the champagne and good company making us loose and happy.

Suddenly, Mia clears her throat, her expression turning serious. "Hey, there's something you all need to know. About the wedding."

We sober up, leaning in.

"One of Nate's brothers ... well, he's kind of famous." She cringes a little. "Actually, like, really famous."

My eyebrows shoot up. "What?! Why haven't you mentioned this before? Who is he?"

Mia takes a deep breath. "Sorry, it was need-to-know only. He doesn't want to disrupt the wedding, so Nate and I thought it would be best if you knew beforehand." She pauses. "Nate's youngest brother is Evan Edwards."

There's a beat of silence, then the room erupts.

"Evan Edwards? *The* Evan Edwards?" Penny squeals, waving her hands for emphasis. I've never seen her so animated.

"Holy shit, Mia!" Joanie exclaims. *Joanie*, who is impressed by practically nothing, is clearly just as surprised and interested as the rest of us.

I'm certainly stunned, anyway. So much that I sit there, shocked into silence.

Evan Edwards. The man whose movies I've watched a hundred times. Whose posters graced my college dorm room walls. Nate's *brother?* I did not see that coming.

But now that she's said it ... actually, I can see it. They have the same tall, broad-shouldered build. The same artfully messy light brown hair and hazel eyes. Though from what I've seen in his movies, Evan's physique leans more like a swimmer — all lean, long muscle. Nothing like Nate's bulky bodybuilder frame.

"I need you all to be cool about it," Mia says, her tone pleading. "Please don't make a big deal. He's just Nate's brother, okay?"

We all nod, murmuring our assent.

But inside, I'm fangirling so hard I can barely breathe.

As the others start chatting again, Mia pulls me aside. "One more thing. Evan will stay at our place while we're on our honeymoon. And for a couple weeks after, too."

My heart stops. "Okay," I manage to squeak out.

"I was hoping you could make sure to include him in things. You know, so he doesn't feel lonely or left out."

I nod, not trusting myself to speak. Me? Hang out with Evan Edwards? For weeks? Why is she asking me to do this like it's a chore? I want to squeal as loud as Penny did and start jumping up and down. But Mia asked us to play it cool. I can go nuts later when I'm alone.

"Of course," I finally say, my voice miraculously steady. "I'd be happy to."

Mia hugs me, clearly relieved. "Thank you, Carrie. You're the best."

I hug her back, my mind reeling. As we settle back into our spots, the conversation flowing around me, I'm only half-listening.

The other half of my brain is spinning, imagining all the ways I could potentially embarrass myself in front of Evan freaking Edwards.

But beneath the nerves, there's a thrill of excitement. This is a chance to get to know the man behind the movies. To maybe, just maybe, become friends with someone I've admired from afar for so long.

Suddenly, I'm looking forward to Mia's wedding for a new reason. As I sip my wine, grinning at a joke Rae just told, I can't help but feel like my life in Alpine Ridge is about to get a whole lot more interesting.

CHAPTER SEVEN

EVAN

The sun is just beginning to set as I drive into Alpine Ridge, painting the sky in stunning shades of orange and pink. I'm immediately struck by the town's beauty, nestled among the towering evergreens and rugged mountains. It's like something off a postcard.

My awe grows as I wind my way up to Nate's house. The modern, glass-walled structure seems to blend seamlessly with the surrounding forest, making you feel fully immersed in nature. I can imagine how peaceful it must be to live here, far from the chaos of Los Angeles. I'm starting to understand why my big brother left and never looked back.

I park my rental car and head to the front door. I knock, but there's no answer. After a minute, I decide, fuck it, this is my brother's house, and he's expecting me, so I try the door handle. Not surprisingly, it's unlocked. Why bother locking your door this far from civilization?

I head inside, following the sound of animated voices around the corner to a large living room where I find Nate's "bachelor party" in full swing. And by that, I mean Nate, our other brother Dylan, and a third guy, and they look like they've just been lounging around, drinking beer, and chatting. Not that I blame them. The large, tan leather couches and crackling fire look mighty appealing, especially after half a day of traveling.

"Hey," I greet them. All three look my way. Nate hops up. "Sorry, I'm late. My flight was delayed." I hold up a bottle of expensive scotch. "But I come bearing gifts."

Nate grins, pulling me into a bear hug. "No worries, man. I'm just glad you made it."

When he releases me, Dylan steps up and slaps me on the back. "Good to see you, Ev."

"The Edwards brothers, together again," I proclaim. "So, what kind of trouble are we getting into tonight?" I shake the bottle of booze for effect.

Nate smirks. "Unless you want to go find a bear to fight or something there isn't any trouble to be had here. One of the things I like best about this town." He gestures to the other guy. "This is my friend, Greg. Greg, this is my brother Evan."

Greg rises and steps forward to shake my hand. "Nice to meet you," he says casually. No fawning. No questions or comments. I like this guy already.

"You too," I reply. "You like scotch?"

Greg laughs and nods, so Nate takes the bottle and pours glasses for us all. We sit down and I listen as they pick the conversation back up. I don't even engage at first, happy to sip my scotch and mellow out for a bit. As I observe them, I'm struck by how relaxed and happy Nate seems. He's always been laid-back, but there's a new light in his eyes as he talks about Mia and the wedding. I've never seen him this excited, and it warms my heart.

It's great to see Dylan, too. As a cellist with a touring philharmonic orchestra, we usually only catch him around the holidays, and even then, it's hit or miss. But he's here now, regaling us with tales from the road and gushing about the woman in his life.

"I'm planning to take a break from touring," he admits, a soft smile on his face. "Spend more time with her, you know?"

Nate voices his approval, and I nod, understanding the pull of a genuine connection all too well. It's a rare thing.

As the night wears on, the conversation turns to me. Greg, who runs the community and fitness center here and apparently shares my passion for high-intensity interval training, asks how things are going in my world.

I hesitate, the weight of my career worries suddenly heavy again on my shoulders. I hadn't missed the burden. "Honestly? I've been struggling a bit," I confess, the words tumbling out before I can stop them. "Feeling stuck, like I need a change."

To my surprise, there's no judgment in their eyes, only understanding and support.

"Yeah? Is that what this break is about?" Nate asks.

I sigh and nod. "Pretty much. Though I'm not expecting to have an epiphany or anything. I just needed to get away from all the pressure."

Dylan raises a brow. "Pressure to do what?"

I smirk at him. Dylan's always been perceptive. "Rom-coms," I admit. All three men groan in sympathy, and I can't help but laugh. "Yeah, that's pretty much how I reacted, too."

"That may be a far cry from what you're used to, but if anyone can make that work, you can," Nate assures me. "But if you don't want to, that's okay too. You've got to do what's right for you."

Dylan nods his agreement. "You've been doing this a long time, Ev, and killing it. If you want to pivot, great, but it's okay to just take a step back and live your life for once."

Greg snorts, and we all look at him. "Sorry. I just … it's weird hearing them give you advice because I doubt any of us know what it's like to be a movie star," he says, giving an apologetic look toward Nate and Dylan. Then, turning back toward me, he adds, "But I do know what it's like to resist the pressure to do things you don't want to do. It all comes down to what kind of man you want to be. That's hard to remember when someone's breathing down your neck."

My chest constricts at his words. Damn, if he didn't just hit me right in the gut with that one. I nod slowly. "Fuck," I breathe out. "That's exactly what I'm going through. Thanks for that." I clap him on the back.

"Anytime." He holds up his glass. "To being the kind of man you want to be."

"Hear, hear," Nate says. And we all clink glasses and down the rest of our drinks.

I swallow hard, forcing the liquor past the emotion thickening my throat. A rush of gratitude flows through me for my brothers and this newfound friend. In the cutthroat world of Hollywood, it's rare to find people who don't pressure you to be someone you're not. But here, with these guys, I feel like I can breathe again.

We talk and drink late into the night, the worries of the outside world fading away under the camaraderie and laughter.

The next morning, I wake in the guest room to the gentle rustling of leaves and the soft chirping of birds. As I blink away the remnants of sleep, I'm struck again by the serenity of Nate's house. The bedroom's glass walls, which I hadn't noticed in the dark of night, offer a stunning view of the sun-dappled forest. With every passing moment, I gain a deeper understanding of Nate's decision to leave behind his high-powered plastic surgery career in L.A. for this peaceful mountain haven. Maybe I've been buying vacation houses in all the wrong places. Because this is what a vacation should feel like.

Unfortunately, now isn't the time for languishing in self-reflection. Today, my big brother is getting married.

With a smile, I hop out of bed and shower quickly before getting dressed and heading downstairs to help Nate with any last-minute wedding preparations. But it seems like his fiancée set everything out before heading to her own pre-wedding celebration yesterday. So, before I know it, we're driving down to the community center, where the reception will be held, apparently, to meet up with the bridal party.

In the light of day, as we drive into the town proper, it's lost none of its charm. Even the dated-looking wooden buildings are a nostalgic throwback to simpler, more peaceful times. When the world moved more slowly, and family was at the core of everything. It makes me realize how much I've missed mine.

"You all right, Ev?" Dylan murmurs from the passenger side of the backseat.

"I'm great, thanks. It's just so good to be here with you guys."

Dylan gives me an appraising look. "You seem different."

I take a deep breath. "I'm ... I don't know what I am. I've had this feeling for a while. Like I know something has to change. I just didn't think it would mean doing less of what I got into the biz for." I shrug, not sure how to explain it. Not sure I even *understand* it.

"Change is hard," he replies thoughtfully. "I never thought I'd be stepping back from the philharmonic. Yet here we are."

"But you're happy?" I ask, tilting my head.

Dylan, the most reserved Evans brother, *grins*. "Ecstatic, actually. Denise is …" He sighs wistfully. "I love her so much," he admits. "But that doesn't mean it's not hard to step back from what I was doing."

I give him a reassuring pat on the knee. "I'm happy for you, though. And I have no doubt you'll find a similar opportunity locally. Surely, there's a musical outfit in the Portland area that would love to have you."

"Actually, before I even knew Denise was it for me, I'd started looking for something near Mom and Dad. They're getting on in age, so I figured I should be ready to move there if they needed me. Turns out there are several great ensembles that were eager to have me. It took having those options to admit that I wasn't enjoying what I was doing even before Denise was in the picture. Not like I did when I started, anyway."

"Really?" I ask incredulously. "How come you never told me?" Dylan and I were close growing up despite being four-and-a-half years apart, and we still talk often, considering our demanding work schedules.

Dylan huffs. "Because I couldn't admit it to myself. It had become so much a part of who I was I couldn't wrap my head around it not being a good fit anymore. But at the end of the day, I'm not a kid anymore. The on-the-go life was fun for a while, but at some point, I realized I wanted to settle down and plant roots. I just needed a good enough reason to make that leap."

"Denise?"

He nods. "Denise. But you're so much more decisive than me, Ev. You've never needed an excuse or a reason to be who you are and do exactly what you want."

I smile. "So, you're telling me to get in touch with my inner desires and set them free?" I joke.

Dylan lifts a shoulder. "I'm not telling you to do anything, man. Do what you want. When have you not, though?"

I pause, thinking about what he's said. I *haven't* been doing what I want, settling for scripts that came to me, bowing to my manager's "career advice." Maybe that's why this all feels like a slog lately.

I realize suddenly that the car's become awfully quiet. And that we've stopped at what is presumably the community center.

I look up to see Nate gazing back at me from the front passenger seat. He doesn't say a word. He doesn't have to. Being nearly a decade older than me, I've always looked to Nate for his opinion and, to an extent, his approval. So, I know his expressions well. And the look on his face tells me he heard what Dylan said and concurs. All the feelings I've been suppressing for months surge in my chest. I take a deep breath and shove them back down.

"I appreciate the support, guys. But right now, what I want the most is to see my big brother get married." I clap Nate on the shoulder.

Nate grins in response. "Hell, yeah."

A sharp rapping knock sounds on Nate's window. We turn to see our parents outside, and all of us, except Greg, jump out of the car like we're kids again and rush into a family embrace. As my parents' arms wrap around me, another rush of emotion swells, stronger this time, bringing tears to my eyes. I blink them back.

I tell myself it's just being on the receiving end of my brothers' love and support, seeing my parents for the first time in months, and being here for such an emotionally charged occasion. That's all. I'm most certainly not on the verge of an emotional breakdown.

Probably not.

Maybe.

Or … Am I?

Shit. I think I am.

CHAPTER EIGHT

CARRIE

"There," I say, stepping back to admire my handiwork. "You look perfect."

Mia turns to the mirror, her eyes widening as she takes in the delicate crown of white asters nestled in her long, dark waves. "Carrie, it's beautiful. Thank you."

I smile, blinking back the sudden sting of tears. "I just wanted today to be extra special for you. You deserve it, Mia. You and Nate both."

She turns, pulling me into a tight hug. "I love you, sis. I'm so glad you're here with me."

"I wouldn't be anywhere else," I murmur, holding her close.

Another pair of arms wrap around us, and we laugh. "What? You're both too cute not to hug," Joanie says affectionately.

A knock at the door breaks the moment. Rae pokes her head in, her face split in a wide grin. "It's time, ladies. Everyone's here."

Mia takes a deep breath, smoothing her hands over her flowy lace and tulle dress. I likewise adjust my burgundy strapless cocktail dress, and then Joanie and I flank Mia, ready to walk with her toward her future.

As we step out into the main room, I see Nate standing with what is unmistakably his family: four tall men, including Nate, with light brown hair and huge smiles, one of them considerably older and standing next to a small, older blond woman.

Nate's eyes find Mia, and the look on his face steals my breath. It's pure, unadulterated love and awe, tears glistening in his eyes as he takes her in. Mia beams back at him, and for a moment, it's like they're the only two people in the world.

And then my gaze slides to the man standing beside Nate, and my heart stutters in my chest.

Evan Edwards.

He's even more devastatingly handsome in person. His navy suit and white button-front shirt are well-tailored and hug his lean, muscled frame, and his light brown hair is artfully tousled. When his hazel eyes meet mine, I feel a jolt of electricity down my spine.

"Mia's already met my family, but Rae, Joanie, Penny, Carrie, this is my dad, Steven, my mom, Diane, and my brothers Dylan and Evan," Nate says, introducing everyone with gestures.

"So nice to meet you all," Diane gushes with a smile. The warmth in her voice makes me think of hugs and family holidays full of joy. I hope Mia gets both and more with Nate's family because goodness knows we've never had either.

"Now, I've heard talk of Rae before from Nate, but how do the rest of you lovely ladies fit into the picture?" Steven asks with his own gentle smile.

"Penny works with Rae and me at the bakery," Mia offers. "Joanie has been my best friend since law school and is our newest Alpine Ridge townie —"

Joanie scoffs. "Townie? I'm not … okay, actually, fair," she accedes. We all laugh, and Joanie shrugs. "I'm a Seattleite originally. I guess I'm still getting used to it."

"And Carrie —" Mia pulls me close "— is my sister. Since she just got her master's in political science, she's here helping us with the town incorporation elections."

"And they're not twins," Joanie adds. Because we look so much alike, we often get asked if we are. I forget that these days since we went years without spending much time together. Though at just over five foot six, I'm almost two inches shorter than Mia and have our dad's chin.

A wave of sorrow washes over me at the thought of our father. Our parents. As much as I miss them in some ways, it's best they're not here.

"Well, I hate to rush this party, but there will be plenty of time at the reception to get to know each other, and we have some folks waiting for us outside," Rae points out.

"Oh! Of course," Mia agrees, moving forward. She gets as far as where Nate stands by the door before she stops and looks up at him. "Hey," she says softly.

He looks down at her, his eyes sparkling. "Hey." He kisses her lips softly, and Penny and I sigh in unison.

Greg smirks and leads Joanie past them. I feel a hand on my back, and suddenly, Rae propels Penny and me forward.

We step outside to a small crowd of the half-dozen townsfolk Mia and Nate were close enough with to invite to the celebration. I recognize Meg, a sweet blond woman who works at the coffee stand, and I wave hello.

There isn't much time for talking, though, as Greg and Nate lead the way to the field of wildflowers where the ceremony will be held. It's not far, just a few minutes' walk up the path behind the community center.

When we're almost there, Evan falls into step beside me. His presence is both thrilling and unnerving.

"For the record, I think it's obvious you aren't twins," he opens. Hearing his familiar, deep voice sends a wave of goosebumps over my skin. It's really him. Evan Edwards. Here in Alpine Ridge.

Stay cool, Carrie.

"Oh? Why's that?" I ask, looking ahead toward the mass of wildflowers now peaking over the horizon.

"She's taller. You have a heart-shaped face. But mostly, while she's beautiful, you're absolutely stunning," he remarks, his voice low and warm.

My eyes jump to his face to find him watching Nate and Dylan come to a stop in the sea of white, yellow, and purple flowers framed by trees filled with leaves in blazing autumn reds, oranges, and golds.

I feel a flush creeping up my neck from Evan's unexpected compliment.

Stay. Cool.

I let out a flippant laugh. "I'm sure you say that to all the single women at weddings," I tease.

A smile tugs at his lips as he turns his gaze to mine. "I speak only the truth."

"Mhm," I murmur, unconvinced. But even if he's totally just laying on the charm, I can't help the flip-flop of my stomach at the fact that Evan Edwards said I'm stunning. Me.

"So, who's older?" he asks.

I raise a brow. Given that Mia is more than five years older than me, I wonder if that's a compliment to her or an insult to me. "She is," I reply drily. "I'm twenty-six — well, twenty-seven in a couple of months. She's thirty-two."

"That's about how far apart Dylan and I are. Except, I'm thirty-five, and he's thirty-nine, almost forty."

"Are you all close?"

He nods. "Dylan and I especially, since we're closer in age. What about you and Mia?'

I shrug. "She's pretty much my best friend. We've been through a lot together."

His expression softens. "That's special. Family is everything."

I nod, a lump rising in my throat. "It is. Even when it's complicated."

Something in my tone must give me away because Evan leans in close. His smell almost overwhelms me — an intoxicating blend of the ocean and evergreens. "Complicated can be good, though. Means you care enough to work through the tough stuff."

I glance up at him, surprised by his insight. But before I can respond, Dylan calls everyone to order, and the ceremony begins.

I try to focus on the love and joy emanating from Mia and Nate, the beautiful vows they speak, and the tears and love they share. And I do, mostly, though my gaze keeps straying to Evan, to the strong line of his jaw, the way the sun gilds his hair.

I'm starstruck, I realize. Completely and utterly captivated by this man who, until today, existed only on a screen. But I shut it out as much as possible and focus on my sister and Nate.

So, I'm fully in the moment as Dylan declares, "I now pronounce you husband and wife!"

I watch, misty-eyed, as Nate and Mia share their first kiss as a married couple. When they break apart and turn toward us, I don't hesitate, rushing in to hug them both, my heart full to bursting.

After the happy couple has been passed around for hugs, Rae leads us all back to the community center for the reception. I'm suddenly glad as I realize I'm ravenous. I'd been so excited for Mia this morning that I forgot to eat.

Meg finds me for the walk back, linking her arm with mine.

"Is that really Evan Edwards?" she whispers.

I grin and nod enthusiastically. "Yes, he's Nate's brother." We share a look … and then an excited giggle.

"He's so handsome. Even more than on screen," she gushes. "What's he like?"

I shrug. "I don't really know him, honestly. We just met this morning. I only learned they were brothers last night."

Meg throws a hand to her forehead and feigns swooning. "Ugh. You're just so lucky to be related to him now. I'd just *die*. How long will he be here for, do you know?"

Something in her tone rubs me the wrong way. "I'm not sure," I lie, deciding Evan probably wouldn't want us telling everyone he'll be here for a few weeks.

"Well, maybe I can catch his eye at the reception. I wouldn't say no to a fling with a movie star. And lord knows there aren't many eligible men in Alpine Ridge. If he —"

"Speaking of, I'd love to sit down with you soon and talk about the kinds of businesses you'd like to see come to town first. Maybe some that would attract young, single men? More restaurants? Maybe even a mall?" I'm reaching, but hearing her talk about seducing Evan is going to turn me into the green-eyed monster.

"A mall? In Alpine Ridge?" Meg laughs. "That'll be the day. But I wouldn't say no to more restaurants. I'm a hopeless cook, and the tavern's fare barely counts as food, if you know what I mean."

I give her a vague smile. "I know what you mean. Is there even any chicken in the chicken strips?"

"Right? Knowing Jerry, it's probably some low-cost chicken substitute or something. Cheap bastard. Did you know he's thinking of running for mayor?"

I had heard that from Jerry himself, but I lead her down that conversation path as we head into the community center, load up plates, and sit down to eat. Rae and Penny join us not long after, and the distraction is complete.

Except, I'm continually distracted, too, by Evan. I can't help sneaking peeks at him as he mingles with Mia, his parents, and the other guests. I can't hear what's being said, but it's clear he's charming the pants off everyone. Hopefully, not literally.

I'd ask myself why I care, but if I'm being honest, I know why. I would never tell Mia — or anyone — this in a million years, especially not now, but Evan Edwards is a frequent lead in my personal fantasies. Yes, *those* kinds of personal fantasies. I know he's a famous movie star and a supposed playboy. He probably sleeps with tons of gorgeous women. Hell, he likely has one in every town he passes through.

But the idea of him being with someone in Alpine Ridge makes me feel all sorts of things I've never felt — jealousy, for starters. I mean, I've dated. I've had a few boyfriends, including a couple of serious ones. But I've never worried or thought about other women's interest in them. So, I don't know why it bothers me this time because, on the surface, it makes perfect sense that every woman in town has probably seen his movies and would find him just as attractive as I do. And, apparently, as Meg does.

It also makes me feel an intense longing like I've never felt. For excitement and passion. How could being with someone like him be anything but? I've had "nice." I've even had moments of passion. But I know anything I'd experience with him would blow all that out of the water. And my life could use a good dose of that right about now.

I sigh heavily as we all finish our meals but am saved from my own thoughts when Nate stands up to give a speech.

"Thanks everyone for coming," he says. "Obviously, this is a casual affair, so I'll keep this short. But I just wanted to say how much Mia and I appreciate every one of you. We're so lucky to be surrounded by our amazing friends and family as we take this step together. We wouldn't be here without all of you, and we're so grateful." Nate turns to Mia. "And I'm also grateful for this amazing woman, who is now my wife." He clears his throat, clearly fighting tears. I blink against my own. "It took a little tough love from another amazing woman, Mia's grandmother, Dorothy — God rest her soul —but we found each other at just the right time. I love you so much, Mia, and I'm honored to be your husband."

And I can't help it; tears stream down my face as my sister embraces her new husband. As they kiss, their lips once again seal their promise to love and be there for each other no matter what life brings. It makes me feel so many things, and my heart swells to near bursting.

Mia pulls Nate toward the dance floor, where they share their first dance as husband and wife. I'm still crying like a baby when Nate's parents join in, followed by Joanie and Greg. It's only when Dylan asks Rae to dance that it occurs to me that Meg probably hasn't forgotten her quest to seduce Evan. My heart stutters anxiously as my eyes search the room for him. When I can't find him, my breath catches in my throat. Combined with having just finished crying, a little choked sound escapes me.

A handkerchief materializes in my peripheral vision. I look up to find Evan standing beside me. "You look like you could use this," he offers.

I smile gratefully and accept the proffered hanky. "Thank you," I say softly, dabbing at my eyes.

Evan crouches down. "It's my pleasure." He pauses as if hesitating. "Are you okay?"

I sniff deeply and smile. "I'm great. Just so happy for those two," I assure him. It's mostly true, anyway.

He looks over at Nate and Mia, dancing with Mia's head resting on Nate's chest. "Me too," he murmurs. Then he looks back at me and rises, offering his hand. "Dance with me?"

This time, my breath catches for a different reason, and I lose my words. So, I simply nod and take his hand. He tugs me to my feet and leads me to where everyone is dancing. He slips a hand around my waist, drawing me gently against him. My knees nearly buckle being so close to him. I think he knows because he pulls me in tighter, and I have to focus hard on breathing.

"So, Nate says you're going to be my babysitter?" Evan says in a low voice.

I can't help but snicker. "That's one way to put it."

He cocks an eyebrow, and the look is so sexy it makes my heart race. "Is there another way to put it?" he asks with a note of mischief in his tone.

I bite into my bottom lip to master myself. "Mia said I should make sure you don't get lonely," I reply in a husky tenor I don't recognize.

Now, both of Evan's brows raise. "Is that so?" One corner of his lips curls up, and my whole body flushes with heat. "And how would *you* put it?"

My eyelashes flutter of their own accord. Not flirtatiously, just because that's apparently what Evan Edwards does to me. God, I hope I don't faint.

I breathe steadily for a few heartbeats before looking up into his eyes. "I assume you're here to get away and relax. So, I'd put it as I'm here to help make that happen. If there's anything I can do, just let me know. Even if that's staying out of your hair and making sure other people do too," I reply, blushing under his gaze and looking away.

"That's incredibly kind of you, thank you." His tone is different ... raw, and honest, and I look back up at him. This time, he has no sexy smirk or tantalizing raised brow.

I shrug, equally uncomfortable with this more real, down-to-earth version of Evan. He's just as unnervingly charismatic.

I open my mouth to respond when I hear Mia say it's time to cut the cake. Everyone rushes excitedly toward the small but gorgeous confection and watches the couple gently feed each other the decadent Chantilly crème chiffon cake.

"What, she's not going to smash it in his face?" Evan remarks from just behind me.

I turn and give him a look. "You don't actually like that awful tradition, do you?"

Evan gives me a mischievous grin. "Only if it's my brother getting messy."

I chuckle and shake my head. "I am not sad I never had any brothers."

Evan slings his arm over my shoulder, and I'm so shocked by the sudden intimacy that I stare up at him open-mouthed.

"Oh, come on, it's all in good fun," he says, winking at me. "But he's probably too old for that anyway."

Rae starts cutting the rest of the cake and handing out pieces. Evan drops his arm and heads to get one. Meg slinks up next to me.

"He was touching you," she says with wide eyes.

I can't help but let out an off-kilter laugh. Because here I thought that must have been my overactive imagination trying to make my fantasies come to life. "He was, wasn't he?"

"And he looked pretty into you on that dance floor." Meg looks at me meaningfully.

I wave her off. "He's just a flirt."

Meg snaps her fingers in front of my face so abruptly that I flinch. "Wake up, Carrie, the man is *interested*. Don't let that opportunity pass you by because if you don't take it, I will." She gives me an "I dare you" look that still somehow conveys she doesn't really mean it. She's just trying to get me to hook up with Evan.

"If he's interested, he'll say he is. But I'm not about to throw myself at him," I whisper.

Meg rolls her eyes and shakes her head. "Fine, play it safe."

I purse my lips. That's not the first time I've been accused of being too cautious. But I can't help it; it's just how I am. Always afraid of saying or doing the wrong thing and upsetting somebody. And since he's Nate's brother, I don't want to do anything to upset their family by misinterpreting his attention and making a move on him only to be rejected. How awkward would that make holidays for Mia? *I'm sorry my sister shamelessly threw herself at you, but thanks for the scarf.* I shake my head, determined not to mess anything up for my big sister.

But Meg is gone before I can respond, and Evan is back with two slices of cake. He hands me one. "Mia brought this cake to my parents' house at Christmas, and I've been dreaming about it ever since," he admits, taking a huge bite. He jokingly rolls his eyes back in his head and moans deep in his throat.

The sound ripples through me like a physical touch, skating down my throat, over my chest and belly, and settling between my thighs.

I take a subtle, deep breath to fight off the wave of lust. And then I take a bite of cake. "It's good," I admit. "But you haven't lived until you've had her hot cocoa cake. Three words: homemade marshmallow filling."

Evan's eyes widen. "You're joking."

I chuckle and take another bite of cake. "I'm Mia's sister. I don't joke about cake."

"Damn," he swears. "Please tell me you don't bake, too."

My brows bunch together. "I'm more of a cook than a baker. But … why?"

He sets his now-empty plate down on the table next to us. "Because you're already a little too irresistible."

My mouth dries up, which is fine as I've just finished my slice of cake, so I set the plate down and sip my water. Evan looks at me like he knows.

"Feel like another dance?" he asks in a low voice.

I nod mutely and let him lead me back to the dance floor, where we're now the only couple. It doesn't deter Evan, though, as he hauls me against him and leads me to the music.

One of his hands rests on the small of my back, spreading heat up my spine. The other holds my hand in his against his chest.

"I think I'd like it very much if you *didn't* stay out of my hair while I'm here," he murmurs as we sway to the music.

I swallow hard, my brain short-circuiting from his touch and proximity. "I'd like that too."

He rubs his thumb over my palm and pulls me close. As the song switches to a slow ballad, other couples join in. I settle my head on his chest, and he puts his chin on my head. I close my eyes and listen to the steady beat of his heart. I lose myself in it so completely that I don't notice time passing until Rae announces that Mia and Nate are leaving to catch their flight to Hawaii.

As loathe as I am to leave Evan's embrace, I extricate myself, and we follow everyone out. I slip to the front of the crowd to get to Mia. She's removed the outer skirt from her gown, revealing that the top was one-half of a wedding romper. It's so adorably Mia.

I pull her in tight for a hug. "Enjoy the crap out of yourself," I tell her.

She squeezes me back just as hard. "You too," she replies, pulling back and winking at me. I give her a confused look, and she jerks her chin over my shoulder. I turn to see Evan watching us.

"Ah. I will," I reply with a grin.

I don't even have time to hug Nate before they pack into his truck and start the nearly two-hour drive to SeaTac airport.

Once they've departed, so too do all the townies. Nate's family helps Rae, Greg, Joanie, Penny, and I clean up. It doesn't take long with so many of us. Greg and Joanie head out as soon as we're done, followed by Penny.

Steven and Diane turn to their sons. "How about we go for dinner at the tavern?" Steven suggests.

"Rae, Carrie, you're welcome to join us," Diane offers warmly.

Rae smiles. "I need to drop off these leftovers at home first, but I'll meet you there."

Steven nods. "Sounds good." He turns to the rest of us as Rae takes the first load to her Bronco. "We only have room for four. How about we take Dylan with us, if you don't mind giving Carrie a ride?" he asks Evan.

My heart leaps into my throat as Evan grins. "Sure thing." The glee in his tone does funny things to me, and a sort of giddiness settles over me.

The drive to the tavern is charged with a new kind of energy, anticipation thrumming through my veins. Thankfully, it's only a few minutes, as neither of us seems willing to voice what we're thinking.

Dinner is a boisterous affair, especially once Rae joins us. It's filled with laughter, stories about all the boys as kids, especially Nate, and perhaps a few too many drinks. As the night winds down, Evan leans close, his breath warm on my cheek.

"I think I've had a bit too much to drink to drive back to the house," he admits.

"I can drive you back in your rental," I assure him, my pulse quickening. He gives me a skeptical look, and I realize the potential implications. The really forward ones. "I'll stay in Nate and Mia's room, and you can take me home tomorrow morning." Separate rooms aside, my cheeks heat at the idea of spending the night in the same house as him. But there certainly isn't room for him at Rae's, and the B&B is full.

He nods slowly without breaking eye contact before turning back to his parents. "Thanks for dinner, Mom and Dad. I'll see you tomorrow before you head home?"

"Of course, dear," Diane assures him. She glances between Evan and me knowingly. "Drive safe."

I smile innocently at her. "Will do, Mrs. Edwards. Thank you so much for dinner," I reply.

Rae gives me a look and leans around the table. "Text me if you need a ride back tonight. Or anything else," she murmurs low enough so only I can hear. I raise a curious brow. Rae's eyes dart briefly to Evan. "I know it's silly, but he's got a reputation, and I'm protective of you. Sue me."

I huff a laugh and wrap my arms around her. "Thanks, Rae. I'll be fine, though, I promise."

She winks at me, and Evan and I leave as the rest of our party wraps up their business. Evan leads me back to the car, seemingly steady.

The drive to Nate and Mia's is quiet but charged, the air heavy with unspoken desires, at least for my part. And unless everything he said to me tonight was just how he is, I'm hoping for his part, too.

When we arrive, neither of us moves to get out, to break the spell.

"You don't have to stay. You can drive my car back down if you want to go home. I'm sure I can arrange something for tomorrow," Evan suggests. "Though if you do, I promise I'll be a perfect gentleman."

I nod, not voicing that I'd prefer he weren't. "Like I said, I'll stay. It's easiest," I say instead.

I follow him into the house, where he heads straight for the living room. He settles onto one of the behemoth leather couches and pats the cushion next to him.

"Come tell me how a woman like you ended up in a place like this," he says teasingly.

I smile and settle beside him, folding my legs under me. "I'm not sure you had enough beer tonight to handle that story."

I expect him to be flippant, but he reaches out and runs a hand over my knee. "It's okay if you don't want to tell me. I just want to know more about you."

The unexpected tenderness undoes me just a little bit more. I'm not sure I can handle this swoony, sexy movie star also being sweet.

But I also can't resist him.

So, I tell him. Or, at least, as much of the story as it relates to his actual question. That's enough to imply the rest, which is to say a financially secure yet emotionally garbage childhood that's left me terrified to upset anyone ever. Halfway through, Mia's cat, Simba, jumps into my lap. Evan and I lavish him with attention until he's a furry, purring ball between us.

"Wow, your parents are probably the biggest assholes I've ever heard of. And I say this as someone who is an expert in assholes," he says when I'm done.

I can't help bursting out laughing. When he realizes exactly how that sounded, he bursts out laughing too. Our laughter scares Simba, and he darts off the couch.

"Okay, I didn't mean I'm into … *that*," he clarifies, wiping away tears of laughter. "I meant Hollywood is filled with Grade-A assholes, whom I deal with on a daily basis. So your parents are like … Grade AA."

I bite into my lip. I'm not outspoken with people I don't know well. I'm too terrified to offend them. But part of me wants to tell him I'd be okay if he were into *that*.

His eyebrows pinch together at my expression. "What's that face?" he asks.

I shake my head, my cheeks flaming. "Your turn. What brings a man like *you* to a place like this?"

Evan stiffens. "I'll tell you, but first, you have to tell me what you mean by 'a man like you.'"

My chest tightens, and I reach out and touch his hand. "I'm so sorry. I didn't mean to imply anything bad by that at all," I rush to reassure him, kicking myself for upsetting him. "I meant someone as charming, successful, and well-traveled as you. That's all. I know you came for Nate's wedding. I guess I just don't get what else there would be here for you."

The tightness in his posture eases a bit. "Why does anyone come here?" he responds with a shrug. "I needed to get away from it all for a while."

And that's all he says. I can't help but feel like he'd been about to say more but stopped himself for some reason.

Me. I'm that reason: me and my big mouth.

I open said big mouth to apologize again, but he beats me to the line. "Tell me more about this town incorporation thing. I've never even heard of anything like that."

"Oh," I say, surprised. "Um … okay. Well, Alpine Ridge isn't officially a town. It's an unincorporated area of Kittitas County. But that'll all change on election day." I proceed to tell him about all the work Joanie and the others did to file the paperwork, get signatures, and push through the bureaucracy required to set up that all-important vote to officially make Alpine Ridge a town and all the benefits that will bring to the people who live here. Then I explain the part I'll play in the next steps to elect its new mayor and town council and how that plays into my degree and planned career.

He listens intently and asks intelligent questions, but again, I can't help but feel that he's avoiding talking about himself.

Eventually, a yawn escapes me, and Evan glances at the clock. "I should let you get some sleep," he says softly. "I can drive you home if you'd like. I'm sober now."

I shake my head. "It's late, and you're probably tired too. I'll just crash in Mia and Nate's room. You can take me home when it's light out in the morning."

He nods and rises, holding out his hand. I take it and allow him to help me to my feet. My hand lingers in his momentarily as he looks deep into my eyes.

After a few tense moments, he leads me down the hall and up the stairs, his fingers still entwined with mine.

He stops at the threshold of the guest room, and I turn to face him, my heart in my throat.

His eyes darken, his gaze dropping to my lips. "Carrie ..." My name is a plea on his lips.

"Evan," I whisper back, his name a prayer on mine.

He steps closer, raising his hand to brush the hair back from my face.

I draw my lips into my mouth, wetting them almost unconsciously.

His mouth pulls up into a small smile, and he leans in.

His nose touches against mine lightly, and my body sways into his.

His hot breath fans over my face, and it's all I can do not to push into him, to give myself over completely. I want him to take it, so I know it's what he wanted.

But God, I want him so badly.

Like slow torture, he draws in a breath as if trying to inhale my desire. A small whimper escapes my lips.

And then his mouth is on mine, his kiss searing, branding, setting me ablaze.

As tentative as he was, he's just as demanding now as he pulls me roughly against him.

I melt into him without thought, my hands fisting in his hair, pulling him closer. He bites into my bottom lip, then soothes the sting with his tongue. The swipe drives me so wild that I grind against him.

This kiss is everything I've imagined and then some. Heat and passion that makes me ache for more.

But before I can deepen the kiss, Evan pulls back abruptly, his breath ragged. "Goodnight, Carrie," he murmurs, his thumb brushing my cheek.

And then he's stepping into the guest room, the door closing softly behind him.

I stand there for a long moment, my fingers pressed to my tingling lips. Then, on shaky legs, I go up to the third floor to Mia and Nate's room. Mechanically, I change into a set of Mia's pajamas and rinse my face and mouth with water. It'll do for now.

I climb onto their crazy comfortable bed and use a throw blanket to cover myself. My mind races as I lie in the dark, staring up at the star-strewn sky through the glass ceiling. Did I do something wrong? Misread the signals? I'd been so sure he wanted me, too. And he's certainly got a reputation that suggests he'd have taken what I was so clearly offering if he'd wanted it.

But then, as much as he's every inch the heartthrob I'd always fantasized about from afar, up close and personal, he's ... more. So maybe he's more than his reputation, too. More than the tabloids and gossip sites make him out to be.

With startling clarity, it hits me that that's probably what made him withdraw earlier ... the idea that I might think "a man like him" meant he was a sure thing. That I'd reduced him to a conquest that I could brag about to my friends later.

I cover my face with my hands, feeling like an idiot. Of course, that's what he was worried about. And I did nothing to reassure him with how I reacted to his kiss. I practically mauled him for crying out loud.

Still, I realize there's hope. Because he wanted to hear about me. Wants to spend time with me. *Kissed* me.

Maybe, just maybe, he feels this connection between us, this pull that's both thrilling and terrifying. All I can do is hope that he does and do everything in my power to let him know that I want to get to know him, too.

I don't want to be another person that reduces him to his fame. He came here to disconnect from all of that. To just be. And he wants to just be with me these next few weeks. It's the perfect opportunity to get to know the real Evan. Just Evan. Not Evan Edwards, the action movie heartthrob. Because from what he's shown me so far, Just Evan is a great, down-to-earth guy. Someone worth getting to know. Someone I could see myself falling for.

With my racing thoughts, sleep is a long time coming. But when it does, my dreams are filled with searing kisses, strong arms, and the promise of something real.

Something worth waiting for.

CHAPTER NINE

EVAN

The aroma of sizzling bacon rouses me from sleep, and I smile before my eyes even open. Carrie. She not only stayed the night but now she's making breakfast. This woman is something else.

As I lie in bed looking out at the sunlit forest, memories of last night flood my mind. Her openness, her intelligence, her undeniable sexiness. That she didn't push me to talk more about myself, something I'm thoroughly sick of, and is a huge red flag for me with a woman because it usually means they're only interested in my celebrity lifestyle and status.

But Carrie is different. She's warm and caring and achingly beautiful. It took every ounce of my self-control not to take her to bed after that kiss. But I want to do this right. I have a few weeks here, and I don't want to rush whatever this is between us.

But damn, if she's out there cooking me breakfast, my resolve might not last much longer.

I dress quickly in jeans and a black henley and head downstairs, my stomach rumbling in anticipation. And there she is, standing at the stove, a vision in the morning light. Her long, dark hair is pulled back in a low ponytail, and her pink sweatpants and white tee must be Mia's. Either way, she looks fantastic. And she's adding hot, fresh pancakes to plates stacked with bacon and eggs. I can't even remember the last time someone made me breakfast. Well, someone I wasn't paying to do it anyway.

"Morning," I say softly, not wanting to startle her.

She turns, and though her dark blue eyes light up, there's a shyness in her smile that wasn't there last night. "Good morning. I hope you're hungry."

"Starving," I assure her, but I'm not just talking about the food. Best to keep those thoughts to myself, though.

We settle at the table, and as we eat, the air is filled with a strange tension.

"Did you sleep well?" Carrie asks, pouring syrup over her pancakes. There's a formality to her tone that has me worried. Is she having second thoughts about last night?

"Fantastic. You?"

She takes a prim bite and nods. "I slept well, thanks."

We sit in awkward silence as we eat for a minute.

"This is delicious," I finally say, breaking the silence. "Thank you."

Carrie shrugs, her cheeks pinkening. "It's nothing."

God, I just want to reach out and run my thumb over that blush on her face. But I resist.

"Clearly, you've never seen me attempt to make breakfast."

That gets a small smile out of her, and I grin back.

As I finish eating, I decide I'll push just a little. I'm only here for a few weeks. What do I have to lose?

When I'm done, Carrie is staring out the dining room window at the trees. I rise and get her attention with a hand on her shoulder. She looks up at me with big blue eyes, and something lurches inside me.

"I'll just … clean this up and then take you home, okay?"

She chews on her bottom lip for a moment before nodding. It reminds me of biting that lip last night and how it made her press against me. I retreat to the sink so she doesn't see the effect the memory has on me.

After I'm done, I drive her home, and we don't speak but for Carrie to direct me to the house she's apparently sharing with Rae on the other side of downtown Alpine Ridge. I turn to her when we've stopped in front of the cute one-story rancher.

"I really enjoyed spending time with you last night."

Her brows raise. "I enjoyed it too."

I give her a skeptical look. "But?"

Carrie's nose wrinkles, and I think she's … self-conscious?

"No 'but.' I just feel like I may have offended you. I didn't mean to."

My brows draw together. "Offended me? How?"

"By making it sound like I assumed you were a certain type of man. Because while you're everything I expected you to be, you're also different. Good different. And I know you're more than the face you show the world." She reaches out and places her hand on mine. "I should've said that last night instead of rambling about myself the whole time."

I huff a laugh and shake my head, turning my hand over and intertwining my fingers with hers. "You have no idea how much that means to me," I murmur, lifting her hand to my mouth and kissing it. "But you didn't offend me in the least, and I loved hearing about you. It's just … difficult to talk about myself. I have to do it so much. I guess I get a little defensive at times."

Carrie lets out a sigh of clear relief. "I … was about to say I understand, but I probably don't. I'm just glad I didn't upset you." She beams at me, and it's like the clouds parting to reveal the sun.

"Quite the opposite." My eyes flick down to her lips, but I don't want to start something I can't finish right now. "I should let you get home, and I have some errands to run to get settled here. I'll call you later, okay?"

She squeezes my hand and withdraws. "Okay. Bye, Evan."

And I can't help it. I lean forward and capture her lips with mine. Ever so briefly. She sighs contentedly against my lips, and I smile. "Bye, Carrie."

And then she's gone, and I'm relieved that I hadn't pushed too far, too fast.

Feeling good, I head to the grocery store. I'm browsing the produce section when a familiar voice calls out.

"Evan! Hey, man."

I turn to see Greg, a huge grin on his face, his dark hair curly and messed like he just rolled out of bed. "Hey, Greg. You look like you had a good night," I tease.

His grin somehow widens. "I proposed to Joanie. She said yes."

"Congrats, man! That's amazing." I clap him on the back, genuinely happy for him even though it feels like everyone is dropping the settling-down bombs this weekend.

"Thanks. I didn't expect to see you. Sticking around for a bit?"

I nod. "I'm taking some much-needed time off, but don't get too used to me being here. I'll only be staying for a few weeks."

"Hey, I'll take the company any which way I can get it. And since you'll be around for a bit, I'm down a workout partner. Are you up for it, or is this a vacation from everything?"

I smirk. "Oh, I'm up for it."

"Good. I don't have any clients until eight-thirty on weekdays. I usually start my workout at seven. You're welcome to join whenever."

"Seven it is. Thanks, man. It'll be great to have some semblance of a routine," I reply. "And hey, while I've got you here. I was thinking of exploring the area a bit. Any suggestions?"

"Sure, of course. There's always Leavenworth. It's a kitschy Bavarian-style tourist trap, but it's a lot of fun. It's about forty-five minutes north. And if you're headed that way, Lake Wenatchee is another half hour past that. Fantastic hiking and water sports, though it's probably still pretty busy since the summer weather seems to be sticking around." He shrugs. "Oh, and there's always Ellensburg, the closest actual city. It's still small but it's got all the hallmarks of civilization. Shopping, entertainment, restaurants, and a few fantastic breweries."

"Those sound great, thanks. I'll probably try them all at some point. Though today, I hoped to go somewhere nearby to enjoy the scenery."

"Ah. Well, in that case, there are some great trails behind the community center," he tells me. "Past the wildflower field where the wedding was. Lots of good hiking up there."

"Perfect. Thanks, man."

We part ways, and I finish shopping, my mind already on the trails. Hiking has always been a great way to clear my mind and put my life back into perspective. And fuck knows I need a heavy dose of that right about now.

I set out a couple of hours later, following the path Greg described. It's not all easy strolls through fields of wildflowers. It's nearly vertical at several points, but the burn in my legs and the warm air tinged with the scents of fall are invigorating. As I approach a ridge and the peaks of the Cascades begin to unfurl around me, I decide the views are worth it.

When I round the bend and reach the ridge, I spot an old lookout post at the peak. After a few more minutes hike, I climb the stairs to the doorless, sturdy structure. As I look out of the large opening facing the valley beyond, the vistas seem to stretch forever. Clearly, there's still plenty of water here because the bases of the mountains are green and lush, though their peaks are rocky and bare. White, puffy clouds drift across the blazing warm sun, and birdsong fills the air. It's paradise, really.

I can't remember the last time I felt so peaceful. Out here, I can hear myself think.

I use the opportunity to mull over the discontent I feel in the city — well, with my whole life, really. It's been a couple of years since I was really excited about a project. Since I felt like a part was a good fit, something I could be proud of.

Despite what Rick, my agent, seems to think, it doesn't seem to be for lack of opportunities. There's always someone shoving a script my way or requesting that I audition for a part. So, it feels like there are always options, even if none seem all that appealing.

Which makes me wonder ... maybe it's me. Maybe I'm just not that excited about all of this anymore.

There's something to that, I decide. At this point in my career, it's starting to feel like I'm playing the same part over and over.

Holy shit. It *is* me. I'm what's different.

I'm tired of the same old roles, the same interviews, and the same off-camera persona I have to uphold to project the same old image.

Maybe Rick has a point, and it's time to try something new. But ... rom-coms?

I shake my head, unsure I want to go there yet unwilling to dismiss anything at this point. If I'm going to try something new, I know I'll need to keep an open mind.

Rick will be thrilled with this sudden willingness to accept a new group of scripts.

I chuckle as I track a hawk's progress over the valley. I watch until the sun starts to sink toward the horizon, faint oranges and pinks starting to mellow the sky.

My chest aches a little, and it takes me a minute to realize ... it's because I'm alone. This is the kind of sight you share with somebody. Somebody special.

Someone like Carrie.

I smile to myself at the thought of her. There's something so pure and kind about her. I wasn't just trying to pick her up at the wedding; the moment I saw her, I was stunned by her beauty. Only as I get to know her do I realize it's more than the kind that's skin-deep.

I'm attracted to her in a way I haven't been to anyone in a long time. Because she's not like anyone I've been around in a long time. Being immersed in the movie business doesn't put you in contact with many genuine people. And Carrie is nothing if not genuine.

I don't know where this thing between us will go. Or where it can go, given that she's here and I'm based in L.A. But I'm also not giving up on it just because of geography.

I once believed that what was meant to be will be. It was how I handled the initial rejection and climb to the top. Well, that and a shit load of hard work. But if that isn't a good parallel to finding love, I don't know what is.

So, as soon as I make the descent and find my way back to Nate's, I call her.

"You called!"

I chuckle. "That's quite the opener," I tease.

"Sorry. It's just ... 'I'll call you later' is classic guy speak for 'you'll never see me naked,'" she jokes. And then she gasps. "Oh my god, that was so inappropriate. I didn't mean —"

And now I'm really laughing. "Carrie. Stop. It's fine, really."

"Oh, good. Still ... sorry," she says in a small voice.

"Do you always apologize this much?"

Carrie is silent for a moment. "Yeah, I guess I do," she finally admits. "I'm a recovering people-pleaser; it goes with the territory."

Well, I didn't expect that. "I know a little about that," I admit. "But hey, I'm calling because I found something I want to show you tomorrow. Can you meet me at the community center around eight-thirty?"

"In the morning?" she asks.

"Later is fine," I allow.

"No, that's okay, I was just making sure. Yes, of course. I'm curious now. Are we talking like ... a dead body or a really cool tree or something?"

I let out a sharp laugh. "Or something," I respond mysteriously.

After an invigoratingly grueling session with Greg the next morning, I'm using the stretching bars alongside the center when Carrie walks up. She's wearing sleek black leggings and a light blue fitted sporty top, with her long hair tied in a high ponytail.

Bright-cheeked and smiling, she looks ready to go.

"Ready for an adventure?" I ask, offering my hand.

She takes it without hesitation. "Always."

I grin, and we walk hand-in-hand up the path.

"So where are we going?" she presses.

I laugh and shake my head. "You just can't handle surprises, can you?"

She bounces a little on the balls of her feet. "Nope," she agrees. "But I get the sense you enjoy taunting me with it, so I'm going to stop asking."

I grin so wide I'm sure my dimples are showing. "I promise you'll like it. No dead bodies," I swear.

She smirks and allows me to lead her onward. As we hike, we talk about everything and nothing, including our likes and dislikes. She loves kayaking; I prefer running. She's an avid reader; I can't remember the last time I had a hobby outside of work and exercise.

"Okay, favorite book. Go," I prompt.

She laughs. "I could never choose."

"Come on, you have to pick one."

She thinks for a moment. "Fine. I'll go with *Pride and Prejudice*."

I nod approvingly. Even I've read that one. Didn't hate it. "Classic. Okay, your turn. Ask me something."

"Favorite movie — one you're not in," she adds quickly with a smile.

I groan. "You're killing me. I refuse to choose."

"Hey, you made me pick. Now it's your turn, mister."

I sigh dramatically. "Have a point then. If I had to pick just one ... it'd be *From Russia with Love*."

Her eyebrows lift. "A Bond fan, huh?"

"Only if it's Connery," I reply with a grin as we step around the bend that allows a full view of the ridge. And the lookout.

Carrie looks up. "Is that a lookout post?"

I nod. "I think so." I lead her the last few hundred feet and propel her up the stairs before me to take in the view.

Her breath catches. "Evan, this is ... wow."

"Right?" I agree softly, stepping up behind her and wrapping my arms around her. "I had to share it with you." My eyes travel over the sunlit trees, and I see a small river winding through the valley I hadn't noticed before. The sun glints off its rippling surface, even from this distance. The view is every bit as beautiful as yesterday. Even more so with Carrie in my arms, warm against my chest, my nose buried in her coconut-scented hair.

She looks back and up at me, her eyes soft. I lean in and gently kiss her. She lets out a breathy sigh that makes me smile. A feeling of rightness settles deep in my chest.

She tips her head back to look at the horizon. "I can't believe I never knew about this place," she murmurs.

I squeeze her gently. "You've only been here, what, a few months? I'm sure you would've found it eventually."

She shakes her head and turns to me with tear-filled eyes. I turn her to face me, cupping her cheek in my hand. "What's wrong?'

She's quiet for a moment. "I used to come to Alpine Ridge often as a kid to visit my Gran. She and my Gramps lived here for years. But as I got older and got busy with my life ... I visited less and less. Then, she got sick, and Mia came to take care of her. But Mia and my parents were fighting, and I didn't want to get in the middle of it, so I figured I'd visit again when everything settled down. Except, before I even knew how sick she was ... Gran was gone. And I regret not coming more. Not spending more time in this place, with her, while I could."

I pull her into my arms, holding her close as silent tears stream down her face. We stay like that for a long time, just holding each other, the world falling away.

Eventually, she pulls back, wiping at her eyes. "Sorry. I didn't mean to turn this into a therapy session."

"Don't apologize," I murmur, brushing a strand of hair from her face. "I'm glad you shared that with me." It just underscores what a big heart she has, and I find myself drawn to her even more.

She smiles softly. "Thank you for listening. And for bringing me here. It's perfect."

She goes up on her toes to kiss me. But this time, it's different. I don't know if it's her confession or the connection it made me feel to her, but we come together with an intensity that knocks the air out of my lungs. Until her lips moving with mine is my oxygen. Her hands skating up my arms and twining around my neck is all I can feel. Until my hands sliding over her lithe body is the resurrection I didn't know I needed.

I back her against the wall as our kiss turns desperate. My mouth trails down her neck as her hands fist in my hair. The slightly painful tug turns me on even more, and I suck the spot where her neck meets her shoulder hard.

In seeming response, she wraps her legs around me, and I groan into her chest, reaching up to palm her breast as I return my mouth to hers.

Another few minutes of fevered kisses has me hard and wanting. But I know I need to stop. She's so willing and ready for me, but I can't take her here. Hell, I *shouldn't*. Not this soon. Not like this.

So I slowly trail off, easing her legs back down to the ground as I catch my breath.

"You're incredible," I whisper in her ear. She shudders against me, and I bite back another groan.

She rests her head on my chest, and I wrap my arms around her. Seconds later, the moment is broken by an outrageous rumble from my stomach.

"Sorry. Breakfast was a while ago," I say sheepishly.

Carrie laughs. "Let's head back and hit the tavern for lunch," she suggests.

A smile tugs at my lips. "I think that'd be a good idea," I agree.

We walk back down the trail, and Carrie doesn't let go of my hand once.

Not long later, we sit at the tavern, chatting while consuming some well-earned bar food and beer.

But as we're eating, the inevitable happens. A group of people approach our table, eyes wide with recognition.

"Oh my god, are you Evan Edwards?" a small, older blonde asks.

I plaster on my best movie star smile. "Guilty as charged."

The next few minutes are a blur of autographs and selfies, me slipping into the well-worn role of charming celebrity. But the whole time, I'm acutely aware of Carrie watching, of the discomfort on her face.

As soon as the last fan walks away, I lean in close. "Can we get out of here?"

She nods, relief evident in her eyes.

We escape, and Carrie suggests heading to the bakery. Though I'm wary of being noticed again, I agree.

And I'm damn glad I did. As soon as I bite into the slice of huckleberry pie Rae brought out for us to share, I sigh contentedly. In equal parts because it's freaking amazing and because we're the only people here. Well, besides Rae and Penny, of course.

"This was a fantastic idea," I mumble around a mouthful of whipped cream-laden heaven.

Carrie snorts and swallows her own bite. "I figured you could use a pick-me-up after that ambush," she replies wryly.

I sigh and set my fork down. "I'm sorry about that. I thought maybe it wouldn't be an issue here," I say quietly. "The whole celebrity thing can be a lot."

She studies me for a moment. "Is it always like that? The persona, the forced charm?"

I shrug. "Kind of comes with the job. Acting doesn't just happen on screen."

She nods, understanding flickering in her eyes. But I know it doesn't sit well with her because she demolishes the rest of the pie. Even I know what it means when a woman drowns herself in sugar.

So, once I've driven her back to her car at the community center, I take a chance to try to push past this with her.

"Carrie, will you go out with me? On a real date?"

She tilts her head, confusion clouding her features. "I thought this was a date."

"It was. Is. I just ... I want to do this right. Take you out, someplace nice."

Her smile is blinding. "I'd love that."

A weight lifts from my shoulders, knowing she's still up to see where this goes.

So, we make plans for Wednesday, after her video call with the campaign manager she's researching for. Watching her drive away, I'm already counting the hours.

Wednesday arrives, and I pick Carrie up, my nerves buzzing with anticipation. I've chosen Ellensburg, hoping the distance from Alpine Ridge will give us space to be together without thinking about anything else.

We walk through a riverfront park, the conversation flowing easily. Then we catch a movie, some big-budget sci-fi blockbuster, our hands intertwined in the dark. Next, we head to the Whipsaw Brewery for dinner, per Greg's recommendation.

Holding her hand as we walk up, everything feels right. Being with Carrie is the easiest thing in the world, and I'm happier than I can remember being in a long time.

Until we walk in the door.

And that's when the illusion shatters.

Immediately, the whispers start, and the surreptitious phone cameras start coming out. I do my best to ignore them and focus on Carrie, but it's impossible.

Finally, I excuse myself and spend the next half hour smiling for pictures, signing autographs, and talking with star-struck fans.

"Who's the girl?" one woman asks, eyeing Carrie speculatively.

"A friend," I say smoothly, the lie tasting bitter.

When I finally return to the table, Carrie is sipping a beer, her expression unreadable.

"I'm so sorry," I say, reaching for her hand. "I know this is one of the least fun parts of dating a celebrity."

She looks up at me, her eyes searching mine. "Are we dating? I heard what you said to that woman. You called me your friend. So, is that what we are? Friends?"

I sigh. "You know it's not. At least, not just that. But if I said you were my date, the attention on you would be a hundred times worse. Paparazzi, tabloids, social media. I didn't want to subject you to that."

She nods slowly, still seeming down. "I guess I hadn't really thought about what dating you would mean. The scrutiny, the lack of privacy."

My heart sinks. This is it. The moment she realizes I'm not worth the hassle, the headache.

But then she surprises me, her hand tightening around mine. "It's okay. I can't say I love it, but I'm not going anywhere."

Relief crashes over me in a wave, followed closely by a swell of emotion for this incredible woman.

We go ahead and order food, and the rest of our time there is blessedly uninterrupted. I suspect the staff is largely to thank for that, and I make a mental note to tip handsomely. But Carrie is reluctant to talk, and conversation is stilted, trailing to nonexistent.

Even the drive back to Alpine Ridge is quiet. Both of us seem lost in thought. When I pull up to her house, I turn to her, ready to apologize again.

"If you'd rather, we don't have to go out in public again. I know it's a lot to deal with."

She tries to smile, but I can tell her heart isn't in it. "It is weird and definitely not something I'm used to. I think I just need some time to acclimate. How about we stay in tomorrow, though? I can make dinner, and we can just ... be."

"That sounds perfect," I murmur, leaning in to kiss her.

The press of her lips against mine is electric, and it takes every ounce of willpower I possess to keep it chaste, to pull away before I can't.

I get out of the car and round the front to open the door for her, then walk her to her front door.

"Goodnight, Carrie," I whisper, resting my forehead against hers.

She leans up and gives me a gentle kiss. It soothes the anxiety swirling inside me over subjecting her to what my life is like so soon. I'd hoped for more anonymity on this trip, but obviously, that won't happen in this lifetime. At least there haven't been any paparazzi. Yet.

"See you tomorrow, Evan."

Watching her walk inside, I know with bone-deep certainty that I'm falling for this woman. I have to shake off the unease that comes with that because I can't say dating a non-celebrity has ever worked out well for me. I snort at my own thoughts as I get back in the car. Even dating celebrities hasn't worked out all that well but for different reasons. Normal women usually hate the attention I get. Famous women usually live for it. Neither bodes well for a stable relationship.

It would take one hell of a woman to handle the insanity that is my life. But just as I know I'm falling for Carrie, I know she's that and so much more.

360

CHAPTER TEN

CARRIE

I push my cart through the grocery store, my mind whirling with recipe ideas. Tonight's dinner with Evan needs to be perfect, a balm after the awkwardness of our public date. I want to show him that staying in can be just as special. Just as romantic. Maybe even more so.

As I stroll through the produce, I spot a beautiful mound of eggplants and settle on a menu—eggplant parmesan and maple-roasted carrots served with fresh rolls from the bakery. For dessert, pistachio cannoli. Also from the bakery. Mia's taught me well: Always play to your strengths in the kitchen. For me, that's definitely cooking, not baking. Though, really, it's thanks to her that I've discovered my talent for it.

After finishing at the grocery store, I quickly stop at the bakery and head up to Nate and Mia's house. As I drive, I hum happily to myself, noting Evan's car in the driveway as I pull up.

Arms laden with bags, I let myself in. Simba greets me by bumping up against my leg, but there's no sign of Evan. I head into the kitchen, which is a dream, all gleaming countertops and high-end appliances. I set to work, losing myself in the familiar rituals of chopping, sautéing, and seasoning.

I'm so focused that I don't hear Evan approach until his arms are around my waist, his lips on my neck.

"I didn't hear you come in. Smells amazing," he murmurs, his breath tickling my skin.

I lean back into him, savoring the moment. "It'll taste even better. But only if you let me finish cooking."

He spins me around, capturing my lips in a searing kiss. It takes every ounce of willpower I possess to pull away. And the fitted acid-washed jeans and white V-neck T-shirt he's wearing that show off his amazing body aren't helping me resist him either.

"Evan," I warn, my voice husky. "Behave, or no cannoli for you."

He grins, holding up his hands in surrender. "Okay, okay. I'll be good. For now."

With Herculean effort, I turn back to the stove, determined not to let his distractions derail dinner.

We're seated at the table an hour later, with the fruits of my labor spread before us. Evan takes a bite of the eggplant parmesan and lets out a moan that should be illegal.

"Carrie, this is incredible," he says, his eyes closing in bliss.

Pride swells in my chest. "Thanks. I wanted tonight to be special. To make up for ... well, you know."

He reaches across the table, taking my hand. "You don't have to make up for anything. But I appreciate this more than you know."

We eat in comfortable silence, punctuated by appreciative murmurs and contented sighs. When the cannoli emerge, Evan's eyes light up like a kid on Christmas.

"Have I told you yet that staying in was a brilliant idea?" he asks, biting into the crisp shell.

I laugh at how excited he seems by a simple dessert. "No, but I'm glad you're enjoying yourself."

He grins around the half-cannoli in his mouth and I shake my head, smiling, as I nibble at my own.

Once we're done, we clean up together, hips bumping and hands brushing as we rinse the dishes and load the dishwasher. It's domestic and intimate, and I can't remember the last time I felt this at peace.

"So, what's next on the agenda?" Evan asks, hanging the dish towel.

I shrug. "I thought maybe a movie?"

He shakes his head. "I'd rather not."

"Fair," I admit. Then, an idea strikes me. "Nate and Mia have a ton of board games. You up for it, or are you afraid to get your butt kicked by a girl?"

His eyes sparkle with mischief. "Pfff. You wish. Prepare to lose, Anderson."

We start with Clue. Evan, of course, wins handily, his actor's instincts giving him an edge.

"Best two out of three?" I challenge.

He smirks. "You're on."

Next up is Cascadia, a strategy game set in the Pacific Northwest. As we place our tiles and build out habitats, I can't help but appreciate how into this Evan is. Who knew the famous movie star was giddy over board games?

Still, I beat him soundly. It feels pretty good after my Clue loss. I'm not gonna lie.

"Shall we pick another, or are you ready to admit defeat?" I tease.

Evan sighs dramatically and leans back into the couch. "I know when I'm beaten," he replies resignedly. Then he smiles and gestures for me to join him. "Get your gorgeous ass over here and comfort me in my loss, will you?"

I laugh but crawl over the couch and settle next to him. "So, is this what movie stars really do to let loose? Play board games? Ooh, I bet you all love playing Scene It."

"Hardy har," Evan deadpans, wrapping his arms around me. "Being a movie star is definitely not all fun and games."

I trace a finger up his chest. "Tell me about it," I urge gently.

He looks down at me, his hazel eyes swirling with warmth and affection. "I don't want to bring down the mood."

I shake my head lightly. "You couldn't if you tried. I want to know what your life is like, Evan. I get the sense that you're avoiding something by being here. Am I crazy?"

He lets out a long sigh. "No. You're right on the money." He rests his head on his fist, his elbow on the arm of the couch. "I came here to escape the fact that I've been miserable, and apparently, according to my manager, my career is flagging."

My mouth drops open. I suspected he was having something of an existential crisis based on the few comments he'd made, but I didn't expect that.

"How is that possible? You're hot. Hotter than hot. Everybody loves you."

Evan snorts. "I wish. But even if they do, I don't love me. Or action-star me, anyway. I haven't done anything I've been really proud of in *years*. It's just been the same stuff over and over. It doesn't help that there's a lot of game-playing — not the good kind — backstabbing and politicking in Hollywood. It's gotten tiresome."

"And the fact that you can't go anywhere without being recognized," I add quietly.

Evan smiles bitterly. "Can't forget that." He sighs. "Until recently, I didn't want to admit that I'm ready to move on to something else."

I scooch up to a sitting position and look at him incredulously. "What do you mean by 'something else'? You're not quitting acting, are you?"

He reaches out and runs a hand down my arm. "No. Not yet, anyway. My agent has been pushing me to branch out. And, like I said, I'm tired of playing the same mediocre roles. So, I think my agent might be right. A change of pace could be good for me. He wants me to read some rom-com scripts."

"I think you'd be amazing in any genre. You have so much range, so much talent."

He gives me a skeptical look. "Even rom-coms?"

I grin. "Especially rom-coms. You'd be the perfect romantic lead. Charming, handsome, with a hidden depth just waiting to be uncovered."

"You're just saying that because you like me," he teases.

I roll my eyes. "Every woman in America with eyeballs likes you if you hadn't noticed."

"Mmm," he murmurs noncommittally. "Unfortunately for them, I only have eyes for you."

My cheeks heat. "See? That's the kind of thing a romantic lead would say," I deflect.

His eyes darken, his voice dropping to a whisper. "Yeah? Maybe I should practice some of my *other* romantic lead skills on you."

Heat floods my cheeks. "Oh, really?" I aim for nonchalance, but my voice comes out breathy.

Evan stands, taking my hand and pulling me to my feet and into his arms.

"Carrie," he murmurs, his hand cupping my cheek. "From the moment I saw you, I knew you were special. Your beauty, your kindness, your spirit ... you've captivated me, body and soul."

I melt into him, my hands fisting in his shirt. "Evan ..."

"I'm falling for you, Carrie Anderson. Harder and faster than I ever thought possible."

I can't help the whimper that slips out of me. "I'd give you an Oscar for that performance," I say, fighting the shaking in my knees.

"Who says I'm performing?" he asks huskily, lowering his face to mine.

My eyes close at his words, a tremor of emotion rippling through me.

But before I can gather my wits, his lips are on mine, and I'm lost. Lost in the taste of him, the feel of his body against mine.

When he pulls back, I have to blink hard several times before the fog of lust clears. "Seriously. Rom-coms. Do it."

He smiles at me and strokes a hand down my back. "I'll think about it. But also, I meant everything I said just now."

My breath catches in my throat as I absorb that. "Really?" I whisper.

He dips his chin. "Really. I haven't ever opened up to a woman like that." He reaches up and strokes a thumb over my cheek.

My eyes search his, but all I see is truth and vulnerability. "Why me?" I didn't mean to ask out loud, but now there's no taking it back.

"Weren't you listening?" he teases. "Maybe I need to demonstrate what you do to me, Carrie." He guides my hand to the hard length between his legs, and I suck in a sharp breath.

Heat spreads outward from my center, and I arch against him. This gorgeous, amazing man, who millions of women would die to sleep with, wants *me*. I can't wrap my head around it. But mostly, I can't believe he finally opened up to me. I knew he'd been holding back something.

Hearing his doubts, fears, and concerns ... I know this is real. He trusts me. Wants me. And God, do I want him. So badly.

"Too much?" he asks when I don't respond.

I blink, pulling myself back out of my head. "No. Not enough," I respond. Feeling emboldened, I unbutton my jeans and slide his hand down my panties. "Feel what *you* do to *me*, Evan."

Evan's pupils dilate, and he groans, slipping his hand further down to my core, his fingers lightly tracing over my very slick center. He sucks in a sharp breath at what he finds.

"Fuck, Carrie," he breathes. And then his mouth is devouring mine. His fingers slip deep inside me, causing me to cry out. I cling to him as my knees shake against the onslaught of his now-pumping hand. His thumb flicks against my clit, and I moan.

"Take me to bed, Evan. Now," I say, uncharacteristically direct.

He withdraws his hand and lifts me up. I wrap my legs around him and cling to him as he carries me up the stairs, into his room, and sets me gently down at the head of the bed.

His initial urgency gives way to a slower, more deliberate pace as he methodically removes his shirt and then his jeans. Revealing the fact that he wasn't wearing any underwear. I bite my lip hard as his perfect cock slaps against the flat plane of his stomach. At the lean, strong muscles of his chest, arms, and legs. I remove my own shirt and toss it at him. With a predatory grin, he takes the challenge, slowly approaching and crawling over me.

As I lay under a very naked Evan Edwards, I can't even imagine how this is real. But I'm not going to waste a moment. I run my hands down the hard muscles of his chest as he stares deeply into my eyes.

He leans down and kisses my neck. Then down my chest. He uses his teeth to pull back the cups of my bra, my breasts spilling out. He sucks each nipple for a moment before groaning his approval as he continues to move down my body, placing light kisses as he goes. I watch in fascination as his large, warm hands pull at my unbuttoned jeans and panties, working them down my legs until I'm almost as naked as he is. I prop myself up on my elbows, pop the clasp to my bra, and then toss it away.

Evan sits back on his haunches at the end of the bed.

"You're beautiful," he murmurs, his eyes drinking me in.

"I'm yours," I breathe.

A soft smile graces Evan's lips. He rises and retrieves a condom from a bag that sits on the chair in the corner of the room. I watch with hooded eyes as he rolls it on. I lick my lips in anticipation as he returns to me. Settles over me. Looks at me like I'm the sun and stars in his sky.

"And I'm yours." He reaches down and seats himself at my entrance, pausing for my approval.

I bite into my lip and give the softest of nods. And then he's sliding in, stretching me, filling me. He returns his mouth to mine, the warmth of his body cocooning me. I wrap my arms around him as he hits home, fully seated inside me. I squeeze his hips with my legs, wanting more.

Of his body, yes. But also of his words. His adoration. Just … him. Just Evan. As much as he'll give me.

"Mine," I whisper back, tilting my hips.

He nods and starts to move.

"God, yes," he breathes.

He buries his face in my neck as he takes me. I wrap myself around him, my whole body lit up by the joining of our bodies and hearts. It's almost more than I can bear as he takes his pleasure. I lose myself to our rhythm until I hear his breaths coming faster, and it sends bolts of desire rippling through my whole being. His pace increases, and it pushes me to the edge of bliss.

"More," I beg. "Please, Evan."

His lips find mine as he crashes home over and over. Because that's what this feels like. Home. Who knew that the place I felt most at home wasn't a place at all but in his arms?

It's the last thought I have before I tip over the edge into mind-numbing pleasure as Evan finds his alongside me, as I'm ruined completely by what I feel for this man.

After, as we lie tangled together, Evan's heartbeat is steady beneath my ear. As he strokes a hand up and down my arm, it hits me like a freight train.

I'm falling so hard for this man.

The thought should terrify me. We've known each other for such a short time, and our worlds are so different. He doesn't even live here. But then again, I only intended Alpine Ridge to be a temporary stopover, albeit longer than his. I have no idea how long I'll be here or where I'll end up after this.

But as I gaze up at him, I feel a sense of rightness. Of inevitability. Home. The word chants in my mind to Evan's heartbeat.

Still, ever the worrier, doubts pull at me. Maybe he doesn't feel the same way. Maybe he'll go back to L.A. and forget all about me. Maybe someone better will capture his interest and his heart. Maybe I'm not enough.

"Carrie?" Evan's voice cuts through the darkening room and through my troubled thoughts.

"Yeah?"

He slides closer, pulling me against him. "That was incredible." His lips meet mine briefly, gently.

I allow myself a small smile. "It was," I agree. I put my hand on his cheek. "You're incredible."

He squeezes me closer. "Stay with me?" The tenderness of his plea cuts straight to my heart.

I resist saying what I really want to — always. I'll always stay with him if that's what he wants. This all feels too fast, too unreal. Like I'll wake up in the morning, and it'll all have been a dream. But if it is, I'll dream it a little longer.

"Of course," I murmur.

He leans in and kisses me, soft and unhurried, before pulling the blanket over us. He falls asleep before I do, his deep, even breaths soothing the pounding of my heart.

I breathe in his ocean and evergreen scent and settle my ear over his heart, drifting off to its beat. I have two more weeks to soak up as much of him as possible. Instead of focusing on the fact that he'll eventually leave, I decide to make the most of my time with him.

With a smile on my lips, I fall asleep in his arms.

CHAPTER ELEVEN

EVAN

The first rays of dawn are just beginning to filter through the curtains when I wake, Carrie still sleeping peacefully beside me. I prop myself up on one elbow, watching the gentle rise and fall of her chest, the way her dark lashes fan out against her cheeks.

Last night was a big deal, I realize. Not just the incredible sex but the connection and the vulnerability we shared. I'm falling for this woman, hard and fast. The thought of leaving her in two weeks, of returning to my life in L.A. while she stays here, leaves a hollow ache in my chest.

But that's a problem for later, I decide. We'll figure it out. Together.

The idea of being part of a "we" and having someone to navigate life's challenges with ... well, it brings a smile to my face. I reach out, brushing a strand of hair from Carrie's forehead, marveling at the softness of her skin.

The buzzing of my phone shatters the quiet moment. I glance at the screen, noting two things: first, it's barely after five a.m., and second, it's Rick, my agent.

I contemplate letting it go to voicemail, but I know that will only make things worse later. With a sigh, I slip out of bed, padding quietly into the hall so as not to wake Carrie.

"Rick, it's five in the fucking morning," I greet him, my voice rough with sleep.

"Evan, you need to get your ass back to L.A.," he says without preamble. "I've got the audition of a lifetime for you. They're looking for a new James Bond. And they want you to come in and read for them. Today. Two p.m."

I'm glad I'm leaning against the wall because my knees go weak. James Bond. The franchise I grew up idolizing. The reason I got into action movies in the first place. I never dreamed I'd be considered for such an iconic role.

"James Bond? Are you serious?" I manage to croak out.

"As a heart attack. This is huge, Evan. Career-changing. You can't pass this up."

He's right. As much as I'm falling for Carrie, as much as I want to explore what we have ... this is why I became an actor. To have opportunities like this. To bring to life the characters I've admired since I was a kid.

I close my eyes, a war raging in my heart. But in the end, there's only one choice I can make.

"Okay. Book the flight. I'll be there."

"Already done," Rick says, and I can hear the grin in his voice. "You're on a ten a.m. out of SeaTac. So get your ass in gear and get to the airport."

I let out a slow breath. I have just under an hour to get ready and head out to make it through security in time.

"I'm on my way," I tell him, then hang up.

For a long moment, I stand there, the phone clutched in my hand, my heart pounding. I'm thrilled about the audition, but the thought of leaving Carrie, of walking away from what we've just started ...

I contemplate not waking her and just leaving a note. But I can't do that to her. It would make me the world's biggest asshole. She deserves better.

Squaring my shoulders, I head back into the bedroom ... and find Carrie awake, sitting in bed, the sheet clutched to her chest, her face pinched with unhappiness.

"I heard," she says softly, her eyes meeting mine. "You have to leave."

I nod, swallowing hard. "Carrie, I'm so sorry. It's this audition, it's —"

She holds up a hand, stopping me. "It's James Bond. I get it. You have to go."

The understanding in her voice and her willingness to put my dreams before her own desires make me fall for her more.

I cross the room in two strides, taking her face in my hands. "We'll make this work," I promise. "We can talk every day. I'll come back as soon as I can. And you can visit me in L.A. anytime you want."

She nods, but I can see the doubt in her eyes. The fear that this is it, that what we have won't survive the distance.

"Carrie, I ..." The words stick in my throat. I want to tell her how I feel, to make her understand that I don't want this to be the end of us. But the clock is ticking, and I know I need to move.

"It's okay," she whispers, pressing a finger to my lips. "Go. Be amazing. I'll be here when you get back."

I kiss her, pouring everything I'm feeling into the press of my lips against hers. Then, reluctantly, I pull away.

I jump in the shower, somehow feeling nervous excitement and devastating loss all at the same time.

Carrie is gone when I get out of the shower, and my heart sinks. But after I've packed, I head downstairs to find her in the kitchen, a travel mug of coffee and a bagel wrapped in foil waiting for me.

"For the road," she says, her smile not quite reaching her eyes.

I pull her into my arms, holding her tight. "Thank you. For everything."

She nods against my chest, and I feel her take a shuddering breath. "Go kick some ass, okay?"

"I will. I'll call you when I'm out of the audition."

One more kiss, one more moment of holding her, breathing her in. And then I'm out the door, my heart heavy even as my mind races with possibilities.

As I pull out of the driveway, I glance back at the house, at the window where I know Carrie is standing, watching me go.

I'm leaving behind something amazing, something real. And given how new it is, how fragile ... I know the odds of us making it work long-distance aren't great.

But I have to try. Because Carrie ... she's worth fighting for. Worth rearranging my life for. And if I get this role, if my career takes off in a new direction ... I'll find a way to make room for her. For us.

With a newfound determination, I point my car towards Seattle and the future that awaits. It's a future full of uncertainties, but one thing I know for sure.

Carrie will be a part of it. Somehow, some way ... we'll find our way back to each other. Back to this moment, this feeling.

Back to the start of something incredible.

CHAPTER TWELVE

CARRIE

The house feels emptier than it should, given that I've only known Evan for a short time. But as I move through the rooms, tidying up for Mia and Nate's return tomorrow, his absence is a palpable ache in my chest.

I pause in the kitchen, my hands gripping the edge of the counter as I try to steady my emotions. I'm happy for him, truly. The chance to play such an iconic role is a dream come true, and he deserves it. But I can't shake the feeling that this is the beginning of the end for us.

We hadn't been together long enough to develop a bond that could withstand a separation. I know that, logically. But my heart hasn't quite caught up to that reality.

Simba winds around my ankles, meowing for attention. I scoop him up, burying my face in his soft fur. "At least you're not going anywhere," I murmur.

As the day wears on, I keep glancing at my phone, hoping to see Evan's name light up the screen. But it remains stubbornly silent. By the time I crawl into bed that night, the pit in my stomach has grown. He said he'd call after the audition. The fact that he hasn't ... well, it speaks volumes.

The next evening, I'm in the kitchen making tea when I hear the front door open.

"Hello?" Mia's voice calls out. "We're home!"

I plaster on a smile and go to greet them. Mia and Nate look tan, happy, and more in love than ever. It's beautiful to see, even as it makes my own heartache more acute.

"Welcome back!" I say, hugging them both. "How was the honeymoon?"

Mia's eyes light up. "Oh, Carrie, it was amazing. The beaches, the food, the sunsets ..."

As she launches into a detailed account of their trip, I notice Nate glancing around, puzzled.

"Hey, where's Evan?" he asks, interrupting Mia's story about their snorkeling adventure.

My stomach drops. Evan didn't even tell his own brother he was leaving. "Oh, um, he had to go back to L.A. yesterday," I say, trying to keep my voice light. "There was an important audition. So, I came up and stayed to look after Simba for you."

Nate's brow furrows. "He didn't mention anything about an audition before we left."

I shrug, aiming for nonchalance. "It was kind of last minute. You know how these things can be."

Mia looks at me intently, and I can tell she's not buying my casual act. But I don't have the energy to get into it right now.

"Well, I should get going. Let you two settle back in," I say, grabbing my bag. "We'll catch up soon, okay?"

I make my escape before Mia can corner me with questions I'm not ready to answer.

It's not until Sunday that Evan finally calls. My heart leaps when I see his name on my screen, but I temper my excitement.

"Hey," I answer, trying to sound casual.

"Carrie, hi," he says, his voice warm but distracted. "I'm sorry I didn't call sooner. It's been crazy here."

He launches into an explanation about being wined and dined by studio execs after the audition. Then, yesterday, he spent time with his agent, going over paperwork and the next steps.

"It's not official yet," he says excitedly, "but it's looking really good. I've still got more work to do to lock it down, though, so I probably won't be able to call every day."

"That's okay," I say, even as my heart sinks at my fears coming to fruition. "I understand."

We chat for a few more minutes before he has to go. As I hang up, a feeling of dread settles over me. And so, it begins.

The next few weeks prove my fears right. Evan calls maybe once a week, if that. He talks my ear off about the part, the director, and everything related to his new adventure. To his credit, he asks how I'm doing, but it's not like I have much to report besides missing him. I text occasionally when something reminds me of him, but his replies, when they come, are brief and infrequent.

Then, at the end of the month, he calls with news.

"It's still a secret," he says, his voice barely containing his excitement, "but I've officially got the part. They need me to start filming as soon as possible. I'll be in remote locations for the next two months, but I'll try to call when I can."

"That's wonderful, Evan," I say, genuinely happy for him even as my heart breaks. "Congratulations. You're going to be amazing."

We talk for a few more minutes, but it feels like we're speaking across a vast distance, and it's not just the miles between us.

When we hang up, I know, with a certainty that settles in my bones, that he won't call again.

And he doesn't.

As the days turn into weeks, I throw myself into my work. I focus on the upcoming elections and on helping Alpine Ridge become the town it deserves to be.

The November election proves my hunch, and Alpine Ridge is officially voted into townhood. We all take a break to celebrate, including a small party for my birthday, but then it's back to the daily grind.

I spend time with Mia, Nate, Rae, and the others. I find myself building a life here, piece by piece.

But sometimes, in quiet moments when I'm alone, I think of Evan. Of what might have been. Of the whirlwind romance that felt like the beginning of something extraordinary.

And I wonder if, somewhere out there, as he films his dream role, he ever thinks of me, too.

CHAPTER THIRTEEN

EVAN

The scorching Abu Dhabi sun beats down on me as I crouch behind a sand dune, prop gun in hand. Sweat trickles down my back, and my muscles ache from holding the position. But I push the discomfort aside, sinking deep into the role of an international spy.

"Action!" the director calls, and I spring into motion, rolling out from my hiding spot and firing a series of shots. The stunt coordinator had drilled this sequence into me for hours, and I nail it perfectly.

"Cut! That's a wrap for today," the director announces, and I let out a relieved breath.

As the crew starts to pack up, I glance at my watch. It's Thanksgiving back home, I remember, with a pang. The thought of my family gathering around the table without me, of Carrie celebrating with my brother, her sister, and their friends in Alpine Ridge, hits me harder than I expected.

I trudge back to my trailer, peeling off the sweat-soaked costume. My body feels like one giant bruise from weeks of grueling physical training and stunt work. The producers want me to do as many of my own stunts as possible, which means every spare moment is filled with martial arts lessons, fight choreography, and endless repetitions of complex action sequences. It's the kind of training I'm used to, just not on such an intense, accelerated schedule. But then, they didn't expect to have to switch Bonds right before production started, and I'm not the only one scrambling to adjust.

As I step into the shower, letting the cool water soothe my overheated skin, I can't help but marvel at how different my life is now compared to just a few months ago. The role of James Bond is everything I ever dreamed of and more. It's challenging and exciting, and it will undoubtedly catapult my career to new heights.

But it's also all-consuming. The filming schedule is relentless, with early mornings and late nights blurring together. We're constantly on the move, jetting from one exotic location to another. It's exhilarating but also exhausting.

And in the quiet moments, in those precious few seconds before sleep claims me each night, my thoughts inevitably turn to Carrie.

I miss her. It's strange, considering we only spent a week together, but the ache in my chest when I think of her is undeniable. I miss her laugh, her subtle wit, and the way she saw past my Hollywood persona to the real me.

As I towel off and collapse onto my bed, I can't help but feel a wave of guilt wash over me. I've essentially ghosted her, letting the demands of the role push her to the periphery of my life. It wasn't intentional, but the result is the same.

I reach for my phone, thinking maybe I should call her. But what would I say? I'm sorry for disappearing? That I think about her constantly, even as I'm living out my dream? That I hope she'll still be there when this whirlwind finally slows down?

My thumb hovers over her name in my contacts, but I can't bring myself to place the call. It's the middle of the night in Washington, and besides, a phone call feels inadequate after so much silence. It's the same battle I fight with myself every time, and I always lose.

I set the phone aside with a sigh, staring up at the ceiling. I won't make it home for Christmas either. The shooting schedule is too tight, the locations too remote. Another holiday away from family and friends. And the first in a very long time that there's a special someone I want to spend it with. Carrie.

She said she'd be there when I got back, but I know that's not a promise she can keep forever. Life goes on, and people move on. And I've given her every reason to do just that.

But still, I hope. I hope that when this is all over, when I can finally catch my breath and return to some semblance of normalcy, she'll still be willing to give us a chance. I hope I haven't irreparably damaged what we started to build in those few precious days in Alpine Ridge.

As sleep begins to claim me, my last conscious thought is of Carrie. Of her smile, her touch, the way she made me feel more like myself than I had in years.

I'll make it up to her, I vow silently. Somehow, some way, I'll bridge the distance I've created between us. To show her that what we had — what we could have — is worth it.

With that promise echoing in my mind, I drift off into an exhausted sleep, dreams of snowy mountains and a dark-haired beauty waiting for me on the other side.

CHAPTER FOURTEEN

CARRIE

The crisp winter air nips at my cheeks as I make my way down Main Street, my boots crunching on the light dusting of snow. Alpine Ridge has transformed in the past few months, both literally and figuratively. The newly revamped grocery store, courtesy of Greg's cousin Sera, is a testament to the changes sweeping through our little town. That particular change was made possible by Greg's aunt and uncle fleeing from the fallout of their creeper son Ned's misdeeds against certain town residents and subsequent imprisonment. I say good riddance on all fronts, especially when the place, nay the whole town, is now leaps and bounds better for it.

I pause to admire the sleek facade, remembering the dingy, outdated building it once was. Sera has worked miracles, turning it into a modern, inviting space that wouldn't look out of place in a much larger city. Yet, by strategically leaving some of its original embellishments, she's managed to maintain that small-town charm that makes Alpine Ridge special. Who knew wagon wheel décor could look chic?

I chuckle as I push through the doors. The warm air envelops me, carrying the scent of fresh bread and coffee. The aisles are stocked with an impressive array of products, from organic produce to gourmet international foods. It's a far cry from the limited selection we used to have, and thankfully, the prices lean more Trader Joe's than Whole Foods.

"Carrie!" Meg calls out, waving from behind the customer service desk. Her bright smile is infectious, and I can't help but grin back. I can see how happy she is to have moved on from the coffee stand.

"Hey, Meg. Gosh, the place looks great," I say, approaching her.

She beams. "Doesn't it? I can't believe what the new owner has done with it. And you know, I heard she owns a bunch of other land in Alpine Ridge that she's planning to develop come spring. I can't wait to see what else she'll build."

I nod, genuinely excited to see what Sera will do next. "Me neither. In fact, the whole town is buzzing about it."

She gives me a friendly smile as I move along. While I gather my groceries, my mind wanders to the upcoming elections. The incorporation of Alpine Ridge has set off a whirlwind of political activity, and as the person overseeing the process, I'm right in the middle of it all. It's hard to shut out, even when I'm technically off the clock, so to speak.

But I can't shut it out for long anyway, as later that afternoon, I find myself in the community center, surrounded by a sea of campaign posters and eager candidates. The air is thick with anticipation and the faint smell of coffee from the machine in the corner.

"All right, everyone," I call out, my voice cutting through the chatter. "Let's go over the debate format one more time."

As I explain the rules and time limits, my eyes scan the room. Jerry, the crusty old tavern owner, looks smug in his ill-fitting suit. He's running for mayor, to absolutely no one's surprise. After all, he'd claimed to be running the town once before — well, with the help of some of his friends — so I'm not the least bit shocked that he's throwing his hat in the ring to *actually* run it. I suppress a sigh, reminding myself to remain impartial. But secretly hoping he doesn't make the cut for candidates after the first vote in just over a month.

My gaze lands next on a familiar face, and my spirits lift. Brandon Thompson, my childhood friend, is leaning against the wall, listening intently. His blond hair is just as unruly as ever, throwing me back to his teen self, but his jaw is covered with a layer of golden stubble, and he seems taller and broader. He caught me off guard when he showed up a few weeks ago, announcing his candidacy for town council.

I remember the summers we spent together when I was an awkward preteen and how he always looked out for me like a big brother. Now, he's all grown up, and his boyish features have matured into a rugged handsomeness that speaks of his years traveling the world as a photographer and aid worker. We haven't had much time to talk, but I've meant to catch up with him.

Thankfully, after the meeting, Brandon approaches me, his easy smile bringing back a flood of memories.

"Hey, campaign manager," he teases, bumping my shoulder with his.

I roll my eyes good-naturedly. "I'm not anyone's campaign manager, Thompson. I'm just here to make sure everyone plays fair."

He chuckles. "Always the diplomat. Some things never change."

We fall into step together as we leave the community center, the cold air a shock after the stuffy interior.

"So, international aid worker to small-town council member," I muse. "That's quite a career change."

Brandon shrugs, his breath forming small clouds in the frosty air. "I've seen a lot of the world, Carrie. Done what I could to help. But I realized I wanted to make a difference closer to home. This town ... it's special. I want to be part of shaping its future."

His words resonate with me, echoing my own feelings about Alpine Ridge. "I get that," I say softly. "It's why I'm doing this, too."

We walk in comfortable silence for a moment, and I'm struck by how easily we fall back into our old friendship despite the years and miles that have separated us.

"Hey," Brandon says suddenly, turning to face me. "Want to grab a coffee? Catch up properly?"

I hesitate for a moment, my mind, for some reason, flashing unbidden to Evan, like having coffee with another man is a betrayal of our relationship that couldn't be. But I quickly push the thought aside. Evan made his choice, and I need to move on. And Brandon's just a friend anyway.

"Sure," I reply, smiling. "I'd like that."

Since it's closest, we head towards the coffee stand, and I feel lighter. The past few months have been a whirlwind of activity, barely giving me time to breathe, let alone dwell on my heartache. Between advising candidates, compiling data on the town's needs and desires, and getting to know the residents, I've found a sense of purpose I never knew I was missing.

Brandon and I swap stories over steaming mugs of coffee, sitting in the little heated cubby on the side of the stand. He tells me about his travels, the people he's met, and the challenges he's faced. In turn, I share my experiences in Alpine Ridge, and the ups and downs of the past year. I skate over the mess with my parents, not wanting to wade too far into that swamp. Not when there's so much to be excited about with everything happening here.

"Sounds like you've found your calling," Brandon observes, his eyes warm.

I nod. I hadn't thought of it that way before, but … he's right. "I have. This is what I've always wanted to do, you know? Help shape government structure and make sure people's voices are heard. My dad wanted me to focus on public policy to support his law practice. But this feels right."

Brandon reaches across the table, giving my hand a gentle squeeze. "I'm happy for you, Carrie. You deserve this."

As I look into his kind eyes, I feel seen. It's nice to have him as a friend again.

But I should've known our chat wouldn't go unnoticed in this small, hungry-for-gossip town. Later that night, as I crawl into bed, my phone buzzes with a text from Mia.

MIA

Saw you with Brandon today. Spill the tea, sis!

I shake my head but resist teasing Mia about making assumptions. I know she means well. But I also can't betray what Brandon shared with me all those years ago. It's probably no longer a secret, but I'm not about to make assumptions of my own and share that Brandon and I will never be more than friends because I have a vagina.

Just catching up with an old friend. Nothing to spill.

But as I set my phone aside, I can't help but wonder when there *will* be something to spill about someone special. Because truly, I know I need to move on and date someone else. Alas, there aren't many someone elses to date in this town.

At least I have plenty to focus on for now.

For the first time in a long time, I drift off to sleep without thoughts of Evan haunting my dreams. Instead, my mind is filled with campaign strategies, debate formats, and the warm brown eyes of a childhood friend.

The next evening, I find myself at Greg and Joanie's place for our weekly game night. The living room is warm and cozy, a stark contrast to the frigid air outside. Mia and Nate are cuddled up on the loveseat while Rae sprawls comfortably in an armchair. Greg and Joanie are busy in the kitchen, the clinking of glasses and the aroma of freshly popped popcorn filling the air.

Joanie's voice carries from the kitchen as we wait for her and Greg to join us. "Greg, have you given any more thought to running for town council?"

I perk up, remembering our earlier conversations on the subject. Greg emerges from the kitchen, a bowl of popcorn in his hands, his expression thoughtful.

"I have, actually," he says, setting the bowl on the coffee table. "And I think I'm going to do it."

A cheer goes up from our little group, and I can't help but feel a surge of excitement. Greg would make an excellent council member, with his deep ties to the community and genuine desire to help people. He also owns a fair amount of land here, so it feels right that he should have a say in town matters.

"What about you, Nate?" I ask, turning to my brother-in-law. "Have you reconsidered running?"

Nate shakes his head, his arm tightening around Mia. "I appreciate the thought, but I have to pass. It's our first year of marriage, and I want to focus on that." He pauses, a smile playing on his lips. "Plus, I've been considering getting re-licensed to practice medicine."

"Really?" Mia asks, surprise evident in her voice.

Nate nods. "Yeah, I think I want to go ahead and add a walk-in medical clinic to the wellness center. It's something the town could really use." Mia gives Nate a loving look that makes my chest ache.

I clear my throat. "That's fantastic, Nate," I say, genuinely impressed. "I know you've been concerned about helping the large elderly population here. The town would definitely benefit from that."

"What about you, Mia?" Rae pipes up. "Are you thinking of throwing your hat in the ring?"

Mia laughs, shaking her head. "No way. You know the bakery keeps me busy enough as it is. I'll leave the politicking to the rest of you."

"And don't even think about asking me again," Rae adds with a grin. "I'd bet dollars to donuts Jerry carries the vote for mayor, and there's no way I'm working with that blowhard ever again."

Greg snorts, and Joanie smirks.

As we settle into our game night routine, the conversation naturally flows to the upcoming elections. The energy in the room is palpable. Everyone is excited about the changes happening in Alpine Ridge.

"I can't believe how much is going on," Joanie remarks, shuffling a deck of cards. "Between the elections, Sera's development plans, and now Nate's clinic idea ... this town is really coming alive."

I nod in agreement, feeling a warmth spread through my chest. "It's amazing, isn't it? There's so much potential here."

As I look around at my friends — my found family, besides my sister, who is actually family — I'm struck by how content I feel. The pain of my parents' rejection has faded to a dull ache, and thoughts of Evan, once so consuming, have become less frequent. Instead, I'm filled with a sense of purpose and excited about my role in shaping Alpine Ridge's future.

"You know," Mia says, catching my eye as if she can read my thoughts, "I'm really proud of you, Carrie. You've thrown yourself into this election stuff, and you're doing an amazing job."

I feel my cheeks warm at her praise. "Thanks, Mia. It feels good to be doing something I'm passionate about."

"And it shows," Greg adds. "The candidates all respect you, and the townspeople trust you to keep things fair. You've found your niche here."

I blush, brushing them off and refocusing on the game. As we get absorbed in it, the room is filled with laughter and playful competition, and I can't help but feel grateful. Alpine Ridge has given me more than just a place to stay — it's given me a home, a purpose, and a chance to be the person I've always wanted to be — something I hadn't even dared to dream about not that long ago.

The elections might keep me busy, but moments like these, surrounded by people who care about me and filled with a sense of belonging, remind me that there's so much more to life in Alpine Ridge than just politics.

Alpine Ridge's future is bright and full of possibility. And maybe so is mine.

CHAPTER FIFTEEN

EVAN

The roar of the jet engines fades as we touch down at SeaTac Airport, and I let out a long breath. After months of non-stop filming, reshoots, and living and breathing James Bond, I'm finally free. Well, as free as I can be before the publicity storm hits.

I check my phone and see a text from my manager.

RICK

Announcement set for Monday. Lay low this weekend.

A grin spreads across my face. Lay low? That's the plan. Just not in L.A. — but I didn't bother telling Rick about the detour on my way home for fear he'd try to talk me out of it.

After I collect my luggage, I secure a rental. Climbing into the driver's seat, my heart races as I punch the familiar route to Alpine Ridge into the GPS. I'm going to see Carrie. Finally.

The drive passes in a blur of anticipation and nervous energy. What if she's moved on? What if she doesn't want to see me? I push the doubts aside, knowing torturing myself over it won't change anything, and focus on the road ahead.

It's late when I make it to Alpine Ridge. The January evening is every bit the frigid, snow-filled landscape I expected it to be. But at least the main roads are plowed, and Carrie's place is just off Main Street. As I pull up, I see lights glowing warmly in the windows, so someone is still up. Hopefully, it's Carrie because I'm not sure if Rae knows about us, and if she doesn't, I'm not sure this is how Carrie would want her to find out. There are so many things that could go wrong here.

I take a deep breath before approaching the door. And I knock, my stomach in knots.

The door swings open, and there she is. Carrie. Her eyes widen in shock, her mouth forming a perfect 'O'.

"Evan?" she breathes like she can't believe I'm real.

"Hi, Carrie," I say, drinking in the sight of her. She's even more beautiful than I remembered, her dark hair loose around her shoulders, her blue eyes bright in the porch light. She's wearing the most adorable pink and blue waffle pajama top and matching long johns.

She blinks, seeming to come back to herself. "What are you doing here?"

"I ... Can I come in?" I ask, suddenly aware that we're standing in her doorway and my wardrobe choices were based on a much warmer climate. These jeans, tee, and light jacket aren't doing anything to keep me warm.

She hesitates, then nods, stepping back to let me in. "Sure. Rae's out anyway." Well, that's a relief. One thing that could go wrong off the plate. On to the next.

When I've barely stepped inside, the words tumble out of me. "I'm so sorry, Carrie. These past couple of months have been insane. The filming schedule was brutal, and then there were reshoots, and I was jumping from one location to another ..." I run a hand through my hair, frustrated with my own excuses. "I know I should have tried harder to call. But for what it's worth, I couldn't stop thinking about you. I flew straight here from our last reshoot in Australia."

Carrie sinks down on the couch, her expression guarded. "Evan, I ..." She trails off, seemingly at a loss for words. Or perhaps she has so many she can't decide which to say first.

Hesitantly, I sit carefully beside her, unable to resist the pull between us. "I missed you," I murmur, reaching out to touch her cheek.

She leans into my touch, almost unconsciously, and that's all the encouragement I need. I close the distance between us, capturing her lips with mine.

For a moment, she's still. Then, like a switch has been flipped, she's kissing me back with a fervor that matches my own. Her hands fist in my shirt, pulling me closer.

We break apart, both breathing heavily. "I missed you too," she admits. "But Evan ..." She trails off again, shaking her head — definitely too many words.

"I know," I assure her, stroking her cheek. "I know I messed up. I know we can't magically pick up where we left off. But fuck, Carrie. I thought I missed you before we kissed. Now?" I draw in a shaky breath, willing myself not to rip her clothes off right this second. I run my thumb slowly down her neck. "I didn't realize how much I *need* you."

She takes my meaning instantly and lets out a small moan. She closes her eyes. "This doesn't change anything."

I lean and kiss her, saying softly against her lips, "I know."

She rises, pulling me by the hand down the hall and into a small bedroom. Her messy queen-sized bed takes up most of the space, with barely room for a nightstand and dresser. She closes the door behind us.

"Show me how much you missed me, Evan," she breathes. Despite her bold words, she looks as nervous as I felt coming here.

Despite my near-animalistic need for her, I approach slowly, stopping so there's barely a breath's distance between us. I look down into her big blue eyes and cup her cheek before meeting her lips with mine.

I go slow, waiting for her to respond. She wraps her arms around my neck, and I pull her close, breathing in her sweet coconut scent. I deepen the kiss, pushing into her mouth with my tongue. She opens to me with another tiny groan that has me aching for her.

As I explore her mouth with mine and her body with my hands, I slide them under her and lift her gently against me. Her legs wrapped around me is like coming home. I carry her to the bed, laying her down softly under me without breaking our kiss.

Just being here with her like this is already driving me crazy. And I can't help myself anymore; I grind into her soft center. She gasps, her head tilting back with pleasure. I use the opportunity to kiss down her neck as I run my hands under her top. Only to find she's not wearing a bra.

"Fucking hell, Carrie," I groan, lifting her shirt to reveal her perfect tits. I can't help myself; I lean in and suck a nipple into my mouth. She arches against me. And I lose it. I rip the top off her, then shuck my jacket and shirt. I climb off her and kick off my shoes, then rip off my pants and boxers. I was going to do Carrie's next, but she's already there, tossing her own over the side of the bed.

And it's at that moment I realize she's completely, gloriously naked and laying there looking at me with lust-filled eyes.

And it's the next moment when I realize … I don't have a goddamn condom.

"Shit," I curse. "Do you have any protection?' She rolls over, opens the nightstand drawer, and then holds up a foil packet. Relief rolls through me. "Thank fucking God." I snatch it from her and roll it on in a blink.

"Hurry," Carrie says desperately.

A shiver of anticipation rolls down my spine, and my balls tighten. I climb between her legs, running the tip of my cock through her wet folds. She whimpers, and I can't take it. I slam into her. She gasps in surprise. I look up at her, and she nods, so I unleash.

It's been a long time since I was so turned on. Since I let go so completely. I grasp Carrie's hips as her warm, slick grip sends electricity gliding along my skin, coiling behind my cock. I'm not going to last long.

"Fuck, Carrie, I missed you so damn much," I groan. I rub my thumb in circles over her clit as I take her, pushing her toward orgasm. She cries out and tilts into me. My cock thickens as she works her hips with mine. It's too much, and I collapse on top of her, meeting her mouth with mine as I continue to pump in and out. Her lips feast on mine greedily as her nails scrape down my back. The pleasurable pain sends me ricocheting over the edge, groaning my release into her neck.

Unfortunately, I know she hasn't come yet, but thankfully I'm still hard. So, I pump faster. It doesn't take long before she's clinging harder to me, and her walls clamp down on my cock, her moans now muffled against my neck.

I finally slow to a stop and then roll off her. Our bodies are sticky with sweat, and the scent of her coconut shampoo mixed with *her* has me taking deep breaths, desperate to remember this moment forever. That was by far the most intense sex I've ever had.

Still … I roll back toward her and trace a finger down her shoulder. "I'm not sure I did how much I missed you justice."

Carrie shoots me a wry look. "I think you did pretty well."

My lips tip up in a half-hearted smile because I can feel the skepticism radiating off of her, even now.

"Carrie … I won't make promises I can't keep this time," I say. "But I hope you believe that I never stopped thinking about you. You were the first thing on my mind when I woke up and my last thought before I went to sleep at night. Unfortunately, almost every moment between, I had to focus on everything that was being thrown at me. I know any relationship I have isn't going to be conventional, but I hope that once things settle down, we can find a way to make this work."

"But do they ever settle down?" she asks wistfully.

My stomach sinks because it's not a question with a good answer.

"This shoot was particularly intense because of the last-minute change and everything I, and the rest of the crew, had to do to make up for that. But … no, my life while filming isn't conducive to maintaining a relationship. Still, that's only a few times a year for a month or two."

Carrie turns to me with a raised brow. "*Only*? So, for a quarter to half of the year, you're filming. And the rest? What about promoting? Don't you go on a tour of sorts for every movie?"

I press my lips together. She's not wrong.

"I do," I admit. "It would be a challenge, I know." I sigh in frustration and roll onto my back.

Carrie scoots in, molding her body to mine and laying her hand on my chest. "Just … stay and hold me. I wasn't expecting you to show up, but now that you're here, we might as well make the most of it."

I fold my fingers over hers and squeeze. I'd expected the worst, and this is far from it, so I'll take it. In any case, I'm too exhausted to do anything else as the jetlag catches up with me, and I fall asleep with Carrie in my arms.

The next morning, we agree to keep things under wraps for now because, as I suspected, she didn't tell anyone what had happened between us the last time I was here. Thankfully, I manage to sneak out without Rae catching me. I head into Ellensburg to have breakfast and pick up some more seasonally appropriate clothing, and then I text Nate to let him know I'm headed his way for a surprise visit on my way back to L.A.

He suggests we meet at the bakery, so I start the trek back.

When I get there, I enter to find Nate, Carrie, and Joanie sipping coffee at a table while Mia and Rae are working the counter.

"Evan!" Mia exclaims, rushing out from behind the counter to hug me. "This is a wonderful surprise. What are you doing here?"

I grin, hugging her back and, in turn, accepting hugs and handshakes from the others. "Just wanted to see my favorite people before things get crazy with work again."

We spend the day catching up, with Greg joining us once he's done at the community center. Through an afternoon of pastries, hearing about the happenings around town, and the general camaraderie, I'm struck by how much I've missed this group. How much I've missed feeling like just Evan, not James Bond or Hollywood star Evan Edwards.

Even though they ask about the shoot and how I'm feeling about my new venture, it's all coming from a place of interest and caring for me. It's a nice change. They're even super supportive and understanding when I admit that as excited as I am for the upcoming announcement, I'm terrified at the thought of filling such big shoes. Even if people have loved me as an action star, there's just no knowing how the public will react to my taking such a monumental role. But even just saying it out loud makes me feel better, and the conversation moves swiftly along.

That evening, we all head to Nate and Mia's for dinner. Throughout the night, I catch Carrie's eye across the room, the air between us charged with our secret. It's thrilling and maddening all at once. Eventually, the others take their leave, and it's just Nate, Mia, Carrie, and me.

Just being around Carrie today, watching her listen intently to her friends and be her sweet, supportive self, has me right back where I was when I left. Totally smitten.

Watching her laugh at something Mia says, I let out a small, happy sigh. Carrie's eyes shift to meet mine. I smile. She smiles back. And there must be something of how I'm feeling in my gaze because she blushes. Suddenly, the image of her post-orgasm-flushed face flashes through my mind, and my thoughts drift in that direction.

I meet her gaze again and flick my eyes up the stairs in invitation. She blushes harder but gives me a subtle nod.

When Mia yawns a few minutes later, Carrie seizes the opportunity. "Well, that's my cue that you guys want me to get the heck out of here," she says with a chuckle.

"Oh no, you don't have to," Mia protests. "Though I guess I should get to bed." She gives Nate a meaningful look. Carrie smirks at her sister and rises to give her a hug.

"I'll see you guys later," she says to Mia and Nate. "It was nice to see you again, Evan. Hope you have a good trip back home."

"Thanks, good seeing you too, Carrie," I reply casually. With a small wave, she's gone. Thank God for my acting skills because it was all I could do just then not to give into my caveman instincts and drag Carrie up the stairs by her hair.

"I won't be around when you leave, but I agree, it was so good to see you, Evan. I hope you come back soon," Mia says warmly, suppressing another yawn.

I rise and hug her. "Thanks, Mia. Me too."

Nate slaps me on the back. "See you in the morning, bro."

I nod and follow them upstairs, slipping into the guestroom as they continue upward. I pull out my phone to find a text from Carrie.

CARRIE

Are they upstairs yet?

With a grin, I reply.

Just. Get your gorgeous ass in here.

I grab a condom from the box I purchased this morning, and then I strip and lay on top of the comforter in the center of the bed, completely naked. It's only a couple of minutes before she slinks in the door. Her eyes widen as she sees me.

Without looking away, she kicks off her shoes. "And here I thought we were just going to talk," she says quietly with a smirk. And then she rips off her sweater and bra in one motion, followed by a similar trick with her pants and underwear. She saunters over to the bed and climbs onto the end, prowling toward me, her hair and breasts swinging. My semi goes to a full-on in an instant. She eyes it with interest.

And before I can speak, she takes me in her mouth. "Oh fuck," I whisper.

She gives one more deep suck before pulling away. "Okay," she says, uncharacteristically boldly. She takes the condom and rolls it down my length, then climbs over me, lowering herself slowly onto my dick. Every inch that slides into her tight pussy makes me harder and harder. Finally unable to take it anymore, I grab her hips and thrust up, burying myself completely inside her. The look on her face as I sink in to the hilt is pure bliss.

But despite my initial eagerness, our lovemaking is slower and more deliberate after that. She's clearly enjoying using my body to pleasure herself, and I'm happy to watch. It's more than pleasurable for me, too. Watching her ride my cock is next level.

Still, I try to pour everything I'm feeling into every touch, every kiss as our bodies work together, and we both gasp and pant quietly in pleasure. I want her to understand how much she means to me, even if I can't find the right words to fix what I've broken.

Her pace starts to stutter, the tilt of her hips becomes more erratic, and I know she's close. I hold onto her and pick up where she left off. Her gaze meets mine, and I nod.

"I've got you, baby," I assure her softly.

An almost pained look of pleasure crosses her face as she puts her hands on my chest and leans forward. I use the slight change in position to piston my hips under her. She nods her encouragement, so I continue until she shatters. Until she's strangling my cock with her pussy. Until she's biting back screams before slumping down onto my chest.

I stroke my hands up her sides and hold her against me, rolling us both over. I reposition her legs so I can keep taking her. I go slow, though, as she's still coming down from her orgasm, waiting until the slickness between her legs builds once more. Until she's writhing again under me.

The sight of her undone, with my cock sliding in and out of her ... it does things to me. My chest aches with how much I want to please her. I test different depths and speeds until I find a stroke that has her gripping the bedspread and biting her lip so hard I'm afraid she'll draw blood. Her walls start to flutter around me, and the low ache behind my cock swells.

"Come for me again, Carrie," I whisper, reaching down to stroke her clit as my base need overrides my slow pace, as I start to fuck her hard and fast, chasing my own orgasm.

She whimpers and nods, her eyes rolling back in her head, lowly moaning, "Oh god, oh god, oh god."

And then she's coming, and the sensation is too much. I explode, biting the inside of my cheek to stave off the roar I want to let out. But I can't help it when I collapse on top of her and groan "Holy shit" against her skin.

With our bodies pressed together, still buried completely inside her, I know I've missed her on more than a physical level. I want so much more than sex with this woman, but I also know that this was the safest, and possibly only, way for her to allow me back in.

So after we clean up, I don't protest when she gets dressed. I don't bother, hoping it'll lure her back in, even though, deep down, I know it won't.

"I should go," she says, settling on the edge of the bed.

"Stay," I plead.

She shakes her head. "Evan, this was ... it was amazing if I'm being honest. But I can't do this." She gestures between us. "I can't let myself get attached again only to end up sitting around waiting for you to remember I exist."

Her words hit me like a punch to the gut, but I get why she feels that way. "I know it seemed like that these last couple of months, but I could never forget you exist." I sigh heavily, scrubbing my hands down my face. "I know it's not easy trying to have a relationship with me. Hell, that's where the whole playboy image came from. I didn't bother *trying* to have a relationship with anyone. I haven't even wanted to for a very long time. Not until you."

Carrie's bottom lip trembles and my heart breaks. "If this is what a relationship with you looks like, I hope you understand when I say I just can't do it. Don't get me wrong. On some level all I want is to be with you, and I waited for you far longer than I probably should have. But I can't live with waiting for you half of the time. I'm not built for that."

I nod slowly. "I know. And you deserve so much more than secret sex and broken promises." I turn my head as tears fill my eyes. "You deserve someone who is as selfless and caring as you are. Who can be here for you and give you back just as much as you have to give."

A soft, warm hand presses against my cheek, returning my gaze to hers. "You deserve that too. And I have no doubt that when you're ready to settle down, you'll have your pick of amazing women."

Now it's her turn to look away, but she's not fast enough, and I see the tears fall.

But I have nothing to say to soothe her. I can't tell her she's the only woman I want. It's unfair. Selfish. And because I care for her so deeply, I can't do that. I have to put her feelings before mine.

"I'll see you around?"

She gives me the smallest of smiles. "Yeah. Sure. See you around."

And with that, she slips out of the room and out of my life once again.

I don't sleep much despite my bone-deep exhaustion, and when I do, it's fitfully. So, I hear Mia when she comes down the stairs just after four a.m. Once she's been gone for a bit, I give up trying to sleep.

I rise and pack my bags to head back to L.A., unable to shake the feeling that I've lost something precious.

But the show must go on. In just over twenty-four hours, I'll be unveiled as the new James Bond and will have publicly achieved the dream this journey was based on.

So why doesn't that feel like enough anymore?

CHAPTER SIXTEEN

CARRIE

The crisp January air bites at my cheeks as I make my way down Main Street, my mind a whirlwind of conflicting emotions. It's been a week since Evan left, and I still can't shake the memory of his touch, his scent, the way he looked at me like I was the only person in the world.

I shake my head, trying to clear my thoughts. Just when I thought I was moving on, putting the whole affair behind me, he showed up and turned my world upside down again. His explanation for his absence made sense on some level — I can only imagine how grueling and all-consuming filming a movie must be. But at the same time, it didn't. How hard is it to send a text? To make a quick call?

I sigh, my breath forming a small cloud in the cold air. The truth is, I couldn't resist him. The moment he touched me, all my resolve crumbled. I remembered what it felt like to be in his arms, to be wanted by him, and I was powerless against it.

But now, in the harsh light of day, I'm upset with myself for allowing it. Twice. I let myself be vulnerable and opened myself up to the possibility of more heartache. Even so, a small part of me is proud that I found the strength to close that door. To tell him that I couldn't do it anymore, couldn't live half a life waiting for him.

As I push open the door to the bakery, the warm, sweet scent of freshly baked goods envelops me, momentarily pushing my troubled thoughts aside.

"Hey, sis," Mia greets me from behind the counter, her smile not quite reaching her eyes.

I raise an eyebrow, hanging up my coat. "Hey. Everything okay?"

Mia sighs, gesturing for me to join her and Nate at one of the tables. Joanie's there, too, nursing a steaming mug of coffee.

"I just finished the financials for last year," Mia explains once I'm seated. "Business did a bit better around the incorporation approval, but now it's stalled."

My brows jump. "Well, that's no good," I murmur. "But it's winter, right? Maybe that's why?"

Mia shakes her head. "We're surrounded by ski resorts. The traffic is there. It's just not stopping in Alpine Ridge. If we can't get more people into town both permanently and as tourists, this place isn't going to last much longer."

Nate reaches out, squeezing Mia's hand. "It's not like we can force people to move or visit here, though. Maybe we can cut costs or something. We'll figure it out."

I open my mouth to suggest that with the upcoming elections, surely there's a way for us to leverage that for more traffic, but before I can speak, Joanie pipes up, a mischievous glint in her eye.

"I have an idea," she says, leaning forward. "Actually, it's something that occurred to me a while ago, but I figured I'd wait until after the elections. It could still work in our favor now, though." She pauses, presumably for dramatic effect, because Joanie is nothing if not dramatic. I smirk at the thought. "What if we get someone famous to live here? Part-time, anyway, since the ultimate plan is to make this an upscale second-home destination. It's like dominoes: get one on the hook, and other famous and rich people will want to move here. And then everyone else will want to visit to catch a glimpse of the famous people and see what all the fuss is about."

Nate's brow furrows. "Someone famous? Like who?"

Joanie gives him a disbelieving look. "Really, Nate?" She shakes her head. "I think we all know someone famous who seems to like it here."

My heart stops as I realize where she's going with this. Please, no.

"You mean Evan?" Nate asks.

"You bet your ass I do," Joanie confirms.

I wait for Nate to shoot down the idea and point out all the reasons why it wouldn't work. Surely there are reasons besides my secret desire never to be tempted by him again? But to my horror, his face lights up.

"That could actually work," he says, excitement creeping into his voice. "And it would be awesome to get to see my brother more often."

"I say go for it," Rae pipes up from behind the counter. "Old Jerry would have a heart attack if a celebrity came knocking on Alpine Ridge's door looking to stay a spell. And if that didn't do it, the media coverage and fanfare might." She grins wickedly at the thought.

Joanie chuckles. "Is it bad that I don't even care if it pisses off some of the geriatrics in the town if it saves my bestie's business?" she adds airily.

Nate smirks. "Not in my book. We're all in at this point on breathing life into this place. There will be some people who don't like that, no matter how we go about doing it. At the end of the day, we need to do what's necessary to keep things moving in that direction, or the town won't make it."

Mia nods in agreement. "While it's good to keep in mind, I agree that we can't let the possibility that people won't like it stop us. Ultimately, though, there will be matters they have a say in and things they don't. This is definitely the latter because it's not up to them who lives here and who doesn't."

Nate nods, and I sit there, frozen, as he promises to call Evan and ask what he thinks about the idea. My mind is racing, torn between what's best for the town and what I can handle emotionally.

They're not wrong — having someone like Evan buy property here would be great for Alpine Ridge. It would put us on the map and draw attention and further investment. But can I really handle Evan having a home here? Can I handle him coming and going constantly? The many emotions I've felt from his last two visits were hard enough. The thought of experiencing that rollercoaster on a regular basis makes my stomach churn.

But as I look around at the hopeful faces of my sister, brother-in-law, and friend, I feel the familiar weight of expectation settling on my shoulders. I can't let my personal feelings wreck the town's chances of growing or deny Nate the opportunity to be closer to his brother.

So, like the people pleaser I am, I keep my mouth shut. I smile and nod as they discuss the possibilities, all while my heart aches in my chest.

As I help Mia clean up later, she bumps me with her hip, a knowing look in her eye. "You're being awfully quiet about all this," she says. "I thought you'd be excited about the prospect of Evan being around more."

I shrug, focusing intently on wiping down the counter. "It's a good idea," I say, aiming for nonchalance, as I often seem to have to do when talking about Evan. "If he goes for it, it could be really great for the town."

Mia's quiet for a moment, and I can feel her studying me. Oh no. Her Spidey senses are tingling. I can just tell. "Carrie," she says softly, "is something going on between you and Evan?"

And there it is. Curse my super perceptive big sister. For a split second, I consider telling her everything — the stolen moments, the passion, the heartache. But I can't bring myself to do it. It feels too raw, too personal, and admitting it out loud might make it all too real. Besides, it's over … right?

"No," I lie, plastering on a smile. "We're just friends. I'm worried about you and Nate, but at the same time, I'm also worried that we may pin our hopes on this only to have it not pan out. Evan's a busy guy, after all. He might not have time to deal with something like that right now."

Mia nods, seemingly satisfied with my answer. "Fair point. And it might be too distracting to have him here while you're trying to manage the elections."

My brows jump. "I wouldn't be distracted," I protest a little too quickly. However, as soon as I say it, I realize she might not have meant me. Because it certainly could be distracting for the townsfolk, and the candidates, adding a complicating factor to a fledgling process. In any case, I can see the suspicion on Mia's face at my defensiveness.

"Mhm," she hums, clearly unconvinced. And as she turns away, I see doubt in her eyes. That makes two of us.

That night, as I lie in bed staring at the ceiling, I can't help but imagine what it would be like if Evan did have a place here. Would I be as weak as I was this last time and fall back into his arms every time he visited? Or would I have to watch him from afar, pretending that my heart doesn't skip a beat every time I see him?

I'm not sure I'd have the willpower to resist him if he's here often. And I know having to constantly deny what I feel is a recipe for heartache. Really, both scenarios are equally terrifying.

I almost wish we'd never hit it off in the first place before I admit to myself that's just not true. When we're around each other, there's something like magic between us. That's impossible to deny.

But it also feels selfish to wish he didn't have a big, shiny career that's more important than the potential between us.

Though … maybe I should be more selfish. Or at least admit to myself that what I really wish is for it to somehow work out that Evan and I can be together while we're both able to pursue our passions in a way that doesn't interfere with that.

A girl can dream, anyway.

And as I finally drift off, I do dream of Evan. Of the tender look in his eyes when he called me "baby" while we made love. Of how it made me feel cherished and wounded in equal measure. It's, unfortunately, a feeling I'm all too familiar with. The acknowledgment causes the dream to change, and Evan's face is quickly replaced by those of my parents. In the dream, I run through darkness and rain to escape their hurled accusations and cold indifference until I'm safe, though alone. But better alone than subjecting myself to feelings of constant rejection and disappointment.

Apparently, even in my dreams, I know I need to protect myself better.

CHAPTER SEVENTEEN

EVAN

The California sun streams through my office window as I settle into my chair, ready to tackle the mountain of scripts Rick's been sending me. But before I can even open the first one, my phone buzzes. Nate's name flashes on the screen.

"Hey, bro," I answer, leaning back. "What's up?"

"Evan! Got a minute to talk?"

There's an excitement in his voice that piques my interest. "Sure, shoot."

Nate launches into an idea that has my eyebrows climbing higher with each word. A vacation home in Alpine Ridge? It's like he's read my mind. It sounds like it would help push the town in a good direction, and I've been considering a West Coast getaway, somewhere to escape the L.A. madness. This could be perfect for so many reasons.

"What do you think?" Nate asks, his enthusiasm palpable even through the phone.

I can't help but grin. "I think it's a fantastic idea. I've been toying with the idea of a new vacation home, and having one closer would give me a solid reason to get out of L.A. more often."

As I say the words, an image of Carrie flashes through my mind. Being closer to her, having a legitimate reason to see her more often ... it's almost too good to be true. But I push the thought aside. It's not something Nate needs to know.

"Great. I was hoping you'd be into it. It'd be awesome to have you around more."

We chat for a few more minutes about development around town and all the land that's still available, and an idea forms in my mind.

"You know what? Instead of buying a place, I think I'd love to buy some land and build something custom. Maybe something like your place, but bigger."

Nate's all for it, and by the time we hang up, he's promised to send me some contacts to get started. As I set down my phone, I can't shake the feeling that this is more than a coincidence. Could this be fate nudging me in the right direction?

The next week is a whirlwind of activity. Between the Bond announcement, the many potential new opportunities it brought, and starting the process for my new home, I barely have time to breathe. But it's exhilarating. I have video conferences with an architect, a builder, and a realtor, outlining my vision for the perfect Alpine Ridge retreat.

When the property listings come in, I immediately forward them to Nate for his input. His local knowledge proves invaluable as we work together to narrow the options. Things start coalescing, and the idea takes a more definitive shape. I'm excited about that in a way I can't even explain, and I can't wait to get my feet on the ground and make this happen.

Before I know it, I'm back in Alpine Ridge, just days before the next election. I step out of my rental SUV, ready to meet with my team and make some decisions. Even if February seems to have brought even more snow than when I was here a month ago, it makes the whole town even more picturesque, if possible, and at least the 4x4 vehicle I rented can handle it.

We tour several properties before settling on the perfect site. It's one peak over from Nate's place and is secluded with stunning mountain views, yet close enough to town to not feel isolated. As the architect unfurls the preliminary sketches and walks me through the layout, I can already envision lazy mornings on the expansive deck, watching the sun rise over the peaks.

"What do you think?" the architect asks, a hint of nervousness in her voice.

I nod, impressed. "It's a great start. I love the open concept and the way you've incorporated the views. But can we make the master suite a bit larger? And maybe add a home gym?"

She jots down notes, nodding eagerly. "Absolutely. We can adjust the layout to accommodate those changes."

The builder chimes in with a ballpark cost that makes me wince internally — only because I come from a working-class family that had little to spare with three growing boys to feed — but given the millions I've made in my career, I can certainly afford it, and I have a gut feeling it'll be more than worth it.

He estimates they can break ground in late March or early April, depending on weather and permits, which, for the time being, are still being handled by the county. Apparently, that will work in our favor. I'm thrilled to hear it can start so soon, though he cautions that it'll take about six months to complete, possibly more. Though they'll definitely finish before winter sets in again.

Exhilarated by the progress, we wrap up mid-afternoon and I head to the bakery to tag up with Nate and Mia.

"Hey, you," Mia greets me with a grin. "How'd it go?"

I can't help grinning back, but I also want to wait until Nate's here to share the good news. "Oh, you know, not bad. When will Nate be done at the wellness center?"

Mia checks her watch and shrugs. "Should be any time now. Want a cup of coffee or a snack while you wait? It'll be a while before our usual Saturday night dinner party."

I raise a brow. "Dinner party?" That's got my interest. I'd been hoping to see Carrie while I was here, and that sounds like the kind of thing she'd attend.

Mia nods. "Yep. The whole gang will be there. If that's okay? You've probably had a long day."

"That's perfect," I say enthusiastically. "And you know what?" My eyes scan the glass display case, weighing the options from what's left this near to closing. "I'll take a caramel apple cupcake."

Mia gives me a mischievous grin. "Oh, I've got just the thing that'll go with that." She plates the cupcake and then goes into the back for a moment, emerging with a partially filled brandy snifter.

"Cupcakes and brandy?" I ask with a laugh.

She hands me the glass and plate. "Trust me."

I shrug and take it to the nearest table as Rae emerges from the back.

"Evan! What the hell are you doing back in this dump?" she teases.

I chuckle. "Good to see you too, Rae."

"He's here to look at properties," Mia explains.

A look of understanding passes over Rae's face. "Ah, yes, that. I didn't think he'd actually go for it, though. I'll be damned. You gonna move here, sugar?" she teases me with a wink.

"Wouldn't you like to know," I reply with a return wink. Then I bite into the cupcake … and let out an involuntary groan. The sweet, smooth caramel buttercream is balanced by a tart apple undertone, and the yellow cupcake is moist and crumbly, with more of the apple flavor — freaking perfection. "Well, if I was on the fence, I'm not anymore. I'd move here just for the cupcakes." Mia smiles knowingly and gestures at the snifter. So, I take a sip. The caramel and apple taste still on my tongue meld with the brandy to create an amazing blend of flavors that's indescribably rich, oaky, and sweet all at the same time. "Holy. Shit. I thought you were joking with this combo but *damn.*"

Rae peers over the counter. "Oh yeah, that's one of my favorites of Mia's drink and cupcake pairings."

I nod as I continue to eat. "I never would've thought to put those two things together, but this is phenomenal, Mia. You could clean up in L.A. with this concept."

Mia beams under the praise. "Thanks, though I'm hoping to clean up here. It's one of my ideas to bring in more business — evening events, parties, even weddings someday."

"Bonus, it'll piss off Jerry if Mia's serving booze better than his," Rae adds.

"Jerry?" I ask, taking another bite of cupcake.

Mia shoots Rae a look. "She's kidding, I'm not trying to piss anyone off," she says, more to Rae than me. Then she turns her gaze back my way. "Jerry is … well, that's a long story. Short version, he owns the tavern and is running for mayor." Rae raises her eyebrow. "And Rae's got it out for him." Rae rolls her eyes, and Mia shrugs.

I chuckle at their antics, but Nate's arrival saves me from trying to figure out what the full deal is with this guy.

Nate slaps me on the back and takes a seat across from me. Mia scoffs. He chuckles and stands, leaning over the counter to give her a kiss. "Hey, babe."

She smiles as he pulls back. "Hey, yourself."

Nate settles back in the chair and raps his knuckles on the table. "I see Mia's converting you to her cupcake and booze ways."

I snort as I polish off the remaining brandy. "It wasn't a hard sell, that's for sure."

"So, how'd it go?" Nate asks.

I glance between him and Mia. I'm tempted to make them wait until I can tell everyone, but I'm not that big of an asshole.

"I put in an offer on the second parcel we were talking about," I admit.

Nate lights up and holds out a fist. I bump mine against his and laugh. "That's *fantastic*," he says. "Damn. You hear that, babe? My little brother's going to have a house in Alpine Ridge." Nate runs a hand through his hair and laughs. "Man. I can't believe it."

I huff a laugh of my own. "Really? It was your idea," I point out.

He shakes his head. "Actually, it was Joanie's."

"Well, I'll have to thank her at dinner when I give her the good news."

Nate smiles. "You do that." He shakes his head again, laughing like he really can't believe it. And to be honest, I'm still a little in shock at how quickly this seems to be coming together. It just goes to show that when something is meant to be, all the doors open at the right time.

Back at Nate and Mia's that evening, I head downstairs after changing for the dinner party. I didn't know if there'd be a dress code, but I figured a fresh shirt never hurt anything. Since I only planned to be here through tomorrow morning, I didn't bring many clothes, so the navy henley I'm wearing with a nice pair of jeans will have to do.

When I get downstairs, I find Mia in the kitchen chatting with Joanie.

"Hey, Joanie," I greet her.

"Hey, studmuffin," she replies flippantly. And I'm so shocked, I don't know what to say in return.

Mia laughs and points at me. "You totally have surprised Pikachu face right now."

"I guess I just wasn't expecting that greeting," I say, a little thrown off by Joanie's forwardness.

"Oh, that's just Joanie's way of treating you like one of us," Mia explains.

"If you have another suggestion, I'm all ears," Joanie offers, batting her eyelashes.

Mia rolls her eyes. "Greg, come handle your woman. She's hitting on Nate's brother."

Joanie cackles as Greg appears from the direction of the living room. "Hey, Evan, good to see you," he says. Then, to Joanie, "Baby, we've talked about this. Ask first before assigning pet names."

Joanie pouts. "Fine," she replies with a sigh. "But I did say I was open to suggestion."

Greg smirks at her. Mia gives me a look. "Well, now that Joanie's flirted shamelessly with you, you're really part of the gang. Hope you're okay with being constantly teased and a total lack of regard for personal privacy," she says drily. "And that's just Joanie."

Greg fails to stifle his laugh and Joanie smacks him on the chest teasingly. "You know you love it."

He shakes his head, still laughing. "Not rising to that bait. Come on." He pulls her behind him toward the living room.

"Wow. So, I guess my trial period is up," I joke to Mia after they're gone. "Good to know."

Mia starts to reply, but a voice from the hall cuts over her.

"Hey, Mia, we're here."

And I'd know that voice anywhere. Carrie. I stand up taller as she walks into the kitchen. All long, wavy dark brown hair, big blue eyes, and a snug sweater that matches the pre-dawn night sky shade of her irises. And then a blond dude trails in behind her. He's about six inches shorter than me but he's broad-chested and fit, and he's standing way too close to Carrie for my liking.

I'm so distracted by him that I don't notice the silence that's fallen for a moment. I look back at Carrie to find her staring at me with wide eyes, her mouth popped open in surprise.

"Evan. What are you doing here?" I don't miss the note of panic in her voice. "I mean … hey. Good to see you." She pauses. "What are you doing here?"

Mia and the blond guy exchange a confused look.

I extend my hand toward him, ignoring Carrie's question. "Hi, I'm Evan, Nate's brother. And you are?"

The guy gives Carrie a look before he reaches his hand out to take mine and meets my gaze for the duration of our brief handshake. "I'm Brandon, a friend of Carrie's." He studies me for a moment. "You look familiar. Have we met before?"

Carrie lets out a tinkling laugh laced with nervous energy. "Excuse us for a moment," she says, hauling Brandon behind her toward the dining room.

My heart is thudding in my chest, but I do my best to casually turn to Mia and ask, "New boyfriend?"

Mia shrugs. "Supposedly, they really are just friends. But they were inseparable for a few summers when we were younger, and since he returned to town a couple of months back, they've been spending a lot of time together." She scrutinizes me, and I hold tight to my blank expression.

"Well, good for her either way," I respond. Joanie saunters back into the kitchen. "Hey, Legs, have you given Carrie's new boyfriend a nickname yet?"

Joanie gives me a feline grin. "Legs. I like it." I smirk back at her. She's short, but she does have shapely, long legs for her frame, and despite my initial astonishment, I'm happy to show her I'm all right with a little harmless flirting. And I'm also totally fishing for information on this dude. Joanie turns to Mia. "Carrie has a new boyfriend?"

Mia doesn't look at her, her gaze still firmly locked on me. "He means Brandon."

Joanie pulls a face. "Oh, him. Nope. Only met him a couple of times." She grabs a handful of almonds from the bowl on the counter and pops one in her mouth. "When's dinner? I'm starving."

Mia rolls her eyes. "We can eat when Rae gets here, Jo."

"Damn that woman and her fashionable lateness," Joanie grumbles, heading back toward the living room.

Mia finally breaks her gaze and steps to peek into the dining room. She turns back to me and folds her arms over her chest. "I get the sense Carrie's going to hide in there until you leave the kitchen," Mia says quietly. Pointedly.

I force my brow into a confused furrow. "Did I do something wrong?"

Mia narrows her eyes and shakes her head.

She's totally onto me.

"Oookay. If I'm not in trouble, is there anything I can do to help with dinner?" I offer.

"Thanks, but I've —"

"Helloooo," a female voice calls from the front of the house.

"Fucking finally!" I hear Joanie exclaim.

Mia and I share a look before we burst into laughter.

When we finally sit down and enjoy the amazing Beef Wellington, garlic mashed potatoes, and roasted Brussels sprouts Mia prepared, the conversation quickly turns to the upcoming election.

"So, Greg," I say, reaching for the mashed potatoes, "how are you feeling about your chances for town council?"

Greg grins, a mix of excitement and nervousness on his face. "Pretty good, I think. But ask me again after the votes are counted."

Joanie nudges him playfully. "He's being modest. He's got this in the bag."

"And Brandon, I hear you're also running for town council?" I prompt with a raised eyebrow.

Brandon nods, setting down the glass of wine he'd just sipped from. "I am. I was traveling a lot for work, but my contract was up, and I thought it would be a great opportunity to settle down a bit and get behind making this place even better."

Carrie, who is sitting beside him, pats his hand. "Brandon is a professional photographer. He was working for an international aid organization and did relief work for them, too."

Fuck. He's talented and a do-gooder. Most women would probably go for a movie star first, but I know Carrie well enough to know that that would tug on her big, soft heart.

"How nice," I say blandly. "So, you have family here?"

"Yes, my grandfather. Who's getting on in years, too, so it'll give me the opportunity to be here when he needs me," Brandon replies.

I internalize a groan. Well, this just keeps getting better and better.

"How's John doing, by the way?" Mia asks.

"Still healthy as a horse," Brandon assures her. "He's all up in arms over the upcoming election. He has very strong opinions on how things should be run."

Carrie rolls her eyes. "Doesn't everyone?"

I chuckle and use the opportunity to speak to her. "Townsfolk giving you a hard time, Carrie?"

Her eyes flit to mine ever so briefly before she looks down to play with the food on her plate. "It's challenging, but I know what I signed up for."

"Don't let Ms. Modest over there fool you," Rae breaks in. "I've gone to a couple of the debates, and she handles it like a pro. Sweet as pie, and she's got them all wrapped around her little finger."

Carrie blushes crimson. "I'm just focused on making sure everything runs smoothly and fairly." Brandon reaches over and squeezes her hand. She smiles at him gratefully.

I nod along with everyone else, fighting the urge to round the table and haul her into my arms. To claim her, mark my territory, in case this Brandon guy thinks he has any sort of a chance with her. Being this close to her, yet having to maintain this façade of casual friendship, is harder than I expected. But I know she wants to keep things platonic, so I'll do my best to respect that. Because she's not mine, and I have only myself to blame for that.

"So, you missed out on the news earlier, Carrie," Mia says a little too casually. "Evan just put in an offer on some land in town. Operation Bring Someone Famous to Alpine Ridge is full speed ahead."

Carrie looks up in shock, first at her sister, then at me. And I can practically see the progression of emotions behind her eyes: from shock to horror, to the realization that she needs to not show how upset she is by the news, to having to put on a mask of fake enthusiasm.

And I'm pretty sure Mia sees it, too.

"That's … wow. How fantastic for the town," Carrie says, her voice abnormally high. "And for you, Evan. I'm … so … happy for you." She gives me the saddest excuse for a smile.

My heart breaks a little, and suddenly, I have the urge to contact the realtor and call this whole thing off because Carrie is obviously not okay.

"Evan Edwards!" Brandon exclaims, drawing everyone's attention. "I knew I recognized you. Holy shit!"

Joanie rolls her eyes. "You're a little late to the 'Nate's brother is a movie star' party there, Brandon." Her sarcasm is unmissable.

I'm starting to really like Joanie.

"Am I?" Brandon asks cluelessly. He turns to Carrie. "A little heads up would've been nice."

Carrie gives a feeble shrug. "Sorry? I've had a lot on my mind lately, and I didn't exactly know he'd be here tonight." Carrie shoots Mia a look.

"Well, this is awkward as ass, and I'm pretty sure everyone's done eating. How about we move on to the next portion of the evening?" Joanie suggests abruptly.

I chuckle appreciatively as everyone rises, and we all help Mia clear the table. Once that's done, we head into the living room, trying to decide on a game to play.

"Well, we have a couple of newer members to the group, so why don't we just take turns asking icebreakers?" Rae suggests.

Joanie nods. "Ooh, I like that idea."

Greg snorts. "Nothing too personal, babe."

"Spoilsport," she grumbles jokingly.

"I think that's a great idea," Mia agrees. "We each take turns asking, and everyone has to answer." There are nods and sounds of agreement all around. "All right, I'll go first. Sweet or salty? I think we all know what I'd pick."

"Ditto here, sweet all the way," Rae says.

Joanie smirks. "You bakery babes would choose sweet. Me? I pick salty."

Nate and Greg both concur.

"That's a hard one, but I'm going with salty," Brandon says thoughtfully.

"I'd pick sweet every time," I offer, my eyes flicking to Carrie. She looks up and meets my gaze.

"Me too," she says softly.

I don't miss Joanie shooting Mia a look. I break my gaze from Carrie, determined to stop giving her loaded looks before *everybody* knows there's something between us. Or there was, anyway.

"Okay, I've got one," Nate says, completely oblivious to the furtive glances happening around him. "What skill or trait do you think everyone should have? For me, it'd be critical thinking. It's fundamental to self-improvement and practically every profession there is." I smile at my serious, brainy big brother. He may not practice medicine anymore — for now anyway — but he still manages to sound like a doctor.

"Oooh, that's a good one," Greg says.

"Confidence," Joanie adds immediately. Confidently. Mia smirks at her.

"I was going to say basic first aid," Greg chuckles, "but that's better."

"Resiliency," Mia says. "You'll never achieve anything if you always give up."

Rae raises her hand. "Communication. There are eight billion people in this world. You won't get far if you don't know how to talk to them."

"And yet, without creativity, what use is communication?" I interject. "Otherwise, we'd all go around saying and doing the same things, thinking the same way."

"Good point," Rae concedes with a grin.

"Empathy," Carrie says quietly. "Because you can't have creativity or real communication without it."

Brandon looks at her with such deep admiration that it makes me grind my teeth. He then adds, "I say the ability to be grateful. I've seen a lot of the world through my work, and most people have no idea how good they have it. Life has little meaning without gratitude and understanding how blessed we are."

As one, Carrie, Mia, and Rae sigh. The expressions on their faces remind me of the heart-eyed emoji. Greg and Nate smirk at each other. For my part, I fight not to roll my eyes.

"Yeah, yeah, yeah, enough of this heavy shit," Joanie says. "I want to know everyone's hidden talent."

She doesn't add anything, and Greg gives her a look. "Aren't you going to say yours?" he prompts.

Mia pinches the bridge of her nose. "I'm sure she didn't for a reason. You did tell her not to get too personal."

Joanie grins. "My lovely bestie speaks the truth." Then she leans in and stage-whispers to Greg, "I'll show you later."

"I can't unhear that," Nate mutters, and we all laugh.

"What's yours, Mountain Man?" Joanie asks Greg.

He raises an eyebrow. "I can talk to dogs."

Joanie's brows pull together. "Like … Doctor Dolittle?"

Greg laughs. "No. They just … get me. And I get them." He shrugs.

"Oh, we're getting a dog so you can show me this trick."

Greg looks intrigued.

"I can fold napkins," Mia offers. Everyone, myself included, gives her a questioning look. She waves her hands in the air, miming folding. "Like … into pretty things. Flowers, birds, that sort of thing. I haven't done it in a long time, though. But I guess now I'm obligated to bust it out for the next dinner party."

"Man, even I didn't know that," Carrie admits. "Mine is kind of lame. I can solve Sudokus like nobody's business. I smash records on every app I've been able to find."

I can't help grinning at her cute, nerdy admission. Figures though. She's a smart woman.

"I can speed read," Nate says, though that's no surprise to me. "I learned to survive medical school."

"I'm a polyglot. I speak four languages," Brandon says. Because, of course, he does.

"Ooh, which ones?" Rae asks.

"English, of course, and Spanish, French, and Swahili."

"Impressive," Carrie says, looking at him all-too-starry-eyed. He returns her look with a gentle smile.

I'm going to need new teeth at this rate.

"Oh, I know Rae's," Joanie exclaims.

Rae waves her hand dismissively. "Everyone knows I can sing, Jo. Though unless you count being able to touch my tongue to my nose, I can't say I have any actual hidden talents."

We all chuckle, but Nate says to me, "I'm going to out you, Ev, because we're all friends here." And then to everyone else, "Evan sings, too."

I scrunch my face and drop my head in my hands, groaning. "Why you gotta sell me out like that, Nathan?" I look up and sigh dramatically.

Rae perks up. "You sing? What style?"

I shrug. "Anything? I did musicals in high school, but I'll sing ballads, classics, pop … you name it."

"Done any duets?" she asks with a mischievous grin.

I can't help but return it. "No, but I wouldn't say no to doing one." I give her an assessing look. She looks to be in her mid-to-late forties, so I know just the song to tempt her. "You look like a woman who'd appreciate An Officer and a Gentleman." Rae grins, and I know I've got her.

"What's going on here?" Joanie murmurs to Greg.

"I think they're about to —" Rae sings the opening line to "Up Where We Belong," and Mia nods. "Yep. They're going to sing."

I rise and join Rae, holding her hand while waiting for my cue. And soon, we're singing together, our voices blending beautifully, bouncing off the high ceilings of Nate and Mia's living room. It feels good to belt out a song again. I usually save it for the shower, but there's nothing like performing for a live audience.

And everyone stares at us, mouths dropped open. Carrie's most of all, and I can't help giving her a wink. What can I say? I live for the limelight. And having Carrie's eyes on me is more satisfying than anything I've experienced in a long time.

Even filming a James Bond movie.

As the song winds down, the realization hits me like a ton of bricks. And I know I can't give up on Carrie. Not yet. Even if I have to play the role of her friend for a while, the show's not over yet. Not by a long shot.

CHAPTER EIGHTEEN

CARRIE

As the last notes of "Up Where We Belong" fade away, I realize my mouth is hanging open. I quickly snap it shut, but I can't shake the awe that's coursing through me. Who knew Evan could sing like that? I certainly didn't. And when he leans in to kiss Rae on the cheek after sharing such a romantic ballad duet with her ... a surge of emotions I don't want to feel crashes over me.

Jealousy. Longing. Regret.

I push them down, reminding myself that Evan and I agreed to just be friends. But as the evening progresses, I find myself struggling more and more. It's not just his sudden reappearance or the bombshell announcement that he's buying property in Alpine Ridge. It's how impossibly hard it is to be in the same room as him and pretend we've only ever been friends.

And I know I'm doing a terrible job of it.

Every time our eyes meet, I feel a jolt of electricity. When he laughs at something Joanie says, I have to fight the urge to stare at how his eyes crinkle at the corners. And don't even get me started on how my body reacts when he casually stretches, his shirt riding up just enough to reveal a sliver of toned abs.

I'm a bundle of nerves by the time the evening winds down. I practically jump at the chance to walk Brandon out to his car, desperate for a moment to collect myself.

The cool night air is a welcome relief as we step outside. Brandon is quiet for a moment, then turns to me with a serious expression.

"Carrie, what's going on between you and Evan?"

I freeze, my heart pounding. Am I that transparent? I consider lying, but something in Brandon's eyes tells me he'd see right through it. With a sigh, I decide to come clean.

"We had a ... thing," I admit, keeping my voice low. "But it's over now. And nobody else can know about it, okay?"

Brandon nods slowly. "Why is it over?"

I let out a humorless laugh. "Because I can't handle a movie star's lifestyle. The crazy schedule, the fans, the fact that his entire life is in L.A. ... it's just not meant to be."

He studies me for a long moment. "That's not what I saw tonight," he says gently. "Not the way he was looking at you."

My chest tightens at his words, but I shake my head. "It doesn't matter. We agreed to just be friends."

Brandon doesn't look convinced, but he doesn't push it. He hugs me before getting into his car, leaving me alone with my swirling thoughts.

Taking a deep breath, I head back inside, determined to have a word with my sister. I find Mia cleaning up the last of the dishes in the kitchen.

"Why didn't you tell me Evan would be here?" I demand, my voice sharper than I intended.

Mia turns to face me, her expression a mix of exasperation and concern. "Carrie, I think we both know there's something going on between you two. It would have really helped to know that before I threw you together at a dinner party."

I deflate, the fight going out of me. "I'm sorry," I mumble. "You're right. I should have told you."

With a sigh, I lean against the counter and come clean ... well, mostly. I tell her about hooking up with Evan during her honeymoon, and then again when he showed up after New Year's. But I keep it vague, making it sound like it was all physical, leaving out the depth of emotions involved.

"But that was the last time," I assure her. "We agreed to just be friends going forward. It'll just be awkward for a bit while we try to forget what each other looks like naked."

Mia raises an eyebrow, clearly not buying it. "Care-bear ..."

"Please don't tell anyone else," I plead. "Not even Nate. I don't want to cause trouble, and Evan fits in well with everyone. I don't want him to feel uncomfortable when he's here, even if it probably won't be that often."

Mia sighs but nods. "Fine, I won't say anything. But Carrie, you weren't exactly subtle tonight. I'm pretty sure at least Joanie knows something's up."

I groan, covering my face with my hands. "I'll deal with it if people figure it out. I promise I'll try to do a better job of being cool around Evan. It'll be easier going forward, I think. This was the first time I'd seen him since we agreed to be friends."

Before Mia can respond, Rae pops her head into the kitchen. "Ready to head home, Carrie?"

I nod, grateful for the interruption. "Yeah, just give me a minute."

As I gather my things, I run into Evan in the hallway. My heart flips, but I force myself to stay calm.

"Goodnight, Evan," I say, aiming for casual. "It was good to see you."

He smiles, and it's so warm and genuine that it makes my knees weak. "Goodnight, Carrie. Take care."

And that's it. He's so chill, so effortlessly casual about it all. As I follow Rae out to the car, I feel a mix of relief and ... disappointment? No, I can't let myself go there.

I climb into the passenger seat, my mind racing. I can do this. I can be Evan's friend. I can pretend I didn't get a taste of everything I ever wanted.

I have to.

Because the alternative — admitting how much I still want him, how much it hurts to see him and not be with him — is too painful to contemplate.

As Rae starts the car and pulls away from Nate and Mia's house, I close my eyes and take a deep breath. One day at a time, I tell myself. That's all I can do.

Thankfully, with the primary election on Tuesday, I have plenty to keep me busy. After that, there's round two of helping the chosen candidates, research, debates, and everything in between, and then the final election at the end of April.

I brighten at the thought. I only committed to managing the elections. So, if the situation with Evan being in and out of town becomes untenable, I only have to ride it out for a few more months. I'm not a prisoner here, after all.

Except I'm far from it. In fact, Alpine Ridge feels more like home than ever. But with so much change, who knows how I'll feel in the future?

I shake my head, refocusing on my new mantra.

One day at a time.

CHAPTER NINETEEN

EVAN

The Los Angeles sun beats down on me as I step out of my Audi, but it doesn't lift my spirits like the Alpine Ridge air. I miss the crisp mountain breeze and the scent of pine, and most of all, I miss Carrie.

I shake my head, trying to clear my thoughts as I enter my sleek, modern house. Despite the expensive furniture and state-of-the-art entertainment system, it feels empty. At least I have good news waiting for me — an email confirming that the permits for my Alpine Ridge property have gone through. Now, it's just a waiting game to see when the weather will allow construction to begin.

My phone buzzes, and I groan when I see it's Rick, my agent. "Evan, my man!" he practically shouts when I answer. "I've got great news. We're going to capitalize on this Bond buzz and set you up with a little publicity boost for your movie premiere next month."

I know that tone. He uses it when he's about to suggest something I'll hate. "What did you have in mind?" I ask warily.

"I've set up a little arrangement with Kelly Cook. You know, from that hit sitcom? She's looking for a profile boost, too. It's a win-win!"

My stomach sinks. A fake relationship. I hate this part of the business, the artifice, the manipulation. But Rick's never steered me wrong before, and he knows the industry better than anyone. "Fine," I sigh. "Set it up."

The next day, I find myself at a trendy café, waiting to meet Kelly at a semi-private booth in the back. She sweeps in, all long blond hair, perfectly round fake tits, and designer sunglasses, looking every inch the Hollywood starlet. As she air-kisses my cheek, I catch a whiff of her overpowering perfume and can't help but think of how much I prefer Carrie's subtle coconut scent.

"Evan, darling," Kelly purrs, sliding into the seat across from me. "I'm so excited about this. We're going to be the hottest couple in Hollywood!"

I force a smile, already exhausted by her enthusiasm. We chat about our careers and our "relationship" strategy, and I find myself zoning out as she rambles about her latest juice cleanse and the benefits of crystal therapy.

As our meeting winds down, Kelly leans in, her voice dropping to a sultry whisper. "We could make this arrangement even more ... mutually beneficial if you're interested." Her hand slides across the table, fingers brushing mine.

I pull back, keeping my tone light but firm. "I appreciate the offer, Kelly, but I think it's best to keep this strictly professional."

She shrugs, seemingly unbothered. "Your loss. But the offer stands if you change your mind."

Over the next two weeks, Rick and Kelly's agent, Sarah, orchestrate a series of "dates" for us. We're photographed leaving restaurants, attending gallery openings, and even taking a "romantic" stroll on the beach. Each outing feels more forced and fake than the last.

As I pose for another "candid" shot, Kelly's arm wrapped around my waist, a wave of disgust washes over me. This isn't me, and this isn't what I want my career to be about.

That night, I find myself staring at my phone, Carrie's number pulled up on the screen. I want to call her, to hear her voice, to tell her about this ridiculous charade I'm caught up in, just in case she's paying attention and is in any way hurt by it. But I don't. I can't. Because I know if I hear her voice, I might just throw it all away and run back to Alpine Ridge. Even if that's what I want, it's not what Carrie wants.

Instead, I pull up the plans for my new house, losing myself in thoughts of the life I could have there — a life with real connections and genuine relationships, a life with Carrie in it.

It's not lost on me that I've suddenly got more bandwidth to think about her and plan a new life close to her now that she no longer wants that. But if I'm persistent and demonstrate that I can show up, maybe she'll see that and change her mind.

But that's sure as hell not going to happen while I'm fake dating Sitcom Barbie. As I fall asleep, I make a silent promise to myself. This fake relationship will be over when the press tour for my upcoming movie is over, and it will be my last. From now on, I'm going to do things my way, industry expectations be damned, because life's too short for fake smiles and empty embraces.

I want the real thing and know where and with whom I can find it. It's just a matter of getting her to find her way back to it, too.

CHAPTER TWENTY

CARRIE

The crisp spring air carries the scent of blooming wildflowers. It's early April, and Alpine Ridge is finally shaking off the last vestiges of winter. The town seems to be coming alive, not just with the changing seasons but with the buzz of the upcoming election.

I can't help but smile as I pass by the numerous campaign posters plastered on storefronts and lamp posts. The race for mayor has narrowed down to two primary candidates: Jerry, the crusty tavern owner, and Arthur Burton, another of the town's older residents. Despite being a decade older than Jerry, Arthur is surprisingly sprightly and far less grumpy, though he does have a tendency towards pomposity.

I'll never admit it out loud, but I'm secretly rooting for Arthur, partly out of loyalty to Rae, who's made no secret of her dislike for Jerry. I also believe Arthur has a better vision for Alpine Ridge's future.

As for the town council, we have about twenty people vying for the seven available spots. Greg and Brandon made it through the initial cut, which doesn't surprise me. They're both passionate about the town and have a lot to offer.

I've also been spending a lot of time with Brandon lately. Some of that is due to the election — he often seeks my advice on campaign strategies — and genuinely enjoying his company. But if I'm honest with myself, it's also because I've been avoiding everyone else. I'm afraid that if I spend too much time with them, I might let something slip about Evan.

Evan. Just thinking his name sends a pang through my chest. I've been trying not to dwell on it, but the truth is, I've been upset ever since I found out he immediately jumped into bed with one of the hottest actresses in Hollywood right after leaving Alpine Ridge. I know I was the one who ended things, but I can't help feeling hurt that I was so easy to move on from.

I shake my head, trying to clear my thoughts. I need to focus on my work and on the election. That's what's important right now.

As I reach the community center, where I've set up a makeshift election headquarters, I'm greeted by the sight of Brandon poring over some polling data.

"Morning, Carrie," he says, looking up with a warm smile. "Ready for another exciting day in the world of small-town politics?"

I laugh, feeling some of the tension ease from my shoulders. "Always. What've we got on the agenda today?"

As Brandon fills me in on the day's schedule, I can't help but feel a surge of excitement. Despite the complications in my personal life, I'm truly passionate about what I'm doing here. In fact, I've been thinking more and more about my future in Alpine Ridge.

What I really want is to work for the town as a political planner. I know I have to wait until the town government is established, but given all the work I've done and the good relationships I've built with the candidates, I'm hopeful I can convince them of my worth in helping structure the town government and planning over the next few years.

The idea is exhilarating, and the thought of a new life where I'm more independent and career-oriented is exactly what I need to stay focused on myself and my goals. And despite everything, I love Alpine Ridge. The complicating factor of Evan building a home here ... well, that's something I'll deal with if and when I have to.

"Earth to Carrie," Brandon's voice breaks through my reverie. "Are you okay? You seemed lost in thought there for a minute."

I smile, shaking off the last of my musings. "Sorry, just thinking about the future. There's so much potential here, you know?"

Brandon nods, his eyes lighting up. "I know exactly what you mean. That's why I came back. Alpine Ridge is on the cusp of something great, and I want to be part of shaping that future."

As we dive into our work for the day, I feel a renewed sense of purpose. My heart might still be healing, but my mind is clear. I have goals, dreams, and a town full of people counting on me.

Evan Edwards and his Hollywood drama can take a backseat. I have an election to run and a future to plan. And for the first time in a long time, I'm genuinely excited about what that future might hold.

CHAPTER TWENTY-ONE

EVAN

The fresh mountain air fills my lungs as I step out of my rental car, a welcome change from the smog-filled Los Angeles atmosphere I've left behind. Alpine Ridge stretches before me, the snow-capped peaks in the distance a stunning backdrop to the budding spring foliage.

I'm here for a final walk-through of my property with the architect and builder before construction begins, but my heart races with anticipation for an entirely different reason. Carrie. The thought of seeing her again, even if just for a moment, sends a thrill through me.

The walk-through goes smoothly. As I stand on what will soon be my deck, overlooking the breathtaking vista, I can almost picture a future here — a future with Carrie by my side. But first, I need to convince her to give us another chance. I know I should keep playing it cool, but something is telling me to try again one more time.

After wrapping up with the building team, I make my way into town. I spot Carrie leaving the community center, her arms full of what looks like campaign materials. Taking a deep breath, I approach her.

"Hey, Carrie," I call out, trying to keep my voice casual.

She looks up, surprise flashing across her face before she schools her features into a neutral expression. "Evan. I didn't know you were in town."

"Just got in," I explain, falling into step beside her. "Final walk-through of the property before construction starts."

She nods, not quite meeting my eyes. "That's great. I'm sure you're excited."

We walk in silence for a moment, the tension between us palpable. Finally, I can't take it anymore. "Carrie, I was hoping we could talk. About us."

She stops abruptly and turns to face me. "Evan, there is no 'us.' We agreed to be friends, remember?"

"I know, but ..." I take a deep breath, steeling myself. "I can't stop thinking about you."

Carrie's eyes flash with something — hurt? Anger? — before she shakes her head. "I'm not someone you can use for fun whenever you come to town, Evan. And I'm sure your famous actress girlfriend wouldn't appreciate that either."

My heart sinks as I realize she's seen the tabloid photos with Kelly. "It's not what you think it is," I explain quickly. "What we had though, Carrie ... what we could have ... it's real."

She laughs, but it's a hollow sound. "Real? You left town and immediately hooked up with one of the hottest actresses in Hollywood. How does that make this —" she gestures between us "— real?"

I run a hand through my hair, frustrated. "That's not ..." I step closer and drop my voice. "My relationship with her is fake, Carrie. We're not really together. It's all a publicity stunt to boost both of our careers." Carrie's mouth drops open in shock, but she still steps back. I run a hand through my hair, frustrated. "I'm trying to show you I can be more accessible and willing to make changes. But I understand if you don't want someone who can't always be here."

Carrie's expression softens slightly, but she still shakes her head. "Evan, I appreciate what you're trying to do. But it's not just that. I can't be with someone whose life is so ... public. So unpredictable. I need stability and consistency. And let's face it, you can't offer either."

As much as her words sting, I can't help but feel a surge of pride. This is the Carrie I know she wants to be — strong, assertive, not settling for less than she deserves. "I understand," I say softly. "And I'm proud of you, you know. For standing up for yourself. I know that's not always easy for you."

A flicker of surprise crosses her face, followed by a small smile. "Thanks. I'm ... working on it."

We stand there for a moment, the weight of what could have been hanging between us. Finally, I nod, taking a step back. "Well, I should let you get back to work. But I meant what I said about being friends. I hope that's still on the table."

Carrie nods, her smile a little more genuine now. "Of course. Friends."

As I watch her walk away, my heart aches with the loss of what could have been. But I remind myself that this isn't the end. I'm building a home here. There's still time to show Carrie that I can be the man she needs, the man who deserves her.

For now, though, I'll respect her wishes. I'll be her friend. And I'll keep hoping that someday, she'll decide what's between us is worth dealing with the challenges. Challenges I have no doubt we could overcome together. If she's willing.

That's the part that worries me because she's been consistently clear that my life — the crazy schedule and the unrelenting media attention — is a dealbreaker for her.

As I stand in the middle of the street alone, a thought occurs to me that I've never considered before. Asking Carrie to bend is not only unfair to her, but it's also selfish in that it means I don't have to.

So maybe the real question is: How much am *I* willing to give up to be with *her*?

My stomach sinks because I know I'm not ready to walk away from the industry. Not now that I've achieved the success I've been striving for all these years — a success I'd like to maintain for at least a few more.

Fuck.

It's not Carrie that needs to change her mind. It's me.

Maybe she was right all along, and this just wasn't meant to be. At least, not right now.

I suddenly understand the phrase "timing is everything" all too well.

And our timing, Carrie and me? Complete shit.

I trudge back to my rental car, shoulders down, heart in my shoes. I set out to convince Carrie to give me a chance. But I realized that I'm the one keeping us from being together. And I have no fucking clue what to do with that right now.

CHAPTER TWENTY-TWO

CARRIE

As I walk away from Evan, a mix of emotions swirls inside me. His visit has left me with a lot to process, as usual. I've seen more of him lately than I expected, and I can't deny how drawn I feel to him every time he reappears.

I had convinced myself that Evan was happy with his new blonde bombshell Hollywood girlfriend and that his increased presence in Alpine Ridge had nothing to do with me. But his words today ... they've shaken up my world. The realization that Evan still thinks about me as much as I do him, that he hasn't really moved on as I thought, is both comforting and unsettling.

Still, it's also made me realize I know myself better now. I'm already prone to insecurity, and trying to be in a relationship with someone whose availability changes like the wind truly isn't going to work for me, no matter how much my heart might wish otherwise. And I refuse to let myself be a doormat for anyone ever again.

I'll happily give my heart and soul to someone when they've shown me they'll cherish them. Unfortunately, Evan can't love me the way I deserve to be loved. And I'm not going to settle for less than I deserve. Not anymore.

So, with a deep breath, I refocus on what I need to think about right now: the elections. There's still so much work to be done. While I have my own opinions and desires regarding who runs the town, I'm determined to remain impartial until all the townspeople have had their say. It's what they deserve and what I need to do to prove myself in this role.

As April rolls on, the excitement in Alpine Ridge builds to a fever pitch. Finally, election day arrives, and the results are in: Arthur Burton is voted mayor, with Greg, Brandon, and five others elected to the town council. Rae, for one, is beyond ecstatic, though most of the town seems to be in a celebratory mood.

To that end, Greg has even thrown a post-election bash at the community center. Streamers and balloons festoon the walls, and the air is filled with laughter, the clinking of glasses, and upbeat pop music on low in the background. Everyone is congratulating the winners, and half of the town seems to have turned up to celebrate. As I survey the room, pride swells in my chest. I've been working towards this, and it's finally here.

"May I have this dance?" Brandon's voice breaks through my reverie. I turn to see him holding out his hand, a warm smile on his face.

"Absolutely," I grin, taking his hand and letting him lead me to the makeshift dance floor.

As we playfully dance to the music, I can't help but ask, "Are you happy, Brandon? With how everything turned out?"

He nods, his eyes twinkling. "Incredibly. But what about you? Obviously, I see a future here in Alpine Ridge, but what kind of future do you see?"

I consider his question. "I see potential. For the town, for myself." And despite the truth of those words, my heart aches for more than that.

It must show on my face because he asks slyly, "And where does Evan fit in?"

I grimace. "He doesn't. I wanted him to, and you weren't wrong; he still has feelings for me. But we're living separate lives. It's just not in the cards." I sigh heavily despite the liveliness around me. "What about you? Is there anyone special you've left behind in your travels that you're pining for?"

Brandon chuckles. "Not really. My work wasn't conducive to relationships, so it's been hookups for a while. Which was fine, but it's part of why I wanted to settle down. To find someone."

I don't miss the parallels to Evan's situation. It must show on my face because Brandon raises an eyebrow.

"What?" he asks.

I shrug. "It's just ..." I trail off, deciding against discussing Evan further. "I don't know. Why settle here, then? Don't you think finding someone in Alpine Ridge might be hard? It's not exactly a bustling metropolis."

He smiles enigmatically. "You never know. The doors opened in this direction, so I walked through them. I have faith that it will lead me where I need to be. Maybe a nice guy will move into town someday, and we'll hit it off, fall in love, and build a life together."

His words strike a chord in me, and I find myself hanging on every word as he continues.

"Sometimes you have to take risks, Carrie. Pay attention to the doors that open, do a gut check whether it's what you want, and if it is, walk through with confidence. Maybe it'll be *the* door, or maybe it'll just be *a* door on the path you're supposed to walk. But you'll never know unless you try."

As the song ends, he pulls me into a quick hug, kissing the top of my head. It's reassuring, and I'm grateful for his advice and friendship.

Brandon's words echo in my mind when we take a break to grab drinks. Could it really be that simple?

It turns out he may have been on to something after all, when the following week, as I'm packing up my makeshift office in the community center, a knock on the door frame startles me. I look up to see Arthur Burton, our newly elected mayor, standing there with a smile.

"Ms. Anderson," he begins, "I was hoping we could talk about your future here in Alpine Ridge."

"Of course, come in," I offer, gesturing to a chair next to the tiny desk I've been using. "But please, call me Carrie."

"And you can call me Art," he returns as he settles in. "Now about that future …"

My heart races as he outlines the position he wants to create: a political planner for the town. It's everything I've been working towards, everything I want.

Brandon's words come back to me as I listen to him speak. A door is opening. All I have to do is walk through it.

"So, what do you think, Carrie? Would you like to continue doing the fine work you've been doing so far? While I can't offer concrete terms until the financials are established, I plan to compensate you well. You've been invaluable throughout the election process, and I have no doubt your expertise will be crucial to establishing Alpine Ridge's government."

"I'm … flattered. Thank you so much," I reply. I take a deep breath. "I'd be honored, Mayor Burton."

The next few weeks pass in a whirlwind. With my new job secured, I take another leap: I use the money Gran left me to put a down payment on a custom townhouse in one of Sera's new developments. As I sign the papers, a sense of rightness settles over me. This is where I'm meant to be.

The first thing I do after that is head to the bakery to share the news with Mia. If she was proud when I got the job with the town, she'll be over the moon that I'm establishing firm roots in Alpine Ridge. Nothing says "I plan to be here a while" like buying property.

Walking down Main Street toward the bakery, I can't help my silly grin. I'm finally taking control of my own life, committing to this town that has come to mean so much to me. Being here reminds me of Gran, and my sister and found family are here. The history and love I have here can't be found anywhere else.

And who knows? Maybe someday, a nice guy who gives me butterflies will move into town … and stay. The thought of Evan flits through my mind, but I push it away. If it was meant to be, it would have been. And even if the nameless nice guy never finds me in this tiny town? Well, I'll just have to be awesome all on my own. Given the life I'm finally building for myself, I feel pretty good about the future either way.

CHAPTER TWENTY-THREE

EVAN

The flashing lights of the paparazzi's cameras are relentless as I attempt to drive through the crowd outside my L.A. home. I should've known better to take the convertible today. Their shouted questions blend into a cacophony of noise, but a few phrases cut through:

"Evan! Did you supply Kelly with drugs?"

"Are you going to rehab, Evan?"

"What do you have to say about Kelly's accusations?"

I grit my teeth, refusing to engage as I slowly but surely make it onto my property and into the garage. As soon as the door rolls shut behind me, I let out a long, frustrated sigh.

How did everything go so wrong so quickly?

Just a week ago, I was riding high. My latest movie had opened to rave reviews and impressive box office numbers, and the promotional tour had been exhausting but exhilarating. Then, out of nowhere, Kelly got arrested for drug possession with intent to traffic.

That alone would have been bad enough. But then she had the audacity to claim *I* was the one who'd given her the drugs. Me. The guy who barely even drinks, let alone does anything harder.

Now, I'm caught in a maelstrom of accusations and investigations. Even though I know I'll eventually be exonerated — because they can't prove something that never happened — the damage to my reputation feels irreparable.

My phone buzzes. It's Rick.

"Evan, my man," he says, his voice tight with stress. "We've got a problem."

I laugh humorlessly. "You think? What now?"

"The studio is discussing cutting you loose from the Bond contract."

The words hit me like a physical blow. Bond. The role I've dreamed of since I was a kid. The pinnacle of my career. And now it might be snatched away because of a lie.

Part of me wants to find Kelly to force her to answer for what she's done to me, to get her to take back her story. Why would she make such a serious accusation against me? Why me at all? Is it just because I've repeatedly rejected her advances and kept our fake relationship, well, fake? It's the only thing I can come up with because surely she can't have thought it would stick enough to save her from the trouble she's in. In any case, I doubt they'd let me see her, and it probably would do more harm than good anyway. The whole situation is infuriating.

"That's not all," Rick continues, his voice grim. "Multiple other projects have retracted their scripts. They're distancing themselves until this blows over."

I close my eyes, feeling a wave of despair wash over me. "So, what do we do?"

"I'll handle it," Rick assures me, though I can hear the uncertainty in his voice. "For now, I think it's best if you get out of L.A. and go somewhere else for a while until this passes."

"Can I do that?" I ask. "I mean, legally?"

"You've already talked to the Feds, and there haven't been any formal charges. They did ask us to notify them if you were leaving town so they'd know where to find you." He pauses, heaving a sigh. "So, where you gonna go, kid?"

Finally, a question I can answer. An image flashes in my mind: mountains, fresh air, and a half-built house overlooking a stunning vista.

"Alpine Ridge."

"What? Where the hell is that?"

"Washington State. In the Cascade Mountains. I've got a house being built there. I can oversee the construction, lay low for a while."

Rick agrees, and we quickly make arrangements. Within hours, I'm on a private plane, leaving behind the chaos of Hollywood for the tranquility of the mountains.

As the plane touches down, I feel the weight of the past week settling heavily on my shoulders. The unfairness of it all burns in my chest. I've worked my ass off for years, built a career I'm proud of, only to have it threatened by a lying, drug-addled starlet.

By the time I reach the construction site of my new home, a plan is forming in my mind. Maybe I don't go back. Maybe I just ... stay here. Take a long break, or even retire altogether. The thought is tempting, almost intoxicating in its simplicity.

As I stand on what will soon be my deck, overlooking the breathtaking landscape of Alpine Ridge, I feel a sense of peace wash over me for the first time in days. With its quiet beauty and lack of prying eyes, this place feels like a sanctuary.

And it's not just the views. My brother is here. He's been there for me from the start, and I know he'll have my back no matter what. And, of course, there's Carrie. She's here, too. And while I know she's made it clear that we can't be together, the thought of being near her, even just as friends, relieves some of the tension tightening my shoulders.

I take a deep breath of the fresh mountain air, feeling better than I have since Kelly's arrest. I don't know what the future holds. But for now, I'm here. And that feels like a step in the right direction.

As I turn to head to Nate's, I make a silent promise to myself. No matter what happens with this scandal or what becomes of my career, I will use this time to figure out what I really want. Because if there's one thing this whole mess has reminded me of, it's that the glitz and glamour of Hollywood isn't all it's cracked up to be. There's good there, but there's so much more that's not worth it.

Maybe it's not where I'm meant to be anymore. Maybe real happiness is waiting for me somewhere else. Maybe even right here in Alpine Ridge.

CHAPTER TWENTY-FOUR

CARRIE

On Sunday afternoon, I'm lounging on Mia and Nate's couch, sipping tea and chatting with my sister while Nate reads in the armchair beside us, the buttery early June sunshine slanting through the windows, when the front door swings open. My heart skips a beat as Evan walks in, looking tired but relieved to be here.

"Honey, I'm home," he says jokingly, dropping a duffel bag in the hallway before kicking off his shoes.

Nate doesn't seem surprised to see him, rising to greet his brother with a warm hug. "Hey, man. Glad you made it."

Okay, I guess Nate knew Evan was coming? I shoot Mia a look, and she shrugs. But then, I shouldn't be surprised. Of course, we'd all heard the news. We even talked about it earlier today — the scandal involving drugs, Evan, and his fake actress girlfriend, Kelly Cook, that has been splashed across every tabloid and news outlet for days. If it were me, I'd get the hell out of dodge the first chance I got, too.

"Evan, I'm so sorry about what's happening," Mia says, genuine concern in her voice as Evan flops down on the other end of the couch.

"Thanks," he says with a sigh. "I'm just glad to get away from it all for a while."

"Well, you know we're always happy to have you here," Mia replies. "But I also know your name will be cleared soon. I'm surprised it hasn't been already, honestly."

Evan's shoulders relax slightly. "I love you for not asking whether I was involved."

Nate scoffs. "Anyone who knows you at all would know better than to believe those accusations," Nate reassures him.

I nod in agreement. "Absolutely. You're the least 'celebrity' celebrity I've ever met. You don't act entitled or arrogant, and you certainly don't seem to be living the crazy Hollywood lifestyle."

Evan's eyes meet mine, a ghost of a smile on his lips. "Thanks, Carrie. That means a lot."

Nate asks for an update, and Evan explains that he's talked to Federal Agents and there's an ongoing investigation, but no charges yet. "Hopefully, they'll resolve this soon," he sighs. "I'm being dropped like a hot potato and might lose my Bond contract."

Mia and I gasp in shock.

"No! That's crazy! I'm so sorry, Evan. What can we do to help?" Mia asks, ever the nurturer.

Evan shakes his head. "I don't even want to think about it. I just want to be here and have as normal a life as possible."

Nate nods. "I understand. Why don't you help me at the wellness center this week? It's physical work. Good for taking your mind off things."

"That sounds perfect," Evan agrees, looking relieved.

As they continue to chat, I can't help but feel concerned for Evan, but I'm thankful Nate will be keeping him busy. I have my own job to focus on, and while I think I can handle seeing Evan at game nights and the weekly dinner party, that's about it. I make a mental note to ensure I'm busy enough not to run into him too often.

The next week, I spend a lot of time working and hanging out with Brandon, even skipping game night. But there's little excuse to skip the weekly Saturday night dinner party since Brandon is in Seattle for the weekend, and I know I have to face the music sometime.

I arrive a little early and pull Mia aside. "Can you help run interference while I get used to having Evan around?" I ask quietly.

Mia gives me a curious look. "I mean … I can. But — and forgive me if this is overstepping — why don't you just use this opportunity to see where things go between you two? It seems like he'll be around for a while this time."

I shake my head. "You and I both know that this will blow over, and then Evan will go back to L.A. I don't want to start something I can't maintain, and while Evan's a great guy, I'm not interested in a long-distance relationship with a famous movie star."

Mia nods thoughtfully. "Honestly? I probably wouldn't want that either if I were in your shoes. Okay. I'll do what I can."

"Thanks, sis." I give her a peck on the cheek. "Can I help with dinner?"

"You want to be in the kitchen with my bossy butt?" she teases.

I smile, knowing exactly how she can be. "There's nowhere else I'd rather be."

She rolls her eyes. "You can't avoid Evan all night, Care-bear."

I chuckle. She knows me too well.

To my surprise, the night ends up being really great. Evan is friendly but doesn't give me longing looks or try to touch me, and I find we can get along really well in the group setting with that pressure gone. We joke and laugh, and I have a genuinely good time.

Encouraged, I show up for game night and the Saturday night dinner party the following week. Things continue to go smoothly. Evan has folded seamlessly into our group, and Nate is thrilled to have his brother around, not to mention the extra help at the wellness center. Evan has even pitched in to help Greg with the increase in personal training requests on the weekends. I'm happy for him, seeing how well he's adjusting to life here.

The next week, however, throws me for a loop. I arrive for game night a little early … and run into Evan coming downstairs in just a towel. He freezes and gives a deer-in-headlights look that I'm sure is on my face, too.

He points down the hall toward the laundry room. "Hey. I … was just going to grab a pair of pants from the dryer," he explains awkwardly.

I nod, my face burning with embarrassment. "Of course. Um … no worries." I hate that I'm this flustered. But the long expanse of his taut, golden, muscled torso throws me back into memories I wasn't prepared to relive. Sexy ones. Very, *very* sexy ones.

"It's not like it's anything you haven't seen before," he replies. And I can tell he meant it to sound casual.

Except, it doesn't. Not even a little bit. Because the husky tone of his voice tells me he remembers me seeing him naked, too. And is probably now remembering me naked as well.

For a few long moments, the air between us is thick with tension and chemistry so strong I can practically taste it. Or maybe that's just a fresh dose of Evan's ocean and evergreen scent. Either way, it's making me a little dizzy.

"Hey, Carrie, when'd you get here?" Mia asks, popping out of the kitchen.

I turn to face her, grasping for words. "I … That … Just a minute ago."

Evan takes the opportunity to continue down the hall. Mia watches him go. She turns back to me with a raised brow. "Everything okay?"

"Great. Everything's great." I smile innocently, resisting the urge to fan myself to beat back the heat on my cheeks.

She gives me a knowing look but doesn't say anything and heads back toward the kitchen. "Good. Then get your booty in here and help me prep."

I let out a sigh of relief and follow her into the kitchen. As I help her prepare snacks for game night, I'm reminded that no matter how much I pretend, I clearly still want Evan on some level. But I'm determined to deal with that because Evan is happy, Nate is happy, Greg is happy … everyone's fine with the situation, so I will be too.

Someday.

For now, I'll keep my distance as much as possible, continue focusing on my work, and hope these feelings fade with time. After all, I've built a life here that I love. I won't let my lingering attraction to Evan derail that.

As we rejoin the others in the living room, I paste on a smile and throw myself into the game night festivities. I can do this. I can be Evan's friend. I have to.

Because the alternative — giving in to how much I apparently still want him — is just a recipe for heartbreak.

As soon as I step into the living room, however, I'm distracted from my own troubles by a tiny creature whizzing around my ankles.

"What in the hell?" I set down the platter of chips and guac on the coffee table before I drop it.

"Oh, look, Bruiser likes you!" Joanie exclaims from her place on the loveseat next to Greg.

The small critter finally stops long enough for me to realize it's a dog. A chihuahua, to be precise. Named Bruiser. I look up at Joanie.

"You didn't."

She grins widely. "Totally did."

I look at Mia, who has her hand over her mouth to stifle her laughter. I shake my head in disbelief. "I was about to say you're no Elle Woods, but ..."

"I'm better?" Joanie teases.

I burst out laughing. "Yeah, actually." I squat down and offer a hand. Bruiser smells it with interest and then licks it. I laugh and scratch under his chin. "He looks just like his namesake, too."

"Well, duh. I knew he was it when I saw him at the shelter."

I rise, still chuckling, as Bruiser follows me to the couch. "Greg? How do you feel about this?"

Greg shrugs. "Joanie's happy, I'm happy." Bruiser runs over to Greg, hopping on his leg, his own little legs too short to make the jump to his lap. Greg reaches down and scratches the dog's head fondly. "He is pretty cute." Then to the dog, "Not now, Bruiser. Go play."

And like the damn dog understood, he runs for the corner where a knotted rope lays and starts attacking it.

"Holy crap, you *are* a dog whisperer," I say, laughing.

Greg raises his hands in a shrug. "Guess it's a hidden talent no longer," he jokes.

"Hmm. I'm still not convinced," Mia says. "Tell him to do something else."

Greg sighs heavily. "Hey, Bruiser." The dog looks up, his adorable ears perked toward Greg. "Go give Evan loves." Greg points toward where Evan is now sitting in Nate's armchair. Evan claps his hands together, encouraging Bruiser to come.

Bruiser looks between Greg and Evan for a split second before darting toward the latter. Evan scoops him up, and Bruiser proceeds to jump on his chest and lick every inch of his face. Evan laughs, petting the dog while it smothers him with doggy kisses.

Greg crosses his legs, leaning back into the cushions with a smug look on his face. "Do you believe me now?"

I look back at Mia, whose jaw is hanging open.

"I didn't believe it either at first," Joanie offers.

Mia shakes her head in disbelief. "That's ... wow."

My eyes flick to Evan, who is still soaking up the dog's affection. The silly grin he's giving the dog is adorable. And some doggie snuggles are probably just what Evan needs these days. Animals are good for the soul, after all.

As I watch Bruiser curl up on Evan's lap, I try not to notice how sweet they are together.

"Boy, he really likes you, Evan," Mia says.

"And I really like him. He's such a sweetheart," Evan says, emphasizing his words with belly rubs for Bruiser. Bruiser's little tongue lolls out as he rolls onto his back to allow Evan better access. Evan laughs. "Dogs are the best."

"You should get one," Joanie adds. "I wish we had sooner, honestly, and we've only been dog parents for three days."

Evan nods contemplatively. "I've thought about it. But I've always traveled too much to be able to commit to having a pet. Though it seems like things might be changing, so maybe I'll be able to soon," he says with a shrug, his tone equally sad and hopeful.

My heart twists in my chest as everyone else moves on like nothing just happened. But I can feel Evan's struggle from here. His despair at the sudden tumble that his career has taken warring with his hope that things might still be okay, whether that means a return to normal or an opportunity for something new. His strength and resilience in the face of adversity aren't lost on me, even if nobody else notices.

As if he hears my thoughts, his gaze lifts to meet mine. He gives me a melancholy smile, and I give him a supportive one in return. His eyes sparkle, and I know he picks up on my message: I see you.

And though it would open too much of a can of worms to voice the words, I hope he knows that no matter what we are to each other, I'm always in his corner.

CHAPTER TWENTY-FIVE

EVAN

These last couple of weeks in Alpine Ridge have been exactly what I needed. A calm environment with no pressure, no paparazzi, and no time to worry about contracts or scripts. Nate's been working me hard, but it's been good. I feel useful and clear-headed for the first time in a long time. I'd been looking for this late last year when I planned to take a break. I guess it took an *un*planned disaster to make it happen. I'm almost grateful for it. Almost.

Though as unburdened as I feel here, I still haven't been able to force myself to think about what I want for my career. I need to see how this mess with Kelly plays out first and then consider my options. Ultimately, it's hard to make a decision when you don't know what your choices will be.

In the meantime, Joanie had the brilliant idea to take a day off and go play tourist in Seattle. Nate and Mia vetoed Friday since it's one of their busiest days. And Carrie begged us to do it over the weekend so she could come too. So here we are on Sunday, the early morning sun glinting off the hood of Mia's SUV as we pull out of Alpine Ridge, headed for Seattle.

I'm in the back seat, with Nate driving and Mia in the passenger seat. Greg, Joanie, and Carrie are following in Joanie's Subaru. Despite the cloud hanging over my career, I can't help but feel a surge of excitement. It's been years since I've played tourist anywhere, so this feels like a vacation within a vacation.

I brought my hat and sunglasses, hoping they will offer some anonymity. The last thing I want is for my presence to disrupt our day.

It's nice to be a passenger as we make the two-hour drive. I've only ever been the driver on this trek, and watching the winding mountain paths transition to a sweeping descent into the Seattle area is a lot of fun. There's so much to look at between the lakes, changing cityscape, and even Mt. Rainier, clearly visible to our left. I'd seen it from the plane, but viewing it from the ground gives you a better sense of its sheer scale.

The sight of the Seattle skyline as we cross yet another lake has me itching to get there and explore. Thankfully, traveling with natives pays off, and Mia directs us seamlessly to a parking garage a stone's throw from the Space Needle.

"Hope you're not afraid of heights," Mia says with a grin as Greg, Joanie, and Carrie join us.

I grin back. "Bring it on."

As we ascend in the elevator the five hundred and twenty feet to the observation deck of the iconic structure, I feel a childlike thrill, bouncing on the balls of my feet.

Carrie laughs and shakes her head. "Trust me, it's not *that* exciting."

I bump her with my shoulder. "Says you. You've probably been up here tons of times."

"Okay, fair," she allows. "Still. I find it helps to keep your expectations low, then you're always pleasantly surprised."

I give her a look and open my mouth to say something about how that explains so much, but the doors open, and I'm so distracted by the view that all I can do is gape as we exit the elevator.

"Well, this definitely exceeds my expectations," I say, impressed. The view from the top is breathtaking — the city sprawls below us, Elliot Bay a glittering expanse in the distance. A walk around the circular deck unfurls more vistas of the city as well as lakes and distant mountains, including Rainier.

"I guess it is pretty amazing, huh?" Carrie's voice is soft beside me.

I nod, not trusting myself to speak. Our arms are almost touching on the railing, and I'm even more aware of her presence than usual. It takes me a minute to realize it might have something to do with what happened the last time we shared a beautiful view. I take a deep breath and try to brush it off.

The natives let me linger for a while, enjoying the view, though I can tell they got bored after a few minutes. Still, I snap a few selfies at various points, then insist on one of the group before we make our way back down, out of the clouds.

Next, we make our way toward the Olympic Sculpture Park so we can walk along the waterfront. The weather is perfect as we stroll, big puffy white clouds dotting the otherwise clear blue sky. The sun shines brightly, but the morning temperatures are still comfortable.

The sculpture park turns out to be an unexpectedly wild experience. It's a blend between a showcase of seriously cool and totally out-there contemporary sculptures of all kinds and is also surrounded by beautiful backdrops with the bay and Space Needle flanking it, each on either side. But we don't linger long and are soon heading down Alaskan Way. The smell of the ocean air makes me feel at home.

As we pass the Edgewater Hotel, Carrie nudges me. "See that? That's where the Beatles were famously photographed fishing out of one of the windows."

I grin, impressed by her knowledge. "No way! That's so cool."

"Yep. They don't allow fishing anymore, though. Just in case that gave you any ideas." She winks at me, and I laugh.

"I'm not big on fishing, but thanks for clarifying."

We walk in comfortable silence for the most part, though Carrie points out the sights as we go. We pass a huge sailboat docked just off the piers, the aquarium, with tons of little kids running around outside squealing, and then another set of sculptures less ostentatious than the first ones we saw but still interesting. Finally, I spot a sign on one of the larger piers for Miner's Landing ... and the Seattle Great Wheel. The childlike excitement returns as I eye the monstrosity at the end of the pier that, even from a ways away, dominates the skyline.

"Okay, studmuffin, this may not be as tall as the Space Needle, but I promise you won't be disappointed," Joanie says, gesturing to the pier just ahead of us.

"No worries on that front, Legs. It's already delivering," I say without hesitation, looking at it in awe. As we turn onto the pier and approach it, I have to crane my neck back to take it in. It may not be as tall as the Space Needle, but it's the biggest fucking Ferris wheel I've ever seen.

Since it's a Sunday, we have to wait a bit, but it's not too bad. My excitement levels as we're locked in the climate-controlled gondola are off the charts. The cabin is lined with two benches. Nate, Mia, and Carrie sit on one side, Joanie, Greg, and me on the other. But we're all turned outward toward the horizon, anticipating the coming views.

The views rise with us, the Ferris wheel halting occasionally for others to disembark and board. Within a few minutes, downtown lies sprawled out behind us, the ferry-dotted bay beneath us, and mountains in the distance still have white at their tips.

"How is there still snow on those mountains?" I ask in awe.

"They're tall," Joanie says with a shrug.

I smirk at her. "Gee, thanks."

"They're the Olympic Mountains. They're not as tall as the Cascades, but they sometimes get snow in June. Same as we do," Carrie offers.

Mia smiles and squeezes her sister against her. "You said 'we'," she points out.

Carrie blushes. "I did. Guess I've officially joined the Alpine Ridge cult."

Greg chuckles at that.

My eyes search Carrie's face. I was pretty sure she hadn't been back here since the fiasco with her parents, but based on the vibe I'm getting off of her, now I'm almost certain. "Is it weird being back in Seattle?" I ask.

She blows out a slow breath and turns back to the horizon that's slowly slipping out of view. "Super weird," she admits. "I can't believe I spent my whole life here, yet I've been away for almost a year."

I reach out and touch her on the knee, bringing her eyes to mine. "It's okay to not miss it, you know."

Her mouth drops open. "How did you ..." She shakes her head. And then, hesitatingly, she asks, "Am I a bad person if I don't?"

I consider that for a moment. "I think we don't miss places so much as we do the people who made them feel like home. So no, I don't think it makes you a bad person that you don't miss a place where people didn't appreciate you the way you deserved." I remove my hand from her knee, realizing that, though I meant it as a comfort, it could be seen as pressure. And that's something Carrie doesn't need more of. She's been under pressure her whole life. To meet her parents' expectations, to be something she didn't want to be, to please everyone around her. I know firsthand that even when pressure comes from within, that doesn't mean it's easy to switch off. In fact, sometimes, it's easier to cut off external pressure. That, you can walk away from. It's harder to rewire yourself after years of behaving a certain way.

Carrie is silent for a while. And so am I, as the others start to chat about where to have lunch. Because while my thoughts were directed at Carrie, I realize they are just as applicable to me. There's nobody in L.A. that makes it feel like home to me. Not a single fucking person. And yet, I've stayed for my career. I've persisted against the odds. It's just how I am. I do what needs doing. Unfortunately, I can do nothing about Kelly's accusation and the chain of events it started.

But the thing with Kelly doesn't depress me as much as realizing I don't have any true friends in Los Angeles. Even though I'm not there for friends. Still, it's odd that I can't claim a close friend in all my years there. Sure, I have tons of "friends" — in solid air quotes. They're the Hollywood kind of friends. Surface level. Fun to hang with at parties. But they're not the kind of people who are really there for you when you need them.

Not like this group, right here, plus Dylan and my parents. Oh, and Rae, who I can't leave out just because she couldn't join us today. They're my people. And maybe the fact that I'm always too far from them isn't helping my career struggles. Because how can you push through the hard stuff without a support network? One that can work out with you and lend an ear while you do. Or hand you a cupcake and a glass of brandy. Or go on a hike with you and make you feel like you're the only person in the world that matters.

My heart aches in my chest. As the revolution continues and the horizon returns, Carrie looks back at me with a smile. And I realize I've been staring at her, lost in thought, this whole time. I pull my gaze away, only to find Mia watching me. I give her a sheepish smile and look down into my hands. But I can still feel her sharp gaze on me, seeing more than I'm ready to admit to. Thankfully, she doesn't say a word, though.

"So, what do you think, Ev? Do you want to hit someplace on the waterfront, or should we have lunch at Pike Place Market?" Nate asks.

I look up, sensing that they'd just been discussing both options. "I'm the noob here, so whatever you guys agree on is good with me," I offer, snapping back to reality with a smile.

"And the vote carries for Pike Place Market," Joanie says with a victorious wiggle.

That gets Carrie's attention, too, making it clear she also wasn't listening. "Pike Place? Really? We should've gone there first, then," Carrie groans.

Joanie gives an exaggerated shrug and grins. "Gotta earn that burger, Carrie."

I raise a brow. "What does that mean?"

Greg claps me on the shoulder. "It means … it's a good thing you're a beast on the Stairmaster, my friend."

"Noooo, not the Hillclimb," Mia protests.

Nate shakes his head and laughs. "You want me to carry you?" he offers.

She brightens at that. "You would do that for me?" He leans in and kisses her in answer.

"Great. Guess I'll be suffering by myself then," Carrie jokes. I open my mouth, but her eyes snap to me. Something in them tells me *not* to make the offer I was about to. I press my lips together to keep from laughing. Damn, she's stubborn.

I lean back and watch the views for our next two rotations as the girls bicker amongst themselves, Carrie and Mia trying to convince Joanie out of climbing what is apparently a fuck ton of stairs. But with the glacier-and-snowcapped Rainier on one side, the glittering bay filled with ferries on another, and amazing views of everything downtown from the Space Needle to the aquarium to the other iconic buildings dotted everywhere, it's hard to pay attention to anything but the peace I feel being right here, right now.

When we finally disembark, I'm disappointed. Being up in the sky felt like being apart from everything for a while. It was nice.

But I am hungry, so I'm glad when Joanie leads us off the pier across multiple converging lanes of traffic and starts up a set of zig-zagging concrete steps that seem to go on forever.

After the first set of stairs, we cross another, smaller road and wait for Carrie and Mia, who decided to hoof it on her own, I suspect to keep Carrie company.

Then we head up *another* lengthy set of stairs.

Nate and I reach the top first, followed closely by Greg, then Joanie. My leg muscles burn but I feel better for the exercise. Though we have to wait for Carrie and Mia again, this time, there's plenty to keep me busy because we've emerged smack in the middle of the famous Pike Place Market. My eyes can't take everything in fast enough, from the fishmongers to the sea of flowers in buckets to wares of every kind sprawled out across what seems like endless stalls. The street outside is crowded with pedestrians and lined with restaurants and shops. Smells of roasting fish, pastries, coffee, flowers … it's a feast for the senses, and the vibe is borderline overwhelming but also exhilarating.

There's so much to see that I can't possibly take it all in, and it's only whetted my appetite for more by the time Carrie and Mia appear, puffing and panting.

"No … comments … about … out of … shape," Mia pants toward Nate. He just grins and, in one swift move, loads her up onto his back, where she promptly flops her head on his shoulder like a ragdoll. It's disgustingly adorable.

As we walk out, I look back and realize the iconic Public Market Center sign was above us the whole time.

"Will you guys hate me if I take a few pictures?" I ask.

Joanie smirks. "Of course not. I think Carrie and Mia would be thrilled for the breather, honestly."

Greg snorts, and I laugh. "All right, it won't take long, though, promise."

I quickly take a few selfies with the sign in the background, then have them all join me for a group pic.

"Thanks for humoring me," I tell them as Joanie and Greg lead us into a bar and grill across from the market entrance.

Joanie shrugs. "No problem. I forget how novel this is to some people."

"I feel that. When I first moved to L.A., it was like this. Everything was new and exciting. It wears off quickly, I know."

"Ah, but some things quickly become favorites, too, and the joy goes on," Nate says, setting Mia down in the waiting area. "Speaking of which … it's Boom Boom Shrimp time, sweetheart."

Mia gives a tired smile. "Thank God."

I slip off my hat and sunglasses as we get seated. We immediately order a round of appetizers — Mia's Boom Boom Shrimp (fried shrimp with a Thai chili sauce), a smoked salmon sampler, and oysters on the half shell — plus a beer bucket, which turns out to be just as much fun as it sounds. As we eat and drink and wait for our main courses, Mia and Carrie take turns giving me Seattle history lessons in disjointed pieces — the origin of the Space Needle (built for the 1962 World's Fair), the Smith Tower (which was Seattle's first skyscraper and, at the time, the tallest building in the West). They've just started on Seattle's Underground when our food shows up.

As intriguing as a whole section of the city still existing in a spooky tomb-like underground area is, my attention is wholly occupied by the fish and chips that are put in front of me. Basic, perhaps, but simple food can sometimes be the best. And as I eat the flaky, tender battered fish dipped in tartar sauce, I don't regret it.

Though everyone ordered something different, so we all swap bites of each — best of all worlds. Carrie's seafood pasta is okay but a little all over the place for me. Mia's chicken and waffles is an unexpected menu item, and not as good as Roscoe's back in L.A., but it's still all right. Nate, who I know isn't all that into seafood, ends up with a perfectly cooked New York Steak, and Greg's Dungeness Crab is melt-in-your-mouth delicious.

I lean back in my chair, groaning after the decadent indulgence of the meal. "Hope you guys are prepared to roll me out of here," I joke.

"You and me both," Mia agrees.

"What, no dessert?" Carrie asks Mia with a mischievous twinkle in her eye.

"Oh, oh, oh," Greg interjects excitedly. "We've got to stop by the Dahlia Bakery. My cousin Sera got me hooked on it last year. Their coconut cream pie is to die for."

Mia gives him a strange look and then bursts out laughing. "Who are you, and what have you done with the real Greg?" she asks, wiping tears of laughter from her eyes.

To everyone's surprise, Greg blushes, and now we're all laughing.

"Seriously, though, he's not wrong. It was always one of my favorites, too," Mia admits. "It's only about a ten-minute walk from here."

"Oh, but aren't we going to explore the market before we go?" I ask hopefully.

Mia hits herself on the forehead. "Duh. Yes, of course, we can totally do that. Sorry. Greg said 'coconut cream pie,' and I got distracted."

We settle up and head out, with me doing my best to tamp down my little kid level of excitement. I'm giddy today from all the normalcy and good times.

I should've known it wouldn't last. As we step back outside, I realize I left my hat and sunglasses in the restaurant. I don't even have time to vocalize that before I hear a familiar excited shriek followed by, "Oh my God, it's Evan Edwards!"

The shout comes from somewhere to my left, and suddenly I'm surrounded. Fans push for autographs and selfies, but most hurl questions about Kelly and the scandal.

"Evan, do you really do drugs?"

"Are you and Kelly still dating?"

"Is your career over, Evan?"

The questions come rapid-fire, each one a painful reminder of why I escaped to Alpine Ridge in the first place.

"All right, that's enough!" Joanie's authoritative voice cuts through the chaos. She grabs my arm, pulling me through the crowd and around a corner to a street where a couple of cabs are dropping people off. "Evan, Carrie, Nate, get in this taxi. We'll go in that one —" she points behind us "—and meet you at the parking garage near Seattle Center."

Before I know it, I'm in the back of a cab with Carrie, with Nate riding shotgun, watching the crowd recede through the rear window.

"I'm so sorry, Evan," Carrie says softly, her hand on my arm.

I let out a frustrated sigh. "Even when I'm an outcast, I can't have a normal life."

"Hey," she says, her voice firm but gentle. "This will pass. And you're not an outcast. Not to us."

I meet her eyes, seeing nothing but sincerity there. The rest of the world fades away for a moment. It's just me and Carrie, and I'm overwhelmed by the concern in her gaze. She laces her fingers with mine, giving me a reassuring squeeze. I can't help the small smile that tugs at my lips, or tracing my thumb over her palm, or staring back at her. She's sweet and kind and so caring, and being here with her like this ...

The taxi jerking to a stop breaks the spell. I look up and realize that we're at the parking garage.

As we climb out and into our separate cars for the drive home, I'm disappointed our day was cut short. But a small part of me is grateful for the reminder. That Carrie feels for me, even if it's not how I want. That even though things fell apart, I can just be a normal guy sometimes, even if it's only for a little while. That I have a group of people who have my back, no matter what.

Even being mobbed by fans and reminded of the mess that is my life and career right now ... well, it doesn't seem so bad when you don't have to face it alone.

CHAPTER TWENTY-SIX

CARRIE

The aftermath of our Seattle trip hits Alpine Ridge like a tidal wave. What started as a fun day out for our little group has morphed into a media frenzy, with paparazzi and tourists descending upon our quiet mountain town in droves. Evan's brief public appearance sent the vultures circling, desperate to uncover where he's been hiding.

For the first week, it's chaos. Evan hunkers down at Nate and Mia's while the rest of us navigate the sudden influx of outsiders. Thankfully, the paparazzi lose interest quickly when they realize Evan isn't coming out to play. The tourists, however, prove more persistent.

As I walk down Main Street, I can't help but notice the changes. There's a steady stream of unfamiliar faces, all seeming to vibrate with excitement at the mere possibility of catching a glimpse of Evan. Watching them take selfies in front of our modest storefronts as if they're posing before famous landmarks is surreal.

The town's reaction is mixed, to say the least. Mia is thrilled; the bakery is busier than ever, with lines stretching out the door most days. But for every happy business owner, there's someone like Batty Betty McDonald, who cornered me yesterday to rant about a tourist trampling her prized begonias.

As I approach the makeshift town hall — currently just a conference room in the community center — I brace myself for what's to come. Arthur asked me to prepare budget outlines and timelines for our first quarterly town hall meeting, but I have a sinking feeling those topics will be quickly overshadowed.

"Carrie," Arthur greets me as I enter, his normally cheerful face creased with worry lines. "Are you ready for the meeting?"

I nod, forcing a smile. "As ready as I'll ever be. But Arthur, I should warn you — I don't think we will get very far with the budget discussions. People are going to want to talk about the tourist situation."

He sighs, running a hand through his thinning hair. "I know, I know. But there's not much we can do except capitalize on the business and use it as a learning exercise for everything else. We'll just have to roll with the punches."

As expected, the meeting quickly derails from Arthur's planned agenda, with barely an acknowledgment that we've broken ground on the new town hall building to be finished by the end of the year and have a fiscal plan and schedule for setting up police and fire services by next year. But the room is packed with angry residents ready to explode over their tourist troubles, and it doesn't take long for the complaints to start flying.

"They're parking wherever they damn well please!" one resident shouts.

"I found three of them in my backyard yesterday, taking pictures!" another chimes in.

"The noise at night is unbearable! Don't these people sleep?"

I cringe, glad at least that they didn't bring pitchforks and torches. Thankfully, Greg, ever the voice of reason, speaks up. "Perhaps we can consider clear, designated parking areas and more signage for public versus private property?"

Brandon nods in agreement. "We could also institute local ordinances for noise and trespassing."

Janet, one of the older council members, adds, "While we haven't had any major traffic issues yet, I've noticed plenty of confused drivers. We should discuss improving our transportation infrastructure."

It seems to mollify the townspeople, for now at least. As the meeting winds down, I can't help but feel a mix of frustration and pride. Yes, we're facing challenges, but watching our fledgling town government tackle these issues head-on is oddly inspiring. In a way, this might have been a blessing in disguise.

The next evening at game night, nobody feels much like playing. Instead, we fill Evan in on what happened at the town hall meeting.

"I'm sorry I'm causing waves," Evan says, his brow furrowed with concern. "Maybe this wasn't such a good idea after all."

Mia leans forward, her eyes sharp. "Are you going to keep going forward with building your house here?"

Evan hesitates. "I've gone too far not to finish the build, but if it comes down to it, I can always sell."

"That would be dumb," Joanie interjects, her tone matter-of-fact. "This is exactly what we hoped for when we asked you to live here — attention for the town. So what if not everybody is happy? Tough shit."

We all laugh, and I can see some of the tension leave Evan's shoulders.

"I'm with Joanie," Rae pipes up. "A good number of people in this town just like to complain. The way I see it, we gave them something juicy to bitch about." She shrugs.

"For sure," I agree. "But even beyond that, it showed us exactly the issues we will need to address if we want to manage a growing population and increased tourism over the next few years. Better to know these things now while we're still in the planning stages for the town."

"You think?" Evan asks, and the vulnerability in his voice gets me right in the chest.

"Yeah, I do," I assure him. "I know it doesn't feel like it right now, but I think this will turn out to be a good thing."

Everyone's silent as they process all that's been said.

After a minute or so, Greg clears his throat. "If we're done with the depressing stuff, I have some good news." We all turn to him expectantly. "Joanie and I have set a wedding date. December tenth, the second anniversary of when we met."

"Oh, yay!" Mia is the first to exclaim. "Congratulations, guys." She rises and pulls Joanie into a hug.

"Congrats, man," Nate says, leaning in to fist-bump Greg.

"Well, that is good news," Rae adds. "Congratulations, you two."

"That's fantastic! I can't wait to be at *that* party. I mean, if it won't mess things up," Evan says, and I feel a flutter in my chest at his certainty.

"Are you kidding? It wouldn't be a party without you, studmuffin," Joanie replies with a wink.

Despite the lightness in the room, I feel ... odd as I offer Joanie and Greg a smile and a "Congratulations." Really, though, I don't have to work hard to figure out why. It's because Evan seemed so sure that he'll be there. Which makes me wonder ... does he plan on *still* being here, or is he assuming he'll be back in L.A. at that point but is set on being here for their special day anyway? Certainly, the latter is more likely. Which makes me think that ... maybe, even once he goes back to L.A., Evan will be around more. He seems genuinely attached to this town, to all of us.

A small kernel of hope blossoms inside me, but I quickly tamp it down. Fools rush in, as they say, and I've had enough of being a fool for one lifetime. For now, I'll wait and see. After all, we've got a town to run and, apparently, a wedding to plan.

CHAPTER TWENTY-SEVEN

EVAN

The call comes on Monday afternoon, just as I'm finishing up for the day at Nate's wellness center. My phone buzzes insistently, and when I see the unfamiliar number with a D.C. area code, my heart leaps into my throat.

"Mr. Edwards?" a crisp, professional voice greets me.

"Yes?" I reply, my voice surprisingly steady.

"This is Agent Carlson from the FBI. I'm calling to inform you that our investigation has concluded, and you've been cleared of all accusations related to Ms. Cook's drug charges."

Relief washes over me like a tidal wave. "Thank you," I manage to croak out. "That's great news."

As soon as I hang up, I try to call Rick, but it goes straight to voicemail. I leave a message, my voice shaking with excitement and relief.

The next afternoon, Rick finally calls back. "Evan, my man! I heard the good news. Sorry I couldn't get back to you yesterday — it's been a madhouse here."

"What's going on?" Despite being cleared, I'm suddenly nervous that something else has happened.

Rick chuckles. "You won't believe this. Over the holiday weekend, another A-list actor got caught in a DWI scandal that outed his severe alcoholism. All eyes are off you now, kid."

I let out a low whistle. "That's ... unfortunate for him, but I can't say I'm not relieved."

"You should be," Rick says. "Because I've also been working overtime to placate the studio. They're willing to move forward with the Bond contract but want you back in L.A. ASAP. We need to do some damage control, get you back in the public eye in a positive way."

I feel a pang in my chest at the thought of leaving Alpine Ridge. But I know I can't hide away forever. "All right," I sigh. "I'll head back tomorrow."

"Why not tonight?" Rick pushes.

I snort. "I can be in your office by noon tomorrow. They'll never know the difference."

"You wanna take that risk?"

A headache starts pounding at my temple. "Fine. I'll see what I can do."

"Good. Text me your flight info when you have it." And with that, he hangs up.

Fuck. Just like that, I'm back in the fast lane.

I hang up, letting out a long breath. Nate looks up from cleaning up after a session. "Headed back to L.A.?"

I nod slowly. "Yeah. First flight I can make out, actually." Nate grimaces. "I know. Though I should've expected that's how it would go down." I sigh heavily. "Thanks for … everything, man. This has been great, really."

Nate walks over to me and claps me on the shoulder. "It has. But don't talk like you won't be back. Don't forget, you've got a house being built."

I give him a half-hearted smile. "I haven't."

He nods. "Go say your goodbyes. I'm sure I'll talk to you soon."

A wave of emotion rolls over me, and I grab my big brother into a bear hug. "Yeah, you will." I release him quickly and turn away, blinking back tears as I grab my gear bag and head out to my rental.

I stop in the bakery on the way, the bell on the door jingling as I enter. Rae looks up from frosting a tray of cupcakes.

"Hey, sugar," she greets me.

"Hey, Rae," I respond. "Came to say goodbye. The studio wants me back ASAP, so I'm outta here."

She looks back up in surprise. "Mia!" she calls toward the back. Then she sets the frosting bag down, wipes her hands, and rounds the counter to give me a hug. She smells like vanilla and sugar, and it's kind of making me hungry. "You go back there and kick some ass."

I chuckle. "Thanks, Rae. You keep everyone in line while I'm gone, okay?"

She snorts. "I'll do my best."

"What's going on?" Mia asks, appearing behind Rae.

I pull back and give her a rueful smile. "I'm headed back to L.A."

Mia's jaw drops. "No! Really? Like, right now?"

I shrug. "They say jump, I say how high."

Mia frowns. "Well, we're sure going to miss you, Evan." She holds out her arms, and I pull her in for a hug.

"Thanks for everything, Mia. I'm going to miss you too. And your cupcakes and booze."

Mia chuckles against my shoulder. "You know you're welcome to come back for more anytime."

I pull back. "Count on it. Carrie still working out of the community center?"

Mia nods. "Yep."

"Cool. I'll say goodbye to her and Greg at the same time. Tell Joanie I'll see her and her fantastic legs later?" I say with a smile I don't feel.

"Of course," Mia returns with a similar forced smile.

I turn and walk away before I can get all emotional again. I make it out in one piece, though I know I won't be so lucky with my next stop.

To save time, I drive to the community center but sit in the SUV for a few minutes, psyching myself up. I finally take a deep breath and hop out, heading for the front door. I notice Greg on the other side of the building, hosing down the outdoor equipment.

"Hey, man," I call.

Greg looks up and grins, then turns off the hose.

"Evan, my man, what's up? Does Nate need something for the wellness center?"

I shake my head. "Nope. I'm headed back to L.A. Came to say goodbye."

Greg nods, the smile dropping off his face. "Well, glad you didn't just cut and run. We'll miss you, man." He reaches in for the hand clasp and bro hug. And I start to get teary again.

"Anyway, I'm going to go in and say goodbye to Carrie quickly, then I gotta run. I'm sure I'll see you soon. Gotta come back to check on the house and all." I say, sniffing as subtly as I can.

But I can tell Greg isn't fooled. Still, he only says, "Sounds good. Have a safe trip back."

I nod, stuffing my hands in my pockets as I head into the community center.

I find Carrie in one of the back rooms that's been turned into a small office. She's turned mostly away from me, so she doesn't notice I'm there. I take the opportunity to observe her for a minute. Her dark hair is swept up into a loose bun on her head, with a pen sticking out of the dark mass. She's chewing on her lip as she reads something, her heel-clad foot tapping on the metal leg of the chair. She's beautiful. And I'm going to miss her like crazy. A pang hits me in the chest; oddly, I already miss her. I clear my throat, partly to dislodge the thickness that's suddenly welled there, partly to announce myself.

Carrie looks up distractedly. "Evan? What are you doing here?" She turns and rises, and I notice she's wearing a tan pencil skirt and a white button-front top that shows a hint of her cleavage. My mouth dries up, and I lose my words.

"I ... I'm ..." I swallow hard. "I came to say goodbye." I lift my eyes to hers, willing myself not to continue ogling her. But Jesus, why did she have to look like hot business right now? As if leaving wasn't hard enough.

Her brows pull together, her dark blue eyes clouded with confusion until she realizes what I mean. And if it was hard before, seeing the disappointment seep into her face nearly undoes me. But she hides it quickly, so I try to do the same.

"Oh. Well ... guess it had to happen sometime," she says with a resigned sigh.

My jaw tightens. She's not wrong, but it just makes me realize ... Carrie's been waiting for me to leave again. I'm proving once more that even if I'm here, it's only until L.A. calls me back. This time, it just took longer.

"Guess so," I agree softly. "I'll be back, though."

"When?" she asks, looking down at her hands, fidgeting with the pen she's holding.

She cares. I shake my head, frustrated. "I wish I knew. If absolutely nothing else, I'll be back when the house is done, which is supposed to be sometime in October."

Carrie nods. "Well, that's only a few months." She looks up to meet my gaze. "We'll all miss you. You're one of us now, you know." She gives me an honest but sad smile.

"We?" I ask softly. "What about you, Carrie? Will you miss me?"

She swallows hard. "Please don't ask me that."

I nod, tears pricking at the backs of my eyes. "Sorry." I swallow back the words, "I'll miss you." I don't think she wants to hear it, either. "Well, I wish you all the best with the new job. I'll see you when I see you."

I should leave. Fuck knows I can't kiss her, no matter how badly I want to. If I do, I won't go. Or she'll hate me for it. I don't know. I just know that no good can come from pursuing her when she's not ready. If she's ever ready.

So, we simply stare at each other, the air thick with unspoken words and suppressed feelings.

At the same moment, we both seem to snap, coming together. Carrie slides into my arms and wraps hers around me. I bury my face in her hair and hold onto her like she's my lifeline. But really, she's so much more than that.

Neither of us speaks. We've said it all before. Nothing we say will undo the reality of what is.

I kiss her on the top of her head and untangle myself. "Goodbye, Carrie."

She turns back to her chair. "Bye, Evan." The emotion in her voice belies the casualness of her words.

The urge to grab her and kiss her senseless almost overwhelms me. My hands twitch at my sides. My heart aches. My body refuses to move. My frustration peaks, and rather than do something I can't take back, I walk away. I keep it together until I'm back behind the wheel. And then I let the silent tears fall.

❧

The next few days are a whirlwind of traveling, meetings, PR appearances, script readings, and endless hoops the studio wants me to jump through. But even as I throw myself back into the Hollywood machine, I can't shake the feeling of melancholy that followed me out of Alpine Ridge.

I miss the quiet mornings there, the easy camaraderie with Nate and the others. And Carrie. Always Carrie.

But, on the bright side, the scripts coming my way aren't half bad, and I can feel my career getting back on track. It's what I wanted, isn't it? To reclaim my place in La La Land?

Yet, as I sit in my lavish home in the Hollywood Hills, looking out over the city lights, I can't help but feel a disconnect. This doesn't feel like home anymore.

An idea starts to form in my mind. If I can't be in Alpine Ridge, maybe I can bring a piece of it here. Or, more specifically, a certain political science expert.

It's crazy, but I need to do something to assuage this feeling of loss. So, I start making calls, asking around about jobs that would suit Carrie's qualifications. It's not long before I find an open assistant professorship position at UCLA's Luskin School of Public Affairs, with ties to projects for the city of Los Angeles.

I know it's a long shot. I know it won't magically win her over. But if I can get her down here, maybe it's a start. A chance to show her that I care enough that I want to find a way to keep being a part of each other's lives.

I pull some strings, calling in favors until I get them to agree to interview her. Now, there's only one thing left to do.

My hand shakes slightly as I place a call to Carrie.

"Evan? Hey. What's up?" her voice comes through, a mix of surprise and something else I can't quite place.

"Hey, Carrie," I say, trying to keep my voice casual. "I hope I'm not catching you at a bad time. I, uh, I just heard about this job opportunity that I thought might interest you ..."

As I explain the position at UCLA, she asks a few questions, and I can hear the hesitation in her voice. But she doesn't outright refuse, so I count that as a win.

"I'll consider it," she says finally. "Thanks for thinking of me."

I resist the urge to point out that I'm always thinking of her. Instead, I give her the contact info and then we hang up. I lean back in my chair, staring at the ceiling. I know I'm walking a fine line here. I don't want to pressure her or make her feel like I'm trying to uproot her life.

But I can't just not see her for months. Not talk to her. And I can't shake the feeling that if we're ever going to have a real shot, if I'm ever going to get her to give in to how I know she feels, we need to be in the same place. And right now, that place has to be L.A.

As I return to the pile of scripts on my desk, I hope Carrie will be too tempted to pass up the opportunity. Because even as I dive back into my career, I know that success won't mean much without her.

CHAPTER TWENTY-EIGHT

CARRIE

After Evan's unexpected phone call, I sit at my desk, lost in thought. I have to admit, I'm shaken. I thought I'd be at peace when he returned to L.A., but saying goodbye this time was harder than ever before. Somehow, in the month he was in Alpine Ridge, we not only became friends, but our friendship melded with the ever-present attraction I feel toward him and became something more. And it wasn't until I heard his voice just now that I realized how much more. I miss him, plain and simple. Well, really, there's nothing simple about it because my mind hasn't changed.

Though I'm also touched that he has so much faith in my abilities and cares enough to have put me forward for such an amazing opportunity. Despite my heavily mixed feelings and having a job I love, I'm tempted because this position could open all the right doors for an amazing career.

I decide to talk to Brandon about it. I text him to stop by when he has a few, and not even fifteen minutes later, he's poking his head into my closet-sized office.

"You rang?" he teases.

I give him a half-hearted smile. "Thanks for coming so fast because I could really use your advice."

He raises a brow and settles into the folding chair next to my small desk, crossing his legs and gesturing for me to go on. So, I launch into explaining Evan's phone call. The rest — my persistently growing feelings for Evan — he already knows.

"What do you think I should do?" I ask, fidgeting with my pen.

Brandon gives me a pointed look. "Remember what I said about walking through open doors to see where they take you? This seems like a pretty big door, Carrie."

I nod slowly, realizing he's right. "You're right. I know you're right. And I would probably hate myself if I didn't at least try."

"That's the spirit," Brandon jokes.

I huff a laugh. "Thanks," I reply drily.

"Is that all you called me over here for?" he asks with a smile. "Because that was a little too easy, and I'm pretty sure you didn't need me to confirm what you already knew."

"When it comes to Evan Edwards, I'm always second-guessing myself." I shake my head.

Brandon pats me on the knee. "Just keep making the decisions one at a time, honey."

I nod. "You're right. Again. Thank you," I reply sincerely. And while he is, it's certainly easier said than done when all my brain wants to do is constantly churn through every possibility. I sigh.

He winks at me. "I love hearing those words."

"Thank you?" I ask, confused as my mind had wandered.

He grins. "No. 'You're right.'" I chuckle, and he slaps my knee gently. "Now come on. You're going to take a break, get some fresh air, and then you're going to call about that interview."

I stand up, and he does, too. I bump my shoulder against his and smile, grateful for his reassurance.

And he's right again. After taking a breather in the sunshine, I feel much more level-headed and prepared. So, I call the number Evan gave me and schedule an interview for the following Friday. Then I make travel plans and text Evan to let him know that I'll be headed his way in one week. And then I try not to vomit from nerves. Nerves I wish were only about the interview.

After a relatively uneventful plane ride, I arrive in Los Angeles the following Thursday night, pick up my rental car, and make my way slowly through traffic to get to my West L.A. hotel. The whole time, I replay the reactions I received to this little trip. Mia's horror that I might move to Los Angeles, despite my reassurances that I had no real plans to do that, as this whole thing was a long shot. Joanie's encouragement to jump Evan's bones while I was there because my mood after Evan's departure led me to confess the situation to her, though I knew she'd suspected it anyway. Rae's support of whatever I wanted to do, even if that meant losing a friend and roommate. And, of course, Brandon's gentle encouragement to walk through the doors with faith in my heart that it's all part of my path. As if having my own jumble of mixed-up thoughts and emotions swirling around in my brain wasn't enough.

By the time I enter my hotel room, I'm mentally and physically exhausted and beyond ready for a good night's sleep. Thankfully, I'm asleep almost as soon as my head hits the pillow, only remaining lucid long enough to wonder ... what if I *do* get the job? My dreams seemingly attempt to answer that question and are filled with visions of prestige, success, and ... Evan. Because only in my dreams can we be everything I wish we were.

I spend the next morning going over my notes on the position, school, department, everything. I feel as prepared as possible when I head to UCLA in the afternoon for my interview. The campus is stunning — a beautifully landscaped oasis with incredible architecture amid the bustling city.

My interviewer, Stephanie, is a department chair and tenured professor about my mother's age. She's an absolute delight, and we hit it off immediately. She's had a career I can only dream of, and I know I could learn so much from her and the position. The interview is challenging but good. At the end, Stephanie leans forward, her expression kind but serious.

"Carrie, I want to be honest with you," she begins. "While I think you're knowledgeable and have the right education, you lack sufficient experience on the teaching side to be a great fit for this particular role. But I've enjoyed talking with you today and think you'd fit in well here, so we'll keep you in mind if a more entry-level position arises."

It's a rejection but a kind one. Still, I'm not sorry I tried. Now, I don't have to wonder.

"I understand, and I appreciate your candor. I enjoyed getting to know you as well. Thank you so much for taking the time to meet with me," I reply warmly.

We rise and shake hands, and she walks me out, making small talk. In the hot July Southern California sunshine, I meander happily back to the car and realize ... I'm relieved. While it was an undeniably amazing opportunity, I'm glad I get to go back to my quiet, simple, small-town life. I wonder for a moment if maybe I'm *too* happy with the status quo. But then, it's not like I've settled. I pursued the job I wanted and got it, and I'm living in a place I love. Still, I make a mental note to continue to stretch my skills purposefully as Alpine Ridge grows and beyond.

I also text Evan on the way back to my car. He replies quickly, suggesting we meet for dinner at a restaurant called Craig's in West Hollywood in a couple of hours. When I get to the car, I plug it into the GPS. Supposedly, it's less than thirty minutes away, but given it's already after four p.m. and my small amount of experience thus far with L.A. traffic, I decide to leave now.

It was a smart idea, because it takes me almost twice as long to get there and find a place to park. I decide to sit in the car and call both Brandon and Mia to let them know how the interview went.

The time-filler works a little too well, as I'm still talking to Mia when it's about to hit six, so I end the call abruptly, scrambling out of the car as I'd had to park a couple of blocks away.

Walking down Melrose Avenue, I can't help feeling like I'm a character in a TV show. The neighborhood seems unassuming, but the simple storefronts belie their luxury interiors. There's a good mix of restaurants, shops, and other buildings, and as I approach Craig's, it looks modest but classy with its logoed awning.

But a bunch of guys with cameras wait outside, looking up hopefully as I approach. They return to what they were doing once they see me, but it underscores the surreal feeling. Because I'm headed to meet a famous movie star at what is apparently one of Los Angeles's celeb hotspots, on Melrose freaking Avenue. I shake my head, chuckling to myself.

I walk in and note the modest yet classy feel continues inside. It's both modern and what I'd imagine a classic Hollywood hangout to look like. It has a relaxed vibe despite the literal white-tablecloth service in one part of the restaurant and the low, dark, decadent-looking curved booths in the other.

At one of the latter, I spot Evan all the way in the back corner, far from prying eyes but just the right distance from the kitchen. One of the perks of his status, I presume.

I smooth my hands over my lavender Ralph Lauren linen shirtdress, hoping it's not too wrinkled from my interview and being in the car.

Evan grins widely as I approach, rising to wrap me in his arms. "Hey, you," he greets me warmly. He looks fantastic in an all-charcoal suit and smells even better as he envelops me in his arms. Even in heels, my head hits under his chin. The hard warmth of his body against me is soothing in a way I don't want to think too much about.

"Well, hello," I say, surprised. "You're hugging me. In public." I keep my tone light to let him know I'm joking. Mostly, anyway.

He pulls back and gestures for me to take a seat. I slide onto the supple leather seat, unable to resist running my hands over the buttery soft material as I do. While the restaurant has an effortlessly simple look, it still has luxury touches.

"The paps aren't allowed in, and the windows are tinted," he explains, retaking a seat. "And the only thing the diners are allowed to take pictures of is their food. Why do you think it's so popular with celebrities?" He winks at me. "So, I'm dying to hear how the interview went."

I open my mouth to respond, but our waiter appears.

"Good evening, miss. May I get you something to drink?" he asks me. I glance at Evan and notice he already has what appears to be whiskey.

"Oh, um …" I pick up the menu and fumble to find the drinks section.

"Try the Gozzer Lemonade," Evan offers. "It has huckleberry syrup, and I know how you Washingtonians love your huckleberry."

I smirk and glance over the cocktail menu. The drink also includes red berry vodka and lemonade. It sounds good to me. "I'll take that, please," I tell the waiter.

He nods. "Of course, miss, I'll be right back with that for you."

Evan grins, leaning forward on his elbows and intertwining his fingers. "I didn't mean to pounce on you. Why don't you take a minute more to look at the menu? I bet you're hungry."

The corner of my mouth tips up. He's so thoughtful, and I realize he's right — I'm ravenous, having been too on edge to eat lunch earlier today. So, I flip to the dinner portion of the menu.

"Since you're full of suggestions tonight, what entrée would you recommend?"

Evan leans back into the booth, taking a thoughtful sip of his drink. Definitely whiskey, by the smell.

"I'm partial to the Chicken Parmigiana. Though the New York Steak is damn good, too."

I drop my eyes to the menu and try not to react to the prices. They're not outrageous, but they're higher than I expected.

"My treat, of course," he says smoothly, reading my discomfort.

I look up and smile. "No, no," I object. "I wanted to treat you as a thank you for getting me the interview." I snap the menu shut and set it aside, having decided to go with his suggestion of the Chicken Parmigiana.

Evan leans forward and tucks a loose strand of hair behind my ear. His fingers linger on my cheek for what feels like a fraction of a second too long to be casual, and I feel heat creep up my neck.

"I suggested the restaurant," he counters. "And it was nothing, Carrie. I'm just so glad you're here. You don't even know."

I chew anxiously on my bottom lip. "Evan ..."

"Carrie," he replies in a teasing voice. "I missed you. I miss *all* of you, so I jumped at the first opportunity to bring a piece of Alpine Ridge to L.A. to tide me over. So just let me buy you dinner, okay?" His tone is light and pleasant, but his eyes are intense. And I feel like he's trying to play off the tension I feel between us.

"Okay, fine," I agree. "Thank you."

Our waiter returns with my drink and takes our orders. Evan goes for the steak. While he orders, I take a sip of the cocktail. It's delicious.

"So," Evan says once the waiter's gone. "The interview?"

"It went great, but they were looking for someone with more teaching experience."

"Damn. I'm so sorry, Carrie."

I reach out and squeeze his hand. "Don't be. I'm not disappointed," I assure him. "It was still a great learning experience, and I'll spend some time playing tourist before heading home. This is my first time in L.A., after all."

Evan perks up at that. "I have a meeting in the morning, but if you want some company, I'd love to join you for the afternoon."

"Oh, you really don't have to do that," I assure him. "I'm sure you have more important things to do." Except, part of me yearns to spend time with him. I know it's my heart. Because my head is saying this dinner is already a little too intimate, and spending more time just me and him could lead down a path I swore I wouldn't go.

This time, Evan reaches for my hand, running his thumb over the back. "There's absolutely nothing that's more important than spending time with one of my favorite people," he murmurs, his hazel eyes roving my face.

Warmth spreads through my body, and I know it's not just the alcohol. I swallow hard. This. This is exactly why it's a bad idea. Because even a light touch on my hand makes me want more. Makes me *remember* more.

I pull back and clear my throat, then take another sip of my drink. "Well, then it's settled," I say, attempting a casual tone. "This is great, by the way."

He nods. "I know."

I laugh, shaking my head. Only Evan can still sound charming while being cocky.

Our food arrives in short order, and Evan and I take turns catching each other up. Me on what's been happening in Alpine Ridge, which is to say, not a lot he didn't already know. Him on all the hoops he's had to jump through to get back in the good graces of the studio, the fans, and the media. He also lets me have a bite of his steak, which is almost as heavenly as the perfectly cooked cheesy goodness that is my Chicken Parmigiana.

But even more amazing, no one approaches the table the whole time we're there. Sure, there are a few looks and whispers, but it's a surprisingly normal meal. Well, aside from how distracting it is to have Evan Edwards' full attention. He's intense but in a good way. A little too good.

So, after we've finished eating and paid, I'm hesitant when Evan asks if I want to take a walk around the neighborhood.

"Won't the paparazzi follow us?" I point out. Yeah, that's why I don't want to take a romantic stroll around the block with him.

He smiles mischievously. "Not if we don't go through the front door."

I laugh. "You have an answer for everything, don't you?"

The smile slides off his face. "I wish." He huffs a laugh. "Come on." He rises and holds out his hand. "You in?"

My heart races as I look up at him. He's handsome and charming, and now that I know him better, I trust that he won't push me to do anything besides what he's offering. It's my own self-control I'm worried about, really. And I'm not ready to say goodbye to him just yet. So, I slide my hand into his and rise.

"I'm in."

Evan signals our waiter, who shows us to the staff entrance through the kitchen. Once we leave, the door closes to silence, a few parking spots, and a service alleyway behind the restaurant.

Evan takes my hand, leading me behind the row of businesses toward the main block. I contemplate extricating my hand because friends don't hold hands ... but it feels so good and seems relatively harmless.

"How come there are no paparazzi back here?" I whisper.

"They're not allowed," he explains with a shrug. Then leans in and says in a mock whisper, "So you don't have to worry about them finding us." He squeezes my hand and chuckles.

I nudge him with my hip, thankful he's looking ahead so he doesn't see me blushing. Though still not convinced ... surely, they're wise to celebrities pulling this kind of stunt?

But as the alleyway dumps out onto a regular city street, with cars whizzing by and people milling up and down the sidewalks, I see not a photographer in sight. Huh. It worked.

"So, what do you think of L.A. so far?" he asks nonchalantly. But despite his attempt at it, I can tell he cares about my answer. Something about the tone of his voice or the careful way he doesn't look at me when he asks ... it's hard to say.

"It's busy," I reply lamely. "I don't know. The traffic is insane. But the UCLA campus was beautiful, and that was a fantastic meal. Thank you, by the way. For dinner."

We stop at a traffic light, waiting to cross. Evan strokes his thumb over my hand again. "You're welcome." His eyes sweep over me. "You look beautiful in that color."

I blush hard but can't seem to break my gaze from his. "Thank you."

We're so wrapped up staring at each other that we almost miss the light turning. We're cued only when another pedestrian passes us to cross. Evan leads me across and then across again as the light changes the other direction.

"It seems like you have a destination in mind."

The corner of Evan's lips tips up. "There's a park just down a bit. I figured we could sit and talk."

I can't help laughing. "Is that your master plan to get me to fall in love with Los Angeles? A park? Well, I hope it has swings."

Evan chuckles. "Damn, that should have been part of the plan." He gestures to the right, where a walkway branches out, and leads me down it. "But no, no swings. I figured I could show you that there are quiet places here and there despite all the hustle and bustle."

A strange sight appears on our left. "What … is that?"

Evan smirks. "Art," he says simply.

I raise a brow. A large, concrete circle like the ones that would usually hold a fountain or plants is filled with strange, elevated reflective prisms. "I … can see that," I allow.

He pulls me toward the installation, settling on the wide, circular concrete lip around it.

"What do *you* think of L.A., Evan? Do you like it here?"

Evan's brows rise. "I don't think anyone's ever asked me that." I give him an expectant look, and he pushes out a breath. "Honestly? There are things I like about it. But it also wears on me at times. After so many years, the traffic, the paparazzi, not being able to go out in public without being recognized … hell, even the fact that it's *always* sunny. That sounds insane, I know. But sometimes a guy just wants a little rain or snow, you know what I mean?"

I smile. "I do."

He chuckles. "I really enjoyed being in Alpine Ridge. It reminded me what it's like to be normal. I thought maybe if I brought a piece of that here," he nudges me playfully with his knee, "it might bring back that feeling."

"Is that all that this was all about?" I ask suspiciously.

He shrugs. "That, and I genuinely wanted to help you."

I chew at my bottom lip, trying to make sense of this. "Did you pull strings to get me that interview, Evan?"

His lips turn down ever so slightly. "Would you be upset if I did?"

A pang shoots through my chest. And I have to think about why. Am I upset that they agreed to interview me only because of his influence?

No, I realize. I'm not. Because it was obvious that I was qualified, mostly, anyway. Surely, they wouldn't have interviewed me if I weren't? I almost laugh because that was a stupid thought … I know they most certainly would've. But still, I'm not upset. Because he was trying to do something nice for me.

And beyond that … I look up at Evan in shock, realizing he was hoping I'd get the job. That I'd move here. Which means he's still struggling with this as much as I am. He still wants me in some way.

"I'm not upset. But … why me?" I ask, wanting to laugh at the absurdity of someone like him pursuing someone like me. Especially after I'd laid out my boundaries about long-distance relationships. Especially how hard I'd friend-zoned him while he was in Alpine Ridge.

God, he's trying to work *within* my boundaries, I realize. Except, part of that wasn't just distance. It was also his career and the attention that goes with it.

Evan searches my face. "Fuck, Carrie, isn't it obvious?" he murmurs, cupping my cheek and running his thumb down the line of my jaw. The touch sends tingles down my neck and arm.

I close my eyes against the wave of emotion that washes over me. I reopen them. And I pull back. A pained look flashes over his face for a fleeting moment before it's replaced by his usual casual smile.

"It isn't," I admit. I take a deep breath. "But either way, it's probably for the best this didn't pan out. I put a down payment on a townhouse in Alpine Ridge, Evan."

Evan's eyebrows shoot up. "Really? That's ... wow." He stares at his hands for a moment before looking back up at me. And if I didn't know him as well as I do, I wouldn't notice the fakeness of his smile. "It sounds like you're really making a life for yourself there. I'm happy for you, Carrie."

"Thanks," I reply softly, unsure what else to say.

He rises, this time not offering his hand. "Come on, I'll walk you to your car."

I nod and follow him. Once we're back on Melrose, I regain my bearings and lead him to my rental car.

"Thanks again for dinner." I lean against the driver's side door as he towers over me, looking up into his face. His features are pinched with an emotion I can't quite place.

"Anytime. I'll call you tomorrow when I'm done with my meeting?"

I nod, pushing off the car to a standing position. Before I can turn to get in, he pulls me into his arms and gently kisses me on the forehead.

"Drive safe," he murmurs against my skin.

And then he's walking away.

I don't watch. I can't. There's already a hole in my chest from shutting him down tonight, and if I watch, it'll just get bigger.

So, I get in the car and focus on doing exactly as he said. It's tough, as my mind is filled with conflicting thoughts.

He still wants me. But this is where his career is.

I still want him. But his best attempt to lure me close wasn't enough.

Even if it had ... even if we both lived in Los Angeles ... I don't fit into his world here.

The thought sets off an avalanche of yearning. Because if his month-long stint in Alpine Ridge showed me anything, he fits a little too well into my world there. Unfortunately, just as I've made it clear I can't be in a long-distance relationship, he's made it clear he has no plans to leave L.A.

Once I return to my hotel room, shower, and slide into bed, my last thought is to do my best to keep him at a distance tomorrow. I slipped tonight, letting him too close, physically and otherwise. It's not a mistake I can make again. Not if I want to keep my sanity and my heart intact.

CHAPTER TWENTY-NINE

EVAN

I 'm sitting in a meeting with my PR team, but my mind keeps drifting back to my conversation with Carrie last night and the fact that she's bought a place in Alpine Ridge. The news shouldn't bother me as much as it does, but I can't shake that she's putting down roots. Roots that don't include me.

"Evan? Are you with us?"

I snap back to attention, forcing a smile. "Sorry, just thinking about the upcoming press junket. Please, continue."

As the meeting drones on, I make a concerted effort to focus, but it's a struggle. When we finally wrap up, I practically bolt from the room, pulling out my phone to text Carrie.

Hey, you up for some company this afternoon?

Her reply comes quickly.

CARRIE

Sure! I'm at the Santa Monica Pier right now.

Perfect. I'll meet you there for lunch.

I arrive at the pier to find Carrie waiting near the entrance, her hair windblown and cheeks flushed from the ocean breeze. Wearing a white and blue striped shirt-short combo, she looks beautiful, and I have to remind myself to keep my distance. I was a little too handsy with her last night, and I could tell it spooked her.

"Hey," I greet her with a smile. "How's your morning been?"

"It's been great. I spent some time at the theme park, which was fun. There's a restaurant down at the end of the pier that looked nice for lunch."

I know the place she's talking about — a Mexican restaurant that's decent, but there are better places in L.A. to get Mexican food. I gesture to the Bubba Gump Shrimp Co. behind us. "The food's better here, and the view is just as good. But — fair warning — we should decide quickly if you don't want to deal with paparazzi."

Carrie nods, suddenly looking a bit overwhelmed. "Bubba Gump it is, then."

We settle into a table with a view of the ocean, and I can't help but notice how Carrie's eyes keep drifting to the waves. The ocean is one of my favorite parts of living here, and I wonder if its magnetic power is working on her, too, despite what she said last night.

"So, what else did you do this morning?" I ask, trying to keep the conversation light.

She turns back to me, her expression a mix of disappointment and curiosity. "I walked down the Third Street Promenade, but it was kind of sad. So many closed shops."

I nod, remembering how vibrant it used to be. "Yeah, rising rents really killed it. It's a shame."

As our food arrives, I tell her about my meeting, but fans constantly interrupt us asking for autographs and photos. I can see Carrie growing increasingly uncomfortable, picking at her food and avoiding eye contact.

Finally, I decide enough is enough. "I'm sorry, folks, but I'm trying to have lunch with my friend. I appreciate your support, but I'd like some privacy now."

As the last fan walks away, I turn back to Carrie. "I'm so sorry about that. How about we get out of here? I have an idea for a more relaxing afternoon."

She nods, looking relieved. "That sounds great. What did you have in mind?"

"How about Griffith Park? It has an observatory and a zoo, and you can see the Hollywood sign. It'll take about an hour to get there, but I think you'll like it."

Carrie's face lights up. "That sounds perfect."

As we drive through the L.A. traffic, I can't help but steal glances at Carrie. She's looking out the window, taking in the city, and I wonder what she's thinking. Is she enjoying her trip? Or is she counting the hours until she can return to Alpine Ridge?

I'm thrilled to see Carrie's excitement when we arrive at the zoo. As we wander through the exhibits, she's like a kid, her eyes wide with wonder.

"There are so many more animals than I expected," she says, grinning. "Even more than the Woodland Park Zoo in Seattle."

We stop at the elephant exhibit, and I watch as Carrie's face softens. "The elephants were always my favorite at Woodland Park," she explains. "But they closed that exhibit years ago. This is amazing." I stand next to her, watching the gentle creatures spraying themselves and each other with water to keep cool, and I can't help but agree. They're fascinating animals.

As we continue, Carrie coos over the sloths and koalas, but it's the gorillas that truly captivate us both. I am drawn to the glass, making eye contact with one of the massive creatures on the other side. As I mimic its movements, and he does the same, I feel a connection that's hard to explain.

I turn to see Carrie watching me, her expression a mix of awe and something else I can't quite place. "That was beautiful," she says softly.

The look on her face kills me, and I want nothing more than to pull her close and kiss her. But I hold back, reminding myself of the boundaries she's set. Instead, I offer her a smile and suggest we move on to the next exhibit, all the while wondering if I'll ever be able to bridge the gap between us.

But watching Carrie stop and marvel at every animal gives me unexplainable joy. I've never seen an adult so happy at a zoo. And I only get stopped a couple of times for autographs, which Carrie seems to tolerate better here in the open, with the animals to keep her busy.

In fact, her delight is infectious, and seeing the animals through her eyes is a connection I hadn't thought to look for on this outing. She's caring and affectionate in the way some women are with babies, and it tugs at a part of my heart I didn't even know existed. I rein myself in, determined not to think about how Carrie is with babies. Because I know how much she feels and does for others.

Imagining Carrie as a mother? I can't go there, or I'll abandon L.A. without a second thought. Ironically, thinking about why I can't think about it cements my resolve. I'm so done here. Because my heart isn't in it anymore; it belongs to Carrie now.

As the sun begins its descent, I steer her toward the exit, and then we make our way to the Griffith Observatory. The twenty-minute drive is filled with comfortable silence, both of us lost in thought after our zoo experience.

We grab a quick, light dinner at the café before exploring a few exhibits. But the real excitement comes when we join the line for the Zeiss telescopes. As we wait, I can feel Carrie's anticipation building.

When it's her turn, I watch as she peers through the eyepiece. Her gasp of awe is audible, and when she turns back to me, her eyes are wide with wonder.

"It's incredible," she breathes. "I had no idea how much more you could see with one of these. How much more there even *is* out there." She shakes her head. "We're really less than ants in this universe, aren't we?" The observatory's guide smiles patiently, likely having been present for many such humbling revelations.

Having never looked through such a powerful telescope either, I take my turn ... and I'm equally blown away. The vastness of space, the pinpricks of light representing entire worlds ... it's equal parts unbelievably stunning and a stark reminder of our place in the universe, just as Carrie said.

"And remember folks," the guide pipes up. "Many of the stars you see in the night sky will have died before their light makes it to us. So, in a way, what you'll see with the telescope is a snapshot of the past."

Carrie and I share an awed look. And it hits me that we aren't just small and insignificant in the grand scheme of things; our lives are also so fleeting. I stow the observation and its consequences in favor of paying attention to the guide as he continues to explain what we're looking at. I let Carrie take another turn before my time ends, sensing her yearning to get one more look.

After the telescopes, we find a spot on the grass in front of the observatory. As we sit side by side, watching the stars emerge in the darkening sky, I mull over the many deep thoughts the past couple of days have inspired.

Life truly is a miracle in the vastness of the universe. And our individual lives are just a blip on the cosmic radar, too short in the grand scheme to hold meaning on a universal level. All the meaning we have in this life is what we make.

Sure, I make movies that millions of people enjoy. Once that brought meaning to my life. But now? It seems like not enough.

It wasn't until I was back in Alpine Ridge, starting with my brother's wedding, surrounded by my family, that I remembered how meaningful deep connections to others are. That's how acting started for me, too. But the more successful I became, the more difficult it was to connect.

But what I feel for Carrie goes beyond anything I've ever experienced. In the bigger picture, it's miraculous to have found someone who sees me for me, cares for me, and who I've come to crave on a level I didn't even know existed before.

Suddenly, I understand why her buying a townhouse in Alpine Ridge bothers me. It means that if I want to be with her, it needs to be there.

I need Carrie. My universe is dark without her. She's my sun, my guiding star. And I'm off kilter not having her at the center of my universe.

Something shifts inside me, and emotion floods me so fast and hard I have to close my eyes. I'm not going to let go of this connection we've found. I've had a great career, and while it doesn't have to be over for good, I'm willing to set it aside for now. I'm willing to risk it might not be there when I return. As I open my eyes and watch her profile as she stares up at the stars, I can't deny that Carrie means so much more to me. I was just too stubborn to admit it and to make the necessary sacrifices to shift what my world revolved around. I was a fool to think that once I found her, anything could have meaning without her.

I want to tell her all this, to pour my heart out right here under the stars. But I hold back. I want to put everything in place first, to show her with actions, not just words. I want her to know it's not just empty promises or an attempt to get her into bed on her last night here.

Though, God, do I want to take her to bed. It's all I can do not to run my hands over her soft skin. To not lace my fingers through the long, dark hair tumbling down her back. To not lay her back on the grass and cover her body with mine and kiss her senseless.

Instead, I sit and watch her, drinking in the sight of her profile silhouetted against the night sky. "What do you think of L.A. now?" I ask, my voice soft.

She's quiet for a moment, considering. "It's been fun exploring, and it's been good to see you," she begins. "But," she shoots me an apologetic look, "I still feel the same as I did yesterday. L.A. isn't for me. The traffic, the crowds, the noise ... it's all so much. But even if it were, my life, my family is in Alpine Ridge."

Her words both sting and soothe. They confirm what I already knew, but they also reinforce my decision. If Alpine Ridge is where her heart is, then that's where I need to be.

"I didn't ask to see if you'd changed your mind," I clarify. "Just wondering if you saw more of what I saw in it now."

She smiles, her eyes wandering over my face. "There are some wonderful things here," she says, her voice thick. And it's all I can do not to touch her. Because I'm fairly certain she's not talking about the zoo or the stars but about me.

If her seemingly conflicted responses to me this weekend have told me anything, there's a good chance she still cares for me the way I do for her. The temptation to kiss her and test the theory is strong. But I'd rather go for the grand gesture — the all-in moment. If I'm misreading her, and it doesn't work, I'll have no regrets.

We reluctantly decide it's time to leave as the night grows cooler. Like the previous night, I drive her back to her car. But this time, our goodbye feels different. Heavier. More significant.

We embrace, and neither of us seems willing to let go. I breathe in her scent, committing it to memory. When I finally pull back, I gently kiss her forehead. Same as last night, it's the most I can do without losing control.

"Have a good trip, Carrie," I murmur, my voice thick with emotion.

"Goodbye, Evan," she replies softly, her eyes shining in the streetlight. This time, I feel stronger, so I stay and wait for her to get in her rental car.

Watching her drive away, I'm filled with a sense of purpose I haven't felt in years. I know what I need to do. I turn and walk to my car, my mind racing with plans. It's time to make some changes. It won't be easy, but Carrie is worth it. She's worth everything.

CHAPTER THIRTY

CARRIE

The insistent beep of the hotel's alarm clock jolts me awake. For a moment, I'm disoriented, the unfamiliar surroundings throwing me off balance. Then reality sets in — I'm in Los Angeles, and it's time to go home.

I pack my bags methodically, my mind still fuzzy with sleep and the remnants of last night's dreams. Dreams filled with stars, gentle gorilla eyes, and Evan's warm smile. I shake my head, trying to clear the images away.

The drive to the airport is surprisingly smooth for L.A. traffic, though I suppose that's the benefit of an early Sunday morning flight. As I return the rental car, I can't help but feel a sense of relief. No more navigating unfamiliar streets or dealing with the constant traffic.

Once through security, I settle into a seat at my gate, watching as the sun rises over the airport, painting the sky in hues of pink and gold. It's beautiful, I have to admit, but it doesn't stir the same feelings in me as an Alpine Ridge sunrise.

Before I know it, I'm boarding the plane, finding my window seat and buckling in. As we take off, I watch the sprawling metropolis of Los Angeles drop away beneath us. The city seems to stretch on forever, a concrete jungle interspersed with pockets of green and the glittering blue of the Pacific.

I reflect on my whirlwind trip. I'm glad I walked through this open door, as Brandon suggested. The interview was a great experience, even if it didn't pan out. And spending time with Evan ... well, that was both wonderful and heartbreaking in equal measure.

But as the last glimpse of the city disappears beneath the clouds, I realize I'm not sad to be leaving. With its constant noise, endless traffic, and frenetic energy, Los Angeles is truly too hectic for me. I crave the quiet of Alpine Ridge, the sense of community, and the slower pace of life.

So why does it feel like I'm leaving a piece of my heart behind?

As much as I can be in denial sometimes, I know the answer: Evan.

I close my eyes, leaning back in my seat. Despite my best efforts to maintain boundaries, keep things friendly, and nothing more, I can't deny our connection. The way my heart races when he's near, the comfort I feel in his presence, the way he looks at me like I'm the only person in the world.

But I remind myself why we can't be together. The distance, his career, the public scrutiny — nothing has changed. No matter how much my heart aches, my head knows this is for the best.

As the plane levels off and the seat belt sign dings off, I take a deep breath. It's time to focus on the future — my future in Alpine Ridge. I have a new home being built, a job I love, and friends who have become family.

I'm blessed, and it doesn't do any good to focus on what I don't have. If I'm lucky, maybe someday I'll find love, start a family, the works. But for now, I'm going home.

And there's no place like home.

CHAPTER THIRTY-ONE

EVAN

I take a deep breath as I stand outside Rick's office, steeling myself for the conversation ahead. I'm about to tell him I'm exercising the exit clause in my Bond contract, wrapping up my other commitments, and leaving L.A. for the foreseeable future. It's a big move, but after my weekend with Carrie, I know it's right.

Before I can even open my mouth, Rick waves me. "Hey, kid, glad you're here. Sit down. I've got some news," he says flatly.

I settle into the chair across from him. My curiosity is piqued despite myself.

"Got an email from the studio over the weekend," Rick continues, leaning forward. "Looks like your tenure as Bond will conclude with just this one film. They're planning to go in a totally different direction after that. They're thinking about a female Bond if you can believe it."

I blink, taken aback. This isn't at all what I expected.

Rick barrels on, clearly trying to soften the blow. "But don't worry, I've already got other opportunities lined up for you. There's a prime role in a rom-com with one of the hottest directors in the genre. It has a great cast and a very famous female lead. It's perfect for branching out, just like we talked about."

I can't help it. I laugh. The irony of the situation is just too much.

Rick's brow furrows. "What's so funny?"

I shake my head, still chuckling. "I'm glad they canceled my Bond contract, Rick. And I won't be auditioning for the rom-com. Or for anything else, for that matter."

"What are you talking about?"

"I came here to tell you I'm going on indefinite hiatus. I'm focusing on my personal life for a while."

Rick's face darkens. "Are you out of your mind? You can't just walk away now.

If you want to stay big, you need to be here, branching out. I'm not here to wait for actors who can't make up their minds."

I lean back in my chair, suddenly feeling lighter than I have in years. "I have made up my mind, Rick. This is what I want."

"If you do this, I'll drop you as a client," he threatens.

I stand up. "No need. You're fired."

I leave the office, ignoring Rick's spluttering protests behind me. As I step into the elevator, my phone buzzes with notifications from my PR company. My stomach drops as I read the message: pictures of me getting cozy with a mysterious brunette at the zoo have been splashed all over the tabloids this morning. I click the link to see a photo of Carrie and me at the gorilla exhibit, inches apart, staring into each other's eyes.

Fury bubbles up inside me as I read through the piece. They don't know who she is yet, calling her "the Hollywood Playboy's new toy." I know there's not much I can do, but it doesn't make it any easier. All things considered, it could be a lot worse, but I know the speculation has already begun. It's only a matter of time before they figure out who she is and start digging for dirt.

I dial Carrie's number as soon as I'm in my car.

"Hey," she answers, her voice surprisingly calm.

"Carrie, I'm so sorry. I just saw the tabloids. Are you okay?"

There's a pause, and I can almost hear her shrug. "I've seen them. It's not great, but ... honestly? I'm not upset. They didn't even say anything unflattering. Just the usual general B.S."

Her reaction throws me.

"I'm glad, but you should know that it'll just get worse once they find out who you are," I warn her.

"Thanks, but what are they going to do? Report on my boring life as a political consultant? Talk to the like, half dozen people I'd consider friends who would never give them jack shit? Good luck with that."

I snort. "Fair point," I allow. I pause, briefly considering telling her what's happening with my career, but I'm not quite ready. There are still a few more things I need to do. "Let me know if anything changes, all right?"

"Of course," she agrees. "Oh, and Evan?"

"Yeah?"

"Thanks again for everything. This weekend was ... well, it was great seeing you."

My chest aches, and I'm dying to hold this woman. Soon. "It was great seeing you, too, Carrie. I'll talk to you soon."

After we hang up, I respond to my PR company, instructing them not to respond for now but to keep me updated on any developments and to put out the word that I'm looking for a new agent.

I take a deep breath as I put my phone down and start the car. It's been a whirlwind of a morning, but I feel more certain than ever about my decision. The road ahead might be uncertain, but for the first time in a long time, I'm excited about where it might lead.

CHAPTER THIRTY-TWO

CARRIE

Tabloids who? If I didn't care before, I don't have time now as I'm buried in budget proposals for the new property tax levies we plan to introduce to keep funding town growth. As if that wasn't headache enough, I'm interrupted by raised voices near the community center's entrance. Curiosity piqued, I step out of my tiny office to investigate. The scene that greets me makes my blood run cold.

Greg is trying to de-escalate a shouting older couple, and with a jolt of recognition, I realize … it's my parents. Their faces are red with anger as they rant about the changes to Alpine Ridge.

"What the hell have you done to this town?" my father bellows, waving around what appears to be the Sunday edition of the Seattle Post-Intelligencer. Oh. Shit. I'd forgotten they were printing a piece about the development of Alpine Ridge. My eyes flick back to my father's face. The fury etched there tells me they've come for blood. "Dorothy's house is a bed and breakfast now? Who the hell approved that? And what about all this new construction?"

My mother chimes in, her voice shrill, her features just as violently angry. "I've never seen so many cars in town. What exactly is going on here? We demand to know who has allowed all of this … this … *change*."

Greg attempts to explain the community center's temporary use for town offices, but they steamroll right over him. Then their eyes land on me, and all hell breaks loose.

"You!" my father snarls, getting in my face and shaking the newspaper in his fist. "You and your sister are behind this, aren't you? Ruining your grandparents' town!"

I'm frozen, old habits of shrinking away from their anger kicking in. But before I can find my voice, Joanie, Mia, and Nate burst in, followed closely by Arthur and Brandon, finally back from lunch. Thank God.

My parents turn, and their eyes widen. I can tell they're about to unleash their wrath on Mia, but Arthur steps in, his voice calm and authoritative. "Excuse me, sir, ma'am, I'm the mayor and —"

"You stay out of this," my mother snaps, not bothering to look at him. "My daughters will answer for ruining Alpine Ridge. I *know* it's their fault."

Arthur physically steps between my parents and Mia. "Now, folks, there's no need for this. The residents are thrilled with the changes coming to Alpine Ridge. It's not anyone's 'fault' — it's progress."

My mother's eyes narrow dangerously, continuing to ignore him in favor of glaring daggers at Mia. "Our family has been in this town for decades. My mother would be rolling in her grave if she saw what you've done to her home!"

Something inside me snaps. Years of pent-up anger and hurt come rushing to the surface, and suddenly, I find my voice.

"You don't know a damn thing about what Gran would have wanted," I spit out, surprising even myself with the venom in my tone. "You treated her like garbage, just like you treat everyone else. Especially us."

My parents' jaws drop, but I'm not done. "You want to know what Gran wanted? Ask Mia. She was there in Gran's final days — you know, while you were busy disowning a daughter who only wanted her own life and trying to manipulate me into taking sides. You know what? Never mind. I can tell you what she wanted since I'm finally free of your toxic bullshit and don't give a shit about your approval anymore. It was Gran's last wish that Nate and Mia start their businesses and change this town for the better."

It's the first time I've seen my parents rendered speechless, and it empowers me in a way I never could've imagined. I take a step closer, my voice low and dangerous. "So, you can take your opinions and fuck right off. You're not welcome here. You're horrible, miserable people who don't deserve to be part of this amazing community. Neither Mia nor I give a flying rat's ass what you think."

"Me neither," Joanie pipes in. Greg snorts.

"Same here," he adds, wrapping his arm around her waist in solidarity.

My parents start to bluster, but Nate, Greg, and Brandon step up and form a protective wall around me.

Nate's voice is ice cold as he says, "I think it would be best if you left without causing a further scene." He folds his massive arms over his powerful chest, and I've never seen him look so forbidding.

But my mother, ever the instigator, steps forward and points her finger a dangerous few millimeters from his chest. "This is public property and —"

Greg opens his mouth to contradict her, but a new voice beats him to it. "I believe my brother asked you to leave."

We all whirl around to see Evan standing in the doorway, his presence commanding and unmistakable. My parents' eyes widen in recognition, their protests dying on their lips. Nate smirks, and Joanie grins. Everyone else looks like they're holding their breath, waiting to see how my parents react.

"Fine. Ruin this town. Just like you two ruin everything," my mother says imperiously toward Mia and me. And then she turns and leaves, dragging my father behind her.

The sound of the door behind them makes me deflate like a balloon.

In the stunned silence that follows, Mia and Brandon envelop me in a hug. "I'm so proud of you," Mia whispers, her voice thick with emotion.

"You did good, honey," Brandon agrees, rubbing my back gently.

I'm trembling, adrenaline coursing through my veins, but beneath it all, I feel ... proud. So damn proud for standing up for myself, for this town, for the family I've chosen.

My eyes find Evan's across the room. He's looking at me with a mixture of admiration and something else I can't quite name. I offer him a shaky smile, surprised but grateful for his unexpected appearance.

As the others discuss what happened, I only have eyes for Evan. What is he doing here? I mean, I'm glad he's here since his presence clearly helped get rid of my parents. The shock of seeing an A-list celebrity standing up for their traitorous daughters was clearly more than they could handle. I don't know if I should thank him first or ask him why he's here now, less than a week after I saw him last.

One thing I do know is that in this moment of triumph, something has shifted inside of me. I've embraced the strength I never knew I had until recently. Fully and completely. I know I never have to compromise what I need for what someone else wants ever again.

Evan takes a step towards me, and for the first time, I'm not afraid. And the absence of fear ... well, it makes me realize how much I missed him. Not for being apart for only five days. But for being apart in *that* way for all these months. And as he stops in front of me, I have to work hard to remember why I've kept him at arm's length all this time. I have a feeling that also had a lot to do with fear.

CHAPTER THIRTY-THREE

EVAN

The tension in the room is palpable as Carrie's parents storm out. I can see the adrenaline still coursing through Carrie, her body trembling slightly as she's embraced by Mia and Brandon. Pride swells in my chest at her strength and her ability to stand up to people who put her through years of manipulation and abuse.

Carrie's eyes find mine as the others start to disperse, discussing what just happened in hushed tones. She offers me a shaky smile, and I feel my heart skip a beat. I move towards her, drawn by an invisible force I can no longer deny.

"Thank you," she says softly as I approach. "For backing us up."

I shake my head, unable to keep the admiration from my voice. "Carrie, I'm so proud of you. What you just did ... that was incredible."

A blush creeps up her cheeks, but there's a new confidence in her posture that wasn't there before. "Thanks," she murmurs. Then, curiosity overtakes her features. "What are you doing here, Evan?"

I hesitate, glancing around at the others still milling about. "We don't have to talk about it right now. You've been through a lot today. It can wait."

But Carrie shakes her head, determination in her eyes. "No, I want to know. Please."

I take a deep breath, steeling myself. This is it. The moment I've been building towards since I left L.A. "I walked away from Hollywood, Carrie. I'm here to stay."

Her eyes widen in disbelief. "What? But... your career, the Bond film..."

"I'll still have to do some promotion for Bond. It's in my contract. But I'll do only what I absolutely have to, nothing more. And then I'm done. I've got a new agent who understands that's the deal."

Carrie stares at me, her brow furrowed as she processes this information. "But why? Why would you give all that up?"

I can't help but chuckle, remembering our conversation in L.A. "Fuck, Carrie, isn't it obvious?"

A small smile tugs at her lips, and there's a look of understanding in her eyes. But she doesn't let me off the hook. "I need to hear you say it."

I step closer, close enough to see the gray flecks in her blue eyes. "I'm here for *you*, Carrie. This thing between us ... it's more important than anything. More important than fame, more important than Hollywood. I want to see where it goes. If you'll have me."

I watch as a myriad of emotions flicker across her face — surprise, joy, and something that looks a lot like hope. But there's hesitation there, too, and I understand. We've been down this road before, and I know I have a lot to prove.

"Evan, I ..." she starts, her voice barely above a whisper.

"You don't have to say anything right now. This is a lot to take in, especially after what happened with your parents. I'm not going anywhere, Carrie. We have all the time in the world to figure this out."

"I appreciate that, but it's mostly just that ... well, I'm still technically at work right now," she points out.

I shake my head, laughing at myself. "Of course you are. I'm so sorry. I forgot with all the commotion."

She smirks. "How about we meet for dinner when I'm done?"

I nod, relief coursing through me. "Deal. Tavern at six?"

Carrie smiles a real, genuine smile that lights up her entire face. "Count on it."

As I turn to leave, I feel lighter than I have in years. For the first time in a long time, I'm exactly where I'm supposed to be. And no matter what happens next, I know I've made the right choice.

Alpine Ridge is my home now. And Carrie ... well, I hope she'll be my future.

CHAPTER THIRTY-FOUR

CARRIE

I'm still in shock as I watch the clock tick slowly towards quitting time. Evan's declaration echoes in my mind, a constant loop of "I'm here for *you*." It seems too good to be true, and I can't quite shake the nervousness that's settled in my stomach.

As soon as I'm free, I rush home to freshen up before heading to the tavern. Evan's already there when I arrive, looking devastatingly handsome in a simple blue button-down and jeans that tells me he's just as nervous as I am because he freshened up too. He stands as I approach, and I feel a flutter in my chest.

We order food and drinks, then settle into a quiet corner booth. For a moment, we just look at each other, the weight of possibility hanging between us.

Finally, I take a deep breath. "Evan, I want to see where this goes too, but ... we need to take it slow. It's hard to believe you'll just walk away from your career like this."

He nods, understanding in his eyes. "I know it's a lot to take in. What do you want to know?"

"What are you planning to do while you're here?" I ask, curious about how he sees his life in Alpine Ridge.

Evan leans forward, excitement clear in his voice. "I talked to Nate about that this week. He's close to getting back his license to practice medicine. We discussed the possibility of me taking over management of the wellness side of the practice while he expands to include medical and urgent care."

I raise an eyebrow, impressed. "That sounds like a great opportunity. But are you sure it's enough for you?"

He reaches across the table, taking my hand. "I really enjoyed working with Nate when I was here before. And honestly? It feels more fulfilling than anything I've done in Hollywood lately."

I nod, still trying to wrap my head around this new reality. "Where are you going to stay until your house is finished? Surely not with Nate and Mia for months?"

Evan grins. "Actually, I talked to the builder. I'm paying for a night crew, which was an option, given how remote the building site is. We were already ahead of schedule, so the house should be done within the month."

My mind reels. He's really thought of everything. "Wow," I breathe. "You've clearly thought this through. You're serious about this."

"I have and I am," he says, his gaze intense. "I know it's a lot to absorb, but I'm all in, Carrie."

I take a deep breath, feeling something shift inside me. "I've let fear rule me for a long time. I don't want that anymore. You've taken this huge step, and … I think I can take a smaller one."

Hope blooms in Evan's eyes. "What are you saying?"

"I'm saying … let's try again. For real this time."

His smile is radiant, and I feel an answering warmth spread through me. We spend the rest of dinner talking and laughing, the tension from earlier melting away.

As Evan walks me to my car at the end of the evening, there's a new energy between us. He stops, turning to face me, his eyes searching mine. Then, slowly, just like I've wished for and feared at the same time, he leans in and kisses me.

I wrap my arms around his neck, my lips melding with his. For once, he's unhurried, and his kiss is soft and sweet and perfect. Warmth and happiness spread through me as he pulls me close, kissing me until I'm dizzy with everything he makes me feel.

It feels like coming home.

CHAPTER THIRTY-FIVE

EVAN

Being back in Alpine Ridge is everything I needed and more. Nate and I start right in on redesigning the wellness practice for the upcoming changes. Carrie and I take things slowly, which is helped by how busy we both are. Still, we see each other a few times a week, including the weekly game night and Saturday night dinner party, which are even more enjoyable as a couple. Really, just being near her takes years of stress off my shoulders.

Before I know it, the end of the month arrives, and with it, the completion of my new home in Alpine Ridge. I've done the final walkthrough and am ready to show Carrie. To prove that this is all very real. As I drive with her up the winding road to the property, I can't help but feel a mix of excitement and nervousness. This house represents so much more than just a place to live — it symbolizes my commitment to this town, Carrie, and our future together.

We pull up to the house, and I hear Carrie's sharp intake of breath. The modern structure stands proudly against the backdrop of towering pines and rugged mountains. With glass walls everywhere but the garage, it's a mirror to Nate and Mia's house, just larger. It's everything I'd hoped for and more.

"Evan, it's beautiful," Carrie says, her eyes wide with wonder.

I take her hand as we walk through the front door. The interior is even more impressive—open and airy, with floor-to-ceiling windows showcasing the breathtaking views. We move from room to room, Carrie's enthusiasm growing with each new discovery.

"It's huge," she remarks, "but it doesn't feel overwhelming. Whoever designed this really knew what they were doing."

I nod, relief washing over me. "I used Nate's architect, in case that wasn't obvious. I've never seen anything like his ability to make you feel like you're outside when you're inside. It's perfect, isn't it?"

She turns to me, her smile radiant. "It really is. Though it could use some furniture," she adds with a laugh.

I pull her close, wrapping my arms around her waist. "I was hoping you might help me with that. You've got great taste, and I want this to feel like your home, too."

Carrie's eyes soften. "I'd love to help. We can make it cozy and inviting."

As we stand there, surrounded by empty rooms full of possibility, I'm struck by how right this feels. Carrie in my arms, in our home — because that's what I want it to be, ours. But I don't voice that yet. Things have been going so well. I don't want to overwhelm her. And I know we'll get there.

"Come on, I want to show you the deck," I say, pulling her toward the back of the house. I open the glass door, letting her pass through in front of me. And get an eyeful of the view.

She gasps, hands flying to her mouth. "Oh my god," she breathes. She walks to the aluminum-framed glass barrier that serves as railings and leans against it, taking in the full view of the valley floor below us, where you can see the buildings of Alpine Ridge dotted amongst the trees. "It's *beautiful*."

I approach her from behind, wrapping my arms around her. "Not as beautiful as you," I murmur in her ear. I feel a shiver roll through her.

It sends my nervous system haywire. Because this is the first time we've been alone together, given that I've been staying with Nate and Mia, and she's still rooming with Rae while she waits for her townhouse to be finished.

I can tell Carrie is aware of it, too, as she sighs and leans back against my shoulder, her backside squirming against me.

"Careful," I murmur.

She turns in my arms and places her hands on my chest. "Or what?"

I cock an eyebrow. "I think you know what," I respond, leaning in and running my nose up her jawline. She angles her head with a breathy sigh, giving me full access to her neck. Her hand reaches for me, finding the hard length under my jeans. I suck in a sharp breath and pull back. Only to meet her eyes and see that they're filled with fire.

"I'm ready, Evan. You've been more than patient these last few weeks. And as hard as it was to believe … this is all real, isn't it?"

I close my eyes, and my lips part in a sigh as emotion rips through me. "It's real," I confirm, reopening my eyes to gaze back into hers. "And I'm not going anywhere."

We stare at each other for a moment, soaking in this moment. It feels significant. I knew it would be, but the reality is even more intense than I anticipated. It's the culmination of everything I promised her when I came back. Of my own journey in realizing what's important in life. And for me? It's only Carrie. Always Carrie.

Then, like a tether has snapped, Carrie launches herself at me. Her arms wrap around my neck, and our lips meet, hot and hard. Her tongue sweeps into my mouth as her hands explore my chest, my arms, my back. I don't know where this confident vixen came from, but in an instant, I'm aching from her touch, her kiss.

In a flash of inspiration, I turn my back to the view, sinking down against the glass as I pull her with me. So she can fully enjoy the view while I fully enjoy her. She settles on my lap, her mouth never parting from mine. I match her energy, exploring her mouth with my tongue and running my hands under the crop top she's wearing, teasing at the clasp of her bra.

"Do it," she says against my lips, circling her hips over mine in a grind that sends sensation shooting through me.

"Fuck, Carrie," I groan. She's so sexy this way I can barely stand it. I do as she says, unclasping her bra and shoving it, along with her shirt, up over her breasts, baring them to the warm summer air. I lean in and take one of her nipples in my mouth as I pinch the other. She arches into me, causing her hot center to press harder against mine. I glance down and note that her pencil skirt is now bunched around her waist.

"Sex with a view," she muses, smirking down at me. "I could get used to this."

I lose all my words at the idea of taking each other right here. I reach up, pulling her mouth back to mine. Our lips work together with renewed enthusiasm as Carrie reaches between us, unbuttoning my jeans and freeing my cock.

"I don't have protection," I say, swearing internally. I did not expect this at all.

"We don't need it," she replies. "You know I'm on the pill."

I nod. "And there hasn't been anyone else for me since I met you, Carrie. There isn't anyone else for me but you."

She bites her lip, and her eyes take on a glassy sheen. "And there isn't anyone else for me but you," she echoes, shifting upward.

I reach between her legs, moving her panties to the side and feeling the slickness there. My cock aches, knowing how ready she is. I position her over me, and she sinks down.

We both groan as I fill her, as she stretches around me.

I take her nipple in my mouth, grasping her backside with both hands and encouraging her as she starts to move on top of me. Her eyes lock onto mine as her whimpers become more desperate, so I move my mouth to hers. Her lips are feverish, her tongue devouring. It's almost too much, and I pull back, afraid that kissing her while she fucks me will push me over the edge too soon.

Though even just watching her take her pleasure has me hanging on that edge. Normally, I like to be the one in control, but between Carrie initiating this and seeing her own her confidence, this may be the sexiest and most intimate moment of my life.

"Fuck, Carrie, you are the most beautiful thing I've ever seen," I tell her. Her lips tilt up, followed quickly by her brows bunching together. And I know she's close. I move both hands to her breasts, kneading, pinching, and pulling. "Come on, baby. Come for me."

Carrie whimpers and her hips grind against my own in a slick, hard rhythm that has her clenching around me in seconds. I drop my hands to her hips as her pace stutters, as the edges of my vision go white, rubbing her center over me until we're both crying out in orgasm.

Carrie collapses into me, her head resting on my shoulder. I run my hands up and down her back lightly as I come down from the high.

Even after the intensity of my orgasm has faded, with Carrie nestled in my arms, I feel a sense of peace and satisfaction that I've never known before.

In my sex-addled state, the truth becomes startlingly clear.

This is home.

This is where I belong.

465

CHAPTER THIRTY-SIX

CARRIE

The last few weeks have been some of the best of my life. Evan and I have shopped relentlessly to fill his glass mansion and promptly christened every piece of furniture delivered. Despite the constant distraction, it's coming along and starting to feel like a home.

Work has also been busy, but we're making huge leaps toward establishing town services, and it's the most satisfying feeling. I feel useful, and I can't wait to see the town become all that I know it can be.

All in all, life is good.

And it's about to get even better since I just picked up the keys to my newly finished townhouse and immediately dragged Evan with me to check it out.

I can hardly contain my excitement as I unlock the door. Evan stands beside me, his presence a comforting warmth in the cooling late September air.

As we step inside, I'm struck by the newness of it all — the fresh paint smell, the plush and freshly cleaned carpets, the blank canvas waiting for me to make it my own. Mine. The first place that's truly my own. I haven't missed Evan's hints that he'd love having me live with him, but I needed to cement my newfound confidence by living on my own for a while.

"It's *perfect*," I breathe, practically giddy.

"I'm glad you're happy with it," Evan says from the living room, where he peers out the window. "It's a great location. Your value will skyrocket as everything gets built up around you."

I huff a laugh and shake my head. He can be practical, but me? I'm daydreaming of homey touches, cozy fires, and happy nights spent cooking and making love.

As I walk through the gleaming kitchen, I run a hand lovingly over the quartz counters and glance out the big, wide window over the sink. It lets in plenty of light and has views of the tops of the trees surrounding us.

With a happy sigh, I turn to find Evan giving me a mischievous grin. I roll my eyes, instantly understanding where his head it at. "You probably associate new houses with *special* celebrations now, don't you?"

He chuckles, a warm smile spreading across his face. "That's not exactly what I had in mind, but I'm game if that's what you want."

My eyebrows rise in curiosity. Because I do want that, but the implication that he had something else in mind intrigues me. "Oh? What exactly did you have in mind, then?"

Evan takes a deep breath, his expression turning serious. "I was planning to tell you how proud I am of you, Carrie. How amazing these last few weeks have been."

My smile softens, but then I notice the hesitation in his eyes. "And?"

He sighs, approaching and pulling me into his arms, stroking a hand over my back. "And ... I just heard from my manager that the Bond press tour is starting a bit earlier than planned, and I'll be gone for an extra week."

"When do you leave?" I ask, my voice quiet as disappointment settles in my chest. Even though I knew this was coming, having it moved up means less time before I have to let him go.

"Sunday," he replies, watching my face carefully.

I nod, understanding but unable to hide my disappointment. Two days. "That's soon. But ... you've gotta do what you've gotta do." I shrug, trying to act as if I'm okay with it.

"I know, but I'm still sorry," Evan says, moving his hands to cup my face. "There's something else I wanted to tell you."

I look up at him expectantly, my heart racing, unsure whether it's a good something or a bad something. "What is it?"

Evan's eyes lock with mine. "I love you, Carrie," he says, his voice filled with emotion.

For a moment, I'm speechless. Then, joy bubbles up inside me, spreading through my body like warm sunshine. I knew he cared. And I knew long ago that I'd fallen for him despite trying to deny it. But to know he feels the same ... it takes the sting off his announcement. But mostly, it allows me not to be afraid to admit what I know I feel.

I bite my lip, looking up into his warm, hazel eyes. "I love you too, Evan."

He grins and kisses me so tenderly it makes my heart ache. The thought of Evan leaving for three weeks still stings, but now it's tempered by the knowledge that he loves me — that we love each other.

Still, I'm nervous about this separation. The anxious part of me wonders if he'll be reminded how much he left behind. How exciting it is to be in the spotlight, adored by millions. But he's given me no reason to doubt him these past couple of months and every reason to trust that what we have is more important than what he gave up.

Even so, this will be our first test as a couple. And part of me is terrified that this has all been too good to be true. But as I pull him into the brightly lit living room with soft, cushy carpets and let him make love to me in my new home — because all joking aside, I can't resist this man — it's hard to think of anything but how right I feel in his arms.

CHAPTER THIRTY-SEVEN

EVAN

The juxtaposition of centuries-old architecture and the bright lights of the Parisian red carpet is a familiar sight, but this time, it feels different. As I go through interview after interview ahead of the French release of my Bond film, I find myself genuinely enjoying the experience. Knowing it's my last major promotional tour for a while adds a bittersweet quality to each moment.

After another long day, I finally make it back to my hotel room. I pull out my phone and dial Carrie's number without even bothering to take off my suit jacket. Her voice, when she answers, instantly soothes the weariness from my bones.

"Hey, you," she says, and I can hear the smile in her voice.

"Hey yourself," I reply, sinking onto the plush hotel bed as I undo my bowtie. "God, it's good to hear your voice."

We catch up on our days, Carrie filling me in on the latest developments in Alpine Ridge. I share some stories from the press tour, including a particularly funny moment when a French journalist's translation went hilariously wrong.

"Oh, and then a British interviewer asked me an interesting question."

"Yeah? What?"

"She asked what my favorite unscripted moment was. You know, the stuff actors ad-lib that ends up in the movie," I explain.

"I get what you mean. What did you say?"

"Something that my agent is going to kill me for," I admit. "I know the interviewer was talking about the movie, but I said that my favorite unscripted moment was when I quit Hollywood. That this would be my last movie for the foreseeable future."

Carrie gasps, "You *didn't*."

I laugh. "Totally did. And I don't regret it. But it's true, even more than I realized at the moment. I've always been fed lines. For movies, interviews, red carpets … my whole career has been scripted. But the best things in my life have been unscripted. Quitting acting. And falling in love with you. I never saw either coming."

"Oh, Evan," Carrie says, her voice thick with emotion. "You know what? I feel that way too. I mean, I'm not an actor, but I let other people tell me what to do, think, and say for so long. Living unscripted has been a gift. For us both." She pauses. "Has your agent ripped you a new one yet?"

I snort. "I wish that's all she did," I reply. "She told me I owed her for dropping that bomb when and how I did. She also told me that I shouldn't write my career off completely and, as my penance, she wants me to agree to read scripts in the future that fit the exact roles I'd like to play. To consider coming back for the right project."

There's a pause on the other end of the line. "What did you tell her?" Carrie asks, curiosity evident in her tone, though I can hear her hesitancy, too.

I chuckle. "I told her I'd have to talk to my girlfriend about it."

Carrie's laughter fills the line, warming my heart. "I have to say," she admits, "this is all going more smoothly than I expected, so ... maybe? I mean, I didn't expect you to call this much. Not that I'm complaining."

"Is it too much?" I ask, suddenly worried.

"No, not at all," she assures me quickly. "We don't talk every day, but every two or three days feels just right. Somehow, I feel closer to you for it. I guess absence really does make the heart grow fonder."

I feel a weight lift off my chest. "I'm glad to hear that. I miss you like crazy, but knowing we're making this work, even though I know you weren't thrilled ... it means everything, Carrie."

"I miss you too," she says softly. "And you know what? If you only had to do this every so often, I think that would be okay. But it's up to you if you want to stay connected to that world."

I consider her words carefully. "It's an intriguing idea," I admit. "But for right now, I'll be happy to be done with this and be with you without having to leave again for a while."

"I know, me too," Carrie says, and I can hear the understanding in her voice.

We talk for a while longer, neither of us wanting to hang up. Finally, regretfully, I glance at the clock. "I should probably get some sleep. Early call time tomorrow."

"Of course," Carrie says. "Go get some rest, superstar."

I laugh at the nickname. "I love you, Carrie. I'll be home soon."

"I can't wait," she replies softly. "I love you too. Goodnight, Evan."

As I hang up the phone, I'm struck by how different this feels from any other press tour I've done. The excitement of the Bond premiere, the thrill of the interviews — it's all there. But now, there's something more. *Someone* more, as it were.

For the first time in my career, I'm not looking forward to the next big thing. I'm looking forward to going home.

With a contented sigh, I finally shrug off my jacket and prepare for bed. Tomorrow's another day of interviews and photo shoots, but now, each day brings me one step closer to home. To Carrie. And that gives every move I make, every word I say more purpose.

I grin at the realization that I had to walk away from something I thought would give my life meaning to find what truly means something: the love of an amazing woman and the support of people who don't measure my worth by my performance at the box office — proving that sometimes the path you take isn't the path you're meant to stay on. Sometimes unscripted is the way to go in life and love. Because I know now, deep in my bones, the only path for me is the one that leads back to Carrie. To Alpine Ridge. To the life we're building together.

EPILOGUE

CARRIE

Alpine Ridge is a winter wonderland draped in a pristine layer of snow that sparkles under the mild December sun. Thanks to our resident snowplow hero, who has formalized his role, much of the town is accessible despite the heavy snowfall. It's perfect timing since today is Greg and Joanie's wedding day.

The community center, recently returned to Greg's care after completing the new town hall, buzzes with activity. Rae, as usual, takes charge of the decorations and catering, while Mia, Brandon, and I assist where we can.

"You know, Rae," I tease as we hang fairy lights, "you might have a future as the town's official wedding planner. First Mia, now Joanie ..."

Rae chuckles. "Oh, honey, I've done way more weddings than that. Back in the day, my Grams used to cater weddings at the Alpine Ridge Chapel. My momma and I would help with the decorations."

The room falls silent. "Wait," Brandon says, voicing what we're all thinking, "You're telling me there used to be a church here?"

Rae's smile fades slightly. "Sure am. But it burned down when I was sixteen. There wasn't money to rebuild." Her tone makes it clear she doesn't want to discuss it further, so I quickly change the subject, and the conversation moves swiftly on as we finish our work.

But, as we put the final touches on the reception area, Joanie joins us, looking gorgeous in a simple white silk sheath wedding dress that clings to her every curve.

"Damn, Rae, you're good at this. Remind me why you haven't been snapped up for your own wedding yet?" she asks in classic blunt-Joanie style.

It's the first time I've seen Rae's good humor falter.

"Not everyone's cut out for marriage," she says quietly. "But I'm happy for you and Greg."

Joanie looks chagrined for the first time since I've known her. She puts a hand on Rae's arm. "I'm sorry, Rae. I didn't mean to upset you. That was tactless of me."

Mia and I exchange an incredulous look.

Rae's whole demeanor shifts. "Oh, sugar, don't you worry about me. Go on, enjoy yourself while we finish up here." And off she bustles to do … well, I'm not sure what since we're basically ready for the ceremony.

Joanie slips on a white fur stole and loops her arm in Greg's. He's wearing an all-white suit and tie that, as a pair, makes them look like the King and Queen of Winter. Surprising no one, Joanie unconventionally requested that all the guests wear white as well, which makes sense now as we make our way to the field behind the community center for the ceremony. It's where Joanie and Greg first started falling in love during the Winter Festival two years ago. And with us all matching the snow, it's a romantic ode to winter, to be sure.

Without Dylan here to officiate, this time, Nate has gotten internet ordained. He handles the ceremony, which is short, by necessity, given the temperature, and intimate, much like Nate and Mia's wedding. In addition to our core group, Joanie's parents, the town council, and some other townspeople have gathered to celebrate. It warms my heart to see how everyone has accepted Evan, treating him like any other resident, now that the shock of having a celebrity in our midst has worn off.

Though short, the ceremony is sweet, if a bit steamier than I'm used to when it comes to the kiss. But that's Joanie and Greg for you — passionate in everything they do.

Afterward, at the reception, Evan and I sway gently to the music.

"You know," he says softly, "I was wondering if you've ever thought about moving in with me?"

I smile, noting his careful phrasing. "I have," I admit. "But … would you be upset if I said I'm not quite ready yet?"

His embrace tightens slightly. "Not at all. I don't want to pressure you. I love you, Carrie, and I see us growing old together. So, I guess it doesn't matter when you move in if we've got forever, right?"

Tears prick at my eyes. "Right," I whisper. "We've always done things on our own timeline, haven't we?"

Evan settles his forehead against mine. "We have. But you're it for me, Carrie. Always."

I close my eyes, a tear of happiness escaping down my cheek. "Promise?" I ask.

He slides a finger under my chin, forcing me to open my eyes and look at him. "With everything I am. And when you're ready, I'll say it with a ring, a wedding, kids, and whatever else makes you happy. I want it all with you, Carrie."

I bite into my bottom lip. It all still feels too good to be true. But I'd be lying to myself if I didn't admit I felt the same.

"I want all of that with you too, Evan. But don't wait forever."

He chuckles and leans in, kissing me gently. "I won't. But for now, I want to dance with you. Then take you home — yours or mine, I don't care — and make love to you." He doesn't even let me respond, his lips covering mine once more until I'm afraid we're the ones who are pushing the limits of how steamy it's okay to get at a wedding.

We break apart, breathless and happy. And as we continue to dance, surrounded by our friends and the twinkling lights, I'm filled with love and contentment.

Alpine Ridge has become more than just a town — it's become a home, a community, and a future for both of us. And with Evan by my side, I know that whatever challenges come our way, we'll face them together.

In this moment, watching Greg twirl Joanie across the dance floor, seeing Mia lean her head on Nate's shoulder, feeling Evan's steady heartbeat against my cheek, I know one thing for certain: love, in all its forms, is what makes a place truly special. And Alpine Ridge? It's brimming with love.

ELUSIVE LOVE

A SMALL-TOWN SECOND CHANCE SINGLE
DAD ROMANCE

CONTENT WARNING

Elusive Love is a small-town second chance single dad romance novel that includes elements that might not be suitable for some readers, including the use of profanity, open-door sex scenes, and other potentially sensitive topics. Visit https://melanieasmithauthor.com/elulcw.html for a full list (warning: may include spoilers).

PROLOGUE

RAE

The snow-covered fields around the Alpine Ridge community center sparkle under the December sun as I bustle around inside, readying everything for Greg and Joanie's wedding reception. I've always enjoyed decorating for special occasions, a skill I discovered helping my Grams with weddings back in the day. She may have owned the bakery, but she took care of everything for weddings in town — food, flowers, décor, music — and loved every minute.

Weddings bring more complicated emotions for me, so it's a bittersweet nostalgia that tugs at my heart today.

Still, the mood is lighthearted, as it should be. And as I hang fairy lights with Carrie, she teases, "You know, Rae, you might have a future as the town's official wedding planner. First Mia, now Joanie ..." Mia, Carrie's sister, smirks from where she's adding white winter roses to the cake our bakery made for the wedding.

I give a small good-natured laugh, but the sting of memories burns deep at her words. "Oh, honey, I've done way more weddings than that. Back in the day, my Grams used to cater weddings at the Alpine Ridge Chapel. My momma and I would help with the decorations."

Carrie, Mia, and Brandon all stop helping hang decorations and stare at me, jaws dropped.

Then Brandon voices what they're all thinking, "Wait, you're telling me there used to be a church here?" While Brandon recently returned to Alpine Ridge after a dozen years away, he grew up here. So, I expect the knowledge is even more shocking to him. But the church was before his time. If only just.

The smile drops off my face as I recall the day the church burned down, and the fallout that meant losing my dreams of marrying the love of my life. I internalize a sigh and shove all the emotions back down.

"Sure am. But it burned down when I was sixteen. There wasn't money to rebuild," I explain matter-of-factly.

Carrie, using her diplomatic skills hard-earned while running Alpine Ridge's town elections, changes the subject, clearly seeing my desire not to dwell on the past, and they talk about everything that's left to do.

Joanie joins us just as we're finishing up, radiant in her white silk dress, her dark hair tumbling down her back in sleek waves. "Damn, Rae, you're good at this. Remind me why you haven't been snapped up for your own wedding yet?" she quips.

Her words hit me like a punch to the gut. Not because they remind me of the wedding I wanted, the one I was just reminded of. No, they remind me of the wedding I got. Which was much shabbier and to the wrong man. As evidenced by my subsequent failed marriage.

Still, I know she meant no harm. She's just blunt and forward by nature, which I'm sure doesn't hurt when you're a lawyer.

I force a smile and respond as honestly as I can. "Not everyone's cut out for marriage. But I'm happy for you and Greg."

Joanie, uncharacteristically chagrined, apologizes for her tactlessness. I brush it off, not wanting to dampen the mood on her special day.

Thankfully, there's no time to dwell on it. As the ceremony begins in the frigid, snowy field outside, I watch Greg and Joanie, king and queen of winter in their white formal wear, exchange vows, their love for each other palpable. While Joanie is a more recent addition to the town, Greg has lived here for several years and, having run the community center, he's connected with so many people in town, me included. So, it's good to see him overwhelmed with happiness.

It's infectious, really, and, for a moment, I allow myself to imagine what could have been — a life with my high school sweetheart, a simple but happy home, children of our own. But I quickly push those thoughts aside. That ship sailed long ago. And it was a dream I never could've achieved for so many reasons.

At the reception, as couples sway on the dance floor, I busy myself with serving drinks and food. Though I can't help but overhear snippets of Carrie's conversation with her movie star boyfriend, who also happens to be Mia's brother-in-law. Their talk of moving in together and promises of forever send a pang of envy through me, followed immediately by guilt. They deserve happiness, and I truly wish them well.

I see Nate and Mia on the other side of the room, their eyes locked as they move in perfect unison. Husband and wife. It's a catching condition in Alpine Ridge these days. I'm happy for them, too.

For all of them. Truly.

As the night winds down, I find myself lost in thought, memories of the past mingling with the joy of the present. Alpine Ridge has seen me through my highest highs and lowest lows. It's a place of love and loss, of painful endings and new beginnings.

But as I watch my friends — my chosen family — celebrate and support each other, I realize that this town, with all its heavy history, is still full of love and light. And there's hope in that thought that carries me through the darkness that's tugging at my heart.

CHAPTER ONE

RAE

TWO MONTHS LATER

The scent of freshly baked pie wafts through the bakery as I wipe down the counter for what feels like the hundredth time this afternoon. It's slow, which isn't unusual at this time of day. With Alpine Ridge getting more traffic these days, most folks come in first thing in the morning to snap up Mia's most popular goodies. But that makes for a boring closing shift and gives me too much time to think about the visit to my momma I have planned later and the pile of laundry waiting for me at home afterward.

The bell above the door chimes, and I look up, ready to paste on my best customer service smile. But as soon as I see who it is, the smile dies on my lips.

Jerry.

The crusty old bastard I worked for most of my life until Mia came along with a better offer. We've got history, Jerry and I, but it's at best lukewarm. And at worst … well, I try not to think about that.

Either way, I sure don't miss his grimy tavern, and I don't miss Jerry.

His eyes move around the tables, checking to see who's here. In his usual plaid shirt and faded jeans, he looks as out of place in Mia's cheerful bakery as a vulture at a garden party.

Without a word, I turn on my heel and march into the back room, where Mia is pulling the pie I smelled earlier out of the oven.

"Am I allowed to refuse service to people?" I ask, my voice tight.

Mia raises an eyebrow and purses her lips, setting the tray on the cooling rack. "To who? Why?"

"Jerry," I reply without further explanation. She knows why. Partially, at least. Enough, anyway.

Mia's expression softens into a knowing, sympathetic grimace. "No need. I can serve him. Or …" She chews on her lip. Nervous as to what she has in that devious, intelligent mind of hers, I pop my hands on my hips and look at her expectantly. "Or you could just have it out with him. Alpine Ridge is a small town, Rae. You can't avoid him forever."

I blink, surprised. "You're telling me I can give him a piece of my mind? Even though he's a customer?"

Mia shrugs. "Why not? You've been holding onto this anger for a while now. It might do you some good to let it out. If he doesn't like it, he can go buy prepackaged pastries at the grocery store."

A slow smile spreads across my face. And not just because, after striking a deal recently with the owner, said prepackaged pastries are also from Mia's bakery, so she gets his money either way. But because she's got a point. It's about damn time I let him know what I think of his latest bullshit. I'm not sure why I held back so long, now that she's pointed it out. Especially now that I'm being encouraged to do it.

"You know what? You're right. Thanks, sugar."

She sets the pie on a cooling rack and gives me a teasing salute.

I march back out to the front, squaring my shoulders as I approach the counter where Jerry stands, examining the pastry case with feigned interest.

"Well, well, well," I drawl, crossing my arms. "Look what the cat dragged in."

Jerry's head snaps up, his bushy eyebrows rising in surprise.

"You've got some nerve showing up here," I continue, not allowing him to speak. "After lying to me and everyone else in this town, pretending to be on a town council that didn't even exist yet. And then you had the audacity to run for mayor. Now you waltz in here like nothing happened?"

Jerry's weather-beaten face creases into a frown. "Now, Rachel Lynn Donovan—"

"Don't you full name me, Jeremiah James Allen," I cut him off, shaking my head. Honestly, what kind of parent gives their child three first names? "And I wasn't finished. You know what really gets me? That you had the balls to come in here at all. Did you think we'd forgotten? And don't even get me started on the petition signatures that were stolen. I *know* you had something to do with that."

To my surprise, Jerry's shoulders slump. "I didn't come here to cause trouble, Rae. I came to apologize."

I fold my arms over my chest and fix him with a skeptical look. "Apologize? You?"

He nods, his eyes meeting mine. "You were the best bartender and server I ever had — a loyal employee." I scoff. Of course Jerry only thinks of me as an employee. Even after all these years. But he continues, undeterred by my obvious disdain. "I shouldn't have tricked you or anyone else like that. I understand why people didn't want me as mayor." He lets out a breath. "And I swear, I didn't steal the signatures. But … I may know who did." He huffs out a defeated sigh.

My eyebrows fly up, not having expected him to admit anything. "And?" I prompt.

He fidgets, avoiding my gaze. "Look, I'm not here to go throwing anyone else under the bus. Let's just say it was someone who thought it would impress me." His eyes meet mine. "And it most certainly did not. I'm real sorry it came to that, and I'm glad the town is getting what it needs now, even if I'm not in charge."

I stare at him, waiting for the punchline. When it doesn't come, I narrow my eyes. "Are you pulling my leg?"

"No, I'm not," Jerry says, his voice gruff but sincere. "I know we've had some bad blood in the past, but I'm too old for that kind of shit anymore." He looks up at the ceiling. "I'm sorry, Rae."

I blow out a disbelieving breath. "Well … all right then, I forgive you, I guess." I furrow my brow, still skeptical. Jerry has *never* apologized, despite having done far worse.

He nods contritely. "Good." He pauses, as if hesitant to go on before doing exactly that. "I … was also hoping to speak to Mia about selling her pastries at the tavern. People … well, they miss having your huckleberry pie after a meal."

Ah. There it is.

Jerry is eating crow so people can eat my pie, or my Great Grams's pie, as it were. Though as false as his apology now seems, I have to admit I'm glad he's at least willing to cop to his mistakes. Even if he only did it to shut people up about the pie. It's more than I would've thought him capable of, anyway.

I take a deep breath, letting some of the tension ease from my shoulders. "Well, I'll be damned. I never thought I'd see the day Jerry Allen apologized."

A ghost of a smile flickers across Jerry's face. "Yeah, well, don't get used to it."

I snort. "Wouldn't dream of it." I jerk my thumb towards the back. "I'll go get Mia for you."

As I head to the back room once again, I can't help but shake my head. Miracles really happen. If only they could erase more than some stupid political bullshit. Because despite his apology, I was only partially mad because of his latest stunt. All the ones before? Well, I may forgive, but I don't forget.

By the time my shift ends, all I want is to go home and collapse into bed. But it's Sunday, which means my standing date with Momma.

I swing by the grocery store, still not used to how much nicer it is since the renovation last fall, picking up the usual supplies — TV dinners (because Lord knows Momma won't cook for herself), some fresh fruit (which I'll probably end up eating myself next week before it goes bad), dinner fixings, and a box of her favorite tea.

The drive to Momma's little house on the outskirts of town is as familiar as breathing. I pull into the cracked driveway, noting it needs shoveling and salting again. Driving on it is nothing my Bronco can't handle, but if Momma needs to go out, her old Toyota Corolla isn't going to be able to. Add that to the list of things to take care of next week. Thankfully, it's almost March, so winter will be on its way out soon.

"Momma?" I call as I let myself in. "It's me."

"In here, sugar," comes the reply from the living room.

I find her in her usual spot, curled up in her recliner with a romance novel in her lap. Pamela Donovan might be pushing seventy, but she still has a girlish glint in her eye when it comes to her bodice rippers. I cast a quick eye over the shabby furniture, noting that the crocheted blanket covering her chair could use a washing. But not much else has changed. It all still looks the same as it has my whole life, seventies pinks and browns and all.

"How are you feeling today?" I ask, bending to kiss her cheek.

"Oh, same old, same old," she says. "How was work?"

As I bustle around the kitchen, putting away groceries and starting dinner, I fill her in on the day's events, including Jerry's surprise visit.

"Well, I'll be," Momma says, shaking her head. "Wonders never cease."

"Indeed," I agree. "Oh, and they fixed that pothole on Main Street. The new transportation department is getting things done. I hear tell they're working on setting up police and fire departments next."

"Never thought I'd see this place come back to life," Momma remarks, setting aside her book to set the table, as usual.

"Me neither, but I'm proud to be a part of it," I respond. Even though Joanie did most of the work on the incorporation paperwork, and Carrie handled the election process, it was nice to be part of the team, organizing events and having a say in how it all came together. And though the rest of it is out of my hands now, it's still exciting to see our efforts pay off as our tiny town gets the services it has so desperately needed for years.

We eat dinner together — a simple meal of grilled chicken, rice, and vegetables, with enough leftovers to last her until my next visit. As I tidy up the house, Momma settles back into her chair, flipping on the TV to reruns of her favorite game show.

I join her on the couch, handing over a plastic container of her favorite peach crumble, leftover from the bakery. As I dive into my portion, my mind drifts as Alex Trebek's voice fills the room. It has been an almost typical day save Jerry's abrupt change of heart. But I'm pleased with all the positive changes that came with the town's incorporation. And I'm glad Jerry came to his senses so I could bury that particular hatchet with the old bastard. I can't say I respect him after everything we've been through, and especially all those years of pretending to be something he wasn't just for a power trip, but at least we'll be able to be civil to each other from now on. Hell, we've found our way around worse over the years.

Once Momma falls asleep in her chair, I do a final cleanup, gently kiss her forehead, and cover her with a blanket. Then I head back to my house just off the other end of Main Street.

I open the door to darkness. But even with the lights on, the small two-bedroom home feels empty and forlorn. It's cozy enough, I suppose, with its mismatched thrifted furniture and colorful, though cheaply framed art hanging on the walls, but I sure miss having Carrie living here. She wasn't here long, but we became close. But she's happy in one of the new townhouses Greg's cousin built last year, and it's probably best she's got her own place now that she and Evan are together. Lord knows I don't need the constant reminder of what good sex sounds like.

I sigh, setting my things down and collecting all the laundry of the past week, dumping it into the ancient washer, and starting it up. A step I always forget before leaving for work. Now I'll be up late.

Resigned, I settle onto my old saggy couch and grab the fantasy book I'm reading. Momma may like her romance, but I prefer to disappear into another world for a while. Give me epic heroes, impossible quests, and mythical creatures. But then, both take you into their own worlds, I suppose. I just like being as far away from reality as possible. Somewhere I don't have to pretend that watching everyone around me find love and settle down doesn't hurt.

Who knew it was possible to be bursting with happiness for someone else's joy and desperately sad and lonely at the same time? But that's me and my big old soft heart. Too many emotions for my own good sometimes. But we can't all get swept off our feet like Mia, and her handsome doctor with the body of a fitness model. Or like Joanie with her rugged secret millionaire. Or like Carrie, with her famous movie star boyfriend who gave up his glamorous life to be with her.

But I'm forty-six, and I've been through the wringer a time or three, and I know not everyone gets their happy ending. Even if there were any men for me in Alpine Ridge — which, after having lived here most of my life, I can definitely say there are not — I've been through enough to know that not everyone finds their soulmate. My ex-husband sure wasn't mine. And my father left my momma. She's the best woman I know. Loving, beautiful in her day, beautiful *still*, inside and out. If she can't make it work, there truly are no guarantees in this life. Though it's not like mine is bad.

I've got Momma, a group of friends I love, and my own interests that I'm free to pursue. Most of the time, I'm content. But sometimes, despite knowing how wrong things can go, I just want … more. So apparently, I'm also a glutton for punishment.

CHAPTER TWO

LUKE

Being back in Alpine Ridge after thirty years away is a trip, to say the least. As I drive down Main Street, I'm hit with a wave of nostalgia so strong it nearly knocks the wind out of me. The bones of the town I remember are there — the old buildings, the layout — but there's a freshness to it all. Fresh paint, new businesses, new life.

When I left, being in Alpine Ridge was the source of all my family's problems. And now it may be the answer to them. I've been pushing to get the fire chief position in my South Seattle fire station for years. Despite proving myself in the field and being more than qualified, it's eluded me anywhere in the Seattle area, even with station hopping over the years. On top of which, my twelve-year-old daughter, Zoe, has been struggling in school. I've been wanting to pull her out and homeschool her for a while and get her somewhere a little more mellow.

And as much as my exit from Alpine Ridge was a mess, my childhood here was pretty good. At least, I enjoyed being able to roam and explore as I pleased. And I know Zoe will, too. So, this opportunity to transition out of my stressful role as assistant fire chief and help Alpine Ridge establish its first-ever fire department is a great one. It's a long time coming for both me and the town. I will work, but at a much slower pace for at least a year before the department is established. And even once it is, I doubt it'll be as hectic as my current job. Even if it is, it's an opportunity I couldn't pass up. It means so much more to me than a title, in ways I'm not ready to face just yet. One thing at a time.

I park in front of the newly constructed town hall, a modern building that stands out among the older structures. Inside, I'm directed to a conference room where I find two people waiting for me: an older gentleman with a kind face who I assume is the mayor, and a striking young brunette.

"Mr. McMillan," the older man says, standing to shake my hand. "I'm Arthur

Burton, the mayor. And this is Carrie Anderson, our city planner. We conducted your phone interview. It's a pleasure to meet you in person."

I shake both their hands, noting the warmth in Carrie's smile. "Please, call me Luke," I say, though there's something familiar about Arthur that tells me we've probably met before, back when I was a kid. I imagine I'm going to have a lot of that feeling as I settle in here, seeing people who I knew as a child but whose faces have changed over the years.

It makes me think of one particular face I'd like to see soon.

Focusing back to the present, I follow their lead, and we take our seats. Arthur recaps our discussion from my interview the previous week. Carrie chimes in with details about the proposed location for the fire station, showing me land surveys of the selected parcel.

"As we explained," Arthur says, "you'll be overseeing the design and build of the station itself, then take on the active role of fire chief once we're up and running. The county will be involved, letting us know our minimum requirements for building, equipment, and staffing, but otherwise, everything will be at your discretion."

I nod, having already mentioned that I've witnessed this process before, though not in a role of leadership. I'm practically itching to take the reins.

Carrie slides a folder across the table to me. "This outlines the compensation package we can provide during the planning stages, and then once the department is operational."

I flip through the paperwork, nodding as I go. It's all in line with what we'd discussed before, and honestly, it's more than fair given the cost of living here compared to Seattle.

"This all works for me," I say, looking up at them both. "I'm honored to be back in Alpine Ridge and to oversee the creation of such an important part of its infrastructure."

Arthur beams, pulling out a pen and sliding it across the table along with a contract. "Then let's make it official."

I sign on the dotted line, feeling a mix of excitement and trepidation. This is really happening.

After we wrap up the meeting, I head out to check on my old family home. My dad put it in my name during the divorce from my mom all those years ago, and even though we haven't spoken since not long after, I know he'd never come back here. Given all that he took over the years, I have no qualms about keeping it. Though I don't know what shape it's in. I inhale and exhale slowly, reminding myself not to borrow trouble. It will be what it will be.

As I drive down the long, gravel driveway and break through the trees, I'm surprised to see that the old place is still standing proud. Admittedly, it needs repainting, and the yard needs tending, but it's far from the dilapidated wreck I'd envisioned as the worst-case scenario.

I unlock the front door, my key still fitting perfectly after all these years. Just the fact that I kept it makes me realize that on some level I knew I'd find my way back here someday.

The musty smell of disuse hits me as I step inside, but beneath that, there's still the faint scent of home — pine and cinnamon, just like I remember.

Turns out, it isn't too bad; nothing I can't fix, anyway. And in the meantime, all it will need is a few repairs and new appliances to be livable. The rest will be an excellent project while I'm working on establishing the fire department. A good hands-on learning experience for Zo, too.

I wander through the rooms, memories flooding back with each step. Here's where I scraped my knee learning to roller skate indoors. There's the spot where my mom used to measure my and my sister's heights each year. And in the kitchen, I can almost see my dad at the table, poring over the newspaper like he did every morning.

Taking out a notepad, I jot down measurements and make a list of what needs to be done. New fridge, definitely. The ancient, yet still functional, stove can probably stay for now. The bathroom will need a complete overhaul, but that can wait.

As I work, I envision how Zoe and I will fit into this space. Her room will be my old one, with the big bay window overlooking the backyard. Maybe we can set up a little study nook in one of the spare rooms for her homeschooling.

It's going to be a change, no doubt. Trading the bustle of the city for the quiet of small-town life. Swapping my hectic schedule for a more laid-back pace. But as I stand in the doorway, looking out over the waist-high grass to the mountains beyond, I can't help but feel like I'm exactly where I'm supposed to be.

I head back to my truck, my mind racing with plans for the move to Alpine Ridge. There's so much to do — packing up our Seattle apartment, figuring out Zoe's homeschooling program, coordinating the move itself. But for the first time in a long time, I'm excited about what lies ahead.

As I drive back through town, I catch sight of the bakery on Main Street. It's clearly still open, the lot half full of vehicles.

My heart races with anticipation, wondering if she's still there, too. Could it be that easy to find her? Am I even ready for this?

I take a deep breath and turn into the parking lot. Because really, why not? She probably won't even be there. With that voice of hers, she's probably got a singing career that takes her around the world. Though I've looked for her over the years and found nothing, that doesn't mean it hasn't happened for her. Maybe she performs under a stage name. I hope so. She damn well deserved to make it, even if I was never there to see it happen like I promised. Something else I blame my father for.

If nothing else, I could use a cup of coffee before I hit the road back to Seattle, right?

CHAPTER THREE

RAE

The bell above the bakery door chimes, and I look up from the register, a smile plastered on my face as usual. But as soon as I see who's walking in, my smile freezes and my heart pounds like a jackhammer.

Luke McMillan.

My high school sweetheart.

I blink hard, trying to decide if I've had so much sugar today that I'm seeing things.

But I'm definitely not.

My next thought? What in the hell is he doing back here?

Still, despite my shock, I can't help noting that he looks the same yet different all at once. His dark blond hair is still thick, but now it's peppered with silver. His brown eyes crinkle at the corners when he smiles — a new addition, along with the laugh lines around his mouth. And the well-trimmed beard is definitely a surprise.

But his stocky build is bulkier now, his muscles more defined under his fitted T-shirt. Thirty years have been kind to him.

Too kind.

"Rae Donovan, as I live and breathe," he says, his deep, rumbling voice familiar yet a different, older version of itself all at the same time.

I swallow hard, trying to find my own voice. "Luke. Wow. What brings you to town?" I aim for polite but professional, but even I can hear the strain in my tone.

I give myself points for not asking him where he found the balls to waltz back into town like he didn't cheat on me and father a child, abandoning us both for the last thirty years.

He leans against the counter, his smile widening. "I guess gossip doesn't travel around town as fast as it once did," he teases. "You're looking at Alpine Ridge's new fire chief."

"Oh. Congratulations?" I manage, my mind reeling. Luke, back in Alpine

Ridge? I feel faint as my mind whirs into overdrive, trying to process what that will mean.

"Thanks." He nods, his eyes roaming over my face. "You look great, Rae. Haven't changed a bit."

I resist the urge to roll my eyes. My golden blond hair might be courtesy of L'Oréal these days, but my face certainly bears the signs of age just like his. Though I don't point that out. But I realize … he's clearly not aware that everyone found out about his little indiscretion.

Wait … does he even know about Brandon?

He can't *not* know, can he?

I freeze, wondering whether I should bring it up.

No. There's no way I'm asking him that. Nope. Not going near that with a ten-foot pole.

And yet, if he sticks around too long, I know I won't be able to keep my trap shut.

Time to get him back out of that door.

"Thanks," I mutter, grabbing a to-go coffee cup. "The usual?" The words slip out before I can stop them while I fill the cup with black coffee and cap it. A reflex from a lifetime ago while my mind is fixed on getting rid of him.

Luke's eyebrows rise. "You remember my order?"

I curse myself silently. Of course I remember. Just like I remember every detail of our time together, every first, every whispered promise of forever.

The memories that once warmed me now twist like a knife in my gut. Because what I remember most is his betrayal.

"Lucky guess," I lie, ringing him up and handing over his coffee.

An awkward silence falls between us. Luke looks like he wants to say something more, but I cut him off with a brisk, "Well, thanks for stopping by. I have to go take care of some things in the kitchen, but I'll see you around."

He blinks, clearly taken aback by my abruptness. "Right. Sure. It was good to see you, Rae. See you around."

I nod curtly, slipping through the door behind me and leaning against the wall beside it until the bell chimes again, signaling his departure.

Covering my face with my hands, I wait for my heart to stop racing. Good god, could it have been more obvious that I couldn't get away from him fast enough?

I'd imagined seeing Luke again over the years, but always pictured myself as indifferent, unaffected. I never expected the rush of hurt and anger that is coursing through me now.

How could I not feel this way, though? He came out of nowhere. And I never got to rip him a new one for cheating on me. Probably pointless since he clearly either thinks he got away with it or maybe just doesn't care, thinking it in the past.

The thought sends another bolt of agony ripping through me, and something deep down knows this shouldn't hurt so much. But that's what I get for shoving things down and not dealing with them. They all come bubbling back up, fresh as the day they were born.

"Rae? Everything okay?" Mia's voice snaps me out of my spiral. I drop my hands and look up to find concern etched on her face, dark wisps of hair escaping the bun she's always got her long hair tied in while she works.

I wave her off, forcing a smile. "Yeah, it's fine. Just a long day. Ready for game night, that's all."

She looks unconvinced but doesn't push. "Okay. If you're sure." She heads back to the long table beside the ovens, clearly going back to some experiment of sugar and flour and butter she'd been working on.

I take a deep breath and steady myself. As I go about my closing tasks, I ignore the implications of Luke's return for my sake, and my thoughts drift to Brandon.

If this blindsided me, it's nothing compared to how Brandon might feel. But then, I assumed since everyone in Alpine Ridge knew about Brandon's parentage, that so did he.

Since Luke himself didn't act like anything had happened at all, like he hadn't cheated on his girlfriend, knocked up someone else, and abandoned her and his son … maybe neither of them knows? I shake my head, not even sure how such a thing could be possible. It's old news from the rumor mill. Part of the town's fabric.

And yet, if I've learned anything today, it's that sometimes the past can jump out and bite you when you least expect it.

As I go home to clean up ahead of traveling up the mountain to Mia and Nate's house, I can't decide what, if anything, I should say to Brandon. Maybe I know more about him than he knows about himself? He sure doesn't know me all that well.

I left Alpine Ridge when he was still a kid, and he was gone when I got back, only returning recently to claim his place in town as one of our new council members. As far as he knows, I'm just the kooky lady that works at Mia's bakery.

I won't say a word, I decide. It's not my place.

Besides, even if Brandon doesn't know, he won't miss how alike he and Luke look. Or the whispers that will surely start up again. He has his grandfather, John, who can explain anything he wants to know.

Still, doubts plague me as I make my way to Mia and Nate's that evening. I could save him the element of surprise. Give him the heads up. I shake my head and push the thoughts aside, deciding to focus on the comfort of being with my friends. But they linger like an unpleasant taste in my mouth.

The entire gang is in the living room by the time I arrive, fashionably late as usual. Though there's nothing fashionable about it, I'm just scattered as hell, and I always feel like I'm ten steps behind where I'm supposed to be. Always have. But now's not the time to worry about that, so I shove that thought down, too.

I shake off the chill of outside as I step into the toasty living room. Since the snow drifts remain outside and the chill of winter has been clinging to the end of February, Nate is stoking a good-sized fire in the massive fireplace.

Joanie and Greg sit on one couch with Bruiser, their chihuahua mix rescue. As usual, they're a little too handsy for polite company, but that's part of their charm. Evan and Carrie sit on the floor in front of the fire, with his arms wrapped around her from behind. Mia is nowhere to be seen, probably working on food in the kitchen.

"Rae, thank god, come be my date," Brandon calls from across the room, patting the loveseat cushion next to him.

Normally I'd take that comment and run with it, but right now I can barely manage a weak smile. Still, I cross the room and settle next to him, patting him on the knee. Resisting the urge to point out that I'm old enough to be his mother, for so many reasons. Besides, I lack the … ah … equipment that he's really looking for in a date, anyway.

"Are we lavender dating now?" I tease, digging deep to be my usual peppy self.

Brandon raises a dark blond brow in an expression that is so like his father it physically hurts me. The reaction surprises me, though it shouldn't. I thought I'd long gotten over his resemblance to his father. And I shouldn't be after what happened today. I should've expected seeing him to hit that nerve again, really.

"I'm impressed you even know what that is," he admits. "But no. That would imply I want people to think I'm hetero." He smirks, and I can't help letting out a wry laugh.

"Oh good, you're here, and you're happy," Mia says brightly from across the living room, walking in with a tray of sugar cookies. Of course.

Carrie frowns and looks between us. "Why wouldn't Rae be happy?"

And now Joanie perks up. "Rae's not happy? Why?" She turns to me. "Did someone drop a proverbial turd in your hot cocoa at the bakery today? Tell me who and I'll fight them. You know I can roundhouse kick a bitch like nobody's business."

I snort a laugh. These ladies. I love them for their loyalty and sass, truly. "Nothing. I'm fine. Really." I give Mia a pointed yet joking glare.

She sets the tray down and raises her hands as Greg and Evan both dive for cookies. Joanie gives Greg a look when he emerges with a precariously balanced stack in hand. "What? Ev and I are working out in the morning, it'll be fine," he says defensively. He shrugs and downs half a cookie in a single bite. Since he runs the community and fitness center and is the epitome of in-shape, I don't know why she's worried.

Joanie shakes her head and turns her attention back to me. "I've heard more honesty from opposing council defending a habitual re-offender," she says drily.

Brandon scoffs. "Speak human, Jo Jo."

Joanie tips her head to the side. "Huh. No innuendo, and I still like that nickname."

I roll my eyes. "She means she can tell I'm full of shit," I explain, then sigh. "I'm just …" I search for a plausible explanation. Anything that will save me from having to open the Luke McMillan can of worms. "I'm still thinking about my conversation with Jerry yesterday."

"Jerry had the balls to speak to you?" Greg asks, incredulous.

I smirk. "That he did. He even gave me a full apology for pretending to be on a town council that didn't exist at the time and said that he's glad the town is doing well even if he's not in charge. *And* he told me he knows who stole the town incorporation petition signatures at that St. Patrick's Day event we held a couple years back."

Everyone gasps. I suppress a smirk at successfully baiting them with a distraction.

Mia tuts. "Which was great until he showed his actual cards. He only wanted discounted pie."

Joanie scoffs. "No offense, Mia, but who the fuck cares about pie? I want to know who stole the signatures." Joanie turns to me expectantly.

I shrug. "He said he didn't want to 'throw anyone else under the bus'," I reply with air quotes. "But that they did it to impress him."

"I know that happened before I got here," Carrie hedges, "but that has Batty Betty McDonald written all over it."

Carrie may not have come to Alpine Ridge until the summer before Nate and Mia's wedding, just after the incorporation petition signature theft, but she was crucial in wooing all the townspeople into being involved in the election process. I saw how hard she worked to get to know people and listen to them. Betty McDonald included. So, if anyone had a good sense of her during that time, it's Carrie.

Though I've also known Betty my whole life. Both she and Jerry lost their spouses five to ten years back. Even if she's a good twenty years older than me, I know her well enough to know she'd pull some shady moves to woo someone.

"I agree," I reply succinctly. "But we re-collected the signatures, and the incorporation went through. So, I'm going to try to just let it go."

Everyone's silent for a moment, presumably processing that.

"She comes into the wellness center for massages once a week," Evan pipes up. "I could have Dana, you know, go a little rough on her next time." He wiggles his eyebrows in a way that lets us know he's joking.

Probably.

Everyone laughs, anyway.

"You just hired Dana," Nate objects. "Let's not ask her to do anything sketchy for at least six months."

Mia settles next to him on the couch and smacks his arm. "Nate!"

He grins at her. "I'm just kidding, babe." But he winks at Evan when Mia turns away, and I snort.

"I'm a big believer in karma," I say. "So, nobody needs to do a damn thing. Betty has a pile of karma coming her way, don't you worry."

"But it's so much more fun when you get to watch it happen," Joanie says.

Greg laughs. "This is normally where I'd try to balance your vicious tendencies, city girl, but Betty is … special. And in this case, I agree completely."

"We are not manufacturing a way to make Betty get hers," Carrie interjects firmly. "Even if I agree, we're trying to build a community here, not piss off its long-time residents, no matter how irksome they may be." She perks up. "Oh! And speaking of building the community, we officially hired the new fire chief today."

My heart drops into my stomach.

No. No, no, no, no, no. I worked so hard to avoid exactly this conversation.

"His name is Luke McMillan," she continues. "He grew up in Alpine Ridge." She turns to Brandon. "And I swear, he looks just like you, B. Is there any chance you could be related?"

I can't imagine I'm hiding the horror on my face. Every word out of Carrie's mouth … it was like a series of horrible accidents I was powerless to stop. And now … the wreckage.

I turn to find Brandon's face strangely blank.

And everyone else is looking between me, Carrie, and Brandon, clearly confused about the vibe in the room.

It's at that point I realize … I'm the only one here who knows. The only Alpine Ridge resident that was around when it happened. When the gossip was flying around town. When Luke's indiscretions came to light. When what was left of my world fell spectacularly and completely apart.

Brandon sighs, running a hand through his hair. "He's my biological father."

His words break through the paralyzing fog I've been wrapped in.

"I wanted to warn you, but I didn't know whether you knew," I say.

Brandon's brown eyes meet mine, and all I see there is warmth. The tightness I hadn't realized was seizing my chest loosens.

"What?" Carrie asks, eyes widening. "Wait. Rae, you —"

"Knew Luke. Know Luke," I correct. "Yes. He stopped by the bakery today."

Brandon nods resignedly, at what I'm not sure. Acknowledgment of his father's presence, I suppose.

"Well, this is going to be awkward as ass," Joanie mumbles.

Mia leans over, placing her hand on Brandon's knee. "Are you going to be okay having him back in town?"

Brandon drags in a deep breath and shrugs. "Yeah, sure. I mean, I couldn't care less that he's here," he says flatly. "My grandfather told me about him years ago. But Luke's never been involved in my life. That says all I need to know about my sperm donor."

I blanch at the frankness that I can't argue with.

"You seem … mad," Carrie points out tentatively.

Brandon shrugs. "That would require caring. Which … okay, I can't honestly say I don't care but I also don't want to care, you know?" He gives another agitated shrug. "But I'll deal with it, and I'm sure if I ever have to interact with him, we'll both be polite. Clearly, we're not going to be best buds or anything."

Greg sets down his crumpled napkin. "Speaking as someone who has a piece of human garbage for a father," he opens, "sometimes you just need to tell someone exactly what you think of them so you can mentally move on. Even if you don't expect or want a response, all those feelings you have … you've got to let them out, man, or they'll fester."

Brandon shifts uncomfortably. Greg is usually on the quiet side, so we're all a little taken aback by his frankness. I mean, most of us know what a blow-hard his dad is, but to hear him summarize it like that … well, I can see his point. It makes me want to give Luke a piece of my mind. I'm not sure if that's on my behalf or Brandon's. Both wouldn't go amiss.

But Brandon still looks unsure.

Carrie, ever the diplomat, seamlessly reassures Brandon with a hug and moves everyone into our first game of the evening. It's somber at first, but eventually everyone loosens up and things return mostly to normal.

Despite putting on my own "normal" face, I still can't shake my unease. Knowing that Brandon is aware of his connection to Luke doesn't make me less anxious. If anything, it makes it worse.

Because I know the gossip mill in Alpine Ridge. Luke's return and his link to Brandon will be all anyone can talk about for months. And while Brandon might be able to shrug it off, for now at least, the idea of reliving the pain of Luke's betrayal, of having to hide it from my friends ... it's already wearing me down.

I thought I'd put that part of my life behind me. But with Luke back, the past is threatening to swallow me whole. And I'm not sure I'm strong enough to keep my head above water this time around.

CHAPTER FOUR

LUKE

The two-hour drive back to Seattle gives me plenty of time to replay my interaction with Rae in my mind. The way her smile froze when she saw me, her chilly reception ... it's clear she's not thrilled about my return to Alpine Ridge.

I got caught up in the idea of catching up with my first love, wondering if she still thought about me like I do about her. But I didn't consider that she may, just not in a good way.

I can't say I blame her.

Thirty years is a long time. And despite our promises to keep in touch, to keep our connection alive until we could reunite in the two short years we had until adulthood ... well, I didn't. In fact, even though I think of her often, I haven't spoken to her since the night before I left all those years ago.

In my defense, my father went to great lengths to keep me isolated from everyone in Alpine Ridge after the fire. Moving meant a new phone number, which he didn't want given out, and he also intercepted my mail and even threatened to pull me out of school and move across the country if I tried to reach out. And since my mother had left us by that point, I didn't have her normal intervention to save me from his strictly enforced rules.

And he was stricter — and angrier — than ever, so I feared crossing him. He said the town had ruined us, and to have anything to do with it was an insult to our family. While I didn't buy into that, I also had enough on my plate not to fight him on it.

Once I hit eighteen, I wanted a quick and easy way out of what had become a hellish situation. So, I joined the military. I'll admit, I didn't even think about contacting Rae at that point. I'd made my decision, and I assumed she'd moved on.

Or maybe it was easier than facing the truth — that I'd let her down. That I'd broken the promises we'd made to each other.

Well, I'm facing it now. Because she's still in Alpine Ridge, and now I will be, too, permanently it seems. I'll have to tell her what happened and beg her forgiveness.

Hopefully she'll give me the chance.

I push the thoughts aside as I pull up to Danny's house. As I head up the steps, Danny pops out of the front door, running a hand over his jet-black hair absently. I note he's gotten a fresh high and tight fade on our day off. He'd look sharp but for the exhaustion written all over his face. I'd say it's from the twenty-four hour shift we just finished but I can tell it's more than that.

I raise my brows. "Hey, man," I greet him.

"Hey, Luke," he replies somberly.

I stop beside him, putting my hands on my hips. "I'm guessing you're not out here to talk me into rattling the pans next shift."

"Well, I am a shit cook, but no," he replies, then sighs. "The girls had a big fight at school. Thought you should know what you were walking back into."

"Ah," I say, heaving a sigh. "About what?"

Danny's head swings side to side, even though I know he, like me, probably knows what it was about. "Don't know for sure. Neither will talk. To us or each other."

I rock back on my heels. "Okay. Are we talking fistfight here or …"

Danny smirks. "Just cattiness, I think. No blood or bruises that I can see, anyway. Still … Zo's been crying when she thinks we aren't listening. Nia tried talking to her a few times with no luck."

I shake my head and slap him on the shoulder. "Thanks for the heads up. And for having her. I hope it didn't disrupt things too much for you guys. I can look for someone else to stay at the apartment with her while I get things set up in our new place."

"You know I love her, but honestly I think she'd be happier that way." He pauses, assessing me. "So, new place, huh? That mean you're out of here?"

I nod. "As soon as I can work it out with the chief."

"What's the town called again?"

"Alpine Ridge."

Danny smirks. "You must really want that chief title to leave Seattle for some Podunk town in the Cascades, man." His grin says he's teasing, but the comment lands a little too hard.

"Come on, you know I wouldn't do it just for the position," I respond defensively. "I'm *from* that Podunk town, you know."

"Oh shit, sorry, I guess I missed that part," he murmurs. He pops the door and leans in, shouting up the stairs, "Zo, your dad's here." He leaves the door ajar and turns back to me. "So full circle opportunity, huh?"

I heave out a sigh. "More than you know. My family left there because of a fire."

I chew on my lip to keep the rest of the story from spilling out. That it was a fire that burned down so much more than my father's church. It burned down our family, metaphorically. And, unfortunately for my sister, literally.

"Damn. Well, I'm happy for you," Danny offers as I hear Zoe come crashing down the stairs.

She pops out, her sparkly purple backpack slung over one shoulder, a well-worn book in the other hand. Her dark brown curls are in disarray and her right alabaster cheek is ruddy, the puckered scars covering her left cheek paler and starker than usual; by itself, not concerning. But the real tell is her red-rimmed brown eyes. I deflate a little at the evidence of Danny's warning, and how often this seems to happen lately.

Zoe coming home from school upset.

Zoe fighting. *Zoe.* My little pacifist who used to tell me not to yell at people who cut me off in traffic because, *"Maybe they're just having a bad day, Daddy."*

Zoe crying and inconsolable. My little Zen warrior. It kills me.

"Hey, kiddo," I say softly. "Ready to go?"

I can tell she's trying not to look directly at me, so I don't see the evidence full on, but her eyes betray her, darting my way as if she's thinking about folding herself around me like she did when she was little.

"Yeah."

One quiet syllable is all I get. I sigh and give Danny a curt nod.

"Thanks again. See you day after tomorrow."

"Sure thing, Luke."

Zoe dashes on ahead of me to the truck, climbing in the passenger seat. I head around and get in.

As I start the engine, she ever so nonchalantly asks, "Did you get the job?"

I nod solemnly. "I got the job. We're moving to Alpine Ridge."

Zoe closes her eyes and lets out a sigh of relief. She reopens them and turns her big, beautiful brown eyes on me. "When can we go? Tomorrow? Please say tomorrow."

I try not to let my concern for her show on my face. "I'm sorry, Zo, but no. It might take a few weeks, maybe even a couple of months. I need to get the old family house fixed up first and give notice at my job."

Her expression falls. "So ... I'll have to stay with Danny, Nia, and Piper again?"

"No," I assure her. "You don't. We'll figure something out." I pause, unsure of how far I want to push my luck. "Do you want to tell me what happened today?"

And while Zoe's mother and I were only a couple for about five minutes, we did work together, so I knew her enough that the resolute expression that settles over Zoe's features makes her a mirror of her mother in every way. It's moments like these that make me hurt for her loss the most. Not for myself but for Zoe, and for Virginia too, who would've loved every minute of this pre-teen phase. Certainly, her sass would've been a much better match for the stubbornness I know is coming right now.

"Are you asking me to relive my trauma?" she says haughtily.

"I would never," I assure her in as serious a tone as I can manage.

"Good. Because my answer is *no*," she says firmly, lifting her chin and looking away.

A ghost of a smile pulls at my lips at her theatrics. But this isn't my first time trying to get information out of her. I pull into traffic and let the silence do its work.

When we're almost home, it pays off. Zoe lets out an epic, world-weary sigh.

"They were making fun of me again. For being weird. For my scars ... and for not having a mom," she adds quietly, looking down into her lap. Out of the corner of my eye, I catch a fat tear drop hit her thumb.

"Piper, too?"

She looks up, sniffing deeply and shaking her head. "No, but she didn't say *anything*."

"Maybe she was afraid they'd make fun of her, too," I offer, playing devil's advocate.

This time I feel Zoe's sharp gaze before I turn to see it. "Then she's a coward," she says acidly. Then she deflates just a little. "I would've stood up for *her*."

A sad smile crosses my lips, and I reach over to pat her knee. "I know you would've, Zo. But unfortunately, most people are too afraid or nervous to stand up for what's right."

"Guess I am weird because I don't understand that at all," she grumbles as I pull into an open spot on the street in front of our apartment building.

"You say that like being weird is a bad thing," I reply lightly. "You march to the beat of your own drum. Someday you'll be glad for that."

"Not today," she says, folding her long arms over her chest.

I huff a dry laugh. "Fair enough."

She turns abruptly. "Can't I just come with you while you fix up the house?"

I hesitate. The house isn't in top shape, but it's not unsafe either.

And having Zoe with me would make the process a lot more bearable.

And clearly, she's even more miserable here than I thought …

"Tell you what," I say, tugging at one of her curls. "I'll talk to the chief, see what I can do. But we haven't even started packing, so it still might be a couple of weeks, okay?"

Zoe sighs dramatically. "I guess it'll have to do."

I blow out a breath as she jumps out of the truck. Oh boy.

And she's not even a teenager yet.

⊱⊱⊱⊰⊰⊰

Turns out the department was about to furlough someone because of budget cuts so, while they would've rather gone with someone less senior, given the circumstances it only made sense that it be me.

So, to Zoe's great relief, here we are, not quite two weeks later, standing in the driveway of our new home, surrounded by boxes, furniture, and a scant dusting of snow that has fallen.

Well, the house is new to Zoe, anyway. The place is full of memories for me, which is going to make this process extra challenging, because some of them aren't great. The two-story Victorian needs a lot of work. Not least of all a fresh coat of paint. Even if it weren't peeling, the sickly yellow color was never my favorite, but mostly it reminds me of how my parents argued over it.

A sigh escapes me as I try not to get overwhelmed thinking about all the work that needs to be done to the inside.

Bright side, come Monday morning, I'll officially start as Alpine Ridge's fire chief. And maybe I can finally right some wrongs of my past.

"Well, that's the last of it," I say, unhitching the moving trailer from my truck. "What do you say we head to the tavern for dinner? I'm starving."

Zoe's eyes light up. "Yes, please! I want to see more of the town."

I grin as she jumps into the truck with glee. She's been like a different kid since I pulled her out of school.

Or, more accurately, like her old, carefree self. She's reading less and drawing more. Before we left, she didn't hide in her room at all like she had been, choosing the apartment's furnished balcony to sketch trees, squirrels, and passers-by. I was relieved to see her happy again. I can only hope she continues to be happy living here.

As we drive the few minutes to the tavern, I can't wait to see what she thinks of the house's yard. Well, after we clean it up a bit, anyway. I want to share it with her because at least the outside of my childhood home holds plenty of wonderful memories for me, thankfully.

As does the tavern, which looks practically the same as I remember when we pull in. Funny, since I'd have expected it to look shabbier with the years but clearly, it's been maintained. Recently, by the looks of it, I notice as we step out onto a walkway freshly swept of snow while Zoe rapidly fires questions at me about the town that she doesn't wait for answers to.

"And why is it snowing?" she asks, swinging the door open. "It's March!"

I chuckle and follow her in.

"Welcome to Alpine Ridge," I murmur. Snow in early March really isn't all that unusual here. But thankfully Zoe will be spared the full winter snow experience for a while. As a born Seattleite, she's not exactly used to tons of the white stuff.

Instantly, my focus shifts as the weight of curious stares from the other patrons in the tavern lands on us. It's to be expected — Alpine Ridge is a small town, and my return is bound to be big news. And Zoe definitely stands out.

In any case, she seems oblivious to the stares and whispers as we find a table in the semi-crowded dining area. It's Friday night, but it's still early, so we're lucky to snag a two-seater in the corner. Zoe continues prattling on about her plans to explore the local hiking trails and start "unschooling" — a concept we stumbled on that seems tailor-made for her curious, self-directed nature.

It's pretty much what it sounds like; exactly the opposite of traditional schooling with no set structure, expectations, or limits, directed only by the student's interests. Zoe is thrilled to direct her own learning and escape public schools with their cliques and mean girls.

For my part, I know she'll learn loads. Besides, she's only twelve. There's time to worry about test scores and college applications, but I think both of us need this unstructured approach as we figure out our new life here.

After perusing the menus left between the ketchup bottle and saltshaker on the table, I head up to the bar to order since it seems there aren't any wait staff.

The old guy behind the bar looks terribly familiar. I know the Allen family owned this bar once upon a time, and he has their look about him. He has their average height and build, but he also has their look ... it's something about the shape of their faces that I can't quite put my finger on. The two sons were a good ten to fifteen years older than me though, so I don't remember their names or which one this might be.

"What can I get for you?" he asks curtly.

"Hi," I say pointedly, "I'm Luke. My daughter and I would like a couple of cheeseburgers, fries, and cokes, please."

The old guy tips his head to the side. "You're Luke McMillan, Pastor McMillan's boy."

I hesitate only for a fraction of a second. Shit, he put that together fast.

"Sure am."

He narrows his eyes, assessing me. "Well … welcome back, I guess." He leans into the cracked door behind him and shouts down our order before turning back to me. "So just visiting?"

My eyebrows bunch together. How has the gossip not traveled around by now? Am I even in the right town? But then … it was really only Arthur, Carrie, and Rae that I've seen, so clearly all three can keep things to themselves. Good to know.

"Nope. I'm here to get the Alpine Ridge Fire Department up and running." I smile winningly. "And you are?"

There he goes narrowing his eyes again. But after a moment he sticks out a hand. "Jerry Allen."

Jerry. That's right. And his younger brother was Perry.

I hold back a snort as I reach out and shake his hand.

"Pleasure. Be seeing you around, Jerry."

He dips his chin, and I head back to the table. Zoe is swiping around on her phone, probably learning things about the town even I don't know yet.

"Did you know there's no library in Alpine Ridge?" Zoe asks. She turns her phone to show me a map. "The closest one is in a city called Ellensburg."

I smirk. "Honey, this is a *very* small town. I warned you. When I lived here, there was this tavern, a gas station, a history museum, a bakery, a church, and a general store."

Zoe's jaw drops. "Wow. Well, I'm glad it's got more than that now at least."

I nod. "Arthur told me there are plenty more businesses coming soon. You'll see. We'll get to watch this town take on a new life."

"Okay, but first can we go to the library in Ellensburg? I need to make my reading list."

I can't help but smile at her enthusiasm. Zoe has always been a voracious reader, devouring books well above her grade level. It's one of the many things that makes her unique. Special.

"Sure thing. We need to go into Ellensburg tomorrow anyway to order new appliances and pick up some building materials."

Zoe bounces in her seat excitedly. Which at first I think is because of what I said, but I'm quickly proven wrong by Jerry arriving with our food.

"Thank you, thank you, thank you," she says gleefully in his direction as she dives on her fries.

Jerry gives her a bewildered but amused look. "Well, you're welcome, young lady."

I smile and pop a fry in my mouth, giving him a thumbs up.

As he heads back behind the bar, I'm also pleased that everyone else in the room seems to ignore us. Like we're just part of the town.

I laugh a little. Could it really be that easy?

"What's so funny, Dad?" Zoe asks around a mouthful of burger.

"I think we're going to do just fine here, that's all." I say, then I point a fry at her. "And don't talk with your mouth full."

I should've known it was all too easy. On the way home, Zoe spots the bakery.

"Ooh, there's the bakery you mentioned! Can we get dessert? Please?"

Anxiety churns in my gut at her innocent request.

"Not tonight, kiddo, it's already closed," I reply. Since checking the hours was the first thing I did after I walked out last time so I knew when I could come back and try again with Rae. "But I'll bring you another day, I promise." Suddenly my burger and fries aren't sitting so well.

Zoe looks a little crestfallen, which isn't a surprise given that she's visited every bakery in Western Washington, but she immediately starts asking questions about what other businesses might come in next.

I'm glad she quickly moved on from talking about the bakery because I'm not sure I'm ready for Rae to meet Zoe. Not yet. It feels ... complicated.

It takes me a while to figure out why. It's not until I watch Zoe skipping up the front steps into the house that it clicks. Something about watching her come back to my childhood home.

Introducing Zoe to Rae would flaunt a life I've built without her. A life that was supposed to be ours, here in this town.

It was supposed to be our daughter skipping up the steps, racing to see her momma after a night out with her pops.

A sadness I haven't felt in a long time tugs at my heart.

But then I remember the tavern, the curious looks from the other diners. In a town this small, Rae is bound to hear about Zoe soon enough. Whether I'm ready or not.

That night, as I tuck Zoe into bed, she asks for a story, *"Like when I was little."* The request catches me off guard — it's been years since our bedtime story ritual. But something about the new house, the big changes in our lives, seems to have brought out a neediness in her I haven't seen in a while. It pulls harder at that feeling in my chest.

And as I sit on the edge of her bed, spinning a tale about a brave princess on a quest, my mind drifts to Rae. To the life we'd dreamed of together all those years ago. A life filled with love and laughter. A house echoing with the sound of little feet.

It further occurs to me that's why I don't want to let Rae see this part of my life. Because in a way, it's more than what could have been. It feels like ... a betrayal. Like I'm living the future we'd planned, just ... without her.

The thought sits heavy in my chest as I kiss Zoe goodnight and slip out of her room, settling into my own freshly made bed. I know it's ridiculous — it's been thirty years, after all. For all I know, Rae has built a beautiful life of her own, with a husband and children and a home filled with happiness.

I shift uncomfortably, even though it's my same old mattress.

But I know it's not the bed that's bothering me.

It's the idea that Rae has a whole life that I wasn't a part of either.

It's hypocritical.

It shouldn't bother me.

But it does.

I shake my head, as if I can physically dislodge the thoughts. I can't go down that road. Not now. Not when I have so much on my plate already.

Get settled. Fix up the house. Make sure Zoe has everything she needs. That's what I need to focus on. The rest ... well, I'll just have to figure it out as I go.

One thing at a time.

CHAPTER FIVE

RAE

Another day, another round of pretending (badly) that I'm not worried Luke will pop out from behind every corner. I'm fooling no one at this point, myself least of all. So, I'm not surprised at all when I'm at the sink in the customer-facing area of the bakery, washing up with a little more force than necessary, when Mia corners me. A mix of concern and determination fills her big blue eyes, and I know she won't let me avoid this conversation.

"So," she begins, dusting flour off her hands, "I've been giving you some space, but it's clear you're not coming out of this funk on your own. I think it's high time we talk about Luke and whatever happened between you two that has you so upset."

I sigh, my shoulders sagging. "Mia, I've been quiet about it for a reason. It's in the past; I'd really prefer that it stayed there."

Mia raises an eyebrow. "Really? Because from where I'm standing, Luke is very much in the present. He's the new fire chief, and whatever it is with him is obviously affecting you. So, spill."

I close my eyes briefly, knowing she's right. "Fine. Luke and I ... we were high school sweethearts. But then he left town, and that was that." I bite into my lip as I dry my hands. Because that *so* was not that.

Mia scrutinizes me for a moment, and I can practically hear the wheels turning in her head. And I definitely see it on her face when it clicks. Her eyes widen as understanding dawns on her features. "Oh my god! He cheated on you, didn't he? And Brandon ... he's the result of that?"

I nod, my throat tight. "Bingo." It was only a matter of time before she figured it out, even without my help, but it still hurts to hear the words spoken out loud. To remember the raw feelings of losing the love of your life ... only to find out that he'd been going behind your back with your best friend.

Mia's expression softens, and she reaches out to squeeze my arm. "Oh, Rae, I'm so sorry. I can't imagine how difficult it must be, having that reminder constantly in your face, what with Brandon's return and now Luke's."

I take a shaky breath in. "It's been a challenge," I admit. "But I adjusted to Brandon being back. It helped that it wasn't his fault. I'll adjust to Luke being back, too. Might just take a bit longer."

"I can't imagine what that must've done to your ability to trust people," Mia says, studying me. Then, softly, she asks, "Is that why you never got married or had kids? Because of what happened with Luke?"

I side-eye her, debating how much to reveal.

Well, in for a penny, in for a pound.

With a sigh, I mutter, "I *was* married, actually. Once upon a time."

Mia's eyes go wide again, and she opens her mouth to ask more questions that I'm not prepared to answer, but before she can, the bell above the bakery door chimes. We both turn to see Betty McDonald walking in.

I glance over at Mia with an arched brow. She gives me a small nod, having already convinced me to help karma along when the chance arose.

Now it's a double win for me: getting out of a conversation I don't want to have and taking this old bat down a peg or two.

"Hi, Betty. The usual?" I greet her, keeping my voice as casual as possible.

"Yes, and it best be *fresh* this time," she replies imperiously, looking down her nose at me. I fight back an eye roll and give her a sugary sweet smile.

"Of course," I murmur. But as I pack up her order, I lean in, smiling invitingly while lowering my voice. "By the way, a little birdie recently told us who stole those town incorporation petition signatures St. Patrick's Day before last."

And I've never seen someone pale so fast in their life. She turns her head, pretending to look at, well, anything but me.

"Why would I care about old gossip?" she sniffs.

I chuckle. "Oh, I think you know why." I pause for effect. "I didn't take you for a thief, Betty," I say mock-sadly, shaking my head.

She sputters, her face reddening as her wide, enraged eyes return to meet mine. "How dare you accuse me? As if I would ever do such a thing!"

Setting her bag down between us, I give her a razor-sharp smile. "Oh, I think we both know you would. And did," I reply firmly. "But like you said, it's old news, and it didn't stop the incorporation from happening. So, I'd be willing to forgive and forget … *if* you were to apologize."

"I have nothing to apologize for!" she insists indignantly. "And … and even if I did — which I *don't* — there isn't a world where I'd ever owe an apology to an uppity piece of trash like you."

Despite knowing that's exactly how she's always thought of me, the words still sting, and I blanch as she snatches the bag from the counter.

Mia steps forward. "No charge for that today, Mrs. McDonald."

A smug smile crosses Betty's face, and she turns her nose up at me. "As well there shouldn't be! I can't believe you let the help speak to customers like this. She'd better be fired!"

Mia tips her head to the side. "Oh, I'm sorry. I didn't mean to imply that Rae did a damn thing wrong. In fact, I think she's being gracious even giving you the chance to redeem yourself. I sure wouldn't. But it's her call, since she had to do all the work to replace the signatures you stole." Mia shakes her head. "No, I was saying I don't want your money *or* your business until you do as she asks." Betty sputters, but Mia holds up a hand to show that she's not done. "But now I think that since you've been so insulting, we're going to need a *public* apology before you're permitted back here ... or in any of the businesses that our family runs in this town. And make no mistake, Mrs. McDonald, Rae is my family." Mia turns to me. "So, that's also Nate's new medical practice, Evan's wellness center, Greg's community center, Joanie's new law practice, Brandon's new art gallery ... hmmm ... I'm missing someone ..."

"Sera's new realty office," I offer, lips twitching, presuming she didn't mention Carrie because, while she's the town planner, she doesn't actually own a business.

"Ah, yes, Greg's cousin. She's definitely part of the family. Oh! And she owns the grocery store, too. Goodness me, well, that's pretty much everything but the tavern and the gas station!" Mia says with feigned alarm.

"And the mail place, since Jerry owns that now, too," I correct, stifling a laugh.

"Ah. Yes, and the mail place," Mia agrees with a serious nod.

"You ... she ..." Betty's eyes flick between us as she sputters incoherently. "Your pastries are barely tolerable, anyway!" With a frustrated noise, she throws the bag with her maple bar on the floor, *stomps on it*, and storms out.

For a moment, we silently stare at the crushed pastry bag and bits of donut that have scattered out of the top.

"Well. I'd best let everyone know what went down as soon as possible," Mia murmurs. She looks over and gives me a small, self-assured smile. "Hope she has fun driving into Ellensburg every time she needs something."

I can't help but laugh. "Thank you for talking me into doing that. It was the most satisfying thing I've done all year." I pop around the counter with a broom and quickly sweep the mess into a dustpan.

"That *was* more cathartic than I expected," Mia agrees. "And it was a good message to send. The new Alpine Ridge won't put up with any bullshit."

With a chuckle of agreement, I dump the mess into the garbage can and put back the broom.

Then I turn to Mia, untying my apron. "That seems like a perfect note to end the day on. And anyway, Arthur asked me to stop by town hall this afternoon."

Mia nods, her expression a mix of concern and curiosity. "Okay. But don't for one minute think I'm going to forget you told me you've been married before. We're definitely finishing that conversation later."

I give her a sweet smile, grab my purse, and walk toward the door. "Not if I can help it," I call over my shoulder as I head out the door.

I hop in my Bronco and drive the short distance to the new town hall, windows down, so the slightly less frigid March air can blow away my worries. Dodging yet another conversation about my past with Mia. Betty's stinging words. Thoughts of Luke.

It kind of works, as I'm a bit perkier when I step out onto the newly paved walkway to the building, breathing in the crisp, clean mountain air. One of my favorite parts of living here.

I enter the building to the smell of new. Like the subtle aromas of paint, brass, and paper mixed, and I find I like it. It's the smell of progress.

I wave at Meredith, the newly hired office manager.

"Here to see Mayor Burton?" she asks with a bright smile.

"Sure am," I confirm. "Is he in his office?"

She shakes her head, her beautiful curly ginger locks swaying. "He's in the conference room. He should be just wrapping up a meeting. If the door is open, you can go on in."

I nod my thanks and slip a pastry bag to her on my way by. "For you."

She opens the bag and inhales deeply. "Oooh, one of Mia's chocolate croissants," she breathes. "Thanks, Rae."

"Anytime, sugar," I reply with a wink.

I head down the hall, appreciating the classical architecture. Simple, understated columns line the main hall, each topped with domed lighting, ending at the sizeable meeting room. The decoratively paneled double doors give the relatively small space a sense of importance and grandeur.

It all just feels so … official. A swell of pride moves through me at getting to be a part of making this town grow into something even better.

Since one door is propped half-open, I peek inside. I find Arthur, Carrie, and Greg at the opposite end of the long, black walnut conference table. They all look up at my arrival.

"Were you ready for me?" I ask Arthur tentatively.

A warm smile spreads over his friendly, wrinkled face, and he gestures for me to enter. "Nearly. Please, come in. We're just about done here."

I step inside tentatively. "Is it okay to ask how everything is going with setting up the town?" I ask. "Fire chief aside, of course. I think we all know about that." I give my best impression of a smile, but it feels more like a grimace.

Carrie's smile, however, is radiant, as she brushes her long dark waves behind her shoulders and smooths her cream pantsuit. Clearly, she's quite pleased with herself, but understandably so. "I'm working on the police department next," she offers. "We're making good progress."

Greg nods in agreement, his blue eyes lit up. "And I've just agreed to run the parks and rec department."

"Well, I'll be. Congratulations!" I say, genuinely happy for him. I slink up and squeeze his shoulder before taking a seat. "So, what does that entail?"

"Well, first, cleaning up and maintaining the hiking trails. But also establishing parks, running events, that sort of thing," he explains.

"How does the community center fit into that?" I ask with a frown. "I know how hard you worked to get it set up. Surely, it'll be part of the plan?"

Greg smiles indulgently. "I'll split off and continue to run the gym portion. We just agreed to hire someone to run the other side for workshops, special programs, and events."

Arthur chimes in, "That's actually why we asked you here, Rae. The young lady who will take on the role is based in Leavenworth and will only come on an as needed basis until she's able to move permanently in a couple months. We'll need someone to show her the ropes and help run things until then. And since you've been the driving force behind many of our events, we were hoping you could help. The St. Patrick's Day event this year should be a good way to get Layla up to speed and kick things off. We'd like to pay you as a consultant."

"Oh, gosh, I wouldn't say I've been the driving force," I demur. "Greg has really been at the forefront —"

Greg snorts. "I own the space, show up, and do what I'm told, Rae. You absolutely make those events shine. You're who *everyone* looks to when planning an event around here. Give yourself some credit."

I wrinkle my nose. "Okay, fine, I *might* have already come up with ideas for that event …"

Carrie chuckles and Arthur smiles knowingly.

I sigh. "All right, all right. I'm in."

"Excellent," Arthur says, clapping his hands together. "Now, if that's all —"

"Did I miss the party?" a deep voice asks from behind me.

We all turn toward the door to see Luke standing there, looking uncertain. My eyes involuntarily trail down his body, taking in the fitted polo and slacks he's wearing that show off his toned physique spectacularly.

I swallow hard as my stomach does an uncomfortable flip.

"Ah, Luke," Arthur says. "You're early."

"Before you move on, Arthur, I have one more thing I'd like to talk to you about," Greg says.

Carrie rises, and I follow suit, all too happy to get out of any room Luke is in. "Of course, we'll give you all the room," I say with a smile in Arthur and Greg's direction.

Arthur dips his chin. "We'll reach out soon."

I nod and follow Carrie out. She's already headed back to her office, and I'm making to leave when I hear someone call, "Rae, a minute, please." I turn to see Luke has also stepped out of the room and closed the door behind him, presumably to give Arthur and Greg privacy. But that also leaves me alone in the hall with Luke.

Shit.

I take a subtle deep breath and plaster on my best impression of a smile. Even though my palms are already sweating.

"What can I do for you, Fire Chief McMillan?"

Luke gives me a look. "Well, if I didn't suspect you were upset with me before, that would've done it," he responds drily.

"I don't know what you're talking about," I reply airily, lifting my chin.

He cocks an eyebrow and my insides curl tightly. "It's been a long time, Rae, but I can still tell when you're lying."

I clench my jaw. The audacity of him to pretend like he still knows me. But I presume Meredith is listening, so I do my best not to lose my cool.

"Don't be silly," I reply with a forced laugh.

"Rae, we should talk about —"

"So, you're a firefighter," I blurt out, hoping to head off wherever he was taking this conversation, as I'm certain it's somewhere I don't want to go. Not here. Not now. Probably never.

His deep brown eyes examine my face for a moment before he replies. "Just registered that, did you?" he murmurs, a hint of teasing in his tone.

I lift a shoulder. "I was too busy being shocked that you were back for it to fully sink in."

He raises a brow. "It was long overdue. Me coming back, I mean."

I snort derisively. "That's sure one way to put it." My first instinct is to be horrified at showing my irritation and anger, but I realize I'm not the one here who has something to be ashamed of.

"And how would you put it?" he asks, curiosity lacing his tone.

I frown, unsure of how to frame this, given that I don't know if he knows about Brandon. But Mia's encouragement seems to have freed my inner thoughts lately.

"It is what it is, and I have no interest in gossip. Never did. So, I wouldn't put it any way. But the townsfolk … well, as you can imagine, they've got their own opinions."

His brows pull together. "What? Why?" he demands.

My own brows pop up. It seems like he doesn't know … yet I find that hard to believe. So, I can't resist putting out one more piece of bait.

"You didn't think they'd find out?"

An unnatural silence settles over the hall. Now I *know* Meredith is listening. It's so quiet I'm afraid Luke might hear the rapid pounding of my heart as I wait breathlessly for his response.

His brow furrows deeper. "Why would they care that we broke up? That my father made damn sure I could never speak to you or anyone here after we left? At least until it didn't matter anymore, anyway," he replies gruffly.

I let out my breath, and my chest constricts as his words sink in. Pastor McMillan stopped him from speaking to anyone in town? Well, that would sure as hell explain a lot. But … why?

"I'm sorry. I'm not sure I understand. He did what?" I pull back, distracted by this new information. "Why would …" I shake my head "… but even if he did, that's not … I'm not talking about us, Luke." My hands ball into fists at my sides, and I can't help the frustration in my voice.

But now it's Luke's turn to shake his head. He's clearly bewildered. "Then I have no idea what you *are* talking about, so you're going to have to clue me in."

I couldn't imagine how he wouldn't know. But … he *doesn't*. Holy shit.

My stomach drops as certainty settles over me.

"You really don't know," I whisper, more to myself than him.

"I don't know what, Rae?" he asks tightly.

The blood drains from my face. I put a hand over my mouth, shaking my head. I can't do it. I can't be the one to tell him. That he has a son. That he's missed out on Brandon's whole life. That he created a reputation for himself he's going to have to contend with. That I know of his betrayal.

It's so much. Too much. I never should've gone down this road. Never should've had this conversation. It's none of my business. Hasn't been since he stepped out on me. This is between him and Brandon.

Thankfully, Greg comes out of the meeting room, and I seize the opportunity to leave the conversation.

"Greg!" I cry in relief. "I need to talk to you alone for a minute." I give Luke a tight, fake apologetic smile and drag Greg away.

I can practically hear Luke's teeth grinding, but he doesn't stop me from leaving. He just watches as I loop my arm through Greg's and practically drag him down the hall.

Greg looks at me questioningly, clearly missing the tension. "What's up, Rae?"

I take a deep breath as we exit the building, pausing just under the awning and turning toward him. I realize all at once that I have to stop letting my past control me. That the only way I can stop caring about Luke and what he knows is to just let go.

"I've been mulling over something for a while," I tell him. "And it just came together for me. You said you'll only have half the community center for the parks and rec department?"

"Yes?" he says uncertainly.

I take a deep breath. "Surely you could use more space?" I offer.

He tilts his head back and forth. "I mean, yes, but I figured we'd just build it. Lots of that happening right now, anyway." He shrugs.

I huff out a breathy, on-edge laugh, preparing to get rid of the only part of my past I have control over. "Sure. Or you could use the museum." I lick my lips nervously. "I've decided it's time to let go of it."

Greg's eyebrows shoot up. "Really? I mean, that'd be great, but are you sure?"

Am I sure that I want to get rid of the museum my daddy ran once upon a time — the unexpected inheritance I received when the man who'd abandoned us died, hopefully alone and miserable? Even before he caused the fire that broke our family apart, he did awful things, and I've never mourned him. The better question is, why have I held onto it this long?

I'd laugh, but I'm already teetering on insanity with everything that's happened. And it's time to do something to stop it.

That museum doesn't just hold Alpine Ridge's gold rush history, it also represents everything that went wrong during that time of my life when both of the men I loved left me. I can think of no better symbolic gesture than getting rid of it. And maybe it'll give me the courage to let go of all of this hurt and anger, too.

I meet his gaze, my voice steady. "I'm sure. It's time I let go of the past."

CHAPTER SIX

LUKE

I stare after Rae's retreating form, her sudden departure leaving me reeling. What the hell is she talking about? What don't I know? I rack my brain, trying to unearth some long-buried memory, but come up empty. Unease settles in my gut like a lead weight.

Shaking my head, I turn my focus to the task at hand. I have a fire department to establish, and that will require all my attention. Pushing thoughts of Rae aside, I step into Arthur's office to discuss the next steps.

Arthur is all business as we go over the preliminary research that I've done on the county regulations. We discuss how to work with them to grease the wheels for getting everything approved smoothly. He recommends I talk to Carrie first, as she's established contacts there, but cautions that it can't be tomorrow, as he's asked the rest of the town council to meet us in the morning so he can introduce me to them. Then he plans to take me on a full tour of the town so I can familiarize myself with what building sites and projects will be upcoming as I prepare to take responsibility for fire department coordination and inspections of new builds.

By the end of our meeting, I'm a little overwhelmed, but not in a bad way. Aside from being the perfect distraction from whatever this unknown drama is, it's exciting to sink my teeth into this huge new responsibility. Having always been on the periphery of it, I underestimated how involved the process is. And this is just the tip of the iceberg. I'm equally thrilled by and terrified of that fact.

That evening, my mind is so busy working on the events of the day that once I dry the last dish after cleaning up from dinner, I'm staring out the kitchen window, gazing blankly at the near-dark sky when Zoe pokes me in the side.

"Earth to Dad," she teases, waving a hand in front of my face.

I turn to her with a smirk. "What's up, kiddo?"

She raises a sassy eyebrow. "You were going to teach me how to use the escape ladder?" she reminds me.

Shit. That's right. We replaced the old smoke detectors and installed new carbon monoxide alarms over the weekend but hadn't gotten around to a full emergency drill. Since we lived in an apartment building with external fire escape stairs, she's never had to mount and navigate a hanging ladder, so that's definitely job number one this evening.

"Sure am," I respond. "Follow me." I toss the towel I'd been holding on the counter and take her upstairs.

I talk her through hanging the ladder herself and have her go down it several times until she's comfortable with the less-sturdy feel from what she's used to. She doesn't complain once, but she never does with these things. She and I, of all people, know how important fire safety is.

Not that it saved her mom, who, being a firefighter herself, knew it all. Knew it and pushed too far to save others, dying herself in the process.

My thoughts are so distracting I don't even notice Zoe packing up the ladder until she stops and approaches, wrapping her arms around my middle.

"I miss her when we do this, too," she murmurs into my chest, clearly understanding where my head is at.

I wrap my arms around her and rest my chin on her head. "Gosh, you're getting tall," I respond evasively. And then, so she doesn't think I'm ignoring her, I add, "She would've been so proud of you."

"Thanks, Dad."

Zoe's deep sniff tells me she's crying. It's been a while since she did, about her mother, anyway. At least that I know of. She was so little when the fire that leveled their apartment building took Virginia and left Zoe with third-degree burns on the left side of her face, neck, and shoulder. As if the burns themselves weren't bad enough, they also got her teased and bullied mercilessly from the moment she started school. Bullying that didn't relent, even when we transferred her to a top-shelf private school. And yet, here she is, as sweet as ever.

"I'm proud of you, too," I add. "I know things at school were rough before, but this is a whole new era. One in which I hope you can learn to love and appreciate the gentle person you are. Because it's your superpower, Zo."

She snorts and pulls away, wiping at her cheek. "As if," she scoffs.

I tap her under her chin. "I'm serious. What you've gone through would send most people spiraling to a terrible place. Yet you stay so positive. And empathetic. In this world, that's definitely a superpower."

Zoe rolls her eyes so hard I have to work not to laugh. "Puhleeease," she groans. "You're being embarrassing, Dad."

But I see the little smile on her lips. "Fine," I concede. "Let's practice our escape routes and then we can have dessert, okay?"

Zoe bounces on the balls of her feet, waiting for my direction. I call a series of emergencies, from a fire in different places in the house to an earthquake to power outages. By the time we're done, we've thoroughly earned the banana splits we make ourselves. I use mostly banana, but Zoe piles hers high with everything, naturally.

"So ... am I allowed to ask why there's so much stuff left in this house from when you were a kid?" Zoe asks tentatively. "Like ... why didn't you guys take it all with you?"

I take in a deep breath and set my empty dish down on the new coffee table we bought this weekend. But the sofa we're sitting on is vintage eighties, as is much of the furniture in the house.

I haven't told Zoe much about my family, save that I'm not in contact with any of them. But I knew the questions would come someday. I'm not exactly surprised she's asking now, given our surroundings.

"It's ... complicated," I say, not sure how to answer her without dumping more on her shoulders than she wants, or needs, to know.

"I hate when grown-ups say that," she groans. "Try me."

I smirk. "Okay, Miss Mature," I tease her. "You know my father was a pastor. One night, there was a fire at the church."

Zoe's eyes go wide. "Was everyone okay?"

My heart clenches. As a burn victim, of course that would be her first question. God, I should have thought this conversation through better.

"No," I say sadly. "A fallen storage cabinet trapped my little sister. They got her out, but by then, she'd inhaled so much smoke."

Zoe sets down her half-finished dish, clearly having lost her appetite. "What happened to her?"

"Well, Alpine Ridge is pretty far out. So, there weren't any medical services for miles and miles. They called my mom, who came and took her to get help while my dad and another man tried to save the place. They did what they could, but she couldn't breathe like she used to. And while they had things that could help, they didn't have as many options as they do now. Though even if they did, she was pretty bad off. She died within the year." I let out a shaky breath as I note Zoe's frown.

"I'm sorry, I didn't know. We don't have to talk about it anymore," she says.

"Hey, it's okay," I assure her. "I probably should have told you a long time ago." I shake my head. "Anyway, back to your question. With the accident, and my sister being in the hospital, my mom moved out first, only taking what she needed to stay with my sister. And then my dad and I left not long after, since the town didn't have the money to rebuild the church. We didn't have the means or need to take much."

I shrug, trying to feign nonchalance when in reality my skin is crawling with terrible memories of that time. Of all I lost. Of all I left behind. Because to hell with furniture. I left the community I'd known my whole life. Friends. And the girl I'd planned to marry.

"So, the house just ... sat here?" she asks, drawing her legs against her chest and wrapping her arms around them.

I nod slowly. "And it's ours now. If you want, we can get rid of everything and make it all new. All us."

Zoe considers that. "I think we can do some of that. It'd be nice to have a dishwasher, at least," she replies. I laugh, resisting teasing her. It's not like she's had to do the dishes, anyway. "But ... I think it's good to keep the memories that make you stronger. So, I guess it's up to you."

My brows jump. Well, damn. Maybe she *is* Miss Mature. God, she's growing up so fast.

"You're wise beyond your years, Zo," I commend her. "That's a good plan. I'll keep it in mind. And speaking of good plans, I set up an appointment for Thursday to get satellite internet installed."

Zoe jumps to her feet and does a happy dance. "Yes, I can't wait!" she cries with a fist pump. "I haven't watched YouTube or played *Dress to Impress* in like a week!"

Chuckling, I rise, taking both of our dishes toward the kitchen. But Zo stops me with a hand on my arm. "I think I'll finish mine after all," she says, taking her bowl back.

I ruffle her hair, partially out of affection and partially because I know she likes it even though she pretends it exasperates her.

At the end of the evening, Zoe trots off to bed all on her own. She doesn't ask for a story like she has been the last few nights. She barely even hugs me goodnight. Clearly, despite the slightly somber tone of earlier this evening, she's feeling good about life. More secure.

I'm glad but, unfortunately, I can't say the same. As I lie in bed, sleep eludes me and my mind fitfully refuses to settle, wondering what I'm missing about my exit from town. I try to dismiss it as perhaps Rae's own hurt at my departure seeming like a bigger deal in her mind ... but even as a teenager, she wasn't that prone to those sorts of theatrics. But maybe she is now?

I know there's no point in worrying about it, so it's only after reminding myself that whatever it is ... well, it's nothing compared to what I've already lived through. It'll be fine. One way or another.

The next morning, I arrive at town hall, ready to meet the council. But instead of the meeting room, I find myself ushered into Arthur's office. It has plain ivory walls and crown-molding detailed to match the rest of the building, but is otherwise simple with a black walnut desk, a few padded chairs, and a couple of filing cabinets. No other décor graces the walls, though there is a framed family photo on Arthur's desk.

Arthur looks up at me without expression as I enter.

"Have a seat, son."

I raise a brow at the terseness and lack of greeting but sit across the desk from him.

"I hope you're not offended, but I overheard your conversation with Rae yesterday," Arthur continues. "And I did some thinking after our meeting. While I'd heard some rumors when your family left town, I despise gossip and did my best to — forgive the language — stay the hell out of it." I smirk despite the churning anxiety I have for where this is going. "After some deliberation, I decided that a bit of well-intended intervention was worth a shot."

"I'm not offended, but I also have to admit I have absolutely no idea what this is all about," I admit, wiping my sweating palms on my dark jeans.

Arthur nods and sighs. "I surmised as much. And there's no easy way to do this." He leans forward and presses a button on his phone. "Meredith, can you bring Brandon to my office, please?"

My brows pull together. "I've heard his name mentioned. He's on the town council, right?"

"Yes, he is. I'm trying to convince him to take on Public Works. He was an aid worker, and he's shown a very good understanding of the basic infrastructure needs of a developing area. But —"

A knock on the door interrupts him and a blond head pokes in. Attached to a familiar face with familiar brown eyes. And as the younger man walks fully into the room, my breath catches in my throat. The resemblance is uncanny, like looking in a mirror that shows the past. I'd peg him at about thirty. Some quick mental math makes my pulse race, and I rise on unsteady legs.

"Luke, this is Brandon," Arthur says, gesturing toward the man. "Brandon, Luke."

Neither of us makes a move toward the other. Me because I'm so stunned. But as the shock wears off, I wonder why he hasn't.

"I'll just give you gentlemen some time," Arthur says after a few painfully silent moments. He rises and leaves, closing the door behind him.

And I still don't know what to say.

Brandon breaks the silence first. "So, what do I call you? Dad seems a little too familiar, don't you think?" His tone is acerbic, clearly communicating a lifetime of feeling rejected. Thirty years of it.

I feel queasy and breathless, like someone punched me in the stomach.

I have a son?

I have a son.

What else could he be? We even *sound* similar. It's almost eerie.

"We're going to need to back up here, because I don't understand what the hell is going on," I manage at last. "I had no clue … I swear I …" I shake my head, my thoughts jumbled and confused. I take a deep breath, willing my mind to settle. "Why didn't your mother tell me I have a son?"

Brandon shrugs and takes a seat in the chair closest to the door. "She was sixteen and pregnant by a guy who'd just left town. What was she supposed to do? It's not like social media existed back then. She had no way of finding you."

I scrub my hands down my face. "Fuck," I swear. But things are clicking into place. "Well, that explains why she's so pissed off."

Brandon's brow furrows. "Excuse me?"

"Your mother. She's clearly furious with me and I had no idea why until you —"

Brandon holds up a hand. "Whoa there. My mother is dead. Who in the hell are you talking about?"

I blanch at his words. "Your mother isn't Rachel Donovan?"

"Who?"

"Rachel Donovan … Rae Donovan," I repeat.

"Oh," he says. "Rae? God. No. My mother was Bethanny Thompson."

And now I'm back to shock. *Bethanny Thompson?* Rae's *best friend?*

I shake my head vehemently. "That's impossible. I never had sex with Beth Thompson."

Brandon's eyes narrow. "Then why do you look like me with an aging filter?"

I shake my head, baffled as I try to answer that myself.

I've heard of women getting themselves pregnant from used condoms, but Rae and I didn't use them. I'd blame it on the small-town potential for our parents finding out, but honestly, we were just dumb kids. And short of Beth climbing in my bedroom window and looking for used tissue ... no, that train of thought leads to wild speculations. That's way too far out there. So ... how? How could Brandon look *so* much like me?

When I ask it like that, the truth quickly crashes over me like a tidal wave. I sink into the chair I'd been sitting in, my legs no longer able to support me. Brandon's face, his voice, hell, even his *mannerisms* are so like my own. It all slots into place with sickening clarity.

I feel like puking, and it must show, because a look of concern crosses Brandon's face. "What?" he prompts.

"My dad," I choke out. "It must have been my dad." My eyes flick up to meet his. "I look just like him. And so do you." Though now that I'm looking, there are some differences. Brandon's nose is narrower, his jaw a little rounder. He's a little stockier, too, though with the same fit build as my father and me.

"Wasn't your dad a pastor?" Brandon asks hesitantly.

I blink. "How'd you know that?"

Brandon looks away and shrugs. "I might've done some research after you came back to town."

I huff out a dry laugh. "Yes, he was a pastor," I agree. "And a hypocritical piece of shit." And apparently a philandering predator who then convinced his victim to tell everyone I'd knocked her up and left her to deal with it. But I don't need to say that part out loud. "We can get a blood test done to make sure."

"Well, since apparently everything I knew is wrong ... that's probably a good idea," he agrees.

I nod absently, my mind still processing everything. Anger churns in my gut while the betrayal burns like acid in my veins. My dad, the man who preached about morality and sin, fathered a child with a teenage girl and pinned it on me. I knew he was a hypocrite. Preaching about God's plan and the kindness of Christ while unleashing his anger verbally and physically on his family. Forcing us to do what he said, when he said it. Ruling by fear. His actions had an enormous impact on me in my formative years. I thought that part of my life was over, but apparently, I was wrong.

My thoughts continue to whirl with the staggering implications of this revelation.

But now I get what Rae meant about the town's opinions. If that's the person they've thought of me as all these years, that's sure not going to make stepping in as the Fire Chief any easier.

More importantly? That means Rae thinks I cheated on her. That I abandoned my child.

Now I also get why she can't stand the sight of me.

I pull myself out of my thoughts to find Brandon looking at me with an equally contemplative stare. He must be reeling as hard as I am right now. And it finally sinks in that he mentioned Beth died.

"What happened to your mom?" I ask softly.

Brandon's gaze drops to the floor. "She passed when I was five. Overdose. My grandpa raised me."

I search my memories for anything on her father. John, I think? He was a single father, his wife having died in childbirth, if I recall correctly. Not having a mom messed Beth up pretty badly. John seemed like a great father, but I've seen firsthand the emotional toll it takes on a girl to lose her mother.

My brain wants to take that commonality and run with it, but Beth was quiet and kept to herself. The kids in town constantly teased her for her antisocial behavior. Now, as an adult, I understand she was probably depressed. Zoe, however, is compassionate, connected, and expressive. Though many burn victims struggle with depression and anxiety, Zoe has shown no signs of either given her natural positivity and an excellent personal and professional support system that wasn't available to Beth given where she was. So, I don't think for one minute Zoe will meet the same fate as Beth.

But right now, all of my other concerns aside, my heart goes out to the man in front of me, for the mother he lost, for the family he never knew. Including me.

Assuming my guess is correct, and I'm reasonably certain it is, Brandon is my brother.

A fierce protectiveness surges through me. I've lost one sibling. I will not lose another.

For his part, Brandon is silent, so I know this must be hitting him hard.

"I'm sorry for your loss, Brandon," I say sincerely. "If there's anything I can help you figure out about our family, I'm here, okay?"

He nods solemnly. "Thank you," he murmurs. He breathes in deeply and looks up at the ceiling. "Where is our father?"

I frown.

"Honestly? I don't know. I haven't spoken to him in years. But I'm sure as hell going to track him down now."

Brandon nods, a glimmer of hope in his eyes. "Good. Let me know what you find out."

"Of course. I'll figure out how we can do that blood test, too."

"Why don't you let me take that one? I have a friend who might help," Brandon offers.

As we've clearly both had enough for one day, we exchange numbers, a tentative bridge spanning the chasm of years, before calling Arthur back in.

Arthur re-enters his office, his expression guarded. "I'm sorry to have sprung this on you two, but I'd hoped that cutting to the chase right away would be best for you both. And if it wasn't, please know that if you'd prefer not to work together, we can accommodate that," Arthur says.

I smirk at the slightly pompous speech that I know is well-intentioned. "We're good," I reply. "But thank you."

Arthur looks surprised but pleased. "Brandon?" he asks, turning toward him.

Brandon nods. "I'm still a little shocked, honestly. I came in expecting to meet my father, and I'm leaving with a brother." He shakes his head as if he can't quite believe it.

"I'm sorry. Did you say Luke is your *brother?*" Arthur asks, his weathered brow scrunching.

"We think so, yes," I reply. "To be confirmed soon. And I know you don't like gossip, so I'll let you know as soon as it's proven."

"Oh, that won't be necessary. I don't intend to spread your business around," Arthur protests.

I rise and pat Arthur on the back. "Given the false version that's been circulating all these years, look at it as helping me set the record straight."

"Us," Brandon pipes up. "Helping *us* set the record straight."

I meet Brandon's eyes, and a warmth passes between us.

Brothers.

I don't have a son … I have a brother.

I have so many emotions about that I can't even begin to unpack right now.

"Are we still meeting with the rest of the council?" I ask Arthur.

He shakes his head. "I've requested with the rest of the council to reschedule for Friday. I figured this took priority, as well as whatever came of it."

"You're a good man, Mayor Burton. Thank you," I tell him. I reach out and shake his hand. "If we're done here, I have something important to take care of as soon as possible."

"By all means," Arthur responds.

Brandon eyes me speculatively. "Since you're my brother, you should know I'm terribly nosey," he says with a mischievous twinkle in his eye.

I laugh loudly and honestly. "You got something to ask, kid, just say it," I reply.

Brandon grins. "Where are you going?"

"To set things right with someone who has every reason to be angry with me."

Brandon nods. "You know, I came in thinking *you* were a hypocritical piece of shit, but now I'm thinking you might be a good man, Fire Chief McMillan," he says.

"Glad to hear it," I say sincerely. "I look forward to getting to know you, Brandon. I'll see both of you later this week." A thought halts me as I head for the door, and I turn back to Brandon. "Oh. I have a twelve-year-old daughter named Zoe. You're an uncle."

Brandon grins, but I don't wait for a response. Instead, I stride out of the office, determination quickening my steps. I have a record to set straight with Rae. She thinks I cheated on her. That I fathered a child with her best friend. The betrayal she must have felt ... I can't even imagine. Well, actually, given my father's betrayal, I have some idea. But that's different. She's had to live with it all these years, whereas I'm just finding out.

I practically run to my truck, jumping in and hurrying out of the parking lot. I need to see her, to explain. To tell her it wasn't me. That I never betrayed her. That I never stopped loving her.

CHAPTER SEVEN

RAE

I'm just putting a fresh batch of chocolate chip cookies into the display case when Evan pops into the bakery, a mischievous grin on his handsome face, his light brown hair artfully disheveled, oozing movie star charm. And his wellness center uniform fits against his swimmer's body in a way that should be illegal. I try not to ogle too hard. It'd be a shame to drop a cookie.

"Hello, ladies, what's good today?" he asks, knocking his knuckles on the counter.

I wave a cookie at him. "Just out of the oven. Want a booze pairing or just the cookies?" I ask.

He laughs. "Just the cookie. Two, actually. I have a break between appointments, so no alcohol for me. Though I am curious what booze Mia pairs with chocolate chip cookies," he replies.

Mia pops out of the kitchen as I bag his cookies. "A Frangelico cocktail," she offers, answering his question. "What's got you in such a good mood?"

Evan grins. "Oh, you know, one of my famous friends may or may not be building a house in Alpine Ridge soon," he announces, leaning against the counter.

Mia's eyes widen. "What?! Who? Tell me, tell me!" she pleads, practically bouncing on her toes.

Evan shakes his head, his grin widening. "Nope, not saying a word. It's all very hush-hush."

Mia narrows her eyes as I hand him the bag. "Does Carrie know?"

"Of course she does. She's the town planner, after all," Evan replies with a wink.

Mia huffs. "Fine. I'll just get it out of my sister later, then."

Evan laughs and waves as he heads out the door with his treats. "Good luck with that!"

"It's a shame Penny left to go to school in Seattle. She'd love to see more celebrities around here," I say as I head back into the kitchen to put the baking tray away.

Mia nods, a thoughtful look on her face, following me through the door. "True, but who knows? Maybe she'll come back at some point."

The bell above the door chimes again, and Mia perks up. "I bet that's Evan, coming back to spill the beans," she says, hurrying back out to the front.

But a moment later, she pops her head back into the kitchen, her expression unreadable. "Luke's here. He wants to talk to you."

My stomach does an uncomfortable flip. I'm not ready for this conversation, not by a long shot.

"Tell him I'm at work," I protest weakly.

Mia levels me with a look. "I can handle things here for a bit. There, now you have no excuse to deal with it. Which you definitely should do, because this is a small town, and you can't avoid him forever."

"Fine, have a point," I grumble. Reluctantly, I untie my apron and hang it on the hook by the door. I take a deep breath, steeling myself, and step out into the front of the bakery.

Luke is waiting at a table, his hands clasped in front of him. He looks up as I approach, his brown eyes filled with a mix of apprehension and determination.

"What can I do for you, Fire Chief McMillan?" I ask brusquely.

He winces. "Can we talk?" he asks, his voice low.

I contemplate him for a moment. I could say no, but Mia's right — nothing keeps in a town this small. Plus, I'd always wonder what he was going to say. Though, while I may begrudgingly agree, I also don't want anyone who walks in to hear whatever he's got to get off his chest, either.

"Guess we'd better. But not here." I glance out the window, remembering the chill in the air as I walked in today. It's gotten cold again, winter not quite ready to release its grip.

"We can sit in my truck. It's probably still warm," he offers, rising.

I glance out the window at what I presume is his vehicle. It's nice, if not well-loved. Mostly, I'm thankful it's not the same truck he drove back in the day. Though being in any truck with him is bound to bring back memories. Still, it's probably our best option.

"Fine," I agree tersely, grabbing my coat off the hook by the door and slipping it on.

Luke leads the way out. As I climb inside the truck, he starts the engine, presumably to have the heat running to keep us warm.

But as soon as I slide in, a subtle but acrid smell hits me. "It smells like smoke in here," I comment.

Luke shrugs. "Comes with the firefighter gig."

"Didn't you shower at the fire station or at least change clothes or something?"

He looks at me for a long moment. "It sinks into everything. Even your skin."

I shudder at the tone that implies he's talking about so much more than the smell. I hadn't thought too hard on how difficult a job it must be.

An uncomfortable silence settles between us as he seems to gather his thoughts. Finally, he takes a deep breath and meets my gaze head-on.

"I talked to Brandon," he begins.

My brows pop up. "Well … okay. That was unexpected," I admit.

"Arthur thought it best that we confront the issue head on. The issue you apparently couldn't tell me about? The one where everybody talked about me having a son and abandoning his mother?" He casts me a look that holds no anger, just hurt.

"I wanted to," I admit. "But I didn't think it was my place." My insides churn.

"Beth was your best friend. In what world wasn't it your place to call me out for that?" he asks candidly.

I'm a bit taken aback. "What good would it do now? He's grown. She's gone. Everyone has moved on." I shrug, uncomfortable with skating so close to the well of anger inside me.

"In the spirit of confronting the issue head on …" he says warily. I feel myself shrink away from whatever else he's about to lay on me. But he looks me straight in the eyes anyway. "I'm not his father, Rae. I didn't sleep with Beth."

I can't help it. I let out a sarcastic laugh. "Really? That's the story you're going with? I mean, you saw Brandon, right?" I shake my head. Unbelievable. It took me a long time to come to terms with how little I really knew Luke, and I think part of me still didn't believe it. But the gall of him denying it is astounding.

A muscle in his jaw flexes as his gaze turns hard. "Did you ever consider that there's someone else who could've had a child that looked just like me?"

I stare at him, baffled. Is he serious? And who the hell could that even be? The only other man in his family … my chest constricts at his implication.

No. He cannot possibly mean who I think he means. I speak before I can even fully process what I'm saying.

"You've got to be joking. Your dad? Are you really that desperate to avoid taking responsibility? Is the idea of being a parent so bad?" I ask accusatorily.

Luke's nostrils flare. "Not at all. I *am* a parent, Rae. I have a daughter. And if Brandon was my son, you bet your ass I'd claim him in a heartbeat. But he's not. And in case it's not crystal clear, I also didn't have sex with your best friend." He shakes his head angrily.

My heart pounds in my chest and my palms go clammy. Luke has a *daughter?* How have I not heard this yet? Maybe she's grown, too, and didn't move here with him, so nobody knew? God, that would have to mean he knocked Beth up, then not long after knocked someone else up. My stomach churns at the thought.

"You're … serious?" I stare at him, struggling to accept what he's telling me. But by far the hardest story to swallow is him pinning this on his dad. "You're saying your father — a married man, pastor, and pillar of this community — slept with a sixteen-year-old girl?" I ask, my voice laced with disbelief.

Luke sighs heavily, staring down at his clenched fists. I can't tell if he's exasperated or exhausted. "That's exactly what I'm saying. And honestly? I was horrified when I figured it out, but not at all surprised. He's not a good man, Rae. I've always known that, even if I never told anyone. But that was part of his brainwashing: best face forward, always. Be the perfect family. And after we moved away … our family fell apart. Then things got even worse."

He looks at me with tears in his eyes and despite my anger, my heart twists.

"But that … that's another story. What I'm worried about right now is making things right with you. I guess I hoped you'd listen. That you'd believe I'd never do that to you. I loved you, Rae. I was devastated when I had to leave you." His eyes roam my face, his lips pulled down in a frown. "And now I'm devastated to know you still believe the worst."

I close my eyes, trying to process everything he's thrown at me. It's too much, too fast.

"When you left, my world shifted," I admit. "And then when Beth herself told me …" I turn away, staring out the window. I can't relive that day out loud. My best friend claiming that the love of my life had only ever wanted her. That I was just easy sex. I shake my head, refusing to dwell on the part of me that died that day, or the rage that took its place. "It took me a long time to come to grips with yet another new reality. And now … I'm being told it was all a lie." I look back at Luke. His anguish is written in the lines around his down-turned mouth. Defeat in the slump of his shoulders. "This is a lot to take in. I'm going to need some time."

We stare longingly at each other for a few moments that do no justice to the years of heartache I can tell we've both suffered. Not for the first time, I wish I'd been stronger than my pain all those years ago.

Maybe I can be now. But not right away. Not right this moment.

"I understand," Luke finally says softly. "For what it's worth, Brandon and I are getting a blood test done. That should give you some reassurance that I'm telling the truth, at least. I guess I kind of hoped you wouldn't need it, though."

My throat tightens under his disappointment. Not because his opinion matters, though I can't deny it does. But because I feel like my entire life has been one disappointment after another since he left.

But right now? There are too many words to say. Most of them wouldn't mean anything to him, anyway. So, I make a noncommittal noise and crack the door open. "I'll see you around, Luke."

He huffs a sharp breath and nods. "See you around."

I hop out of the truck and swing the door shut behind me. The metallic snap feels like an echo of another heartbreak. I practically stumble back into the bakery, torn between deciding to hate him and his desperate lies for the rest of eternity … and accepting his version so I can go back thirty years and do my life over with hope in my heart.

But there's no going back. So, I push through the bakery door. The bell tinkling heralds a choice made. The choice to walk away from Luke. For now, at least. I have to in order to protect myself.

I look up to meet Mia's concerned gaze. She takes one full look at my face and ushers me into the back room, sitting me down on a stool.

"What happened?" she asks quietly.

I relay the conversation to her, my voice shaking.

She says nothing at first, and I don't ask whether she believes him.

"How are you feeling?" she eventually prompts.

I shake my head. "I want to believe him, but the betrayal I thought had happened ... it changed how I viewed things. That's hard to undo."

Mia is quiet for a moment. "Is there something more going on here?"

I throw her a sharp look. "What does that mean?"

One slender brow raises on her forehead. It says she knows I'm full of shit. "I think you know exactly what that means. And while I know you're hurting right now, I wouldn't be a good friend if I didn't point out that your trust issues seem to go deeper than this thing with Luke." She pauses. Not like she doesn't want to say whatever is on her mind, but like she's trying to figure out how to word whatever truth she's going to hit me with next. "Does this have anything to do with why your marriage ended?"

I flinch as if she's slapped me, even though I should've seen it coming. "That was different," I snap.

But Mia's gaze is unwavering, and I feel my defenses crumbling. Because I'd never thought about it before. But now she asks ... well, she may not be wrong.

"I couldn't have children," I admit, my voice barely above a whisper. "So, my husband cheated on me with my best friend, who we were trying to use as a surrogate. That's why we split." I tip my head back, blinking back tears, realizing I was wrong; it's not different. And that she's right.

"Oh, Rae. I'm so sorry." Mia's eyes widen in horror as she makes the connection. Because I make it, too.

I don't know how I could've missed it before. Two men I loved cheating on me with and impregnating my best friend. It just shows how deep I'd buried both hurts, that they didn't even sit in my mind long enough for me to make the connection. To realize I might disbelieve Luke because, while I didn't catch him in the act, I sure as hell caught Sam. I didn't consciously make the association but apparently my brain did.

And I suddenly get that that's exactly what happened. Seeing Sam fucking Tanya on the couch my mom gave us as a wedding present was irrefutable proof that they were both awful, lying assholes. So, my mind filed Luke and Beth in the same category. Damn.

"Thanks, sugar," I say with a sniff. "But now I think on it, it really isn't different at all. Now that I think about it, catching my ex-husband in the act is very different from believing someone you knew to be a liar." I look over at her and see the confusion on her face. "Beth was ... unstable. She lied for attention loads of times. I should've known to question her about it before believing her."

Mia's eyes soften with pity. "Well, I'd say everyone wants to believe their best friend, but ..."

I wipe an errant tear off my cheek. "But?" Mia chews on her lip. I huff a dry breath out and gesture at her. "Out with it."

"But maybe, deep down, you wanted to believe the worst? That somehow you deserved to be cheated on? Or that you didn't deserve Luke?" My brows bunch together angrily, and she holds her hands up. "I'm just saying, it's easier to believe things that reinforce our own fears, Rae. It would explain why you didn't question it."

I open my mouth to give her a what-for ... but close it when I realize she may be right. Luke always loved me in a way I didn't think I deserved.

"Shit. You might have something there."

Mia smiles sadly and squeezes my hand. "I have a great therapist I do teletherapy with. Would you like her number?" she offers.

I sniff deeply and chuckle. "That might be a good idea," I agree. "I've got a lot to unpack." I shake my head. "Forty-six years of baggage, really. Because lord knows there was plenty of it even before Luke and Beth." I take in a deep breath. "We should get back to it. Someone's liable to come in." I'm deflecting, but I've had enough.

Thankfully, Mia seems to get it, as she nods. "Just … one more thing before that?" she asks tentatively.

"Mia, sweetheart, I love you to death, but I don't want to talk about Luke anymore," I reply wearily.

The corner of her mouth tips up ever so slightly and she shakes her head. "No, it's not … I just wondered … why couldn't you have children?" Mia asks softly.

I look at her, my brow furrowing. That's a whole other can of worms, but I sense she's got a purpose behind the question, and I'd rather not get into my fertility struggles and the surrounding mess. Best to cut to the chase of whatever she's really after.

"Why do you want to know?"

Mia bites her lip, looking away. "Nate and I … we've been struggling to get pregnant. I'm … afraid of seeking answers in case they tell me I'll never have children."

My heart clenches. I know that pain. I've lived that pain. I reach out, taking her hand in mine. "Mia. Look at me." She meets my eyes reluctantly. "You need to go get that information. Living in doubt of your own body, the fear every month as the clock ticks down, the devastation of starting to bleed …. even in my day, there was so much they told me they could do depending on how things turned up." I sigh, opting not to add that in my situation, that meant surgery that ended my dream of having a baby. But even in that knowledge, there was comfort. However, it's Mia's journey that's important right now. "Trust me, taking the chance is better than living in the hell of not knowing what could have been."

Mia meets my gaze with a sad smile. "You're right. I know you're right. Thank you." She bumps her shoulder against mine. "You know, that applies to you and Luke, too."

I sit back with a resigned sigh. She's right, of course. Again. As much as I want to cling to the hurt and anger of the past, I know I need to ask all the questions this time. To get all the information I can. To give Luke a chance to prove himself. To give myself a chance to heal and accept the truth, whatever that may be.

Though this whole situation has felt like yet another round of pain and doubt and fear, maybe it's the fire I've got to walk through to find peace and happiness again. I'm suddenly reminded of a quote. One I think we could both use right about now.

"We must accept finite disappointment but never lose infinite hope."

Mia smiles. "Martin Luther King Jr. … Does that mean you're going to give Luke a chance?"

I smile back. "Yeah. I think I am. What have I got to lose?" My stomach flips. Because I've got a lot to lose. It makes me wonder … is it worth the chance?

But Mia cuts off my train of thought with a shake of her head. "I think the question is: what do you have to gain?"

I close my eyes as her words pierce through me.

I open them again and consider her for a moment.

I grab my apron and whack her with it before slipping it back over my head. "I think I've had enough of you being right for one day. Let's go eat some of those damn cookies."

Mia laughs and gestures for me to lead the way. "I think we both could use a few," she agrees. "But Rae?" I turn back and give her a questioning look. "I'm queen of using humor to deflect. But you should know I'm always here for you, no matter what, okay?"

Touched, I pull her into a hug. "I know. Me, too, sugar."

She pats me on the back. "And I promise not to sleep with your next boyfriend."

I bust up laughing. Then we go eat a good chunk of the fresh cookies. And I realize, Mia is just one of my "no matter what" people. I've got a whole family of friends now. So, no matter what truth comes out of this thing with Luke, I know I'll be okay.

CHAPTER EIGHT

LUKE

Yesterday was a heavy day. I wake up still reeling from everything I learned and obsessing over everything I wish I'd said or done differently, particularly with Rae. But I won't change her mind by chasing her, so I get my ass out of bed hoping to distract myself as much as possible.

Unfortunately, I'm almost immediately hit with another letdown. Before Zoe has even come downstairs, I'm having my morning coffee when Arthur calls to let me know he has to postpone our Friday meeting to introduce me to the town council due to scheduling conflicts. I'm disappointed as I was eager to meet everyone and share what I've put together so far, but I understand. Life happens.

Instead of wallowing, I spend the morning setting Zoe up on a website she discovered called Outschool where she can take classes on almost any topic. Naturally, she's selected a drawing class. I'm thrilled, as there are a bunch of other kids her age in it and, listening while I do some minor repairs in the kitchen, it sounds like the teacher really knows their stuff and is great at keeping the kids involved.

Once the repairs are done, I'm still fidgety. I make lunch for Zoe and me before she heads outside to take advantage of the warming weather. Apparently, her instructor wants them to practice drawing trees. Good thing we're surrounded by them.

Alone in the house for a rare moment, I decide to use the time to track down my father. I really don't want to talk to the bastard, but I might as well get it over with. Even though in my mind he's Brandon's father, I want to hear it from him. It's not even about the facts. The blood test will give us those. I want the fucker to know he didn't get away with throwing me under the bus. That I know the truth. Brandon knows the truth. And soon the whole town will know the truth, too.

It takes some digging, and several calls to old friends in Marysville, but I eventually wind up with a phone number. My hand shakes as I dial, my heart pounding in my chest.

He answers on the third ring. "Hello?"

My gut clenches at his familiar voice. The awful memories it brings.

I'm silent a beat too long and he says, "Hello, who is this?"

I swallow hard, my throat suddenly dry. "It's Luke."

Silence. Then, "What do you want?"

No *"Son, so good to hear from you,"* or *"I'm so glad you called."* Then again, deep down, I didn't really expect that.

I take a long breath. "I know about Beth Thompson."

He scoffs. "And what do you think you know?"

I roll my eyes to the ceiling. "That you cheated on Mom with her. Or I guess I'm hoping it was consensual, anyway." A shiver trails down my spine. I hadn't even thought of the alternative, and I'm not prepared to go there. I've got to stick to what I called for. "And I also know you blamed it on me."

After another beat of silence and some rustling, he finally says, "I don't know what you're talking about. The girl's father called me and said you knocked her up. I did what I had to do to protect our family."

Suddenly, all my anger rushes to the surface. "She had a boy. Did you even know that? And he looks just like us. I know I didn't have sex with her. So, I think you *do* know what I'm talking about, and you did what you had to do to protect *yourself*," I snap. "Never mind what you did to that poor girl. Or your other son." I resist the urge to tell him what a great guy Brandon seems to be. How much he missed out on. He doesn't deserve to know. He does, however, deserve to know how pissed I am. "Or me. Did you think I'd never go back? That I'd never find out the whole town thinks I'm a piece of shit? It wasn't enough to ruin my childhood — all of your children's childhoods — you had to make sure we inherited your legacy of lies and ruin?"

"We're all sinners, Luke. Repent and be saved."

I almost laugh at his false piousness. "That's rich. Because if anyone needs to repent, it's you. But repentance requires regret and change. Two things you're obviously incapable of. Also, if you think that's what it takes to be saved, you clearly never really got the heart of Christianity. Ironic, given your line of work. All you need to be saved is Jesus. I'd introduce you, but I'm pretty sure you've been shitting all over His word while you were cheating on your wife and, at best, committing statutory rape, all while stealing from the churches you were supposed to be shepherding. I'm not the least bit surprised you can't even admit to any wrongdoing. I'm just glad I get to tell you I now know exactly how much of a fucking asshole you are, and I hope you get exactly what you deserve. My only regret is that I won't be there to see it happen, because if I wasn't done with you before, I most definitely am now."

He starts to sputter a protest, but I've had it. This conversation is obviously going nowhere, and I'm only getting madder by the moment. So, I hang up. It makes me miss the days of analog phones. My cathartic rant could've only been improved by the ability to slam the handset down when I hung up on his pathetic ass.

I'm so upset, I stand at the counter, chest heaving, tightness bunching my shoulders inward. Breathing deeply, I close my eyes and meditate until I relax.

I'm tempted to chastise myself for not keeping my cool better. Because it made an already high-stakes conversation even more difficult. But while I may not have gotten what I wanted out of it, I ended up getting what I needed.

Still, the more I think about it, the little he said all but confirms his guilt. I blow out a final, slow breath before calling Brandon.

He answers immediately. "Hey, Luke. What's up?"

I fill him in on my conversation with our father. He's quiet for a moment.

"So, he didn't admit it?" Brandon asks.

"Not directly, no. But I know him. 'We're all sinners' was code for 'so what if I did?'" I explain.

"Okay. I can buy that. But what does 'I did what I had to do' mean?" he presses. "Obviously he said or did something that made my grandfather and my mother let you just walk away from any responsibility," he muses.

"Damn. That's a good point. I hadn't picked up on that," I admit. "I guess my anger blinded me."

"I don't blame you at all," he responds. "Do you think he'd talk to me about it?"

My brows jump. "Do you even *want* to talk to him?"

Brandon chuckles. "Good point. Not really, honestly. But I do want to know how it all played out. Guess I'm too curious for my own good."

"Have you ever asked your grandfather?"

"Huh. Not in a very long time. Since I was still a kid, basically."

"Seems like a good place to start," I respond.

"It's Wednesday, so he's home. Are you busy right now?"

"You want me to come?" I ask incredulously.

"You deserve answers as much as I do," he points out.

I think about that for a moment and decide he's right. And it wouldn't hurt to have a conversation with John, man to man, to clear the air.

"All right. I'm in. I'll let Zoe know I'll be gone for a bit and then I'll head on over."

"I mean, you can bring her if you need to. Can she even, like … be left on her own?" he asks tentatively.

I laugh. "She's twelve going on twenty-five. She'll be fine. Plus, I think this may not be an appropriate conversation for her to be privy to," I point out.

"Ah. Gotcha. You're probably right. Okay, well, I'll see you soon, then?"

"Yep. Bye."

"Oh, hey, one more thing," he adds. "My friend Nate runs the medical clinic. He said we can stop by anytime for a blood test. So, we can do that after if you have time."

"Sounds perfect. Thanks, Brandon."

It takes me almost an hour to meet Brandon, given that I had to look in fifteen trees before I found Zoe. I can't be mad, though. She's curious and intelligent, and I'm thrilled that she's so happy here.

But finally, I pull up to John Thompson's house, a tidy little bungalow on the outskirts of town. I knock, and Brandon answers.

"Sorry it took me so long. Took a while to find Zoe. She was up a tree twenty feet from the house."

Brandon frowns. "No worries, but she should be careful. We get bears and wolves up here."

"Hm, good point. I forgot about that, thanks. I'll head back and have a conversation with her about it when we're done here."

Brandon nods. "As long as she's not still out at dusk, I'm sure she'll be fine. It's just something to keep in mind."

"Guess I've lived in the city too long," I admit with a sheepish grin.

"And I've been in remote locations that make the Cascades look like a petting zoo. Guess it's made me extra cautious," he admits. "Anyway, come on in. I just got here a few minutes ago. I was helping Grandpa use the bathroom." He gives me a loaded look.

"Is he okay?" I ask quietly as I follow him inside.

Brandon nods. "He fell and hurt his hip yesterday, apparently. It doesn't seem too bad, but he's embarrassed as hell. He says only old farts fall and break a hip."

"I can hear you," a voice calls from the room at the end of the hall.

Brandon and I share a conspiratorial chuckle as we enter a cozy living room crowded by a deep red overstuffed couch and recliner set surrounding a long, low knotty pine coffee table. A news program is paused on the wall-mounted flat-screen TV.

"Luke McMillan," John says, struggling to stand.

"Hey now," I say, approaching and holding out a hand. "Don't get up on my account."

John fixes me with an indecipherable look but reaches out and shakes my hand. "Appreciate that, son. Good to see you."

"Good to see you, sir," I reply in kind, taken aback by the warmth of his greeting. Given he apparently thinks I knocked up his daughter and never looked back.

John shoots a look at Brandon. "So, what can I do for you boys?" he asks, settling back into his recliner.

Brandon and I exchange another glance, this one more nervous. I clear my throat. "We wanted to ask you about Beth. Well, more specifically about what happened when you spoke with my father after you found out she was pregnant."

John's weathered face grows somber. He sighs heavily. "Beth insisted you were the father, so I felt like I had to try, even though I knew your family had troubles of its own. But when I contacted your dad ... well, instead of making you take responsibility, he paid Beth off to go away."

I feel like I've been sucker-punched. "He what?"

John nods. "It was a sizeable sum. Too much money to hand a sixteen-year-old. Hell, I'm not sure how she could even legally sign the agreement his lawyer sent over, but I couldn't stop her. She was strong-willed and had dollar signs in her eyes. But I held onto the money until she was legally an adult. And I was right to. Wish I could've held on to it longer. As soon as she turned eighteen, she took off with the cash and her new boyfriend. Used it to buy drugs. It took her a full three years to snort through enough cocaine to kill her." His voice is heavy with old pain.

I swallow hard. "I hate to ask this, but ... did you ever suspect that maybe I wasn't the father?"

John meets my gaze, understanding in his eyes. "I had my suspicions. I knew you enough to have a sense of you, and you seemed like a good kid. And once Brandon started growing up, it was obvious he looked like you and your pa. But Beth ... even before the drugs, she lied as much as she told the truth, and I don't think even she could tell the difference sometimes." He pauses. "Are you trying to tell me you're not Brandon's father?"

"I am," I agree. "I never ... Beth and I were just friends, and mostly just because of Rae. There was no ... physical component to our relationship." I could not feel more awkward than I do in this moment.

We sit in heavy silence until finally, John speaks again.

"I didn't think so. So, that leaves Pastor McMillan. And honestly, just by the way he handled the whole thing, I'd suspected as much. But once Beth was gone, I didn't see the point in pushing the issue. I was more than capable of raising Brandon. I didn't think dragging it all up would change anything."

Brandon nods slowly. "It may not change anything for you, but I guess I needed to know what really happened. So, thank you."

"The truth will set you free. John 8:32," he says to Brandon. Then to me, "Just wish your father practiced what he preached."

"Me, too," I murmur.

"But would I be here if he did?" Brandon muses.

We both look over at him in surprise. John chuckles. "Guess not, kid. Guess not."

Despite both John and Brandon's seeming acceptance, I can't help but feel awful that my father did this. I turn to John. "I'm sorry for what my father did to your daughter. If I'd known I —"

"It's not your burden to bear, son. Put it down." John looks me square in the eye.

And his words remove a weight from my heart I hadn't known was there. "Thank you," I say, my voice thick with emotion.

Brandon pats me on the shoulder. "Next stop, blood test?"

I nod. "Let's do it."

Brandon points at John. "I'm calling the home nurse service to get someone to hang out with you until your hip is better. Don't do anything stupid until they get here, okay?"

John glowers for a moment before growling, "Fine." And then he resumes his news program.

With the clear signal that he's done with the conversation, we head toward the front door. As I leave, I feel a mix of anger and relief. Anger at my father, at the lies and betrayal. But relief, too. Relief that truth will prevail.

A short time later, we meet up at Nate's clinic and the nurse calls us each back in turn for the blood draw. I go in first, and before she takes the sample, she lets me know the results could take a week, and that we might get them faster if we went to the hospital in Ellensburg. Brandon and I already discussed that option and agreed there was no hurry. That getting the ball rolling was enough for now. So, she goes ahead.

After, I feel lighter.

As we leave the clinic, I turn to Brandon.

"I need to head back and make sure Zoe wasn't eaten by bears. But given the time, I'll probably just be bringing her back down here for dinner at the tavern. Want to join us?" I offer.

"I'd love to," he agrees. "But — and this might sound weird, so feel free to say no — is it okay if I ride back with you? I have a couple more questions I don't think you'd want to answer in front of Zoe, and I think I'd rather meet her for the first time not in public."

I nod slowly, having not even thought about that aspect.

"I think that's a good idea, because there's something you should know before you meet her."

Brandon's eyebrow quirks. I gesture toward my truck and we both get in. Before I start the engine, I turn to him. "Zoe and her mother were trapped by an apartment fire when Zoe was little. Her mother got her out but … she didn't make it. And Zoe was burned badly. She has facial scars that … well, I think she's mostly okay with them now. It's other people that have been a problem."

Brandon covers his mouth in horror. "Oh god. I can't even imagine what they've said. Kids can be awful," he says with a bitterness that implies he's suffered being bullied, too. "Thanks for the heads up, though. I'm sorry you lost your wife."

I shake my head and start the truck. "Ginny and I were never married, and by then we'd long since gone back to being just friends. We were barely ever more than that, really," I admit. "That's not to say it didn't hurt. I cared about her a lot. Zoe was devastated, of course. It was a hard time for us both, but mostly for Zo." I take in a slow, deep breath.

"So, not to pile on …" Brandon says nervously.

I huff a wry laugh. "Dude, we're already rolling around in the mud. I'm obviously not afraid of getting dirty."

Brandon chuckles. "That's … apt." He takes a deep breath of his own. "So, our dad … is he really that bad?"

I glance at him warily. Because obviously my gut answer would be "no, he's worse." But I try to put myself in his shoes. I'd be concerned just learning that my biological father is … well, my biological father. So, I guess I'm the best person to answer his questions. Unfortunately, I'm not great at sugar coating things.

"I'd love to tell you that there were good parts of him. But honestly? I can't remember any. He's not a good man, Brandon. Everything was always about him. We all walked on eggshells because he'd explode at us for the slightest inconveniences. Behind closed doors, anyway. At church and in public, he was the doting husband and father. Righteous and patient and kind. As a kid, even I bought the act, so I always felt like I deserved his punishments. Because clearly, I must've been doing something wrong. Everyone thought he was an amazing man." I shake my head at the memories.

"What made you realize he wasn't?" Brandon asks solemnly.

I snort. "The fire started it. I was sixteen when the church burned down, and we left Alpine Ridge. I should've taken divorce filing from my mom as a clue that something was very wrong. He only got meaner after that. Especially because it took him a long time to get a new job. And things were ... rough. Financially and otherwise." I let out a heavy sigh. "Then he got a new job at a church up north of Seattle. Not long after, he started coming home with piles of cash. It didn't take much to figure out he was stealing from the Sunday tithe collection. I remembered times like it when I was younger, when he'd take us all out to a fancy dinner on Sunday nights, and I realized he'd probably been doing that all along."

"Shit."

"Yeah. I should've known his deceit went further than that." I pause as we pull into the long driveway. "I'm sorry for what happened to your mom. For the role he played in it."

Brandon is quiet for a moment. "I'm not sorry I was raised by my grandpa. He's a good man. And my mom ... what I remember of her ... she was too young. Too selfish. Too unstable. She wasn't ready to be a parent."

I reach over, squeezing his shoulder. "Well, you've got a brother now. And a niece. We're here for you."

He gives me a grateful smile as we pull up to my house. Zoe bounces out the front door, demonstrably not consumed by a wild animal. I let out a nervous laugh as Brandon and I get out.

She looks warily between Brandon and me as we approach.

"Hey, Zo, I've got someone for you to meet," I say, giving her a reassuring smile.

"Okay," she replies, clearly unsure.

I have the urge to crouch slightly to her level, like I did when she was younger. I shake it off. She's far too mature for that. I think it's just my urge to protect her from the nastier aspects of this revelation.

"This is Brandon Thompson. I just learned yesterday that we're related."

Brandon gives me a fleeting, confused look. I shake my head subtly. "Well, duh," Zoe says. "I mean, he looks almost exactly like you."

Brandon and I both laugh. "I guess it doesn't take a genius to see that," Brandon admits. "Nice to meet you, Zoe."

She looks him up and down. "Nice to meet you, too," she says, still with a note of skepticism. Then to me, "So, is he my cousin or something?"

"Well, that's a good question," I reply carefully. "We think he might be your uncle. But we're working on figuring that out."

"Hm," she hums. "How old are you, Brandon?"

Brandon's brows flatten. "I'm thirty."

She scrunches her nose — her thinking face — before declaring, "Okay, I guess you're old enough to be an uncle."

Brandon smirks. "Glad that's settled."

"So does that mean you'd be okay if Brandon came to dinner with us?" I ask her.

Zoe thinks about that for a moment. "Yeah, I guess that'd be cool."

I press my lips together to hold back a laugh. "All right then. Shall we?"

We climb into the truck and Brandon turns around as Zoe's buckling in. "So, Zoe. I hear you're twelve and that you're an artist."

She looks up, her eyes alight.

"Oh boy. Now you've done it," I murmur teasingly.

Zoe spends the drive talking Brandon's ear off about her favorite drawing media, her new class, and the sketch of a bough of fresh pine needles she did this afternoon. As we walk into the tavern, she's describing the softness of the newer needles compared to the older ones lower to the ground.

We get seated and Brandon takes the opportunity to talk to her about the woods around the house and how to keep an eye out for animals — bears and wolves especially — and that she should never go out around dawn or dusk for her safety.

Zoe listens to him in a way she doesn't even listen to me, and while we wait for our food, I'm happy to watch their surprisingly already strong bond solidify.

It's not until Zoe is chowing down on her chicken tenders, a new favorite, that I'm able to get a word in edgewise.

"So, I hear you were an aid worker?" I prompt.

Brandon nods. "It actually started with photography. I wanted to be a photojournalist for natural disasters. But once you see the destruction they cause and the desperate need of the people affected, it's impossible not to want to help."

"I know a little something about that," I murmur.

"So, the church fire made you want to be a firefighter?" he asks gently.

I glance at Zoe, who is listening raptly. I've told her about Hannah now, but she doesn't know details about my life before her.

"Sort of," I admit. "I had a little sister. She got caught in the fire and sustained extensive lung damage from the smoke. She died not long after. It devastated our family. My mom …" I breathe deeply, slowly. "I think it broke her. She left, and it was just Dad and me."

"I'm so sorry," Brandon says.

I push my partially eaten plate away and lean back. "Thanks. It was a long time ago. Anyway, I guess I thought it could have been prevented. That even if I couldn't go back and undo it, I could save someone else's sister. Someone else's family. So, when I graduated high school, I joined the army and trained for fire-fighting missions. Then once I was out, I went through the Seattle Fire Department's recruit school and bing-bang-boom. Firefighter."

Zoe leans over and wraps her arms around me. "I'm sorry about your sister, Dad."

"I know, sweetheart. And I'm sorry about what happened to you and your mom. Just goes to show that even when there are firefighters in the equation, it doesn't always work out like we want. Though you know if I could've saved you both, I would've."

"I know," she says quietly.

Brandon shakes his head. "I'm so sorry for you both."

I shrug. "If I've learned anything, it's that you can't save everyone. No matter how much you want to. And as devastating as the losses have been, I've found solace in that. So, I do my best, and the rest isn't up to me."

"Alpine Ridge is lucky to have you as its new fire chief," Brandon replies.

"And its lucky to have you as a town council member. It sounds like you've got experience this town is going to need," I reply.

Brandon blushes. "I don't know about all that. But I'm excited to be part of establishing the new Alpine Ridge. I can't wait to see what this town becomes."

I nod. "Me, too."

"I just hope we get a library soon," Zoe pipes in.

Brandon laughs. "I will pass that on to the mayor and city planner," he assures her.

Zoe claps her hands. "So, until that happens, what is there to do for fun around here?"

"Well. There's the bakery. And my friends have regular game nights and a weekly dinner party. But honestly, I spend most of my weekends away," Brandon admits.

"Oh? Where?" I ask, with an arched eyebrow, sensing there might be a reason involving a special someone. I may have been lucky, but I know it's probably hard to date in such a small town.

"At first, I visited Seattle a lot. But these days I'm spending most of my time in Ellensburg. I'm ... seeing someone there," he replies.

Zoe grins and makes that "oooooh" noise kids do when they're teasing each other about their crushes. I hide my smile behind my glass as I take a sip.

"What's her name?" I ask as nonchalantly as possible.

"*His* name is Alex," Brandon corrects gently, blushing even harder than before. "He owns an antique shop. We met when I was setting up my art gallery and looking for pieces with local history to include."

I feel like a complete ass. "I'm sorry," I say. "I shouldn't have assumed."

Brandon waves off my apology. "No worries. It's an understandable mistake."

I'm about to ask how long they've been dating when Zoe bursts in, clearly unable to contain herself. "You have an art gallery? Can we see it?"

Brandon smiles at her enthusiasm. "Sure, we can go when we're done here."

And so, after Zoe finishes eating at record speed, we head over to the gallery. It's a small space, but Brandon has filled it with an impressive array of local artwork. Photography, wood carvings, fiber arts, paintings ... it's a celebration of Alpine Ridge's unique beauty and creative spirit.

"This is amazing, Brandon," I say, marveling at a stunning photograph of a line of pine trees just visible under the snowy Cascade peaks at sunset with deep oranges, pinks, and purples highlighting the rugged landscape.

He ducks his head, looking pleased. "Thanks. It's a work in progress, but I'm happy with how it's coming together."

I gesture at the photo. "Is this yours?"

"It is," he admits.

"It's gorgeous. There are so many pieces here I'd love to get for the house. Once Zoe and I finish fixing it up, anyway."

Zoe nods her agreement. "I like the paintings," she says, gesturing to the far wall filled with watercolor renderings of native wildflowers.

"Good eye," Brandon says encouragingly. "They're painted by a Chinook tribe descendant who lives in town. She's one of our oldest town residents."

Zoe's eyes go wider than I've ever seen them. "There's a woman here who *paints?*"

I chuckle. "I don't think you realize what you just started," I tease Brandon.

"I'm glad she's excited. That's why I started this place. To showcase the beauty and talent of the townsfolk, not just the landscape itself."

He finishes showing us through the displays, and when we leave the gallery, I can't help but feel a swell of pride. My brother, building something beautiful in the town we both call home.

Friday morning, I'm just finishing up breakfast when my phone rings. It's Nate.

"Hey, Luke, hope you don't mind my calling," he opens.

"Not at all," I respond. "What's up?"

"I've got your test results," he says. "You and Brandon are definitely half-siblings. Same father."

I blow out a breath. I'm … relieved. That my assumption was correct. That my assessment of my father was dead on. That rumors can now be replaced by facts.

"Wow. Okay. Thanks. That was … fast."

"I went ahead and expedited it. If it were me, I'd want to know."

"Thanks, Nate. I appreciate that." We only met briefly at the clinic, but my sense that he's a standup guy was dead on.

"No problem. I'll make sure you get a copy of the results. Also, we're having a dinner party tomorrow night. Brandon's coming. Why don't you join us?"

"Really? Are you sure? I'd have to bring my twelve-year-old daughter. I wouldn't want to intrude."

"Absolutely. We'd love to have you both. Mia lives to feed people. She'll be thrilled."

I hesitate for a moment. Because if Mia, who I'm pretty sure is the bakery owner, will be there, then Rae probably will, too. And I'm not sure if she'd want me there. Last I checked in, she still needed time. But the thought of spending more time with Brandon, of getting to know Nate and their friends better … it's appealing. And we can always leave if it makes Rae uncomfortable.

"Yeah, okay," I agree. "We'll be there."

"Great. I'll text you the address."

"Thanks, Nate."

"Sure thing, Luke."

After I hang up, I sit at the kitchen table, thinking. I figured I'd be worried about seeing Rae tomorrow, but my brain keeps sticking on the blood test, and the fact — *fact*, mind you, no longer just speculation and rumor — that Brandon is my brother.

It throws everything into a new light. My parents' marriage. My parents' divorce. My mother's subsequent distance. I always assumed it was because of my sister's death, but now …

I find myself searching for my mother's address. It takes some digging, courtesy of the internet and what little I remember of the names of family members on her side, but I eventually track her down in Spokane. It's a shot in the dark, but given everything I've been through lately, I find I'm valuing family more than ever.

So, before I can talk myself out of it, I sit down to write her a letter. It pours out quickly as if I'd been writing it in my head for the past thirty years.

Dear Mom,

I know it's been a long time. Too long. But I've learned some things recently that I think you should know. I know about Dad and Beth Thompson. About their child, and how he told everyone it was mine. I know his unfaithfulness was probably part of why you left. I'm so sorry you had to go through that and losing Hannah alone.

I have a daughter now. Her name is Zoe, and she's twelve. She reminds me so much of Hannah. She has the same smile, the same laugh. I think about Hannah, and you, every day.

Believe it or not, I'm back in Alpine Ridge, as their new fire chief. I went into firefighting to save people, families, like ours. I'm building a fire station here. Trying to make something good out of all the pain.

I hope you're doing well. I miss you.

Love,

Luke

I add my phone number at the bottom of the letter and fold it carefully, sliding it into an envelope. I don't know if she'll write back. If she'll even want to hear from me after all these years. But I have to try.

For her. For Zoe. For the family I'm piecing back together, one truth at a time.

CHAPTER NINE

RAE

S aturday morning arrives in a flurry of activity. It's go time for preparing the St. Patrick's Day event, which we decided to hold on Sunday to ensure as much of the town can attend as possible, even though the actual holiday is on Monday. One less day to make the shamrock adorned festivities a reality. On an already short schedule, that has me feeling the pressure. Thankfully, that's when I do my best.

I arrive at the community center early, expecting to get some time to work on my own. But to my surprise, I find Greg, Joanie, Brandon, Carrie, and Layla already hard at work.

While I've spoken to Layla on the phone a few times this past week, this is my first time meeting her in person. It's easy to pick her out, as hers is the only fresh face. And it's an intimidating one; she's beautiful, with big, jewel-green eyes, flawless deep sienna skin, and thick, curly black hair.

"You must be Rae," she says warmly, approaching and wrapping me in a hug.

"Oh!" I exclaim in surprise. She's nice, too. Goodness. "And you must be Layla," I reply, giving her a squeeze before taking a step back. "You're here early. You're *all* here early."

Carrie grins. "You always do so much work for town events, so we wanted to surprise you by taking care of as much as we could. We cleaned the whole place, and we're moving the tables out now."

I put a hand to my chest, moved by their thoughtfulness. "You guys are the best, thank you," I gush, setting down my overstuffed tote bag. "I brought the lightest bits in first, but I wouldn't object to help bringing in the bigger boxes from the Bronco."

"On it, boss," Greg says. I toss him the keys as he and Brandon head outside.

I rub my hands together, eager to dive in. "All right, Layla. Are you ready for your first Alpine Ridge extravaganza?" I joke, considering Leavenworth's event traffic is probably light years beyond ours.

Layla laughs, her dark curls bouncing. "As ready as I'll ever be. I'm just glad we're having it inside, given how unpredictable the weather's been."

I nod in agreement. "True. But we've got plenty of space here, and you've all done a great job of getting started setting up."

"So, what's the plan?" Joanie asks, planting her hands on her hips like she's about to run a race.

I chuckle. "You'll see once the guys bring the boxes in. First, I want to go through what we have to make sure I accounted for things correctly."

First, I give Layla a high-level overview of the events we run. She listens and asks good questions.

"So, your permanent population is how many people?" she asks, tapping a long, slender finger to her chin.

"A few thousand, but we're pretty spread out," I respond.

She nods. "That's about how many permanent residents Leavenworth has, but our events are more geared toward the larger tourist population."

"Ours will be eventually, too, I hope," I say. "But until now, it's mostly been locals. We usually get a few hundred people, give or take. The key is to be flexible and roll with the punches. Weather, turnout, last-minute changes ... I treat it as part of the fun."

Layla mumbles to herself while jotting down notes. "Sounds a lot like the festivals we have in Leavenworth, too. It's always an adventure!"

I take Layla with me to the supply closet and go over what we have. It doesn't take long, and after we're done, I get ready to distribute the boxes I brought. I call everyone back together in the main room.

"Okay. Are you all ready for your assignments?" I ask. Everyone grins and hoots in response, and I can't help but chuckle at their excitement. "Excellent! Greg, I need you to set up a dance floor in the corner with a CD player." I dig through my tote.

"A CD player? Huh. Okay. We might still have one somewhere," he replies skeptically.

I fish out the CD I was looking for and hand it to him. "Mr. O'Reilly will teach traditional Irish Céilí Dancing, and he gave me this for the music."

He takes the CD. "Well, now I *have* to find a CD player. This sounds too good to miss out on."

I wink at him and grab another box. "Carrie, you're on Shamrock Bingo duty," I inform her. "Oh, and you're still bringing the mini shepherd's pies, right?"

She grabs the box. "Absolutely. Evan and I will make them tonight after the dinner party, so they're as fresh as possible."

"Sounds like my kind of after party," I respond. "Brandon, since I already asked you to do a photo booth, the cat's out of the bag on that one." I gesture to the largest box, sitting by the door. "There's a green photo backdrop and a whole pile of St. Patty's Day themed props in there. Let me know if there's anything else you'd like me to scrounge up for you."

Brandon nods. "A few stools wouldn't go amiss, but I think I saw some in the closet."

"Sounds good," I agree. "Mia will provide everything for the Pot of Gold cookie decorating table, along with Guinness cupcakes with Bailey's icing. But for the food table itself —" I nudge a large box toward Joanie with my foot "—Joanie, if you could arrange these platters and serving ware, I'd be much obliged. There are some beverage containers and cups that will go on the drinks table Jerry will be running."

"Can do," Joanie agrees. I give her a look, waiting for her to say more. When she doesn't, everyone else's heads, save Layla's, swivel in our direction. Joanie throws up her hands. "What? I don't *always* have to be sassy. I can be cooperative sometimes."

Everyone laughs except Greg, who looks like he's trying not to. It's sweet that he doesn't want to seem like he's making fun of her, even though I know she wouldn't care if he did.

"What's Jerry bringing?" Brandon asks curiously.

"A non-alcoholic Irish cream liqueur drink and elderflower cordials," I reply.

"Damn. I was hoping for some Guinness," he laments.

I shrug. "Guinness isn't cheap, and Jerry's nothing if not frugal," I point out. "I have no doubt he came up with drinks that would use ingredients that don't move at the tavern. But I'm sure you can go there after and get one."

"Hm. I might do that for lunch because now that I've said it, I kind of want one right now."

"I'm down," Greg offers.

"Babe. Really? Before noon?" Joanie says, poking him in the stomach.

"Well, not right this exact moment, obviously," Greg responds. "Maybe we can all grab lunch when we're done."

"Oh, that sounds good," Carrie agrees. "I'll text Evan to see if he'll have time to come after his morning appointments." Nobody brings up inviting Mia and Nate, as both will be swamped on a Saturday, and we'll see them at tonight's dinner party, anyway.

"I'm not saying no, and I can't believe that I'm the one who has to say this, but can we please focus here?" I tease.

Layla's brows bunch together. "Are you not usually on task?" she asks me quietly.

I lift a shoulder. "I'm easily distracted." Then to everyone else, "So, I get it. But if you want lunch and beer, we're going to have to get this done." I glance at my watch. Considering it's almost eleven, it'll be a late lunch at best. "Anyway. I'll be running the raffle and setting up the prize table, and Layla and I will handle general decorating and coordinate anything you need or the attendees need. Sound good?" Noises of agreement bounce around the room, and I nod, satisfied. "All right, let's do it!"

"I love your ideas, Rae," Layla says as everyone splits off to start their tasks. "This is going to be a lot of fun."

"It is. I really hope as the town grows, we can keep the small-town community feel to these events. It's what makes them so rewarding, knowing my friends and neighbors are enjoying themselves," I admit.

"I know what you mean. You just have to learn to think of the visitors to town as new friends. That's how I do it."

I smile. "That's a lovely way to frame it."

As morning passes into midday, the community center transforms into a sea of green and gold. Shamrocks, leprechauns, and pots of fake gold decorate every surface, and laughter and excited chatter fill the air.

Once Brandon finishes setting up the photo booth area, he meanders over while I'm arranging the raffle prizes.

"You're doing an amazing job, Rae," he says, rubbing my back. "As always."

I smile up at him. I keep the smile fixed on, even though lately I get that gut punch when I look at him. It happened a lot when he first came back, but I thought I'd gotten used to it. Or, I suppose I had, until Luke returned, anyway.

"Thanks, Brandon. I really appreciate your help. Especially given everything that's been going on lately. How are you doing with all the Luke stuff?" I ask as nonchalantly as I can. With the event preparation, I have had little time to dissect my discussion with Luke or check in to see how Brandon was doing. But if he's feeling anything like I am, "overwhelmed" probably doesn't even begin to cover it.

"Honestly? I feel fantastic," Brandon says, to my surprise. "I spent my whole life thinking Luke was the father who rejected me. So, when I heard he was moving back here, I was terrified of whatever would come next. Now I don't have to worry about that, and I also have a brother and a niece who both seem pretty awesome. It's great. I'm great. But thank you for being concerned."

I smile, my heart faltering at his description of Luke. Because his description reminds me that I also found Luke pretty awesome once. More than awesome. Once, Luke was the most important person in the world to me. Which is why what I thought he did hurt me so much. And why, even now, I still have feelings for him. Convoluted ones, but still, feelings.

"I'm happy for you, Brandon." I pause, unsure of whether I should ask, but too curious not to. "So, it's confirmed then? You're brothers?"

Brandon's chin dips. "It is. Nate was kind enough to get us the blood tests results quickly. Brothers with the same father."

I try to smile again, to share his clear relief and joy, but it's a weak attempt.

I can tell Brandon sees right through me. Proven when he says gently, "Look, I know Luke told you all of this, and I know it was probably shocking. Just in case you're not ready to deal with it yet, you should know they'll both be at the dinner party tonight. Luke and his daughter, Zoe."

My stomach does a little flip. Nerves, anticipation, a lingering hint of the anger I pushed down for years ... it's a complicated mix. One I'd like to let go of but am afraid of what that might mean. The unknown is ... scary. Though I know at some point, I'm going to have to deal with it.

"Thanks for the heads up," I manage. "I'll be fine. And I'm sure they'll fit right into the group."

"Hey, Brandon, will you please come help me mount this speaker?" Greg calls from the opposite corner of the room.

Brandon kisses me on the top of my head and goes to help Greg, leaving me distracted and unsettled. I look down at the beautiful baskets I'd put together this week, trying to focus on the joy of bringing joy to others. For the first time in a long time, it doesn't feel like quite enough.

I think about not going. Then I think about going and pretending everything's fine. *Then* I think about going and having the heart-to-heart I know Luke and I need. And that's when I go back to thinking about not going.

Yet here I am, standing on Mia and Nate's doorstep, late, as usual, a bottle of wine in hand. Going won, obviously, but I'm still not sure if I'm going to act like it's not happening or face it head on. Guess there's only one way to find out.

I step inside to the sounds of dishes clattering in the kitchen and multiple conversations going on in the living room across from it. All I have to do is step forward and round the corner into the living room.

I have to force my feet to cooperate. Setting my coat on the rack, I hang my purse over it and force myself down the hall.

As I stop at the entrance to the living room, I take a deep breath. But nobody looks up. Brandon and Carrie are talking to each other by the fireplace. Greg and Joanie are watching a dark-haired girl who, I assume, is Zoe playing with Bruiser on the floor. And Nate and Luke appear to be deep in conversation, leaned against the back wall.

Since nobody's paying attention, I take a moment to really look at Luke. I've avoided it so far, maybe because I feared getting caught, or maybe because I didn't want to remember how attractive he is. Because the reality is that he looks good. Really good. The same yet different, but the gray in his hair, the laugh lines around his eyes ... they suit him.

He's somehow even more handsome than when we were kids. I shake myself, trying to tear my gaze away. And in doing so, I realize Mia and Evan are both notably absent. Since I have a pretty good idea where Mia is, and my nerves are getting the better of me, I turn and head into the kitchen.

As I expected, Mia is busy at work pulling dishes out of the oven.

"Need any help?" I offer.

Mia looks up, little pieces of her dark hair sticking to her neck. "Rae! Hey! Didn't hear you come in." Surprise laces her tone. She blows a piece of hair out of her eyes. "Yes, please." She jerks her chin toward a stack of plates and cutlery. "Mind setting the table?"

"Not at all," I agree, heading to the sink to wash my hands first.

As in the bakery, we work seamlessly in tandem to get everything set up. It smells heavenly; pork roast, buttered fingerling potatoes, garlic rolls, and roasted asparagus sprinkled with lemon and parmesan.

"Cheese?" I ask curiously as she finishes sprinkling the asparagus. "Since when does Nate eat cheese?"

Mia smirks. "A while now. I think I've tempted him into eating most of his food no-nos at this point. But he's on his feet all day at the clinic, so he says he's not worried about the calories." She shrugs, then turns to me and hands me a bowl of steaming rolls. "Go by the living room on your way to the dining room. That ought to get their attention."

I chuckle and do as she says. This time, the second I appear at the wide arch entrance of the living room, everyone's heads perk up, Bruiser's included.

"Dinner's ready," I trill, continuing on to the dining room. I don't miss hearing the excited cries and shuffle of feet as everyone follows. I chuckle to myself as I set the bowl in the center of the long table.

They've all poured into the dining room and are taking seats when Evan finally shows his face.

"Damn, it smells amazing down here," he says, looping an arm around Carrie's waist and giving her a kiss.

I briefly wonder what he was doing upstairs but am distracted by Zoe, who was about to take a seat next to her dad and stops cold, her jaw dropping and her eyes getting hugely round.

Oh shit. Someone forgot to mention the movie star to the newbies.

Mia comes in with the pork platter, the last dish, and sets it down with an, "All right, everyone, let's eat!" just before Zoe screeches, "Omigod, Evan Edwards!"

The room erupts into laughter, and to my surprise, Evan blushes bright red, rubbing at the back of his neck. "Wasn't expecting that," he mutters as I slide into the chair next to him.

Mia props her hands on her hips. "Nate, did you forget to tell Luke and Zoe about your brother?" she asks accusingly.

Nate scrunches his face. "Sorry, babe." He turns to Luke. "Hey Luke, Zoe. My brother is Evan Edwards. You know, the movie star. Try not to make a big thing of it?"

Mia rolls her eyes and swats him on the arm.

Luke's jaw had dropped, too, but he promptly shuts it and nods. "Sure, of course, no problem. It's nice to meet you, Evan." He sits and pulls Zoe into the chair beside him. "Right, Zo?"

Zoe thunks down onto the chair, her big brown eyes still wide and excited. "I love your movies! You're so cool! Why are you here? Is she your girlfriend? Do you, like, live here now? Oh my god, I live in the same town as Evan Edwards!" She makes a little squealing noise and wiggles in her chair.

Okay, so clearly Zoe's not ready to chill. I chuckle. It's pretty cute to see her honest, awed response. I know I had that reaction internally when we found out Evan was Nate's brother and that we'd be meeting him at Mia and Nate's wedding. Thankfully, he's such a down-to-earth guy, that it didn't take long to just see him as one of the gang. I'm sure Zoe will get there with time.

Nate sighs and puts a slice of pork roast onto his plate, triggering the rest of us to dive in as well.

"Wow, well, thanks," Evan replies. "And, to answer your question, yes, I live here. Welcome to Alpine Ridge." He smiles warmly at her.

"So, Luke, Zoe, what do you think of the town so far?" Carrie asks, drawing their attention away from Evan, who I notice rubs her leg under the table gratefully as he starts eating. Guess he's still over all the attention that came with his former gig.

"It's already leaps and bounds better than when I left," Luke admits. "I can't wait to see how things continue to develop."

Carrie nods. "We have so much more planned. I think Arthur intends to take you through it all at some point."

"Is there going to be a library?" Zoe pipes up.

Carrie raises a brow. "You know what? I don't think we've talked about that yet, but I love that idea. I'll put it on the agenda for our next meeting," Carrie says to Zoe. "What do you like to read?"

"I like dystopian. My favorite books ever are the *Hunger Games*, but I like *Red Queen* and *Divergent*, though that series ended kind of bad. But I also like fairytale retellings like *A Curse So Dark and Lonely* and *Cinder*."

"I love all of those," I offer. "I'm Rae, by the way."

"Nice to meet you Rae," Zoe says.

"So you like fantasy, too, then?" I ask.

Zoe taps her lips. "A bit. Why, do you have some suggestions?"

I hold back a smile. "*An Ember in the Ashes* is a fantastic series, or if you like Greek mythology, there's always *Percy Jackson and the Olympians*. You also can't go wrong with *The Hobbit* or the *Inheritance Cycle* series. Or if you're looking for something a little quirkier, *The Eyre Affair* series is fun, and —"

"Okay, okay," Carrie holds up a hand. "Damn, Rae, sounds like you could get the library started yourself with all of those books."

I give a guilty smile. "Sorry, I didn't mean to overwhelm you," I tell Zoe. "In case it wasn't obvious, I read a lot, too, and you're always welcome to borrow my books."

Zoe grins, then we all eat for a few minutes in happy silence. Mia's food is delicious as usual, and everyone tells her so.

When Nate finishes, he leans forward on the table. "So, guess who came into the clinic today?"

All heads turn toward him, even Luke and Zoe's.

"Big Bird?" Joanie asks dryly. I assume it's her sarcastic commentary on Nate's inability to cut to the chase like she would.

Nate smirks. "Close. Betty McDonald."

"No!" I gasp.

"Yes," Nate confirms. "She said to Maura — that's our receptionist," he adds for Luke and Zoe's benefit, "that she wanted a copy of her medical records for her new doctor in Yakima. Because — get this — she's *moving there*."

Now everyone else gasps. I slam a hand down on the table. "Hallelujah!" I shout, keeping it clean since Zoe is present. "Finally!"

Luke's brows jump. "You're talking about Mrs. McDonald? The one who used to chase us away from her 'prize winning' flower beds?"

Carrie chuckles and I nod emphatically. "One and the same. She really crossed a line a couple years back, only we just found out recently. I might have given her a piece of my mind and made it less than comfortable for her to stick around."

"Sounds like she had it coming," Luke says drily. "Even when we were teenagers, she would yell at us for 'hanging around looking like we were doing nothing.'"

I roll my eyes. "Do you remember the time she told our parents we were delinquents because we were out after nine p.m.?"

"How old were you?" Zoe asks with a grin.

"Fifteen!" Luke responds. "She was ridiculous."

Luke and I share a smile. The warmth in his eyes hits me right in the chest. And

I remember. Those nights we'd wander around, just so we could hold hands a little longer. That's all it was at that age, anyway. Though sometimes, when Pastor McMillan would work late, we'd climb the church's bell tower stairs and clamber onto the roof to stargaze and make out. That part became … more about a year later.

My eyes drop to his lips as I remember. The warmth of his body. His strong hands groping clumsily under my shirt. Gosh, we were so young. So in love. And so naïve, as you always are that first time.

"Well, there's one less thing to worry about," Joanie says dismissively, snapping me out of my trance. "How about we celebrate with dessert?" She rises to help Mia clear the table.

Carrie and Brandon join them, and I make to help, but Mia waves me off, shaking her head and looking pointedly at Luke.

I grimace at her and sit back down. I'll give her a piece of my mind for trying to force us together later.

"So, what *haven't* you seen around town yet?" Greg asks.

"The gym, for starters. And I hear you're just the guy to talk to about that," Luke says.

Greg grins. "You're more than welcome," he says, spreading his hands out. "Though I'm curious if the new fire station will have its own workout equipment."

Luke nods. "Of course. That's a staple. We've got to keep in tip-top shape," he agrees. "But until it's built, you'll be seeing a lot of me."

I swallow hard, trying not to imagine exactly how good of shape he's in under those clothes that more than hint at the already mouthwatering physique he's clearly honed over the years.

"We haven't been to the bakery yet!" Zoe interjects. "Dad keeps putting me off for some reason, but I'm *dying* for pie."

"Did someone say pie?" Mia asks, bringing in a tray of what looks like her mini chiffon pies.

Zoe's eyes go wide. Then Carrie walks in with a tray of mini chocolate cream pies, and Brandon with a tray of mini strawberry rhubarb pies, a newer experiment of Mia's.

"Everyone needs to try the strawberry rhubarb mini pies," Mia announces. "I'm tweaking the recipe for the bakery, so I want to hear what you think."

"Please. They'll be amazing. Stop fishing for compliments," Joanie teases as she pops one in her mouth. She groans. "See? Fucking delicious." Her eyes widen and move to Zoe, then to Luke. "Sorry." She blushes and hides behind her napkin.

Greg bursts out laughing. "We had a conversation about learning to not swear when kids are around, but clearly it didn't stick."

Zoe lifts her chin as she delicately takes a strawberry rhubarb mini pie. "I'm twelve, I'm not a kid. It's not like I've never heard the F-word before. Dad says it plenty."

Luke's cheeks turn pink. "I don't say it *that* much," he protests, popping a chocolate cream mini pie in his mouth.

Zoe turns around to face Mia. "They *are* delicious. If I had anything to offer as a suggestion, maybe the strawberry flavor could use a boost? It's kind of being overpowered by the rhubarb just a teeny bit. Maybe you could add some lemon or nutmeg?"

Mia raises an eyebrow and smirks. "Funny enough, I was thinking the same thing, Zoe. You've got a good palette there."

Zoe beams under Mia's praise, but it's Luke that responds. "She should. Zoe loves baking shows, and she made me take her to every place that sells pie in the Seattle area so she could compare and contrast them —" he holds up his hands "— her words."

Mia is visibly shocked. "Wow. That's … there are a *lot* of bakeries and pie shops in Seattle."

"There are. But there's one pie I miss that can only be found in Alpine Ridge," Luke says, his eyes fixing to mine. "And I hear tell you're still making it."

I smirk. "If you're talking about my Great Grams' huckleberry pie, then you heard right." I turn to Zoe. "You like huckleberry pie, sugar?"

"Love. I *love* huckleberry pie," she replies.

"Well, that settles it. You *need* to come to the bakery. Luke, why haven't you brought this young lady by yet?" I demand. It was meant to be teasing, but the stricken look on his face answers my questions.

He hasn't brought his daughter to the bakery because of me. Or how things are between us right now. Damn.

"You should bring her soon," Mia says softly, taking the sting out of the moment. "She can have a slice on the house for her excellent taste buds." Mia winks at Zoe and she grins, blushing at the praise.

Mia takes a seat and starts in on her own dessert.

Luke looks over at me and asks quietly, "You sure?"

My heart twinges that he'd need to ask. "Of course. You're both welcome anytime," I assure him. "So. Zoe. What are you doing for school now you're here?"

Zoe launches into a lengthy explanation of her plans to "unschool," including classes she's found online, "field trips" around the area for things like hikes and shopping, and so much more.

As we chat, I can't help but marvel at how easy it is to talk to her. She's bright and curious, with a surprisingly mature outlook for a twelve-year-old. I can't help but wonder if the scars she bears have forced her to grow up faster than she would've otherwise. Kids can be cruel. But I push that thought aside and focus on my new young friend and her undeniable sparkle. I can already tell she's going to bring something special to Alpine Ridge.

I also don't miss that down the table, Mia is grilling Evan about the mysterious celebrity who's apparently building a house in Alpine Ridge.

"Come on, Ev," she wheedles. "Just give me a hint. Is it someone from one of your movies?"

Evan shakes his head, grinning. "My lips are sealed, Mia. They're locked in on a property now, too. You'll find out, eventually."

Carrie laughs. "Oh, you know it's someone good if Evan's going to such lengths to keep it quiet."

Mia groans dramatically. "You're killing me here! Both of you!"

"Wait ... is there another famous person moving here?" Zoe asks me in a hushed voice.

"I don't know," I admit, then raising my voice, I add, "I kind of think Evan and Carrie might just be screwing with Mia." I raise an eyebrow in Evan's direction and the table erupts in laughter, and for a moment, everything feels normal. Easy.

Like maybe, just maybe, we can all find a way to coexist in this new normal.

But then my gaze catches Luke's, and the laughter dies in my throat. Because beneath the surface, there's still so much left unsaid between us. As demonstrated by the fact that he felt like he had to avoid bringing Zoe to the bakery. Or even coming himself, given that I haven't seen or heard from him since he dropped a reality bomb on me. Then again, I did tell him I needed space.

And I did. But I'm realizing ... maybe I don't need it anymore. Maybe I'm starting to accept that things aren't what I thought, and that it doesn't have to be a big thing.

After dinner, we're cleaning up and I decide that once we're done, I'll talk to Luke. But before I can, Mia pulls me aside, her expression nervous.

"What's up?" I whisper.

Her eyes dart around, making sure nobody is within hearing distance. "I made an appointment," she says quietly. "With a fertility clinic in Seattle. For early April."

I put my hands over my mouth to stifle a joyful sound. Tears prick at the back of my eyes.

"Oh, Mia. I'm so proud of you. I know it's scary, but you're doing the right thing." I wrap my arms around her, trying to convey how much I feel for her. How much I know what it's like to be where she is.

She nods against my shoulder. "I just ... I'm terrified of what they might say. What if they tell me I can never have kids?"

I pull back, looking her in the eye. "Then we'll deal with that together. But don't borrow trouble, okay? Take it one step at a time. And remember, no matter what happens, you have so much love in your life. Nate, me, all of us ... we're here for you." I brush a lock of hair out of her face and cup her cheek. My heart aches, and I wish I could fix this for her.

Mia gives me a shaky smile. "Thanks, Rae. I don't know what I'd do without you." She takes a deep breath, seeming to steel herself. "You know, you should talk to Luke. I think it would be good for you. For both of you."

I bite my lip and nod. "Already decided to, sugar."

She smiles and gives me one last squeeze before slipping away, leaving me with my own demons to face.

So, I reach deep and find my courage. And I go look for Luke. I find him in the dining room, talking to Nate about the architecture of the house, specifically the glass window wall they're standing beside, and how it was designed to make you feel like you're outside even when you're inside. It's one of my favorite things about being in this house, honestly, so I'm not surprised it grabbed Luke's attention. It's hard to grow up in Alpine Ridge and not love the towering pines, snow-capped mountains, and endless blue skies.

"Hey," I say softly. "I'm sorry to interrupt. Luke, can we talk?"

Surprise flickers across Luke's face. "Of course. Would you please excuse us, Nate?"

"Of course," Nate replies graciously, stepping out of the room and pulling the door closed behind him.

For a moment, we just stand there, the silence stretching between us.

"I'm sorry," I blurt out. "For believing people I should've known better than to trust. It's just ... it always upset me so much because I thought I knew you. I couldn't imagine you doing any of those things."

Luke's expression softens. "Rae —"

"And then my ex-husband," I continue, words I never intended to say tumbling out in a rush. "He cheated on me. With a friend. And I think ... I think I unfairly lumped you two together. Assumed the worst because it was so similar to what I thought you'd done, even though I didn't recognize that's what I was doing at the time."

Luke's eyes widen, a flash of anger sparking in their depths. "Your *husband* cheated on you? God, Rae, I'm so sorry." He runs a hand through his hair angrily and turns to look out the window.

I shrug, suddenly feeling self-conscious about the confession even I didn't expect. "It is what it is. But I'm realizing now that I let it color the way I saw you; like him, a liar and cheater to the core. It's what made it so hard to make the mental shift from what I thought I knew. And that wasn't fair. To you or to me. We both deserve better."

Luke is quiet for a moment. "I understand," he says at last. "And for what it's worth ... knowing that's what you thought of me was hard. Not just because I loved you then, but because as soon as I saw you again, I realized I still did. I don't think you ever stop feeling that for your first love. It becomes a part of you. And thinking you hated me?" He puts a hand over his heart as a pained expression crosses his handsome face. "I couldn't let that go on. I had to set the record straight, even if it didn't change anything else."

"I don't hate you, Luke. I'm not sure I ever did. I was hurt, too," I admit.

He steps forward, looking down at me with an intensity that takes my breath away. "I know the truth can't erase years of hurt. But I hope it can help you heal. Because honestly? I can't imagine being back here and not having you in my life, Rae."

The deep tenor of his voice rumbles through me, straight to my heart. I close my eyes, emotion welling, clogging the back of my throat.

"Don't say things like that," I whisper.

I feel his finger slip under my chin, tilting my head up. "Look at me," he implores. The gentle plea leaves me with no choice but to do as he asks. His warm, liquid brown eyes dart between mine, drinking me in just as surely as mine are him.

"It's just the truth. I'm still drawn to you. I don't think I ever stopped being drawn to you. But I'll take whatever you're willing to give. We can be the kind of friends who only see each other at the weekly dinner party." His thumb strokes under my chin and it makes my knees weak. "We can be friends that spend time together. Lunch at the tavern. Hiking with Zoe." He leans in, his breath fanning over my face as his thumb traces down my neck and across my collarbone, sending pleasant shivers down my spine. "Or we can be more. More than friends. Even more than what we were capable of at sixteen." He steps back, withdrawing his hand. And the absence of him leaves a hole in my heart that I can't deny. "Whatever you want."

I close my eyes, my heart aching. Because part of me wants nothing more than to fall into his arms, to pick up where we left off all those years ago.

But I know I can't. Not yet. Maybe never. I'm too damaged. I swore off serious relationships long ago because of everything I can't be for a man, and never finding one that could be true to me. And while this new reality may change that … we're not there yet.

"I don't think I'm ready for *more*," I reply honestly. "Let's start with friends."

Luke smiles, a sad, understanding smile. "Friends." He looks at me, clearly purposely not asking what kind of friend. "I'd like that."

I nod, afraid that speaking will break the hold I have on all the emotions I feel right now.

But he's as good as his word. Because even as we rejoin the others, I can feel the tentative new beginning taking root between us in the way he talks to me amongst our group. With care and respect for my boundaries.

I feel a glimmer of hope. Because maybe there's still a chance for us to heal. To find our way back to each other, even if it looks different from what it was before.

Only time will tell.

CHAPTER TEN

LUKE

I stand in front of the mirror, adjusting my green bowtie for the third time, wondering if it'll be enough. But strangely, it turns out it's the only green piece of clothing I own, so it'll have to do.

Zoe bounces into the room, wearing a green pajama onesie, a shamrock headband perched jauntily on her head. "Come on, Dad! We're going to be late!" she exclaims, tugging at my arm.

I chuckle, letting her pull me away from my reflection. "Okay, okay. I'm coming, my little leprechaun."

Zoe rolls her eyes at me, and I chuckle. But joking aside, as I grab my keys and head out the door, I can't shake the nerves fluttering in my stomach. All I can think about is seeing Rae again after our conversation last night. The way she opened up to me, the vulnerability in her eyes ... it gave me hope. Even her request that we "start with friends." Because that implies that she's open to ending up somewhere else.

Which is good, since I don't want to be just her friend. I want so much more. But I meant what I said — I'll take whatever she's willing to give. Even if it means tamping down my own feelings, giving her the space she needs, and spending time with her platonically.

The community center is already bustling with activity when we arrive. A shamrock garland hangs around the outside of the entryway, music and laughter pours out the doors, and the smell of frosting hits us hard as we enter. I note the cookie decorating table close to the entrance, piles of colored frosting bags and undecorated cookies beckoning.

But to my surprise, Zoe makes a beeline for the Irish Céilí Dancing lessons, her eyes sparkling with excitement. I follow more reluctantly but soon find myself swept up in the infectious energy of the room. We dance in groups of four, led by an elderly Irishman with a thick brogue and a twinkle in his eye. I don't remember him from when I was a kid.

When Carrie and Evan show up and start dancing with Zoe, she's so over the moon she forgets I'm even there, so at the next break in the routine, I join him. "So, Mr. O'Reilly —"

"Call me Ronan, lad."

I smile. "Ronan. I'm —"

"I know who you are, Luke," he says with a smirk. "I remember you and your gang of begonia-stomping hooligans getting Betty riled every other day." The twinkle in his eye tells me he likely shared my feelings toward Mrs. McDonald.

And it makes me laugh so hard it hurts.

"Wow. All right then, well, that answers my question about whether you lived here when I was growing up."

"The O'Reilly clan has been in Alpine Ridge for sixty years now," he says as the others continue to whirl and stomp. "Brought a bit o' the old country with us, we did." He smiles fondly at the dancers.

"It was kind of you to share it," I reply. "That's my daughter —" I point her out "— Zoe. She needed this kind of joy, I think."

"Well, in that case, tell her she's welcome to come by my home anytime for a spot of fun. I'm just off Main on Mountain View Drive. Mine's the one with an Irish flag. Can't miss it." He pats me on the shoulder. "Good to have you back, son. You'll make a fine fire chief." He gives me a look I've seen before. The pitying kind that tells me he remembers very well why my family left, and why I'm returning as fire chief. It normally chafes, but this time I find myself touched by his empathy and confidence.

Unfortunately, I don't have time to reply, as Zoe whirls to a stop in front of me and pulls me back into the throng, even though it throws off the pairings. But everyone redistributes and we figure it out. As the music winds down, I realize maybe it was the kind of joy I needed, too.

After the lesson, Zoe and I grab some drinks — a non-alcoholic Irish cream liqueur for her, a Guinness for me — and Zoe gets a cupcake and Lucky Charms marshmallow treat to boot. I'm going to have to make her eat broccoli for the next week to account for all the sugar she's eating.

Brandon appears at our side, grinning. He holds up his own beer, clinking it against mine.

"Cheers to the beer that almost wasn't. I had to convince Jerry, the cheap old fart, that it wasn't a St. Patty's Day festival without Guinness," he says by way of greeting.

"Well, thanks," I reply. "You're not wrong."

Brandon nods sagely. "Hey, Zoe, want to come play Shamrock Bingo with me?" he asks.

Zoe nods eagerly, shoving the last of her cupcake in her mouth as the two of them head off, leaving me alone.

I scan the room, my heart skipping a beat when I spot Rae manning the photo booth. She's wearing a vibrant emerald green dress and her shoulder-length blond hair is swept off her neck with a sparkly shamrock clip holding it in place. She's laughing with the group getting their photos taken, and her smile hits me right in the heart.

I make my way over, trying to appear casual. "Having fun?" I ask, leaning against the booth.

Rae looks up, a smile still playing at the corners of her mouth. She taps my bowtie with a finger and grins. "Tons. You?"

"Absolutely. Though I think I might need to practice my jig a bit more."

She laughs, and the sound warms me from the inside out. "Well, lucky for you, there's a photo booth right here. We can document your progress."

Once the folks that were there head off, Rae and I spend the next half hour taking silly photos, first of me attempting an Irish jig, which is hilariously awful. Then we play with the oversized buckled green hats and goofy sparkly gold and green glasses. For a moment, it feels like old times — the two of us, laughing and joking, the rest of the world falling away. Maybe this friends thing isn't so bad, after all.

When Zoe finds us later, her cheeks are flushed with excitement. "I won Bingo! Look at all the chocolate truffles I got!" she exclaims, holding up a small black plastic pot filled to the brim with gold-wrapped candies.

"Great job, sweetheart," I say, congratulating her with a high-five.

"Ah, yes, the truffles. They're my favorites. And the one thing Mia doesn't make at the bakery," Rae comments.

"Want one?" Zoe offers.

Rae laughs. "I've had a good half dozen already today. But you're a doll to offer to share."

"I'd give them *all* to you for a slice of huckleberry pie," she says with a mischievous glint in her eye.

Rae smiles and shakes her head. "Your gold is no good here, sugar. Like Mia said, you come on by whenever you want and get a slice, free of charge."

Zoe turns to me. "Dad, when can I?"

I rub my jaw. At first, I'd avoided taking her so as not to crowd Rae. But now, well, this week is going to be pretty busy.

"I don't know, Zo. I've got a lot on my plate this week," I hedge.

"Even more reason to bring her by. You can drop her off. I'll feed her and …" Rae winks at Zoe "… I may even teach her how to make my Great Grams's famous huckleberry pie while I'm at it."

Zoe's jaw drops. "No! Really? Would you really teach me?" She bounces on her toes excitedly.

Rae smiles wide at her enthusiasm. "Absolutely." Then to me, "How about tomorrow? Our morning rush is usually over around ten."

"That would be amazing, actually," I admit. "Thank you."

I've been a little reticent to leave Zoe alone so much, but between repairing the old house and gearing up on planning the fire department, I haven't exactly had a lot of time to research activities for her. And this way, I get to see Rae again.

Rae waves me off. "It's nothing. Mia will be thrilled to have her, too. It's a win all around."

"Speaking of winning," Brandon says, sidling up with Joanie, Greg, Mia, and Nate in tow. "Has everyone entered the raffle? Miss Rae here put together some fantastic prizes. And the proceeds will go toward a development project of the townspeople's choice."

"I love that idea," I reply. "Do we vote for one when we enter?"

Brandon shakes his head. "We'll see how much we end up with and match it with town funds, then put together a list of the projects people have asked for that fit the budget it allows."

"How terribly practical," Joanie says drily. She taps her chin. "I have the sudden urge to go buy a few hundred raffle tickets." She winks and heads off toward the raffle table, dragging a laughing Greg along with her.

"Oh, hey, speaking of practical," I say, pulling Nate aside as Rae, Mia, and Zoe start to talk baking. "You mentioned at dinner last night that the clinic is already pretty busy?"

Nate nods. "On the urgent care side, mostly. Which is fine, since a lot of folks already have a primary care physician and don't want to make the switch, so the routine appointments side is slow enough to where that's fine for the time being. But I'm definitely concerned for the future."

"Well, for what it's worth, I'm a trained paramedic, so if you need any help in that regard, don't hesitate to call me," I tell him.

"Really? That'd be amazing. A tremendous weight off my mind, actually. We've had to send a couple of folks to the ER in Ellensburg. But if we had more basic triage in town, it would make a huge difference," he admits.

"I get it. And once the firehouse is up and running, all the guys on my crew will be at least EMT level, if not full paramedics, which most firefighters choose to do. Plus, we'll have a rig that can transport patients," I add.

Nate scrubs a hand down his face. "Damn. Well, that just made my year. I feel a lot better. Thanks, man."

I clap him on the back. "That's what I'm here for. And who knows? If the town grows quickly enough, we may get a full hospital sooner than we think." I laugh, because I know it's possible, but imagining Alpine Ridge being that big is wild.

Nate laughs along with me. "That would be something, but let's not get ahead of ourselves. Eat the elephant one bite at a time, as they say."

"Hey, Dad!" Zoe says, grabbing my arm. "Can we do cookie decorating?" She bats her eyelashes at me. "Pleeeeease?"

I laugh and shake my head. "How can you still want cookies after cupcakes and Lucky Charms treats?"

Zoe shrugs, grinning. "There's always room for cookies."

"She's a girl after my own heart," Rae teases.

"Mine, too," Mia adds, giving Zoe a fond smile.

I shake my head, marveling at her bottomless appetite, but gesture for her to lead the way. Mia takes us over to the cookie decorating table, where we settle in.

She demonstrates how to pipe both the easier shamrock-shaped cookie with thick green buttercream frosting, and the more difficult royal-icing and fondant pot of gold cookies. Zoe tries to go straight for the bigger challenge, but Mia makes her do the shamrock cookie first as a "test" she has to pass to go on. Zoe eats that challenge up faster than the cupcake from earlier.

Naturally, Zoe nails both, though she struggles a little with painting luster dust on the fondant coins and placing them on the pot. Still, the results are impressive, looking extremely similar to Mia's examples.

Despite my best efforts, my cookies come out looking more like blobs than shamrocks. But I sit and watch Zoe, with Mia's patient guidance, create an entire tray of picture-perfect treats. By the time she's done, Mia is gushing over her work, and Zoe is on cloud nine.

As the event winds down, Layla takes the stage to announce the raffle winners. But before she begins, Brandon joins her, holding up a hand for quiet.

"Before we get to the prizes, I have a quick announcement," he says, his voice carrying across the room. "As many of you know, Alpine Ridge is getting a new fire chief. I wanted to take a moment to introduce him to you all. Ladies and gentleman, my brother, Luke McMillan." My jaw drops, but I quickly close it. Damn, I wish he would've told me he was going to do that. Good thing I work well under pressure.

A murmur ripples through the crowd as I stand, feeling a rush of emotion. As I walk toward Brandon, his encouraging smile makes me realize what he's doing. He's trying to reverse the rumor mill and put me on a good footing with the town at the same time. Damn. That's both thoughtful and brilliant.

I clear my throat, nodding at the sea of curious faces. "Thank you, Brandon. I'm honored to be here." I take a subtle, deep breath and decide to lean into it hard. "As many of you know, I grew up here in Alpine Ridge and only left because a fire burned down the town's only church, taking away our father's livelihood as the church's pastor. But that event affected more than my family; it affected the entire town. It's what made me want to be a firefighter. To save families and communities from the fate that befell all of us all those years ago. I'm grateful for the opportunity to return with a wealth of knowledge and experience that I didn't have then that I can use to serve this community."

To my surprise, everyone applauds when I finish. I can feel my ears burning as I step down and Layla takes the mic.

As I head back to my seat, every person I walk by smiles at me. Many whisper greetings and thanks for being here. Each interaction bolsters my confidence in the decision I made to come back and my gratitude for this opportunity.

When I sit back down, Zoe leans over and whispers, "That was really nice of Uncle Brandon."

"Yeah," I agree, my throat tight. "It really was."

The rest of the event passes in a happy blur of raffle prizes, final treats, and hugs goodbye, and before I know it, Zoe and I are heading home, our arms laden with cookies and prizes.

Once the sugar rush has finally worn off at the end of the evening, I tuck Zoe into bed and she yawns, her eyes heavy. "That was the best St. Patrick's Day ever," she mumbles.

I brush a stray curl from her forehead, smiling. "It really was, wasn't it?"

And as I close her door, I realize that for the first time in a long time, I feel like I'm exactly where I'm supposed to be. All the hard work I've done to get to chief. All the risks we took leaving our life in Seattle behind. All the drama I didn't know was waiting for me. It wasn't for nothing. For the first time in a long time, I feel like my life is finally coming together.

CHAPTER ELEVEN

RAE

Monday morning brings the usual wave of caffeine and sugar seekers, but it's who I know is coming after that has nervous energy coursing through my body the whole time.

At ten on the dot, Luke and Zoe walk through the bakery's door. Nerves aside, I can't help but smile at the sight of them, their cheeks flushed from the crisp, almost-spring morning air.

"Happy St. Patty's Day," I greet them, wiping my hands on my apron.

Zoe grins and bounds up to the counter. "Happy St. Patrick's Day!" she returns. "What have you got that's green?" Her eyes start scanning the cases and I laugh.

"Zoe, you're here to make and eat pie. Don't you think that's enough? Especially after yesterday?" Luke admonishes her with a sigh.

"Dad. It's *all* green," she says in a shocked whisper, seemingly oblivious to what he'd said. She looks up at me. "Food coloring?"

"Matcha," I reply with a wink. Then to Luke, "Off to town hall today, then?"

He nods. "Yep. I shouldn't be too long."

Mia pops out from the kitchen, her face lighting up when she sees Zoe. "Hey, guys!"

"Take all the time you need," I assure Luke. "I think Mia's got big plans for Zoe."

Zoe grins, bouncing on her toes. "Yes! I'm going to learn how to make huckleberry pie today, right?"

"You sure are," Mia agrees. "But that's Rae's specialty, so she'll handle that part. But I definitely have things for you after that."

Zoe's eyes dart back to her father, then to me. She gestures for me to lean close, then when I do, she whispers in my ear, "Can we bake a huckleberry pie for me to take home, too? Dad says it's his favorite."

I chuckle, reaching out to tuck her hair behind her ear. "I think we can manage that," I agree with a wink.

When I look up, Luke's eyes meet mine, and for a moment, the world seems to slow. There's a warmth in his gaze that makes my heart flutter, a tenderness that makes my knees weak.

"I'll leave you lovely ladies to it, then," he says softly. "Thank you. For everything."

I swallow hard, nodding. "Anytime."

As Luke leaves, I turn to Zoe, clapping my hands together. "All right, Miss Zoe. Ready to get baking?"

Zoe nods eagerly, and we head into the kitchen. I walk her through the steps of making my Great Grams' famous huckleberry pie, from rolling out the crust to mixing the filling, to creating the perfect lattice top. She listens intently, her brow furrowed in concentration as she follows my instructions flawlessly.

By the time we put the pie in the oven, Mia has started making lunch. She lets Zoe help her prep the ingredients for panini, though Mia handles pressing the sandwiches because apparently letting non-employees, kids especially, handle heated appliances is a big insurance no-no. Still, Zoe helps to assemble the sandwiches, then plates them afterward, getting a quick lesson in presentation.

As we eat our deliciously gooey cheesy veggie panini, Zoe chatters excitedly about all the things she wants to learn to bake next.

"Slow down there, sugar," I tease her. "We couldn't possibly do all of that today. I think we're going to have to make this a regular thing if you want to learn it all."

"Really? I can come back again?" she asks, her eyes wide and hopeful.

My heart melts, realizing that since her mom died when she was so young, and her dad isn't the baking type — unless something has seriously changed, because he was always hopeless at it when we were kids — that Zoe hasn't had anyone to indulge her passion for baking. To guide and instruct her in it. It's clear she's done some on her own, but there's so much more we can teach her.

I decide that's exactly what we're going to do.

I give Mia a look. She nods. "Of course you can, Zoe," Mia agrees. "In fact, you can come every day this week. We can always use an extra set of hands around here."

Zoe's face lights up like a Christmas tree. "Oh my god, are you serious? That would be amazing!"

"I'm so serious that I think we should clean up our lunch and start making the cookie dough we're going to need for tomorrow," Mia replies.

Zoe quickly grabs all our plates and ferries them to the sink, rolling up her sleeves to begin scrubbing.

I man the front while Mia teaches Zoe. They get through the cookie dough quickly, then Mia shows her how to prepare all the various fruit toppings, compotes, and syrups that we use.

I pop my head in occasionally to join them between customers. As I watch them work, I can't help marveling at how quickly Zoe has learned today ... and how she's made her way into our hearts just as quickly. Her intelligence, enthusiasm, and unbelievable natural talent are hard not to love.

When Luke returns to pick her up, Zoe can barely contain her excitement. "Dad, guess what? Mia said I can come help every day this week!"

Luke raises an eyebrow, looking between Mia and me. "Really?" he asks skeptically.

"Really," I assure him. "She's a natural in the kitchen. So helpful and such a joy to have around."

Luke smiles, pride shining in his eyes. "That's my girl."

Zoe slips her hand into her dad's, leading him out as she starts to tell him all about her time with us.

"Zoe?" I call after her, retrieving the pie box we'd stashed under the register. She turns back with wide eyes. "Don't forget this," I mock whisper, sliding the box across the counter.

She leans up and wraps an arm around my neck and squeezes. "Thanks, Rae, you're the best."

I squeeze her back. "Right back atcha, sugar."

I let her go only to find Luke looking at me with an expression on his face that makes my cheeks flush. It's sweetness and gratitude and something … more. Something I'm not quite ready to acknowledge.

Zoe grabs his hand again, teasing him about her surprise.

"Thanks again, ladies. We'll see you tomorrow?" Luke calls back. But I'm still too stunned by the look he gave me to respond.

"See you tomorrow," Mia agrees when I don't say anything.

After they leave, Mia turns to me, her expression curious. "Are you really okay with seeing your ex and his kid every day? I mean, I know you and Luke are trying to be friends, but you look a little shell-shocked right now."

I shake myself out of it and take a deep breath, considering her question. "Honestly? It's kind of a reminder of all the things I wanted, that's for sure. But in a way, I feel like I get to have them now. Luke and I are friends, and it's good to have him back in my life. Especially now that I know he didn't cheat on me and father a child with my best friend."

Mia nods, understanding in her eyes. "And Zoe is a pretty exceptional kid."

"She really is," I agree, smiling.

But even as I say the words, I feel a twinge of sadness. Because as much as I'm enjoying having Luke and Zoe in my life, there's a part of me that wishes it were different. That wishes Luke was my husband and Zoe was our child, the way I'd always dreamed it would be.

I push the thought aside, focusing on the present. On the joy of teaching Zoe to bake, on the warmth and gratitude of Luke's smile. It's enough, I tell myself. It has to be.

Thursday afternoon finds me at town hall, fidgeting nervously as I wait for Arthur to see me as he'd requested. When he finally calls me into his office, I take a deep breath, steeling myself for whatever he has to say. Wondering if I did something wrong with the St. Patrick's Day event. If it wasn't what he'd hoped for.

"Rae, thank you for coming," Arthur says, gesturing for me to sit. "I wanted to talk to you about the St. Patrick's Day event. It was a huge success, and everyone loved it."

I feel relief and a flush of pride at his words. "Thank you. I'm glad everyone enjoyed themselves. I sure did, anyway."

Arthur nods, leaning forward on his desk. "As did I. I particularly liked the dancing. Who knew Ronan still had that in him?" He chuckles to himself before continuing. "I also wanted to discuss the future of the community center events. Layla enjoyed helping out, but she's decided to take another opportunity that will occupy her full time. She won't be able to manage future events on her own, though she's still open to assisting when she can."

My heart sinks. "So, who will handle them then? And what happens to the community center?"

"Well, we've talked to Dana — who is currently a masseuse at the wellness center — and since her current position is only part-time, she's interested in running the community center if she can also do that part time. Which we're fine with, for now. But in any case, she wouldn't have enough time to handle the events as well. Which is where you come in."

I blink, surprise washing over me. "Me?"

Arthur smiles. "I'd like to continue hiring you as an independent contractor to run the events. But to do that, we'd need to make things a bit more official. At minimum that would mean you'd need a registered business name, a tax ID number, and liability insurance."

"So basically, you want me to start an event planning business," I say slowly, the pieces clicking into place.

"More or less, yes. I understand it's a big decision, and I want you to take some time to think about it. But Rae, you have a genuine talent for this. You bring something special to the town events that nobody else can provide."

"Wow, Arthur, that's incredibly kind of you to say, thank you," I reply, touched. But then my brow furrows. "You're not just trying to sweet talk me so I agree to do it, are you?"

Arthur chuckles. "A little, but it's still the truth," he admits. "Truly, though, Rae, I'm merely asking you to formalize what you already do. It doesn't have to be more than that."

I nod. "Thank you, Mayor Burton. You've given me a lot to think about. I'll let you know soon."

He rises and extends his hand. I rise in kind and shake it. "It was a pleasure speaking with you, as always," he says, then sees me out the door. With one last smile, I walk away slowly in a daze.

I leave town hall with my head spinning, Arthur's words echoing in my mind. An event planning business. Me. It seems impossible ... even if it's something I've secretly always wanted to do. But I already have a job. And left to my own devices, I'm awful at time management and expense tracking and filing all the paperwork that running a business would require. It's crazy ... yet, I didn't say no.

That night, we gather at Greg and Joanie's house for game night. It's Luke and Zoe's first time joining us, and I can sense their nervousness. But everyone goes out of their way to make them feel welcome. Mia brings a batch of mini pies specifically for Zoe to try, while Greg and Joanie present her with a new toy to play with Bruiser. I can tell Luke is touched by their efforts to make her feel at home.

We start the evening with a game of Clue. Surprising no one, Joanie's strategic mind and competitive nature lead her to victory. Next up is Apples to Apples, where Evan's wit and creativity shine through, earning him the win.

The room is filled with laughter, jokes, and playful banter, but I find myself going through the motions, unable to fully engage. My mind is elsewhere, replaying the conversation with Arthur, his offer, and the weight of the decision bearing down on me.

Eventually, Brandon notices my distraction and calls me out. "What's going on, Rae? You seem preoccupied."

I sigh, realizing there's no point in hiding it. "Arthur wants me to start an event planning business to handle future town events."

A chorus of excitement and encouragement erupts from the group.

"Rae, that's fantastic! You'd be amazing at it! I mean, you *are* amazing at it," Mia says.

"Totally. I've leaned hard on you over the years, and you always deliver," Greg agrees. "So, what's worrying you?"

I sigh. "It's just … running a business is a big deal, right?"

Joanie shakes her head. "Misconception. It doesn't have to be a big thing, just a shell company if it's only for town events. You could make it a sole proprietorship with a DBA and get an EIN from the IRS. Boom, you're done. Well, except for the insurance, but that's no biggie either. I'd go umbrella if it were me."

I stare at Joanie with confusion. "Are you speaking English?" I ask.

Everyone laughs. "I think what Joanie is trying to say is that it's not as much work — or paperwork — as you think," Carrie explains gently.

I shake my head, finding that hard to believe.

Luke catches my eye and, ever so gently, says, "Rae, you've *always* had a knack for this sort of thing. Even your Grams asked your opinion on everything, and she was the pickiest woman this side of the Cascades. I think you should go for it."

Somehow, of all the voices in this room of encouragement, it's his words that really strike a chord. I'd forgotten how important Grams had made me feel, because she didn't dole out praise easily.

Maybe I do have a knack for event planning. No, I definitely do. I know that. I don't know why I'm questioning that when it's the rest I'm worried about. I bite my lip, uncertainty swirling inside me. Uncertainty that's creeping into other parts of my life. Maybe pushing through this would stop it.

"I wouldn't even know where to start," I admit helplessly.

Brandon leans forward, a supportive smile on his face. "My boyfriend has an MBA and has started multiple businesses. He helped me start up the art gallery, too. I couldn't have done it without him. He was great at walking me through things step by step, so I didn't get overwhelmed. I'll bring him to dinner on Saturday, and maybe we can all brainstorm together?"

I nod, because how could I say no to that? While I'm overwhelmed, I'm also touched by their faith in me. If nothing else, their unwavering support should encourage me.

And yet, even as the games continue, I can't help feeling like I'm still drowning. In information. Doubt. Anxiety.

A second round of Apples to Apples does little to quell the storm brewing inside me, so I excuse myself abruptly and step outside for a breather.

I've taken exactly three deep breaths of the cold, clear air when Luke walks out onto the porch.

"Hey," he says, his eyes filled with concern. "I'm sorry if we overwhelmed you in there earlier. You should know you don't have to do anything you don't want to."

I take a shaky breath. "It's not that I don't want to. I'd love to. But Luke, I can barely keep track of my own life. How could I possibly run a business?"

He takes my hands in his, his touch warm and reassuring. "If you want to, you can do this, Rae. I know you can. And you won't be alone. I'm here for you and so are all our friends." He smiles fondly at the statement, and I realize I'm clearly not the only one grateful for that crazy bunch.

I'm also happy that Luke has quickly found his place here with these people. With my people. With me.

Emotion wells up in my chest, and for a moment, the air between us crackles with a palpable attraction. My eyes drop to his lips, and he takes a hesitant step forward. My breath catches in my throat as my eyes meet his again. They're dark and warm and inviting, and I sway forward.

But before either of us can act on it, Zoe interrupts, popping her head out.

"Dad, come see the new trick I taught Bruiser!"

I inhale sharply, realizing I almost crossed a line I'd sworn not to. "Go on," I encourage him. "I'll be back in soon."

"You sure?" he asks skeptically. And though the years have changed us both, I can tell he still knows me enough to know I'm still reeling. I'm touched that he clearly doesn't want to leave me. To make me feel alone.

"I'm sure," I reply firmly. "Thank you." I swiftly reach out to squeeze his hand, then let go just as quickly.

They go into the house, and I shift my gaze to the stars as I finish my breathing exercises. Once I've calmed down as much as I think I will, I head back inside.

The games have broken up and everyone is chatting and finishing off Mia's mini pies.

As I watch Luke and Zoe interact with my found family, a bittersweet mix of relief and disappointment washes over me. I can no longer deny my growing feelings for Luke, the desire for something more than friendship. Or that I wish we'd had that all along. That life hadn't torn us apart. But that's not how it happened, and no amount of wishing will change that.

Too soon, Luke takes Zoe home, citing preteen bedtime. We can only exchange casual goodbyes, surrounded as we are, but it feels like a part of my heart goes with him, along with all my unsaid words.

I settle back onto the couch and Carrie sinks down next to me.

"Hey, you," she says with a sympathetic smile that tells me she might know exactly where my head is at.

"Hey, sugar," I say, sounding every bit as tired as I am. "How's things?"

"Oh, you know, working my dream job, doing life with my dream man," she says. "So, it's all right."

We both laugh.

"And Evan? How's he adjusting to small-town life after being an international movie star?" I'd ask him, but the man's as much of a people-pleaser as Carrie, so best to get the facts from her.

She chuckles, shaking her head. "Surprisingly, he's really happy. This move has been good for him, for both of us." She pauses. "Am I allowed to ask what's between you and Luke? There's history there, right?"

I take a deep breath and nod, over keeping the truth from everyone except Mia. "He was my first everything. Then, he left. Afterward … someone told me he cheated on me and fathered a child with my best friend, but turns out it was *his* father that did the fathering …" I trail off and grimace. "That made more sense in my head."

Carrie smirks. "I got what you meant. That sounds … messy."

I give her a vague smile. "That's an understatement. Having him back has been an emotional rollercoaster, I'm not going to lie."

"I could tell," she replies honestly. I groan and tip my head back. She pats me on the arm. "Only because I know you so well. I think the only other person who suspects is Mia."

I sit upright and give her a guilty look. "I may have already told Mia."

Carrie feigns indignation. "You mean you told her first? We were *roommates*, Rae. *Roommates.*"

I laugh. "I'm sorry! I couldn't even admit to myself how messed up I've been. I had two more partners after Luke who cheated on me and between that and the fact that my daddy left my momma right after Luke left me?" I shake my head and sigh. "Honestly, I didn't realize how much it shattered me until recently. Or that I've been so afraid of ending up like my mother." It's the first time I've voiced the thought, and it underscores how little I understood why I've been feeling this way.

Carrie's blue eyes are filled with empathy. "I understand how trauma can shape you, but Rae, we're not destined to repeat our parents' mistakes. Look at Mia and me. If we were bound by our family's past, we'd be lost. But we've chosen different paths."

Just as Luke's did earlier, her words strike a chord. I've been living under the assumption that I would inevitably face the same heartbreak as my mother, but that doesn't have to be my fate.

"I can choose a different path," I say out loud. Then I laugh at the simplicity, the absolute freedom of that idea.

"Rae, if I know anything about you, it's that you are capable of so much more than you let yourself believe. I wish you saw yourself the way we do. You're strong, smart, and you have a huge heart. You could rule the freaking world if you wanted to," Carrie teases. But I can tell she believes what she's saying.

"I guess I just need to learn to believe that, too," I say.

"Hey babe, ready to go?" Evan calls to Carrie from the other side of the living room.

Carrie leans in and hugs me. "There's no rush. Stop overwhelming yourself with what you think you can or can't do and focus on what you *want*. Because I love you and I want to see you happy, okay?"

I kiss her on the cheek. "Love you, too, wise woman. Good night." And then I raise my voice toward Evan, "And good night to you, too, hot stuff."

Evan chuckles, but Joanie beats him to the punch.

"Oh good, Rae's feeling sassy again," she comments. "Now I don't have to feel bad about telling you guys to get the hell out so Greg and I can fu—"

Greg clamps his hand over Joanie's mouth in the blink of an eye. "Well, it was great having you all. Rae, I'm glad you're feeling better about things," he says with a nervous laugh.

I can't help laughing myself as I rise while Evan and Carrie hightail it out the door. "Thanks for having me. You two feel free to go at it," I say as I show myself out.

I shake my head, still laughing at Joanie as I climb into the Bronco. She may be brash, but she has an honesty about who she is that I admire.

Maybe Luke is right. Maybe they're all right. I'm surrounded by people who care about me. People with different strengths than me. People I admire, trust, and lean on. Maybe I can lean on them for this, too.

As I drive the short distance home, I feel a glimmer of hope. A sense that I can finally break free from the shadows of my past and embrace a future filled with success, happiness, and even love.

CHAPTER TWELVE

LUKE

On Friday morning, I wake with a sense of nervous excitement. And it's not because I'm meeting the rest of the town council today, though I'm glad that's finally happening.

No, I'm all worked up because of last night. Because of how close Rae was to letting me back in. I could practically taste her yearning on Greg and Joanie's porch. Not just for me to kiss her, but for me to comfort her, despite her fears. Or maybe because of them. Our attraction has always been deeper than physical. She's always gotten me, and I her. It's encouraging how quickly we're making our way back to that, but I realize now how important letting her set that pace is. I almost forgot that while I rediscovered how much she pulls me in.

I close my eyes, a swell of desire rippling through me at the memory of her lips parting with want, the moonlight gilding her hair. She was so beautiful, and I wanted to kiss her so badly. And I know she wanted it just as badly. Whatever magic existed between us all those years ago is still there. And if I thought I'd felt hopeful before ...

I take a deep breath and force myself out of bed. There's no time for the kind of wallowing I want to do in those memories. If I don't get up now, I'll be late for the meeting.

I push through my morning routine quickly and encourage Zoe to do the same. On the drive to the bakery, she talks my ear off about how fun game night was, how she thinks we should get a dog just like Bruiser, and all the things she wants to do today.

The dog idea catches my attention. I've always loved dogs. I haven't had one in years, since it didn't feel right living in an apartment and working the schedule I do, but I admit I wouldn't mind it. But I don't say that to Zoe, because we're not there yet. The house isn't there yet. The yard definitely isn't there yet. And maybe I'm not *quite* there yet either. A dog is a big responsibility, and I'd like things to settle down a bit more first.

When we get to the bakery, I don't go in with Zoe like I have been. I know if I do, I'll for sure be late. Though I can't help a longing look past Zoe as she walks in, hoping to catch a glimpse of Rae. But the morning sun is reflecting off the glass front of the bakery, and I can't see much of anything.

With a sigh, I put the truck in gear and drive onward to town hall. In a couple minutes, I've pulled in, parked, and am heading through reception. I wave hello to Meredith and head down the hall to the meeting room.

As I walk through the door, I breathe deeply to settle myself. While I already know Arthur, Brandon, and Greg, the other five members people seated around the long table don't look familiar.

To my surprise, they greet me with warm smiles and enthusiastic handshakes. I quickly realize they are all long-time residents that, with some reminiscing, I *do* remember from my childhood, because clearly, they sure remember me. And they welcome me with open arms and fond memories, assuring me they always doubted the rumors about Brandon's parentage.

"We knew you were a good kid, Luke," Janet Henderson says, patting my hand. "Never believed a word of that nonsense."

"I always said it was awfully suspicious to blame you, given that your family had just been forced to leave town after the accident," Archie Bennett adds in agreement.

"Now, now, there's no need for any of that. It's all water under the bridge," I reply, though I end up having to repeat myself in various forms as more of them jump to my defense.

I'm touched by their kindness, though I'm fully aware they're probably only saying these things to make me feel more at ease. All that matters to me is that we can all move forward now.

Arthur gives a high level of what the council's role is. Which is to say, it's not terribly well-defined yet. They're taking things as they come and learning as they go.

Which works for me, because I have ideas of my own, including one I've been mulling over that I share with everyone — I want to offer home and business fire inspections to anyone who'd like them while we work on building the fire station, including offering a limited amount of free equipment from basics like smoke and carbon monoxide detectors, or even just batteries to more extensive tools such as extinguishers, escape ladders, and the like. It'll be a year or two before the fire station is operational, so in the meantime, I want to keep the community engaged and catch any potential issues that could save lives. After all, the town was largely built in the '70s, and fire safety standards have improved by leaps and bounds since then.

To my relief, everyone thinks it's a brilliant plan. Carrie suggests we go talk to her contact at the county next week to discuss moving forward with the fire department build process. I readily agree, feeling a sense of purpose and excitement as things finally start to move from theory and planning to action.

After the meeting, Arthur takes me to lunch, then on a tour of the town, pointing out all the new developments and upcoming projects. The townhouse complex with commercial units housing Joanie's law office, Sera's realty office, and Brandon's art gallery. A new bank and drugstore in the works. Sites that are being cleared for more housing, plots for sale that the council hopes to fill with restaurants, entertainment venues, retailers, and so much more. It's incredible to see how much Alpine Ridge is growing, and I'm thrilled to be a part of shaping its future.

When we get back to town hall, I'm standing next to my truck, ready to offer my thanks before heading over to pick up Zoe when Arthur leans toward me with a somber expression.

"Luke, there's something I need to tell you. Something I should have told you a long time ago," he says in a low voice.

I furrow my brow, concerned by his sudden change in demeanor. "What is it, Arthur?"

He takes a deep breath, as if steeling himself for a tough conversation. "I was part of the church leadership, overseeing the finances, when your father was pastor there. When ... the accident happened."

My heart skips a beat at the allusion to the church fire, the memories of that painful time still raw after all these years.

"Before the fire, the church was being audited by the IRS," Arthur continues, his voice heavy. "And when I reviewed my records, I realized someone had altered them. I investigated and discovered it was your father. David had done the tampering."

The revelation punches me in the gut, knocking the wind out of me. How deep does this rabbit hole with my father's transgressions go? On some level, it's hard to believe one man could do so many bad things.

"My dad? Are you sure? I mean ... I knew he wasn't ... honest, but it's hard to swallow him doing something that bad." And yet, once the words are out of my mouth, it's not that hard to believe. I'm just surprised he did something with such a high risk of being caught. Though, again, that's not really a first for him either. Going so far as to tamper with records isn't that far from stealing from your congregation. Hell, they probably went hand in hand. I guess I'll never get used to learning of the awful things he's done.

Arthur nods grimly. "I confronted him about it. He said he did it for the good of the church, to avoid what little tax we would've had to pay. I pointed out that would be tax fraud, but he didn't seem bothered."

A fresh wave of disappointment washes over me. My father, who was supposed to be a man of God, who I looked up to for most of my young life, truly was a lying bastard. On levels I probably haven't even realized yet and may never even know about.

"He seemed so unbothered, in fact, that it made me realize he wasn't the man we thought we'd hired. Which, in turn, made me wonder if there were other ways he may have taken advantage of the church. So, I dug deeper," Arthur continues, his eyes filled with regret. I have to work not to flinch at whatever is about to come out of his mouth. "I found evidence of theft from the church funds that could only have been your father. I also learned there was a mortgage on the parsonage that shouldn't have existed. The house was owned by the church, funded by a group of Alpine Ridge residents, including myself, who jointly purchased the land and had both built. Your father wasn't part of that group. We hired him after completion to lead the church and we gave him use of the house so long as he held that position."

I shake my head, a sudden realization hitting me. "During the divorce, my father put the house in my name, to keep it from my mother. He said it was because she was trying to 'take him to the cleaners' as revenge for what happened to Hannah. I never knew the house was supposed to belong to the church." I'm spinning, yet again, not just from what he did, but for what this could mean for me and Zoe. How can I keep a house that was never supposed to belong to me?

Arthur sighs heavily. "We didn't know he'd somehow transferred it to his name until it was too late. Until the IRS closed the audit case shortly after your parents' divorce. I noticed their final report omitted the parsonage as part of the church's assets. It didn't take much digging with the county to discover that was because it no longer belonged to the church and hadn't for over a year at that point. And that further, it no longer belonged to your father, either.

"Between the fire, your family moving away, and the fact that your father didn't even legally own the property anymore … well, the remaining investors and I decided to let it go. There was no hope of rebuilding the church, so what did we need a parsonage for?" Arthur twists his fingers anxiously, belying that this still bothers him as much as it does me. "There were only three of us left at that point, and the other two have since passed away. I'm the only one who knows the truth now, but I felt you deserved to know, too."

I shake my head, my mind reeling at the depth of my father's deceit. The house I grew up in, never truly ours. The life I thought I knew, built on a foundation of dishonesty. But that part's nothing new. My stomach churns with disgust and shame.

"Arthur, I … I don't know what to say. I'm so sorry for what my father did. The house … I can give it back to you. I *want* to give it back. If not to you directly, to the town. It's the least I can do."

But Arthur shakes his head, placing a hand on my shoulder. "I didn't tell you this to take the house back, Luke. I told you this because you deserve to know. Because you're a good man, and I know that if anyone can redeem that house, make it serve the town as it was intended, it's you. Your father's sins are not yours to bear. I trust you'll do right by Alpine Ridge. Maybe God saw that the house went to you for that very reason."

Tears prick at the corners of my eyes, the weight of Arthur's words settling over me like a warm blanket. In this moment, I feel a sense of purpose, of belonging, that I haven't felt in years.

"Thank you, Arthur," I manage, my voice thick with emotion. "I promise I'll do everything in my power to make this town proud. To be the man my father should have been but never was."

Arthur offers a small smile, a glimmer of hope in his eyes. "I have no doubt you will, Luke. No doubt at all."

We part ways and I'm so disoriented by what I've learned that have to sit in my truck for a solid fifteen minutes before I'm able to drive the short distance to pick

Zoe up. But I compartmentalize it to examine it later. Right now, I have other responsibilities.

I head to the bakery, going inside before I can think about whether it's a good idea to see Rae in my current condition. But turns out she's gone for the day, anyway, so I'm spared having to worry about her seeing right through me and asking what's up. Which is good, because I'm going to need more time to process this before I talk to anyone about it.

In any case, I let Mia know I'll be gone longer on Monday for the county meeting but that I can make other arrangements for Zoe if she's not able to stay at the bakery the whole time. Much to Zoe's delight, Mia assures me it's no problem. I can't help but feel a surge of gratitude for her support and friendship. Especially given the deep hurt and confusion I'm feeling over things my father did. How can near-strangers be kinder than the man who raised me? This whole thing is messing me up badly.

We're almost home when I get over myself long enough to realize Zoe is also uncharacteristically quiet. Besides greeting me when I picked her up and a cursory "it's fine" when I asked how her day's been, she hasn't said anything since we climbed into the truck. I glance over at her, concern etched on my face.

"What's up, kiddo?" I ask gently.

She fidgets with her seatbelt, avoiding my gaze. "Nothing," she mumbles.

I frown, unconvinced. "Zoe, you know you can talk to me about anything, right?"

She nods but stays silent. I decide not to push, giving her space to open up when she's ready.

It's not until we pull up to the house that she finally speaks, her voice thick with emotion.

"Mia let me help in the front today, serving customers," she mumbles.

My heart clenches, a pang of worry shooting through me. My mind goes to the worst-case scenario: someone said something cruel about her scars. The thought brings out my papa bear instincts in a flash, but I focus on not overreacting without the facts. At the very least, I'm going to need to know who I'm going to have to have words with.

"Did something happen?" I ask carefully, trying to keep my tone neutral.

To my surprise, Zoe shakes her head. "No, nothing happened, not like you're thinking, anyway. That's the thing, Dad. Nobody here makes fun of me. Only one person even asked about my scars all day, and they were so nice about it. They told me I'm beautiful, scars and all."

Tears start to stream down her face, and I reach over to take her hand, my own eyes stinging, but my heart lifting with gratitude and relief that it's not what I thought at all.

"Then why the tears, sweetheart?"

She sniffles, wiping her nose with her sleeve. "Because I never thought I'd find a place where people didn't treat me badly because of how I look. Where my scars could make me feel closer to someone, instead of like an outsider. I don't ever want to leave here, Dad."

I swallow hard, a lump forming in my throat. I'm overjoyed that Zoe is finding acceptance and kindness here, but a part of me knows it might not always be this way. That someday, someone might not be so nice. And I wouldn't be a good parent if I didn't caution her of that, but … not right now. For now, I'm just grateful she's getting a respite from the cruelty she's faced for so long. That we're both getting a reprieve from our troubles.

That night, as I'm fixing the leaky faucet in Zoe's bathroom, my mind drifts to the future. Like her, everything that's happened since we moved here has made me appreciate this town more every day. And I can see staying here for a long time. Watching it grow. Being part of a community again. It's already begun.

So maybe it's okay to start putting down roots. Maybe it's okay to want more. Zoe deserves more. She's growing up so fast, and I know the teenage years will bring a whole new set of challenges. She hasn't even had her first period yet, and the thought of navigating that minefield alone terrifies me.

I've always felt like a part of her needed a mother figure, someone who could guide her through the complexities of womanhood in a way I never could. But as I tighten the last screw, a realization hits me.

Ever since Zoe's mother passed, everyone questioned how I could be a single father. How could I possibly raise a daughter alone? How could I let Zoe go through life without a mother? How will *I* go through life alone? Virginia's parents, Zoe's counselors and teachers. Hell, even my own friends have all expressed these concerns over the years.

While I may not have a partner to help me raise Zoe, maybe … maybe I don't need to feel the pressure to find one anymore. Because here, I'm not alone. We have Mia and Rae, who have already unexpectedly taken Zoe under their wing, forming a special bond with her. And then there's Joanie and Carrie, both strong, kind women.

If things between Rae and I become more, and I hope they will, I'd have everything I ever wanted. But I don't need to put pressure on myself, or her, to make it become more for Zoe's sake. I can't remember the last time I pursued a woman without that thought pushing at the back of my mind. It's … a relief. And it means if it works out, it'll be for all the right reasons.

For the first time in a long time, I feel a sense of peace wash over me. Zoe will have the support and love she needs to grow into a confident, compassionate young woman. She's already well on her way. And I'll have support, too.

And maybe we'll both end up with so much more than we ever thought to hope for.

As I drift off to sleep, I say a silent prayer of thanks for this chance at a better life, for the amazing people who have welcomed us into their hearts.

Alpine Ridge isn't just a fresh start for me and Zoe. It's a chance to heal, to build something beautiful.

And I can't wait to see what tomorrow brings.

CHAPTER THIRTEEN

RAE

It's Saturday night, weekly dinner party night, and I find myself arriving late once again. And once again, with a stomach filled with butterflies. This time it's not because I know Luke will be there — well, not just because of that anyway — but also because Brandon is bringing his boyfriend with the hope that he can help me break down starting my own business into something I feel like I can actually manage.

I dig deep and walk inside, instead of giving in to my fear, running back to the Bronco, and hightailing it the hell out of here at the thought of exposing how clueless and incapable I am.

As soon as I enter, a wall of aromas hits me: tomatoes, garlic, and cheese. It reminds me of my Grams's lasagna, and I'm instantly soothed. I pop my jacket onto a hook and kick off my boots, then head into the living room. Because I'm a big girl, and I don't have to hide in the kitchen every time my anxiety rears its anti-social head.

I'm rewarded with everyone turning my way with excited faces. "Rae!" the cheer goes up. I laugh and step down into the cozy room, packed with my favorite people.

"I know you're all just excited because that means we can eat now," I tease.

Everyone laughs.

"Damn straight," Joanie agrees from the couch. I smirk at her, and she blows me a kiss.

Then, my eyes land on Brandon, who is sitting on the love seat just beyond the couch. And then on the man next to him. As soon as they do, I can see why Brandon is so smitten. His boyfriend is unobtrusively handsome, with a thick shock of dark brown hair, lively dark brown eyes, and a warm smile topped with a well-manicured moustache that's giving off some serious Pedro Pascal vibes. But it's the fact that he's gazing adoringly at Brandon that tells me everything I need to know about my friend's new love.

"Rae, you're late to the meet-my-boyfriend party! Get your cute butt over here," Brandon calls, gesturing for me to join them. "Alex, this is Rae."

I smile and approach, perching myself on the arm of the loveseat next to Brandon. "Hi, Alex, it's nice to meet you," I say, offering a hand.

Alex reaches out and shakes it. "It's a pleasure. Brandon has told me so much about you. About all of you, really," he replies warmly.

"Well, he hasn't kept you a secret or anything, but he hasn't exactly told us much either. So, I want to hear all about you," I respond.

Mia's voice interrupts from the arched entrance of the living room, rising over the murmur of multiple conversations. "I feel like I should have a cow bell or something, but dinner's ready."

We all laugh and head in to sit down, starting on the manicotti and salad Mia's prepared. It doesn't take long before everyone starts firing questions at Alex. Where'd you and Brandon meet? Where are you from? What made you want to open an antique shop? The questions go on for a while before Brandon good naturedly ends the barrage, though Alex seems unperturbed. Quite the opposite, actually, especially when Zoe asks him where he and Brandon went on their first date. She's such a cute kid.

And Alex is friendly and easygoing, fitting right in. I can see even more why Brandon likes him so much. And given the groans when asked to stop the impromptu game of twenty questions, I can also see why Brandon waited to introduce him to the gang. Brandon and Alex seem solid enough to handle it, though, exchanging sweet glances and smiles.

"So, is it my turn now?" Alex teases.

"You bet," Mia agrees. "Just don't ask Joanie anything."

Everyone laughs, but Alex looks puzzled. "Why not?"

Joanie smirks and raises an eyebrow, but Greg beats her to it. "Because she has absolutely zero filter, and she's just waiting to give you a raunchy nickname." Zoe's eyes widen and Greg shoots Luke an apologetic smile.

Without missing a beat, Alex turns to me. "So, Rae, Brandon tells me you're an incredible event planner. And that you're considering starting your own business?"

Laughter echoes around the room once more and even I chuckle at his hilarious handling of Greg's comment, though I also feel my cheeks flush at the compliment. "I don't know about incredible, but I do enjoy it. The business side of things is what scares me, to be honest."

Alex nods understandingly. "It can seem daunting at first, but from what I hear, you've got real talent."

I know this is why Brandon suggested he come tonight, but suddenly I'm not so sure. "I know Brandon probably asked you to talk to me about starting a business, but I don't want to dump you into the deep end —"

"Nuh uh. If you won't, we will," Joanie taunts before taking a sip of wine.

Mia shrugs. "I'm with Jo. We all want this for you, Rae."

Brandon gives me an apologetic smile. "What she said. But you've got to want it for yourself, too."

I give Alex an unsure look and he gives me a reassuring smile in return. "I'm happy to use what I know to help. Really. The business aspect isn't as complicated as it might seem. I promise." His calm demeanor and warm smile would melt a stronger woman than me.

Still, I hesitate, my doubts creeping in. "That's so kind of you, but I'm just ... I'm so scattered, always running late, constantly forgetting things. I don't know if I'm cut out for running a business."

"I highly doubt that," Alex says gently.

"Rae, you've seen me learning the ropes of owning a business at the bakery," Mia offers. "He's right. You can totally do it."

"While I appreciate the vote of confidence," I say quietly, "you have a law degree, Mia." I gesture around the table. "And Joanie runs her own business ... and also has a law degree. And Nate, too, with his medical degree. Seems like it takes some serious smarts, if you ask me."

I deflate like a balloon, but Alex just looks at me. "And I've got a bachelor's in art history and a Master's in Business." He shakes his head. "All that means is I paid a lot of money for someone to teach me things I used for the first five minutes of a real job. The rest I had to learn."

"Does that mean I don't have to go to college, Dad?" Zoe whispers to Luke.

Luke face palms and mutters, "We'll talk about it later."

"When?" she whispers back. Carrie snickers at her sass.

"In about five years," Luke hisses, exasperated.

I huff a dry laugh, then turn back to Alex. "That's easy to say when you had a good, solid foundation under you," I say tensely. "School was never my strong suit. Don't get me wrong, I tried a few community college classes after I realized I wasn't going to make it as a singer. I took some French. An accounting course. Then, when neither of those clicked, I went into the nursing assistant program."

"Really? I didn't know you were a nurse's assistant," Nate says.

I scoff. "I wasn't. You think I'm late now? You should've seen me then. I didn't finish the program, what with showing up halfway through class more often than not. So, I dropped out. After that, the only jobs I could ever keep were ones where I worked more than I didn't, and being 'late' wasn't even a thing when the only thing I didn't do was sleep there." I shake my head. "I love you all to death, and I appreciate the point you're trying to make, Alex, but I'm ... different. I don't have what it takes. Not like you all." I gesture widely around the table.

Alex tilts his head, studying me for a moment. "Rae, have you ever considered the possibility that you might have ADHD?"

I blink, taken aback. "ADHD? Isn't that for kids who can't sit still in class?"

Alex chuckles. "That's a common misconception. Adult ADHD often looks a lot like what you're describing — difficulties with organization, time management, forgetfulness. There are treatments available that could help you manage it. It might boost your productivity and your confidence."

"I had a classmate with ADHD," Zoe offers. "We all knew when she hadn't taken her medication."

"How?" I ask, curious.

Zoe lifts a shoulder. "She'd show up after the bell and she wouldn't listen to a thing the teacher said. She didn't move around a lot or anything, she just seemed to daydream a lot more than usual."

I sit back, reeling at Zoe's words. Because daydreaming was my main hobby in school. And there goes my stereotype of ADHD kids being fidgety.

Could it really be that simple? Could this explain the struggles I've faced my entire life?

"I ... I never even considered that," I admit.

"I'm ashamed I never thought of it either," Nate admits. I can hear the frustration with himself in his voice. He's certainly known me the longest of those present, save Luke, of course. "If you want to come into the clinic next week, I can get you a referral for a therapist who can evaluate you."

I take a deep breath, my eyes darting around the table uncertainly. But all I see looking back at me is love and encouragement. My eyes well with tears as they settle back on Nate.

"Okay. Yes. Let's do it," I agree. Then, to Alex, "Thank you."

He smiles warmly. "Of course. I'll give you my number before I leave tonight. I'm happy to start helping anytime, in any way I can."

The conversation moves on, but I'm quiet as it does. I feel overwhelmed ... yet encouraged and supported at the same time a newfound sense of possibility taking root in my chest.

Later, as I'm helping Mia clear the dishes, Luke approaches me, his expression soft.

"Hey," he says, leaning against the counter. "That was some heavy out there. Are you okay?"

I smile as I rinse plates. "Yeah, actually. Knowing there might be an explanation for the way I am has me hopeful that I might be able to fix it."

Luke's eyes scan my face. "Understanding yourself is an important part of accepting yourself. I hope it helps you on both counts. Because there's nothing to 'fix'. You're perfect just the way you are, Rae."

I smirk. "I am, aren't I?" I ask airily.

Luke laughs, and tingles erupt over my skin. "Hey, I've been meaning to ask — how's Zoe been doing at the bakery?"

I can't help but smile, darting a glance back toward the living room to make sure she's out of earshot. Not because I have anything bad to say, but because I don't want to embarrass her with praise. "She's an absolute delight, Luke. Such a quick learner, and so eager to help. You've raised a wonderful young woman."

Pride shines in his eyes. "That means a lot, coming from you. I'm just glad it's working out. Zoe adores spending time with you and Mia, and it's been great for me to have a consistent rhythm to get things done without feeling like I'm neglecting her."

I nod, though I can't even begin to fathom the balancing act of single parenthood. I can barely handle my own needs most of the time. "It must be tough, though, getting time for yourself."

Luke shrugs. "It can be, but I manage. Actually, I've been wanting to check out this brewery in Ellensburg that Greg keeps raving about. I don't suppose you'd want to join me sometime?" He looks away, clearly feigning nonchalance. I remember that look. It means he's dying for me to say yes.

I don't know how this gorgeous, successful man could still be interested in me after all these years, but I realize … he is.

My heart skips a beat, but I force myself to play it cool. "Luke, that sounds an awful lot like a date."

He raises his hands in mock surrender, a playful grin on his face. "Hey, I didn't mean it like that. I just … I've missed spending time with you, just the two of us. The more I see you, the more I remember how much fun we used to have together."

I bite my lip, considering. The idea of an afternoon alone with Luke, away from the prying eyes of Alpine Ridge, is undeniably appealing. I miss him, too. And it doesn't have to be anything but two old friends catching up, right?

"Okay," I say at last. "Let's do it. How about the middle of next week? Zoe can hang out with Mia while we're gone."

Luke's face lights up. "Perfect. It's a plan."

As he winks and walks away, my tummy is tied in knots for a whole new reason. First over starting a business, then over a possible explanation for all the things I've struggled with my whole life, and now I've agreed to spend time with Luke. Alone. With alcohol.

I fan myself with the dishtowel, wondering how I got myself into all this. And yet, somehow, it's all a little thrilling. The possibilities. The hope. I breathe deeply, holding onto both hopes gently in my heart, praying they don't slip away like they always do. Praying that this time is different.

The next day, I find myself at my momma's house, the conversation with Alex still fresh in my mind. As we sit at her kitchen table, sipping tea, I decide to broach the subject.

"Momma, did you ever notice any ADHD symptoms in me when I was a kid?"

She frowns and sets down her cup. "Like what?"

I shrug as nonchalantly as I can. "Forgetting stuff. Being easily distracted. Difficulty being on time. That sort of thing."

She waves a dismissive hand. "Oh, Rae, that's how all kids are."

"Yeah, I guess," I agree reluctantly. "But was I … more like that than other kids?"

She shrugs. "How should I know? I only had you."

I roll my eyes. "Surely you saw how other kids behaved at some point."

She lifts her cup back to her lips, taking a slow, deep sip before responding. "It's not the same when they're not yours," she finally says. "You seemed like a normal child." She says it in a final tone. Like she doesn't want to keep talking about it.

So, I refrain from pushing. From pointing out that those traits followed me into adulthood, making everything from schooling to relationships to work more difficult than they seemed for everyone else.

Because I know my momma, I take a deep breath and change the subject.

"There was something else I wanted to talk to you about. I'm thinking about starting an event planning business. Nothing big, just enough to formalize the work I'm already doing for the town."

Momma purses her lips. "A business? You?" She eyes me skeptically with her critical gaze. "What about the bakery?"

My heart drops. "I don't know. I guess I'll have to see how well it does. But I'd keep working there, for now at least."

She huffs out a breath. "Rae, honey, you're good at planning events, thanks to your Grams, but that seems like a lot to take on. Wouldn't you rather focus on carrying on the family legacy at the bakery? Grams would be so pleased to know you brought it back to life."

I press my lips together to stop myself from pointing out it wouldn't have had to be brought back to life if she hadn't run it into the ground. That maybe she's projecting, assuming I can't run a business because she couldn't. But I don't want to be spiteful.

"Mia's doing that just fine," I reply tightly. "I may work there, but she's the one running the show. I'm just trying to find something I'm good at."

Momma pats me on the hand patronizingly as she rises to refill her cup. "Well, you are good at planning your little parties," she says condescendingly. "But, sugar, that's not a business. Don't get me wrong, it's lovely that you help the town out. That's something you can do here and there. But a whole business?" She shakes her head. "No need to get too big for your britches. Stick to what you know."

Her words hit me like a slap, and suddenly, I see the stark contrast between my momma's well-intentioned but limiting beliefs and the endless encouragement of my friends.

All my life, Momma has urged me to play it safe, to think small. But my friends? They push me to dream big, to reach for more. And maybe it's that small thinking that's been holding me back all along.

I've always thought I was just like Momma, destined to follow in her footsteps. But in this moment, I realize that perhaps we're not as alike as I once believed.

Because deep down, I know I want this. I may be forty-six, but it's never too late to go after what you want. And what I want is to build something of my own, to challenge myself and grow. And I want to explore the possibility that there might be a reason behind my struggles, that with the right support, I can learn to manage them.

I'm tired of accepting things as they are. I'm ready for more.

The next morning, I stop into Nate's clinic as soon as they open and make an appointment to get that referral. I'll have to wait two days to see Nate, but it lifts my heart to know that he is doing so well that the clinic is already struggling to accept walk-ins.

With a few minutes left on my break, I call Alex, who agrees to come to next Saturday night's dinner party early so we can start talking business.

While these are small steps, they feel monumental.

As I head back into the bakery, the sun rising behind me, the flicker of hope in my chest that started last night blooms into something more. A desire to do this. To understand myself. To see if starting a business is possible. To see if having Luke back in my life, as something more than a friend is possible. To take one step at a time toward the kind of happiness I never thought I deserved.

And for the first time in God only knows how long, I tell myself I can do this.

CHAPTER FOURTEEN

LUKE

From the moment I wake, anticipation courses through me. I'm taking Rae out today. Maybe we aren't calling it a date, but my hopes are high. The more time I've spent with her, the more I realize that everything I once felt for her is still there … and more. She's kind, and funny, and so damn sexy it literally hurts. I have to push extra hard during my morning workout to tame those particular feelings.

I know even Zoe senses something is off as we drive into town, but she doesn't say anything, jumping out as usual as soon as we park at the bakery. I trail behind, watching with a smile as she embraces Mia and Rae in turn before heading into the kitchen with Mia.

I stop just inside as Rae steps out from behind the counter. In a blue and white gingham dress with a jean jacket, she looks like a sexy, grown-up version of the proverbial girl next door I fell in love with. And never fell out, as it happens. Because the sight of her, the small smile on her face, the nervous energy as she brushes her short, blond hair behind her ear … I just want to take her in my arms and show her how much I hadn't realized I missed her.

Instead, I opt for, "Hey, Rae." I grin at her.

"Hey, Luke," she responds, her cheeks pinkening.

"You look like Spring and my teenage fantasies all at the same time," I tease in a low voice meant only for her.

She wrinkles her nose. "That's not the kind of thing you say on a not-date," she points out.

I laugh. "Did I say it wasn't a date?" She nods slowly, and I shrug. "Ready to go?"

Rae smiles and shakes her head but contradictorily says, "Definitely." She turns and leans over the counter. "Mia, we're headed out."

Mia and Zoe pop out of the kitchen. "Have fun," Mia says with a knowing smile.

"Be good, Zo," I tell my daughter.

Zoe wiggles her eyebrows. "You, too, Dad."

She disappears back into the kitchen too quickly for me to respond, so I'm left standing there with my mouth hanging open.

Rae approaches and places a finger under my chin, snapping my jaw closed. "Come on, before you catch a fly," she teases.

"She's just so sassy. Have you been giving her lessons?"

Rae smirks as we exit the bakery. "Oh, she came to us like that."

I open the truck door for her, and she raises a brow, but hops in without further comment.

With a grin, I round the truck and get in.

I was worried a half-hour-plus drive would be awkward. That it's been so long since we were alone — well, when she didn't think I fathered a child with her best friend — that we'd have nothing to talk about. But I was as wrong as could be.

As we drive, we talk easily, with Rae pointing out all the subtle changes I'd missed while I was focusing on re-orienting myself with the area and keeping Zoe entertained on the drive. New power line runs. Expanded highways and new local roads. Empty fields with "land for sale" signs where farms once existed. Subtle but telling changes of development.

By the time we walk into the tavern, it's like we've somehow both stepped back in time thirty years and brought our previous relationship forward into a new era. It's the best of both worlds. I can't help but feel a mix of nerves and excitement wondering if she feels the same way.

We settle into a booth, making small talk about the food and drinks as we peruse the menu. Once we've ordered, Rae tells me about her appointment with Nate tomorrow, to get a referral to see if she has ADHD.

"I did some reading online yesterday," I admit. "And apparently, ADHD can present differently in girls than in boys. Looking back, I think you definitely showed signs as a kid."

Rae's eyebrows rise in surprise. "Really? Like what?"

I shrug. "Like … you didn't have a lot of friends and shied away from groups. Or how hard it was to get your attention sometimes when you'd zoned out. Which you did a lot. But you never acted out, so I guess I didn't think much of it at the time."

She nods slowly. "I never acted out because I hated disappointing my parents."

The mention of her parents sparks my curiosity. I'm dismayed to realize I hadn't even thought of them since I'd returned, and she hasn't said anything about them. Given that her father was blamed for accidentally starting the fire that burned the church down, surely it affected them.

"Speaking of your parents … is it okay to ask what happened to your dad after I left?" I ask carefully.

Rae's face falls, and I immediately regret bringing it up. But she takes a deep breath and shakes her head.

"No, it's fine. As you can probably guess, the town ostracized him for starting the fire. My parents fought constantly over it, and eventually, he just … left. And my mom … well, she was a mess, especially once the divorce was finalized.

Honestly, between their split and finding out that you had cheated on me and gotten Beth pregnant, I was a mess, too."

I flinch at the mention of my supposed infidelity, the old accusation still stinging even though we both know the truth now.

"I was so angry," Rae continues. "At the townspeople for how they treated my dad, at my dad for leaving us, at Beth for what I thought she'd done, at you for … well, you know. I got into fights, vandalized property. I earned a well-deserved reputation as a troublemaker that's followed me to this day."

She shakes her head, lost in the memories. "Anyway. Without my dad's help, the bakery struggled, too. Momma had to shut it down the next year. She took a job at the grocery store, and I started working at the tavern. We barely made ends meet."

My heart aches for her, for the hardships she endured in my absence. And I can't help it. I reach out and wrap my hand over hers. She looks up, blinking rapidly against the sheen of tears in her eyes. "Rae, I'm so sorry. I had no idea it would be that bad."

She gives me a sad smile. "It's in the past."

"I'm still sorry." I pause. "Wait, the bakery closed?"

She nods. "Mia only reopened it recently. Her grandmother had bought it from my momma."

I blow out a breath, still stroking my thumb over the back of her hand. "That bakery was everything to your family. Your Great Grams must've been so disappointed."

Rae huffs a breath out of her nose. "She was devastated. But not for long. She started to lose her faculties shortly after." She sniffs deeply, clearly troubled by the memory. And I understand why. Once the bakery was gone, her Great Grams had no reason to keep going. "She passed when I was twenty. That's when I left Alpine Ridge."

I take a deep breath and nod slowly, recalling something she'd said previously about moving to Seattle to try to make it as a singer.

"To pursue your singing career?" I prompt.

Rae nods. "I got some small gigs at clubs, but I never hit it big. And then I met my ex-husband. We wanted a family, so I had to give up on being a struggling artist. I worked full-time, and there was no room for singing anymore. And … well, you know the rest."

"He cheated on you," I say softly, shaking my head. "Why would *anyone* cheat, much less on you?"

Rae sighs. "Turns out I couldn't have children … but she could." She looks away.

I start to respond, my heart breaking for the dreams she lost after I left. My gut twists knowing I was probably one of them. But our food arrives before I can, and she changes the subject to Alpine Ridge's development, a topic we thoroughly discuss over our meal.

After, we decide to take a walk around downtown Ellensburg, the quaint, colorful shops and the warming spring day too inviting to deny.

We walk in silence, our hands brushing together. The tension has me so amped up I have to say *something*. "Isn't Alex's shop around here somewhere? Maybe we should drop in and say hello."

"It's closed Mondays and Tuesdays," she responds. "But he's coming to Mia and Nate's weekly dinner party again this Saturday."

"Oh yeah? That's great. He seems like a good guy. Brandon seems happy, anyway, and that's what matters most," I reply.

Rae pauses in front of a boutique and looks at me thoughtfully. "Is it weird to have a brother? After ..." She trails off, her cheeks turning red.

"After Hannah died?" I offer. She nods. "It's okay to talk about her, Rae. And no. It's not weird. I miss Hannah every day. I'd like to think she'd be excited to have another brother. I am, anyway, despite the circumstances. Brandon and I just ... click." I smile down at her. "Kind of like you and me."

Rae's blush deepens, but she doesn't look away. "We always did. Even when you were just the scrawny pastor's kid." She smiles fondly at the memory. "And then you grew up."

I nod, remembering the day I came into the bakery after being away for a summer at my grandparent's house. I'd grown a good three inches, and my voice had dropped. And I remember the look on her face that day. The day she saw me as *more*.

"I've grown up even more since the last time I saw you," I point out.

Rae tips her head back and laughs. "You sure have, Luke McMillan." Her eyes trail over me and my skin hums under her gaze.

"I have to admit, part of why I came back to Alpine Ridge was the hope of spending time with you. To see if there was more than just a click."

Rae bites her lip, a playful gleam in her eye. "And? What do you think? Is there?"

I look at her. Really look at her, gazing deep into her eyes, noting her hesitation but willing her to see everything I'm feeling and can't quite put into words. Because Rae and me? We fit in a way I'd never found before her.

Back then, I was in love with her before she ever even noticed me. And I was an idiot to think I could leave a love like that behind and never look back. Because Rae's still a part of me. And she still draws me in. Possibly even more now for having been away from her so long. Too long.

Her lips part as her eyes soften. And it's the permission I didn't know I needed. I raise a hand to her cheek, stroking my thumb over the delicate skin. Her breath catches and I smile.

"So much more," I murmur, leaning in. I close my eyes and run my nose along hers, waiting for her to give me full permission. Full access to her luscious mouth.

She hesitates for a moment, and I start to think I've misread her. But then she mumbles, "Fuck it."

We both stop holding back, our lips crashing together in a kiss so heated it's almost frantic, with lips quickly giving way to tongues, hands wrapping around each other until there's not an inch of space between us. Her body molds to mine, and I groan into her mouth at the familiar feel of her in my arms.

God, I missed this. I missed her. I missed *us*.

When we finally pull apart, foreheads still touching, we're both breathless.

"So much for this not being a date," she breathes.

I chuckle. "I'm not mad about it." And then I kiss her again, slower this time, relishing the feel of her soft lips against mine.

But when we break apart this time, she pulls back, and I see uncertainty again in her expression.

"Is this a good idea?" she asks.

I run a thumb down her jawline. "Why wouldn't it be?"

She breathes in, slow and deep. "It's ... I'm not good at relationships. And this one? There are bigger stakes here."

I draw my head back and furrow my brow. "Such as?"

She gives me an incredulous look. "Zoe, for starters. Don't get me wrong, I already love her to death. But I don't want her to think I'm trying to take her mother's place. And then there's you."

I huff a laugh. "What about me?"

Rae shifts uncomfortably, pushing away gently. "You seem so certain I'm what you want, but you've only been back a few weeks. You don't even know who I am now. I'm afraid you're interested in the idea of me more than who I actually am."

I reach out, taking her hand in mine. "Rae, slow down. We're just starting again. At least, I hope we are. We can take this as slowly as you need. And Zoe adores you. She'll be thrilled that we're spending more time together. And if it wasn't obvious, I'm pretty into you, too. You. The you who, yes, is still a lot like the girl I knew. But you've grown up, too," I point out. "And I see that. It's not like we haven't spent time together. Everything I've learned about who you are now has brought us to this moment. And I hope I get to keep learning about where you've been, what you want, and what we might be together at this stage of our lives. Because I'm still drawn to you, Rae. And I don't want to pretend that I don't think about you all the time anymore."

Rae takes a shaky breath. "Honestly? I think about you all the time, too." She looks up at me, stepping back in and allowing me to take her hand. "You're right. I'm sorry for being silly. I just ... I don't know how to navigate this."

I give her hand a squeeze. "For a woman with so much heart and so much talent, you're awfully unsure of yourself. Maybe you need someone to remind you every day how amazing you are."

Rae's eyes shine with unshed tears, and I realize with a pang that she probably hasn't had enough of that kind of support and encouragement.

"I do limit myself," Rae admits softly. "But no more." She lifts a hand to my face. "Do you want to go steady with me?" She bites into her bottom lip, fighting a smile.

I laugh. "I'd love nothing more than to pick up where we left off," I murmur, drawing her toward me with a finger under her chin and kissing her softly.

She pulls back with a happy sigh. "Let's look at it as starting fresh," she suggests. "I feel like there are so many things I believed to be true that weren't. About you. About myself. About life. I want to start something new. Something better."

My heart swells with ... yes, with love. Damn. I bite back the words, determined to make sure I'm not getting caught up in the moment. But I'm filled with love for her right now. Amazed by her bravery, her honesty, and her heart.

"And I'll be right here beside you, every step of the way," I promise.

As we continue walking hand in hand, I feel a sense of rightness settle over me. I know with every fiber of my being that I'm exactly where I'm meant to be.

I can't wait to see where this journey, this new start, takes us.

CHAPTER FIFTEEN

RAE

After Luke drops me off at the bakery and leaves with Zoe, Mia corners me, her blue eyes sparkling with curiosity. "So, how was the date?" she asks, a knowing smile playing at her lips.

I feel my cheeks flush. "It wasn't supposed to be a date," I protest weakly. But then I sigh, a grin tugging at my mouth. "But yeah, it kind of turned into one. A *really* good one."

Mia squeals, clapping her hands. "I knew it! Congratulations on finally giving in to your feelings."

"My feelings. For Luke."

Mia smirks. "Did you not know? Because it was obvious, to me at least."

I raise an eyebrow. "Obvious? I've spent the last few weeks going from being angry with him to dealing with the confusing fallout of what really happened." I shake my head, trying not to dwell too much on the whirlwind that has been Luke's return to town. Because I can't deny my feelings anymore, and right now I'm tired of looking at them too closely.

Mia huffs impatiently. "Rae, even when you were furious, you still looked at him with love in your eyes. And only someone you truly love can hurt you that badly."

Her words hit me like a ton of bricks. She's right. I can't deny the truth of it. I probably do still love Luke, even though there's an enormous chunk of his life I've missed. Yet he seems like the same guy I fell for all those years ago. Despite thinking he'd done something awful, I think deep down I always knew who he was. Still, there are a lot of blanks to fill in.

"Maybe. But I don't know him anymore, not really. Though I guess I'll get the chance to learn about all of that while dating him," I muse aloud.

Mia grins. "Exactly. It's like having your cake and eating it, too."

We both burst out laughing, the sound echoing through the empty bakery, and my empty heart. Well, not so empty anymore.

*

The next day, I find myself sitting across from Nate in his office, nerves fluttering in my stomach as I await the referral to see a therapist about possibly having ADHD.

Nate gives me a reassuring smile. "You know, this appointment is mostly a formality for the insurance company," he says gently. Then his expression turns contrite. "But honestly, it's also a chance for me to apologize. As your friend, I feel like I should have noticed the signs sooner. I'm sorry, Rae."

"I didn't realize, how could you?" I reply dismissively.

He shrugs. "I'm a doctor. It may not be my specialty, but I should've picked up on it."

"Don't beat yourself up," I say. And then I add nervously, "Do you think I really have ADHD?"

Nate leans forward, clasping his hands. "You have all the hallmarks — difficulty being on time, getting easily distracted, feeling overwhelmed and anxious, among other things. But most adults with ADHD are so used to masking their symptoms to appear 'normal' that they don't even think about it."

I lean back in the surprisingly comfortable office chair opposite Nate's old oak desk and absorb that. "Masking," I repeat. "That's ... yes, that fits." I nod, mostly to myself. The pretending to be paying attention. Setting a slew of alarms to be on time so nobody would realize how hopeless I was at keeping to a schedule. Forcing myself into social situations that sent my anxiety spiraling, all while pretending to have fun. "So, what will the therapist ... do?"

Nate smiles patiently. "If seeing a therapist is too daunting, that's okay, Rae. These days, lots of people self-diagnose," he assures me. "But all a therapist will do is ask questions to confirm the diagnosis and maybe make you fill out some questionnaires. The real benefit to going the official diagnosis route is access to treatment. Though it can take time to dial in what works for you. But even just having an official diagnosis and the treatment options that go with that can give you a mental health boost."

Nate looks down at a form, checking a few boxes and then signing the bottom before handing the top copy to me. "Here's your official referral. We'll fax a copy to the therapist's office this afternoon and they should be contacting you within a few business days. That'll give you some time to think about whether you want to proceed."

I let out a breath, grateful that he understands my reticence. But anxiety aside, I've already made my decision. "Thanks, Nate."

"Anytime," he assures me, rising and walking me out to the waiting room. He leans in and drops his voice. "I'd give you a hug, but then everyone else would want one, too." He winks at me and straightens up.

I chuckle. "No worries, I'll just go get one from your wife," I tease with a wink back.

Nate laughs and waves goodbye, heading back toward his office.

I leave, referral in hand, feeling supported and relieved. I'm finally walking the path to understanding myself better.

Am I anxious about convincing a complete stranger how badly I struggle sometimes? Honestly, yes, I am. But you can't be courageous without fear. And I seem to have somehow finally found my courage.

At the end of the day, Luke stops by the bakery a bit earlier than expected. Zoe and Mia are still in the kitchen formulating some new cupcake concoction.

"You're early," I say after sending Janet on her way with her daily chocolate chip muffin.

He grins, leaning over the counter. And since Janet was the only customer left, I lean in and meet his mouth with mine. Warmth floods me as his lips work against mine, his tongue lightly teasing me.

When he pulls away, I have to take a moment to compose myself. It's been a damn long time since I've been kissed period, much less in a way that makes me dizzy. I remember long make-out sessions with Luke when we were teenagers but even kisses while on the giddy high of first love don't compare to how his kisses make me feel now. If it's any indicator, Luke has developed some incredible skills and I'm trying very hard not to think about what kind. I'm determined to take this slowly.

But then, I was determined not to date him at all. I give what I'm sure must be a dazed smile as I fill a cup full of decaf for Luke and hand it over.

"So, how was your day?" I ask, knowing he'd started interviewing architects.

Luke runs a hand through his gray-streaked dark blond hair. "Boring as hell. And not nearly as important as your meeting with Nate. How'd it go?" He takes a sip of coffee and gives an appreciative rumble that makes me shiver.

I blink a couple of times while I try to remember his question. Oh. Yeah.

"It was good. I've got the referral. They're supposed to call me in a few days."

"Is there a reason you're waiting for *them* to call *you*?"

I chew on my lip. "I ... no. There's no reason. I'll call them once I'm off." I nod resolutely.

"Good. You deserve answers."

I lift my chin. "I do, don't I."

Luke laughs, and the sound warms me from the inside out. "Look at you, already more confident. And I haven't even told you how gorgeous you look today," he murmurs, his eyes scanning down my powdered-sugar-covered apron.

I snort. "Got a thing for hot messes?" I tease.

Luke smirks. "Got a thing for you, Rachel Donovan."

I blush hard at the suggestive look on his face.

"I don't remember you blushing so much," he says slyly.

And I blush harder. "I'm just flushed. Hormones." I shrug even though I know I'm not convincing anyone.

"Hormones," he repeats skeptically.

"You've never heard of perimenopause? Hot flashes? Sweating?" I know I sound nervous because I am. And I also know he sees right through me.

Luke chuckles and sets his coffee down on the counter, pulling me forward by the hand and running his nose down the column of my neck. Shivers erupt across the sensitive skin and my whole body flushes with heat.

"Then why does it happen when I do this?" he murmurs huskily against my skin, kissing just under my ear.

"Definitely hormones," I mumble, craning my neck to give him better access. He chuckles against my skin and the warm puff of air has me tingling all over.

We hear feet shuffling and voices coming toward the kitchen door and we spring apart.

"To be continued," he promises.

I bite into my bottom lip to hold back a grin as Zoe emerges and gives Luke an earful about her day. He manages a quick thanks to Mia and a brief goodbye before she's tugging him toward the truck, still chattering nonstop.

He's such a wonderful dad. And she's such an amazing kid. I can't screw this up.

As the week goes on, Luke makes a habit of coming early to pick up Zoe so we can talk. It's hard to get in much besides how our days are going, so we end up texting between things late into the night until it's time for bed. Apparently, texting is easier, since talking on the phone with Zoe around is nearly impossible. Like most twelve-year-old girls, she's — in Luke's words — nosy as hell. I correct him that she's got an inquisitive mind, which is a good thing.

Still, texting it is. Which I've never been big on, but it's a surprisingly good way to ask random questions about his life, and vice versa. I learn about his time in the military after high school. How he hasn't talked to his mom since his sister's death. That one gets me, and I can't help asking how she could walk away from her other child. He says he doesn't know, but he suspects it has to do with his dad, and the fact that Luke himself made sure it wasn't easy to find him so that once he cut contact with his dad, he couldn't be sucked back in.

Still, his family situation pulls at my heart. Then again, it's not like mine's any better. Even though our fathers had very different roles in the fire and what came after, it seems the results for their families were equally disastrous. It's strange bonding over shared pain like that, but ... cathartic. It's not something I even share with folks who don't know, much less feel like they could ever understand. But Luke does.

It's not all heavy, either. I learn his favorite food is takeout Chinese. When he can find the time, he loves rock climbing — in nature, not at a gym. And his goal has long been to become a fire chief, to look after a town, city, or even county to ensure the safety of as many families as he could.

Apparently, after training in first response, rescue, and firefighting in the military, he used the GI bill to go to school for occupational safety and leadership, then started working his way up the ranks of the Seattle Fire Department. But chief always eluded him. While the guys are used to working as a team, according to Luke, they can be savage in competing for promotions. And Luke is many things, but cutthroat is not one of them.

We must send hundreds of messages over the week. He asks to see me on Friday night, but Saturday is an early day at the bakery, so I have to decline.

> I have to be at work at 4 am. But I'll see you tomorrow night at Mia and Nate's, right?

His reply is swift.

LUKE

You bet your sweet ass.

I chuckle.

> If anyone around here has a sweet ass, it's you. I can't wait to see it in uniform.

I watch the dots bounce on the screen, biting my thumb nail as I sink under the covers and switch off the light.

LUKE

I'd much rather you see it out of uniform.

I nearly swoon at the response and my whole body flushes with heat once more. It's been happening more and more these days, but Luke has a next-level ability to trigger it.

> That image isn't going to help me sleep.

LUKE

Mmm. I can think of a few things that could, but you won't come over.

I fan myself with one hand as I respond with the other.

> What's gotten into you?

LUKE

You don't like it?

My insides tighten at the response I can almost hear him whispering in my ear. God, this man is going to be the death of me tonight.

> You know I do.

Or maybe he doesn't remember how much I liked it when he'd whisper those sorts of things to me as we made love. If he even remembers. Because I sure do. Clumsy and unskilled as our trysts may have been, he always had a knack for getting me so worked up I could barely think straight. Clearly, he hasn't lost it.

> LUKE
>
> Do I? It's been a while. I think I need you to remind me what you like and how you like it.

God. Damn.

> This is taking it slow?

But as soon as I send the message, I know what he's going to say. Because clearly, he's in that kind of mood.

> LUKE
>
> Oh, I'd be happy to take it very slow with you. I've got all night, Rae.

Forget fanning myself. I throw off the covers and get out of bed, cracking the window open to let the chilly night air in. I'm tempted to strip, too, but I don't want any reminders of being naked, and what can happen in that state.

> You're playing dirty. And don't make that sexual!

I chuckle as I lay back down, my feverish skin finally cooling under the icy breeze from outside. My phone buzzes, so I lift it back up.

> LUKE
>
> Fine. I'll be good. For now. Sleep well, beautiful.

I grin, putting my phone on the charger and closing my eyes. I'll bask in this part while it lasts. Because we'll either keep getting to know each other, and we'll get there eventually, or … well, I don't want to think about the alternative. I don't want this to end in disaster like every other relationship I've ever had. Because it's been a long time since I've even let myself take this chance. All I can do is hope it's worth it.

The next evening, I arrive at Mia and Nate's house even earlier than I told Mia I'd be meeting Brandon and Alex there. More than a little proud of myself for managing it, I knock but get no response, so I let myself in, as we're always told to do.

When I step inside, Mia's voice floats down the hall. "But what if the tests say —"

"Don't what if this," Nate interrupts. "Whatever the results are, we're in this together. And no matter what, I love you. Understand?"

I pause, holding my breath as I realize they must be discussing their visit to the fertility specialist. I knew they'd headed there after the bakery closed early yesterday, but I'd forgotten until just now.

Not wanting to intrude, I quietly reopen the front door, then loudly slam it closed, calling out a greeting. "Hey guys, I'm here!"

Mia's head pops out of the kitchen. "Rae! You're early!"

I leave my coat and shoes at the door, trekking down the hall to join her. One look at her puffy eyes tells me she has, indeed, been what-iffing herself to death. I haul her into my arms and squeeze her tight. "Hey, sugar. You okay?"

Mia squeezes me back. "I'm … no, not really."

I let go, holding her at arm's length. "Let's cook and you can tell me all about it."

Mia smiles at me gratefully and, with some prompting, tells me about their visit. Which is to say, not much. They were informed of the full barrage of testing that is their routine, but Mia clearly took that to mean they'd already concluded something was horribly wrong with her. I gently insert that I went through this, too, and that it's all standard. That this doesn't mean anything is wrong with her, and to do what they say and hope that it'll show an easy fix. Because it very well may. And that I'd happily cover for her that day at the bakery, and she shouldn't worry about a thing.

By the time the roast is in the oven, Mia is clearly doing better. We're getting started on side dishes when I hear voices at the door heralding Brandon and Alex's arrival.

I step out of the kitchen to go meet them only to run into Nate, who I quickly realize had probably never stopped listening after he left the kitchen.

"Thank you," he mouths, his eyes darting toward Mia.

I shake my head to say that there's nothing to thank me for, then I pull the big, muscly lug into a hug of his own. And damn if he doesn't hug me back just as hard. I pat him on the shoulder reassuringly before heading toward Brandon and Alex.

"Hi, guys," I greet them enthusiastically, suddenly excited for what's coming.

"Rae, darling, you look fabulous as always," Brandon says, kissing me on my cheek.

I pinch his cheek in return. "You're my favorite."

"And I'm here to give him a run for his money," Alex teases, pulling me in for a hug.

"Oh good, you're a hugger," I reply, squeezing him back. "Why don't we go into the living room?"

We troop down the hall and settle around the coffee table. As usual, there's a fire roaring in the fireplace, making the room warm and cozy. I sit on the floor at the corner of the table, flexing my bare toes in the long, cushy pile of the plush beige rug.

Alex settles down and pulls a laptop out of his bag, opening it up on the coffee table so we can all see.

"So, before we get into it, I just want to say that you should think of the business plan as mostly for you at this point. Your first plan doesn't have to be long or detailed. It's more a way for you to organize your thoughts and get an idea of what it would take to do what you're thinking about doing and then decide if you want to keep going. Make sense?"

I tip my head to the side. "Yes, actually, and that sounds way less scary than I thought."

Brandon chuckles. "Alex can make anything approachable."

Alex gives Brandon a loving smile. "I wish. You're just smitten with me."

Brandon grins. "Damn straight." He leans over and gives Alex a sweet, chaste kiss.

"Aww, you two are just too damn cute. Can we focus now?"

They both look at me in shock. "Are you already on meds?" Brandon jokes. "Because *you* just told *me* to focus."

I laugh. "I'm not, though maybe soon. And to be fair, if my boyfriend were here, I'd probably have trouble focusing, too."

Brandon raises a brow. "Boyfriend?"

Shit.

I smile innocently and turn back to Alex. "So, you were saying about the business plan?"

Alex looks between us for a moment as if trying to decide which one of us to side with.

"Yes, the business plan," Alex finally agrees, turning the computer toward me. "I'm going to cut to the chase so as not to overwhelm you. Before you can start, there are five questions you should answer."

I arch a brow. "You're giving me homework?"

He shrugs. "I mean, yes? Even if you know the answers now, it would still be good to think about them and actually write out your reasoning, since they'll be the core of the rest of the plan."

I shrug. "Okay, Yoda, show me the ways of the force."

Brandon snorts and Alex turns the screen to me, reading the questions aloud. They really are simple, but I see how they'll be key to making a plan.

"What is your service and why is it unique?" he reads. "The former is a straightforward answer, but I'd encourage you to really think about the latter part. Maybe even look around at what other event planners do, that sort of thing."

I nod, pulling out my phone and taking notes. I glance up at the next question. "Who will be my customers? At least that one's easy."

Alex nods. "And the one after, too — how will you reach your customers? You're lucky in that your business is serving an existing customer. Though if you decide to expand, you'll want to revisit that question."

My eyebrows fly up. "Whoa there. One thing at a time."

"Sorry," Alex says sheepishly. "I don't want to overwhelm you, but honestly, if you're going to have a business, it's better to plan for growth from the start than pretend like it could never happen."

"Straight facts," Brandon says in agreement.

I blow out a slow breath. "Okay. Noted." I can do this. I. Can. Do. This.

"Next question: how will you make money?" Alex reads, then turns to me with a thoughtful expression. "Have you made money on the events you've run so far?"

I shake my head. "We don't charge attendees, so no. But honestly … since my friends often end up pitching in, I've thought about what I would have to charge to have the events pay for themselves, at least, so they didn't have to keep dumping their own money in. So even though it'll be the town paying, I have some idea of what I'd need to charge."

Alex nods. "That's a great start. Have they talked to you about payment for your services?" he asks.

I lift a shoulder, fighting against the discomfort of a lifetime of authority figures and employers telling me never to discuss compensation. "Arthur paid for everything for the St. Patrick's Day event and I received a non-employee compensation check that was way more than I thought I deserved," I admit.

Alex's eyes narrow. "We're going to talk industry rates at some point. But I'm glad they're clearly willing to pony up the necessary cash."

I huff a laugh. "Now I just have to get used to talking about money," I mumble.

"You're going to have to get comfortable talking about a lot of things," Brandon adds. "But not all right this second, so tell that anxiety I can see on your face to shut the fuck up."

This time I full-belly laugh. "Damn, B, you just said a mouthful." I shake my head, wiping away tears of laughter. "I'll work on it. All of it."

Alex smirks. "Which brings me to the last question: what does your team look like?" He pauses. "I know your friends have pitched in, but if you're going to run a business, you need employees, not just friends."

My heart sinks. This. This is the part of running a business that really freaks me out. I'm so used to doing everything myself, only allowing others to pitch in under very carefully controlled circumstances. But hiring and managing people I don't already know and trust? I can already feel my anxiety levels jumping back up.

"I take it by your silence that this is the hardest one," Alex says delicately. I nod, unable to respond with words, to explain. "Allow me to offer a solution?"

My brows bunch together. "What do you mean?"

Alex's eyes dart to Brandon, who has an equally confused look on his face. Alex clears his throat. "If you're open to a business partner, I would be interested."

My jaw drops. "You're joking," I gasp.

"I'm not," Alex says plainly. "The antique shop is practically running itself these days. I'd been thinking about opening another here, but it doesn't feel like Alpine Ridge is quite ready for that. So, in the meantime, I'd love to have a heavier hand in your event planning business. You bring the event planning experience, I bring the business experience. And we can learn from each other as we go." He darts another nervous look at Brandon. "And that means I can be here more. So, you'd really be doing me a favor."

Brandon stares at Alex, and by the heave of his chest I can tell he's close to hyperventilating. I lean back, unsure if he's upset or … Brandon launches himself at Alex and gives him a full-on, open-mouthed kiss.

Okay, he's happy.

I chuckle with relief.

They break apart and Brandon caresses Alex's face. "You'd do that for me?"

Alex swallows hard. "For us," he breathes. Then, to me, "And for you, Rae. I feel strongly that I could be there to help you get off the ground … and slowly fade out when you're ready for me to. Does that sound like it would work for you?"

Now it's my turn to be speechless. So, I take a cue from Brandon, knocking Alex over with a hug. Brandon and Alex both laugh.

"I'll take that as a yes," Alex murmurs in my ear as Brandon joins in on the hug.

I nod, tears brimming over. "Yes," I choke out. "Thank you."

"Are we having a hug party?"

I barely have time to look up before a smaller body crashes into us and Zoe joins our pile.

I pull back, laughing as I wipe the tears away to find Luke standing in the entryway to the living room, looking unsure.

I grin and gesture for him to join us. "Alex and I are going into business together," I explain.

Luke's brows jump in surprise. "Really? That's … wow, that's great. Congratulations to you both," he says, reaching over and shaking Alex's hand.

There's not much time for talk as the rest of the gang arrives and the house fills with laughter and lively conversation. Followed by even more over another amazing meal from Mia, followed by the cupcakes that Mia and Zoe perfected this week.

Everyone praises Zoe's creativity at the flavor combination — lavender, lemon, and blueberry. She beams under the praise, and I'm so damn proud of her. She's already a better baker than I ever was, which I tell her. Her surprised look and wobbly lip tell me that my approval means something to her. The realization is simultaneously flattering and heavy. Because I'm seeing her father now. I brush off thinking about the implications of it, which is good, because everyone has already moved on to discussing what they want to do after dinner.

I help Mia clean up and miss most of that conversation. That is, until I vaguely hear Carrie make a comment to Evan, the only part of which I pick up is my name, causing Evan to turn to me with a mischievous grin.

Oh, no. I'm not sure I like whatever's going to happen next. I look at him warily.

"Rae, darling," Evan says winningly, sidling up to me and slinging an arm over my shoulders. "We're thinking a little after-dinner music would hit the spot. And it's been brought to my attention that it's been way too long since we sang together."

I blanch, totally surprised. We did one duet forever ago, that I hadn't even remembered until now.

I look at him skeptically. "Now? Really?"

But then Zoe pipes up, her eyes wide and pleading. "Please, Rae? I want to hear you sing!"

Well, damn. How can I say no to that face? "Okay, okay," I relent. "One song."

Evan rubs his hands together gleefully. "How about 'Don't Know Much'?"

I snort. "Too serious. Let's do 'Don't Go Breaking My Heart' instead."

He laughs. "Okay," he agrees, then leans in and stage whispers, "But your age is showing."

I swat at him playfully. "Shush. That song came out the year I was born. It's a classic."

We launch into the duet, our voices blending together like they were made to harmonize, just as before. And I'm once again blown away that Evan is a handsome, talented actor and an amazing singer. It seems like too much for one person to be good at.

As we sing, I lose myself in the music, memories of belting out tunes with my hairbrush as a microphone while imagining my bright future as a famous singer flooding back.

When we finish, the room erupts into cheers and applause. Zoe bounces up and down, grinning from ear to ear.

"Wow, Rae! You should have been a superstar!"

Her words simultaneously thrill and sting, a bittersweet reminder of the dreams I once chased. Still, I smile and take a little bow, basking in the warmth of my friends' praise.

Joanie suggests we do full karaoke in the living room, and Evan can't get there fast enough, taking most of the gang with them, including Zoe who, if she wasn't smitten before she knew he could sing, too, may now never leave his side.

While I stay to help finish clearing out plates, Luke appears, his hand grazing the small of my back. He tilts his head towards the dining room, and I follow him in, curiosity blooming in my chest.

Once we're alone, he turns to me, his brown eyes soft and filled with wonder. "Zoe's right, you know," he says quietly. "Your voice is even more beautiful than I remember." He reaches up, tucking a strand of hair behind my ear.

"You don't have to say that," I admonish him.

"Even if it's true?" He smiles down at me, his eyes full of emotion. "Do you remember when you used to sing to me, Rae? Because I do."

I swallow hard, nodding. It was his favorite kind of foreplay. We'd find an empty field and lay a blanket on the grass. I'd sing while we watched the stars. Then we would make love. A fact I hadn't remembered until just now. And suddenly I'm feeling very weak in the knees.

"I still dream about those nights under the stars," he admits. "And somehow you're even more beautiful now than you were then."

"Luke." I can't tell if his name on my lips is a protest or a plea.

"Rae," he whispers as his lips capture mine in a slow, sensual kiss. I melt into him, my hands coming up to rest on his broad chest. The rest of the world falls away, narrowing down to just the two of us, lost in a moment of pure, perfect bliss.

"Ahem."

We spring apart at the sound of a throat clearing. Zoe stands in the doorway, a huge, triumphant grin on her face.

"I knew it!" she crows. "I knew you two liked each other!"

Heat rushes to my cheeks, and I bury my face in Luke's shoulder, mortified at being caught making out like teenagers.

"We do," Luke admits. "Is that okay?"

"Okay?" Zoe asks incredulously. "That's *awesome!*"

Luke chuckles and I manage to beat back my mortification enough to lift my head and offer Zoe a feeble smile. "Did you need something, Zoe?"

Zoe gives me her most winning smile. "Will you come sing some more, please?"

My smile broadens as my anxiety relaxes. "Sure thing, sugar. I'll be right there."

"Yes!" Zoe cries triumphantly, turning tail and heading back to the living room.

Luke kisses the side of my head as I stare at the spot where Zoe was standing. "See?" he says. "She's thrilled."

I turn and look at him. And the happiness on his face hits me right in the heart. I realize in this moment that despite his reassurance, I was still afraid she might object to me and Luke being together. But the sheer joy that was radiating from her tells a different story. She's happy for us.

And just like that, one more piece of the puzzle clicks into place. With Luke by my side, Zoe's approval, and the unwavering support of my friends, I feel like all of the hurts of the past are being healed by the joy of the present.

Luke and I can do this slowly, and I don't have to fear a relationship with him. Zoe isn't worried about me taking her dad's attention away or seeming like I'm trying to be a mother figure. And Alex, in what should qualify him for sainthood, has offered to start a business with me, meaning I won't have to do this alone. I feel like in this new world, there's nothing holding me back. Nothing I can't do. And everything to look forward to.

CHAPTER SIXTEEN

LUKE

Spending time with Rae every day when I pick up Zoe from the bakery has quickly become the highlight of my days. On Wednesday, we don't get to spend as much time together as usual since Rae is covering for Mia. But on Thursday, Mia makes it up to us by giving us some extra time alone.

We decide to go on a walk, our hands intertwined as we stroll down Main Street. Spring is in full bloom, and the evergreen hills are dotted with budding maples, cottonwoods, and willows; shades of bright greens splayed over deep emeralds, contrasted against the clear blue sky. Rae looks beautiful in a flowy green polka dot dress that shows off her toned calves.

The conversation flows easily between us, ranging from who is the better cook — we agree it's her, since my attempts to cook for Zoe and me have been feeble at best — to how we hope all the changes to the town shape its character — with both of us hoping that more families with kids move in and bring new life and energy with them.

At one point, Rae turns to me, her hazel eyes sparkling with curiosity. "What's it really like being a firefighter?" she asks. "I mean, beyond the hero stereotype."

I take a deep breath, considering my response. "It has its ups and downs," I admit. "Obviously, there's a lot of good — saving people, their homes, their livelihoods. But it's not all about saving people and rescuing kittens from trees."

I go on to explain how, everywhere I go, I can't help but notice potential fire hazards. Lit candles left unattended, missing or non-functional smoke detectors, blocked fire exits I feel compelled to clear. It's a constant state of vigilance that I can never quite turn off.

"And sometimes," I continue, my voice growing quieter, "in my dreams, I can't unsee some of the horrors I've witnessed on the job."

Rae squeezes my hand, her expression sympathetic. "But you bear that burden so that others don't have to," she points out softly. "Luke, I'm so proud of you for turning a tragedy into a lifelong career of helping people."

Her words wrap around my heart like a warm blanket. She understands, perhaps better than anyone, the impact of the fire that changed the course of my life.

I clear my throat, needing to be fully honest with her. "The reality is, being a firefighter can be hard on relationships, too," I confess. "The crazy shifts, the danger, the emotional toll ... it's a lot for someone to handle."

Rae stops walking and turns to face me fully, her hand coming up to cup my cheek. "We can deal with that when we get there," she says firmly. "Together."

"You said *when*," I point out, my heart expanding at her obvious message: she's in this for the long haul. I already knew I was but hearing her talk that way does things to me.

She grins. "Yeah. I did."

In this moment, gazing into her eyes, I know with absolute certainty that I love her. That she's the one that got away all those years ago, and I'm sure as hell not letting that happen again.

But I hold back the words, not wanting to overwhelm her when we're supposed to be taking things slow. Instead, I lean down and capture her lips in a tender kiss, pouring all my unspoken feelings into showing her. As she kisses me back passionately, I can't help but feel like this can't be real. It's just too good to be true.

On Friday, as I'm going over the architect's notes for the new fire station schematics, my phone rings with an unfamiliar number. I mentally note that's a firefighter tic I didn't mention — I never let calls go to voicemail in case it's an emergency. So, I pick up.

"Hello?"

"Luke? It's ... it's your mother."

I nearly drop the phone in shock. "Mom?" I manage, my voice strangled.

She takes a shaky breath. "I got your letter. I wrestled with whether to respond, but... I decided you deserved to know the whole story. The truth about why I left your father."

My chest tightens with anticipation and old hurt as I listen to her explain what really happened the night the church burned down. How Rae's father caught her mother having sex with my father in the church. How the two men fought, knocking over a candle, which started the fire. How my father threatened Rae's dad into silence, forcing him to go along with the story that Chet accidentally started the fire by flicking his cigarette butt into the bushes in front of the church.

She also confirms what Brandon and I discovered — that my father was the one who got Beth pregnant, not me. Apparently, he paid her off and got her to blame it on me during their divorce proceedings, which is how my mother found out. Her lawyer also uncovered evidence of my father skimming from the church's tithe for years.

I'm not surprised by my father's actions, having known him for the fraud and liar he is. I share with my mother how Arthur had already figured out the financial misdeeds.

"Thank you for telling me all this," I say sincerely. "But Mom ... why did you never reach out before? After the divorce, after I joined the military ... I thought ..." I trail off, unable to voice the abandonment I'd felt.

"Oh, Luke," she sighs, her voice thick with tears. "I tried. The divorce gave me visitation, but your father blocked me at every turn. And then you were off serving, and I couldn't find you. I assumed ... I thought maybe you didn't want to be found. That you were angry with me for leaving. I'm sure your father spun it that way."

"He did," I confirm. "But I never believed him. And I'm not angry, Mom. Not anymore. I understand now, and ... I'd really like to have a relationship with you, if you're open to it."

"I want that more than anything," she whispers.

We end the call with tentative plans to meet up soon, and I lean back in my chair, absorbing everything she revealed. On one hand, I feel a sense of relief, a few more missing pieces of the puzzle clicking into place. But on the other ...

My father was responsible for the fire that ended up killing my sister. And he used God only knows what against Chet to get him to take responsibility. Probably convincing him that nobody would believe him over their pastor. Chet had a reputation for cheating. On his wife. People out of their money. Even at simple card games. He was an easy target for my piece of shit father.

Sadly, none of that is what's really upsetting.

What I'm really worried about is Rae.

God, how am I going to tell her about her mother's role in the fire? The implications are staggering, the potential fallout for our burgeoning relationship terrifying.

But she deserves the truth, no matter how painful.

With shaking hands, I text her, asking if I can come over tonight. She agrees readily, and I call Brandon to see if he can watch Zoe for the night. He agrees, asking that I drop her off at his place. She'll be thrilled. Rae? She'll be devastated. I scrub my hands over my face, steeling myself for my world to potentially come crashing down around my ears in a few hours.

When I get out of my truck at Rae's place, I stand staring at the small, quaint house. All I can think is that I never wanted to see her home for the first time under these circumstances. I'd pictured coveted time alone. Dinner. Conversation. And, honestly, taking her to bed.

As soon as Rae opens the door, her face falls at what I'm sure is my somber expression. The first words out of her mouth are, "Luke? What's wrong?"

"Can I come in?" I ask.

She frowns, but steps back. "Of course."

I step inside into the living room. It's cozy and eclectic, with bright colors and interesting art, and it smells like sugar and vanilla. Or maybe that's just Rae.

I guide us to the couch and take a deep breath, steeling myself. "I'm not sure if I mentioned, but after I spoke to my father about Brandon, I … well, I tracked my mother down and sent her a letter."

Rae puts a hand on my knee, which I cover with my own. "You didn't. Did she respond?"

I nod. "She called me today." I give her a wary look. "You're not going to like what she had to say."

Rae lifts her chin. "Don't handle me with kid gloves, Luke. Give it to me straight."

I huff out a humorless laugh. "Okay." And I do. I tell her exactly what my mother told me about the night of the fire. About her parents.

Rae listens in stunned silence, her face growing paler with each revelation. When I finish, she stands abruptly, pacing the small living room.

"I can't … I don't …" She shakes her head, pressing her hands to her temples.

"I know," I agree. "It's a lot."

"It's … I can't believe it," she mutters.

I grab her hand as she paces by me. "I understand that. And maybe …" I quickly go back over my mother's claims. "Maybe my mother only knew what my father told her. I don't know when she got there that night and what she did or didn't see, or if it was just her lawyer that told her. Maybe you should talk to your mother about it. Ask her what the truth is."

Rae continues her pacing, shaking her head. I don't feel ignored. I can tell she's completely overwhelmed by this. After a few minutes, I rise, and she stops abruptly before she runs into my chest.

"What do you need from me?" I ask gently, aching to touch her but not wanting to add to her turmoil.

She shakes her head again. "I don't know. I … I think I just need some space. To process all of this."

My heart sinks, but I nod in understanding. "Of course. Take all the time you need." I press a kiss to her forehead. "I'm here when you're ready to talk, okay?"

She gives me a brittle smile, and I let myself out, my mind whirling with worry and what-ifs.

As I drive home, I can't shake the feeling that just when things were finally falling into place, the secrets of the past have once again thrown us into chaos. I can only hope that, once she's had some time to process this, Rae and I will weather the storm together.

Because I'm not giving up on us. Not now, not ever.

CHAPTER SEVENTEEN

RAE

I'm overwhelmed. My mind is spinning with the implications of what Luke just told me about my mother's role in the church fire. I feel like an asshole for shutting him out, but I just need some space to think this through. Though my head is already full of thoughts and starting to ache. But I can't stop now that I'm spiraling.

Hearing that my mother cheated on my father with Luke's dad, causing the fire and everything after … that would change everything. I've looked up to her my whole life. I knew my dad was no saint, and that they'd had problems, but they always seemed to make it work. Until they didn't.

Unfortunately, if this is true … well, it would make my father's actions after the fire make so much more sense. The anger, the fighting with Mom. And thinking more on it, I can see my mom cheating, knowing that my father was unfaithful, too. She may want to put on a proper front to save face, but I've seen glimpses of her selfishness before. I just thought everyone had a bit of that. But could it really run this deep?

I don't even know if Mrs. McMillan was there or if this is all just hearsay, even if it fits. I'm so upset that I know I need to talk this out with someone before I confront my mother and say all the wrong things.

I consider talking to Mia or Carrie, but that doesn't seem quite right. Maybe Nate, since he's known me so long? But that doesn't feel right either. None of my friends really understand everything I've been through, and I don't want to relive it all on top of this.

Then it hits me. It's Luke who has known me the longest, who understands what this all means to me. Who was there when it happened and has also suffered the fallout. Though after all but kicking him out, it would be selfish to bring him back just to dump my feelings on him. Especially since he's going through it, too. But mostly? I'm worried it'll strain what we've rebuilt. A relationship that is already resting on the unsteady foundation of the ashes of our shared past.

Caught in my own anxieties, I do nothing but pace and worry and cycle through the same negative thoughts, spiraling until I'm too exhausted to continue. Then, feeling overwhelmed and alone, I lie down and cry myself to sleep.

I wake to my six a.m. alarm with swollen eyes and a scratchy throat. I know I'm not really sick, it's just from crying, but either way I'm in no state to deal with my perky best friend-slash-boss and demanding customers. So, I decide to do something I've never done while working for Mia and call in sick.

"Hey, Rae, what's up?" Mia answers, sounding distracted. I hear shuffling that sounds like pans going into the oven.

"I'm so sorry to do this to you, sugar, but I'm not feeling up to coming in today," I say, sounding every bit as awful as I feel. Emotionally, anyway.

"Oh, Rae, you sound horrible," Mia replies. "Of course, don't worry about it."

"I'm sorry to leave you in a lurch," I apologize sincerely.

"Gosh, no, I'll be fine. I'm sure Carrie or Joanie can come pitch in. You just focus on feeling better. I can drop off some food for you on my way home if you want, since you obviously won't be making it over for dinner?" she offers.

And now I feel even more like an ass. She's too good to me. But I know even if she had all the facts, she'd probably still say the same. I'm lucky to have a friend like her.

"I'm good here, don't you bother about me," I assure her. "But thank you. I'll see you on Monday, hopefully."

"I hope so, too, but like I said, just focus on getting better, and let me know if you need anything, okay?"

Tears well in my eyes, my emotions still so near the surface. "Thanks, Mia," I reply thickly. I hang up more abruptly than usual. But it was necessary, as I start bawling, Mia's kindness a stark demonstration of a level of support I never realized I wasn't getting from my own mother all these years. Making me realize maybe I haven't seen her for who she truly is, idolizing her simply because she's my mom. And that maybe she really is capable of worse.

That evening, I'm still deep in my pity party, wrapped in a blanket on the couch, enjoying a threesome with Ben and Jerry, when there's a knock at my door.

A glance through the peephole tells me it's Luke, and my heart drops. I swing the door open, stricken.

"Luke, is everything all right?" Surely, he must be here because something so bad happened that he didn't want to tell me over the phone. Oh god. Or maybe he's come to end things with me, thinking maybe I'm just like my mother.

Luke's brown eyes scan me from head to toe, and I'm suddenly very self-conscious that I haven't showered today and probably look a mess from sleeping like crap and wallowing all day.

"Thank God, you're okay." He shakes his head. "Everything's fine. I came because I showed up at Mia's for dinner and she said you were sick. I thought … I don't know what I thought," he admits. He takes a tentative step toward me, running a hand through his hair. "I was just worried about you."

I let out a breath. Fucking anxiety. I'm over here catastrophizing and he's making sure the latest drama in our saga didn't make me ill, or worse.

"I'm … fine," I say lamely, stepping back and gesturing for him to come in. He crosses the threshold and grabs me as I swing the door closed, pulling me into a crushing hug.

"You went into self-protection mode, didn't you," he murmurs into my neck.

I blink back tears. "Yeah, I guess I did."

He pulls away, cupping the back of my neck with his hand. "I get it. I've been tempted to do the same. The one upside of being a single parent — wallowing is not an option."

I huff a dry laugh. "That's an upside?" I bunch my brows. "Where is Zoe, anyway?"

The corner of his mouth tips up. "When Mia realized I was leaving to take care of you, she offered to have Zoe sleep over. And naturally, Carrie and Joanie jumped in saying they had to make it a full girls' night. After that, Zoe couldn't get rid of me fast enough," he says, rolling his eyes.

My heart nearly bursts with gratitude. That my friends jumped in to care for her. That they knew it was so Luke could care for me. That Luke is here. Though I'm a little sad that I'm missing out on that party. I blink against fresh tears and Luke sees where I'm at in an instant, pulling me back into his arms.

"Whatever you're feeling right now, it's okay," he murmurs soothingly. "You're allowed to feel all of it. I sure am."

I tip my head back to look at his face. The creases in his forehead are more pronounced and the corners of his lips are pulled down. "Are you mad at my mother for her part in Hannah's death?" I ask bluntly.

Luke closes his eyes. "Honestly? Yes," he breathes. "But I'm angrier with my father."

I pull him toward the couch, sitting down and drawing him next to me. He hauls me into his lap so he can keep me wrapped in his arms, like he needs it as much as I do. But then again, I imagine he does.

"I'm sorry," I whisper.

He shakes his head slowly. "It's all shades of disappointment. It was a new addition to an already awful situation. I already knew my dad was a cheat and a liar. I'm mostly upset for *you* having to learn that both of your parents were, too, though in different way. In any case, you most definitely do not have a damn thing to apologize for."

"I'm not apologizing, I'm empathizing," I clarify.

Luke gives me a vague smile that affects me no less than usual for its sadness. He's beautiful, even in our shared grief for the continued loss of faith in the people who were supposed to be protecting us and setting the example of what being a good human looks like. I can't imagine failing my own children as badly as they failed me. Not that I'm going to have any of those, but still.

"What are you going to do?" he asks softly, breaking me out of my thoughts.

I sigh. "I guess I have to talk to her, don't I? Even though I've realized it's probably all true … she's my mother. I should at least give her a chance to tell me her side of the story."

Luke nods. "That's how I felt about my father, and you know what his response was. I wouldn't expect much more from your mother."

I lift a shoulder, deciding against explaining that I've been trained to expect the bare minimum. Instead, I say, "Expect the worst, hope for the best."

Luke kisses my collarbone. "I guess in this instance I can understand that philosophy." He looks up into my eyes. "But I'm here to get you used to expecting the best and getting it. Because you deserve it."

I melt at his words. I was so, so stupid not to call him back sooner. Because he's saying exactly what I needed to hear. Reminding me that I do deserve good things.

I put my hands on his face. "I don't know what I did to deserve *you*, but I'm so damn happy you're here."

He nuzzles into me and pulls me in tight, holding his ear against my heart. I stroke his thick hair, running my fingers through the almost indistinguishable intertwined strands of blond and gray.

"Me, too," he murmurs. "Just tell me what you need, Rae. I want to be here for you through this."

I crack my first smile since before I knew. "A proper dinner would probably be a good start. Because a pint of ice cream sure isn't it."

Luke looks at the empty carton on the coffee table and chuckles. "Probably a good idea since I left before I could eat at Mia's. Tell me what you want, beautiful, and I'll do my best to make it happen." His voice is so husky and sincere, it does things to me.

I bite into my bottom lip and the sudden dirty thoughts that run through my head. How can I possibly be thinking about sex right now? Then again, my emotions are all over the place, and I am tightly pressed up against the taut muscles of Luke's chest and thighs, wrapped in his strong arms.

I push off his lap and put some space between us to cool down my dusty libido, heading toward the kitchen.

"I'm sure I've got something I could whip up."

He follows, wrapping his arms around me from behind as I stare into the open fridge. "I'll help."

The feeling of him pressed against me … that definitely won't help us focus on food. So, I decide what we'll make and put him to work, so he's at least not touching me while I'm trying to think clearly.

We work together seamlessly to throw together a simple meal and, as if by unspoken agreement, we don't mention my mother, the fire, or anything else related for the rest of the night.

We talk late into the night about anything and everything else, though. I don't realize how late until I crack a deep yawn.

"I should go," Luke murmurs, rubbing my knee like he wants me to move it so he can get up.

"Stay," I find myself saying. Then I blush hard at the look he gives me.

"Are you sure?" he asks.

I take a slow, deep breath, trying to decide how to put this. But it's Luke. So, I let him see the tears I was tempted to hold back.

"I don't want to fall asleep alone and crying again tonight," I admit.

Luke's expression falls. "Oh, Rae —" I put a finger to his lips to silence him, unable to handle the heartbreak in his voice.

"Don't. Just … stay," I plead.

He nods and lets me lead him to the bedroom. Since I never got out of the joggers and tank top I sleep in, I climb into bed. Luke kicks his shoes off and slides in on the other side, pulling me against him. He wraps his arm around my waist, threading his fingers through mine.

"I'm here," he assures me in a whisper against my ear. "You're not alone."

My eyes drift shut like they were waiting for his words. His embrace. And the safety I feel being with him.

My eyes open to full daylight, and it takes me a moment to realize I'm not late for work. It's one of the rare Sundays I've had off, and it's a good thing I do. Because I also remember my new reality. And that I'll need to talk to my mother today, since I'm supposed to go over for my weekly visit.

A sleepy groan behind me reminds me I'm also not alone like I usually am. I roll over to a sleep-rumpled Luke checking the time on his phone, then putting it back on the nightstand. He rolls back toward me with a lazy smile.

"Well, aren't you just the most beautiful sight first thing in the morning," he says.

My breath catches as he kisses me, soft at first, then with increasing urgency, the lengths of our bodies pressing together. I feel his arousal against my hip and pull back, breathless.

"I'm sorry," he says quickly. "I didn't mean to get carried away. I just wanted to distract you from … everything."

A smile curls my lips. "You succeeded. But don't you have to pick up Zoe?" I ask.

"Not for a couple of hours." He pauses. "But I'm happy with this." He kisses me gently once more. "I don't expect anything more."

I close my eyes against a wave of desire that washes over me. He may not expect it, but I'm ready for *more*. It's been so long since I've wanted a man, much less been with one. And Luke has been here for me in a way I haven't had … well, since he left. He's everything I thought he was before I believed the lie that tainted what we'd had all those years ago.

But there are no more lies between us. No secrets. And the love we shared then hasn't gone. It's just changed. Matured. Grown into something … more. Luke has always owned a piece of my heart, and now he has it all once again.

I reopen my eyes and stare into his. "But you want it?" I ask, slipping my hand over the bulge between us.

He sucks in a sharp breath, his eyes darkening. "I do. But you'd better be sure you do before you do that again," he says huskily.

I bite into my bottom lip and stroke him once more.

And just like that, his tether snaps, and his mouth is on mine, his tongue pushing into my mouth, his hand hauling my leg over his hip as he grinds into me. The hot, hard length grazing my core has me molten in seconds and I gasp into his mouth.

He pulls away, nipping a blazing trail down my neck, his hand now covering my breast, teasing the tip with his thumb.

Well, that went from zero to a hundred in no time at all. And as he pulls my tank top down to expose my breasts, I know it's exactly what I need right now. What *we* need. To feel something *good*. Oblivion. Passion. Connection.

I grind against him, chasing it all.

"Fuck, Rae," he curses. And since he so rarely does, I know he's losing control just as much as I am, and it makes me feral for him.

"I need you, Luke."

He pulls away and makes short work of ripping my tank top over my head and my panties and joggers off after in two quick, powerful moves. He tosses them away before doing the same with his own clothes.

As he crawls back onto the bed, I admire his toned, hard body, shivering in anticipation. He pauses, hovering over me, his eyes full of desire.

"You are so beautiful, Rae," he says in a soft tone that is filled with need.

I reach between us and spread my legs, guiding him home.

"I'm yours," I say simply. "Take me, Luke."

His head tips back for a moment before he sinks in slowly. We both groan at the tight fit, the mind-spinning pleasure, and the feel of skin on skin.

Once fully seated, he pauses. I don't know if it's to give me time to adjust or so he can keep it together. But based on his sharp, panting breaths, he's just as turned on as I am right now. I put my hands on his face until his eyes meet mine.

And then he moves. Slow and deep, he watches me while he brings me more pleasure than I can ever remember having.

I have to break eye contact to tip my head back, my entire body clenching with tightly coiled anticipation as he drives me quickly toward my peak. Everything is heightened by the emotions that have been swirling inside of me, and it seems that's affected me physically, too.

And when he shifts us, his chest now touching mine, his face buried in my neck while he pistons his hips, I can barely stand the intimacy of it.

"This is nothing like it was," he says.

"It's better," I agree.

"It's everything," he whispers against my skin.

I arch against him, my breasts scraping against his chest. "I'm yours," I repeat, tears filling my eyes.

"And I'm yours," he breathes, pumping faster. Harder. His breaths coming more quickly.

Knowing he's close, I start to lose it, grinding into him, chasing my own orgasm. His gasps turn to frantic puffs, a desperate noise escaping him with each. I whimper at the depth of pleasure swirling inside me, as I feel myself approach the edge.

"I need more," I beg.

He sits up, looking down at me with an expression I can't quite place, then takes me harder. Faster. I nod encouragingly, watching his face as he moves inside me.

And it undoes me completely. My orgasm washes over me, unlike any other I've had. Because it's so much more than that. I'm shattered. Broken. Exposed. His.

Luke comes on a cry and fills me, giving a few last shuddering thrusts as he finds his release. Then he leans back down, our sweat-soaked bodies slick against each other. I wrap my legs and arms around him as he sinks down, and everything I was is forever changed. Because this wasn't just sex. I've had just sex. This was so much more than that. I'm wrecked, in the best way possible. Because this was an act of love. I've believed enough pretty lies and had enough meaningless sex to know the difference now.

Luke pulls his head back just enough to look in my eyes. "You okay?"

I give him a lazy, sex-soaked smile. "Perfect. You?"

He brushes a sweaty lock of hair from my face. "Incredible. Words can't even do it justice."

I nod, understanding.

We lay like that a few minutes more before taking the most sensual joint shower of my life. Slippery skin touches and sexy, sated looks that fill a hole in my chest I'd long pretended wasn't there.

When we're done and dressed once more, we stand at the door, preparing to part ways.

"You ready?" he asks softly, running a hand over my shoulder, down my arm, then twining his fingers with mine.

I breathe deeply. "As I'll ever be."

I smile up at him, unable to put to words the deep sense of gratitude I have for him. He's grounded me. His touch makes me feel invincible. And with his encouragement, I know I can handle this conversation with my mother, and so much more.

I go up on my toes and kiss him gently. "Thank you."

Luke laughs, lifting my spirits even higher, somehow. He pulls me against him and the smile drops off my face, my eyes going wide. "I should be thanking you," he murmurs. "That was the best sex of my life."

I huff a laugh. "I wasn't thanking you for the sex, Luke," I say drily. Then, with a smile, "But it was for me, too." I shake my head. "Thank you for being here for me. I needed this to find the courage to face my mother today."

"I'll always be here for you. But you don't need me for that. You've always had courage, Rae."

My brows bunch together. Because I don't feel like I have. "Really?" I ask skeptically.

"Really. Nobody can give you courage. All they can do is help you find what you already have."

I pull him down and kiss him firmly on the lips. "I'll call you later?"

He nods, kissing me one last time. "You'd better." He winks as he opens the door, and we step back into reality.

The whole drive over, I reflect on the things Luke said. I deserve to be treated well. I have the courage to have this conversation with my mother. I have people who love me. I'm not alone. I can do this.

Even though it's earlier than I usually stop by, I don't call ahead to warn my mother I'm coming. I just show up, my heart pounding as I let myself in.

"Rae? That you?" Mom calls from the living room.

I tuck my keys into my pocket instead of putting them on the table like I usually do and leave my shoes on.

I walk into the living room to find her in her armchair, another bodice ripper resting pages down on her lap.

"It's me," I confirm unnecessarily, leaning against the wood-framed entrance to the room and crossing my arms.

"You're early," she replies, picking her book back up.

"Yes, well, I didn't have work today," I say.

She looks up. "Why are you still standing there? Sit down."

I ignore her suggestion, and say instead, "You remember I told you Luke McMillan is back in town?"

Mom sets her book down again. And now that I'm paying attention, I notice her tells. Her pinky taps the cover nervously.

"I do. And I heard tell he didn't actually father the Thompson boy."

I make a noncommittal noise. "No. Pastor McMillan did."

My mother's nostrils flare. "That's a big accusation, young lady."

And now she's deploying the "I'm the boss of you" tactic. God, I never connected that to her deflecting until now.

"It's not an accusation. They got a blood test that proves it." I tilt my head to the side before delivering my first blow in what may be our last fight. "Luke recently reconnected with his mother, too, and she confirmed it. It's part of the reason they divorced after they left town."

Mom huffs. "Guess the fire devastated their marriage, too," she replies, her eyes not meeting mine.

"Oh, she certainly had a lot to say about the fire." I tap my finger on my arm and stare her down. I don't know where this confidence is coming from — or maybe I do, thanks to Luke — but it's clearly keeping her from pushing back. For now.

After a few solid moments, she waves a hand dismissively. "That was years ago. I don't know why she'd dredge that whole mess back up."

I huff an annoyed laugh. Clearly, she has no intention of fessing up, but I'll give her one last chance.

"Is there anything you want to tell me about that night?" I ask plainly.

Now she looks at me. And it's with vitriol I've never seen her direct my way.

"No," she says firmly.

I narrow my eyes. "Really? So, you're saying Dad didn't catch you having an affair with Pastor McMillan that caused him and dad to fight until they knocked over a candle and burned the church down?"

My mother's face pales. "Your dad admitted he started the fire with a cigarette. What would she know? She wasn't there."

My brows raise. "And to know that *she* wasn't, *you* would have to have been," I point out.

Mom's mouth pops open in surprise at being caught.

An inappropriate sense of glee courses through me. And I make a mental note to thank Luke again for helping me be calm so I could give my mother enough rope to hang herself with.

"Now, don't go jumping to conclusions like you always do," she chastises. "Your father was there, wasn't he? You don't really think *I'd* cheat on *him*, do you? Honestly, Rae, I thought you had more sense than that." She shakes her head.

She's good, I'll give her that. If we'd had this conversation a few months ago, I'd feel embarrassed for assuming the worst. But now I see it for the gaslighting it is.

"I'm onto your tricks now," I warn her. "And I notice in that little speech you didn't actually deny anything."

She clenches her jaw and glowers at me. The silent tension is thick between us.

"So, are you going to spread that gossip around like you do all the rest?" she finally asks, lifting her chin.

I scoff and shake my head. "Wow. Really? That's your response?"

Her lips tighten into a frown, and I can see her trembling. "Your father left, and I had to raise you all on my own. You'll forgive me if I don't want the judgmental busy bodies making my life hell over things they only think they know about. If you love me at all, you wouldn't subject me to that."

And now I'm mad again. She's all but admitting it, though she can't even manage that properly. And all she cares about is what other people think of her? Though obviously, I'm not on that list.

I take a deep breath, but it does nothing to quell the anger surging through me. "With all due respect, go to hell, Mom. You cheated on Dad and went along with a lie that destroyed this family. A lie that also cost me thirty years of love with the only person who has ever put my needs first. And the worst part? You were part of the reason Luke's sister died!" Now I'm yelling.

"Hannah's ... dead?" she asks, placing a hand to her throat.

I flinch. Is that ... remorse?

But in a flash, whatever it was is gone and she lifts her chin defiantly once more.

"Whatever happened to her wasn't my fault. I didn't even know she was asleep in the Sunday school room," she protests. "And it wasn't me that knocked over the candle."

"I thought it was a cigarette? Now you're admitting it was a candle?" I shake my head, disgusted by her lack of actually admitting what she did and taking responsibility. "You aren't the woman I thought you were," I tell her, my voice shaking. "You're an awful person. And while Dad wasn't perfect, letting him take the fall was unforgivable. Pretending like you had nothing to do with what happened to Hannah ... to *all* of us is unforgivable."

Her eyes narrow. "Well, you're not the woman I thought you were either. I thought you were a good, loyal daughter."

I laugh bitterly. "You're right, I'm not the woman either of us thought I was. I'm stronger and more capable than I realized. Than you ever let me believe." I push off the frame and march forward, looking down at her. "You always kept me small, and now I know why. Because Pamela Donovan only cares about Pamela Donovan. We can't have Rae getting 'too big for her britches' and having a full life that might take her away from her daughterly duties." I take a deep breath and walk backward. "But I'm done with that now. I'm only going to surround myself with good people who lift me up and encourage me. You are neither of those things."

I stop at the entrance to the living room, waiting for her response. Any response. But it doesn't come. I shake my head, my rage gone, replaced only with disappointment.

"I hope you have the life you deserve, mother."

She blanches at my usual lack of endearment — Momma; the name I called her from the time I could talk. But she's no longer the mother figure she was to me. Despite her obvious distress, she doesn't respond.

So, I leave.

I don't let the tears stream down my face until I get in the Bronco and start driving away. They don't stop until I get home, and only because I pull myself together enough to call Luke.

"Hey. How'd it go?" His warm, concerned voice soothes me.

"About as we expected. She admitted nothing directly and took responsibility for nothing. It's done. I'm done."

"I'm so proud of you, Rae," he says softly. "You did the right thing."

"Thank you," I whisper. "For everything."

There's a noticeable pause before he finally says, "I love you, Rae. I didn't want to say it for the first time again over the phone, but I needed you to know."

My heart swells, tears flowing afresh. For a good reason now. "I love you, too, Luke," I admit with my whole, healed heart. Because he was what it had been missing. "I'm guessing you can't come tell me that in person?"

He pauses, and I know the answer is no. He's a dad. He has responsibilities. "Zoe and I had already planned to take off for the day, and we aren't supposed to be back until late," he hedges. "But I can come home if you need me. Just say the word."

"No, please, don't worry about it, I get it," I assure him. "Go on, have fun."

"Are you sure?"

"I'm sure," I confirm.

"I'll tell you tomorrow, I promise," he says.

"Tomorrow," I agree.

"Get some rest, beautiful."

"Bye, handsome."

As I hang up, my emotions are bittersweet. I'm just starting to mourn the loss of the mother I thought I had … while regaining the love I thought I'd lost.

I'm realizing that sometimes you don't get to pick what shape your life takes. And sometimes it shapes you.

CHAPTER EIGHTEEN

LUKE

Monday morning comes and goes in a blur of meetings and phone calls as we're still deep in the architectural draft phase for Alpine Ridge's fire station. It's not until I'm on my way to pick up Zoe from the bakery that I realize I haven't seen or texted with Rae all day.

When I arrive, Mia tells me Zoe's just finishing up a task in the back. I take the opportunity to steal a few moments alone with Rae.

"Hey," I say softly, pulling her into a hug. "How are you feeling about the confrontation with your mom after sleeping on it?"

Rae sighs, leaning into me, and I notice a dab of frosting on her neck. I resist distracting her by licking it off.

"The anger is fading. It's all in the past, really, and I don't want it to affect my future." She looks up at me with a small smile. "Our future."

My heart swells at her words, at the promise they hold. I was so terrified that "going slow" meant she had too many doubts. That she'd eventually decide it wasn't worth the risk. I've never been happier to be wrong.

"Though I'm disappointed in her and have no plans to speak to her, given that she's clearly not sorry about any of it," she adds, her expression clouding.

I'm about to offer some words of comfort when suddenly, the shrill wail of smoke alarms fills the air. Rae and I exchange a panicked glance before sprinting to the kitchen.

We burst through the door to find a small fire in a pan on the stove, which Mia is already putting out. My gaze immediately seeks Zoe, and relief crashes over me when I see she's okay, standing back from the stove with wide eyes, her face so pale the ridges of her scars stand out.

"What happened?" I ask, my voice tight with concern as I rush over and check Zoe over from head to toe, needing to reassure myself she's unharmed.

Mia gives me an apologetic look. "Zoe just set the oven too hot by accident and the oil in the pan burned. It's my fault, I should have been watching more closely."

Zoe's bottom lip trembles. "I'm sorry, Dad. Are you ... are you not going to let me keep baking now?" Her voice is small, afraid.

I lean in, taking her hands in mine. "Did it scare you, Zo?"

To my surprise, Zoe shakes her head. "No. I know I'm safe here."

Mia nods, offering me a reassuring smile. "Zoe was calm and knew exactly what to do to put out the fire. You've taught her well, Luke."

Pride swells in my chest, temporarily overshadowing the residual fear. A year ago, an incident like this would have triggered Zoe's PTSD, sending her into a panic attack. Hell, it probably would have triggered mine, too.

But as I look at my brave, resilient daughter, I'm struck by how far we've both come. How much stronger we are here, in this place that's starting to feel like home in a way nowhere else ever has.

"No, sweetheart. I would never stop you from doing something you obviously love so much," I assure her.

Zoe wraps her arms around me, squeezing hard. "Thanks, Dad. Let's go home."

I rub her back, my eyes meeting Rae's. She looks relieved as she watches us lovingly. And I realize in a sudden rush I want Rae to go home with us, too. Today, particularly. But ... maybe every day. One thing at a time, though.

"Rae, would you like to come over for dinner tonight?"

Her face lights up. "I'd love to."

When we get back to the house, I can't help noting once again how badly it needs a coat of paint. And I still hate that damn yellow.

At least the yard has been beaten back some, but it still needs the full treatment. Several dead bushes line one side of the house, and the huge maple behind the house needs trimming for sure. But then, I've been focusing on the inside. I'll get there, and though I want the place to look presentable, I know Rae won't really care.

Once inside, I busy myself with getting everything ready, nerves fluttering in my stomach. It's still a work in progress, but I'm proud of how much I've accomplished so far. All the appliances have been replaced. All the plumbing and electrical is now in tip-top shape. The bathroom and kitchen fixtures still need updating, and the décor is ... horrid, honestly. But everything is in working order, finally.

When the doorbell rings, I take a deep breath and go to let Rae in. Her presence immediately fills the space, warm and radiant.

"Hey, beautiful," I say, pulling her in for a hug. But I can't resist sneaking a kiss, too, seeing as Zoe is upstairs in her room.

"Hey, you," she replies, giggling as I kiss down her neck. God, I love her neck. Long and graceful and it's where her vanilla sugar scent is the strongest.

"Let me give you the grand tour," I say, taking her hand.

As I lead her through each room, pointing out the repairs and updates I've made, Rae listens attentively, offering compliments. But when we reach the living room, she pauses, a playful glint in her eye.

"I have to say, Luke, the repairs look great. But ..." She gestures around at the mismatched, dated furniture and decor. The living room is by far the worst, aesthetically speaking. "You really need help with everything else."

I laugh, rubbing the back of my neck. "It could use a woman's touch, huh?"

Rae smirks. "Stop hinting and just ask."

"Okay, okay." I hold up my hands in mock surrender. "Rae Donovan, would you do me the honor of helping me redecorate this disaster zone?"

"God, yes, please. You have to let me get rid of that awful wallpaper," she replies with a sheepish grin.

I flick my eyes up to the faded peach and pale green stripes. She's not wrong. What were my parents — and everyone in the 80s — thinking?

From the top of the stairs, Zoe lets out a whoop of excitement. "Yes! Rae, we can make this place look so good!"

"Zo, have you been eavesdropping this whole time?" I call up.

She charges down the stairs. "Nooo," she replies unconvincingly. "I was just coming down because I'm hungry. When's dinner?"

The oven timer dings and Rae laughs. "Good timing, kiddo."

I roll my eyes. "Why am I not surprised?" Zoe has always had a sixth sense as to when food is going to be ready. I guess it's part of what makes her such a great baker.

Over dinner, Zoe chatters animatedly about all the things she wants to do with Rae now that she's officially my girlfriend. Rae indulges her enthusiasm, suggesting shopping trips, craft projects, and more that have Zoe practically bouncing in her seat.

It warms my heart to see the two of them bonding, to know that Zoe is okay with having Rae in our lives like this.

Later, once Zoe's upstairs reading before bed, Rae and I settle on the couch, her head resting on my shoulder.

"Is it hard being back in this house sometimes?" she asks quietly. "With all the memories it must hold?"

I sigh, considering my answer. "Sometimes I'm reminded of the bad times," I admit. "But there were good memories here, too. And more than anything, I want to make new ones. With Zoe." I press a kiss to the top of Rae's head. "And with you."

She tilts her face up to mine, her eyes shining with emotion. "I can't wait."

As I hold Rae close, the warmth of her body seeping into mine, I'm filled with a sense of contentment, of rightness. Yes, the past held its share of darkness. But the future stretching out before us is filled with light. Rae is my light. My love. And while it's not surprising, I'm relieved to see how well she fits in here. In this house. And with Zoe and me.

Rae is literally everything I ever wanted. Even after we left when I was sixteen, she was the one I compared all of my girlfriends to. And I'm just now realizing that's probably why I never got married. Never stayed with anyone that long. Sure, the job made it tough, but ... none of them were her.

Now I finally realize, I've been waiting for the last thirty years to come back to this place, by her side. We've already worked through some heavy, emotional issues, and her relationship with Zoe absolutely melts me. She fits perfectly into my life. If I have my way, I'll never leave again.

CHAPTER NINETEEN

RAE

As I sit across from the psychologist in her cozy Ellensburg office, my nerves are buzzing with a mix of anxiety and anticipation. I've been waiting for this moment, for answers, for so long.

The therapist, a kind-faced woman named Patricia, who appears to be in her fifties, looks up from her notes and smiles. "Rae, based on everything we've discussed, it's clear to me that the issues you've been struggling with align with an ADHD diagnosis. Specifically, the Inattentive type."

I let out a breath. Hearing it out loud, having it confirmed by a professional, is equal parts validating and overwhelming.

"Okay. And Inattentive type — that means I don't have the fidgety stuff?"

Patricia smiles patiently. "Yes, basically. Nor are you impulsive. Your issues are all around difficulty focusing. And there are plenty of ways to help manage that."

The anxiety in my chest unravels at her reassuring words. We spend the rest of the session discussing strategies for managing my symptoms. Some of it I'm already doing — creating routines, setting alarms, breaking down tasks into manageable chunks. Some of it I'm not — meditation, regular physical activity, and continued therapy with Patricia. All sound perfectly reasonable and manageable. Though I have been doing other therapy, with the woman Mia recommended. I've done a couple of sessions with her to process the issues with my mother, which has definitely helped with the anxiety I've felt since our confrontation. To help continue my progress, Patricia also recommends starting me on a low dose of methylphenidate, better known as Ritalin.

"How long will it take to help?" I ask, trying to tamp down my eagerness.

She chuckles softly. "Oh, about an hour."

My eyes widen in surprise. For some reason I thought you had to take that kind of medication for weeks or even months before seeing results. But knowing that relief could be just around the corner? It's incredibly encouraging. For the first time, I feel like I can get a handle on this, on myself, sooner than I ever thought possible.

Leaving the therapist's office, I'm filled with a renewed sense of hope and determination. And I know exactly where I need to channel that energy.

The bell above the door jingles as I step into Alex's antique shop. He looks up from the counter, a warm smile spreading across his face when he sees me.

"Rae! I wasn't expecting to see you today," Alex greets me from behind a long, oak counter with beautiful scrollwork on its front.

I grin, pulling a folder out of my bag and holding it up triumphantly. "I was in the area. And I come bearing gifts."

Alex raises an eyebrow as I hand him the folder. Inside is the answers to the questions he gave me as homework. But there's also a draft business plan. The result of hours of research and brainstorming since our last conversation. Once I started thinking about it, it was kind of hard to stop. And I'm pretty damn proud of what I put together.

"Is this what I think it is?" he asks, his eyes going wide as he opens it. He gasps. "It is! It's ... a business plan?" He looks back up at me in shock.

"It's just a draft," I hedge.

"That's ... wow. Mind if I skim it really quick?" he asks.

I wave a hand, gesturing for him to go ahead. And instead of letting my anxiety build watching him, I glance around the shop. It's tidier than I'd expect of an antique shop, with well-marked sections for various types of items. There's a full bookcase of old typewriters to the left of the counter, and the entire corner on the other side is full of clocks. But there's too much to take in, and he clears his throat sooner than I'd expected.

"Rae, I'm impressed. This is ... incredibly thorough for a draft. I can tell you've put a lot of thought into this."

I nod, shifting my weight from one foot to the other nervously. "I have. And I know it still needs work, but Alex ... I'm ready to do this. Like, really do this. I even have some money set aside. As you probably noticed in the plan, I include leasing a space for the business, since my house is too small for what I'm thinking."

Alex nods. "I agree. Especially since you included Ellensburg in your target market. Even once I knew what kind of business you wanted to start, I didn't realize until looking at this that Ellensburg doesn't have *any* event planning services. But ... there's something you should know ..." His lips press together and my pulse races.

"Did I mess something up? Or is leasing a space too much too fast?" I ask self-consciously, bunching my suddenly sweaty palms in my skirt.

"No. It's only ... the last open shop space in Alpine Ridge was just leased."

My heart sinks. "Oh. Well, I guess we'll have to look elsewhere then."

But then Alex's face breaks into a grin. "It was just leased ... because I leased it. For us! I'm ready, too, Rae."

My shock gives way to mild indignation and total elation. I reach over and slap him playfully on the arm. "Don't do that to me, Alex!" I laugh. "Are you serious?"

"As the heart attack I apparently almost gave you," he replies with a chagrined smile.

"Well, damn, sugar. I think I need to give you a hug." I reach over and pull him into my arms, squeezing tight. "Thank you."

"No, thank *you*," he says, squeezing me back. Then he pulls away. "Truly. I was feeling … blasé. Like I needed a new challenge. Between that, and Brandon and I getting more serious and commuting back and forth, I knew it was time to make a change. And then Brandon told me his sweet friend Rae was looking to start a business and needed help."

"I didn't expect to get quite this much of it," I admit. "But I'm so grateful, Alex."

"Oh, honey, we're just getting started," he says slyly. "I've been going through my inventory to see what event-related pieces we could use in the new space. Want to see?"

I clap my hands gleefully. "Is that even a question?"

Alex laughs and goes to the entrance to flip the open signed to "be back soon," then he takes me into the storeroom behind the counter. It's not huge but is still crammed with many beautiful objects. He leads me to the ones he's picked out, and I'm speechless. Vintage garden arches perfect for floral arrangements, sets of delicate, ornate china, an array of gorgeous vases … it's like a dream come true.

"Oh, Alex, it's all beautiful. But are you sure?" I ask, fingering the gold edge of one of the beautiful sets of plates.

Alex reaches out and squeezes my shoulder. "Absolutely. These are almost all duplicates anyway. We can keep some here for Ellensburg-based events, and take these to Alpine Ridge for events there," he replies.

I feel tears prick at my eyes. I put a hand to my chest, speechless from all of the emotions I'm feeling right now. I take a few deep breaths and collect myself.

"That's … this is all just *perfect*," I breathe.

Alex smiles warmly. "Can you meet me early again this Saturday? At our new office?"

Happiness so strong and acute thickens my throat and I swallow hard. *Our new office.*

"Absolutely," I agree.

We finalize the details, and I leave, practically floating. All I can think on the drive home is that I can't wait to share the good news with Luke. But I want to wait to tell him in person. This is too big to share over the phone, and I don't want to get emotional while driving. Especially since I have one more stop to make. One more difficult conversation to have today.

When I pull up to the bakery, I sit in the Bronco for a minute, taking in the storefront. Mia kept the original style but had the "Alpine Ridge Bakery" repainted to look fresh. I usually don't pay attention, because it reminds me of too many memories. But now I've made new ones here. Better ones. Though my path is about to take me down a different road, this place will always hold a special place in my heart.

I head inside to find Mia transferring the few remaining pastries for overnight storage in the back. She looks up, surprised and her face lights up.

"There you are! How did it go with the therapist?" she asks eagerly.

"It went great, actually. Better than I expected," I reply, setting my coat and purse down on one of the tables and sitting down.

"I want to hear all about it," she replies. "Need a pick me up?"

I go to decline before deciding … what the heck. "Sure, why not. You choose."

She grins and shuffles around for a minute before emerging from behind the counter with two plated brownies. She plunks one in front of me, then sits across the table with the other.

"So?" she prompts, taking a bite of the oversized chunk of gooey chocolatey goodness.

"Alex was right. I have ADHD." I leave it there, doubting she cares about the details. "She had some helpful tips, and we're going to try some meds. I'll keep seeing her, and hopefully things will get … easier." I shrug, then take a bite of my brownie. It was a good choice, as the combination of nostalgia and chocolate calm my heightened emotional state. It's the perfect reward for everything I've accomplished today.

"That's fantastic, Rae. I actually expected to see you sooner, and I was starting to get worried."

I chuckle. That's Mia. Even though she's like a little sister to me, she still has the tendency to mother me. And everyone around her, really.

"I stopped at Alex's antique shop to talk about moving forward on the event planning business." Mia perks up, clearly curious. "He leased that last retail space next to Sera's realty office. We're doing it, Mia."

"Oh my god," she says, wiping her mouth with her napkin before half-standing to lean over and hug me. Good thing I wasn't taking a bite. I chuckle as she sits back down. "Sorry, I'm just so happy for you!"

"Thanks. And don't worry, I'll stick around until you find someone to replace me here," I assure her.

But Mia waves off my concern. "Oh, don't you worry about that. I'm just thrilled to see you chasing your dreams." She pauses, her expression turning slightly shy. "Actually, I have some good news of my own. The fertility doctor found a hormone imbalance and put me on medication to correct it. We should be able to get pregnant now. Well, at the normal odds, anyway." She smiles softly, her eyes shining with cautious optimism.

I let out a gasp of delight and now it's my turn to leap forward and hug her. "Mia, that's wonderful! I'm so, so happy for you and Nate."

"Thank you," she responds when I pull away. "For being there for me. For encouraging me to get checked out. I don't think I would've done it without that push."

"What are friends for? You did some pushing of your own, too. And I'm grateful for that," I admit, referring to her encouraging me to be honest with myself about my feelings for a certain fire chief.

"How *are* things going with Luke?" she asks, leaning forward.

I close my eyes and smile, my heart swelling with all the joy I feel today.

"Amazing," I admit on a sigh. I open my eyes to her sparkling smile. "It's hard to believe he's only been back a couple of months. There's been so much that's come to light, and we've faced it all together." I shake my head. "You were right. I never stopped loving him, same as he never stopped loving me. And now that we're getting to know each other with all the facts on the table?" I bite into my lip to stop the tears. Mia puts her hand over mine.

"He's The One, isn't he?" she asks softly.

I nod, a tear spilling over my cheek.

"Always has been. Always will be."

Now Mia's eyes are glistening. "Have you told him that?"

I sniff deeply, wiping the tears from my eyes. "Not in so many words," I admit.

Mia squeezes my hand and pulls back. "You finish that brownie and go tell that man how you feel, Rae. Life's too short not to."

I laugh. "You've got that right," I agree. I raise my fork, and she meets it with hers, the small clink a toast to our friendship. Started from a mutual love of pie. But now it's so much more.

As we eat and talk a bit more, I'm struck by how much joy there is in seeing the people you love get exactly what they've been hoping for. It's a feeling I could definitely get used to.

That evening, I'm bustling about getting ready for Luke and Zoe to come over for dinner at my place. For some reason I'm nervous to have them both in my personal space. Even though Luke has been here before, Zoe hasn't. And they definitely haven't together. It feels almost like being interviewed to be part of their family. I shake it off, stirring the pasta sauce. I'm being silly.

Still, I'm nervous when the knock on the door comes. I wipe my hands on a towel and go to answer it. Zoe bursts in as soon as I open the door.

"Rae! We're here, and we brought dessert!" she exclaims, holding out a box.

"Why, that was so thoughtful of you, thank you," I tell her, secretly starting to regret the giant brownie I had this afternoon. Still, always room for more sugar, I suppose, especially if Zoe made it.

Luke comes in tentatively, as if compensating for Zoe's enthusiasm. "Hey, beautiful," he murmurs, giving me a chaste kiss on the cheek. He smells amazing, like soap and pine. "How was the appointment?"

I start to answer, but Zoe has clearly been cataloging sights and smells. "Gosh, your house is so cute! And something smells amazing," she gushes.

I chuckle, ruffling her hair affectionately. "Well, thanks. I hope you're easily impressed, because it's just Spaghetti Bolognese."

"I'm not, but I'm sure it will be delicious because you made it," she replies. "I consider myself a foodie, you know. I might even go to culinary school someday."

That catches me by surprise. I look at Luke, who just shrugs. "Culinary school? I would have thought you'd want to go to pastry school, given your love of baking," I tell her.

Zoe's eyes go comically wide. "There's a separate pastry school?"

"There sure is."

"I thought it was just part of culinary school!" She clutches at Luke's arm, practically vibrating with excitement. "Dad, forget culinary school. I want to go to pastry school!"

Luke laughs, pulling her into a one-armed hug. "Zo, you can do whatever you set your mind to. You're a smart, capable young woman, and I will support you no matter what."

The look of pure joy and pride on Zoe's face is enough to melt even the coldest of hearts. She beams up at her dad before turning to me.

"Oooh, I just remembered you told me you like to read! Where are all your books? Can I pick one?" Zoe asks, switching subjects on a dime like only children can.

I laugh. "Sure thing, sugar. The ones that are okay for you to read are on the white bookshelf," I point to the second bedroom, "in that room. Why don't you check them out while I finish getting dinner ready?"

"Awesome!" she cries, bounding off.

Once she's gone, Luke laces his fingers through mine. "Want to tell me about your day while we work?"

I smirk at his use of "we." He has a lot to learn about how I operate in my own kitchen.

"Sure, I'll tell you about my day while you *watch* me finish dinner and stay out of my way," I tease, leading him toward the kitchen.

He holds up his free hand. "Whatever you say, boss." I laugh. "You look happy, so I'm guessing things went well today?"

I grin. "They did." I stop at the counter and go up on my tiptoes to give him a kiss on the lips. I keep it brief, in case Zoe decides to pop out. "The therapist was great. She confirmed the ADHD diagnosis and put me on some meds. There's more, but that's the gist. In slightly bigger news ..." I chew on my bottom lip and Luke's eyebrows jump. "Alex and I are officially going into business together. I gave him my draft plan ... and he's already leased a space."

Luke's jaw drops and I grin at his shock. "For real?" I nod. He picks me up, spinning me around before placing me gently back on my feet. Then he kisses me much less gently. His mouth consumes mine greedily, his excitement palpable in the rough stroke of his tongue against mine. It lights me up from head to toe, and I'm dizzy and breathless when he pulls back. "Rae, I'm so fucking proud of you," he murmurs huskily.

"Damn, you must be if you just cursed," I tease him.

He smirks down at me. "You have no idea." His gaze is so intense it sends shivers over my skin. "We need to celebrate. A real date, just you and me. What do you say?"

"I say, it's about damn time, Fire Chief McMillan," I tease, giddy with happiness. "Now go sit over there so I can finish dinner. Chef Zoe needs to pass judgment, after all."

Luke chuckles and sits at the stool on the other side of the counter.

As I work, I can't resist starting a conversation I've been meaning to have with him. "You're an incredible father, you know that?" I say, stacking plates to bring to the table.

"I'm just trying my best to be what she needs. It's not always easy, but I got lucky. She's an amazing kid."

I hesitate for a moment, biting my lip. There's a question I need to ask him, but I'm almost afraid to hear the answer. "Luke ... do you think you'll want to have more children someday?"

I can't help darting a glance his way as I head toward the dining room table next to the kitchen. So, I see the understanding that dawns in his eyes. I look away to put the plates on the table and turn back just in time to find him putting himself between me and the kitchen.

He looks deep into my eyes, trailing his fingers down my arms. "Rae, even if you and I hadn't found our way back to each other, I can honestly say that more kids were never part of my plan. I love Zoe with all my heart, and she's more than enough for me."

Relief washes over me, followed by a swell of emotion so intense it nearly takes my breath away. "Good. Because I love you, Luke. I realized I always have. And I want a future with you, more than anything."

His answering smile is blinding. "Rae, before I even came back, you were the love I could never forget. The one I compared every love after to, and they all fell short. Now that I have you back ... well, I've never been happier than I am right now. We've already wasted too much of our lives apart. While I don't want to scare you off ... well, I already know I want to live the rest of my life with you."

He watches me as if waiting for me to run. But why would I, when we clearly found our way back to each other, through lies and secrets and heartache, only to fall right back in love? We're clearly meant to be.

I slide into his arms, tilting my head back to look at him. "Didn't you hear me? I love you, Luke McMillan, and I wish we hadn't wasted time either, so I'll take that offer."

"Are you sure? You haven't lived with a firefighter before," he says, his eyes twinkling. "The smoke smell, the gear everywhere, the schedule —"

I go up on my toes and silence him with a kiss. He smiles against my lips, wrapping his arms around me and pulling me in deeper. His mouth is demanding and giving all at once, loving and sensual, anchoring me to the moment while promising forever. It's a kiss that fills me with a bone-deep certainty that this — Luke, Zoe, the life we're building together — is exactly where I'm meant to be.

And for the first time in my life, I'm not afraid to reach out and grab hold of the happiness that's being offered to me, with both hands and an open heart.

EPILOGUE

RAE

EIGHTEEN MONTHS LATER

I stand at the edge of the crowd, watching Luke interact with the new firefighter trainees and townsfolk at the fire station opening gala. I may have planned this event, but I still can't believe it's happening. Though that, perhaps, has more to do with the rocky journey it took to get here. And I can't help but reflect on how much has changed.

I've moved in with Luke, and waking up next to him every morning fills me with a joy I never knew was possible. Zoe has accepted me into their lives with open arms, treating me like a parent, though I always try to defer to Luke when it comes to the big decisions. We even got a husky that Zoe promptly named Cinnamon. She says we need a white cat now that she plans to name Sugar.

Zoe herself is thriving, having fully embraced the unschooling life, mastering whatever subject catches her fancy and still far outstripping what's expected at her age. She's still firmly set on pastry school, and now that's she just turned fourteen, she can officially work for Mia at the bakery.

My mother, in a perhaps not terribly surprising turn of events, moved out of Alpine Ridge to a senior living community in Ellensburg. Janet Henderson caught the movers in action, who spilled the tea. I can't decide if I'm relieved or disappointed, but either way, it's nice not to have that worry hanging over my head.

On the flip side, Luke's mother moved back to town in a bid to re-establish their relationship. I'm sure having a grandchild she'd never met helped, too. She's here tonight, beaming with pride as she watches her son fulfilling his dreams. Their relationship is still fragile, given the hurts they've both suffered, but seeing them work to mend it warms my heart. Between Luke's ever-strengthening bond with Brandon, and now his mother being here … well, it feels like our family, and our love, just keeps growing.

Speaking of growing ... across the room, Mia is positively glowing at Nate's side as she sips sparkling cider, one hand resting on the swell of her fast-expanding belly. They just found out they're having a girl, and the joy radiating off them is palpable. Mia's hired several new helpers for the bakery, besides Zoe and Penny, who returned from college, and plans to be more hands off once the baby comes. I'm happy she's taking that time. It's all precious, as I'm learning with Zoe.

Joanie and Greg are here tonight, too, but have been jet-setting more often than not these days, determined to see the world. But as Greg confided in me when they picked up Bruiser after their last trip — Zoe has been happily pet sitting when they're gone — it's only to get the travel bug out of their systems before they settle down and have kids. He says he wants four, but Joanie insists they should start with one and see how it goes. I can't help but chuckle at the thought of their future negotiations.

And then there's Carrie and Evan, who shocked us all by eloping at town hall a few months back. Everyone was furious at first, until they explained their desire for privacy, given Evan's celebrity status. We couldn't fault them for that.

Speaking of celebrities, Evan's famous friend who built a vacation home here? Well, we're not supposed to say who it is, and somehow the secret still hasn't gotten out. But Evan let it slip at one of our weekly dinner parties last month when Joanie acknowledged that he couldn't *say* it, but maybe he could do an impression of whoever it is. And as soon as he bellowed "Adriaaaaan!" — besides sending us all into a fit of laughter — it was immediately obvious who it was. And now there's buzz about one of the Amazon execs building a house here, too.

Our little town is certainly growing, and not just in residents. New businesses are cropping up left and right; a drugstore, a bank, a hardware store, a beauty salon ... well, you get the idea. Plus, the police department is being built, having started about six months after the fire department's construction began. And Zoe got the library she'd been after from the moment she moved here. Hell, we may even get that mall Carrie keeps asking for soon.

Though first, Alex and I are going to need a new office. Our event planning and antiques shop has grown to where we're looking to hire. It helps that through therapy and tweaking my meds, I'm more focused and productive than I can ever remember being, and I feel like I can hold my own amongst my much more educated business-owning friends now. I'm *proud*. I'm doing things I only thought of as wild dreams not so long ago. And it's all because of the man of the hour.

Speaking of whom, my attention snaps back to the present as Luke steps up to the podium, his brand spanking new firefighter dress uniform crisp and his eyes shining with emotion. There aren't words for how good he looks up there, and it's not just the uniform. I've got love goggles on big time for this man. He's become my everything, and I've never been happier. The crowd hushes as he takes the microphone.

"Thank you everyone for coming tonight. I'd like to dedicate this fire station to my late sister, Hannah Jane McMillan," he begins, his voice thick with emotion. "Nearly thirty-two years ago, Hannah died as the result of a fire here in Alpine Ridge. It was a tragedy that shaped the course of my life, sparking a passion for firefighting that has brought me to this moment."

He pauses, taking a deep breath. "Becoming Fire Chief, being able to make decisions about fire safety that could truly make a difference … it's the culmination of a dream I worked decades to achieve. And to have it happen in my hometown, surrounded by the people I love? It means more than I can say."

Luke's gaze finds mine in the crowd, and I feel tears prick at the corners of my eyes.

"I want to thank everyone for their support, but especially Rachel Donovan. Rae, your love and encouragement have been my guiding light. I couldn't have done this without you."

As the room erupts in applause, Luke cuts the ceremonial ribbon, officially opening the Hannah Jane McMillan Fire Station.

The party resumes, music swelling and laughter filling the air as Luke makes his way through the well-wishers, shaking hands and accepting congratulations. I smooth my black velvet sweetheart neckline cocktail dress nervously as I feel assessing glances from the people he leaves behind.

When he finally reaches me, there's a mischievous glint in his eye. He grabs a bottle of champagne from a passing waiter and tilts his head toward the back of the building invitingly.

Curious, I follow him outside, the cool evening air a welcome respite from the crowded room.

"What's this about?" I ask, gesturing to the champagne.

Luke grins, handing me the bottle, which I clutch uncertainly against my chest. "A private celebration."

He leads me behind the firehouse, where twinkling lights have been strung up, creating a magical atmosphere. Suddenly, he pulls me into his arms, his lips finding mine in a kiss that steals my breath.

When we part, he reaches into his pocket and drops to one knee. My heart stutters in my chest as he opens a small velvet box, revealing a sparkling diamond ring.

"Rae, I let you go once, long ago, and it was the worst decision of my life. I should've fought for you, for us, and the future we could've had. And while I can't go back and undo the past, I can do better this time around. I know we'll be together no matter what, but I want us to be everything to each other. You were my first love, and I want you to be my last. Will you marry me?"

Tears blur my vision as I nod, a shaky laugh escaping my lips. I try to speak, but my "yes" can't get past the tears choking me up.

Luke raises a brow, his grin widening. "Take a deep breath, love, then let me hear it."

I laugh, breathing in deeply. "Yes!" I yell.

He laughs with me, rising to slide the ring onto my finger. I don't even look at it. I can do that later. Right now, I only have eyes for him. He stares back into mine, and the look is filled with promise and desire. As we lose ourselves in each other, the sounds of the party fade into the background, and I'm overwhelmed by the sense of rightness, of belonging.

And when Luke's lips meet mine, I lose myself in him completely. The heat of his mouth warms me soul deep. The slide of his hands over my back makes me press closer to his strong chest. I feel safe, and loved, and whole in this moment, and I never want it to end.

I always believed this kind of love was an elusive concept that could never be real. And Luke was my most elusive love … until he wasn't. Until he showed me that true love does exist. Though it happens in its own time, and you have to be ready for it.

I never believed I was worthy of love, so it was hard to accept. But Luke helped me realize it's what I deserve. And now I know that this is where I'm meant to be. With Luke, in this town that has seen us through so much.

And as I look to the future, to the life we're already building together, surrounded by family and friends, I know that whatever challenges may come our way, we'll face them hand in hand, heart to heart.

Always.

BONUS MATERIAL

Letters from each female main character to their daughters on what they've learned about true love.

MIA

My darling daughter,

As I write this, you're growing inside me where I can keep you safe, but someday when you're older and facing the beautiful complexity of love, I want you to have these words to guide you. There are things about love I wish someone had told me before I had to learn them the hard way.

First, know that love — true love — will never ask you to shrink yourself. For too many years, I lived a life that wasn't truly mine, working endless hours as a lawyer in your grandfather's firm because I thought making him proud was more important than my own happiness. Real love doesn't demand that you become someone else. When I met your father, he saw me at my messiest, most confused moments, and instead of asking me to change, he gave me space to figure out who I really was.

Great-Grandma Dorothy used to tell me that sometimes we all need a little tough love. I didn't fully understand what she meant until I had to face some hard truths about myself. The toughest love isn't about controlling others — it's about having the courage to be honest with yourself about what you truly want and need.

Don't be afraid to make mistakes. I was so terrified of making the wrong choice that I made no choices at all for far too long. I even tried to run away from your father because I didn't believe I deserved him. The beautiful thing about true love is that it's patient — it waits while you figure things out, even when you stumble.

When you find someone who loves you, make sure they see you clearly. Not just the polished, perfect version of yourself, but all of you — even when you're covered in paint trying to renovate a house with no idea what you're doing. Your father saw me at my lowest points and still thought I was brave. That's how you know it's real.

Remember that building a life with someone isn't about grand gestures. It's in the small moments — your father helping me clean the bakery after a long day, or fixing bunting when I was too nervous about opening day to think straight. Look for someone who shows up, day after day, in ways both big and small.

Don't settle for someone who only loves the easy parts of you. Find the person who holds you when you cry, who listens when you need to talk, and who knows when to simply sit beside you in silence. Your father taught me that vulnerability isn't weakness — it's the foundation of the deepest connections.

Most importantly, my sweet girl, know that you deserve love. Not because you're perfect or because you've checked all the right boxes in life, but simply because you exist. For the longest time, I couldn't imagine someone loving me for exactly who I was. I hope you never doubt your worthiness the way I did.

True love isn't about finding someone to complete you, it's about finding someone who gives you the courage to become the fullest version of yourself. Your father didn't "fix" me; he stood beside me while I found my own way. That's what I wish for you — someone who makes space for your dreams while helping you build them.

Remember that the greatest love stories aren't about two people who found perfection. They're about two people who chose each other, again and again, through all of life's complications. Your father and I have built our love one day at a time, through hard days and tough decisions, through grief and celebration, through misunderstandings and reconciliations.

And if you ever doubt that you'll find this kind of love, remember that it often comes when you're not looking for it — sometimes from the quiet man who shows up to save you from creepy grocery store cashiers when you least expect it.

With all my love and tough love,

Mom

P.S. Never underestimate the power of chocolate mousse made with avocados. Sometimes the way to someone's heart really is through their stomach!

JOANIE

To my surely sassy spawn,

You haven't been conceived yet, but your Aunt Mia is pregnant and hormonal, so she suggested we write letters to our future daughters about what we've learned about true love. I figured, what the hell? Even though right now you're still just a possibility in your father's and my future, I can already picture you — perhaps with his bright blue eyes or my stubborn chin — and I find myself wondering what wisdom I could possibly impart about love that would serve you well.

Before I met your father, I thought I knew everything about relationships. I was the queen of casual, the empress of independence, the absolute ruler of keeping my heart safely guarded. I had convinced myself that this was strength — that vulnerability was weakness, that needing someone was a trap.

I was wrong. So gloriously, wonderfully wrong.

The first thing I want you to know is that true love doesn't diminish you — it expands you. When I met your father in that little mountain town of Alpine Ridge, I was running away from disappointment, looking for a brief distraction. What I found instead was a man who saw all of me — my fire, my fears, my fierce independence — and loved every bit without trying to change a single thing.

Real love isn't about changing yourself to fit someone else's expectations. It's about finding someone who makes you want to be the best version of yourself, while accepting you exactly as you are. Your father never asked me to be less bold, less brash, less me. He just showed me that I could be all those things and still be loved.

The second truth is this: strength isn't found in isolation. For years, I mistook self-reliance for strength, believing that needing no one made me powerful. But there is profound strength in allowing yourself to need someone, in building something together that's greater than what you could create alone.

Don't be afraid to let someone in, my darling. Vulnerability isn't weakness — it's courage in its purest form.

Third: trust your instincts, but don't let fear make your decisions. When I first realized I was falling for your father, I nearly ran away. Fear can be a powerful deterrent, whispering that you're risking too much. But some risks are worth taking. The greatest joys often lie just beyond our greatest fears.

And finally, my fierce, beautiful daughter: know that true love is not a fairy tale — it's better. It's real. It's messy and complicated and sometimes hard. But it's also the most extraordinary adventure you'll ever embark upon.

Your father taught me that love isn't about grand gestures or perfect moments (though there have been plenty of those). It's in the small acts of kindness, the inside jokes, the way he makes my coffee just right, the way he believes in me when I forget to believe in myself.

I hope you find someone who looks at you the way your father looks at me — like I'm both an enigma he'll never fully solve and the answer to every question he's ever had.

I hope you find someone who challenges you, who makes you laugh until you cry, who holds you when you need to be held and gives you space when you need to breathe.

But most of all, I hope you know that you are complete and whole and extraordinary all on your own. Love shouldn't complete you — it should complement you. It should add to your life, not define it.

You come from a long line of strong women, my darling. Your Aunt Mia and I have walked different paths, but we both found men who love us for exactly who we are. Whether your journey leads you to a mountain man of your own or something entirely different, I hope you know that your heart is yours to give freely — not a weakness to guard.

Be brave with your heart, my love. Take chances. Let yourself be seen. The right person won't be scared away by your fire, they'll be drawn to it.

With all my love,
Your mother,

Joanie

P.S. And if someone ever tries to diminish your light, remember that your mother knows taekwondo and your father is not above throwing someone out of a building. Just saying.

CARRIE

My dearest daughter,

I was inspired to write you this letter by my amazing sister, your Aunt Mia, who is about to be a mother. And though it's a dream I hope to achieve someday as well, right now you're still just a beautiful possibility in my future with your father. But I already know there are things I want to share with you about love — truths I had to learn the hard way.

For most of my life, I was the person who tried to make everyone else happy, even at the cost of my own needs. I bent myself into shapes that weren't mine, afraid that if I stood firm in who I was, I'd be abandoned. This is not what I want for you.

The first thing I want you to know is that real love doesn't ask you to make yourself smaller. When I met your father, I was terrified of the intensity of what I felt. I was convinced that his life — glamorous, public, demanding — couldn't possibly have room for someone like me. I pushed him away, certain that loving him would mean losing myself.

I was wrong. True love doesn't demand that you abandon who you are. It celebrates you for exactly who you are.

The second thing I learned is that timing matters. Your father and I almost missed each other because we were in different places in our lives. Sometimes, love isn't enough if you're not ready to meet each other where you are. But that doesn't mean it can't work later. Sometimes the paths that seem to diverge are actually running parallel, waiting for the right moment to converge.

Most importantly, I want you to know that love is worth the risk. For the longest time, I was afraid to trust your father's feelings — afraid that what we had couldn't possibly last. I was so busy protecting myself from potential hurt that I almost missed out on the greatest joy of my life.

Love is scary. It means opening yourself up to the possibility of heartbreak. But living in fear of pain means missing out on the deepest connections this life has to offer.

Always remember that you deserve someone who chooses you, actively and intentionally, every single day. Your father moved mountains to be with me, not because I asked him to, but because he couldn't imagine his life without me in it. Don't settle for less than that kind of certainty.

And finally, know that love isn't just about grand gestures or sacrifices. It's about finding someone who feels like home.

Your journey to love will be your own, with its unique challenges and joys. But I hope that by sharing what I've learned, I can help you recognize love when it finds you, and give you the courage to embrace it with your whole heart.

With all my love,

Mom

P.S. Don't be afraid to take your time. I thought I needed to have everything figured out right away, but some of the best things in life are unscripted.

RAE

Dear Zoe,

As I sit down to write this letter, I'm overwhelmed with all the things I want to tell you about love. It's a journey I've been on for many years, filled with ups and downs, joys and heartbreaks. But through it all, I've learned some valuable lessons that I hope will guide you as you navigate your own path.

First and foremost, know that true love is worth waiting for. I know it's cliché, but it's true. When I was your age, I thought I had it all figured out with Luke. We were young and in love, and I couldn't imagine my life without him. But then circumstances tore us apart, and for a long time, I thought I'd lost my chance at happiness.

What I didn't realize then was that love has a way of finding you when you least expect it. It may not always look like what you thought it would, and it may come with challenges and obstacles to overcome. But if it's real, if it's true, it will be worth fighting for.

That brings me to my second piece of advice: don't be afraid to take risks for love. Opening your heart to someone can be scary, especially if you've been hurt before. Trust me, I know. After Luke left, I experienced even more heartbreak that caused me to put up walls around my heart, and I convinced myself that I was better off alone. But when he came back into my life, I had to make a choice. I could either play it safe and let my fear control me, or I could take a leap of faith and give love another chance.

I chose love, Zoe. And while it wasn't always easy, while we had to work through our past and learn to trust each other again, it was the best decision I ever made. Because love, real love, is worth the risk.

Which leads me to my final point: true love is about growth, both together and as individuals. When Luke and I first reconnected, we were different people than we had been all those years ago. We had both lived lives, experienced joys and pains, and grown in ways we couldn't have predicted. But rather than letting those changes drive us apart, we learned to appreciate and support each other's journeys.

That's what true partnership is about - growing together, challenging each other, and always striving to be the best versions of yourselves. It's about being willing to put in the work, to communicate openly and honestly, and to never stop choosing each other, day after day.

I won't lie to you, Zoe. Love isn't always easy. It takes effort, dedication, and a whole lot of patience. But it's also the most rewarding, fulfilling thing you'll ever experience. When you find that person who makes you feel like you can take on the world, who loves you for exactly who you are, flaws and all ... hold onto them. Cherish them. And never stop fighting for the love you deserve.

You are an incredible young woman, Zoe. You have so much love to give, and I know that someday you'll find someone who will appreciate and return that love in equal measure. Until then, remember these words. Remember that you are worthy of the greatest love, and that it's out there waiting for you.

With all my love,
Rae

P.S. Another cliché, but again, it's true – if you love someone, set them free. If they come back, they were always yours. If they don't, they never were.

Thank you so much for reading! Please take a minute to leave a review on any retailer, goodreads, and/or BookBub. Even if it's just a couple of sentences, your opinion is important to potential readers and to me.

Want more? Check out Melanie A. Smith's *The Safeguarded Heart Series*, featuring Greg's cousin Sera, starting with *The Safeguarded Heart*
http://melanieasmithauthor.com/books-the-safeguarded-heart.html

Sign up for Melanie A. Smith's newsletter to get a FREE book plus all the latest news and more
https://melanieasmithauthor.com/newsletter.html

ACKNOWLEDGMENTS

Tough Love

Some books are hard to write. Some books come pouring out. This one was both as it incorporated some very real emotions I've had in my life that apparently needed to be worked into fiction. In that vein, my sole acknowledgement for this book goes to my own beloved grandmother who recently passed away. She was such a big part of my childhood, and it's impossible to imagine a world without her. But she will live in my memories for the rest of my life, and through her example, hopefully in the life of my child and his children and so on, for not just my own little family but those of all of my siblings, cousins, and the many other lives touched by Ida Marie D'Andreano Butts. May she rest in peace, and forever live in our hearts.

Recklessly in Love

My first and deepest thanks go to my husband and son. Their unwavering support and their ability to give me space when inspiration strikes are truly remarkable. I am endlessly grateful for their acceptance and encouragement in all aspects of my life, especially in my writing journey.

To Erin, without whom, I would have given up writing long ago. Being an author has its ups and downs, but your cheering me on is what gets me through the lows. I'm truly blessed to have found you.

To my #morewordsmay homies, my beautiful betas, Eve Kasey and Jen Morris, thank you for your words: words of encouragement, words of support, and, of course, the words you write. You and your books are an inspiration to me!

To my *Naughty List* readers, your anticipation for the completion of Joanie and Greg's story has been a source of motivation during a challenging dry spell. I sincerely hope you enjoy the rest of their journey as much as I enjoyed writing it!

And to all of my readers, old and new, thank you for being here. I truly hope you enjoyed this story. Stay tuned; there is so much more to come.

Unscripted Love

I wrote this book in a record-breaking twenty-two days. It absolutely came pouring out. And I couldn't have given it the kind of focus that took if it weren't for the support of my family. Because, really, none of this author gig is possible without them, and I'm infinitely and eternally grateful for their love and support.

As I am for my amazing book bestie, Eve Kasey, whose opinion is everything to me and without whose support I would probably have had several nervous breakdowns by now. Thank you for being the glue that keeps my author life together.

To the readers who have loved Alpine Ridge and asked for more. Thank you for living in this small-town world with me.

To the readers who are new here, thank you for taking a chance on this indie author. I hope you've enjoyed Carrie and Evan's story.

And, of course, an immense thank you to all of my readers. While I write for myself first, I publish to share the words and worlds in my head with you in hopes that it brings you joy and escape. Something we all need, and I'm honored to be part of bringing that to you.

Elusive Love

Thank you to my ever-supportive husband and son for putting up with my agonizing over writing. And not writing. And back stories of every character that barely show up in the book. And for just generally putting up with living with an author.

To Erin, my book bestie, for encouraging me, checking in on me, and commiserating with me. Wouldn't want to do any of this without you, you amazing human.

To Anne, who checks on me under the guise of teaching me the most amazing Scottish-isms. I'm grateful beyond words for both. And for giving me the inside scoop on what it's really like to live with a firefighter. As you can see, your insights went straight from your fingertips into Luke's mouth because they were too perfect not to include. I continue to be amazed by how our experiences and lives are intertwined, and I'm thankful for our cosmic connection.

And thanks always to my readers, who with every single purchase, review, share, or message give my author journey meaning and immeasurable happiness. I hope you've enjoyed Rae's story and the Alpine Ridge world.

TRUE Love

So you've come this far … did you notice the Easter egg? That's right, the first letters of each book put together spell "TRUE", and that's the theme of both the series and my acknowledgments. True love is all around us, in so many forms. In romantic relationships, to be sure, but also in the people we lean on every day. The people who support us. The people who are cheering for us. Partners, friends, family, and possibly more. There is so much love in this world, and if we simply looked for the ways we're loved, many of our troubles would be lessened. If we loved *ourselves* even more so. So my wish for you is to acknowledge and accept the love around you. For what it's worth? I love you. I appreciate you. I'm so glad you were here on this ride with me. Because I love creating worlds for people to disappear into where they can feel even more love.

All my love,
    Melanie x

ABOUT THE AUTHOR

Melanie A. Smith is an award-winning, international best-selling author of steamy romance with smart, self-sufficient heroines and strong, swoony book boyfriends with hearts of gold. A former engineer turned stay-at-home mom and author, when Melanie is not lost in the world of books you'll find her spending time with her husband and son, crafting, or cross-stitching.

Connect with Melanie on:

MelanieASmithAuthor.com

facebook.com/MelanieASmithAuthor

x.com/MelASmithAuthor

instagram.com/melanieasmithauthor

BOOKS BY MELANIE A. SMITH

The Safeguarded Heart Series

The Safeguarded Heart

All of Me

Never Forget

Her Dirty Secret

Recipes from the Heart

The Safeguarded Heart Complete Series

Life Lessons

Never Date a Doctor

Bad Boys Don't Make Good Boyfriends

You Can't Buy Love

The Heart of Rutherford: The Complete Life Lessons Series

Alpine Ridge Series

Tough Love

Recklessly in Love

Unscripted Love

Elusive Love

TRUE Love: The Alpine Ridge Complete Series

L.A. Rock Scene Series

Everybody Lies

Finding His Redemption

Stand-alones

Last Kiss Under the Mistletoe

Vegas Baby

Short Stories

Cruising for Love

Hot for Santa

www.ingramcontent.com/pod-product-compliance
Lightning Source LLC
Chambersburg PA
CBHW031640200726

48289CB00004BA/986